CROSSINGS®
Inspirational Romance
READER

INCLUDES:

❤

A FAMILY TO CALL HER OWN

❤

SWEET CHARITY

❤

NIGHT MUSIC

❤

PROMISES TO KEEP

Books by Irene Hannon

Love Inspired

*Home for the Holidays #6
*A Groom of Her Own #16
*A Family To Call Her Own #25

*Vows

IRENE HANNON

has been a writer for as long as she can remember. This prolific author of romance novels for both the inspirational and traditional markets began her career at age ten, when she won a story contest conducted by a national children's magazine. Presently, her editorial position in corporate communications—as well as penning her heartwarming stories of love and faith—keeps her quite busy.

Irene finds writing for the Love Inspired series especially rewarding because, "Inspirational romances allow me to focus on the three things that last—faith, hope and love. It is a special pleasure for me to write about people who find the greatest of these without compromising the principles of their faith."

The author and her husband, Tom—"my own romantic hero"—reside in St. Louis, Missouri.

A Family To
Call Her Own

Irene Hannon

Published by Steeple Hill Books™

Steeple Hill™

STEEPLE HILL BOOKS

FIC
CROSSINGS

4 in 1 ISBN: 0-7394-0528-4

A FAMILY TO CALL HER OWN

foil

Copyright © 1998 by Irene Hannon   6|00

Anyone who welcomes one little child like this in
my name welcomes me.

—*Matthew* 18:5

To Dorothy Hannon,
my wonderful mother and cherished friend,
who gave me Isabel.

Chapter One

"That's a lie!" Zach Wright shot to his feet and glared at the managing editor, bristling with rage. He leaned on the desk that separated them, palms flat, eyes flashing. "That's a lie!" he repeated furiously.

"I'm sure it is," Ted Larsen replied calmly, not at all intimidated by Zach's threatening posture. "But are you willing to reveal your sources to prove it isn't?"

"You know I can't do that!"

Ted shrugged. "Then we've got to play it their way. For now."

"Why?" Zach demanded hotly. "I'm telling you, this information is solid. I wouldn't use it if it wasn't."

"I know that," Ted conceded. "But Simmons is getting pressure on this—big-time. They're threatening to sue."

"It's just a scare tactic," Zach retorted scornfully, waving the excuse aside dismissively with an impatient gesture. "My information is good."

"You're probably right about the scare tactic. But it worked. For the moment, anyway. It's not easy being a lucrative publisher in this day and age, Zach. You know that. Simmons is just being cautious."

Zach gave a snort of disgust. "I can think of a better word for it."

"Look, we'll work this out. I know your information isn't falsified. We just have to prove it." Ted paused, as if carefully weighing his next words, anticipating the reaction. "And until we do, we're going to kill the series."

With a muttered oath, Zach turned away in frustration, jamming his hands into his pockets as he strode over to the window and stared out at the city streets. St. Louis could be a beautiful city, he thought. But on this dreary February day it was just plain ugly—the same as his mood. This whole experience was leaving a decidedly bad taste in his mouth. "Whatever happened to printing the truth?" he asked bitterly. "I thought that was our job."

"It is," Ted acknowledged. "But Simmons's job is to keep the paper solvent. He's not willing to risk a lawsuit."

"So we just let them get away with it?" He turned back to face the editor, his eyes still blazing. "Ted, the corruption in that office is rampant—misuse of public funds, a rigged bidding process based on nepotism instead of price, blatant bribery—what am I supposed to do, forget about it?"

"No. Just lie low for a while. In fact, why don't you take some time off? How many weeks have you accumulated, anyway? Five, six?"

"Eight."

"When was the last time you took a real vacation?"

Zach shook his head impatiently. "I don't know."

"Maybe you're due."

"I don't want to take a vacation!" Zach snapped. "I'm not running away from this story, Ted! I'll stand behind my coverage even if the paper won't!"

"We're not asking you to run away," Ted replied evenly. "Just give it a little time. If you don't want to take some time off, we can assign you to another story while we straighten out this mess."

"Like what?"

Ted pulled a file toward him. "Looks like the St. Genevieve area is going to get hit with another flood. I need somebody down there to cover it."

Zach stared at the editor as if he'd gone crazy. "You're kidding, right?"

Ted adjusted his glasses and looked across the desk at the younger man, the sudden glint of steel in his eyes making Zach wary. Ted had come up through the ranks, done a stint as an investigative reporter himself before taking over the editor job, and his staff respected his skill and integrity. But they also knew that his usual affable, easygoing manner was quite deceptive. He could be unrelenting and as tough as nails when he had to be. And now, as he fixed his razor-sharp eyes on Zach, it was clear that the conversation was over.

"No, Zach, I'm not," he said, his tone edged with iron. "You're overreacting to this situation, whether you realize it or not. You need some time to decompress. Nobody can maintain the intensity, keep up the pace you set, month after month, year after year, without wearing down. You need a change of scene, a different focus, a fresh perspective. You can do that by taking the flood coverage assignment—or by taking a vacation. It's your choice. But those are the only options."

Zach frowned and took one hand off the wheel to flip on the overhead light, then glanced down at the map lying on the seat next to him. His city beat rarely took him more than a few miles south of town, and this part of the state was totally unfamiliar to him. St. Genevieve must be the next exit, he decided, though it was hard to tell in the dense fog that had reduced visibility to practically zero and obscured most of the highway signs.

Zach tugged at the knot of silk constricting his throat and drew in a relieved breath as the fabric gave way slightly. He didn't like ties. Never had. But dinner with the publisher was definitely a "tie" occasion. Even though dinner had ended late, he'd wanted to get settled in and start his interviews for the flood piece first thing in the morning.

At least Simmons had had the guts to discuss the situation with him face-to-face, he thought grudgingly. The publisher had assured him that the paper stood behind him, that they had confidence in his reporting. But they'd still pulled the series. And as far as Zach was concerned, actions spoke louder than words.

Zach flexed the muscles in his shoulders and glanced at his watch. Ten o'clock. It had been a long day, he thought. A very long day. And the only good moment had been Ted's parting words.

"These setbacks happen to all of us, Zach," he said, laying a hand on the younger man's shoulder. "Don't let it get you down. You're a good reporter. One of the best. We'll work this out."

Ted's compliments were rare, and therefore prized. It had been a satisfying moment for Zach. Maybe the most satisfying in his career for a long time, he realized with sudden insight.

Zach frowned. Maybe he'd just stumbled on the source of the discontent, the restlessness that had plagued him for the last few months. His satisfaction used to come from his work, the feeling that it was making a difference. And that's where it should come from. Not from recognition by his boss. Yet Ted's compliment had given him more satisfaction than any of the work he'd done for the past six months.

Zach remembered his early years as a reporter, when he'd fervently believed that he could make a difference, that his writing could right wrongs and make the world a better place. For the first time in his career he seriously questioned that belief, directly confronting the doubts that he now realized had been growing for quite some time. For fifteen years he'd devoted himself single-mindedly to his work—an insatiable, demanding mistress that took all the passion he had to give. And what did he have to show for his zeal and dedication? A few moments of satisfaction when justice had prevailed. But far more moments of frustration when some scumball short-circuited the system through power, money or influence and walked away, laughing in his face.

And he certainly didn't have financial security. His meager savings were eloquent confirmation of journalism's reputation as a notoriously low-paying profession. He had no home, unless you could bestow that generous title on the sparsely furnished one-bedroom apartment he'd lived in for years. And he had no personal life.

All he had at the moment was a depressing feeling of emptiness.

As his precise, analytical mind clicked into gear, Zach tried to pinpoint exactly when his passion for tilting at windmills began to ebb. It might have been three years ago, he thought, when his story on corruption in the building industry blew up in his face thanks to a well-crafted smear campaign that didn't quite discredit him but hurt his credibility enough so that no one took his coverage seriously. Or maybe it was the story he did on teenage prostitution last year, when he spent too many depressing nights on the streets with kids who should have been at pep rallies or studying for algebra exams, not hawking their bodies.

But it didn't really matter when he'd stopped believing that what he did made a difference. The fact was he had. Maybe it was burnout, as Ted had hinted. Maybe he did need a break. It might not be a bad idea, after all, to take some time off when this assignment was completed.

But why had he burned out? Not everyone did. Josef certainly hadn't. Zach shook his head as he thought of his idealistic journalism school classmate, back home now in Eastern Europe, fighting the good fight, as he called it, trying to make his country safe for freedom. Josef's vision had never faltered, even in the face of setbacks and personal danger, and Zach admired him for that. He wished he had more of Josef's conviction and optimism. But he didn't. Not anymore. He'd seen too much and given too much. The well was dry.

Zach thought back to the last time he'd seen Josef. It had been almost eight years since his friend brought his delicate wife, Katrina, to St. Louis for the birth of their daughter. During their six-week stay with Zach, the two men had spent hours talking, debating, sharing. It had been an energizing, invigorating, renewing experience for Zach. Josef, with his serious nature, deep convictions and passionate feelings had always been an inspiration.

Zach recalled one of their last conversations, when he'd asked Josef how he coped with discouragement.

"But, Zachary, I don't get discouraged," his friend replied, clearly taken aback by the question.

Zach looked at him skeptically. "How can you not? Are conditions any better in your country now than when you started? Have you seen any progress?"

"I have not seen much visible evidence of progress, no," Josef admitted. "But we are making inroads," he stated with conviction.

"How do you know?" Zach persisted.

"Faith," Josef replied simply. "In your country, you expect things to get better like this," he said, snapping his fingers. "Patience is not a virtue in America. But in my country, we are used to waiting."

"But for how long?" Zach asked.

Josef shrugged. "Change is slow. But more and more people are on our side, Zachary, and one day there will be freedom for all. Maybe not in my lifetime. But still, I must do my part. Because, my friend, I believe that everything we do does make a difference. It is just that sometimes we do not see the result right away. But no good work is ever lost."

For a long time after Josef and Katrina returned home, Zach recalled that conversation whenever he became discouraged. It always inspired him. But not tonight. Josef was wrong, Zach thought tiredly, lifting his hand from the wheel long enough to wearily massage his forehead. All his years of personal sacrifice while questing for truth and right hadn't made one bit of difference in the human condition. If anything, crime was worse now than it had been when he was an eager cub reporter, determined to change the world. And that acknowledgment left a bitter taste in his mouth.

Would he feel any different if there had been someone to share his life with, to buoy him up on bad days? he wondered. But his passion had always been directed to his writing, leaving little for anything—or anyone—else. The few relationships he'd indulged in had been brief and sporadic. Either he broke them off when he realized the woman was getting serious, or she did when she realized he wasn't.

As a result there was no one who cared if he ate dinner when he came home late—or even if he came home at all. His family in Kansas City was too far away to keep tabs on his daily life, and his only regular companion for the past ten years—a cat—eventually had her fill of his bizarre hours and crazy schedule. One night she went out and never came back.

But Josef had found time for love, despite the demands of his work and his precarious existence, Zach admitted. Political conditions were extremely unsettled in his country, and from what Josef said, they were becoming more volatile each day. But he was a man of deep faith, who truly put his trust in the Lord and was at peace with his destiny. With his faith as a foundation, he had the courage to create a family in the midst of chaos, to share his life with the people he loved. While Zach had always looked upon a family as a distraction, Josef looked upon it as an anchor, a source of strength.

And maybe that's why he hadn't burned out, why he still had the energy to carry on the fight for his principles, Zach speculated. His family sustained him, and in the atmosphere of love and goodness and faith that pervaded his home, Josef found strength and hope and inspiration. Maybe the lack of those support mechanisms in his own life was the reason Zach now felt so emotionally and spiritually depleted.

In a way he envied Josef's deep faith. Living with the seedy side of life for so long had shaken Zach's belief in a loving, caring God. Yet without that foundation of faith, he felt oddly adrift. And as for a wife and family—it wasn't that Zach *never* wanted those things. It was just that he always told himself there would be plenty of time later. But at thirty-seven, "later" was now, he suddenly realized.

A sign for St. Genevieve loomed out of the mist to his right, abruptly interrupting his reverie, and Zach slowed down. This pea soup would do San Francisco proud, he thought grimly, as he cautiously made his way down the ramp and carefully turned left at the bottom.

As he drove along the two-lane road, visibility was so limited that he actually began to feel somewhat disoriented. It was almost like something in one of those old "Twilight Zone" episodes, he thought. He had the weird sensation that he was the last living thing on earth.

Zach's gaze momentarily flickered to the rearview mirror, confirming the absence of other cars or signs of life. While he might not be alone in the world, he certainly was alone on the ghostly road.

But not quite as alone as he'd thought, he realized, when his gaze returned once more to the pavement in front of him. A deer suddenly materialized from the mist and, startled by the headlights, bolted directly in his path. With a muttered exclamation, Zach instinctively jerked the wheel sharply.

The deer bounded off safely, but Zach wasn't so lucky.

As his lightweight, compact car fish-tailed across the unforgiving fog-slicked asphalt, Zach struggled vainly for control. But the vehicle seemed to have a mind of its own, skidding crazily toward the shoulder. His last thought as the car careened off the edge of the road and plunged down an embankment was that he'd forgotten to buckle his seat belt.

Rebecca Matthews stifled a yawn and reached for the cup of coffee in the holder under the dashboard. She grimaced as the cold liquid sluiced down her throat, but she needed the caffeine. It had been a long day and she was bone weary. She glanced at her watch and groaned. Ten-thirty. Make that a *very* long day, she amended ruefully. Maybe she should have taken her brother up on his offer when he'd walked her to the car.

"I hate for you to drive home alone, Becka," he'd said with a frown, looking down at her worriedly. "Why don't you spend the night? We have plenty of room."

"Oh, Brad, I'll be fine," she assured him. "I've done this drive alone a hundred times."

"I know. I just wish . . ." His voice trailed off, and he sighed. "I worry about you being by yourself," he admitted quietly.

Rebecca swallowed past the lump in her throat and forced herself to smile brightly. "Worry should *not* be on your agenda today, dear brother," she chided him gently, striving for a light tone. "You have too much to be thankful for. Anyway, save your worry for someone who needs it. I'm busy and happy. Honestly."

He seemed about to say something else, but refrained, bending down instead to kiss her forehead. "Okay. But promise you'll be careful."

"I always am. Besides, you know I could make this drive with my eyes closed," she kidded him with a smile.

And that's about what she was doing, she thought grimly as she peered through the dense, swirling mist, brought on by a combination of damp ground and unseasonably warm weather. So much for her plan to just switch on autopilot for the familiar route from St. Louis to St. Genevieve. For the past twenty miles the weather had conspired against her, requiring every ounce of what little energy and concentration she had left just to stay on the road. And unfortunately tomorrow's schedule wouldn't bend to accommodate her late-night arrival home. She'd still have to be up no later than six to prepare for the Friday lunch and dinner crowd at her restaurant.

Still, the trip had been worth it, she consoled herself. When Brad called earlier in the day to say they were at the hospital, she'd whipped off her apron and left the restaurant in the capable hands of Rose and Frances. That was twelve hours ago. But if it had been a long day for Rebecca, it had been an even longer one for her sister-in-law, Samantha, who had endured a drawn-out, difficult labor, Rebecca thought sympathetically. And poor Brad had been a wreck. But at seven thirty-five, when Emily Matthews had at last deigned to make her entrance, her parents' pain and concern had quickly been supplanted by joy.

Rebecca was happy for Sam and Brad. The tragic death of Brad's first wife seven years before had left him bereft for months, despite his deep, abiding faith and his vocation as a minister. Not only had he lost his closest companion and friend, but Rachel's death had seemingly destroyed his dreams for a family, as well.

Then Sam had come along, unexpectedly infusing his life with love and laughter and hope. And now they had a child. Tonight, as he'd held Emily tenderly in his arms, Brad had referred to her as "our miracle baby," and they clearly regarded this new addition to their life as a gift from the Lord. Rebecca didn't know the story behind that "miracle" reference, but there obviously was one. So it seemed especially appropriate that Emily had been born today, on Valentine's Day. She truly was a product of Brad and Sam's mutual devotion, and she would bring a new dimension to the love they shared as a couple and the love they would create as a family.

Rebecca sighed. Love—at least the romantic variety—wasn't something she knew much about personally, she reflected sadly. And she probably never would. Regrettably, Valentine's Day had never been a holiday she celebrated. Since opening the restaurant three years ago, she'd had little time to indulge in self-pity or dwell on her loneliness, but Valentine's Day always made her sad. And especially so today, when she'd viewed at such close proximity the circle of love shared by Brad, Sam and their new daughter. It had been very hard to hold back her tears as she cradled the tiny new life in her arms, knowing that it was unlikely she would ever repeat the experience with her own child as a loving husband stood by her side.

At thirty-three, Rebecca was still young enough to have the children she'd always wanted. That wasn't the problem. The problem was finding a husband with enough patience to deal with her problem. But patience was a virtue that seemed to be in short supply these days. And any man who was remotely interested in her would have to possess an incredible amount of patience.

Rebecca sighed again. She hadn't met a man yet who was willing to date her more than a couple of times without expecting some physical closeness. While Rebecca didn't believe in casual intimacy, she realized that at some stage in a developing relationship kissing and touching were appropriate. And expected.

But Rebecca couldn't handle that. Even if she liked a man, her only emotion when faced with physical contact was fear, not desire. And no man she'd ever met could deal with that. In fact, she'd stopped trying to find one who could. It was easier this way. Less humiliating. Less stressful. But certainly more lonely.

Yet seeing Brad and Sam together these past few months, and now watching them with their new daughter, made Rebecca yearn for the same things for herself. Surely there must be a man out there somewhere who could help her find a way to express the love she'd held captive for so long in her heart, she thought with a brief surge of hope. A man who could dispel her fear, patiently teach her how to respond, fan into life the flame of desire buried deep in her heart.

With sudden resolve she promised herself that if a man came along who seemed worth the effort, she would make one more attempt to explore a relationship. It wouldn't be easy, she knew. But maybe, with the Lord's help, she could find a way to overcome her fear and create her own circle of love. And if nothing else, it was a wonderful fantasy for Valentine's Day, she thought wistfully.

But right now she'd better focus on reality, not fantasy, she reminded herself firmly. The fog actually seemed to be growing denser—and more dangerous. It might be better to get off the interstate at the first St. Genevieve exit and take the back road into town, she reasoned. At least there would be minimal traffic, and therefore less chance of an accident. She could barely see ten feet in front of her, and the thought that a tractor-trailer truck could be barreling along only a few feet away, unable to clearly see the lane markings and oblivious to the presence of her older-model compact car, was not comforting.

The exit sign loomed out of the mist unexpectedly, and Rebecca automatically flicked on her blinker, realizing the futility of the gesture even as she did so. She took the exit ramp slowly, with a bizarre sense that the world as she knew it had ceased to exist. Carefully she turned onto the deserted secondary road, her headlights barely piercing the gloom as she crept along. She couldn't remember the last time she'd seen a car, and as she drove through the swirling mist, an eerie feeling swept over her. She didn't spook easily, but the overwhelming sense of isolation was almost palpable. She knew there were homes scattered along the road, but they weren't visible tonight. She had no points of reference with which to mark her progress, and she felt disoriented and vulnerable. Worriedly she glanced at her gas tank, reassuring herself that she had plenty of fuel for the last leg of the trip home. This was definitely *not* the place to get stuck.

Rebecca's gaze flickered back to the road and she gasped as her headlights suddenly illuminated a figure walking slowly along the road, almost directly in front of her car. She swerved sharply to avoid it, then glanced in the rearview mirror in time to catch one final glimpse of the apparition before it was swallowed up in the gloom.

Good heavens, what had she seen? she wondered in alarm, her heart pounding as adrenaline raced through her veins. Surely not a ghost! Of course not, she admonished herself sharply, stifling her overactive imagination. She didn't believe in such nonsense. She forced herself to take several deep, calming breaths and eased back on the accelerator, frowning as she mentally tried to recreate the image that had briefly flashed across her field of vision.

It was a man, she realized, wearing a white dress shirt and a tie, and carrying a suit jacket. Had he been weaving slightly? Or was that just a trick of the swirling fog? she wondered. And why would he be walking along the road at this hour of the night in this weather? Her frown deepened and she lifted her foot off the accelerator even further, slowing the car to a crawl.

There were only a few possible explanations for the man's behavior. Either he was a lunatic, he was drunk or he was in trouble.

The first two possibilities frightened her. She wasn't equipped to deal with them. Not alone on a deserted road. But if he was in trouble or hurt—she thought about the story of The Good Samaritan, who came to the assistance of the stranger on the road, and bit her lip thoughtfully. There was definitely a parallel here. She couldn't turn her back on someone in trouble. If he needed assistance, she had to provide it. But she wasn't going to take any chances, either. She'd just wait until he appeared and then use her best judgment to determine how to proceed.

Rebecca carefully pulled her car over to the side of the road, double-checked that all her doors were locked and that the windows were tightly rolled up, and waited.

As the minutes ticked slowly by and the man didn't appear, Rebecca began to worry. Perhaps he had become disoriented in the fog and wandered off the pavement. Or maybe he'd fallen into the drainage ditch near the shoulder. Or collapsed in the middle of the road, in the path of oncoming cars. Should she back up and . . .

Suddenly the man materialized out of the mist immediately to her left, and Rebecca drew a startled breath. He was less than ten feet away, walking right down the center of the road. In the unlikely event that a car appeared, he would be a sitting duck, she realized. But he seemed oblivious to the danger. He also seemed oblivious to her car. In fact, he didn't seem to notice anything. And he was definitely weaving, she realized. His gait was unsteady, and his head was bowed.

Rebecca lowered her window a mere two inches and called to him. "Excuse me . . . do you need help?"

The man's step faltered momentarily, and he raised a hand to his forehead, but after a moment he continued to walk without even looking in her direction.

Rebecca frowned and quickly put the car in gear, following along slowly beside him. She lowered her window a little further and tried calling even more loudly. "Hey, mister!"

The man stopped again, and this time he glanced confusedly in her direction. Rebecca studied his face, and though it was mostly obscured by the billowing wisps of fog, she could tell that he was fairly young. Late thirties, maybe. He was also tall. Probably six feet. And he looked strong. Very strong. Which frightened her. She would be no match for someone of his size, and on this deserted road anything could happen, she thought fearfully.

But suddenly, as the opaque veil between them momentarily lifted, she realized that her fears were unfounded. The man was clearly injured. His face was gray, and there was a long, nasty-looking gash at his hairline. He was obviously in no condition to walk, let alone attack anyone. She'd be willing to bet that at the moment her strength far surpassed his.

Feeling a little less frightened, she lowered her window even more. "What happened?" she called.

"Accident," he mumbled, gesturing vaguely behind him.

Rebecca hadn't seen a car, and she looked at him suspiciously. "What kind of accident?"

"Deer," he replied, his voice slurred. He didn't appear to be able to manage answers of more than one word.

Suddenly he started to walk again, but after only two shaky steps his legs buckled and he fell heavily to his knees, palms flat on the pavement.

Without even stopping to consider her own safety, Rebecca unlocked her door and dashed toward him, stopping abruptly when she reached his side to stare down helplessly at his bowed head. What was she supposed to do now? Tentatively she reached down and touched his broad shoulder.

"Look, you can't stay here," she told him urgently. "You're in the middle of the road."

He ignored her, and in desperation she tugged on his muscular arm. "Please, try to get up. It's dangerous here. You could be killed," she pleaded.

Her words finally seemed to penetrate his consciousness, and he tilted his head to look up at her. His brown eyes were clouded and dazed, and he seemed to be having a difficult time focusing.

"Dizzy," he mumbled.

"Look, I'll help, okay?" she offered, tugging more forcefully on his arm.

This time he made an effort to stand. And as he struggled to his feet, she realized just how tall he was. At five-five she wasn't exactly short, but he towered over her by at least six or seven inches. And he was well built. And obviously strong.

A wave of panic washed over her, and for a moment her resolve to help wavered. But when she loosened her grip, he swayed, and she was left with no choice but to guide his arm around her shoulders. Stay calm, she told herself sternly. Think logically. The man is hurt. He does not represent any danger.

She took a deep breath, repeating that mantra over and over again as she slowly guided him to the car. He leaned on her heavily, his breathing labored, and she stole a glance at his face. He looked awful, and she wondered if he might have other injuries besides the deep gash at his hairline. Please, Lord, help me get him to the hospital as quickly as possible, she prayed.

When they reached the car, she propped him against the front of the hood and backed up, eyeing him worriedly. "Stay put, okay?" she said slowly, enunciating every word. "I'm going to unlock the car door."

Rebecca had no idea if he understood her words—or even if he heard them. In his zombielike state, she doubted whether very much was penetrating his consciousness. She'd just have to work quickly and hope he was able to remain upright until she returned.

She moved rapidly around the car to the driver's side, and with one lithe movement climbed onto the seat and reached across to unlock the passenger door. She lowered the passenger seat to a semireclining position, then backed out of the car.

The whole maneuver took only a few seconds, but when she emerged, the stranger was trying unsteadily to navigate around the car on his own. Her heart pounding, she raced toward him, praying that he wouldn't fall before she reached him. She didn't know whether he'd have the strength to stand up again, and she couldn't lift him.

Just as she reached his side he stumbled, wildly flinging out an arm as he tried to regain his balance. Unfortunately, Rebecca was right in the path of his knuckles.

The backhanded blow caught her on the chin, and she stumbled back, grabbing at his arm to keep from falling. But that only threw him more off balance, and before she knew what was happening he fell against her, pinning her to the hood of the car under his body.

Dazed from the blow, aware only that she was suddenly immobilized and at his mercy, Rebecca panicked as a wave of primitive fear swept over her. With a strangled sob, she struggled to get free, writhing beneath the man's weight. But he was heavy. So heavy! She could hardly move. But she had to get free! She had to! Summoning up all her strength, she shoved him far enough away to tear her body from beneath his.

The stranger seemed stunned by her action, and he staggered back, his eyes glazed. He wavered, then dropped to one knee, groaning as he raised his hands to his bowed head.

Still reeling from his blow, Rebecca reached up and gingerly felt her tender chin. Her chest was heaving as she drew in one ragged breath after another, and she braced herself against the hood, not sure her trembling legs would hold her up. In fact, her whole body was shaking, she realized. As she struggled to control her irrational reaction, she watched the man touch the gash at his hairline, then stare in confusion at the blood dripping from his fingers.

With a sickening jolt, Rebecca realized that the impact of his fall must have opened the cut again, and a pang of guilt swept over her. Dear Lord, what was wrong with her? The man was hurt, for heaven's sake! He was in no condition to attack her even if he wanted to, which was unlikely. He hadn't hit her on purpose. She needed to get a grip.

Rebecca took several more deep breaths, then knelt beside the stranger and scanned his face. Blood was seeping from the gash, his pallor was alarming and his forehead felt clammy to her tentative touch. The man needed medical attention. Immediately. For the first time ever she regretted that she hadn't invested in the cellular phone Brad was always badgering her to get. It would certainly come in handy tonight.

She drew a deep breath and lifted his limp arm, tucking her head underneath. As she draped his arm around her slender shoulders, his hand brushed her bruised chin and she winced. But the condition of her jaw was the least of her problems. She was more worried about getting the stranger upright. Since he probably outweighed her by a good seventy-five pounds, that wasn't going to be easy. But she had to try. She needed to get him into her car before he passed out, which at the moment appeared to be an imminent possibility.

"Okay, can you try to get up?" she asked. "I'll help. Just lean on me."

Rebecca made an attempt to rise, but it was like tugging on a dead weight. He didn't budge.

"Come on, mister, just try. Please!" she pleaded.

This time when she urged him upward he took the cue, struggling to stand as Rebecca tried to assist him. Once he was on his feet he swayed, and she planted her feet solidly, determined to maintain her own footing. She glanced up worriedly, noting the deep grooves of pain etched in his face and the thin, compressed line of his lips. Despite the chilly air there was a thin film of sweat on his brow, and his breathing was labored.

"We're almost to the door," she encouraged him, trying to keep the panic out of her voice. "It's just a few steps. You can make it."

Half dragging, half pulling, she got him into the car, expelling a shaky breath as she shut the door. She retrieved his suit jacket from the middle of the road where he'd dropped it, tossed it into the back seat, and slid behind the wheel. As she put the car in gear, she glanced over at his semisupine form. She wasn't even sure at this point if he was conscious. But at least he was still breathing, she thought with relief, noting the even rise and fall of his broad chest.

As she drove carefully through the swirling, silent fog, she stole an occasional glance at her unexpected passenger. Although his color was ashen, his clothes stained and rumpled and his hair disheveled, she could tell that he was handsome in a rugged sort of way. His dark brown hair was full and slightly longer than stylish, almost brushing his collar in the back but neatly trimmed. Her eyes traced his strong profile and firm jaw, which seemed to speak of character and integrity. Yet there was a worn look about his face—a sort of deep weariness that had nothing to do with his injuries. For some reason she had the impression that he was a man who had seen it all and now viewed the world with skepticism and cynicism. Despite his world-weary appearance, however, there was a feeling of leashed power about him. Even in his present condition he seemed to radiate energy and vitality and . . . sensuousness.

Rebecca was taken aback by that impression. Yet it was true. The man exuded an almost tangible virility. She stole another glance at him, her eyes lingering for a moment on his firm, strong lips. Her breath stuck in her throat, and she swallowed convulsively, forcing her gaze away from his face and down to his hands. He had nice hands, she thought. They looked . . . competent. As if they could be gentle or demanding or forceful, depending on the circumstance. The kind of hands that would be equally at home chopping wood—or caressing a woman.

Rebecca's gaze snapped back to the road. She was letting herself get way too fanciful. The man was a stranger! None of her speculations were grounded in reality. For example, just because he looked like he had character and integrity didn't mean he did. Looks could be deceiving. She knew that from experience. Caution was more prudent than curiosity in a situation like this, she warned herself.

Yet she couldn't help but wonder about him. Why had he been driving on this road alone so late at night? She ventured another quick glance at his left hand. No ring. That didn't mean anything, of course. He might be one of those married men who preferred not to wear a ring. But for some reason she had a feeling he was single—and unattached. A surprising little tingle ran down her spine at that possibility.

Which was silly, she told herself sharply. In a few minutes they'd be at the hospital and, her duty done, she could finally go home and catch a few hours of much-needed sleep. She'd probably never see the man again. And that was just as well. For some reason he unnerved her, even in this semicomatose state. He was just so . . . male.

Rebecca knew that wasn't a very articulate explanation for her reaction, but it was accurate. His mere presence seemed somehow . . . dangerous . . . and threatening. Threatening to what, she wasn't sure. Certainly not her physical safety, not in his present condition. It was more insidious than that. It was almost as if he was a threat to her emotional safety, to her peace of mind. Which made no sense at all. She didn't even know the man. And she never would. In a few minutes she'd leave him at the hospital, and that would be the end of this little adventure.

But oddly enough, that thought didn't give her much comfort.

"And you didn't see anything else?" the highway patrolman asked after Rebecca finished her statement.

She shook her head, wrinkling her nose in distaste at the antiseptic hospital smell. "No. Like I told you, he was just wandering down the road. He mumbled something about a deer and an accident. But I didn't see a car."

"Well, we'll check it out." He turned to a new page in his notebook. "Now can I get your address and phone number?"

Rebecca frowned. "Why?"

The officer gave her a quizzical look. "If we have any questions later about the statement, we may have to call you. Is that a problem?"

"I'd really rather keep my name out of this."

"We can mark it confidential, if you prefer. But we do need it for the record."

Rebecca bit her lip. "He doesn't have to know, does he?" she asked, nodding toward the examining room where they'd wheeled the stranger.

"No."

"All right."

By the time they'd finished filling out the report, the doctor joined them in the waiting area.

"So how is he?" the officer inquired. "Can I talk to him?"

"He's still pretty groggy. I'm not sure you'll get much, but you can try if you want to. We're going to keep him here overnight for observation."

"But he'll be okay?" Rebecca queried.

"Looks like it."

"Is there someone you can notify?"

The doctor nodded. "He gave us the name of a friend in town."

Rebecca sighed with relief, feeling as if a responsibility had been lifted from her shoulders. She was bone weary, and six o'clock was going to roll around way too soon. "So I can leave?" she asked hopefully.

The doctor looked at the officer, and they both nodded.

"He did ask who brought him here, though," the doctor told her. "I guess he'd like to thank you. Do you want me to pass along your name?"

Rebecca shook her head emphatically as she reached down to retrieve her purse from the plastic chair. "No."

The doctor gave her an understanding look. "Okay. We'll just say it was a Good Samaritan. You're probably wise to be cautious. You can't be too careful these days."

Rebecca nodded. Her earlier flights of fancy about the stranger might have been way off base, but she instinctively knew one thing. This man could disrupt her life. She sensed it with a degree of certainty that startled her. Intuitively she knew she would be a whole lot safer if she just vanished from his life.

And as she stepped outside, disappearing into the fog much as the handsome stranger had appeared out of it less than two hours before, she told herself this was the best way for this bizarre episode to end. She'd just pretend it had never happened. She would put the stranger out of her mind, forget their paths had ever crossed.

But for some reason she had a feeling that wasn't going to be easy to do.

Chapter Two

"Hi, Ben."

The rotund man behind the counter turned, wiped his hands on his white apron and smiled at Rebecca as she climbed onto a stool.

"Hi, there. I was beginnin' to think you were going to skip your coffee again this morning. Missed you yesterday."

Rebecca crossed her arms on the counter and rolled her eyes. "I barely made it to the restaurant in time to get lunch going," she admitted ruefully. "I just don't function well on five hours of sleep. And I don't feel a whole lot better today."

Ben looked at her quizzically, his bushy white eyebrows rising. "Late night Thursday?"

"Uh-huh. My brother and his wife had their baby, and I drove up to be with them. I just didn't expect it to take so long. But babies seem to have their own schedules when it comes to making an entrance," she noted wryly.

Ben chuckled. "That's a fact. Everything go okay?"

"Yes. It was a great day—except for driving home in the fog."

"I heard it was bad," he sympathized. Suddenly he peered at her chin and leaned closer. "Say, that's a nasty bruise," he observed, inspecting the bluish patch of skin on her jaw, clearly visible even under makeup. "What happened?"

Rebecca wrinkled her nose and gingerly touched the tender spot. "That, my friend, is a long story."

She was saved from having to explain by the jingling bell on the door, announcing the arrival of another customer. Ben glanced toward the entrance, then poured her a cup of coffee. "This'll wake you up. I'll be back in a minute."

Rebecca took a long, slow sip of the scalding liquid. Ben really did have a knack with coffee, she acknowledged. Of course, she could easily make her own at the restaurant a few doors away. But three years ago, when Ben had been one of the few people to oppose her request for a permit to open a restaurant, she'd gotten into the habit of stopping by every morning. It had taken a lot of talking on her part to convince him that she was no competition, that they would attract a different clientele. But she'd won him over in the end, and now they were the best of friends. Her early trips for coffee, once peace missions, were now simply an enjoyable way to start the day and catch up on town news.

Rebecca glanced affectionately toward the booth where Ben was conversing with another patron, gesturing emphatically over some point. With his bristly white hair framing a swatch of bald head—the fairway, he called it—he could almost pass for Santa Claus. In fact, he played that role every year at a variety of town holiday functions. And he had certainly been good to Rebecca.

By the time he ambled back to the counter, Rebecca's cup was almost empty, and he reached for the pot to give her a refill. She started to protest, but he waved her objections aside. "I know you usually only indulge in one cup, but you'll have a busy day today, bein' Saturday and all. You'll need it." He reached into the toaster oven behind him and plopped a bagel on a plate, adding cream cheese and a pat of butter. "And have this, too. You need to keep up your energy. Running a restaurant is hard work. I know. Although how you manage to stay so skinny in this business is beyond me. Course, I went the other way." He patted his generous stomach and grinned. "Too much sampling, I guess," he said with a wink.

Rebecca smiled. "Thanks, Ben. What would I do without you?"

He waved her comment aside. "You'd get along just fine. You've got those two old busybodies dithering over you all day at the restaurant."

"Now, Ben," she admonished him gently. "You know I could never manage without Rose and Frances. They're a godsend."

With a snort he reached for a damp rag and began polishing the sparkling counter. Rebecca stifled a smile as she took a bite of the bagel. The friendly rivalry for her affections between the two camps—Ben in the diner, Rose and Frances in the restaurant— always amused her. But she was grateful to be blessed with such loyal friends.

"Well, all I can say is, you make the best coffee in town," Rebecca declared to appease him. She knew he was mollified when he handed her the morning paper.

"Here. Take a gander," he said gruffly. "Probably be the only time all day you sit down."

"Thanks, Ben." Rebecca took the peace offering and scanned the headlines, her attention caught by a story on area flooding. She didn't even look up when the jangling bell announced a new arrival, at least not until Ben leaned down to give her an update.

"Mark's here. Got a stranger with him, too."

Even before she glanced up at the mirror over the grill and saw his reflection, Rebecca knew with uncanny certainty that the stranger with Mark was the man in the fog. She swallowed her last sip of coffee with difficulty, her pulse suddenly accelerating as she peeked above the paper to surreptitiously survey his image. If she'd had any doubts about his identity, the bandage at his hairline immediately confirmed her intuition. And if she'd sensed a power and virility radiating from him Thursday night when he was half-unconscious, today it was at full strength. His attire—worn jeans that sat well on his slim hips, and a dark green cotton shirt that revealed a glimpse of dark brown hair at the open neckline—only enhanced his appeal.

Suddenly Rebecca felt shaky, and though she made an attempt to control her physical reaction to his presence, it proved futile. She didn't have much time to try, anyway, because Mark immediately walked over to her, the stranger in his wake.

"Hi, Rebecca. Can we join you?"

Rebecca turned slightly at their approach and forced herself to smile at Mark, avoiding the stranger's eyes as she struggled to find her voice. "Of course."

Mark climbed onto a stool and gestured toward his companion. "Rebecca, this is a buddy of mine from way back, Zach Wright. He's a reporter—for that paper, in fact," Mark said, leaning over to tap on the section Rebecca was clutching. "He's here to cover the flood. Zach, Rebecca Matthews."

Rebecca could no longer avoid looking at the stranger, so she took a deep breath and turned to face him. The last time he'd gazed at her his eyes had been glazed, unfocused and dull with pain. Now they were clear and alert and warm. And disturbing. Her pulse went into overdrive.

Zach held out his hand, and short of being rude, she had no choice but to place hers in his firm grasp. "It's nice to meet you, Rebecca." He had a pleasant voice, deep and mellow, with just a touch of huskiness.

"It's nice to meet you, too." She tried to think of something else to say, anything, but her mind suddenly went blank. All she could do was stare into his compelling brown eyes.

Zach was equally captivated by the hazel eyes locked on his. Rebecca Matthews was a beautiful woman, with classic high cheekbones accentuated by the French twist hairstyle of her russet-colored hair. Beautiful and, surprisingly, familiar. He somehow sensed that their paths had crossed before. He had a good memory for names and faces—a skill that was essential in his business—and it rarely failed him. But he came up empty on the woman across from him. Although how he could forget someone who looked like Rebecca Matthews was beyond him.

As the seconds lengthened, Zach realized that they were beginning to draw curious glances, and he reluctantly released her delicate hand with an apologetic smile. "I'm sorry . . . I don't mean to stare, but . . . have we met before?" he asked, his eyes probing, quizzical.

Rebecca debated her answer. Originally she'd planned to keep her role in the stranger's rescue a secret because he *was* a stranger. But now that she knew he was a friend of Mark's, remaining anonymous was less important. She'd known Mark for several years, and if this man was a friend of his, he was okay.

She smiled faintly, and a becoming flush tinted her cheeks. "Sort of. Although given the circumstances I'm not surprised you're having a hard time placing me. Between the fog and the accident, I'm amazed you remember anything."

Zach stared at her, the puzzlement in his eyes rapidly giving way to comprehension. "You mean . . . it was you on the road Thursday night? You were the one who stopped to help and drove me to the hospital?" he asked incredulously.

She nodded and glanced away, reaching for her coffee cup. "Yes."

Mark stared at Rebecca, then at Zach. "Are you telling me that Rebecca is the angel of mercy you've been raving about?"

Rebecca's startled gaze flew to Zach's, and he felt his neck redden. But before he could speak, Mark leaned over to examine Rebecca's chin.

"Wow!" he exclaimed. "I just noticed the bruise! What happened? It looks like somebody slugged you."

Rebecca's gaze flickered to Zach, then skittered away. "It was an accident," she said with a shrug, dismissing his question.

There was a moment of silence, and when Zach spoke his voice was troubled. "Why do I have a feeling I'm responsible for that?" he said slowly.

Rebecca turned to find him frowning as he studied the purple bruise shading the delicate line of her jaw. She shrugged again, flushing in embarrassment. "It was an accident," she repeated. "You were hurt. You lost your balance, and I was in the way."

He expelled a long breath and ran his fingers through his hair. "I think I owe you a very big thank-you—and a sincere apology," he said quietly, his intense eyes holding hers captive.

Rebecca dismissed his thanks with a shrug. "I'm glad I could help. And this is nothing," she assured him, gesturing vaguely toward her jaw. "So how are you?" she inquired, feeling increasingly self-conscious under Zach's speculative gaze.

"Doing better. Thanks."

"Twelve stitches and a concussion," Mark elaborated. "Go ahead, Zach. Sit down," he suggested, indicating the stool next to Rebecca.

Zach hesitated, sensing that for some reason his presence was disruptive to the woman beside him, but she smiled politely.

"Please do," she seconded. "I have to leave, anyway." She drained her cup in one long gulp and slid to the ground. "I hope you recover quickly," she said, forcing herself to meet his magnetic eyes.

"Thanks." He grinned disarmingly, once more extending his hand, and again she was left with no choice but to take it. As he enfolded her slender fingers in his firm grip, her heart began to bang painfully against her chest, so strongly she was almost afraid he would be able to feel it through the vibrating tips of her fingers. His eyes held hers—curious, questioning, warm . . . and interested. Which did nothing to slow her metabolism.

"Thanks again for Thursday night." His voice was still shaded by that appealing, husky timbre. "I'm not sure what would have happened if you hadn't come along. I'm just sorry about that." His gaze flickered down to her jaw, and he started to reach up as if to touch the bruise. Rebecca's breath caught in her throat and her heart stopped, but suddenly he dropped his hand, shoving it into the pocket of his jeans instead. Rebecca's pulse kicked back in, then raced on.

"Anyway, I just want you to know that I don't usually go around hitting women," he assured her, his voice even more husky than before.

She cleared her throat, hoping her own voice wouldn't desert her. "I'm sure you don't. I'm just glad you're okay." Carefully she withdrew her hand, and with an effort she tore her gaze from his to look at Mark. "See you later."

"You bet."

"Ben, thanks for the coffee."

"Anytime."

And then she fled.

Zach planted his hands on his hips and watched her leave, a slight frown marring his brow. Clearly she'd wanted to escape from his presence as quickly as possible. But why? It wasn't that she was unfriendly. She just seemed . . . well, skittish. He reached up and rubbed the back of his neck with one hand. He couldn't recall ever meeting anyone quite like Rebecca Matthews. She was poised and polished, yet she seemed somehow . . . untouched. Vulnerable. Fragile. Without hard edges or pretense. She radiated an almost innate goodness, an old-fashioned air of shy sweetness. Those weren't qualities he'd run into often, and he was intrigued—and captivated.

He turned thoughtfully and straddled the stool next to Mark, who was watching him with amused interest.

"Forget it, pal," Mark warned with a grin.

"Forget what?" Zach asked coolly, reaching for the mug of coffee Ben placed on the counter.

Mark chuckled. "I've seen that look before. Had it once myself. Just don't get your hopes up. Rebecca's great—but she has no interest in romance."

"Are you speaking from personal experience?"

"Of course! Do you think a single woman who looks like her could come to a small town like this and not be pursued by every eligible man in the county? But she wasn't interested. Period. In anyone. So I didn't take it personally. We all had to settle for being just friends."

"Hmm."

" 'Hmm' what?"

" 'Hmm' as in, that's interesting but I'm not in the market, anyway."

"Yeah, right."

"Right," Zach repeated firmly. "As my boss told me, I need some time to decompress."

Mark grinned. "I can think of worse ways."

Zach chuckled. "Speaking of which, when do I get to meet your elusive fiancée?"

Mark smiled. "How about dinner tomorrow night?"

"Sounds great."

"Listen, do you mind if I run next door for a minute while you finish your coffee? Then I'll give you the ten-cent tour."

"No problem."

Mark slid off the stool. "Ben will keep you company while I'm gone, right Ben?"

"Sure." A moment later the door jangled to indicate Mark's departure, and Ben ambled over to remove his cup, wiping the counter as he spoke. "Nice girl, Rebecca," he said conversationally.

"Seems to be," Zach agreed.

"Make a good wife for somebody," Ben commented nonchalantly.

"From what Mark says, the lady's not interested in romance," Zach replied, taking a leisurely sip of his coffee.

Ben snorted. "Well, if you ask me, she just hasn't met the right man yet."

Zach had a knack for discreetly ferreting out large amounts of information without people realizing just how much they were divulging. It came in handy in his job—and in situations like this.

By the time he left the diner he knew quite a bit about Rebecca Matthews. She'd moved to St. Genevieve three years before to open her restaurant, "Rebecca's," which was becoming quite popular with both locals and St. Louisans, who often came to the quaint town for weekend getaways. She'd even been written up a few times in area papers—his own included, if Ben's information was accurate. A graduate of the Culinary Institute of America, she'd worked in a couple of prestigious restaurants before striking out on her own. She came from the small town of Jersey, in southern Missouri, where her father still lived. Her brother, Brad—a minister—and his wife, Sam, made their home in St. Louis. She'd been returning from there Thursday night after the birth of their daughter. As far as Zach could tell from Ben's ramblings, Rebecca never dated. And she was apparently doted over by two maiden sisters who worked at her restaurant.

As Mark and Zach started off on their tour a few minutes later, Mark pointed out Rebecca's restaurant. It was a modest building in the historic district, identified only by a discreet awning that displayed the name.

"Rebecca really is a wonderful chef," Mark told him. "The food's great. You'll have to try it while you're here."

"Uh-huh," Zach replied noncommittally. As a matter of fact, he intended to become a regular customer. And not because of the food.

"Rose, have you seen the tube of whipped cream with the star tip?" Rebecca called, her voice muffled as she stuck her head into the restaurant's huge refrigerator.

Rose glanced at the work counter, where the tube lay in clear sight right next to the torte Rebecca was decorating. It was exactly where she'd laid it moments before. Rose glanced at Frances across the counter, and her sister shrugged, mystified. Rebecca was extremely organized, and they'd never seen her flustered. Until this morning.

"It's right here, dear," Rose said, pointing to the tube as Rebecca turned.

"Oh. Well. I guess my brain just isn't in gear this morning. I haven't quite caught up on my sleep since Thursday night," she explained lamely, warm color suffusing her face.

"Frances and I will just finish up in the dining room and leave you in peace to work your magic on that cake," Rose replied, motioning for her sister to follow.

"All right." Rebecca distractedly wiped her hands on her apron and glanced around the kitchen. "Now where did I put that spatula?" she mumbled.

Rose ushered Frances out of the kitchen, and the two older women looked at each other quizzically. With their white hair pulled neatly back into identical soft, motherly buns, the sisters could almost pass for twins, although Rose was the older by two years and stood three inches taller than Frances.

"What do you make of it?" Frances whispered, her voice tinged with concern.

Rose shook her head, frowning. "I don't know," she said slowly, clearly puzzled.

"She almost put cinnamon in the quiche this morning, too," Frances informed her sister worriedly.

Rose considered that for a moment, and then her face grew thoughtful. "Unless . . ."

"Unless what?" Frances prompted.

"Unless it's a man," Rose replied reverently.

"A man?" Frances repeated, her eyes widening.

"Yes," Rose declared, nodding vigorously, becoming more certain by the moment. "I'd bet my prize-winning recipe for pickle relish that there's a man behind this!"

"You mean our Rebecca's got herself a man?" Frances said incredulously.

"How else would you explain what's been happening this morning? Have you ever seen her so disorganized or absentminded?"

Frances shook her head. "No."

"Then there you have it! There's a man behind this, all right," Rose asserted.

"But who?" Frances asked, bewildered.

Rose sighed, her brow knitted in concentration. "I don't know. But maybe that old buzzard, Ben, does. She had coffee there this morning."

"He won't tell us anything," Frances lamented, shaking her head regretfully.

"He will if you drop by with a piece of that torte this afternoon," Rose declared conspiratorially. "He has a sweet spot for you, anyway."

Frances smoothed back her hair and sniffed, pretending indifference. "Well, I suppose I could try."

"It couldn't hurt," Rose agreed.

"So what did you find out?" Rose asked eagerly when Frances returned from her mission later in the day, empty plate in hand.

Frances looked around carefully to make sure they were alone, then leaned close. "There was a stranger in there this morning with Mark," she reported in a hushed voice. "Name of Zach. His car went off the road in the fog, and Rebecca drove him to the hospital. He's a reporter from St. Louis, here to cover the flood. Ben says there was enough electricity flying between the two of them to run his toaster without even plugging it in. Said this Zach seemed like a real nice gentleman."

Rose gave a satisfied nod. "Good job, Frances."

Suddenly the front door of the restaurant opened, and both women straightened up guiltily. A young man carrying a large vase covered with green florist tissue entered the shop and made his way toward them.

"I have a delivery for Rebecca Matthews," he informed the sisters, consulting the card attached to the tissue.

"I'll get her," Rose offered eagerly, bustling toward the kitchen. She opened the door and stuck her head inside.

"Rebecca, there's a delivery here for you."

Rebecca looked up from the soup she was stirring on the stove and frowned. "All our delivery people know to come around back."

"It's not that kind of delivery," Rose replied, her eyes dancing.

Rebecca's frown deepened. "What do you—" But Rose was already gone. Rebecca sighed. She was having a hard enough time concentrating today without all these interruptions, she thought irritably as she pushed through the swinging door.

She stopped abruptly when she saw the young man standing there with what was obviously a vase of flowers, Rose and Frances flanking him on each side like bodyguards.

"Rebecca Matthews?" the boy asked.

"Yes."

"These are for you." He walked over and handed the vase to her. Then, jingling his keys and humming under his breath, he headed back out the front door while Rebecca stared, dumbfounded, at the flowers in her arms.

"Well, aren't you going to open them?" Frances prompted her. "Don't you want to know who they're from?"

Rebecca already knew who they were from. There was no other possibility. Carefully, her heart hammering in her chest, she set the vase down on a convenient table and tore off the green paper to reveal a dozen long-stemmed yellow roses artfully arranged with fern and baby's breath.

"Oh, my!" Frances breathed in awe, reaching out to delicately touch a petal, as if trying to assure herself the roses were real. "Aren't they beautiful?"

"Here's the card, dear," Rose informed Rebecca, extracting it from the flowers and holding it out encouragingly.

Rebecca took it gingerly, suddenly finding it difficult to breathe. She tore open the envelope carefully and slid the card out, taking a deep breath before scanning the message.

"Please accept these with my thanks and apology. It was a memorable encounter. Zach."

For some reason Rebecca suspected that the "encounter" he was referring to had occurred this morning, not Thursday night, and that thought sent a tingle down her spine.

"Well?" Rose prompted.

Rebecca looked up blankly. She'd totally forgotten her audience. "It's just from someone I did a favor for," she explained vaguely, her voice a bit breathless.

"It must have been some favor," Frances commented.

"Yellow roses. Now that's interesting," Rose mused.

Rebecca looked at her curiously. "What do you mean?"

"The language of flowers, dear," Rose replied matter-of-factly. "Yellow roses mean 'I'll never forget you.'"

Rebecca's face flamed and she lowered her head, tucking the note into her apron pocket. "I doubt whether anyone knows that these days," she remarked, striving for an offhanded tone. "It's just a coincidence."

"Maybe," Rose replied, her eyes twinkling. "And then again, maybe not."

"Well, I don't have time to speculate about flower messages," Rebecca declared briskly. "There's too much to do." She picked up the vase and, without a backward look, headed for the kitchen.

The two sisters watched until the door swung shut behind her. Then Frances turned to Rose.

"Do you think they're from him?" she asked eagerly.

"Absolutely. Who else would be sending Rebecca flowers?"

"So our Rebecca really does have a beau," Frances breathed in awe.

"Looks that way," Rose affirmed. "Now let's just hope she gives him a chance."

"Rebecca, some friends of yours are here," Frances announced as she came bustling into the kitchen to pick up the salad course. "That nice couple from St. Louis."

"Nick and Laura?" Rebecca said in surprise, turning from the stove where she was stirring the sauce for chicken Madeira. Normally she checked the reservations, but she simply hadn't had time today.

"Mmm-hmm," Frances confirmed.

"Tell them I'll stop by and say hello at dessert, would you?" Rebecca asked over her shoulder.

"Of course."

Rebecca smiled as she added some lemon juice to the sauce. She didn't get to see her childhood friend often enough. Laura's business as a landscape architect was booming, and her free time was pretty much devoted to Nick, "the man of her dreams," as she called him. And Rebecca couldn't blame her. Nick Sinclair would make any woman's heart beat faster. Rebecca didn't know much about Laura's first marriage, but apparently there had been serious problems of some sort. Serious enough that Brad, who was not only Laura's friend but her minister, had once told Rebecca that he doubted whether Laura would ever remarry. But then along came Nick, who somehow convinced Laura to take a second chance on love.

Rebecca was happy for her. She remembered that even as children, Laura, who was several years older than Rebecca, had always taken it upon herself to watch out for her younger friend and make sure she was included in the games and activities. Rebecca never forgot her kindness, and she was truly happy that Laura had found her own Prince Charming. And she also had Laura to thank for getting Sam and her brother together. If Sam hadn't been Laura's maid of honor, Sam and Brad might never have found each other. The Lord really did work in mysterious—and wondrous—ways, Rebecca reflected with a smile.

An hour later, as Rebecca put the finishing touches on the chocolate mousse with zabaglione, she was glad once again that she limited dinner service to a single seating on Friday and Saturday nights. Until she could afford to hire another chef, one seating was all she could manage. And when she had a full house—as she did more and more often lately—she was a zombie by Saturday night. But it was satisfying to know that her efforts were paying dividends, and not a day went by that she didn't give thanks for her success.

Rebecca stepped back and surveyed the forty servings of dessert, nodding in approval. They were picture-perfect. She shrugged out of her apron, and as Rose and Frances entered the kitchen with two of the high school students who helped out on weekends, she picked up two servings of dessert and stepped into the dining room. Her gaze immediately went to Nick and Laura's "special" table, the same one they'd sat at on their first visit, in the early stage of their relationship. They always asked for it when they made reservations.

As she joined them, Nick rose and pulled out a chair for her.

"Thanks," she said with a smile. "But I'm not staying long. I don't like to intrude on my guests' dinner."

"Oh, Rebecca, we want to visit a little," Laura assured her. "We hardly ever get to see you anymore."

"Life is busy. What can I say?" she replied with a grin. "And I'm not complaining. In this business, busy is good."

"Mmm, I can see why you're busy, with desserts like these," Laura complimented her, closing her eyes as she savored the rich, creamy confection.

"I'll second that," Nick added appreciatively.

"It's a good thing we don't come here too often, though, or my figure would certainly suffer. Not that it will matter soon, anyway,"

Laura said, smiling tenderly at Nick, who took her hand in a gentle clasp, his eyes warm and caressing as he gazed at her.

Rebecca glanced from one to the other as suspicion turned to certainty. "Does that mean what I think it does?" she asked with a smile.

Laura looked back at Rebecca, her eyes shining. "Yes," she replied softly. "Our first little one is on the way."

Rebecca reached over and took Laura's free hand. "I'm so happy for you," she told her sincerely, her gaze encompassing them both. "When's the big day?"

"October 4, according to the doctor. It seems like such a long way off, but I know the time will fly. And I can't wait to decorate the nursery!"

Rebecca felt her throat constrict at the glow of happiness on Laura's face, and she blinked rapidly. She was thrilled for Laura, of course. Just as she had been for Sam. But once again, being in the presence of such a committed, loving couple only served to remind her of her own solitary life. She forced herself to smile, and with one final squeeze of Laura's hand, she stood up. She needed to escape to the kitchen, take a moment to compose herself.

"Well, I'll leave you two alone to celebrate. You obviously have lots of exciting things to discuss."

Nick stood up, as well, and took Rebecca's hand. "It was wonderful seeing you again," he said warmly. "And the food, as always, was superb."

"Thank you, Nick."

"Keep in touch, okay, Rebecca?" Laura requested.

"Of course. And if nothing else, I'm sure I'll get regular updates from Brad and Sam. Good luck, Laura. I'll keep you in my prayers."

"Thanks, Becka," Laura replied warmly, reverting to her friend's childhood nickname.

Rebecca turned away and walked unseeingly toward the kitchen, struggling to hold her tears at bay, berating herself for indulging in such blatant self-pity. She had so much to be thankful for. It was wrong to feel sorry for herself. Just because she'd never found someone who had the key to unlock her heart didn't mean . . .

"Hello, Rebecca."

Rebecca stopped abruptly and glanced toward the voice that had haunted her dreams for the past week. Zach Wright was sitting alone at a secluded corner table. She swallowed and brushed her hand across her eyes before moving toward him, trying to compose herself and discreetly erase evidence of her teary state. Which was difficult to do when her respiration had suddenly gone berserk and her eyes still felt misty.

Zach watched Rebecca approach, his discerning eyes missing nothing as they raked over her face. She was upset. Almost in tears, in fact, although she was struggling mightily to conceal that fact. He'd watched her interacting with the couple at the table across the room, and she'd been smiling and happy then. Their parting had been warm and amicable, as well. But something had prompted this sudden change of mood. He rose as she approached, and indicated the extra chair.

"Could you join me for coffee?"

Rebecca ran her damp palms down the front of her simple, tailored black skirt, trying to still the erratic beating of her heart. Now she was doubly sorry she hadn't taken the time to check the names on the reservation list. It would have been nice to have some warning of Zach's presence. She knew he'd come in for lunch several times since arriving a week ago, but she'd gone out of her way to avoid him, much to the dismay of Rose and Frances. The simple fact was he made her nervous.

Rebecca knew, instinctively, that Zach was way out of her league in the arena of man/woman relationships. Smooth, fast, a man of strong passions—those were the words that came to mind when she thought of him. And she simply wasn't equipped to deal with someone like that. Especially not now, when her emotions were so near the surface. She'd just have to find an excuse of some sort to decline his offer.

"Thank you," she said, her voice sounding shaky even to her ears. "But there's so much to do in the kitchen that—"

"Nonsense, my dear," Rose declared briskly, pausing to refill Zach's coffee cup as she bustled by. "Everything is under control. You sit down and have some coffee with this nice young man. You've been on your feet all day."

Rebecca looked at Rose in dismay, then turned to find Zach watching her expectantly.

"I won't take up much of your time," he promised with an engaging smile.

Rebecca sighed. She might as well give in. Rose had invalidated her best excuse to decline his invitation, and nothing else came to mind. "All right. For a few minutes."

Rose waved to Frances, who hurried over to place a cup of coffee in front of Rebecca. "Now isn't this cozy?" she asked with a satisfied smile.

Rebecca gave the hovering sisters a withering look, but they seemed oblivious.

"If you need anything else, you just let us know," Rose told Zach.

Zach watched them depart, then turned to Rebecca. "They seem very nice," he remarked, his eyes glinting with amusement.

"Oh, they are. Just a little too motherly at times," Rebecca replied wryly. "For two women who have been single all their life, they take an inordinate interest in my—" She started to say "love life," but caught herself, a flush creeping across her cheeks as she gazed at Zach. She had the uncomfortable feeling that he knew exactly what she was going to say, but at least he didn't pursue it.

"Well, I like them," he declared. "But I do feel a little guilty. I didn't mean to railroad you into having coffee with me. I hoped you might *want* to, but I have a feeling I may have caught you at a bad time." He paused and stirred his coffee, frowning slightly. "I hope you won't think I'm being too personal, but you seemed . . . upset . . . when I stopped you. I thought maybe you had some bad news from that couple over there." He nodded toward Nick and Laura.

"Oh, no, not at all," Rebecca assured him. "Just the opposite, in fact." She gazed back at her friends, who seemed oblivious to their surroundings as they sat close together, talking and laughing softly. "I just found out they're expecting their first child, and I'm very happy for them."

"I see." Zach thought there was more to it than that, but he wasn't going to push. Rebecca struck him as a very private person who might easily back off if she felt he was encroaching on her turf.

When her gaze returned to his she found him studying her speculatively, and she dropped her eyes self-consciously, tracing the rim of her coffee cup with one finger. "I'd like to thank you for the flowers," she said softly. "They were beautiful. But it wasn't necessary."

"I wanted to do it. You took a risk, stopping to help a stranger, and I appreciate that. Besides, I still feel badly about the bruised jaw. Sending flowers was the least I could do."

Frances was walking by at just that moment, and she stopped in her tracks. "So those beautiful roses were from you!" she exclaimed. "Rebecca just loved them! She even kept one to dry."

"Frances!" Rebecca rebuked the older woman, blushing furiously.

"Oh, my, I guess I shouldn't have said anything, should I?" Frances murmured contritely. "You're always supposed to keep the gentleman guessing, aren't you? Well, I'll just leave before I put my foot in my mouth again."

Zach chuckled as he watched her hurry off. "I see what you mean about the sisters," he acknowledged.

"Listen, I'm really sorry about that," Rebecca apologized, her face flaming. "Just because a man sends me flowers and then asks me to have coffee, they're jumping to all sorts of conclusions. Most of which are wrong."

Zach took a sip of his coffee, carefully set the cup down and leveled a direct look at her. "Are they?"

Rebecca stared at him. "What . . . what do you mean?" she asked, her voice quavering.

Before she could anticipate his intent he leaned forward and laid his hand over hers. "Exactly what you think I mean," he said evenly.

Rebecca swallowed with difficulty. She'd never met a man quite this . . . frank . . . about his interest. It was just as she suspected. He was fast moving . . . and smooth. "Look, Zach, I . . . I don't date, if that's what you're after."

"That's exactly what I'm after," he confirmed. "Why don't you date?"

For a lot of reasons, she thought silently. None of which she wanted to go into, especially with a man she hardly knew. "I just don't."

"Well, I'm not the kind of guy who gives up easily. Do you mind if I keep trying to convince you to make an exception in my case?"

Rebecca glanced down at the strong, tanned hand, flecked with dark brown hair, that covered hers. She'd like to get to know him better, actually. There was something about him that she found appealing. But despite the promise she'd made to herself on Valentine's Day—to allow the possibility of romance into her life—she wasn't yet ready to deal with someone of Zach's determination and almost tangible virility. It frightened her. Besides, getting involved with a man who was just passing through wasn't at all wise. She could be too easily hurt.

"You'll be wasting your time," she told him with a soft sigh, keeping her eyes downcast.

Zach squeezed her hand, then leaned back and picked up his cup. "Well, I must admit that this isn't exactly great for my ego. You avoid me whenever I come in for lunch, and you won't go out with me. Don't you like me, Rebecca?"

"You seem nice," she hedged.

"'Seem.' An interesting choice of words," he mused. "Do I detect a note of caution in that comment?"

She shrugged. "You know what they say. A woman can't be too careful these days."

"Unfortunately, that's true." He paused and took a sip of his coffee. He sensed there was more behind Rebecca's wariness than mere caution, and he was determined to get the whole story before he gave up on her. "Well, we could bring along a chaperone. How about Rose or Frances?"

Rebecca smiled despite herself. "Now that would be something, wouldn't it?"

"Hey, if it makes you more comfortable, I'm game."

For a minute she was actually tempted. But the fact remained that soon he would be returning to his life in St. Louis, and while St. Genevieve wasn't that far away in distance, she suspected that once enmeshed in his life in the city, it would seem like another planet to Zach. He would forget the small town—and the woman named Rebecca who had simply provided a pleasant diversion while he was stuck there.

Regretfully she shook her head. "I don't think so, Zach."

He looked at her, letting a few moments of silence pass before he spoke. "I'd still like to keep trying."

"Why?" she asked curiously. The man certainly didn't discourage easily, she'd give him that.

"Because I find you attractive. Appealing. Interesting. And very intriguing. And I'd like to get to know you better. So . . . do you mind if I keep at this for a while?"

Rebecca couldn't help but be flattered—and a little overwhelmed—by his compliments and his determination. "Does it matter if I do?" she asked faintly.

He looked surprised. "Of course. I'm not into harassing women. If you want me out of your life, I'll be gone. But I think there's a spark between us. I sure feel it, and I suspect you do, too, whether you're willing to admit it or not," he said frankly. "I'd like to see where it leads. And I'd like to keep trying to convince you to do the same."

This was her chance. She could just tell him to get lost, and he would. He'd said as much. And she suspected he would honor his promise. She opened her mouth to decline his pursuit, but to her surprise different words came out instead. "I just hope you're not disappointed."

Zach smiled, and though his posture had seemed relaxed throughout their conversation, she could feel an almost palpable easing of tension. "I'll consider that a green light. And as for being disappointed—well, let's just say I'm not worried."

"Maybe you should consider it a yellow light," Rebecca countered, "as in 'proceed with caution.' "

"Okay, a yellow light then," he said, laughing.

Rebecca looked into his warm and insightful eyes, and felt her heart stop, then rush on. Zach said he wasn't worried. And she believed him. She just wished she could say the same about herself.

Chapter Three

Zach turned up his collar and took another sip of steaming coffee from the paper cup. The Red Cross tent offered an oasis of light but only marginal protection from the cold drizzle and bone-chilling wind that sliced through the darkness. It had been raining steadily for the past three days, and the river was rising ominously, edging precariously close to danger levels. An urgent call had gone out two days ago for volunteer sandbaggers, and it seemed just about everyone in town had turned out to help with the hard, messy work. Zach had interviewed a number of volunteers as well as National Guard and Red Cross spokespeople, and he was just about to call it a night.

But though he was tired and cold, he was also impressed by the spirit of generosity and selflessness he'd discovered during his ten days in the small community. Having dealt for so long with the selfish, unethical side of human nature, he'd almost forgotten there was a generous, moral side. His experience in St. Genevieve had certainly given his faith in humanity a much-needed boost.

Zach drained his cup, then turned to toss it into a trash container, colliding with a passing volunteer in the process. His hand instinctively shot out to steady the middle-aged man, who was wearing horn-rimmed glasses.

"Sorry about that," Zach said contritely.

The man waved aside the apology. "I'm sure it was my fault. These glasses are so fogged up and wet I can hardly see where I'm going." He took them off and carefully wiped them on a handkerchief, then reset them on his nose and grinned at Zach. "That'll help—for about two minutes."

Zach's mouth twisted into a wry smile of acknowledgment. "Nasty night."

The man looked out into the darkness and nodded. "It sure is. I just hope we can keep up with the river." He turned back to Zach and held out his hand. "I'm Phil Carr. English teacher at the high school."

Zach returned the man's firm grip. "Zach Wright from St. Louis. I'm a reporter, here to cover the flood."

"Oh, yes, Mark Holt mentioned your name."

"You know Mark?"

Phil smiled. "This is a small town. I know a lot of people. Besides, Mark lives down the street from me." He hesitated and looked at Zach earnestly. "I was actually hoping I might run into you."

Zach's eyebrows rose quizzically. "Why is that?"

"Well, I hope you won't think this is too much of an imposition, and I'll understand if you can't do it, but I teach composition and it would be a real treat to have a reporter from St. Louis talk to one of the classes. Do you think you might be able to spare an hour or two before you head back?"

Zach considered the unexpected invitation thoughtfully. He hadn't done anything like that for a long time, and his classroom skills were probably pretty rusty. But it might be fun. "Sure. As a matter of fact, I've always been interested in teaching. I even double majored in college—journalism and education. I just couldn't make up my mind between the two. But I got a good newspaper offer when I graduated, so that sealed my fate. It would actually be nice to get into a classroom again," he mused, warming to the idea as he spoke.

"Great! I'll give you a call. Are you staying in town?"

"Yeah. Let me jot down the information for you." Zach scribbled the name of his motel, as well as his work number on a piece of paper and handed it to Phil. "If I'm not at the motel, just leave me a voice mail at the office."

"I'll do that. And thanks again. The kids will really enjoy this."

He tucked the slip of paper carefully into his pocket and rubbed his hands together. "Well, back to the trenches," he said with a smile.

Zach watched him leave, then turned to survey the scene once more. The ranks were thinning a bit, but it was nine o'clock, after all. Most of these people had put in a full day at work and would have to do the same tomorrow. It was really amazing, he thought. The vast majority of the volunteers weren't personally threatened by the flood, yet they were still willing to help out, even under these miserable conditions. He almost felt guilty for heading back to his warm, dry motel room. But he did have to put this story together and E-mail it to the paper, so he still had a long night ahead of him.

Zach stepped out from under the tent and slowly made his way past the line of sandbaggers, shivering despite his sheepskin-lined jacket. The cold rain was already working its way insidiously down his neck, and his boots made loud sucking sounds as he trudged through the mud. He glanced again at the tired faces as he passed. Sandbagging was backbreaking work, as he'd come to learn in the past couple of days, yet people of all ages and sexes were here to help, from high-schoolers to grandfathers to—

Zach stopped abruptly and stared at a slight figure up ahead in one of the sandbag lines. He could swear that was—

"Zach!"

With an effort Zach pulled his gaze away from the figure and turned. "Hi, Mark."

"Working late?"

"Yeah. But I'm about to call it a night. Listen, tell me I'm wrong, but—" he glanced back with a frown toward the figure that had caught his attention "—is that . . ."

"Rebecca?" Mark finished. "Yeah. She's been helping every spare minute since the call went out for sandbaggers. I've been trying to convince her to go home for the last hour. I even offered her a ride, but she said she wanted to stay."

"How long has she been here?"

Mark shrugged. "I don't know. But she was here when I showed up three hours ago."

Zach felt a muscle clench in his jaw, and he jammed his hands into his pockets. "She must be frozen. Not to mention exhausted."

"Well, why don't you try to convince her to leave?" Mark suggested. "Maybe you'll have better luck. I sure didn't get anywhere. Say, Joe!" he called to a figure in the distance. "Wait up! Zach, I'll see you later."

Zach watched Mark disappear into the darkness, then looked back at Rebecca. Her motions were robotlike, as if she was operating on adrenaline and nothing else. Which was probably the case, he thought grimly. She was too delicate for this type of heavy work, anyway. Couldn't whoever was in charge see that? In sudden decision, without stopping to consider how his actions might be interpreted, he strode over and laid his hand on her shoulder.

She turned, her eyes dull with fatigue, and frowned up at him in confusion. "Zach?"

One searching sweep of her face was all it took for Zach to assess her physical condition—absolute exhaustion—and he glanced around, signaling to a passing National Guard member who held a clipboard.

"Zach, what is it?" Rebecca asked, her voice so scratchy and hoarse it was barely recognizable.

"Hang on a sec, okay?" he replied curtly.

The uniformed man joined them, and Zach nodded toward Rebecca. "Do you have someone who can fill in here? She's had all she can take," he said tersely.

The National Guard member gave Rebecca a quick but discerning glance and nodded. "No problem." He turned and scanned the group on the sidelines, motioning to another uniformed Guard member. "Dave, take over here for a while, okay?" he called.

Zach took Rebecca's arm and gently drew her away from the line. Her legs felt stiff and shaky when she tried to walk, and she stumbled, grateful that Zach reached out to steady her, his hands firm on her shoulders. But why was he bothering her, when there was so much urgent work to do? She looked up at him, still frowning. "What are you doing?" she demanded.

"You're going home, Rebecca."

She stared at him, and even through the haze of her fatigue she was aware of the rigid set of his jaw and the steely determination in his eyes. On one hand, she was touched by his concern. More than touched, actually. No man had ever taken such an active interest in her well-being. On the other hand, she wasn't accustomed to being ordered around. Even if it was for her own good. She straightened her shoulders and glared at him. "Excuse me?"

Zach saw the sudden, stubborn tilt of her chin, heard the indignant tone in her voice, and sighed. *Wrong move, buddy,* he admonished himself. Rebecca was not the type to respond to high-handed tactics. And he wasn't the type to employ them—socially, at least. But for some reason, seeing Rebecca cold and tired and wet had awakened a sort of primal, protective urge in him, and he'd reacted instinctively. And obviously inappropriately. Giving orders was clearly *not* the way to convince her to go home.

A sudden harsh gust of wind tugged several strands of wet hair out of Rebecca's French twist and whipped them across her face, and a visible shudder ran through her body as she reached up to brush them aside. Before she could lower her hand Zach captured it in a firm grip, silently stripping off her wet glove and cocooning her fingers between his palms. Her hand felt like ice, and a spasm once more tightened his jaw. He took a deep, steadying breath, and when he spoke he made an effort to keep his tone gentle and reasonable, though neither of those emotions accurately reflected his mood at the moment.

"Rebecca, Mark says you've been out here at least three hours. You're chilled to the bone, you're wet and you're exhausted. You need to go home where it's warm and dry and get some rest. You won't help anyone if you stay here till you get sick."

Rebecca looked into Zach's concerned eyes, and her protest died in her throat. She couldn't argue with his logic. And he was right about her physical condition. Her legs were shaky, her back was stiff, and her hands and feet were numb with cold. She'd put in a full day at the restaurant, and she had to be up at six tomorrow. It probably made sense for her to call it a night.

With a deep, weary sigh she gave in, her shoulders suddenly sagging. "I guess you're right," she admitted, her voice flat and lifeless with fatigue as she brushed a hand tiredly across her eyes. "Mark said he'd give me a lift a little while ago. I just need to find him."

"I'll take you home, Rebecca."

Her eyes flew to his in surprise. "You?"

"I was leaving, anyway. In a town this size, your place can't be that far out of my way."

Rebecca never took the risk of putting herself in a situation where she was alone with a man she barely knew. But Zach was a respected journalist. He was a friend of Mark's. Ben liked him. So did Rose and Frances. Surely a simple ride home would be safe. Besides, she was just too tired to worry about it tonight. She felt strange—unsteady and shaky—and she knew that if she didn't sit down soon, she was going to fall down.

Zach watched her face, prepared to argue the point if she protested. Under normal circumstances he knew she'd flatly refuse his offer of a ride. But in her state of near collapse he hoped that instead of trying to analyze his motives, she would simply accept them at face value. He cared about her and simply wanted her safe and warm and rested. It was as simple as that. He wasn't sure himself *why* he cared so much about a woman he hardly knew. But he did.

He watched her face, trying to anticipate her response, but before he could come to any conclusions she surprised him by acquiescing.

"All right, Zach. Thank you," she accepted wearily.

He felt a tension he hadn't even realized was there ease in his shoulders, and silently he took her elbow and guided her toward his car. The fact that she didn't protest this protective gesture told him more eloquently than words that she was about ready to drop. He could sense that every step was an effort for her, and when she stumbled a couple of times on the uneven ground he was tempted to just pick her up and carry her. But he knew beyond a shadow of a doubt that the lady *definitely* wouldn't put up with that. A hand at her elbow was one thing. Holding her in his arms was another— even though the idea was suddenly immensely appealing, he realized. In fact, he'd like to do a whole lot more than that. But he quickly—and firmly—reined in his wayward thoughts. Now was not the time to indulge in romantic fantasies.

When they reached his car he pulled open the passenger door, but Rebecca hesitated, glancing down at her muddy, wet clothes and shoes. "Zach, I'll m-mess your c-car up," she protested, trying unsuccessfully to keep her teeth from chattering.

"Don't worry about it," he said shortly, dismissing her concern as he urged her gently into the car.

But she held back stubbornly, resisting his efforts. "Don't you have a blanket or a towel in the trunk that I can sit on?"

He gave her an exasperated look. The last thing he cared about at the moment was soiled upholstery. After all his car had been through in the past ten days, a little dirt wasn't going to hurt anything. But rather than argue the point, he left her standing by the door to quickly rummage through the trunk, emerging a moment later with a rug he kept handy for tire changes. Wordlessly he laid it over the passenger seat, and Rebecca finally slid into the car. *Collapsed* was actually a better word, Zach thought grimly, as he shut the door and strode around to the driver's side. She was all in.

She somehow summoned up the energy to direct him to her apartment, and within a few minutes they pulled up in front of her building.

"I appreciate the l-lift, Zach," she said, her teeth still chattering as she reached for the handle.

"I'll walk you to your door."

She thought about protesting, but by the set of his jaw she knew it would be useless. Besides, she was too tired to argue anymore.

He took her elbow again for the short walk, and this time the protective gesture registered in her consciousness—and also tugged at her heart. Rebecca wasn't sure why Zach continued to bother with her. He'd made no secret about wanting to date her, true, but she'd given him virtually no encouragement. Yet still he'd taken the time to see her home tonight, and she somehow sensed that for whatever reason, he cared about her well-being.

Her door was sheltered by a small porch, barely large enough to accommodate the two of them, and Rebecca was acutely aware of Zach's presence just a breath behind her as she withdrew the key from the pocket of her coat. Her numb fingers fumbled as she attempted to insert it in the lock, and it slipped from her fingers, clattering to the concrete.

With a weary sigh, she started to bend down, but Zach restrained her with a preemptive hand on her shoulder, retrieving the key himself in one smooth swoop. Then he reached past her to insert it in the lock, his other hand still resting lightly on her shoulder. He was only a whisper away now, and Rebecca caught the scent of his distinctive aftershave as he leaned close. When his arm brushed her chest, a surge of yearning unexpectedly swept over her, and she drew in a sharp breath.

Zach turned to her immediately, his concerned eyes probing her face. "Are you all right?" he asked with a frown.

She nodded jerkily, not trusting her voice.

He looked at her appraisingly, noting that she'd wrapped her arms tightly around her body in a protective gesture that said, "Stay away." But, surprisingly enough, her unguarded eyes said something entirely different. They reflected a combination of emotions—longing, fear, uncertainty, confusion, yearning. He doubted whether she realized just how eloquent they were. Rebecca definitely did not have a poker face. She wore her emotions too close to the surface, and her eyes were a window to her soul, communicating clearly what was in her heart.

Zach wanted to respond to the longing he saw, wanted to reach out and gather her into his arms, but he stifled the urge and drew in an unsteady breath. His self-control had never been taxed as much as it was around this woman, who brought out a protective instinct in him that he thought had died years ago. She was the kind of woman who should be cherished and loved and always treated gently, in keeping with her gentle nature.

Unfortunately, Zach didn't have much experience dealing with women like that. Suddenly, desperately, he wished he did, wished he knew how to make Rebecca relax with him, to trust him, to give it a chance. He honestly didn't know where a relationship with her might lead. The physical attraction was definitely there. And maybe that's all there was. But he didn't think so. His gut told him there could be a whole lot more, and he'd learned to trust his instincts. They ought to explore their attraction. But first he had to convince *her* of that.

However, now was not the time. She was cold, aching, tired and wet. What she needed was a dry, warm bed. And rest. And peace of mind. Which—unfortunately—was his cue to exit.

Rebecca was caught in the spell of Zach's magnetic eyes as they held hers captive. He had wonderful eyes, she thought. Trustworthy. Caring. Insightful. Vibrant. Passionate. Very definitely passionate, she realized with a start. She might want rest. He clearly wanted something else—something she couldn't give. Certainly not now. And maybe never. The simple fact was, Zach was a man of intense passions. Rebecca knew that as surely as she knew her reaction to passion. And the two were not a promising combination, she thought bleakly.

Zach saw the sudden melancholy steal into Rebecca's eyes, and without stopping to consider the consequences he slowly reached over and laid his hand against her cheek, brushing his thumb gently over her soft, silky skin. He felt her quivering beneath his touch, but she didn't pull away as he'd half expected. She just stared up at him with wide, vulnerable eyes.

Get out of here before you do something you'll regret, an inner voice ordered. *Now!*

"Take a hot bath, okay?" he suggested.

"Okay," she whispered.

"And get some rest."

"I will."

It would be so easy to just pull her close, to taste her lips, to demonstrate the depth of his attraction to her. It was what he *wanted* to do. Even with her hair in disarray and darkened by dampness, her classic features tinged with fatigue and wiped free of makeup, wearing mud-caked boots and an oversize parka, she did more for his libido than any woman he'd ever met. It didn't make any sense. And if he was confused, she surely would be, too.

Zach didn't usually waste time analyzing his reaction to a woman. He just listened to his hormones and went after what he wanted. But he knew instinctively that Rebecca wouldn't respond to his usual direct approach. And he also recognized that tonight was not the time to explore their attraction. She was too tired and too vulnerable.

Regretfully, summoning up the last reserves of his self-control, he let his hand drop from her cheek and removed his other hand from her shoulder. "Good night, Rebecca."

"G-good night. And thank you."

He hesitated one more second, then, with a last lingering sweep of her face, he turned and strode away into the rain.

Rebecca rose on one arm to peer at the bedside clock, reading the digital display with a groan. One in the morning! She thumped her pillow and flopped onto her back, cringing as her aching muscles protested the abrupt movement. After the last couple of days of backbreaking work she needed rest desperately, but sleep was proving to be elusive tonight. Her sore muscles were just making it too difficult to get comfortable.

But so were thoughts of Zach, she admitted. Tonight she was sure he had been thinking about kissing her. But then, in her exhausted state, maybe she'd misread his eyes. It wasn't as if she had a whole lot of experience to draw on. But there had definitely been . . . vibrations, she thought, for lack of a better word. Surely she wasn't mistaken about that. Yet, in the end, he'd simply walked away.

Rebecca stared at the dark ceiling and tried to think logically. Despite his restraint earlier in the evening, she knew he was interested. He'd made no secret of the fact. He'd been angling for a date ever since their "official" meeting in the diner. She'd put him off, but he didn't seem discouraged. Just more determined. Which made her nervous.

But what made her even more nervous was her interest in him.

Rebecca closed her eyes and drew a deep, quivering breath. She didn't want to be interested in Zach. She didn't want to feel nervous and unsettled every time she was in his presence. She didn't want to wait anxiously every day to see if he'd stop in for lunch so she could at least catch a glimpse of him. But she was and she did. And that scared her. Because she knew that deep in her subconscious she was starting to consider going out with him.

It wasn't that she didn't want to date him. She did. She found him attractive, was flattered by his attention, impressed by his apparent character and integrity. But she was so afraid of what would happen if he . . . A choked sob cut off her thought in midsentence. She didn't have to wonder what would happen. She *knew.* Physical closeness freaked her out. Period. She'd embarrass both of them. He might even be angry. She didn't know him well enough to be able to judge his reaction. But based on past experience with other men, it wouldn't be pretty. No, dating Zach would be a mistake.

Besides, she consoled herself, he'd be leaving soon. This was just a temporary beat for him. He was a city man, used to lights and action and excitement. And he sure wouldn't find those in St. Genevieve. She was better off sticking to her original decision.

But if that was true, then why didn't she feel better off? she cried silently.

Zach typed in the final line of his story, then leaned back and wearily massaged his temple. It had been a long, cold, wet night, and it had taken him what seemed like hours to warm up after he dropped Rebecca off. But at least he had a good story to show for his discomfort, he thought in satisfaction. It uplifted. It reaffirmed. It found goodness even in the midst of chaos and tragedy. It was the kind of story Josef would like, he realized suddenly, a faint smile touching his lips as he thought of his friend.

Zach pulled out his wallet and flipped through the plastic holders, stopping at one that contained a photo taken at Isabel's christening, nearly eight years before. Josef and Katrina had insisted that Zach be the godfather, though he'd protested that the honor should go to a relative. He still remembered Josef's response to his reaction.

"Sometimes ties of the heart are the strongest of all, stronger even than blood, Zachary. You are my best friend, and you would honor us by becoming part of our family in this way."

And so, of course Zach had agreed. He recalled clearly the day the picture was taken. It was right before Zach and Katrina went home, an unseasonably warm late-May afternoon even for St. Louis. They asked him to hold Isabel for the picture, and then stood on either side of him while the minister snapped the photo. Zach had no experience with babies and was almost afraid to grasp the tiny, fragile bit of life, with her flailing arms and kicking legs. But Josef laughingly assured him that Isabel wouldn't break, and in fact she lay quietly in his arms as the picture was taken, staring up at him solemnly with big blue eyes.

Zach glanced at the facing picture, a slightly fuzzy shot taken when Isabel was six. Almost two years ago now. She had turned into a beautiful child, with her mother's long brown hair and Josef's inquiring eyes. Josef and Katrina had gone out of their way to treat Zach as one of the family, despite the distance that separated them, and Zach always remembered Isabel's birthday with some sort of stuffed animal or toy. It would be nice to see them all again, he thought wistfully. He glanced down at the molded pewter ring on his finger that had been their parting gift to him, and recalled the inscription: Friends—Always. And they would be, he knew.

On impulse, Zach leaned forward and checked his E-mail. He hadn't heard from Josef in over two weeks, and he was starting to worry. Though Josef never said it in so many words, Zach knew he was growing increasingly concerned about the deteriorating conditions in his country. He and Katrina rarely went out anymore with friends, and Isabel spent most of her time indoors for safety reasons. Josef's powerful, persuasive writing was also attracting more and more attention from opposing factions, and Zach had begun urging him to use caution. But that word wasn't in Josef's vocabulary, not when he felt he was doing the right thing. Although Zach suspected that there was a very real danger for his friend, Josef downplayed it.

This time, when Zach opened his mailbox, he was rewarded with a note from his friend, and he eagerly scanned it. But it wasn't the kind of message he had hoped for.

Things are not very good for us right now, Zachary. Katrina has had a miscarriage and is very ill. I wish we could be in St. Louis, with good Dr. Anderson, who took such fine care of her when Isabel was born. But that is not the Lord's will, it seems. We must stay here and hope that He will watch over us.

I cannot write much now, my friend. It is not safe here at the newspaper office. We will be moving again soon. It seems that our talk of freedom is causing much distress to the powers that be. But still we persevere, for the torch must be carried.

I hope, Zachary, that all is well with you. I think often of our happy days at Mizzou. It was a good time, was it not? So much hope and enthusiasm and optimism. We were going to change the world, you and I. Remember? And we are, you know. It is just very slow work. But I carry on, firmly believing that this is what the Lord intends me to do.

I will write again when the opportunity arises, my friend. Now I must return to Katrina, who gives my life so much joy. I pray that she will quickly be well again. And I pray also that peace will soon return to our troubled country.

Zach rested his elbows on his desk and steepled his fingers, a frown creasing his brow as he scanned Joseph's message a second time. He hadn't even known about Katrina's pregnancy. He assumed it had been by accident, not design. After her first difficult pregnancy and delivery, the doctors had warned her that attempts to have more children could be extremely dangerous. And Josef loved her too much to risk that.

Zach wished there was some way he could help his friend. Long ago he and Josef had promised each other that should either ever be in need, the other had only to ask and help would be on the way. But Josef hadn't made such a request. Probably because he knew there was nothing Zach could do. Except maybe pray.

But unlike Josef, who was a religious man, Zach's once-solid faith had withered and died in the alleys and slums of St. Louis. Yet he took a moment now, in case there really was anyone listening upstairs, to ask for protection for his friend and his family. Because Zach was beginning to suspect that only a Higher Power would be able to keep them safe.

Chapter Four

Rebecca sighed and reached up to secure a wayward pin in her French twist. The last few days had been tough. She was putting in her usual long hours at the restaurant, then spending every spare minute sandbagging. The rain hadn't abated, and despite the diligent efforts of the townspeople and the National Guard, it appeared that the flooding would be severe and widespread. Rebecca hadn't been in town during the last flood, several years before, but stories of the horror survived. Families homeless, businesses ruined, hundreds of lives turned upside down. She paused for a moment and closed her eyes. *Please, Lord, keep everyone safe,* she prayed. *And help us all realize that lives are more precious than things.*

Rebecca opened her eyes and glanced at the clock, sighing once again. Ten at night was not an ideal time to be getting ready for tomorrow's scheduled bridal shower in the restaurant. But the work had to be done, even if she was bone weary after sandbagging for three hours earlier in the evening. Thank heavens Zach had more or less dragged her off that sandbag line two nights ago! Even though her sleep had been restless that night, disrupted by both sore muscles and conflicting emotions about her "rescuer," at least her body had gotten some much-needed rest. That had helped carry her through the next couple of days. But the reserve was starting to wear thin. Maybe if she worked quickly tonight, she'd get home before midnight, she thought hopefully.

Rebecca checked the consistency of the potato leek soup and, with a satisfied nod, turned off the blender. Now she just had to finish up a couple of special items for the shower and she'd be done.

As she walked toward the refrigerator, a sudden knock on the back door startled her, and she stopped abruptly, glancing toward the door with a frown. Who in the world could be here at this hour?

Leaving the chain firmly in place, she opened the door an inch or two and peered out into the rainy darkness, her eyes widening when she recognized the visitor. "Zach! What are you doing here?" she asked in astonishment.

"I was driving by and thought I saw the light on back here. I just wanted to make sure everything was all right."

"Oh. Yes. I'm fine. Thanks. Just catching up on a few things."

He turned his collar up and dug his hands into the pockets of his coat, propping one shoulder against the door frame as he sniffed appreciatively. "It sure smells good in there."

Rebecca frowned. "Didn't you have dinner?"

He shrugged. "I've been working. And I pitched in for a little while with the sandbagging. Can't you tell?" he asked with a crooked grin, glancing down at his mud-splattered jeans. "Fortunately someone loaned me a slicker, or I'd look a whole lot worse than this."

Rebecca scanned his form in one swift glance. He looked cold and wet and—as her eyes came back to rest on his face—tired. There were lines at the corners of his eyes, furrows on his brow. And his mouth looked strained, as if he was in pain. She frowned and bit her lip. "Do you think you should be sandbagging, Zach? It's been less than two weeks since you had the concussion. Didn't the doctor tell you to take it easy for a while?"

He dismissed her concern with a shrug. "I feel okay. At least I did until a little while ago, when I started to get a headache. I just need some rest and I'll be fine. I'm just going to grab a bite somewhere and call it a night." He straightened up and smiled. "Well, I'll see you around."

"Zach . . ." She couldn't just let him walk away. Not when he was cold and hungry and in pain. It wasn't right. Besides, he'd gone out of his way for her two nights ago and spent this evening helping with the sandbagging. She could at least offer him some soup. It would be the kind thing to do—even if it wasn't the smart thing, she acknowledged. Not when her heart went into overdrive every time she was in his presence. But her conscience prickled, telling her she was being self-centered. With a sigh of capitulation, she shut the door and slid the chain free, then swung the door open. "Would you like a bowl of soup?"

He frowned and dug his hands deeper into the pockets of his coat. "I wasn't angling for a meal, Rebecca," he said slowly. "I just wanted to make sure everything was okay."

"I know. And I appreciate that. I also appreciated the lift home the other night."

"I'm glad. I was afraid you'd think I was a little too heavy-handed."

She shrugged, smiling faintly. "I did," she admitted. "But you were right. Anyway, I just made some soup, and you're welcome to a bowl."

"Well . . ." He hesitated for another moment, then sniffed appreciatively. "Okay. I can't resist that aroma."

She moved aside to allow him to pass, then shut the door and slid the chain back into place. She watched him shrug out of his jacket and hang it on a hook by the door, then rake his fingers through his wet hair. As he did so, she saw the angry red welt near his hairline. It was obvious that the stitches had only been recently removed.

"It's not as bad as it looks," he assured her with a smile.

Her gaze dropped from the injured area to his eyes, and she flushed. "I didn't mean to stare."

He shrugged. "That's okay. I realize it's not a pretty sight. So much for any hopes I might have had for a modeling career," he joked good-naturedly.

The scar didn't mar his rugged appeal one iota as far as Rebecca was concerned, but she decided it was safer to make a quick comment and then move on. "It will fade in time. Why don't you go ahead and sit down while I get the soup."

"I threw a spare pair of shoes in the car before I left the motel, so at least I won't track mud on your floor," he told her with a grin, strolling toward the center island. "But I'm starting to run out of dry clothes."

"Aren't we all," she empathized, heading for the stove. She ladled a generous serving of soup into a bowl, then added a couple of pieces of homemade bread and some butter. When she turned he was sitting on a stool at the counter, and he grinned disarmingly as she set the food in front of him.

"Well, this is a first," he noted.

"What do you mean?"

"Eating in the kitchen. I have to say, I prefer the atmosphere in the dining room, but the company's better here."

Rebecca flushed and turned away to fiddle with a pot on the stove.

"So what are you doing here at this hour, anyway?" he asked, attacking the soup with vigor.

"I'm running a little behind," she explained, reaching up nervously to secure another hairpin. "Frances has the flu, so I'm shorthanded. And I have a special party tomorrow—a bridal shower—which is extra work, too." She was babbling, and she knew it.

Zach paused and studied her with a frown. "Are you still sandbagging?"

She turned to look at him in surprise. "Of course."

"That kind of work is too hard for you, Rebecca," he said quietly.

She shrugged dismissively, though she couldn't so easily dismiss the tingle of pleasure that ran through her at his concern. "I can manage. Besides, every pair of hands helps."

"But do you really have to go every night, after putting in a full day here?"

"These are my friends and neighbors, Zach," she said with quiet sincerity. "This is how life is in a small town. We help each other. It's the best way I know of to put The Golden Rule into practice."

Zach didn't have a rebuttal for that comment. Rebecca clearly took her faith seriously and believed in living the principles, not just talking about them. He admired her for that. But she was pushing herself too hard. "Isn't there some other way you could help that isn't so physically taxing?" he persisted.

"Sandbagging is where the hands are needed," she replied lightly, still touched by his concern. "Besides, it's good for the waistline."

His eyes dropped automatically to the referenced part of her anatomy, then quickly returned to hers. Even under a voluminous white apron, it was clear that her waistline was already in great shape. It was also clear that he wasn't going to be able to convince her to cut back on her volunteer efforts. Nevertheless, he tried once more. "Rebecca, whether you realize it or not, you need more rest."

"I'll be done here soon."

A flash of inspiration suddenly hit, and he smiled. "Well, you'll be done even sooner if I help," he said determinedly.

"Help?" she parroted blankly.

"Sure. I don't mind. What do you want me to do?" He set his spoon down and loosened his cuffs, rolling up his sleeves to the elbows.

"Really . . . you don't have to do that," she protested faintly.

"Oh, give me a chance," he cajoled, his eyes twinkling. "I'm not the world's greatest cook, but I can do simple stuff. I promise I won't poison any of your customers."

"It's not that . . ."

"Look, think about it while I finish the soup, okay? I'm sure you can find something for me to do."

"But you're tired, too. And you haven't fully recovered from the concussion. You admitted you have a headache. You need some rest, Zach."

"The headache's much better now. I think the soup did the trick. Besides, if I help, you can get home a little bit sooner."

When he put it that way, the offer *was* tempting. And why not? she thought. He was already here, anyway. In sudden decision she walked over to the refrigerator and withdrew a bowl of crab salad and some Belgian endive.

"Okay. I just need the endive leaves filled. Here, I'll show you how," she said, deftly demonstrating.

He watched her for a moment, then nodded confidently. "I can handle that," he assured her, taking the spoon out of her fingers. "You go ahead and do whatever else needs to be done."

Rebecca focused on chopping the green part of the leek for the soup garnish, stealing occasional glances at Zach as she worked. His brow was knit in concentration, but he was doing well, she thought, her gaze dropping to his hands—strong, capable, confident. She'd noticed his hands that night in the car, and she remembered her summation at the time—that they would be equally at home chopping wood . . . or caressing a woman.

"So how am I doing?"

Rebecca's startled gaze flew to his, and she flushed guiltily, turning away quickly to hide the telltale blush. "Fine, great," she mumbled, trying to quiet her rapid pulse. Change the subject, she told herself. Get your mind on something else. "I hear you're going to lecture at the high school," she remarked, striving futilely for a casual, conversational tone.

If he noticed that her voice was slightly breathless, he made no comment. He just shook his head and grinned. "I'd say the grapevine is alive and active in St. Genevieve."

Rebecca smiled. "Word does travel fast in a small town. Mark lives on the same street as Phil Carr, who told him, and Mark told me. Being in a classroom will be quite a switch for you, won't it?"

"Mmm-hmm. But believe it or not, I almost became a teacher. In fact, I double majored in college. But when I graduated I was offered a newspaper job that was too good to pass up, so my teaching career ended before it began."

"You usually do investigative work, right?"

"Mmm-hmm."

"That must be pretty exciting."

He shrugged. "It used to be," he replied, methodically working his way through the crab salad as he spoke. "But I was never in it for the excitement. I did it because I thought I could make a difference, change the world for the better. But as I've recently come to realize, that was a pretty naive attitude. The truth is I spent fifteen years tilting at windmills. Nothing I did made any difference," he said, a trace of bitterness creeping into his voice. "I'm actually thinking of taking some time off to reevaluate whether I want to spend the rest of my life doing something that really doesn't seem to matter."

Rebecca frowned. "I have a feeling you're being too harsh on yourself, Zach. I think everything we do makes a difference, even if we don't see the results right away. I really believe that good work is never lost."

Zach sent her a startled look, a strange expression on his face. "That's odd," he remarked softly.

She tilted her head and looked at him quizzically. "What?"

"What you just said. I have a friend who used almost those same words once."

"Really?"

"Uh-huh. He's a reporter, too. In Eastern Europe. Despite the chaos in his country, and the setbacks and lack of visible progress, he still believes his efforts are making a difference."

"He sounds like a man of faith," Rebecca surmised.

"Yeah," Zach replied with a nod. "He is."

"Faith can be a great source of encouragement."

Zach gave her a skeptical look. "Maybe. But somewhere along the way mine evaporated. I guess I dealt with the seamy side of life for too long. There was very little evidence of God on my beat."

"I suppose working in that environment could put your faith to the test," Rebecca conceded slowly. "But you know, that's the beautiful thing about God. We may abandon Him, but He never abandons us."

Zach studied the woman across from him. He admired her faith. Even envied it a little. Much as he envied Josef's. He wished he had their conviction, their certainty. But he didn't, not anymore, and it was too late tonight to even think about it. He reached for a towel and wiped his hands, then stood up and rolled down his sleeves. "Well, are you about ready to call it a night?"

Rebecca nodded. "I just need to turn out the lights."

He picked up the tray of endive. "Where do you want this?"

She opened the refrigerator door. "In here. Top shelf."

As he slid the tray in, his glance fell on a decorated cake on the counter. Although several pieces were missing, enough of the greeting remained to indicate that it had contained a birthday message for Rebecca. "Is today your birthday?" he asked in surprise.

She flushed. "Yes. Frances and Rose brought the cake in, which was very sweet. But to be honest, with everything going on I only had time for a quick sample. Would you like to take a piece with you?"

"No, but thanks." He looked at her thoughtfully. "So what did you do to celebrate?" he asked, knowing the answer even before she spoke.

Other than a phone call from her father, and one from Brad and Sam who invited her up for a belated birthday dinner when things settled down with the new baby, it had been a day like any other.

Special days didn't mean a lot when you lived alone. But she'd successfully kept that thought at bay throughout the day, and she wasn't going to start feeling sorry for herself now.

She forced herself to smile brightly as she answered Zach. "I was way too busy," she replied, striving for a careless, it-doesn't-matter tone. She wasn't sure if she fooled him, so before he could pursue the subject, she hung her apron on a hook and reached for her purse. "Listen, thanks a lot, Zach. I'll just turn out the lights and lock up. Go on home and get some rest yourself."

"I'll walk you to your car first."

Rebecca opened her mouth to protest, took one look at his determined face and closed it. She recognized that look from the other night. "Okay. Give me a minute."

It took less than that, and as she locked the door she nodded toward her older-model compact car parked a few feet away. "I'm right over here," she told him. "And thank heavens it's finally stopped raining!"

"We could do with some dry weather," he agreed.

Rebecca was tinglingly aware of him close behind her as she walked to her car and fumbled with the key. When she at last fitted it into the lock and swung the door open, she breathed a sigh of relief. In a few moments she could drive away, escape from this man who always made her heart behave erratically.

But instead of leaving, as she expected, Zach leaned on top of the door and looked at her, his face deeply shadowed and largely unreadable in the dim light. There was silence for a moment, and although he didn't move, Rebecca intuitively knew that he'd like to touch her. Her nerve endings started to sizzle, and her breath lodged in her throat.

"You know I'd still like to take you out," he said at last, without preamble, his voice deep and husky.

Rebecca dropped her gaze. "I don't date, Zach," she reminded him, her voice uneven. "I told you that."

"And I told you I was going to try and change your mind. You even gave me a yellow light. Remember?"

"Yes," she whispered.

"You do like me, don't you, Rebecca?" he asked gently, his voice soft and coaxing.

She nodded mutely.

"Then why don't you let me in on your secret?"

Startled, her gaze snapped to his and she frowned. "What secret?"

"About why I make you so nervous."

To deny it would be foolish, so she didn't try. "It's getting late," she replied instead.

He sighed heavily. "I guess that's about the response I expected. But I figured it wouldn't hurt to ask."

"Why don't you just give up, Zach?" she asked with a dispirited sigh.

He shook his head slowly. "That's not my style."

Rebecca dropped her gaze and fidgeted with the door lock. She'd assumed as much. Zach was a man of determination and action, who clearly liked challenges. And that was probably all she was to him, she thought bleakly. Which was one more reason *not* to get involved, she told herself firmly. Okay, so she'd promised herself on Valentine's Day that if a man came along who seemed worth taking a chance on, she would risk opening herself to a relationship one more time. And Zach seemed like such a man. But circumstances were against them. First of all, she suspected their natures were quite different. She was slow, cautious and timid. He was fast, impetuous and brash. Patience was not a virtue she would ascribe to him. But it was a virtue that any man truly interested in her would have to possess. Besides, Zach would only be in town for a brief time—not a good omen for a long-term relationship. No, he was wrong for her, she thought resolutely. It was as simple as that.

But his expression when she looked back at him to say goodnight was anything but simple, and her words died in her throat. His eyes held hers with fierce intensity, reflecting a myriad of emotions. Hunger. Frustration. Passion. Tenderness. Confusion. And though the parking lot was only dimly lit, she could also tell from his faint frown that some sort of internal debate was taking place.

Suddenly, with a jolt, she had a feeling she knew exactly what that debate was about. She swallowed convulsively and nervously licked her lips.

Zach's gaze dropped to their ripe fullness, and now it was his turn to swallow with difficulty. Actually, kissing Rebecca wasn't something he'd seriously considered tonight. At least not until now.

Sensing that she'd respond best to casual, nonthreatening behavior, he'd made an effort to keep things pretty lighthearted.

But suddenly he decided to throw caution to the wind, to give her some concrete evidence of his attraction. Words were getting him nowhere. Maybe action was the answer. At least enough action to let her know in no uncertain terms that he was serious in his intentions to get to know her better.

Slowly he moved out from behind the car door until he was standing directly in front of her. His eyes still locked on hers, he reached over and traced a gentle finger across her eyebrow and down her cheek. Then his hand dropped to the side of her neck, his thumb gently stroking the remnants of the bruise on her chin.

Rebecca knew exactly where this was leading. Zach was going to kiss her. She ought to pull away before she freaked out. But for some strange reason she didn't feel threatened. Yes, they were alone. Yes, Zach was a lot bigger and stronger than she was. Yes, he could easily overpower her. But Rebecca didn't sense any ill intent in his touch. It was gentle and caring and tender. Still, she ought to back off, for all the reasons she'd mentally ticked off just moments before. Except that she suddenly couldn't remember even one of them.

Zach studied her eyes, trying to decipher the conflicting emotions in them, attempting to determine if desire was stronger than uncertainty. He couldn't tell for sure. And there was only one way to find out. Slowly, his gaze riveted on hers till the last possible moment, he leaned toward her, his eyes telegraphing a message that even in her agitated state Rebecca couldn't miss. *Don't be afraid,* they said. *I won't hurt you. Trust me. Everything will be all right.* Then, letting his hand drift to her nape, he slowly lowered his mouth to meet hers.

It was a simple kiss, as light as a drifting leaf, a gentle, uncomplicated connecting of lips. But Rebecca's reaction wasn't uncomplicated in the least. A thousand sensations washed over her, and she felt caught in a riptide of sweeping emotion. There was so much to take in! Zach's hand cradling her head, his touch sure and confident. His warm lips, undemanding and gentle, moving over hers, awakening a response that sent her world spinning out of orbit. The woodsy scent of his aftershave wafting around her, and the distant, plaintive echo of a train whistle.

Rebecca knew, deep in her heart, that every time she heard that mellow sound for the rest of her life she would remember this moment. Not just because of the sensory overload that left her breathless and trembling, but because she wasn't afraid. For whatever reason, by some miracle, she didn't panic! She felt shaky and off balance, true, but it was an unsteadiness born of yearning, not fear. It was a new, heady experience for Rebecca, and she did what she never thought she'd be able to do. She responded, returning his kiss as best she knew how.

Zach had imagined how Rebecca's lips would feel against his. But nothing had prepared him for their innocent sweetness. At her age most women generally had plenty of practice in the art of romance. But not Rebecca, whose simple, straightforward kiss was that of a schoolgirl, reflecting absolute inexperience. Zach was stunned—but not displeased. He found her almost-timid shyness refreshing—and extremely appealing.

Other than the soft meeting of their lips and his hand on her neck, Zach didn't touch her. He left his other hand in his pocket, somehow sensing that was the right thing to do. He just savored the moment. At last, with reluctance, he released her.

For several moments she kept her eyes closed, too lost in the magic of his touch to tolerate the intrusion of reality. But finally, with a wistful little sigh that caught at his heart, she opened her eyes and gazed up at him in wonder.

A tender smile tugged at the corners of his mouth. "Happy birthday, Rebecca," he murmured, his voice strangely hoarse.

His hand was still at her nape, his fingers gently stroking the back of her neck, and she was finding it extremely difficult to breathe. "Th-thank you," she stammered softly, her own voice uneven.

"You know, I have an idea," he said softly. Actually, he had plenty of ideas at the moment, only one of which he intended to discuss. "Since you really didn't get to do anything special for your birthday, how about having dinner with me Sunday? Sort of a belated celebration. We could drive up to St. Louis, maybe go to the Hill, if you like Italian. Do you?"

She was staring at him, mesmerized by the tender light in his deep brown eyes. "Do I what?" she asked, trying to follow the conversation, but having a difficult time concentrating on anything but his eyes.

"Like Italian food."

"Oh. Sure."

"Then you'll go?"

Tell him no, her mind instructed firmly. *Think, don't feel. Be rational.* But her heart had other ideas. "Uh-huh."

His smile broadened, and the warmth in his eyes took her breath away. "Great! I'll call to set it up, okay?"

"Okay."

He hesitated for a moment, his eyes caressing her face. Then he leaned forward and once more brushed his lips over hers, the brief contact leaving her yearning for more.

"Good night, Rebecca. Sweet dreams."

She slid into her car, then turned to watch him stride toward his as she sighed contentedly. *No problem, Mr. Wright,* she thought. Sweet dreams are a guarantee.

"My goodness!" Rose said, glancing around the kitchen in surprise. "We came in extra early to help you get ready for that shower, but you've got everything done!"

"Yes. It didn't take as long as I thought," Rebecca replied vaguely, turning to Frances. "How are you feeling?"

"Right as rain," she declared. "Nasty bug, though. I'm glad it's over. Did you work late last night?"

"Mmm-hmm."

"Say, what's this?" Frances asked in surprise.

Rebecca turned. The woman was examining a ring—Zach's ring, to be exact. He must have taken it off when he was helping last night and then left without it, she realized in dismay. Rebecca's face turned bright pink, and she reached for it, dropping it into the pocket of her apron. "It's Zach's. He stopped by last night while I was working," she said shortly.

Rose sent Frances a knowing glance, which Rebecca intercepted. "Now don't you two get any matchmaking ideas," she warned.

Rose smiled at her innocently. "Of course not, dear. Just because the man sends you flowers, comes in three times a week for lunch and happens to drop by late at night—why would we get any ideas?"

Rebecca's flush deepened. "Well, it doesn't mean anything," she stated dismissively. "He's new in town and he doesn't know that many people yet. I'm just a familiar face."

"I'd say that 'familiar' is exactly what he'd like to be," Frances remarked pertly.

"For heaven's sake, you two are hopeless!" Rebecca declared in exasperation.

"Well, that young man is going to start feeling pretty hopeless himself, if you don't give in and go out with him soon," Rose told her.

Rebecca turned away and stirred the soup. It was useless to try and hide the fact that she'd accepted his dinner invitation. People would find out somehow. They always did in a small town. So she might as well be up-front about it, pretend it was no big deal. "Actually, I'm having dinner with him Sunday," she informed the sisters, striving to keep her tone light, hoping to make the date sound inconsequential. But the dead silence that met her revelation told her that she wasn't fooling anyone. Taking a deep breath, she looked over her shoulder to find them both beaming at her approvingly.

"Well, it's about time!" Frances declared. "I'm glad that poor boy's persistence finally paid off. Such a nice young man!"

Rebecca set down the ladle and turned to face Rose and Frances, her hands on her hips, her gaze stern. She needed to stop any rumors before they even started. "Before you get too carried away, remember that Zach and I are just acquaintances. Period. So you better just get these romantic notions out of your heads right now."

"Of course, dear. We certainly will," Rose promised agreeably.

Rebecca congratulated herself, convinced that she'd succeeded in dampening their enthusiasm—until Rose stopped to toss a prediction over her shoulder as she headed for the dining room. "But I don't think it will be easy to convince that young man to do the same."

Rebecca didn't reply. What was the point—when she knew Rose was right?

Chapter Five

❦

Rebecca eyed her reflection critically in the full-length mirror behind her bedroom door and frowned. Was she overdressed? she wondered worriedly. Except for the night in the fog, when he'd been wearing a suit, she'd never seen Zach in anything more formal than khaki slacks and a cotton shirt. He hadn't told her where they were going on the Hill, St. Louis's well-known Italian neighborhood, and the restaurants ranged from corner pizza parlors to elegant gourmet eateries. If they ended up at the pizza end of the spectrum, her beaded white angora sweater and slim wool burgundy skirt were definitely going to be out of place. But worrying wasn't going to solve the dilemma, she thought with a sigh as she reached up to tuck a couple of stray strands of hair into her French twist. If she was dressed inappropriately, she'd find out soon enough.

The more important question was why she'd even agreed to this date in the first place. Logically, it was the wrong thing to do. She knew that. But somehow, in her heart, it *seemed* right. And her heart, rather than her mind, had guided her decision, she admitted. Even now, as she recalled the tender feel of Zach's lips on hers, his hand cradling her neck as he kissed her, a surprisingly intense surge of longing swept over her. She closed her eyes and slowly exhaled a shaky breath. Yes, accepting the date felt right. Because for some reason his touch hadn't frightened her. It was almost like a sign, she thought, an indication that she should give this relationship a chance. Maybe the Lord was trying to nudge her forward. She *had* asked for His help, after all. Perhaps Zach was—

The sudden ringing of the doorbell made her eyes fly open, and she turned with a start toward the sound, her pulse accelerating as she reached up with trembling fingers to nervously smooth her hair one final time. With a silent plea for courage, she drew a long, steadying breath and moved toward the door, turning the dead bolt and unhooking the security guards at the top and bottom with trembling hands.

As she swung the door open, she realized instantly that she was *not* overdressed. Zach wore a charcoal gray suit, which sat well on his broad shoulders and emphasized his muscular physique, and a burgundy-and-silver-striped tie rested against the crisply starched white shirt that hugged his broad chest. He looked impressive, distinguished, suave, incredibly handsome—in other words, absolutely fantastic, she thought appreciatively, her heart banging against her rib cage as she gripped the edge of the door.

While Rebecca completed her perusal, Zach did his own in one swift, comprehensive glance that missed nothing—the glitter of beads on her sweater; the pulse beating in the delicate hollow at the base of her throat; her beautiful eyes, wider than usual tonight as they gazed up at him with a touch of trepidation; and the classic bone structure of her face, highlighted by her sophisticated French twist.

His gaze lingered for a moment on her hair. The style suited her, but he'd love to see what her hair looked like loose and free, the russet highlights glinting as the waves tumbled around her shoulders. He imagined what it would be like to run his hands through those burnished tresses, feel their softness against his fingertips . . .

"Hi," Rebecca said timidly, abruptly interrupting his fantasy.

"Hi," he returned huskily, firmly reining in his wayward thoughts. He let his gaze travel over her once more, not even attempting to hide the appreciation in his eyes. "Has anyone told you lately that you look lovely?"

She flushed and turned away on the pretext of retrieving her purse. "Not that I recall," she replied, striving for a light tone yet secretly pleased by his compliment. "You look very nice tonight, too."

"I don't wear suits often," he admitted as he strolled into the tiny foyer behind her. "Only on special occasions."

So he considered tonight a special occasion, she thought, a delicious tingle running down her spine. *But it could be just a line,* she reminded herself. *Don't get carried away.* She knew he was smooth, practiced, probably very accomplished in the art of seduction. He was the type of man who would know exactly what to say to please a woman. She shouldn't take it too personally.

"Nice apartment," he commented, his gaze traveling around the living room. Chintz-covered couches and chairs, lace curtains, a heart-shaped dried flower wreath on the wall and family pictures artfully arranged in a collection of frames on an end table all combined to give the room a warm, homey feel.

"Thanks. It will do for a while, but eventually I'd like to get a house with some land at the edge of town. My dad is a great gardener, and he got me hooked on the hobby. I miss not being able to work with flowers."

"It doesn't seem as if you have much time for that sort of thing, anyway."

She gave him a rueful smile. "That's true. The restaurant is pretty demanding."

"Speaking of food," he said with a smile. "I have reservations for seven-thirty, so if you're ready we might as well head out."

"Okay. Is it cool enough for a coat?" The weather had been unseasonably mild for the past day or so, providing a much-needed glimpse of spring to the winter-weary, flood-exhausted residents.

"I don't think so. It's a nice night, and that sweater looks pretty warm." And *very* attractive, he acknowledged silently. But he needed to keep such thoughts on ice, he told himself firmly as he stepped aside for her to pass. Later, if things went well, maybe he could allow them to resurface. And perhaps even pursue them.

As they drove into the city, Zach purposely kept the banter light. He knew Rebecca was uncomfortable with this date, had half expected her to cancel. His goal for the moment was to get her to relax, to enjoy his company. Because he didn't want this to be a one-time event.

By the time they arrived in St. Louis, she did seem to be more at ease, but as they pulled up in front of the restaurant her voice died in mid-sentence even as her eyes widened in surprise. He had chosen one of the finest, priciest restaurants on the Hill for tonight's dinner date.

"Zach! I never expected anything like this," she exclaimed, completely taken aback.

He smiled, pleased at her reaction. "I hoped you would like it."

"Like it! That's an understatement! I only know this place by reputation, but I've always wanted to eat here. It's just too expensive." Suddenly she frowned and turned to him. "Zach, this will cost a fortune! I can't let you spend that kind of money on me. We hardly know each other!" she protested.

"Well, I intend to remedy that. Starting tonight. Just think of this as a birthday gift, Rebecca. And I'll let you in on a little secret," he added with a smile, leaning closer to drape an arm casually across the back of her seat, his fingers brushing her shoulder. "It may not be my birthday, but I definitely consider this date a gift. Thank you for coming tonight."

Rebecca was too stunned by his candor to reply. Fortunately she didn't have to. Just then the valet opened her door. Zach winked at her before removing his arm from the back of her seat, and it was all she could do to keep her thoughts coherent as she stepped from the car. He joined her immediately, his hand resting lightly but proprietarily against the small of her back as they walked toward the restaurant, and somehow she knew that no matter what happened in the future between them, she'd always remember this birthday celebration as one of the most special of her life.

The dinner was everything Rebecca had expected—and more— and she even drank a little wine, a rare indulgence for her. But tonight it seemed appropriate, and as the meal progressed she grew mellow and relaxed, smiling and laughing freely. Zach was an ideal dinner companion—witty, well-read, an excellent conversationalist, moving with ease from one topic to another. She found herself telling him about her hometown, about Brad and Sam and their new daughter, about the satisfaction of making her dreams of owning her own restaurant a reality. Zach skillfully drew her out, asking all the right questions, until finally she paused to laugh.

"What's so funny?" he asked with a smile, his fingers idly playing with the stem of his wineglass as he gazed at her quizzically.

She shook her head and grinned ruefully. "I have a feeling you're *very* good at your job."

"What do you mean?"

"You've managed to find out an awful lot about me in a very short time. That skill must come in handy in your work."

He grinned. "I suppose so. But tonight my questions are motivated purely by personal interest," he replied candidly. What he *didn't* tell her was that he hadn't found out the one thing he was most interested in—why she rarely dated. He'd tried a couple of subtle probes, but she'd adeptly sidestepped them. And he didn't think pressing the issue was a good idea.

"So tell me about you, Zach," she said, interrupting his thoughts.

He shrugged. "Not much to tell, really. I grew up in Kansas City, and my mom still lives there. So does my older brother and his family. I went to Mizzou, became a journalist and *voilà!* Here I am."

"Talk about a condensed version of a life story!" she protested. "I guess I'll just have to ask a few questions of my own. What brought you to St. Genevieve? I don't know much about the newspaper business, but a flood doesn't seem like the usual sort of thing an investigative reporter would cover."

"You're right," he acknowledged. "I've been working on a series on corruption in city government, and a couple of the people implicated got wind of it. They claimed I was using falsified documents as a basis for my coverage and threatened to sue the paper if the series ran. So the publisher put a hold on the story while they look into the charges, and sent me off to St. Genevieve for the duration. Mostly to keep me out of the way, I assume."

Rebecca frowned. "No wonder you sounded so burned out about reporting when we talked the other night."

He shrugged. "It wasn't just that. There have been lots of instances through the years when a piece has blown up in my face, or people have found a way to work around the system and get away with murder. Sometimes literally. I think this was just the proverbial straw that broke the camel's back. To be honest, my editor actually realized before I did that a break from investigative work would be good for me," he admitted.

"How do you know?" Rebecca asked curiously.

"At our last meeting he said I needed some time to decompress and regain my perspective. I didn't buy it then. But now that I've been away for a couple of weeks, I have to admit that he's right. In fact, since I talked to that class at the high school on Friday, I'd go even further. I don't just need time away from investigative work. I need time away, period."

"It sounds like a good idea," Rebecca agreed. "Can you manage it?"

He nodded. "I have quite a bit of vacation accumulated. It shouldn't be an issue. In fact, when Ted—my managing editor— called yesterday, I told him that I'm thinking about taking some time off when this assignment is over. Being in the classroom with those kids was a catalyst, in a sense. It reminded me why I was attracted to teaching in the first place—and also that there's a whole world out there apart from journalism and a lot of ways to make a difference in the human condition. I'm going to think about it for a couple more days, but I've pretty much decided that a long vacation would be a good idea."

"It does seem to make sense," Rebecca concurred. Then she propped her chin in her hand and tilted her head as she studied him. "You know, I imagine you'd probably be a really good teacher."

He smiled. "Why do you say that?"

She considered the question seriously, frowning slightly. "Well, you've been out in the real world. You talk from experience. Kids respect that. And you have an intensity . . . a commitment, I guess is the right word . . . plus a real sense of integrity, that would be inspiring to young people. Not to mention the fact that you're obviously an intelligent, well-read, articulate person."

Zach was taken aback by her unexpectedly flattering assessment, and he felt his neck redden. He wasn't a man who handled praise well. It made him uncomfortable. "Well, I think you're being too generous, but I do appreciate the kind words."

She gazed at him speculatively, an idea forming in her mind. "Did you know that Phil Carr hurt his back sandbagging last night?" she asked suddenly.

Zach frowned. "No."

"I found out this morning at church. It sounds like he'll be out of commission for the rest of the semester. They'll be looking for a replacement to come in when spring break ends next Monday."

Zach digested that piece of news in silence for several seconds. When he spoke, his tone was thoughtful. "That suggests some interesting possibilities," he mused. On a lot of fronts, he added silently. A trial run at teaching appealed to him. So did staying close to Rebecca. And he could use some time not only away from reporting, but away from the city, when this assignment was finished. Which would be soon, given that the flood waters had crested. But the teaching slot was probably a long shot. "I'm sure they have people in mind already," he said.

Rebecca shook her head. "I don't think so. At least not on such short notice—*and* for a several-week stint."

"Hmm. Well, I'll have to give that some thought," he said noncommittally. Then he placed his napkin on the table and smiled. "So . . . are you ready to head back?"

Not really, she thought. The evening had been so enjoyable that she hated for it to end. But she couldn't think of any reason to delay the inevitable, so she summoned up a smile. "If I can move, after all that food," she joked. "It was wonderful, Zach. Thank you."

"It was my pleasure."

The ride back was pleasant. The conversation flowed naturally, punctuated by periods of comfortable, contented silence that allowed time for reflection. Zach had proven to be a wonderful companion, Rebecca thought. She couldn't remember the last time she'd been out with a man socially and felt so relaxed.

But relaxation slowly changed to anticipation as they approached St. Genevieve. Would he kiss her good night again? she wondered, her nerve endings beginning to tingle. She had enjoyed their last kiss, much to her surprise, and she wasn't averse to repeating the experience. No, that wasn't quite accurate, she admitted honestly. She *wanted* to repeat the experience. She wanted him to touch her in that gentle, nonthreatening way, wanted to savor the tender feel of his hand on her cheek. She found it hard to believe, after years of avoiding that type of experience, that she was now looking forward to it. She only hoped Zach was, too!

When they pulled up in front of her apartment, he turned off the engine and angled himself toward her, draping his arm across the back of her seat. "Home safe and sound," he announced lightly.

Rebecca tried to smile, but suddenly her lips felt stiff. She had very limited experience in this good night business, and she suddenly wondered if she was supposed to invite him in. But that scared her. It was too . . . intimate. For all she knew, inviting a man in also implied an invitation for more, and she figured she'd better not take the risk. "I had a great time, Zach," she offered, her voice quavering slightly.

"So did I."

His fingers were brushing her shoulder lightly now, back and forth, back and forth, and she suddenly found it difficult to breathe. She tried to discern the intent in his eyes, but in the dim light his expression was unreadable. She dropped her gaze, playing nervously with the clasp of her purse as she searched for something else to say, anything, to break the electric silence between them, but her mind went blank.

Zach knew Rebecca was nervous. It would take a total clod to miss the signs. But he also knew he was going to kiss her. She'd been nervous the last time, too, but she'd responded once he'd initiated the kiss. He hoped she would do the same tonight. Because for the last twenty minutes that had been the only thing on his mind. He wanted to feel her soft, pliant lips against his, wanted to run his fingertips across her silky skin, wanted to hold her so close that he could feel the thudding of her heart against his chest. And Zach was a man used to getting what he wanted. Not that he ever had to push. He had learned through the years to accurately assess a woman's interest and he didn't waste time and energy pursuing unwilling partners. Though he knew Rebecca was nervous, he also knew she was willing. And interested. She just seemed to need a little coaxing.

Zach didn't much relish the idea of kissing Rebecca in the car, however. There was too much in the way. For example, the gearshift would definitely hamper his style, he thought wryly. But she hadn't said anything about coming in. His gaze flickered away from her momentarily to scan the surroundings, coming to rest on a secluded bench discreetly tucked between two pine trees. Thank goodness it was a mild, dry night, he thought in relief.

Slowly he withdrew his arm and smiled at Rebecca. "If you're not in a hurry, we could sit for a while," he suggested casually, his tone giving away none of the anticipatory tension that was slowly beginning to build inside him. "It's a nice night, and there's a convenient bench right over there," he noted, nodding toward the pine trees.

Rebecca swallowed. This was what she wanted, wasn't it? So why did she suddenly feel so nervous and uncertain? Everything would be fine. She was only a few steps from her door, not trapped at a secluded scenic overlook or miles from help, should she need it. Which she wouldn't. *Take a deep breath and relax,* she told herself.

"Okay," she agreed, trying to steady the tremor in her voice.

Zach gave her shoulder an encouraging squeeze, then got out of the car in one lithe movement and came around to open her door. He took her arm as they walked across the uneven ground, the warmth of his fingers penetrating the soft wool of her sweater. When they reached the old-fashioned park bench, she perched stiffly on the edge while he leaned back, draped his arms across the back and stretched his legs in front, crossing his ankles. He seemed totally relaxed and at ease, Rebecca thought enviously. Of course, he probably had a whole lot more experience at this than she did.

Rebecca wasn't sure why she felt so uncomfortable. Maybe because the last time, things had seemed to evolve naturally, spontaneously. She certainly hadn't expected to be kissed that night. And she'd be willing to bet that Zach hadn't planned to kiss her, either. It had just happened. Tonight was different. Tonight she felt intent in Zach's actions. And for some reason that scared her. She shivered suddenly, hoping vainly that Zach wouldn't notice, but she should have known better. His perceptive eyes never missed a thing.

"Are you cold?" he inquired solicitously.

"N-no."

"Well, you *look* cold. Why don't you lean back and I'll warm you up." He reached forward and gently drew her into the protective curve of his right arm, draping it around her shoulder and urging her close. She followed his lead numbly, simply because she didn't know what else to do. And it *was* warmer here—although his proximity did nothing to quiet her pounding heart. She gripped her purse tightly in her lap, aware of their thighs only a breath apart, inhaling the distinctive scent of his rugged aftershave, feeling his warm breath on her temple. She was getting in over her head here and she knew it. But she wanted so desperately to give this a chance! Please, Lord, help me find the courage to at least *try* to relate to this man on a physical level, she prayed fervently.

Zach knew Rebecca was skittish, but he attributed her nervousness to inexperience. She was probably embarrassed by her lack of sophistication, he reasoned. But if he was reading her signals correctly, she did like him. And she'd had a good time tonight, he could tell. He wanted to tell her to relax, to forget about her lack of experience because it didn't matter to him. But maybe, instead of telling her, he needed to show her.

Slowly but very deliberately he let his hand wander from her shoulder to her neck, his thumb playing gently with the lobe of her ear. She went absolutely still, almost as if she was holding her breath, but she didn't protest, he noted with relief. When he lowered his head to nuzzle her neck, he heard her swiftly indrawn breath, could feel the pounding of her pulse against his lips.

"You look very lovely tonight, Rebecca," he murmured softly, his voice husky.

She swallowed with difficulty. "Th-thank you."

He pressed his cheek to hers. "You taste good, too," he whispered, his breath warm against her skin.

This time Rebecca didn't even try to answer. The touch of his lips was now making skyrockets go off.

Gently, he cupped her chin to turn her face toward his. His lips traveled up the slender column of her throat, which she involuntarily arched to meet his kiss, then across her cheek, up to her forehead. Her eyelids drifted closed, and she sighed with pleasure as he kissed each one very gently.

Zach tried to quiet the thudding of his heart, but when he spoke, his voice was hoarse with emotion. "Oh, Rebecca . . ." Without giving her a chance to respond, he cupped her face with his hands and tenderly claimed her lips.

Rebecca found herself responding tentatively to his touch. Her hand crept around his neck and, without consciously deciding to do so, she turned into the embrace, tunneling her fingers through the soft hair at the base of his neck and pressing herself closer. Caught in his spell, she relaxed in his arms as his kiss worked its magic.

Zach felt her trusting response, her willingness to explore their attraction, and with a groan he deepened the kiss. If he felt her sudden surprise, her hesitation, he was too caught up in the moment to notice.

Zach drew her even closer. He shifted so that she was leaning against the back of the bench as he continued to kiss her.

Rebecca didn't know at exactly what moment she panicked. All she knew, quite suddenly, was that she had. The old feelings of terror resurfaced with an intensity that took her breath away. She felt powerless, helpless, suffocating as his pressing weight immobilized her. The kiss that had started out so welcome had suddenly become a thing to be feared; his lips, once seeking now seemed demanding as they imprisoned hers; and his arms felt like steel cables holding her in place. She couldn't breathe, and she clawed at his shoulders desperately as her heart thudded painfully in her chest, hot tears stinging her eyes. But still he seemed oblivious to her distress. Finally, with one last, desperate, superhuman effort she wrenched her lips free, turning her head aside as she gasped for air, struggling to push him away.

Only then did Rebecca's ragged breathing and the frantic pressure of her hands against his shoulders penetrate Zach's consciousness. He hesitated, backing up far enough to look into her face.

That was the only opening she needed. With a strangled sob she broke free of his arms and jumped unsteadily to her feet, dashing blindly for her apartment as tears streamed down her face. She stumbled once, her heels sinking into the rain-soaked earth, but she quickly regained her footing and continued her irrational flight, her thoughts a chaotic jumble, her emotions tattered. She groped desperately for her key, her fingers closing around it reassuringly as she reached her porch. In a moment she would be safe!

But just as she stepped up a hand shot out and grasped her wrist, throwing her off balance. She gasped, teetering precariously on the edge of the concrete stoop, until another hand reached out to steady her.

Once more Rebecca felt trapped, and she tried to shake off the hands, her heart clamoring in her chest. "Let me go, please!" she pleaded, twisting in Zach's grasp.

"Rebecca, calm down!" he said tersely, alarmed at her near-hysterical state.

"Please," she repeated, her voice breaking on a sob. "Just let me go!"

"Not until you tell me what this is all about," Zach said, his voice quiet but touched with steel.

Rebecca could hear the contained anger in his voice as she averted her face. But she missed the underlying concern and confusion as she struggled to control the irrational fear that held her in a vise. *Stay calm,* she told herself. *Get a grip. You're two steps from your front door and a single scream will bring a dozen people running. You're safe.* She forced herself to take deep breaths, fighting the sudden wave of blackness that swept over her, willing her heart to slow down.

"Rebecca, answer me," Zach demanded, gripping her wrist.

"Please—just let go of me," she said brokenly, turning at last to face him.

Zach took one look at her tear-streaked face, at the almost-wild fear in her eyes, and automatically loosened his grip as her sheer panic finally registered. Tension was radiating from every pore of her body, and she was shaking. Badly. Something was very wrong here, he realized with a frown. Okay, so maybe he'd come on a little too strong. But his overzealous ardor shouldn't have induced this frenzied response. There was something else going on, something that had made her freak out at what essentially was just a kiss. And his caveman reaction to her panic certainly hadn't helped the situation, he thought, silently cursing his insensitivity.

Zach released her wrist, jamming his hands into his pockets. He figured that was the safest place for them, considering that his instinct was to reach over and frame her face with them, erase her tears with the gentle brush of his thumbs over her cheeks, taste the salt on her lips as he kissed away her hurt and fear. But he instinctively knew that touching her in any way whatsoever was *not* a good idea. He'd already made a major mistake tonight, it appeared, and he was not about to make another one. He was playing it safe from here on out.

"Rebecca, what's wrong?" he asked softly, gentling his voice considerably, striving to keep his posture nonthreatening.

She shook her head jerkily. "Please, Zach. J-just go. You w-wouldn't understand."

"Would you at least give me a chance to try?"

She shook her head and attempted to swallow past the lump in her throat, praying that he would just leave her alone to mourn the death of her dream of a normal relationship with a man. She had hoped—prayed—that this time it would be different. But it wasn't. And it never would be.

Zach gazed at her, trying to probe her eyes, searching for answers she clearly wasn't going to give. But all he saw reflected in their depths was abject misery, absolute loneliness and utter despair. His gut wrenched painfully as he looked at her, wanting desperately to ease her distress but not knowing how. There were larger issues at work here, issues he couldn't hope to uncover tonight in her present state. All he could do was try to calm her, make her feel safe. But that was going to be a monumental task in itself, judging by her body language. She was poised for flight, hovering only inches from her door, ready to bolt at the slightest provocation.

"Look, Rebecca, I'm sorry," he apologized huskily, trying to communicate with his eyes that he would never purposely hurt or frighten her. "I guess I just got carried away. I scared you, didn't I?"

She hesitated, but finally she lowered her gaze and nodded. Denying the obvious would be foolish. "Y-yes."

"I'm sorry," he repeated, the warmth and tenderness in his voice acting like a balm on her frayed nerves. "That was certainly not my intent. I find you attractive, and I thought the kiss was an appropriate way to demonstrate that. Obviously it wasn't, because you reacted almost like I was attacking you. I want you to know that was the last thing on my mind, Rebecca. I would never force my attentions on any woman."

She knew that, now that the rational side of her brain was finally kicking in. But she also now knew with absolute certainty that she wasn't equipped to deal with a man of strong passions—like Zach. She was sure that any other woman would be flattered by the advances of such a handsome, intelligent, caring man, would welcome his ardor. But Rebecca wasn't like other women. And even though she'd followed through on her Valentine's Day promise to give a relationship one more chance, she'd failed miserably, just as she'd feared.

Much to her embarrassment, a tear silently rolled down her cheek, and she reached up to brush it away with shaking fingers, turning toward the door as she spoke. "It's not your fault, Zach," she told him, her voice catching on a sob. "Just don't waste your time on me anymore, okay?"

"Rebecca . . ." He wanted to reach out and restrain her, and it took every ounce of his willpower to keep his hands in his pockets, balled into fists of helpless frustration.

She finished fitting the key into the lock, then half turned, waiting for him to continue. Except he didn't know what else to say. He wanted to ask her why she was so afraid, but he knew she'd just shut down even more. Yet there was no way he could fight her fear if he didn't know its source. All he could do at the moment was let her know how he felt.

"Rebecca, I care about you," he said slowly, deliberately. "I don't know exactly what went on here tonight, except that I upset you very badly. But I don't want things to end like this. We need to talk about it. Not tonight, I know, but how about tomorrow, in the daylight, somewhere you feel safe? Just name the place and time."

Rebecca's eyes misted again. He was trying, she'd give him that, exhibiting more patience than she had a right to expect after the way she'd rebuffed his embrace, surely denting his ego in the process. But it wouldn't work. Zach didn't strike her as a man who was used to waiting, and she knew his patience would quickly wear thin. To continue to see him would only delay the inevitable.

"I'm sorry, Zach," she whispered, her voice quavering. "It's no use. But thank you for offering. And for not being angry about tonight."

"Rebecca, please let me—"

"Goodbye, Zach," she said, opening the door and slipping inside as she struggled to control the sobs begging for release. "You're a very nice man, and I-I'm sorry," she finished helplessly, her voice breaking as she shut the door with a quiet but decisive click.

Zach stared at the closed door, frowning in confusion and frustration, at a loss for one of the few times in his dating career. He had absolutely no idea how to proceed. But as he turned and slowly made his way to his car, he knew one thing with absolute certainty. He wasn't going to let this intriguing woman slip out of his life so easily. *She* might think their relationship was over, but *he* had other ideas. He hadn't lied to her about not forcing his attentions on uninterested women. But she *was* interested, he'd bet his life on it. Whether she was willing to admit it or not, there were good vibrations between them. Certainly on the physical level, despite what had happened tonight. And on other levels as well. At dinner this evening he'd glimpsed a number of fascinating aspects of her personality that left him hungry to learn more. She had wit and charm and a great sense of humor, and he'd delighted in the sound of her carefree laughter, in the way her eyes sparkled in amusement and deepened with conviction as their discussion ran the gamut from old movies to her strong faith.

Zach had met a lot of women in his life. He'd even been halfway serious about a couple. But none of them had ever sparked his interest in quite the way Rebecca Matthews did. Perhaps it was the combination of social innocence and professional savvy; poise and uncertainty; strength and vulnerability. But whatever the reason, something told him that if he walked away, as she'd asked, he'd spend the rest of his life regretting it. Because he had a feeling that Rebecca was a once-in-a-lifetime kind of woman. And he intended to check out that theory.

Now he just had to convince her.

Chapter Six

❧

Zach stared in shock at the message on his computer screen, trying to absorb the words as a cold knot formed in his stomach, then tightened painfully. Katrina was dead.

He closed his eyes and rested his elbows on the desk, steepling his fingers. A muscle clenched in his jaw as he slowly exhaled an unsteady breath, his mind in denial. He couldn't believe Katrina was gone. It just didn't seem possible. Or maybe he just didn't want to believe it, he thought bleakly. Because although the news might *seem* unreal, the words that stared back at him from the screen when he reluctantly opened his eyes were real enough. He forced himself to read Josef's message again, more slowly this time, finding the content even more jolting—and more final—the second time through.

I do not know how I find the strength to write these words, my friend. Though the outside world goes on around me, my own world seems to have ended. Katrina died two days ago, Zachary. The miscarriage depleted her strength, and infection set in. She was never physically strong, as you know. But she had such inner strength that I thought her light could never be dimmed, that it would always burn brightly to light my way. Yet the Lord has chosen to take her from me, leaving my world in darkness.

I write to you now to request a very great favor. Do you

remember the promise we made to each other, Zachary, so many years ago? A promise to help each other should the need ever arise? I hope that you do, my friend, because the time has come when I must make such a request. I do so with full understanding of the burden it will impose. But if you take the sabbatical you mentioned in your last correspondence, perhaps it will not be so difficult.

Things are not good in my country, as you know. They are especially not good right now. I do not care much for myself, but I worry about Isabel. She is all I have left now, Zachary, Katrina's legacy to me, and I must keep her well. But that is not easy to do. It is no longer even safe for her to go out and play. There are too many random acts of violence and bombings. My work is also putting me at more risk right now. If something should happen to me, I do not know what would become of my precious child. I would turn to my family for help, but my mother is too old and frail to care for her, and my sister can barely put enough food on the table for her own six children.

So, my friend, I ask you from my heart to take Isabel for a few weeks, until things settle down here and it is safe for her to return to me. I know it is a great favor, one I should probably not impose on you. But I do not know where else to turn. There will surely be many details to work out, arrangements to make, red tape to cut through. But I am confident that with your help, we can accomplish this and keep my Isabel safe.

I will wait anxiously for your reply, Zachary. And may God be with you.

With a heavy sigh Zach rose slowly and walked over to the window, folding his arms on the sash and staring pensively out into the darkness, his brow deeply furrowed. It had been quite a night, he thought grimly. First he'd frightened Rebecca. No, more like traumatized her, he corrected himself harshly. That incident had thrown him off balance, leaving him with equal measures of guilt, confusion and compassion. And then he'd come home to be hit with this devastating news. With sudden anger, he slammed his fist against the sash, making the glass rattle, as he railed silently against any Higher Power that might be listening.

Dear God—if You're even up there—how could You do this to Josef? he demanded. *Katrina was everything to him. He's a good man who doesn't deserve to be hurt. He's always lived by Your rules, done the right thing even in the face of personal danger and sacrifice, and how do You reward him? You deprive him of the wife he loved beyond all measure, and You deny his daughter the mother she so desperately needs. It just isn't fair!*

Even as that last thought flashed across his mind, Zach sighed. It didn't do any good to complain that life wasn't fair, he thought resignedly. It was just a fact, plain and simple. He saw proof of it every day in his job. But the truth had just never hit quite so close to home before.

Wearily he walked back to the computer and printed out Josef's message. Somehow it seemed even more real when he held the hard copy in his hands, the black words stark against the white paper. Josef's request seemed more real, too, and more urgent. And therein lay a problem.

Zach remembered their promise, of course. And they'd both meant it, with every fiber of their being, during those heady years in J school that now seemed a lifetime ago. But promises made in the optimism and fervor of youth weren't always easy to keep years later, he now realized. Circumstances changed, life became more complicated. Yet a promise was a promise, a sacred trust not to be treated lightly. His father had always told him that a man was only as good as his word, and Zach believed that. Without integrity and honor, a person was nothing. Zach knew beyond the shadow of a doubt that if circumstances were reversed, Josef wouldn't hesitate to keep their promise. Could he do any less for this man who was closer to him even than his brother?

The answer, of course, was no. Zach stared down again at the letter as he considered the situation. The logistics could be dealt with, that wasn't a problem. He had plenty of contacts from his years of reporting, colleagues all over the world who knew how to cut through red tape. No, that would be the easy part, he thought dismissively. But how on earth would he, a man who had virtually no experience handling young children, cope with a little seven-year-old girl who had just lost her mother and was being sent far away from her beloved father and the only home she'd ever known?

Zach didn't have the answer to that question. And he wasn't sure where to find it.

Rebecca hooked the pepper spray onto her belt, pulled a sweater over her head, secured her long hair loosely with a barrette and locked the car. A good long walk in the fresh air and quiet woods, next to a bubbling brook, would lift her spirits, she told herself resolutely, though in her heart she wasn't convinced it would help. But at least it couldn't hurt. Her spirits were so low right now that the only place for them to go was up.

She struck out purposefully on the state park trail, determined to return to her apartment with some sense of perspective. She'd spent a sleepless night staring at the ceiling, going over and over last night's disaster in her mind. And the more she thought about it, the more she empathized with Zach. *What must he think of her?* she wondered, her face flushing even now. She had overreacted— dramatically—to what, for him, was probably the standard way to end an evening with a woman whose company he had enjoyed.

In retrospect she realized that her attempt to fight off a nonexistent attack had probably not only hurt his ego, but insulted him, as well, by implying that she thought him capable of such an act. Dear Lord, she had really messed things up! If only she could relive that moment! But with a profound sense of discouragement, she admitted in her heart that it would probably end the same. Here, alone, in the fresh air and sunshine, she could think rationally, logically analyze her reaction. But in his embrace, held captive by the strength of his arms and the pressure of his lips, she would panic. It had become an instinctive response through the years, until now it was a self-fulfilling prophecy. She could no more control her irrational panic in that situation than she could stop the flood waters that had slowly but powerfully risen to threaten the town.

Rebecca wished with all her heart that there was some way to overcome her problem. But her hopes seemed doomed and, as a result, so did her dreams of a husband and family.

She trudged along, her gaze fixed on the trail to avoid stumbling over the protruding rocks, so lost in her misery that for once she was oblivious to the beauty of nature around her. In fact, so deep was her introspection that when she glanced up and saw Zach it took a moment for his presence to register.

She stopped abruptly, certain she must be hallucinating. He was just off the trail, sitting on a large flat boulder by the stream, arms around his bent knees. But what on earth was he doing on this secluded nature trail? she wondered in confusion. The state park was usually deserted this time of year on weekdays. She hadn't expected to see anyone, let alone Zach. But it was definitely him, she realized as she stared at the pensive figure not more than twenty feet ahead.

Rebecca considered beating a quiet—and hasty—retreat, but before she could make a move he glanced up, as if sensing a presence, and their eyes connected.

Zach's reaction was much the same as hers—a double take, followed by an "am I imagining this?" look. But he recovered quickly, greeting her in weary voice. "Hello, Rebecca. Fancy meeting you here."

"Hello, Zach."

"Nice day," he commented, tilting his head to look up at the cobalt blue sky, the canopy of branches above him exhibiting the first tender buds of spring.

"Yes, it is. But . . ." She stopped uncertainly, still bewildered by his presence in this unlikely place.

He looked back at her, his lips curving up into the semblance of a smile. "What am I doing here?" he finished for her.

"Yes."

He turned back to gaze down into the stream. "Mark told me about this place a while back. It sounded like a good spot to think."

His face looked haggard, Rebecca thought, as she inched cautiously closer. She knew he was upset about last night's fiasco, but for some reason she had a feeling his subdued mood today wasn't caused by that incident alone. Maybe the much-creased sheet of paper in his hand was the key to his uncharacteristic melancholy, she thought. But whatever the reason, he didn't seem anxious to discuss it with her. Not that she could blame him, considering her behavior last night. Yet she couldn't just walk off and leave, when she sensed that he needed someone to talk to.

"Zach . . . is everything okay?" she asked tentatively, trying to give him an opening.

He turned back to her once more. She had moved close enough now for him to see the dark circles beneath her eyes, eloquent evidence of her sleepless night, and he knew with a pang of guilt that he was to blame. But much as he wanted to work out the situation between them, it wasn't his priority at the moment. He had a more urgent problem to resolve. He glanced back at the letter in his hand and sighed. "Not really. I got some bad news last night."

"A letter?"

"E-mail. It was waiting when I got home."

"Something to do with your family?" She was only a few feet away now, and she paused uncertainly, still unsure of her welcome.

"You might say that." He turned to gaze at her, his eyes troubled. "Look, Rebecca, you don't need to keep me company. You obviously came out here to be alone. I'll work this out myself."

She bit her lip. Was he trying to tell her to get lost? Or just being considerate of her needs, trying not to intrude on her day? There was only one way to find out. "I can be a good listener, Zach, if you want to talk about it," she offered quietly.

His gaze dropped to her belt and he gave a mirthless chuckle. "Well, at least you're prepared today. A blast of that pepper spray should keep me in line."

In the instant before she turned away, Zach saw the shaft of pain shoot through her eyes at his rebuke, and he felt like someone had kicked him in the gut. *Of all the stupid remarks!* he berated himself. Just because he was upset about Josef's situation was no excuse to take it out on this gentle woman who had just offered him a much-needed sympathetic ear.

He rose in one swift movement to follow her, reaching her just as she stumbled on a rock. His hand shot out to steady her, and she reached up to swipe at her misty eyes, trying to clear her clouded vision.

"Rebecca, please forgive me," he implored, his voice raw with pain. "That remark was totally out of line and completely insensitive. My only excuse is that I've had a really lousy twelve hours. Look, stay awhile, okay? I could use the company."

Rebecca held herself stiffly, blinking back the tears still welling in her eyes. She'd always been overly sensitive, wearing her feelings so close to the surface that they were easily hurt. In her heart she knew Zach wouldn't have made that remark under normal circumstances. Something must be terribly wrong. Refusing to forgive him would only add to whatever trauma he was trying to deal with. Rebecca struggled with forgiveness sometimes, often finding it hard to forget callously inflicted hurts. But she needed to learn to let go, and this was a good chance to put that lesson into practice.

She let her shoulders relax and reached up to wipe away the last traces of her tears before she turned to face him. "Are you sure you want me to? I didn't mean to force myself on you."

Zach's own shoulders sagged in relief. He knew his curt remark could have alienated her permanently, considering that they were on shaky ground already. Thank God she was willing to give him another chance! he thought gratefully.

"Believe me, you're welcome," he assured her, the husky timbre of his voice more pronounced than usual. "Come on, let's go back and sit on the rock." He took her arm protectively as they made their way over the rocky ground, releasing it as they sat down on the large boulder. Glancing down at the letter, he drew a deep breath. "Do you remember the friend I mentioned once, the one in Eastern Europe?"

"Yes."

"We went to journalism school together. Mizzou. I can't think of anyone in this world I admire more than Josef. He's a man of deep conviction, impeccable character and great faith. He's always been an inspiration to me when things got tough." Zach paused and picked up a pebble, fingering it absently as he continued, his eyes fixed on a spot across the stream, but his gaze clearly turned inward. "We've kept in touch all these years, despite the distance. About eight years ago he and his wife, Katrina, came to the States for the birth of their daughter, Isabel. Katrina had a problem pregnancy, and was always a little frail, anyway, so Josef didn't want to take any chances. They stayed with me for six weeks, and I was even Isabel's godfather at her christening." He paused to pull out his wallet, flipping to a photo before handing it to Rebecca. "This picture was taken that day."

Rebecca took the wallet and examined the shot. She saw a much-younger Zach, gingerly holding a tiny bundle in white, flanked by an attractive, delicate-looking woman and a slender, dark-haired man with compelling eyes. "They look like a nice family," she said softly.

"Yeah, they were," Zach replied. "That's a more recent picture of Isabel up above."

Rebecca's gaze flickered up to examine the solemn face staring back at her, framed by long dark hair, the delicate bone structure mirroring that of her mother. But it was Isabel's eyes that held her. They were Josef's eyes, no question. But they were also eyes that had seen too much for someone so young, she thought, her heart aching with compassion. No child's eyes should look that wary and vulnerable, so old for their years.

"I got this last night," Zach said quietly, handing her the paper before turning away.

Rebecca looked at his rigid back, knew that whatever this letter contained had brought him great anguish, and wanted to reach over and comfort him. But she held back, not sure that he would welcome her sympathy, and forced herself to read the words on the sheet instead.

As her eyes scanned the page, and the horror of the situation unfolded, she felt her stomach clench, and by the time she reached the end, she wanted to cry. She didn't know Josef or Katrina or Isabel. But in the brief, eloquent note Josef had written she could feel the love and devotion, pain and loss, desperation and fear that now consumed his life. Her heart went out to this grieving man and his cherished child, and she felt suddenly guilty and small for spending so much time agonizing over a personal trauma that paled into insignificance compared to what this family had endured.

"Oh, Zach," she murmured at last, her voice choked. "I'm so sorry. Poor Josef! And Isabel . . . no wonder he's concerned. The conditions sound so awful! And terribly dangerous!"

"Yeah," Zach replied, a muscle clenching in his jaw.

"What are you going to do?"

He sighed and raked a hand through his hair. "I'm going to take Isabel, of course. How can I not? Josef has always prided himself on taking care of his family himself, so I know he would never ask me to do this unless the situation was desperate." He sighed and threw the pebble into the stream in frustration. "But I don't have any experience with children. Especially girls. Then there's the teaching job. I was going to approach the school about it, but I really can't take it if I have Isabel here. I'd like to bring her to St.

Genevieve, though, because I think it would be good for her to spend time in a place like this after the environment she's been in. But I can't afford to keep an apartment here and in St. Louis unless I take the teaching job, and it's not worth closing my apartment in the city for just a few weeks."

The words came out in a long, almost stream-of-consciousness data dump that clearly reflected his turmoil. He paused for a moment and expelled a long breath before finishing. "That's why I came out here today, to try and work things out in my mind."

Rebecca bit her lip and stared down at the letter, an idea slowly forming in her mind. "Zach."

He turned to her, realizing suddenly that for once she hadn't pinned her hair up. Instead, it tumbled freely to her shoulders, held back loosely by only a barrette, the russet strands glinting in the sun just as he'd imagined them. It was a measure of his distress that it had taken him this long to notice the soft waves cascading down her back, he thought wearily.

She looked up at him, her face thoughtful, oblivious to the direction of his wayward thoughts. "Zach, I could help you with Isabel," she said impulsively.

That jolted him back to reality, and he stared at her, taken aback. "But . . . but why would you want to get involved in this?"

"Because these people need help."

"You don't even know them."

"It doesn't matter. I can't turn my back on someone in need."

Zach studied her face, knew she was absolutely sincere in her offer. For her, it was simple. She saw a need, and she offered to help. Period. That was why she'd stopped for him that night on the deserted highway, why she'd pitched in with the sandbagging.

What a remarkable woman, he thought in awe, his admiration for her increasing tenfold. She was completely selfless, more giving and generous than anyone he'd ever met. He knew, if he accepted her offer, that she would throw herself into the care of Isabel, heart and soul. But she had enough to do with the restaurant, he reminded himself. She often seemed to be running on pure adrenaline as it was, and this would be just one more burden on her already-taxed energy and time.

"I appreciate the offer, Rebecca. More than I can say. But you're too busy already."

"But you said yourself that you have limited experience with children. I don't have much more, I'll admit. But together I think we could pull this off. I can watch Isabel at the restaurant while you teach—if you get the job. And I'm off on Monday, so it's really only four days a week that I'd have her. And just during school hours. I don't mind, really. I love children, Zach. I always wanted . . ." She cut herself off sharply, glancing down at the stream as a flush tinted her cheeks. "Anyway, I'd be glad to help."

He looked at her speculatively. It didn't take a genius to fill in the blanks. She'd always wanted children of her own. And she was the type of woman who should have a houseful of children, he realized. With her warm, compassionate nature, she would make a wonderful mother. Yet she'd never married. And after last night, he was beginning to understand why. Which reminded him . . .

"You realize this will put us in close contact, don't you?" he pointed out slowly, loath to bring up the subject but feeling compelled to make sure she understood the implications. "I got the impression last night that was the last thing you wanted."

He was right. Last night, being together *was* the last thing she wanted. But circumstances had changed. A little girl needed their help, and as far as she was concerned, that took precedence over her own wants. She'd just have to deal with their proximity. But maybe *Zach* didn't want to deal with it, she thought suddenly, glancing down with a frown. "I wasn't being very rational last night," she admitted slowly, her voice subdued. "I'm willing to give it a try, though, if you are. But I wouldn't blame you if you didn't, not after what happened."

A large hand entered her field of vision, gently covering her own. "Rebecca, I told you before. I care about you. What happened last night didn't change that."

She risked a glance at him then, and the warmth and caring in his deep brown eyes made her breath catch in her throat. "It isn't that I don't like you, you know," she told him shyly, a blush creeping onto her cheeks.

He smiled and gave her hand a gentle, encouraging squeeze. "I'm glad to hear you say that. I'll admit I was beginning to wonder."

"What happened was . . . I can't— It had nothing to do with you personally," she said disjointedly. "It's . . . it's a long story."

"Maybe someday you'll share it with me."

She looked at him steadily, knowing that she had to be honest. "I can't make any promises."

He returned her look just as steadily. "I'm not asking you to. How about if we just take it a day at a time? Besides, I have a feeling that one little seven-year-old girl is going to require most of our attention and energy in the next few weeks." He tilted his head and looked at her quizzically. "Are you absolutely sure you want to get involved?"

She glanced down at the letter and pictures she still held. "I think I already am. Besides, I have a feeling the Lord wants us to work together to help this family."

Zach wasn't so sure that divine intervention was involved. Then again, maybe it was, he reflected, considering that after last night he figured it would take a miracle to bring Rebecca back into his life. It seemed that such a miracle had just been wrought. He just wished it hadn't come at the expense of his friend.

"How on earth did you manage to arrange everything so quickly?" Rebecca asked in amazement as Zach turned the van onto the highway, heading south.

He grinned. "Chalk it up to my charm and persuasive powers."

Rebecca looked at him speculatively, half believing his explanation. In the past three days he'd interviewed for, and been offered, the job at the high school; arranged to take all eight weeks of his accumulated vacation, plus an additional four-week personal leave; found an apartment in St. Genevieve and signed a short-term lease; and cut through the red tape to get Isabel's paperwork in order. He'd also arranged with a foreign-correspondent colleague who was returning from Eastern Europe to courier Isabel as far as New York and put her on a plane to St. Louis. She would arrive Sunday.

"So what's left to do?" she asked.

"Move some of my stuff from St. Louis. That's on the agenda for tomorrow. And pick up your old bedroom furniture today. The loan of which I greatly appreciate, in case I haven't already thanked you."

"You have," she assured him. "And it's my pleasure. It's just sitting there gathering dust at the house. Dad never even goes into my room anymore, and Brad and Sam use his old bedroom when they visit. By the way, how did you talk Mark into letting you borrow his new van to haul everything?"

He grinned again. "I told you. Charm." When she shook her head and laughed, he sent her a crushed look. "I think I'm insulted," he declared, feigning indignance. "Are you implying that I lack charm?"

On the contrary, she thought, eyeing his strong profile as he turned his attention back to the road. The man had plenty of charm. In fact, it oozed out of every pore in his body.

"No-o-o," she replied with exaggerated thoughtfulness. "I guess not."

"Well, don't be so enthusiastic in your denial," he retorted wryly, then turned to her with a grin. "Speaking of charm, you must have used some yourself to get Rose and Frances to agree to handle the lunch crowd this afternoon."

"They offered," she told him. "Since we didn't leave till noon, most of the prep work was done. It's mostly just a matter of serving and cleanup, and they said they didn't mind." Actually, they'd said a whole lot more, Rebecca thought, a flush rising to her cheeks. At least half a dozen times this morning they'd reminded her to give "that nice young man," as they referred to Zach, some encouragement, waving her off and telling her to have a good time when she left. Even though she'd explained the businesslike purpose of their trip—twice— she knew the sisters remained unconvinced, certain that *Zach's* purpose was romance.

Actually, since the night of their dinner, romance seemed to be the *last* thing on Zach's mind, she reflected. He was attentive and considerate, but she noticed that he not only kept their conversations impersonal and lighthearted, he kept his distance as well. Which was fine with her. She felt safer this way. And she'd actually begun to enjoy their congenial, teasing banter. If the gleam of romantic interest in his eyes had dimmed, she was grateful. Wasn't she?

"So what did your dad say about this?"

Her glance returned to Zach, and she forced her attention back to the conversation. "He thought it was a very nice thing for you to do," she replied. He'd also asked far too many questions about Zach, which Rebecca had sidestepped as much as possible, telling her father only that Zach was an acquaintance she was helping strictly out of Christian charity. She wasn't sure her father bought that explanation, but at least he'd eventually stopped quizzing her. Either he'd lost interest, she'd convinced him, or he was biding his time. Knowing her father, however, she had a sinking feeling it was the latter. He'd always had a propensity for prying into the lives of his children, though always with the best intentions. Maybe she had better warn Zach to expect the third degree.

"Um, Zach, one thing about my father. He's a great guy and all, but . . . well, he tends to ask a lot of questions, and I haven't brought many men to the house through the years, even for an innocent reason like this, so he's apt to jump to a few wrong conclusions and . . . probe . . . a little. I just don't want you to be surprised."

"You mean he's going to ask me about my intentions?" Zach teased her.

"Well, I don't think he'll be quite that direct," she replied, color stealing onto her cheeks.

"So what do you want me to tell him?" Zach asked easily.

She looked at him in surprise. "The truth, of course," she replied. "That we're friends, and I'm just helping you out in an emergency. I've already told him that myself, but he gets these ideas into his head and . . ." Her voice trailed off and she shrugged helplessly.

"Hmm," was Zach's only reply.

Rebecca squirmed uncomfortably, suddenly suspecting that her explanation for Zach's intentions was way too simplistic. But it was the only one she wanted to deal with at the moment.

Fortunately he didn't pursue the subject, and by the time they pulled into the driveway of the two-story frame house with the lattice-trimmed front porch, she was feeling more relaxed again.

"On a day like this Dad's probably in the garden, getting everything ready for spring," she informed Zach, opening her door and sliding to the ground as soon as the van stopped. "I'll let him know we're here."

"Okay." Zach got out more leisurely, watching as Rebecca disappeared around the side of the house, her snug jeans hugging her narrow waist, slim hips and long, shapely legs. Her hair was in its customary French twist today, but for a moment he allowed himself to imagine how it would look cascading down her back. Then he jammed his hands into the pockets of his jeans with a frown. Now was not the best time to be having those kinds of thoughts, he told himself sternly.

He followed Rebecca slowly, reminding himself of the resolution he'd made to bide his time. Now that she had agreed to help with Isabel, he had weeks ahead to woo her, to slowly build her comfort level. He just needed to be patient. Except patience had never been his strong suit, he admitted wryly. But he knew time and patience were the essential ingredients in a successful campaign to win this woman's confidence, and he was determined to give her both. Even if it killed him. Which it very well might, he thought ruefully, as he rounded the corner of the house and another surge of desire swept over him at the sight of her slender, appealing figure.

She was talking animatedly to a spare, wiry man with fine gray hair and a slightly angular nose, who was leaning on a shovel. As Zach made his way toward them, the man glanced his way, said something quietly to Rebecca, then laid down the shovel.

Rebecca turned as Zach joined them. "Dad, this is Zach Wright. Zach, my father."

The older man, who was several inches shorter than Zach, wiped his hand on his slacks, then held it out. Zach took it in a firm grip as their eyes connected, and Rebecca's father gave him a shrewd, assessing look, which Zach returned steadily. When the older man smiled at last, Zach had an odd feeling that he'd just passed some sort of test.

"It's nice to meet you, Mr. Matthews," Zach said.

"Call me Henry. Makes me feel younger. And I'm pleased to meet you, too," he replied cordially.

"We don't want to keep you from your garden, Dad. We'll just go up and sort things out."

"Garden will always be here," he replied with a dismissive wave. "But I don't get that many visitors. Besides, I'd like to get to know your young man a little while you're here."

Rebecca's face turned beet red, but Zach just grinned, proprietarily draping an arm around her shoulders as he spoke. "I'd like to get to know you better, too, Henry."

Rebecca shot him a startled look at the unexpected gesture,

shrugging off his arm as she spoke. "This isn't a social visit, Dad. We just want to pick up the furniture."

"That won't take long. Zach and I will have it loaded in no time. I thought you'd at least have time for a glass of lemonade and some German apple spice cake. I picked one up at the bakery this morning."

"That does sound good," Zach injected hopefully before Rebecca could refuse, as he suspected she was inclined to do.

She planted her hands on her hips and stared from one man to the other. "Why do I have a feeling there's a conspiracy here?' "

"Oh, come on, Rebecca. We can spare half an hour to visit. We'll get back in plenty of time. What do you say?" Zach cajoled. He sensed an ally in Henry, and he intended to use that to his advantage with Rebecca.

With a sigh of capitulation, she gave in. Arguing the point would only make her father even more inquisitive. "Okay. Fine."

"Good, good," Henry approved heartily. "You two go on up and decide what you want to take. I'll just wash my hands and follow you in."

Rebecca strode silently toward the house and up the stairs, turning to face Zach with an accusatory frown when they entered her childhood bedroom. "Why did you do that?" she demanded, keeping her voice low and a watchful eye out for her father.

"Do what?" Zach asked innocently.

"Put your arm around my shoulders."

He shrugged, giving her a bewildered look. "It just seemed like a . . . friendly . . . thing to do. After all, we are friends, aren't we? That's what you told your father."

She eyed him suspiciously, suspecting an ulterior motive. But he *looked* sincere. "That's not the way my dad will interpret it. I told you, he jumps to conclusions."

"Stop worrying, Rebecca," Zach chided her gently. "Your father seems like a reasonable man. I'm sure his perceptive powers are right on target."

That's what she was afraid of, she thought in dismay, as she turned to fold up the bedspread. She wasn't exactly sure of Zach's feelings at this point. But she was very sure of her own. She liked this man. A lot. Despite the disastrous end to their date, she was still attracted to him. And she had a feeling her father knew it, whether Zach did or not.

"Are you sure you don't mind, Rebecca? I hate to ask, but I'm all thumbs with a needle and thread."

"No problem, Dad." Rebecca reached for the suit coat and inspected the spot where the lining had come loose. "This will only take a few minutes."

"Thanks, honey. Listen, Zach, while Rebecca takes care of that, why don't I give you a tour of my garden?"

"I'd like that," Zach replied, depositing his lemonade glass on the wicker table and rising to his feet.

Rebecca glanced up from her seat on the porch swing and gave her father a suspicious look. "There's not much to see yet, Dad."

"The perennials are all coming up," he replied promptly. "And Zach strikes me as a man with imagination. I bet he'll be able to picture what I describe."

She watched them walk down the porch steps, conversing companionably, and frowned. She fervently hoped her father was talking about flowers.

"So you're taking charge of a little girl, I hear," Henry remarked as he led the way toward the rose garden.

"That's right."

"Mighty nice thing to do."

"Josef, her father, is like a brother to me. Considering the situation over there and the loss of his wife, it's the least I can do."

"Pretty bad in some of those places, from what I see on the news."

"I can't even imagine living like that," Zach remarked, shaking his head.

They paused on the edge of the rose garden. "I've got thirty-two bushes," Henry said proudly, nodding toward the bed. "Quite a sight in the summer when they're in full bloom."

"Must be impressive," Zach concurred. "I don't think I've ever seen thirty-two bushes all in one place, except at Shaw's Garden."

Henry beamed with pride at the comparison to St. Louis's well-known botanical garden. "Sam was surprised when I told her how many I had, too," he recalled with a chuckle. "Sam's my daughter-in-law. Married to my son, Brad. They just had a little girl."

"So I hear. Which makes you a proud grandpa now, I guess."

He nodded vigorously, his eyes sparkling with enthusiasm. "Cutest little thing you ever saw. Big blue eyes and a fuzz of the softest reddish hair. Gonna be a carrottop, like Sam, I suspect."

"They sound like a nice family."

"They are," he confirmed. "Course, I never thought it would happen. Brad was married before, you know. First wife died years ago. A real tragedy," he reflected, shaking his head. "I didn't figure he'd remarry. You ever been married, Zach?"

Henry didn't waste any time, Zach thought in amusement, suppressing a chuckle. "No. Never found the time. Or the right woman."

"Hmm," Henry ruminated. "Seems to me like you have to *make* time for some things. Course, you can't be too careful. You sure don't want to make a mistake, pick the wrong partner. That's what I always tell Rebecca. Not that she seems to be looking, anyway. Always been kinda prickly around men."

"I noticed," Zach admitted. "I wonder why?"

"Can't say," Henry replied, shaking his head. "Always wondered about that myself. She's a fine woman. Make someone a good wife. But seems like she needs special handling. Sort of like a skittish colt. Gotta approach her gentle-like, let her get comfortable around you. No sudden moves to spook her, you know what I mean?"

Zach stifled a smile, not at all sure Rebecca would appreciate being compared to a horse. But he got the drift of Henry's comment. And it confirmed the conclusion he'd already come to. "I think you're right. Reminds me of that old saying—good things come to those who wait."

Henry turned and looked up at Zach, placing a hand on the younger man's shoulder as he gazed at him appraisingly. "I know waiting can be hard sometimes," he acknowledged. "I was young once myself. But some things are worth it." He dropped his hand and nodded back to the porch. "Looks like Rebecca's done with that jacket. Let's head on back."

As they waved goodbye to Henry a few minutes later and climbed into the van for the trip home, Rebecca turned to Zach curiously. "What did you two talk about, out there in the garden?"

He chuckled. "Let's just say your dad missed his calling. He'd have made a great investigative reporter."

Rebecca bit her lip and frowned. That's what she'd been afraid of.

Chapter Seven

Rebecca scanned the crowd emerging from the plane's exit ramp, her heart pounding in her chest, her palms clammy. What on earth had she gotten herself into? she wondered in silent panic. When she'd offered to help Zach with Isabel, her heart had certainly been in the right place. But what did she know about taking care of a child? Especially a child who was not only grieving, but had just been sent to live with strangers in an unfamiliar land! She could be in way over her head here. Suddenly, without even consciously realizing what she was doing, Rebecca reached for Zach's hand, seeking courage in the strength and comfort of his touch.

He looked down at her in surprise, hesitating for only the briefest second before willingly enfolding her seeking hand in his warm clasp. "This is pretty scary, isn't it?" he empathized, as if reading her mind.

She looked up at him with a worried frown. "Honestly? Yes."

He gave her hand an encouraging squeeze. "Well, if it makes you feel any better, I'm just as nervous as you are," he admitted.

"Zach—I just thought of something!" Rebecca exclaimed in sudden alarm. "Does Isabel speak English?"

He smiled reassuringly. "Yes. That's one problem we won't have to deal with. Josef is fluent, and he made sure Isabel was bilingual."

Relief flooded her eyes. "Thank goodness! I don't know why I didn't think about that before!"

"You've had a few other things on your mind. Like running a

restaurant and decorating a little girl's room. Quite charmingly, I might add," he said with a smile.

Rebecca smiled as she thought about the way she'd transformed the bare, sterile bedroom in Zach's apartment, hanging frilly lace curtains at the window to complement the pale pink eyelet bedspread, decorating the walls with colorful posters from popular animated children's movies, and attaching fanciful mobiles to the ceiling. She'd even brought along her favorite music box from childhood, a statue of Cinderella that played "Someday My Prince Will Come," to decorate the top of the dresser. "I just hope she likes it."

"I can't imagine any little girl who wouldn't."

As the last of the passengers disembarked, a stewardess appeared in the doorway holding the hand of a petite dark-haired child who was clutching a very raggedy Raggedy Ann doll. Zach drew a deep breath and gave Rebecca's hand another encouraging squeeze. "We're on," he said.

In the brief seconds it took to reach the pair, Rebecca studied Isabel. She wore a pink sweater and a pink and beige striped skirt, and her white ankle socks were edged with lace. Rebecca had a feeling that Josef had dressed his daughter in her "Sunday best" for the trip. Her hair was parted in the middle, pulled up and back on each side, and secured with a pink ribbon that had probably started out crisp but now lay limp and bedraggled. She was smaller than Rebecca expected, pale and thin and delicately boned, and she looked bleary-eyed from fatigue, which wasn't surprising, given the length of her trip and the emotional trauma she had endured.

Isabel watched them approach with large, solemn eyes, looking very much like a little girl who was frightened but trying mightily to be brave, and Rebecca's heart ached for her. As soon as she reached her side, Rebecca dropped to one knee while Zach talked with the stewardess.

"Hello, Isabel," she said softly, giving the waiflike little girl a warm smile. "I'm Rebecca. Zach and I are so glad you came to visit us. Is this Raggedy Ann?" She reached over and touched the obviously much-loved doll.

Isabel nodded. "She's tired now."

"I'm sure she is," Rebecca sympathized with a nod. "It was a long trip, wasn't it?"

"Yes. My papa's far away now, isn't he?" A tremor ran through her voice and her eyes filled with tears.

Rebecca's throat contracted, and she reached over to gently smooth some wayward strands of hair back from the wan little face. "Not if you keep him in your heart," she replied gently.

"That's what he said about my mama, too."

Rebecca swallowed with difficulty. "He's right. The people we love are always with us in our hearts."

Zach knelt down beside Rebecca then, and he smiled at Isabel. "I guess you don't remember me, do you, Isabel?"

Silently she shook her head. "I was just a baby when I saw you the last time," she pointed out matter-of-factly. "But my papa told me all about you. He and my mama talked about you a lot. And I liked the presents you sent me for my birthdays."

"Well, it seems you like that one especially," he noted, reaching out to touch the Raggedy Ann doll he'd sent her two years ago.

She nodded. "I do." She tilted her head and looked at him quizzically. "Are you really my uncle?" she asked suddenly.

"Is that what your papa told you?"

She frowned. "He tried to explain it to me. He said you were his friend, but really more like a brother, so that made you my uncle."

Zach cleared his throat, and when he spoke there was an odd catch in his voice. "That's right."

"So should I call you Uncle Zach?"

"That would be fine."

Isabel turned to Rebecca with a puzzled frown. "But you're not my aunt, are you?"

"No. I'd like to be your friend, though."

"Can I call you Rebecca, then?"

"I think that would be just right."

"Well, why don't we collect your luggage, and then we can all go home?" Zach suggested, standing up.

Rebecca rose, as well, then reached down and took Isabel's hand, giving it a reassuring squeeze. "That's a good idea. Raggedy Ann is tired," she told Zach with a wink. "It's past her bedtime."

By the time they collected Isabel's two suitcases, made their way to the car and buckled the little girl into the back seat, she was fading fast. Her eyes kept drifting shut, though she was trying hard to stay awake.

As Zach slid behind the wheel he glanced back at his new charge. "Are you hungry, Isabel?" he asked.

"No."

He looked at Rebecca, raising an eyebrow quizzically.

"How about a hamburger?" Rebecca suggested, with sudden inspiration.

"A hamburger?" Isabel echoed, her interest piqued. "My papa told me about American hamburgers. He said they were good."

"Well, why don't we let you decide for yourself?" Zach replied.

Fifteen minutes later, as Isabel polished off the hamburger and fries from the drive-through fast-food restaurant, Zach grinned at Rebecca. "Good idea," he complimented her in a low voice.

"Sheer luck," she said with a small smile. "I figured she needed to eat. But actually—" she glanced toward the back seat, in time to catch Isabel yawning hugely "—I think she's more exhausted than anything else. Talk about a day of emotional overload! She just needs to go to bed."

"I appreciate your offer to keep her overnight tonight," Zach said. "I wish I had one more day before school started, but that's just not how things worked out."

"I don't mind," Rebecca assured him. "I'm off, and it will give us a chance to become acquainted. I'll get her unpacked and settled in at your place, too, if you like."

He sent her a grateful look. "That would be great! I'll give you my spare key before I leave tonight."

Rebecca glanced out the window, trying to work up the courage to ask her next question. She'd been thinking about it ever since they decided she would keep Isabel the first night. "Um, Zach, I was wondering . . . since you'll probably be tired after your first day at school, and not in the mood to cook . . . well, Isabel does need to have balanced meals, you know, so I . . . I wondered if you might want to come over for dinner tomorrow night."

He turned to look at her, but she kept her face averted and he couldn't discern her expression in the darkness. To say he was surprised at the invitation was an understatement. But he was also immensely pleased—and touched. "That would be wonderful, Rebecca," he replied, his voice tinged with that husky timbre she found so appealing. "But I feel like I've imposed too much already. Besides, the last thing you need to do on your day off is cook."

"I don't mind, really," she assured him quickly. "And it would probably be good for Isabel to sit down to a nice meal with us her first night in town. It would make her feel more at home and welcome than if you two just grab a bite on the run."

Was concern for Isabel Rebecca's only motivation for the invitation? Zach suddenly wondered with a frown. He tried to read her expression, but again the darkness was her ally. Whatever her motivation, however, she'd made the offer, and he wasn't about to look a gift horse in the mouth. "Well, if you're sure you don't mind."

"Not at all."

"Okay. And thank you. For everything."

Rebecca felt a tingle run down her spine at the intimate tone in his voice. If he was willing to come for dinner, he must not be holding her bizarre behavior the night of their date against her, she thought in relief, saying a silent prayer of thanks. And a "family" type dinner would be good for Isabel. But Rebecca was honest enough to admit that her motives weren't entirely altruistic. Deep in her heart she thought the dinner would be good for her, too. It would give her a chance to be with Zach in a safe, comfortable environment, with Isabel acting almost like a chaperone. And maybe, if she got accustomed to being with him in that kind of setting, without all the pressures incumbent on "dating," she might eventually feel comfortable enough to give a romantic relationship one more try.

If he was willing to take a second shot at it. And that, of course, was a big *if,* she knew. He said he still liked her. But *like* and *attraction* were two different things, she realized. She just hoped she hadn't killed the latter by her performance the other night. But only time would tell.

When Rebecca opened the door in answer to Zach's ring the next night, her eyes widened in surprise at the bouquet of pink tulips, daffodils and baby's breath that he held out to her.

"I thought you might like these," he said with a disarming grin. "You mentioned once that you enjoyed gardening, so I figured you must like flowers."

She reached for the bouquet, smiling in pleasure even as she protested. "Oh, Zach, this is too extravagant!"

"Hardly. Consider it a thank-you for dinner—and for everything you're doing to help with Isabel."

"Well . . . thank you," she said, a delicate flush tinting her cheeks. "Come on in. Dinner's almost ready."

"Can I do anything to help?" he asked as he followed her inside.

"No, thanks. Isabel and I took care of everything, didn't we, sweetie?"

Isabel looked up from the table, which she was setting with great precision and care. "Yes. We're having spaghetti," she informed Zach.

"Mmm. That sounds good."

"I haven't had spaghetti before, but Rebecca says I'll like it," she informed him.

"I think Rebecca is right."

Half an hour later, after watching her demolish a salad, a hearty helping of spaghetti and four pieces of garlic bread, Zach turned to her with a chuckle. "So what did you think?"

She considered the matter seriously. "I think Rebecca cooks real good."

Zach smiled. "I'll second that."

Rebecca's face flushed at the compliments, and she stood up to clear the table. "Well, I'd say it's time for some brownies," she remarked. "Isabel helped me make them," she informed Zach over her shoulder as she headed toward the kitchen to put on the coffee.

"I didn't know you knew how to cook, Isabel," Zach said in mock surprise, turning to the little girl.

"I'm not very good yet," she replied seriously. "But Rebecca said she'd teach me. She has a restaurant, you know."

"Yes, I know."

"She's also very nice," she added in a conspiratorial whisper, leaning close.

"I know that, too," he replied, also lowering his voice. "And I know something else. See that bag over there by the door? I think there's something in it for you."

She looked at him wide-eyed. "For me?"

"Uh-huh. Why don't you go over and take a look?"

She jumped up and scampered toward the door, peeking into the bag eagerly, her eyes lighting up as she withdrew a video of a popular animated children's film. "Is this really for me?"

"It sure is."

She hugged it to her chest, her eyes awed. "Oh, thank you, Uncle Zach. Can I watch it now?"

Zach sent a quizzical look to Rebecca, who was depositing the plate of brownies on the table.

"Well, if your Uncle Zach says it's okay, I guess you can take your brownie into the living room just this once."

"Can I, Uncle Zach?"

"I don't see why not," he agreed. "I'll get it started for you."

By the time he returned to the table, Rebecca had poured their coffee and was sipping hers leisurely. "That was a nice thing to do."

He glanced at the small figure, already enthralled with the video. "I just feel so sorry for her," he admitted helplessly. "I know you shouldn't spoil children, but she's had such a tough time I didn't figure a few indulgences would hurt."

"I agree."

"So how did it go today?"

"That was going to be my next question for you," she replied with a smile.

"You first."

"She slept like a log last night, which I expected. We had pancakes for breakfast, went over and met Ben, stopped for burgers at lunch, then went to your place and got her settled in."

"I bet she liked the room."

Rebecca smiled, a flush of pleasure stealing over her cheeks. "Yes, she did. In fact, she asked me if I could come over tonight and tuck her in. I . . . I didn't think you'd mind, this first night," she said, her eyes anxious and uncertain as they met his.

He reached over and covered her hand with his, his eyes tinged with an intimate warmth that made her tingle all over as they locked on hers. "Rebecca, you are always welcome at our place."

She blushed and looked down, toying with her spoon as she surreptitiously looked at his tanned, lean-fingered hand covering hers. She liked his touch—a lot—in this no-risk setting. Maybe she could eventually learn to enjoy it when they were alone, as well. But in the meantime it was better to move on to safer subjects. "So tell me about your day," she prompted.

He removed his hand, and she missed his touch immediately. "It was good. But a bit overwhelming," he admitted. "The academic world is very different from what I'm used to. I'm glad Phil Carr filled me in a little. And I picked up quite a bit in the teachers' lounge, too. Everyone was very nice and went out of their way to be helpful."

"How were the kids?"

"A little wary. Scoping out the new teacher, getting the lay of the land. But they seem like good kids—in general."

"Why the qualifier?"

He frowned and took a sip of his coffee. "I'm teaching a creative writing class, and I had one kid who didn't turn in the homework. I mentioned his name in the lounge, and it seems he's somewhat of a troublemaker. Rarely does his homework, so his grades are marginal. But he aces out on tests, so he's obviously bright. It's a shame for potential like that to be wasted."

Rebecca frowned. "What's his name?"

"Pete Cramer."

She shook her head slowly. "Doesn't ring a bell."

"I got the impression that he comes from a broken home. Lives with his father, I think, who works at the plant."

"Maybe no one's ever really encouraged him," Rebecca speculated.

"How do you mean?"

She gazed at him earnestly. "Well, if someone took a real interest in him, *made* him do the work, he might blossom."

Zach frowned. "How do you *make* a seventeen-year-old boy do anything?"

"Long-term I guess it's a matter of finding a way to make him *want* to do it," she said thoughtfully. "In the meantime, though, some discipline might do the trick."

He gave her a rueful grin. "Not a popular word in this day and age."

"Maybe not," she agreed. "But being an authority figure isn't always a popularity contest," she pointed out. "I really believe that even though kids may *act* like they resent discipline, they respect it when it's administered by someone who is genuinely concerned about them. And I also think it boosts their self-esteem to know that someone cares enough to take that kind of interest."

Thoughtfully he took a sip of his coffee and eyed her speculatively. "You could be right."

"Well, I certainly don't have any great experience to draw on," she admitted. "But it might be helpful to be firm and set the rules right up front."

"I'll give that some thought," he promised, before turning the conversation to less serious topics.

By the time the video ended, Isabel's eyelids were drooping, and Zach glanced at Rebecca with a smile. "I think it's somebody's bedtime."

"It will take her several days to get over the jet lag," Rebecca replied sympathetically. "I'll just follow you home and get her settled for the night."

An hour later, as Rebecca leaned down to hug Isabel's thin shoulders and place a kiss on her forehead, the little girl clutched at her hand, her eyes wide and imploring.

"Couldn't you stay tonight?" she pleaded.

Rebecca regretfully shook her head. "I'm afraid not, Isabel. This is Zach's apartment."

"I bet he wouldn't mind if you stayed," she tried again, her bottom lip starting to quiver.

Would he? she wondered wistfully, then quickly squelched that wayward thought. "But I don't live here, Isabel," she gently reminded the little girl. "I'll see you in the morning, though. Zach will drop you off at the restaurant on his way to school."

"I . . . I miss my m-mama," Isabel said in a barely audible voice that was tinged with tears, gripping her Raggedy Ann doll fiercely.

With difficulty, Rebecca swallowed past the lump in her throat. "I know, sweetie."

"My papa says I have to be brave and not be sad, because now Mama is with God and she's happy and well again. But I still miss her."

"My mama is with God, too," Rebecca told Isabel, once more hugging her close. "And I still miss her every day, just like you miss your mama. But try not to be sad. I'm sure your mama would want you to be happy. You still have your papa, who loves you very much. And now you have Uncle Zach and me, too."

"W-will you stay till I f-fall asleep?"

"Of course I will. I'll even sing you a little song, how would that be?"

Rebecca didn't know any children's lullabies, so she chose a familiar hymn instead. By the time she sang it through twice, Isabel had drifted off, too worn out to stay awake, despite her best efforts. Gently Rebecca extricated her hand, and once more lightly brushed her lips across Isabel's forehead before rising.

Zach was waiting on the couch in the living room when she emerged, but he'd discreetly eavesdropped on the scene in the bedroom a couple of times. He'd heard enough to realize that Isabel was both homesick and grieving. And enough for his heart to be touched by Rebecca's tender, compassionate interaction with the frightened little girl. He wasn't surprised at the sheen of tears in her eyes when she finally appeared.

"Pretty tough situation for a little kid," he commiserated.

"Yeah." She blinked rapidly, trying to compose herself. "It's hard sometimes to understand why the Lord lets things like this happen."

"It's not just hard, it's impossible," Zach replied, a touch of bitterness in his voice.

"I guess that's true," she admitted. "But it's because we're trying to understand with our finite human intellect. It's almost a sin of pride to even suppose we could understand the ways of God."

"So you just accept everything?"

"Is there any other choice?" she asked quietly.

Zach rose and strode over to the window, staring out into the darkness just as he had the night he received Josef's letter. He jammed his hands into his pockets and sighed. "You sound a lot like Josef. He always accepted everything that happened as the Lord's will, even when he didn't see the reason for it. I guess that's what faith is all about."

"That's part of it, anyway," she concurred.

He continued to stare out into the darkness for a few moments, his brow knit pensively, but finally he expelled a long, weary breath and reached up to massage the back of his neck with one hand. "Listen, I want to thank you for coming over to get Isabel settled, Rebecca. You seem to have acquired an avid fan. I only hope I'll be as lucky." His tone was less than confident as he cast a worried glance toward the half-shut bedroom door.

"You will," she replied reassuringly. It would be hard for anyone not to like Zach, she thought silently—adult or child.

"I E-mailed Josef last night to let him know she arrived, so maybe at least now he'll have some peace of mind."

"That reminds me." Rebecca rose, speaking over her shoulder as she walked toward the coat closet. "I found something you need to see when I was unpacking Isabel's suitcases." She opened the door and withdrew a bulky parcel from the top shelf. "There's a letter taped to it that's addressed to both of us," she told him as she handed over the package and they sat down on the couch. "I was surprised to see my name on it. Did you mention me to Josef?" she asked quizzically.

He'd done a lot more than that, Zach reflected. Josef and he always shared important events in their lives, and meeting Rebecca certainly fell into that category.

"Yeah. I thought it might make Josef feel better to know that a woman would also be watching over Isabel." Which was true. But he'd mentioned Rebecca to Josef long before this situation came up. "Why don't we read it together?" he suggested.

He carefully pulled the white envelope free, then slit it open. As he unfolded the single sheet of paper, Rebecca scooted closer, and the room became silent as they both scanned the contents.

My Dear Zachary and Rebecca,

I address this note to you both because it seems you will share in the care of my precious Isabel. Rebecca, even though we have never met, I feel I know you from Zachary's letters. I am grateful that such a fine, generous and loving woman will be helping watch over my daughter, and I thank you most sincerely for your kindness. Since she just lost her mother, it will be good for Isabel to have a woman's care and special touch.

Zachary, this package is only to be opened in the event something happens to me while Isabel is with you. Otherwise, please return it unopened when Isabel comes home to me. Remember how you always used to tease me about being "buttoned down" when we were in school, about never leaving any loose ends hanging? (See? I have not forgotten my American slang!) Well, I am still that way, planning ahead for all possibilities.

My dear friends—and I now count you among those, Rebecca—I will never be able to repay the great favor you are doing for me. I send you my heartfelt thanks and eternal gratitude. Please know that in the weeks ahead you will be prominently in my prayers. And I ask that you keep me in yours as well. God bless you both.

Rebecca blinked back her tears as she finished reading the note, and Zach's ragged sigh told her he was equally moved. If Isabel's small hand so trustingly placed in hers at the airport yesterday had dispelled most of the doubts Rebecca harbored about the wisdom of her offer, this note banished any that lingered. For reasons of His own, the Lord had put her in a position to offer assistance to this traumatized family. Maybe she wasn't the best-qualified person for the job. She certainly didn't have any experience with children. But she did have a great capacity to love, and perhaps that, more than anything, was what was needed in this situation.

Rebecca thought again about the tragedy and heartbreak endured by the grieving, vulnerable child who now slept peacefully in the next room and by her loving father, driven to extreme measures by their desperate plight, and her heart ached. She couldn't even imagine how difficult it must have been for Josef to put his child, who meant more to him than anything else in the world, on that plane and send her thousands of miles away. His sacrifice was a true measure of the depth of his love, and Rebecca vowed to do everything in her power to give Isabel the comfort and love and stability she so badly needed.

Slowly Zach folded the letter and silently replaced it in the envelope. Rebecca studied his profile, the familiar elements of strength, character and integrity now underlaid with pain, sadness and worry. She had never been blessed with a friendship like Zach's and Josef's, but she realized that the ties that bound them truly were stronger than blood. Strong enough for Zach to feel Josef's pain almost as keenly as if it was his own. Her instinct was to reach over and comfort him, to lay a gentle hand on his arm, but she was afraid to initiate even such an innocent touch. So she let her hands rest motionless in her lap.

As if sensing her scrutiny, Zach turned to look into her sympathetic eyes. "I wish there was—" He stopped to clear his throat. "I wish there was more I could do."

"You're doing everything you can, Zach," she consoled him.

He glanced back at the package in his lap. "Yeah, I guess so," he replied wearily.

"Josef did ask for our prayers. That's something else you could do," she offered quietly.

He shook his head. "I think I'll have to let you do the praying for both of us, Rebecca. I'm sure God will be more likely to listen to a firm believer like you than a wayward soul like me. I haven't prayed with any real conviction in six or seven years."

"It's not too late to start again," she reminded him softly, wishing he would. Because she had a feeling that if he did, much of the restlessness, the searching, she sensed in him would ease.

"It is tonight. I'm beat. It's been a long day for you, too. We both ought to just go to bed."

At another time, under different circumstances, Rebecca might have sensed an innuendo in that remark. But not tonight. It was a simple statement of fact, and judging by the lines of fatigue on his face, Zach really was all in. She was fading fast herself. "You're right," she agreed, rising to retrieve her purse. "I'd better take off."

Zach rose and followed her to the door, still subdued. As she turned to say good-night, she wanted to reach over and smooth the twin furrows in his brow, which spoke more eloquently than words of his troubled thoughts and deep concern. But again she held back.

"Good night, Zach," she said softly.

"I'll walk you to your car."

"I'm right here." She pointed to her older-model car just steps from his door.

"Oh. Well, I guess I'll see you tomorrow morning, then. Is eight-thirty okay? My first class is at nine."

"That's fine. And don't worry about breakfast for Isabel. I'll give her something when you drop her off."

"Are you sure?"

"Absolutely. I'll be cooking, anyway. And Zach," she paused and glanced down shyly. "Thanks again for the flowers."

He smiled, and the concern in his eyes gave way to an intimate warmth that made her pulse take a sudden leap. "I'm glad you liked them."

She looked up at him, her eyes suddenly filled with a wistful yearning that he knew she wasn't even aware of. It made him want to pull her into his arms, to let his lips say good-night in a way that expressed more clearly than words both his gratitude for her support during this difficult time, as well as the depth of his attraction to her. Somehow, the latter had been relegated to the back burner in the past week as they'd both prepared for Isabel's arrival and he'd prepped for his new job. But he didn't intend for it to stay there much longer. Now that he'd settled into his apartment, started his job and Isabel had safely arrived, he could turn his attention back to the most important thing in his life at the moment. Rebecca.

Except that he still needed to be patient and move slowly, he reminded himself, recalling Henry's sound words of advice. So though his hands longed to pull her close, he stuck them into the pockets of his slacks instead and drew a long, shaky breath. "Drive safely, okay?"

With difficulty, she pulled her gaze away from the compelling intensity of his eyes. "Sure. It's not like I have far to go." She tried for a joking tone, but her voice sounded breathless.

"Will you call me when you get there?"

She looked at him in surprise. "Why?"

"I'll just feel better knowing you're home safe and sound."

She was touched by his concern, and a flush tinted her cheeks. "If you want me to," she agreed. "Good night."

As she turned and walked away, her heart felt lighter than it had in years. For the first time ever, she had a man in her life who cared about her and a child who needed her. The circumstances weren't exactly what she'd imagined years ago, when she'd dreamed of a husband and family. But it felt good nonetheless. And right.

Rebecca knew this idyll was only going to last a few weeks. But she resolved to make the most of her time with this special man and charming child. And when it was over . . . well, for once in her life she would follow Scarlett O'Hara's advice. She would worry about that tomorrow.

Chapter Eight

Zach wasn't sure what woke him in the predawn hours. A noise of some sort, he assumed, listening as intently as he could manage in his half-comatose state. But the apartment was absolutely still. With a sigh he turned on his side and hitched the sheet up higher on his bare chest, drifting back to sleep even as he did so. But he was still awake enough to feel the sudden slight jolt, almost as if someone had bumped into his unfolded sleeper sofa bed.

His eyes snapped open and he rose on one elbow, squinting into the dimness as he made a rapid three-hundred-and-sixty-degree scan around the bed. But there was nothing. He frowned. How bizarre! Could that gentle shake, almost like a nudge, have been caused by an earth tremor? he wondered. He knew this area was prone to them. Yet somehow he felt that wasn't the explanation.

Perplexed, he glanced down at the floor—and got his first clue. A blanket trailed along the floor, disappearing from his sight as it reached the bed. He inched closer to the edge and cautiously looked down, his throat contracting at the sight that met his eyes.

Isabel was curled into a ball on the floor, wedged as close as possible next to the bed, her doll clutched to her chest. One bare foot peeked out from beneath the trailing blanket, and even as he watched she scooted closer still to the couch, making it vibrate ever so slightly.

Zach didn't have any experience with children. Had never *wanted* to have any. The idea of being responsible for some little person who was totally dependent had never appealed to him. But the pathetic sight of this tiny, frightened child seeking the comfort of mere human proximity just about did him in.

Moving with extreme care so as not to disturb her, he swung his feet to the floor, then bent down and scooped her up, cradling the reed-thin body in his arms. There was nothing to her, he thought in shock, her featherlike weight hardly registering. She felt like . . . like a wisp, and he was once again struck by her vulnerability. Isabel whimpered slightly, and he held her closer, instinctively rocking her gently in his arms, murmuring soothing sounds as he made his way back to her room. But when he tried to lay her down, her thin little arms snaked around his neck and she held on fiercely, showing remarkable strength for someone so tiny. Short of prying her arms away— and waking her up in the process—there wasn't much choice but to take her back to bed with him, he realized.

He retraced his route, easing himself down and stretching out carefully, Isabel still in his arms. She burrowed next to him as he pulled up the sheet and blanket, and as he looked down at the tiny body so trustingly cuddled against his, his heart was filled with tenderness. It was funny, really. He'd spent his life avoiding commitments that involved women and children. He'd always believed that they would be too demanding, that they would distract him from the really important things in life—like his work. But since arriving in St. Genevieve, he'd been forced to rethink that opinion, reexamine his priorities. He now had a woman *and* a child in his life, both of whom seemed achingly vulnerable and so in need of love. This little one in his arms was totally dependent on him.

And Rebecca . . . well, she didn't need him in the sense Isabel did, to provide food and shelter and the day-to-day necessities of life. But she seemed to need him in other ways. He'd come to the conclusion that for reasons he had not yet discovered, her heart was being held prisoner. But he also believed that it yearned to be free. He could see it in the wistful longing reflected in her eyes. Somehow he felt the key to her freedom was in his hands, that if he was patient he would find a way to release her captive heart.

And so, in different ways, he felt responsible for both Rebecca and Isabel. That sense of responsibility to another person was never something he'd wanted. But the odd thing was, now that he had it, he *liked* it. Caring about them, being committed to their well-being, didn't seem like a burden at all. It seemed like a gift. Because both of these special ladies had already enriched his life in countless ways.

"Pete . . . I'd like to see you for a minute."

The tall, lanky youth looked at Zach nervously, then shot a glance at his buddies, who were waiting in the hall. Zach noted the direction of his gaze, and as the last student filed out of his classroom, he very deliberately moved over to the door and firmly closed it.

"I have to go or I'll miss my ride," the boy said, trying for defiance but not quite pulling it off.

"How far away do you live?" Zach asked, keeping his tone casual.

"About three miles."

"No problem. I'll take you home when we're finished."

"Finished with what?" the boy asked suspiciously.

"Let me ask you something, Pete," Zach replied, ignoring the question as he propped a shoulder against the door and folded his arms across his chest. "Why did you take this class?"

Pete stared at him. "What do you mean?"

"Why did you take this class?" Zach repeated.

The boy shrugged. "It sounded better than another year of English lit."

"You did realize that in a creative writing class you'd be expected to write, didn't you?"

He gave Zach a sullen look, but remained silent.

Zach held his gaze steadily, and finally Pete's wavered, dropping to the floor as he shoved his hands in his pockets and shifted nervously from one foot to the other.

"I'll tell you what," Zach continued conversationally. "I'm new here, and as far as I'm concerned you're starting with a clean slate. You've only missed one homework assignment so far, and I'm going to let you make it up right now."

"Now?" Pete repeated, his dumbfounded gaze jolting up to Zach's.

"That's right. It shouldn't take you long. An hour at the most."

"But what if I don't want to?"

Zach pushed himself away from the door and walked toward the boy, hesitating in surprise for a brief second when Pete took a startled step back, almost as if he expected to be struck. Zach resumed his advance more slowly. "I think you do want to, Pete," he said quietly, his eyes locked on the youth's. "I've heard you're quite a student when you put your mind to it. And Mr. Carr said you have a real talent with words. I'd like to see what you can do."

"Why?" Pete asked suspiciously.

Zach considered his answer carefully, sensing that whatever he said could make or break his relationship with this boy. "Well, I happen to admire good writing," he said frankly. "There's a magic in being able to put words on paper in a way that brings a story to life, whether it's an investigative article or a short story. I think it's a very special gift, and people who have that gift should be encouraged to develop it. One of the best ways to do that is by writing as much as possible. So if you have the gift, I'd like to do what I can to help you develop it."

Pete stared at him for a moment, then looked down and shuffled his feet. "I'm not that good."

"Why don't you let me be the judge?" Zach suggested. "Would a laptop help?"

Pete gave him a surprised look. "Yeah."

"Good thing I brought mine along, then," Zach replied, flashing the teenager a grin. "You okay with Word Perfect?"

"Sure."

Zach retrieved the computer from underneath his desk and zipped open the case. "I'll print your work out at home," he told Pete as he set up the computer on a desk and plugged it in. "You ever work on one of these before?"

"No."

"Let me show you a couple of things, then."

With minimal instruction, and after asking a couple of astute questions, Pete was comfortable with the computer. The boy was sharp, Zach thought, just as the other teachers had said. "Okay, have at it. I'll be up front correcting papers. No hurry."

Fortunately he'd already told Rebecca of his plan, which she enthusiastically endorsed, and so she knew he would he late picking up Isabel tonight. He glanced at Pete, who sat slumped in front of the computer, staring at the screen, his fingers still idle. Suddenly, though, the boy leaned forward and started to type, and Zach settled back to finish reading the papers that had been turned in on Monday. So far so good.

He lost track of time as he made his way through the stack, writing both compliments and constructive criticism on each paper. The students were creative, he had to give them that. But there was plenty of room for improvement in terms of style, grammar and punctuation. Had the school ever considered a journalism class? he wondered. Or an editing class? Both would be excellent ways for students to polish the basics, as well as develop tight writing styles. They would be fairly easy to institute, he mused. It would just require . . .

"I'm finished."

Zach glanced up at Pete, who stood with his shoulders slouched, hands in his pockets, on the other side of the desk. Zach glanced at his watch—just over an hour. At least he'd made some sort of effort and not just blown the assignment off, he thought in relief.

"Great. Go ahead and shut down the computer while I gather up these papers. Then I'll drive you home."

"You don't have to do that. I can hitch a ride."

"A promise is a promise," Zach replied firmly as he stood up and slid the stack of papers into his briefcase.

Pete silently retreated to stow the computer, and by the time he returned Zach was waiting. "So how long have you lived in St. Genevieve, Pete?" he asked conversationally as he led the way to his car.

Pete shrugged. "Too long."

Zach looked at him. "You don't like it here?"

"It's okay, I guess. For a small town."

"You like cities better?"

"Yeah. I'm going to move to Chicago or New York or maybe even L.A. when I get out of school. Someplace where there's more action." He turned to look at Zach. "Are you really an investigative reporter?"

"That's right."

"So what are you doing here? Teaching must be pretty boring after that."

"Depends on how you define *boring*," Zach countered. "Let me tell you something, Pete. I've seen my share of action, and believe it or not, it isn't all that glamorous," he said frankly. "Teaching may not look exciting, but it can be very satisfying. That's why I double majored in college. As for why I'm here . . . it was timing, I guess. I was ready for a break from the fast life in St. Louis, and with Mr. Carr out, it was a good chance for me to get back into teaching, even if it's only for the rest of the semester." Zach glanced over at Pete, in time to catch a fleeting—but grudging—look of admiration in his eyes. "So now tell me about you."

Pete was reticent at first, but under Zach's casual but targeted probing he revealed a great deal. Some things Zach learned by the words Pete said; others, by the words he didn't say.

He came from a broken home, and apparently there had been a great deal of bitterness in the divorce seven years before. His father was awarded custody simply because his mother didn't want him. Zach got the distinct impression that there was no love lost between father and son. It seemed Pete had had a couple of minor run-ins with the law, which had alienated father and son even more. Even in the best of circumstances, however, Frank Cramer did not sound like the nurturing type, Zach thought grimly. He apparently didn't care how Pete did in school, didn't place much value on education, figured if a plant job was good enough for him it ought to be good enough for his son. He especially didn't think much of Pete's interest in writing and literature. In fact, it didn't sound like he thought much of Pete, period. Given that environment, Zach was surprised Pete showed up at school at all.

When they pulled up in front of the tiny house on the outskirts of town, Zach turned to Pete. "I expect you to finish today's assignment on time, Pete," he said, his gaze direct, his tone no-nonsense.

Pete half opened the door, then turned back to look at Zach. "Are you gonna make me stay late again if I don't?"

"Yes, I am."

Pete hesitated, then climbed out of the car. "Thanks for the lift."

"No problem. See you tomorrow."

As Zach pulled away from the curb, he glanced in the rearview mirror. Pete was still standing there, staring after the car, his hands in his pockets, his posture slouched. Zach wasn't sure how successful he'd been with the boy. His plan had been to be firm, to set the ground rules, as Rebecca had suggested. At the same time, he wanted to appear approachable and caring. And it appeared that Pete needed someone like that in his life.

Zach sighed. This teaching business was a whole lot more complicated than he'd expected. He'd always thought of it as classroom work—lecturing, grading papers, that kind of thing. He hadn't expected to get drawn into the lives of his students outside of class. But he now realized it was impossible to separate the two. One influenced the other.

Zach wasn't sure if he'd gotten through to Pete. But someone needed to. Because if what the other teachers said about his intelligence was true, it could very well be his ticket to the larger world he craved.

The challenge was to convince him of that.

"Well, I'll be," Zach said softly as he read the final line.

Rebecca looked up curiously from the board game she was playing on the floor with Isabel. "What's up?"

Zach glanced over at her and shook his head. "I just read Pete's paper."

"And?" she prompted.

"This kid can write," he replied, shaking his head in amazement. "I mean really write. Not high-school-level stuff, either. And this is just something he whipped off in an hour," he added incredulously. "If I hadn't been sitting there while he wrote it I wouldn't believe this was his work."

"Can I see?" Rebecca asked.

"Sure. I'd appreciate a second opinion. I was hoping he'd have talent, so maybe my judgment is jaded. Maybe I'm seeing more here than there really is."

Rebecca took the sheets of paper and reached over to smooth back Isabel's hair. "I'll be right with you, okay, sweetie?"

"Okay. Can I have another cookie while I wait?"

Rebecca smiled. "I think that would be all right."

Isabel jumped up and scampered toward Zach's tiny kitchenette as Rebecca scooted toward the couch and leaned against the front. Zach settled back into the cushions, content for the moment to enjoy the view of her long, shapely legs stretched out in front of her, to leisurely trace the enticing curves of her toned, firm body, to appreciate the endearing way she chewed her lower lip as she read, a frown of concentration on her brow.

When she'd appeared at the door earlier in the evening with a plate of chocolate chip cookies, he'd been taken aback. He'd been desperately searching for an excuse to invite her over, increasingly frustrated by their brief hellos and goodbyes at the restaurant when he dropped Isabel off and picked her up. He wanted to spend time with Rebecca, but neither of their schedules had allowed for that this week. Except for Monday night, when they'd had dinner together, he'd barely had a chance to say more than a dozen words to her. Tuesday night she'd driven to St. Louis to teach a cooking class at a gourmet shop. Wednesday night she had a church function. He'd thought about asking her to have dinner with them tonight when he picked up Isabel earlier in the afternoon, but when he'd arrived Rose told him that Rebecca had gone to the bank. So he'd written off this evening. To say he'd been glad to see her at the door was an understatement. He enjoyed spending time with Isabel, was grateful that she had warmed up to him, but he was desperately in need of some adult company. Preferably of the female variety. And preferably someone named Rebecca.

As he gazed down at her bent head, he thought about how much his life had changed in the past five weeks. He'd gone from hotshot investigative reporter to high school English teacher, from swinging single to pseudo family man. And he liked it. A lot. It was as if a missing piece in his life had suddenly fallen into place. If he didn't know better, he'd think . . .

"Wow!" The single word, spoken in a hushed tone, reassured Zach that he wasn't off base in his assessment of Pete's work.

"So I was right?"

Rebecca turned to look at him, her eyes incredulous. "This is amazing! It's written with such sensitivity, such pathos . . . how old is Pete?"

"Seventeen."

She shook her head. "Incredible. All I can say is, he has a future ahead of him if this is any sample of his ability."

"Can we finish our game now, Rebecca?" Isabel asked.

"Sure thing, sweetie. Then it's off to bed for you." She turned once more to Zach. "It would be wrong to waste this kind of talent. I hope you can get through to him," she said earnestly.

"I hope so, too."

"Hi, Rebecca. How's it going down there in the boonies?"

Rebecca smiled as she recognized the familiar voice of her wise-cracking, heart-of-gold sister-in-law. "Hi, Sam. I hear tell we're going to get running water next week," she replied in an exaggerated country-folk accent.

Sam chuckled. "Touché," she conceded. "But you do seem far away. We never get to see enough of you."

"Well, right now I should think company would be the last thing you'd want. Don't you have your hands full with a little bundle of joy named Emily?"

"She does keep me hopping," Sam admitted cheerfully, clearly not minding in the least.

"So how are you feeling?"

"Tired. But isn't that the story of all new mothers? Otherwise, great."

"How's Brad?"

"Tired," she echoed. "But loving every minute of being a daddy."

"Why am I not surprised?" Rebecca said affectionately.

"Listen, Rebecca, speaking of Easter . . ."

"Were we?" Rebecca asked with a smile, used to Sam's conversational gymnastics—one direction one minute, another the next.

"As long as you mention it, no. But we are now. So what are you doing?"

"Now, or on Easter?" she teased.

"Easter, of course. Stay with me here, Rebecca."

"I'm trying," Rebecca replied with a laugh. That was one of the things she loved about talking to Sam—the other woman always made her laugh. She'd never met anyone with quite as much life and energy as Sam, and her sister-in-law made Brad incredibly happy. Which meant that as far as Rebecca was concerned, Sam was the greatest.

"So? What are your plans?"

"I don't have any yet," she admitted.

"Good. Because we'd love to have you up for the day. Henry is coming to visit for about a week, and we could all go to church together, have a nice dinner. It would be a great chance for us all to catch up."

"That does sound good," Rebecca agreed. But what about Zach and Isabel? she wondered, biting her lip. She hated to leave them alone on the holiday.

"And you're welcome to bring Isabel," Sam added, as if reading her sister-in-law's mind.

"Oh, I think she'd like that!" Rebecca replied with a relieved smile. "She hasn't had a chance to do much since she's been here. We've just been too busy to take her anywhere."

"Zach is welcome, too, by the way," Sam threw in with an air of casual indifference that didn't fool Rebecca for a minute. Rebecca had made it a point to downplay her relationship with Zach, saying simply that she was helping out a friend. But Sam's invitation clearly implied that she suspected it was more than that. Which left only one explanation. Henry.

"What has Dad been telling you?" Rebecca asked suspiciously.

"Oh, not much," Sam replied airily. "Not much at all. Just that you brought a really hot-looking guy down there to pick up the furniture. An *interested* hot-looking guy. No, I stand corrected. Make that a *very* interested hot-looking guy. And that the feeling seemed to be mutual. Of course, this is all secondhand information, you understand. We're only the brother and sister-in-law. Why should you tell us anything?"

The chiding was good-natured in tone, but Rebecca was immensely grateful that Sam couldn't see the crimson color that nevertheless flooded her face. She should have figured Henry would freely offer information—and opinion. She'd better set things straight right now. "I would have been glad to tell you—if there was anything to tell," she pointed out, congratulating herself on her matter-of-fact delivery. "Zach is just an acquaintance, like I've told you all along."

"So then I guess you don't want to bring him along for Easter, this being a family gathering and all," Sam countered innocently.

Rebecca squirmed on her chair, tucking a leg under her. She'd backed herself into this corner, now she had to find a way out. "Well, I hate for him to be alone on a holiday," she hedged.

"That would be a shame," Sam agreed.

"It might be the kind thing to do, to invite him to spend the day with us."

"Yes, I suppose it would."

"Well, I guess I could ask, anyway."

"I guess you could."

"All he can do is say no."

"That's right."

She took a deep breath. "Okay. I'll ask."

"Good. We'll expect you all then. We can meet at church, if that's okay. We'll save you a seat. Look for the redhead with the squalling baby."

Rebecca grinned. "Okay."

"And, Rebecca, one other thing."

"Yes?"

"If this guy is even close to the way Henry describes him, go for it!"

Rebecca's face flamed again. "Sam, I told you that—"

"I know, I know," she interrupted. "But listen, kiddo. I've been there. I was into this let's-be-friends-because-nothing-else-could-possibly-work-between-us mode for a long time with Brad. I fought the attraction as hard as I could, but fortunately your brother persevered. In the end I listened to my heart, and look where I am now? My version of paradise—at least as close as you can get on earth. All I'm saying is that if you're interested, give it a chance. Don't let fear hold you back." She paused for a moment, and when she spoke again her tone was noticeably lighter. "Well, enough lecturing for one day. We'll see you on Easter, okay?"

"Okay."

As Rebecca slowly replaced the receiver, she thought about Sam's words of advice. Rebecca was definitely interested. And she wasn't hiding it very well, either, if her father had picked up on it so quickly. But her fear—that was something else again. How did one control something that was irrational, that had no basis in reality, that was an instinctive response? she cried in silent despair. But no answer was forthcoming. And until one did, the situation was hopeless.

* * *

"Pete? I'd like to see you for a minute."

The boy looked at Zach defensively. "I turned in my homework."

"I know. I want to talk to you about something else. Go ahead and sit down."

Pete hovered uncertainly for a moment, then folded his long frame into a convenient desk, assuming his familiar slouch position. Zach waited until the last student exited, then shut the door and joined Pete, sitting down in the desk beside him. "I wanted to give you your paper back."

He took the assignment out of a folder and held it out to Pete. A look of trepidation quickly swept over the boy's eyes before being replaced by defensiveness. "I had to rush," he protested, his chin jutting out defiantly. "I didn't have a chance to—"

"Look at the paper, Pete," Zach interrupted quietly.

Pete sullenly reached for the paper, his eyes widening in surprise when he glanced at it. "You gave me an A?" he asked incredulously, staring at Zach in amazement.

"You deserved it. Go ahead, read over my comments." He settled back in his seat, waiting as Pete worked his way meticulously through the paper, carefully reading each of the constructive—and complimentary—remarks written in Zach's scrawling hand. When he reached the last one, the teenager read it once, then again, before looking up speechlessly, his face flushed.

Zach leaned forward and folded his arms on the desk. "That is a fine piece of work. You should be proud of it. And it confirms what Phil Carr told me. You do have talent. Very great talent. And I don't want to see it go to waste." He opened the folder again and removed two items, handing them to Hank one at a time. "This is some information on a national short story contest that I think you ought to consider entering. There are monetary prizes involved, but even more important, it would look very impressive on a college application. It would also give you a chance to be published. And this is a brochure about a writing camp being held in Michigan this August. It's for gifted writers, and I think you qualify. Look them both over, and we'll talk about them next week."

Pete stared in stunned silence at the brochures in his hands, then back at Zach. There was a new eagerness, an excitement, in his eyes that transformed his expression from sullen rebelliousness to youthful optimism.

"Do you really think I could do these things?" he asked.

"Absolutely. I wouldn't have given you the brochures if I didn't."

Zach saw the boy's Adam's apple bob, as if Pete was having difficulty swallowing. "Well, thanks," he said, rising suddenly, his face averted. "I'll read them this weekend. See you Monday."

He made his escape quickly, and Zach didn't try to detain him. He knew Pete was overcome by emotion, a tricky situation for a teenager trying to be cool and macho who didn't know quite how to handle such sentiment. He understood. But he also understood something else.

Pete had just been waiting for someone to care, to take an interest, to encourage him. Now that he'd found such a person in Zach, there was a chance he might shape up, might rethink the importance of education, might begin to consider the possibilities that it offered.

Zach knew people's lives didn't change overnight. Fifteen years of investigative reporting had taught him that. But lives *could* change, if people made an effort and learned to believe in themselves. And he had a feeling that Pete had just taken a step in the right direction.

Rebecca added a dollop of whipped cream to the final piece of chocolate torte, deposited the three servings on a tray, then paused, fidgeting nervously. She'd been trying to work up her courage to ask Zach about Easter ever since Sam's phone call two days before, and she still hadn't decided on the right approach. It was a family gathering, after all, and she didn't want him to get the wrong impression. Yes, she was interested. And yes, she hoped at some point she'd find the courage to give dating him another try. But she wasn't at that point yet. And she didn't want him to think she was. She had to find a way to let him know the invitation was only a friendly gesture, that—

"My goodness, Rebecca, that whipped cream is going to deflate if you stand there staring at it much longer!" Rose declared, planting her hands on her ample hips. "Just go ahead and ask the man. I guarantee he'll say yes."

Rebecca was sorry now she'd even mentioned the Easter invitation to Rose and Frances. She had done it in a moment of weakness, and she'd been paying for her lapse all morning. The sisters had been all for it, of course. They'd fallen in love with Isabel, coddling her and loving her like grandmothers, and the little girl had thrived on their attention. And of course they'd been enamored with Zach ever since he sent Rebecca that bouquet of roses. So their employer's reluctance to issue a simple invitation bewildered them.

"I'll ask him for you if you want me to," Frances offered helpfully.

"No! I mean, that's very kind, Frances, but it really should come from me. I was just going in." She lifted the tray and marched determinedly toward the door to the dining room, faltering only when she safely reached the other side and her gaze fell on Zach and Isabel, conversing very seriously and intently at a corner table. She paused to watch their interaction, glad that most of the Saturday lunch customers had departed. He looked great, she thought wistfully, appreciatively noting how his worn jeans and off-white cotton sweater enhanced his rugged good looks.

Just then he reached over to tousle Isabel's hair playfully, and she giggled, the sound of childish pleasure bringing a smile to Rebecca's face. She knew Isabel continued to miss her home and her parents. She talked about them often, excitedly relaying to Rebecca the messages she and Zach received on E-mail from Josef. But at least she seemed comfortable in her new environment, no longer withdrawn and uncertain as she'd been for the first few days.

As Rebecca watched them chatting, she let her eyes rest admiringly on Zach's strong profile. She knew that a child was the last thing he wanted in his life at this particular time. Yet he'd welcomed her without question, honoring a fifteen-year-old promise without hesitation, then constructed his lifestyle to accommodate her. Few men would behave that unselfishly, she knew. He truly was a rare find. Which made it all the harder for her to hide her feelings. But she had to, she told herself resolutely. Because she wasn't yet ready to face anything more than friendship. So, drawing in a deep breath, she put on her best "friend" smile and hoisted the tray into a more comfortable position.

The movement caught Zach's eye, and he turned. His mouth curved up into a lazy smile as he looked at her, and the simmering heat in his eyes was impossible to ignore as his gaze swept her lithe form. When his eyes reconnected with hers she could feel the sizzle of electricity between them, and she knew one thing with absolute clarity. Zach was not thinking friendship.

Flustered, Rebecca blushed, and his smile broadened. It was as if he sensed her discomfort, knew the reason and was pleased. So much for hiding her feelings, she thought wryly. But she had to keep up the pretense. For now.

"Well, are you two ready for dessert?" she asked, moving forward gamely, her voice determinedly cheerful.

"I always like something sweet after a meal," Zach replied, the husky tone in his voice and the look in his eyes implying he had another sort of treat in mind as he rose to pull out her chair.

"Chocolate cake! Oh, goodie!" Isabel exclaimed, reaching for hers eagerly and diving in enthusiastically.

Rebecca no longer had to wonder if Zach's interest in romance had died as a result of her rebuff the night of her birthday dinner. It was alive and well, she realized, suddenly finding it difficult to breathe as she sank down into her chair. Obviously he'd just been distracted during the last couple of weeks. Which wasn't surprising, given all that had been going on in his life. But he wasn't distracted now, she thought, venturing a glance at him as he snagged a piece of torte on his fork, then looked at her. The ardent light in his eyes left absolutely no doubt about his interest. Rebecca literally stopped breathing, her gaze riveted to his.

"This is good!" Isabel pronounced. "I like dessert."

"That makes two of us," Zach seconded, his eyes never leaving Rebecca.

The front door opened, and only when Ben strolled over did Zach finally release her gaze.

"Hi, there," Ben said cheerfully.

"Hi, Ben," Rebecca replied, her voice strained.

Ben looked at her worriedly. "You gettin' a cold?"

She shook her head, a delicate flush tinting her cheeks. "No. I'm fine. What brings you here? Do you want to join us for dessert?" she asked hopefully, thinking Ben's presence might dispel the present mood, which was fraught with overtones she didn't seem able to handle.

"No, thanks. Just taking a break for a few minutes. Thought

Isabel might like to take a stroll with me. What do you say, little lady?"

"Can I, Uncle Zach?" she asked eagerly.

"I don't see why not," he agreed.

"We'll be back in a few minutes," Ben promised, taking Isabel's hand. As he turned to leave, Rebecca saw him glance quickly toward the kitchen door, where Rose and Frances were watching the proceedings with interest. As she caught their eyes, however, the sisters turned away guiltily, and the light suddenly dawned. This was a conspiracy. She should have known that Ben's arrival was too well timed to be a coincidence. The sisters and Ben had conspired to give Zach some time alone with her. The question was, had he been in on it?

She turned to look at him suspiciously, but he held up his palms in protest. "I know what you're thinking. But I had nothing to do with this. Although I can't say I mind too much," he added with a smile, reaching over to cover her hand with his. "I've missed you these past two weeks."

She swallowed, acutely conscious of his hand resting protectively and caringly over hers. "You see me all the time," she protested faintly, knowing that wasn't what he meant.

Don't push, he told himself. *Remember:* Patience *is the operative word here. Play it cool and casual until she's ready for something more.*

"True," he said easily. "But we've both been so busy we've hardly had a chance to say more than a few words to each other. And as much as I enjoy being with Isabel, I could do with some adult company."

Had she jumped to the wrong conclusions? Rebecca wondered suddenly. Misread the spark in his eyes earlier? Maybe he was just glad to have an adult to talk to. She didn't have enough experience with men to know for sure in situations like this whether they were pursuing or platonic.

"So I thought maybe you might join Isabel and me on a few outings now and then," he finished.

"Outings?" she repeated curiously.

"Sure. You know, the state park, the zoo and science center in St. Louis, that sort of thing."

"Oh." Those kinds of things sounded safe enough, she thought. "Sure."

"Great! How about a picnic tomorrow?"

"I can't tomorrow," she declined with honest regret. "I promised to help out at the church supper."

"That's too bad," he said disappointedly. "And next Sunday is Easter, so I'm sure you have plans then."

This was her opening. Now was the time to issue the invitation. She looked down at her uneaten cake, the whipped cream rapidly deflating—as was her courage. *Just ask,* she told herself sternly. *Stop trying to second-guess how he'll interpret the invitation. Remember what Sam said: don't let fear hold you back.*

"You're right, I do have plans," she confirmed slowly. "I'm going up to St. Louis to spend the day with Brad and Sam. Dad will be there, too."

"Sounds nice."

"Actually, Sam said it would be okay if I brought Isabel. And she . . . she said you were welcome, too, if you wanted to come," Rebecca finished in a rush.

Zach tilted his head and eyed her speculatively. His first inclination was to accept immediately. But if it was going to make her uncomfortable with her family, he was reluctant to infringe. "How do you feel about that, Rebecca?" he asked quietly.

She hesitated, trying to frame her answer in a way that wouldn't make him think the invitation was too personal, even if she did want them both to come. "Well, I hate for you two to be alone on a holiday," she hedged.

"So you're inviting us out of sympathy?"

She squirmed in her chair. "No. I . . . I like you both. And it would be a nice change for Isabel."

"You could just take her."

He was putting her on the spot, calling her bluff. He was going to make her admit that she wanted him to come. Or maybe he was being considerate, giving her an out in case having him along would make her uncomfortable. Which it no doubt would, to some extent. But still, she'd like to spend the holiday with him, and she might as well admit it.

"I'd like for you to come, Zach, if you want to," she said softly, keeping her eyes downcast.

He reached for her hand, and when she looked up, she thought she detected a look of relief in his eyes. "I most definitely want to," he assured her with a smile.

She returned the smile tentatively, but a moment later it changed to a frown.

"What's wrong?" he prompted.

"I just remembered . . . You know Brad's a minister, and we're all going to meet at his church for the service when we arrive. But I know churchgoing isn't exactly on your Sunday schedule."

"That's true. But it won't kill me to go on Easter," he replied easily. "In fact, that reminds me. I've been meaning to ask if you would mind taking Isabel to church with you on Sundays. I know Josef would want her to go."

"Not at all," she assured him.

"Thanks. And Rebecca . . ."

"Yes?" She looked at him curiously.

"I want you to know that . . ."

"We're back!" Isabel announced, settling herself in her chair once more.

"We had a nice walk, didn't we, little lady?" Ben remarked.

"Yes. It was fun."

"Well, I'll see you two later," Ben said with a little salute before exiting.

"Rebecca! You didn't eat your cake!" Isabel pointed out in a horrified voice.

"No. I . . . I guess I didn't," she admitted.

"Can I have it?"

"But sweetie, you already had a piece."

"I'm still hungry."

Rebecca glanced at Zach with a helpless look.

"How about if I give you half?" Zach suggested, reaching over to divide Rebecca's neglected cake with his knife. Their eyes met, and she tried to read the end of his interrupted sentence in his eyes. What did he want her to know? But whatever he'd been intending to say, he had clearly decided to save it for another time.

And maybe that was better, she consoled herself. She had a feeling that whatever revelation he'd almost disclosed would only make her nervous. And she was nervous enough already.

Chapter Nine

When Rebecca opened the door on Easter morning, her breath caught in her throat as she drank in the sight of Zach, handsome and distinguished in his dark gray suit, crisp white shirt and blue-and-silver tie, his hair still slightly damp and darkened from the shower. He had such . . . presence, that was the word, she decided. Not to mention charisma and an almost tangible virility. All of which meant he could turn her to mush with just a glance. Especially a glance like the one he was giving her now as his gaze swept over her swiftly but comprehensively, lingering for just a moment on her loose, flowing hair. His smile of greeting remained unchanged during that quick glance, but the warmth in his eyes erupted into a white-hot blaze.

Zach reached up to run a finger around his suddenly tight collar, swallowing with difficulty. He had seen Rebecca in a variety of outfits, but none seemed to capture her essence as well as this one. Zach didn't know much about women's clothes, but for some reason Rebecca's attire gave her an old-fashioned beauty that made him think of afternoon tea or a garden party. From the gracious sweetheart neckline visible beneath the fitted, short-sleeved bolero jacket, to the full skirt that flared out from the tightly cinched waist, the style was eminently flattering to her trim, utterly feminine figure. And the pastel floral cotton fabric seemed to echo the spring hues of the lavender redbuds and pink flowering apple trees now blooming in profusion throughout the countryside.

But the crowning glory—literally—was her hair. Freed from the constraints of her usual French twist, the soft, unfettered waves cascaded past her shoulders, the glorious russet strands glinting in the golden morning sun as they framed her classic features. The wide-brimmed straw hat, adorned with a cluster of silk flowers in the back, was the perfect final touch.

Though Zach had adeptly avoided long-term romantic entanglements throughout his dating career, he was by no means immune to feminine charms. But he was usually drawn to savvy, sophisticated women. The girl-next-door type usually sent him fleeing in the opposite direction, away from all the things she represented—namely, commitment and responsibility and the constraints of a white picket fence.

But despite the fact that Rebecca was definitely of the girl-next-door variety, he wasn't running now—much to his surprise. In fact, just the opposite. There was something about her innate goodness, her straightforward honesty and innocence, that drew him in a way that the sophisticated qualities of the other women of his acquaintance never had.

As he looked at her in the gentle light of morning, his senses suddenly went haywire, and he was tempted to reach over and pull her into his arms, to kiss her sweetly tender lips, to run his fingers through her burnished tresses. It was only with a supreme effort that he restrained those impulses. But there was no way he could disguise the hunger in his eyes. That was out of his control.

Despite her limited experience with men, Rebecca knew desire when she saw it, and she gripped the edge of the door, her legs suddenly shaky. Apparently the Easter outfit she'd splurged on, in an uncharacteristic display of self-indulgence, was a hit. A pulse began to beat in the delicate hollow of her throat, and like a homing pigeon, Zach's gaze dropped to that sensitive area and rested there, the color of his eyes darkening even as Rebecca's mouth went dry.

"Happy Easter, Rebecca," Isabel piped up, her thin, childish voice interrupting the throbbing, electric connection that crackled between the two adults. "Look what Uncle Zach gave me!" She held up a large, stuffed white rabbit for inspection, and Rebecca dragged her gaze away from Zach's mesmerizing eyes, bending down to hug the little girl.

"Isn't that nice!" she exclaimed, her voice as uneven as her pulse. "And don't you look pretty!"

Isabel smoothed the crinolined skirt of her sashed cotton floral dress, touched the lace-edged ruffle at the hem, then reached up to adjust her white straw hat. "I never had a dress like this before. Or a hat, either," she said reverently.

"Well, I think you'll be the most beautiful lady at church today," Rebecca declared. Then she forced herself to take a deep, steadying breath. "Come in for a minute while I get my purse," she suggested breathlessly, backing up to give them access, her eyes touching Zach's briefly before skittering quickly away to escape the heat still radiating from them. "I think there's something on the coffee table for you," she told Isabel with a shaky smile, transferring her gaze to the little girl.

Isabel's eyes widened. "Really?" She scampered into the living room, pausing with a reverent "Oh!" at the sight of the giant basket of goodies, covered with clear yellow cellophane and topped with a big lavender bow. She turned to look at Rebecca, who had followed her and now stood just inside the room. "Is this mine?"

"It sure is, sweetie. Happy Easter."

"Oh, thank you!" she exclaimed, clapping her hands in delight. "Can I open it?"

"Of course."

As Isabel bent down to carefully free one side of the cellophane so she could peer inside, Rebecca felt Zach move behind her, his nearness almost palpable.

"That was very nice of you," he observed quietly.

She turned to find him in the doorway, one shoulder propped against the frame, his arms folded across his chest. She was grateful to discover that the fire in his eyes was now banked to a more manageable smolder.

"What's Easter without a basket—or a rabbit?" she replied, striving for a light tone but not quite succeeding.

"Or an Easter bonnet, as the old song goes," he added lightly, his eyes flickering to her hat for a moment. "By the way, thanks for taking her shopping for the outfit," he added, nodding toward Isabel. "I wouldn't have known where to start. But you were wrong about one thing, you know."

She tilted her head quizzically and frowned. "What do you mean?"

He dropped his voice, and when he spoke, his tone was intimate, caressing. "Isabel isn't going to be the most beautiful lady at church." He reached over and ran a gentle finger down Rebecca's cheek, lifted her soft hair and let it drift through his fingers, then drew an unsteady breath as he rested his palm tenderly against her cheek, his thumb stroking her silky skin, his eyes locked on hers. "I'm looking at the lady who will have that honor," he declared, his voice suddenly husky.

Rebecca's heart stopped, then raced on, her whole body quivering at the heat generated by Zach's unexpected touch—and by the need it inspired. She swallowed with difficulty, surprised to discover that she desperately wanted him to gently claim her lips as he had the night of her birthday, the tender pressure of his kiss stoking the fire in her heart that had languished, reduced to only a few embers, for so many years. She sensed that if any man could coax those embers of passion back to life, this one could. Because while he'd initially struck her as the fast, no-nonsense type who went after what he wanted with aggressive, single-minded determination, he had surprised her by exhibiting a touching gentleness and patience with Isabel. Could he bring those qualities to a relationship with her? she wondered, allowing herself a soaring moment of optimism.

But she stifled the hope quickly and firmly. A child and a woman were two different things, she reminded herself resignedly. And the expectations were entirely different. From a woman he would want responsiveness and satisfaction, and even under the most patient and nurturing conditions, Rebecca wasn't sure she could ever meet the needs of a man like Zach. There was one way to find out, of course—let the relationship progress. But that, unfortunately, involved risk—on a couple of fronts.

There was the risk of a second humiliation, of course—an extremely unpleasant prospect. But even if she could overcome the physical obstacles—and that was a big "if"—there was another, even greater, risk to consider. Zach's sojourn in St. Genevieve was just that—nothing more than a brief interlude. When it was over, he would return to his life in St. Louis, leaving her alone once more, her emotions tattered, her heart aching. It wasn't that he would intentionally hurt her, she knew. It was just that he was probably used to relationships that lasted only as long as the circumstances were convenient.

But a cavalier attitude about involvement wasn't Rebecca's way. She had been raised with solid, traditional values that clearly defined dating behavior and, as a result, had never believed in so-called casual intimacy. For her, kissing and touching were only appropriate in the context of a long-term relationship based on mutual respect and, if not love, certainly deep affection.

Rebecca already felt a deep affection for the man whose gaze now held hers so compellingly. And it wouldn't take much for her to feel even more. In her heart she sensed that her feelings for this man could deepen with very little additional encouragement. Because although Rebecca was uncertain about many aspects of her relationship with Zach, she was absolutely sure about one thing. He drew her in ways no other man ever had, stirring to life the almost cold embers of a long-suppressed passion. But she also knew that if she ever gave her heart to a man, it would be completely and for always. It would be his to cherish—or to break. And the latter possibility scared her to death.

Zach's eyes scanned Rebecca's expressive face. He didn't want to make another mistake with her, but he couldn't handle a strictly platonic relationship much longer. The more he got to know about her, the more he wanted to know. But he had to move slowly, he reminded himself firmly. So he held back, searching her eyes as objectively as he could, trying to discern her feelings. There was uncertainty in them, he acknowledged. And fear. But there was also desire. In fact, unless he was way off base, her eyes were now inviting him more eloquently than words ever could to claim her lips. And it was an invitation simply too tempting to refuse.

He changed his position slightly, a subtle shift that angled his body out of Isabel's view, his thumb still stroking Rebecca's cheek in a manner at once both sensuous and comforting. Slowly, carefully he leaned toward her, making no secret of his intent. He watched her eyes, gauging her reaction, ready to back off at the slightest withdrawal. But he saw only a soft yearning in their depths as he closed the distance between them, his hand moving to her nape to draw her close as her eyelids drifted shut.

"Rebecca, can I eat a chocolate egg?"

Rebecca's startled eyes flew open, connecting with Zach's as Isabel's innocent question short-circuited the electrically charged moment. A flash of frustration, coupled with dismay, swept over Zach's face, and he paused, hovering a mere whisper away from her lips. She could feel the tension radiating from his body, could sense the battle he was waging with his self-control. But in the end he sighed and backed off, giving her a smile that was clearly forced.

"I guess I'll just have to wait until later to finish this conversation, won't I?" he murmured, his voice strangely hoarse.

"Can I, Rebecca?" Isabel repeated.

Rebecca tried to swallow past the lump in her throat. "Yes, that would be fine," she replied breathlessly, her eyes still locked on Zach's, not even sure whose question she was answering.

Zach reached over and trailed his finger down her cheek once more, and his eyes darkened at her sharply indrawn breath. She thought his hand was trembling, but she was such a mass of vibrating nerves herself that she couldn't be sure. In fact, at the moment she was sure of only one thing.

Zach intended to kiss her later.

That realization sent a surge of excitement—and uncertainty—ricocheting through her. She wanted him to kiss her. That wasn't the question. The question was, should she let him? Because one kiss could lead to another, and gentleness would eventually give way to passion. She'd already humiliated herself once with this man. That he was even willing to give it another try seemed like a miracle. But she doubted whether any man's ego would be able to handle that kind of reaction—and rejection—twice. She couldn't count on a second miracle. Just like she couldn't count on her response.

And what of her concerns about the transitory nature of his appearance in her life? And the heartbreak that could result if she let herself get involved with him? Was it worth the risk—or should she just retreat to safety?

Rebecca didn't have the answer to her questions. But maybe in the Lord's house she would find guidance, as well as relief for her deep-seated doubts and insecurities, she thought hopefully. After all, He had always come through for her before, in His own time and way, when she turned to Him for direction with a problem that was too difficult to tackle on her own.

And this one certainly fell into that category.

Rebecca stepped out of the car and gazed up at the deep blue sky with a smile. "Isn't it a gorgeous day?" she exclaimed.

"Gorgeous," Zach agreed, his eyes never leaving her face as he shut the door behind her.

She blushed and reached for Isabel's hand, knowing that his comment wasn't directed at the weather but deciding for the moment it was safer to pretend it was. Although their conversation on the ride to St. Louis had been casual and impersonal, it had still taken her quite a while to recover from those few emotionally charged moments in her apartment. And the look in his eyes right now was stirring up all those unsettling feelings again.

"I always think it's such a shame when Easter is rainy or cold," she chattered nervously as Zach took Isabel's other hand and they made their way toward the church.

Zach gave her a lazy smile that would have warmed her all the way to her toes even if the day had been dismal, and the pink in her cheeks deepened. Sensing her discomfort, reminding himself that he needed to move very slowly, he changed the subject. "I'm looking forward to meeting your brother and sister-in-law," he remarked conversationally.

They were looking forward to meeting him, too, she thought ruefully. Especially Sam, whose imagination had been working overtime. Rebecca's goal today was to convince everyone that she and Zach were just friends. Whether that was true or not was beside the point. She just didn't want her family jumping to any conclusions. Especially when she hadn't reached any herself.

Zach didn't help matters, though, by draping an arm around her shoulders and leaning close to whisper in her ear as they paused in the back of church. "There's your dad," he noted, inclining his head toward the left rear.

Rebecca's head swiveled in that direction, just in time to see Sam and her father exchange a knowing look, and her heart sank. This friendship business was not going to be an easy sell, she thought in dismay. Henry had already formed his opinion, and from the smug look on Sam's face hers had just been cemented. Maybe Brad would be the voice of reason, she thought without much hope.

Rebecca deliberately moved out of Zach's grasp and walked toward Sam, leaving him to follow with Isabel.

"Rebecca, you look absolutely gorgeous!" Sam declared without preamble when her sister-in-law was within earshot. "Doesn't she, Henry?"

"Glowing, that's what I'd say," he pronounced. "You been taking vitamins? Or is there another explanation?" he asked with a twinkle in his eyes.

Sam's gaze flickered behind Rebecca. "This might be the explanation right here," she observed in an undertone, giving Rebecca a grin and an approving wink. When Rebecca blushed furiously, Henry nudged Sam.

"What did I tell you?" he asserted.

"Did I miss something here?" Zach interrupted smoothly, smiling down at Henry.

"No!" Rebecca replied quickly, giving her father a "don't you dare say one more word" look. "It was just . . . just a family joke," she explained lamely.

"Well, are you going to introduce me to this handsome man or not?" Sam asked pertly, when her sister-in-law made no move to do so.

Rebecca turned in time to see Zach's neck redden even as he smiled down at Sam. At least she wasn't the only one being embarrassed today, she thought wryly. She just hoped he hadn't heard the initial exchange between her father and Sam.

"Sam, Zach Wright. He's the *friend* I mentioned," she said pointedly. "And this is Isabel," she added more gently, drawing the suddenly shy little girl forward. "Zach, Isabel, my sister-in-law, Sam. Zach, you already know my father. Isabel, sweetie, this is my papa," she explained.

Zach shook hands with Henry, and Rebecca sat down to peek at Emily's tiny face, framed by a pink bonnet edged in lace. "Oh, Sam, she's so much bigger already!"

"She is growing fast," Sam agreed. "Listen, I hope you don't mind sitting in the back, but I need to be close to the exit in case Emily decides to exercise her vocal cords. I'm afraid to say that I think she's inherited her mother's big mouth," Sam declared with a grin.

"This is fine," Rebecca assured her.

Isabel reached over and tugged on Rebecca's skirt. "Can I sit by the baby?" she asked softly, her fascinated gaze locked on Emily, who was sucking on her fist and watching Isabel with big, round eyes.

"Sure," Sam said. "Emily likes an audience. And that way we can get to know each other better. Just change places with Rebecca," she instructed.

Rebecca wasn't fooled by the apparent innocence of Sam's suggestion. It was clearly a setup. But there was no way out. Left with no choice but to comply, she moved next to Zach. Being only inches away from him wasn't going to help her emotional state in the least, however. Especially when he draped an arm across the back of the pew behind her and proceeded to brush his fingers lightly across her shoulder.

"How've you been, Zach?" her father asked, his sharp eyes missing nothing as he leaned forward to talk around Sam and Isabel.

"Just fine, Henry," Zach replied, his breath warm on Rebecca's temple as he spoke across her. "How's that rose garden coming along?"

"Great! The new shoots are bursting out already. You'll have to come back down and see it in bloom."

"I'd like that," Zach replied with an easy smile.

"So what do you think of my granddaughter?" Henry asked, turning his attention to Isabel.

"She's little," Isabel replied, her tone serious, her face thoughtful. Then she tilted her head and looked at Henry. "Are you really her grandfather?"

"Yep."

"I never had a grandfather," she told him regretfully.

"Well, then, why don't you just pretend I'm your grandfather today?" he suggested. "I could use the practice."

"Really?"

"Sure."

The service started then, putting an end to the conversation—much to Rebecca's relief. Her plan to convince everyone that she and Zach were just friends was already in shambles, and she needed some time to regroup and think about a new approach. Sam and her father clearly had their minds made up about the relationship. Most likely Brad did, too, she thought, watching as he entered, impressed as always by his commanding appearance in clerical garb. Sometimes, when she saw him in this setting, it was hard for her to remember that he was the same big brother who had teased and bullied and protected and encouraged her from her earliest memories to her adolescent years, when he'd left for the seminary. Their relationship changed after that, matured, and in the intervening years the bond between them had grown even stronger.

Rebecca was immensely grateful that Brad now had Sam and the family he'd always wanted. He deserved all the good things the Lord chose to bless him with. In fact, his only "family" worry these days seemed to be her. She knew that he had never understood why she chose to live a solitary life. In his gentle way, he let her know on a regular basis that he was willing to listen if she wanted to talk about it. But even after all these years, her secret was still too painful, too fraught with humiliation and guilt, to discuss.

Rebecca supposed that someone with a less-sensitive nature would have been able to move on, to overcome the shame and embarrassment. But she'd been born tenderhearted, prone to emotional hurt. And so the incident continued to haunt her, leaving her powerless to overcome the debilitating fear that had deprived her of the rich dimension that love could add to her life.

Yet somehow, deep in her heart, Rebecca sensed that there was a chance she could find love with the man at her side. The possibility was there, dangling alluringly just out of her grasp, like the golden ring on a carousel. All she had to do was reach for it. Or, in this case, simply offer some encouragement. But she was so afraid of failure! What if she freaked out again? Or worse yet, what if she didn't, what if she allowed their relationship to develop, only to have Zach reject her in the end as inadequate? How would she ever be able to go on after that?

Rebecca was torn, her heart pulling her one way, her intellect another. But now was not the time to work out her personal dilemma, she told herself resolutely. It was Easter Sunday and she was here to worship, not agonize over her problem. She would simply put it in the Lord's hands, ask for guidance and hope that

He would show her the way. In the meantime she should be listening to Brad's sermon. Determinedly she forced herself to focus on her brother's words.

"And so I believe that the real message of Easter is one of renewal—of new life, of hope, of trust, of a promise fulfilled.

"In our society, Christmas has become the biggest holiday of the year. And it is, indeed, a wonderful event to celebrate. But without today, without Easter, Christmas would have no meaning. Because this is the day when the Lord gave us the legacy of everlasting life. And it is this legacy that gives Christianity its meaning.

"It seems to me that as Christians we can learn much from this day. Certainly it forms the foundation of our beliefs, gives us an incentive to live our lives based on the principles that the Lord taught. And it offers us great hope. Because of Easter, we know that anything is possible with God.

"I believe that the themes of this day—renewal, rebirth, hope, trust—are beautifully symbolized in nature. Consider the tulip. In the fall, when it is placed in the ground, the withered bulb appears to be dead. It lies dormant through the long, cold winter, wrapped in icy fingers. But in the spring it finds new life as the gentle warmth of the sun patiently coaxes it to grow and blossom into a glorious flower.

"In many ways I think the story of the tulip bulb is a good analogy not only for Easter but for a heart that longs for love. All of us here today know from personal experience that the heart is a very fragile thing. We know that it can be easily hurt, it can wither away, it can appear to be dead and empty. But I believe that with warmth and patient nurturing, most hearts can bloom again.

"On this Easter day, as we celebrate the promise of eternal life, let us also celebrate the earthly life given to us by the Lord. Let us resolve not to waste this precious blessing, in all its infinite dimensions. And as we thank God today for the gift of love He gave us through his Son's death and resurrection, let us celebrate that gift by nurturing the love in our own lives. Let us find the courage to seek love if we do not have it, and the wisdom to cherish it if we do. For despite its inherent risks and heartaches, it is still the greatest gift the Lord can bless us with in this life.

"Let us pray. . . ."

As Brad finished his sermon, Rebecca felt her hand being taken in a gentle grasp. She looked up at Zach as he entwined his fingers through hers, and her vision blurred with tears at the tenderness in his eyes and the memory of the pink tulips he'd given her. She didn't know if Brad had intentionally directed the last part of his sermon to her, but it had certainly hit home, she thought, averting her eyes and blinking rapidly to dispel the tears. And he was right. Love was a gift. And the Lord seemed to be offering her a chance for love with the man now holding her hand. Hadn't she promised herself on Valentine's Day that if the right man came along, she would take the risk of pursuing a relationship? Well, the opportunity was being offered. Now it was up to her to take it.

Rebecca knew that she wasn't going to be able to overcome her fear overnight. But maybe, if Zach was patient and understanding, they could find a way to work through it together. It was a long shot, she knew. But for the first time in years she allowed a tender seed of hope to sprout and send out a tentative root.

"Rebecca! Sam! Wait up!"

Rebecca turned at the familiar voice, smiling as Laura and Nick walked toward them hand in hand.

"Don't worry. Brad's still gabbing," Sam replied with a grin. "That's one of the downsides of being the preacher's wife—you're always the last to leave."

"Are you complaining?" Laura asked with a smile.

Sam's face softened. "Hardly. He's worth waiting for any day."

Laura looked up at Nick, her own face softening with love as they exchanged a tender glance. "I know what you mean," she replied. With an obvious effort she tore her eyes away from Nick's and turned to Rebecca, reaching out to take her hand. "It's good to see you, Becka. And this must be Isabel—and Zach," she said, looking from one to the other.

"That's right. Brad, this is Laura and Nick. Isabel, sweetie, these are friends of mine."

While the two men shook hands, Laura studied Zach, frowning slightly. "Have we met before?" she asked. "You look very familiar."

"Not formally," he replied with a smile. "But you two were having dinner at Rebecca's a few weeks ago the same night I was there. I noticed you when Rebecca brought your dessert out."

"That's right!" Laura acknowledged, her frown evaporating as memory returned. "You and Rebecca had coffee together after she talked to us. Remember, Nick?"

Nick grinned sheepishly. "I have to admit I don't. I only had eyes for you that night."

Laura blushed with pleasure as their eyes touched briefly. "Anyway, it's nice to meet you formally," she told Zach.

"The pleasure is mine," he assured her.

"You mean you two had dinner together weeks ago?" Sam asked, eyeing Zach and Rebecca with new interest.

"Not dinner. Coffee," Rebecca clarified.

"But dinner would have been better," Zach interjected with an engaging grin. "Coffee was all I could manage to waylay her for that night, though. And even that was under duress," he admitted candidly. "But fortunately things have improved since then." His eyes sought, held and mesmerized hers.

Rebecca knew that the four adults were watching the two of them with unabashed interest, could sense their rapt attention. She ought to look away, make some flippant remark, carry on the charade that she and Zach were just friends. But she was fighting a losing battle, and she knew it.

"Well, I'm glad to hear it," Henry declared. "Rebecca could use some male companionship."

"Dad!" Rebecca turned to him, her face horrified.

"What's he done now?" Brad asked, his voice laced with tolerant amusement as he came up behind her. But after one look at her crimson face he slipped an arm around her shoulders comfortingly. "Never mind. Don't tell me. I can guess. I have a feeling it has something to do with Zach. And I take it this is Zach?"

"Guilty," Zach replied with a grin.

Brad held out his hand, and Zach took it promptly, realizing that the other man was assessing him even as he smiled. Zach was also aware of Brad's arm protectively around his sister's shoulders. Consciously sent or not, the message was clear: treat my sister with care or you'll answer to me.

Zach respected that, admired it even, and he returned Brad's gaze steadily. "Rebecca's spoken very highly of you. I'm glad we finally have the chance to meet."

"So am I. I try to keep up with the events—and people—in her life. She's very special to me."

"She's very special to me, too," Zach replied candidly, his gaze direct and honest.

Brad held Zach's eyes a moment longer, and when he released the other man's hand there was a satisfied expression on his face.

"Well, we're going to take off," Laura said. "Happy Easter, everyone."

She and Nick left to a chorus of best wishes, and then Brad squatted down beside the silent little girl who clung to Rebecca's hand. "You must be Isabel," he said quietly with a smile. "I'm Rebecca's brother."

"I know. She told me," Isabel replied in a small, timid voice.

"Well, we're glad you came to visit us, Isabel. What do you think of my new little girl?"

"She's pretty," Isabel stated shyly. "And soft."

"Yes, she is," he agreed. "Maybe later you'd like to hold her."

"Could I?" she asked, her eyes growing big.

"I think we could arrange that. You just remind me if I forget, okay?"

"Okay."

"I'd say it's time to head home," Sam declared, shifting Emily in her arms. "This little lady is getting hungry."

Brad stood up. "We'll meet you there, okay?" he said to Rebecca and Zach.

"Sounds good," Zach replied.

As they made their way to Zach's car, he turned to Rebecca with a smile. "You have a nice family."

She smiled ruefully. "Thanks. I love them all dearly. But they can be a little too outspoken at times. Except Brad, of course. He's very diplomatic."

"And very protective."

She looked at him curiously. "What do you mean?"

He shrugged. "He obviously cares about you very much. And he was clearly concerned about my . . . intentions."

She stared at him curiously as he opened the back door and leaned in to buckle Isabel into her seat belt.

"How in the world could you pick that up from such a brief conversation?" she asked when he emerged.

He straightened up and grinned as he shut Isabel's door and opened Rebecca's. "It must be a man thing. But the message was clear, trust me."

As Rebecca slipped into her seat, she frowned thoughtfully. She wasn't sure how Zach had picked up so much when only a dozen words had been exchanged, but she wasn't going to argue with him. Brad *was* protective. He knew her feelings were easily bruised and always did everything in his power to make sure she wasn't hurt. So of course he would be concerned about a man who suddenly appeared out of the fog, admittedly for a brief stay, and who could disappear just as quickly. Because a man like that could easily leave a broken heart in his wake. Her heart. Given the circumstances, it was natural that Brad wondered about Zach's intentions.

As a matter of fact, so did Rebecca.

"Happy birthday!" Sam, Henry and Nick chorused as Sam entered the dining room with a decorated cake topped with flickering candles.

"Is it your birthday?" Isabel asked, turning to Rebecca in surprise.

"No, honey. My birthday was a month ago," she explained, frowning in confusion at the three grinning faces. "What's this all about?"

"Well, you didn't think we'd forget to celebrate your birthday, did you?" Sam asked. "Okay, so it's a little late. Blame it on the little gal now sleeping soundly down the hall."

Rebecca shook her head and smiled. "You guys are too much. I'm going to be spoiled after this year, with two birthday celebrations!"

"Two?" Sam repeated, raising her eyebrows questioningly.

Rebecca didn't even try to sidestep the question. She'd given up the "just friends" pretense hours ago. "Zach took me out for a dinner a couple of days after my birthday," she explained.

"Good for him," Sam asserted promptly. "The fun factor in your life could use a boost. You need to work on that with her, Zach," Sam declared as she deposited the cake in front of Rebecca.

"I try, but she's a pretty hard sell," he admitted.

"Be persistent," Henry advised firmly. "Persistence pays."

"I'll remember that," Zach replied with a chuckle.

"Will you all stop?" Rebecca protested, her face flaming. "I make time for fun!"

"When?" Henry countered.

"Dad." Brad's quietly authoritative voice put an end to the inquisition. "Go ahead, Rebecca, make a wish and blow out the candles," he suggested, turning to her with an understanding smile.

She sent him a grateful look before complying and was rewarded with a round of applause as the last candle was extinguished.

"What did you wish for?" Isabel asked.

"It won't come true if I tell, sweetie," Rebecca replied with a smile.

"Oh." Isabel's face fell. "Well, was I in it?" she asked hopefully.

"In a way," Rebecca hedged.

"Was Uncle Zach?"

Again Brad came to the rescue. "Isabel, how would you like a piece of cake with a big rose on it?" he asked, earning Rebecca's gratitude once more.

Her attention effectively diverted, she nodded her head eagerly, supervising as Sam cut a generous piece with a huge rose in the middle.

When the last bite of cake was consumed a few minutes later, Sam leaned back and groaned. "I'll never lose the rest of the weight I put on with Emily if I keep this up," she lamented good-naturedly.

"You look exactly the same to me as you did before," Rebecca insisted.

"Thanks. But I've still got five pounds to go," Sam admitted ruefully.

"Speaking of new babies . . . have you ever seen a real baby bunny up close, Isabel?" Henry asked.

"No."

"Would you like to?"

"Do you have one?" she asked, enthralled.

"No. But I know where there's a nest, and if we're real careful, I don't think the momma rabbit will mind if we take a quick look."

"Can I, Uncle Zach?" Isabel asked eagerly.

"I don't see why not."

Isabel scrambled to her feet, and Henry stood up and reached for her hand.

"Some fresh air sounds like a good idea," Sam remarked as she also rose. "Why don't you two take a little stroll to the park down at the corner while Brad and I clean up?" she suggested.

"We can't leave you to deal with this mess!" Rebecca protested. "I'll help."

She started to rise, but Brad placed a hand on her shoulder. "Go ahead, Becka. You deal with kitchen work every day. We can manage here. I know we're all fascinating company, but I'm sure Zach won't object to spending part of the day just with you." He looked at the other man and smiled.

"You're right," Zach replied, relieved by the approval he saw in the other man's eyes. Apparently Rebecca's brother had decided that Zach could be trusted with his sister.

"But it doesn't seem right," she protested once more.

"Rebecca, for heaven's sake, just go!" Sam insisted. "You're our guest today. Plus, it's a belated birthday celebration. So you are *not* going to do dishes. Period. End of discussion. That's final." She paused and looked at Brad. "Should I be a little more forceful, do you think?" she asked innocently, her eyes twinkling mischievously.

He chuckled. "I think you made your point. Go ahead, you two. We'll still be here when you get back. And Henry will keep Isabel entertained."

Rebecca looked at Zach. They'd had almost no time alone together since Isabel's arrival, and this opportunity might not come again soon. If she was going to let this relationship progress, now was as good a time as any to start. Besides, things couldn't get that . . . involved . . . in a public park in broad daylight. Or could they? she wondered in sudden alarm, noting the eager, ardent light in Zach's eyes.

"What do you say, Rebecca?" he asked, the casual tone of his voice at odds with the intensity of his gaze.

With sudden determination she stood up. "It sounds like a good idea to me," she agreed, her voice slightly breathless. She turned to look at Brad, whose expression was thoughtful, and Sam, who was grinning like the Cheshire Cat. "We won't be gone long."

"Don't hurry on our account," Sam declared. "You two just have fun."

"We will," Zach promised, smiling down at Rebecca as she joined him in the doorway.

She forced herself to smile back, but as her nerve endings started to tingle, an unsettling question suddenly came to mind. How, exactly, did Zach define *fun?* she wondered nervously.

Chapter Ten

Zach would have reached for Rebecca's hand immediately when they left the house—except that she hid hers in the deep pockets of her full skirt. He knew she was nervous, knew she was probably thinking about the last time they were alone together, and he was determined to put her at ease. He'd just let her take the lead, give her the time she needed to get comfortable.

"I had a note from Josef this morning," he told her conversationally as they strolled along.

"How is everything?" she asked, turning to him with a worried frown.

"No better, unfortunately. Maybe worse. He's not a complainer, so it's hard to tell. But one thing is clear. He misses Isabel desperately."

"I'm not surprised." She sighed and looked up at the canopy of flowering trees above her, the peaceful stillness broken only by the call of the birds. "It's hard to believe on a day like this that somewhere in the world a country is torn apart with strife and terror," she said softly, her voice troubled. "Isabel's only been here a short time, but already I'm dreading the day we have to send her back to that environment."

"I know what you mean," he admitted.

"Does she talk about her home very much when she's with you?" Rebecca asked.

"Only casually. Usually at night, when she's going to bed. How about with you?"

Rebecca nodded slowly, her face thoughtful. "She tells me quite a bit. Enough to give me a pretty clear picture of her everyday life. I know her family didn't have much in a material sense, but it seems they made up for it with love. And she obviously misses her parents. I try to keep her busy at the restaurant, giving her little jobs to do or books to read or puzzles to work on, hoping that will keep her from dwelling on her homesickness. It seems to work most of the time. Actually, I'm amazed at how smoothly she's adapted to such a different environment."

"I think you can take a lot of credit for that," Zach remarked quietly. "Isabel has grown very fond of you—which is easy to understand."

She looked up at him, noted the tender light in his eyes, and averted her glance quickly. "Do you hear from Josef often?" she asked, diverting the spotlight from herself.

"As often as he can get access to a PC, which is every couple of days. Isabel and I check morning and evening for messages, and we send him a note every day when I get home from school."

"Speaking of school, how's your problem student doing?"

"Pete Cramer? He's not a problem anymore. In fact, I heard some teachers in the lounge talking the other day, speculating on why he's suddenly buckled down and gotten serious about his studies."

Rebecca smiled. "I could clear up that mystery in one word—you."

Zach shrugged. "All I did was offer a little encouragement. And some discipline. Very good advice, by the way," he acknowledged with a smile. "Anyway, I think he's going to apply for that week-long writing camp this summer in Michigan that I told you about. The only problem is funding. Which brings me to a subject I've been meaning to raise. Do you hire any extra wait staff in the summer, high school kids?"

"Yes. Do you think he might be interested?"

He nodded. "It would give him something constructive to do, and he could earn the money for camp. Would you consider talking to him?"

"Absolutely. Have him come over someday after school."

Zach gave her a grateful smile. "I appreciate it, Rebecca."

She waved his thanks aside. "I need the help, anyway. And if I can give a job to someone who will really benefit, that's even better."

They reached the end of the block and paused to gaze at the small, deserted park.

"Would you like to sit for a few minutes?" Zach asked, nodding toward a convenient bench.

Rebecca thought about the last time they'd sat on a bench together, and her stomach clenched at the memory. A wave of panic washed over her, and she started to refuse. But as her gaze fell on a bed of colorful tulips in the center of the park, the flowers waving encouragingly to her in the gentle breeze, the words died in her throat. She recalled Brad's sermon, as well as her own promise to herself, and took a slow, steadying breath.

"Yes. That would be nice."

Zach took her elbow as they made their way across the uneven ground, then sat beside her on the wooden bench. "Nice spot," he remarked.

She forced herself to lean back, then folded her hands primly in her lap and glanced around. "Yes. Sam and Brad were glad there was a park close by, with swings and all, so Emily will have a place to play near home when she gets older. Of course, they didn't buy the house because of that. They didn't know then there would even be an Emily. They just liked the house. And that contemporary ranch style suits them, don't you think?" she rattled off breathlessly.

"Mmm-hmm. And I like them a lot. They seem like good people," Zach replied, acutely aware of her unease yet determined not to let that deter him from broaching the subject that had been on his mind for days. "But let's talk about us for a minute, okay?"

Rebecca glanced down, twisting her hands nervously in her lap. After a long pause she spoke softly. "Is . . . is there an 'us'?" she asked, her voice quavering slightly.

"I'd like for there to be."

"Even . . . even after what happened the night you . . . you took me to dinner?" Her voice was tentative, uncertain.

"Let's talk about that, too."

Rebecca forced herself to look up at him, and the caring and kindness—and concern—she saw in his eyes made her throat tighten. She swallowed with difficulty, searching for an explanation that would be enough to satisfy him but not enough to expose her darkest secret. "I-I'm not a woman who likes to be touched very much." Her voice was so soft he had to lean close to hear her.

The obvious question hovered on his lips, but he refrained from asking it. He doubted whether she would tell him why, anyway, not at this point in their relationship. So he'd have to approach her reply from a different direction.

"In general—or just by me?" he asked, striving for a teasing tone.

"In general."

There was silence for a moment, and when he spoke his voice was gentle. "Touching is part of a relationship between two people who like each other, Rebecca."

She was aware of that. It was the source of her fear. "I know."

"Do you like me?"

"Yes." Her voice was a mere whisper.

"Then maybe you should define what you mean by touching," he suggested quietly. He reached over and took her hand, lacing his fingers through hers, stroking the side of her hand with his thumb. "Does this kind of touching bother you?"

Her heart began to pound in her chest as she looked at his strong hand linked with hers, and she drew a shaky breath. "Yes." His thumb stilled, and she hurried on. "B-but not in the way you mean. I . . . I like that."

He resumed the gentle stroking motion, then reached over with his other hand and tipped her chin up, forcing her to meet his eyes as he traced a gentle finger down her cheek. "Do you like this kind of touching, Rebecca?" he asked, the timbre of his voice deepening.

She closed her eyes as his caress sent a shiver of excitement rippling through her. "I . . . yes, I like that," she whispered.

He leaned over then, slowly, and pressed his lips to her forehead, letting them travel gently down the bridge of her nose to her lips. "How about this?" he asked huskily, his breath warm against her face.

Even though it was Easter, the fireworks that suddenly erupted

all around her made Rebecca feel like it was the Fourth of July. "I
. . . I like that, too," she replied unsteadily.

Zach pulled back then, far enough to look into her dreamy eyes
filled with unbridled yearning and ran his fingers through her hair,
brushing it back softly from her face. "Well, I don't see much of a
problem here, Rebecca. You like me, and I like you. And you also
like being touched, whether you realize it or not. So here's my
suggestion. We'll have one simple rule. If I touch you in a way you
don't like, tell me and I'll stop. How does that sound?"

She swallowed, deciding that she might as well be honest with
him up front. "Zach, I . . . touching like this is . . . it's nice. But
I . . . I can't handle the . . . the heavier stuff."

He looked at her speculatively. "Is that why you don't date?"

She nodded mutely, her face suddenly forlorn and sad. "I have
dated a little. But whenever things got . . . close, I . . . I freaked
out. I scared the men to death and embarrassed myself. Needless
to say, they never came back. And I wouldn't have gone out again if
they had."

He frowned, the unspoken question again hovering between
them. What on earth had made her so paranoid of physical closeness? She was not a cold woman. Far from it. She was loving and
warm and kind, and he could see the repressed passion in her eyes,
struggling for release even now. Something had frightened her at
some point in her life—badly enough that she'd denied her desires
all these years, given up her dreams of a husband and family. But
what? Again he almost asked the question. And again he decided
that patience would serve him better. She would tell him when—or
maybe *if* was a better word—she felt comfortable doing so. Forcing
the issue would only make her close down.

He drew a deep breath and took both her hands in his, angling
his body to face her, his eyes intense and serious. "Do you know
what I think?" he asked. She shook her head mutely, and he continued. "I think you've never had a real chance to find out whether
you can handle the heavier stuff."

She frowned. "But I told you, I—"

"Rebecca," he stopped her gently. "Let me finish. I'd be willing
to bet that none of the men you dated went out with you long
enough to give you a chance to feel comfortable with them, to
establish a trust level. They probably got into the so-called heavy

stuff right up front. Sort of the same mistake I made the night I took you out for dinner," he admitted with a disarmingly rueful grin.

She flushed and bit her lower lip. She'd never really thought about that before. "You might be right," she admitted slowly.

"Well, I'm in no hurry," he assured her, even as he silently acknowledged that those words weren't quite true. But he cared enough about this woman to let the relationship progress at whatever pace she set. "We'll just take it a day at a time, okay?"

Rebecca stared at him, finding it hard to believe that at last a man had come her way who not only had integrity, but patience. It seemed too good to be true. Yet the tender touch of his hands and the warmth of his eyes were real enough. How could she refuse?

"All right, Zach. If you're sure."

A smile spread across his face. "I've never been more sure of anything in my life. And by the way . . ."

"Yes?" She looked at him quizzically when he paused.

He touched her nose with the tip of his finger. "You really were the most beautiful lady at church today."

"So did you have a nice day?" Brad asked, coming up behind Rebecca as she stood at the window watching Isabel show Zach the baby rabbits.

She turned, her face filled with a soft radiance that reflected both her new hope and the feeling of being at peace with her decision. "Yes. It was lovely. Thank you."

Brad stuck his hands in his pockets, then gazed out at Zach and Isabel for a moment before turning again to his sister. "I like him," he said simply.

She smiled, and a faint blush colored her cheeks. "So do I."

"Rebecca, I . . ." He paused and expelled a long breath. "Look, I don't want to interfere in your life. Dad does enough of that for both of us," he observed with a quick grin. "But I want you to be happy. I don't know why you've never married, although I'm sure you have your reasons. But I also know that you *should* be married. You have so much love to give, and you'd make a wonderful wife and mother. I hope you . . . well, I hope you give things a chance when the right man comes along."

Rebecca reached over and laid a hand on his arm, her throat

constricting. "Thank you for caring so much, Brad. And I—I'm working on it."

"Well, speaking from personal experience, I can only say that the rewards are great when you find the right person," he replied with a gentle smile.

"I can tell," she assured him. She turned to watch Zach and Isabel making their way back toward the house, her tiny hand trustingly tucked into his powerful one. "I guess I'll just have to ask the Lord to guide me on this one."

He put an arm around her shoulders and gave her a quick hug. "I can't think of anyone better to ask," he agreed. "And I'll do the same."

Rebecca poured Zach's coffee, then sat down at her dinette table.

"This is good cake," Isabel declared, digging into the large rose on top of her piece.

"Well, I'm just glad I could share the rest of it with two of my favorite people," Rebecca said warmly, her eyes meeting Zach's across the table. She'd been floating on a cloud ever since she and Zach had talked in the park yesterday. He gave her a lazy smile as he sipped his coffee, and her pulse lurched into overdrive.

"My birthday is next month," Isabel informed them as she polished off the rose.

Rebecca forced her gaze back to the little girl. "So I hear. And I think we should plan something very special. Don't you, Zach?"

"Absolutely."

"A party?" Isabel asked hopefully, her eyes lighting with anticipation.

"Of course. You can even pick the menu for dinner."

"Spaghetti. And French fries. And corn on the cob. And . . . and chocolate cake!" she declared, ticking off the list without hesitation.

Rebecca laughed. "Well, that's not the most nutritious menu I've ever heard. But it is your birthday, so I suppose we can eat like that for one day."

"Let's see," Zach reflected, reaching for his calendar. "Your birthday is on a Monday. Maybe we could have a picnic Sunday, too. That way we can celebrate for two days."

"I like picnics," Isabel declared. "Mama and Papa and I used to go on picnics sometimes."

Her face clouded, and Rebecca's heart ached for her. She tried desperately to think of something to distract the suddenly solemn little girl. "A picnic would be great," she agreed. "In fact, why don't we have a slumber party, too?" she suggested with sudden inspiration.

"What's a slumber party?" Isabel asked curiously.

"Well, you bring your pajamas over on Sunday night and sleep here with me. We'll make cookies and watch movies and stay up late."

"That sounds like fun!" she exclaimed enthusiastically. "Can Uncle Zach come, too?"

Rebecca almost choked on her coffee, and her gaze flew to Zach, who grinned at her engagingly.

"Can I?" he asked innocently, his eyes twinkling.

"There's room in the bed," Isabel said, her voice eager as she turned to Zach. "Rebecca has a big bed," she told him.

"Is that right?"

By now Rebecca's face was flaming, but Zach ignored the pleading glance she sent him. He actually seemed to be enjoying the situation, she thought in dismay. It was clearly up to her to get out of this. "Isabel, sweetie, slumber parties are . . . they're just for girls," she stammered.

"Oh." Isabel's face fell. "I wish Uncle Zach could come."

He chuckled. "So does Uncle Zach. But Rebecca's right, honey. The kind of slumber party she's talking about is just for girls," he explained, giving Rebecca a wink that made her nerve endings sizzle.

"We'll still have lots of fun," Rebecca promised, her voice slightly uneven.

"Well . . . okay," Isabel capitulated.

They moved on to other, less volatile subjects, and it wasn't until Zach and Isabel were leaving that the situation heated up again. She walked them to the door, wondering how Zach would say good-night, knowing that their options were extremely limited with Isabel there. Which was really for the best, she told herself, though for some strange reason it didn't seem so.

When they reached the door, she glanced at him expectantly,

and although she thought she saw a flame flare suddenly in his eyes, he simply leaned over and kissed her forehead. Rebecca tried to stem the tide of disappointment that swept over her, forcing herself to smile and wave as she watched them climb into the car. Not until she closed the door and leaned against it did her lips droop. It was true that she wanted to move slowly, but at this rate she wouldn't even get a proper kiss until Isabel left. At which time Zach might very well leave, too, she reminded herself, her spirits taking a sudden nosedive.

She was just sliding the second lock into place when a soft knock sounded on the door. Frowning, she opened it to find Zach smiling at her from the other side.

"I told Isabel I forgot my wallet," he explained.

"Oh. Come on in," she said, turning toward the living room. "I didn't see it, but—"

"Rebecca." He cut her off and reached for her arm, restraining her as he slipped inside and shut the door behind him. "I lied."

She turned to him in surprise. "Why?"

Gently he took her hands and urged her toward him, looping his arms loosely around her waist. "Because that brotherly peck on the forehead didn't quite cut it for me as a good-night kiss," he admitted huskily.

Rebecca swallowed and stared up at him, her hands flat against his chest, the pounding of his heart vibrating beneath her fingertips. "Oh," she breathed softly.

"I'd like to kiss you properly, if that's okay."

She swallowed with difficulty, as delicate color suffused her face. "Y-yes. I think that would be n-nice," she murmured.

Zach stared down at her, telling himself to be slow and gentle and attuned to every nuance of her response. Which was extremely difficult, when what he really wanted to do was pull her close and capture her lips in a kiss so thorough that she would be left breathless. But he knew that impulsive approach would end up killing, not creating, desire.

So instead he left one hand resting lightly at her waist while he cradled the back of her head with his other, his eyes burning into hers as he slowly lowered his head to claim her lips.

Rebecca was frightened—frightened of her reaction, frightened of what would happen if things started to move too fast, frightened at the prospect that he might lose control and forget his promise to go slowly. But as his lips closed over hers— gentle, warm and coaxing, demanding no more than she was willing to give—she slowly began to respond. Her kiss was shy, tentative, cautious, but it was given freely. Her hands crept around his neck of their own volition, and she buried her fingers in the hair at the base of his neck. A soft sigh escaped her lips, and she felt the pressure of his hand at her waist tighten ever so slightly. But she wasn't frightened. He seemed in control, and she could handle this level of intimacy.

When at last Zach released her lips, he drew a long, shuddering breath and pressed her cheek against his chest, his chin resting on top of her head. He held her like that in silence for several long moments, his hand rhythmically stroking the small of her back. Never in a million years would he have believed that he could be so moved by just a simple kiss. But Rebecca's shyness, her inexperience, her sweet response just about undid him. He needed a few moments to compose himself. When he'd blithely made the promise to let her set the pace, he'd had no idea how difficult it would be to keep. If nothing else, he would come out of this experience with better mastery of his self-control, he thought wryly.

When at last he spoke, his voice was hoarse and unsteady. "I have to go."

"I know."

"Were you okay with this?"

She nodded. "Mmm-hmm."

"I'm glad. Because I intend to repeat it—as soon as possible. That is, if you're willing." He backed up slightly and looked down at her, his eyes probing.

Rebecca drew a long breath, her lips already tingling with anticipation. "Yes. I—I'm willing," she whispered.

He smiled then, a smile filled with promise and tenderness—and relief. "How about tomorrow night? We'll take Isabel out for ice cream. And I'll think of something else to conveniently forget."

She smiled. "Okay."

He leaned down and brushed his lips across hers once more, then quickly slipped out the door.

She closed it behind him, a dreamy smile on her face. Isabel would enjoy the ice cream tomorrow. But Rebecca was looking forward to a different kind of dessert.

* * *

The phone rang, and Rebecca glanced at the clock in surprise. Since Easter, almost a week and a half before, Zach had taken to calling her every night after Isabel was in bed. She looked forward to those long, rambling, end-of-the-day conversations, but he was a little early tonight. Usually he called about ten, and it was only nine-thirty. Maybe he was anxious, she thought with a smile.

"Rebecca? Zach. Listen, I know it's late, but can you come over?"

Her smile of pleasure changed to a frown of alarm at his taut, tension-filled voice. "What's wrong?"

"It's Isabel. She was just drifting off to sleep when a couple of kids set off some fireworks right outside her window. I guess she thought it was gunfire or something. Anyway, she just freaked out. I can't seem to get through to her," he said, his voice touched with desperation.

"I'll be right there."

As Rebecca dashed for her purse and fumbled for her keys, she sent a silent prayer racing heavenward. *Please help me find a way to comfort this little child! I have no experience with this kind of trauma. But I love her so much! Please show me how to use that love to console her,* she pleaded.

Less than ten minutes later Rebecca stood at Zach's door, her finger impatiently pressed to the bell. Within seconds it was pulled open, and the lines of concern etched on Zach's face made her stomach clench. She stepped into the eerily quiet apartment, then turned to face him as he shut the door.

"Tell me what happened," she said quietly.

He sighed and raked his fingers through his hair. "Like I said, fireworks. I heard her cry out, and by the time I got in there she was huddled on the floor with her doll, shaking. I think she's in shock or something. I tried talking to her, but it's like she can't hear me. She's kind of crying, but there's no sound. I'm sorry to bother you, Rebecca, but I just didn't know what else to do."

"It's okay," she said, placing a hand reassuringly on his arm as she tossed her purse onto a convenient chair. "But I'm no expert at this, either. I just hope I can help."

She moved quickly toward the bedroom, pausing on the threshold. The scene was exactly as Zach had described it. Isabel was huddled against the wall, her knees pulled up, her face pale. Her frail shoulders were shaking, and she clutched Raggedy Ann tightly against her chest. There was a glassy look to her eyes, and although she made quiet crying sounds, there were no tears. Rebecca's heart ached for the frightened, vulnerable little girl, and she moved into the room, dropping to her knees beside her.

"Isabel, sweetie, it's okay. You're safe," she comforted her gently, reaching over to brush some stray strands of hair back from the wan face. She could feel a shudder run through the little body, but Isabel continued to stare straight ahead, as if unaware of Rebecca's presence. "Isabel, would you like me to hold you?" Rebecca asked. Still no response.

Rebecca tried to quell her own growing panic. Zach was right—Isabel appeared to be in shock. She glanced up at him in the doorway, her own worried frown a mirror of his. "Well, how about if I just sit here right next to you?" she asked, turning back to Isabel. "Uncle Zach will sit with us, too, okay?"

She turned again and motioned for Zach to join her, and the two of them sat beside Isabel on the floor. Rebecca looked over at Zach and mouthed the words "touch her" even as she began stroking Isabel's arm. Zach followed her example. "Remember that song I sang to you the first night you were here, Isabel?" Rebecca said gently. "How about if I sing it again?" Without waiting for a reply, Rebecca began to softly sing the words of the familiar hymn. She sang all the verses, and as she neared the end she thought she detected a slight softening in Isabel's rigid muscles. "Would you like to hear another?" she asked, and again she began to sing without waiting for a response.

Rebecca sang for almost twenty minutes, never breaking physical contact with Isabel, and gradually she felt the little girl's muscles go limp, until finally the sobs became more pronounced and the tears began to flow. Suddenly Isabel reached for her, and Rebecca pulled her onto her lap. The thin arms went fiercely around her neck and Isabel buried her face in Rebecca's shoulder. Rebecca closed her eyes and slowly expelled a shaky, relieved breath. Then she gazed at Zach over the little girl's shoulders, rocking her gently.

"I think we'll be okay now," she told him softly.

He nodded, the relief evident in the sudden slackening of his strained features, and he rose slowly. "I'll get her a glass of water," he offered quietly.

Rebecca nodded, then turned her attention back to Isabel, who clung to her tightly.

"I want my m-mama and p-papa," she sobbed.

"I know, sweetie," Rebecca consoled her. "I'm sorry they can't be here with you. But Uncle Zach and I love you very much. And we promised your papa we'd take care of you until it was safe for you to go home."

"S-sometimes it was s-scary at home, when the guns went off," she choked out. "Mr. Ptasnik, who lived on the f-first floor, got shot once. I saw it happen from our window. A-after that my papa would make me get d-down on the floor whenever there was trouble. He told me that there wouldn't be any shooting here, but t-tonight I thought I heard guns."

"It was just fireworks, sweetie, like Uncle Zach told you. You don't need to be scared. We promised your papa that we'd keep you safe, and we will."

Zach reentered and silently handed Rebecca the glass of water, squatting down beside her.

"Would you like a drink, Isabel? Uncle Zach brought this for you."

Isabel turned in Rebecca's arms and looked at Zach. He reached over and touched her cheek.

"Rebecca's right, Isabel. We won't let anything hurt you."

She took a gulp of water and silently handed the glass back to Zach. "I wish my papa was here," she sniffled softly.

"I do too, honey. He misses you just as much as you miss him. But just think of all the stories you'll have to tell him about America when you go home."

She considered that for a moment, and a ghost of a smile flickered across her face. "Just like he used to tell me stories about America."

"That's right."

Suddenly she yawned, and Rebecca smiled. "I think it's way past somebody's bedtime."

Zach reached for Isabel, lifting her easily, then extended a hand to Rebecca, pulling her up in one smooth motion.

"Rebecca, will you stay with me for a little while, please?" Isabel pleaded as Zach tucked her into bed.

"Sure. I'll just lie here right beside you until you go to sleep, okay?"

"Okay."

Rebecca looked up at Zach. "I'll stay for a little while," she said softly.

He nodded. "I've got some papers to read, anyway." He kissed Isabel good-night and walked toward the door, shutting it halfway as he exited. He paused to take a deep breath and massage the tense muscles in his neck. It had been some night, he thought tiredly. Isabel had adapted so well he'd almost forgotten the trauma she'd endured, the terror she'd lived with every day. But tonight's episode brought home very clearly the kind of environment she and Josef coped with on a daily basis.

Zach walked over to the window and stared out into the darkness, shoving his hands into his pockets. What was Josef doing right now? he wondered. Missing Isabel, of course. And mourning Katrina, certainly. He was truly alone now, with only his God and his faith to comfort him.

But maybe that helped more than he realized, Zach acknowledged. Ever since the Easter service, Zach found himself thinking more and more about his abandoned faith. He'd even gone with Rebecca and Isabel to services last Sunday, much to her surprise— and delight. Oddly enough, it gave him a sense of . . . stability and . . . connectedness. He couldn't explain why. But for some reason those worship services seemed to fill a gap in his life, offer him a new kind of hope. Maybe Josef felt the same.

Zach fervently hoped so. Because despite the fulfillment Josef found in his work, despite the commitment to his cause that gave his life so much meaning, he must be struggling right now to hold on to his hope and to deal with his loneliness. *Watch over him, Lord,* Zach prayed silently. *Let him know that we care and that he is in our thoughts and prayers.*

Zach pushed the last paper aside and glanced at the clock, his eyebrows rising in surprise. Eleven-thirty. He stood up quietly and moved silently toward Isabel's door, pausing on the threshold to glance toward the bed.

Rebecca lay on her side, one arm protectively around Isabel, her hair splayed on the pillow behind her. Isabel's back was cuddled against Rebecca, and she still clutched Raggedy Ann. Zach's throat tightened with tenderness as he gazed at them. They both looked so fragile and innocent and vulnerable. And they looked right together, he thought, like they belonged with each other.

Suddenly, with an insight that took him completely by surprise, he wished they belonged with him. Having these two special people in his life these past few weeks had given him a taste of family life. Okay, so it was only temporary. It was just pretend. But despite the fact that he'd spent his life studiously avoiding that kind of commitment, he realized he liked it. A lot.

Rebecca shifted slightly, emitting a soft sigh, and he suddenly wondered what it would be like to have her in his life permanently. That thought had never entered his mind about any of the other women he'd dated. But then again, he hadn't loved them.

Zach frowned. Love? He didn't love Rebecca. At least, not yet. Did he? How did a person know when they were in love?

Zach didn't have the answer to that question. All he knew with absolute certainty was that he cared about Rebecca deeply. And it was becoming harder and harder to imagine his life without her.

Chapter Eleven

Rebecca stretched her jeans-clad legs out in front of her, closed her eyes and tilted her head back to let the warm, mid-May sun caress her face. The capricious breeze gently ruffled the long russet waves of her hair, and she smiled contentedly, looking more relaxed than Zach had ever seen her.

He watched her quietly across the remains of Isabel's pre-birthday picnic, strewn between them on the large, flat boulder where they sat. Since the fireworks incident, their relationship had grown slowly but steadily. Rebecca had become comfortable with his physical expressions of affection, letting her hair down with him—literally and figuratively—as her trust level grew. And as their relationship developed, Zach found the answer to his question. He was definitely falling in love with Rebecca.

It was odd, he mused. He'd been closer to other women physically. But he'd never felt as connected on a deeper, more emotional, level than he did with the woman beside him. Her innate simplicity, warmth and goodness brought a new, rich dimension to his life, and he said a silent prayer of thanks for the blessing of her friendship which he hoped, in time, would evolve into love.

As if sensing his gaze, she opened her eyes and turned to him, tilting her head questioningly at his enigmatic expression. "What are you thinking?"

He considered the question for a moment, debated the merits of telling her how he felt, and decided the time was not yet right. He couldn't risk scaring her off. Waiting was hard, but it was far preferable to losing her by laying his cards on the table prematurely.

"I had some good news this morning," he told her.

"What?"

"My editor called. They're going to run the series on government corruption. One of my sources came forward voluntarily—with plenty of documentation to validate my story."

For the briefest moment, Zach though he detected a look of anxiety on Rebecca's face. But it was replaced so quickly by a smile he couldn't be sure.

"That's great, Zach! You should be very happy."

He nodded thoughtfully. "Yes, I should be. But strangely enough, I don't feel much of anything . . . except vindication. When the phone rang I was getting Isabel ready for the picnic—and looking forward to seeing you—and the call seemed more like a nuisance, an unwanted distraction. I've hardly thought about it since." He paused and glanced at Isabel, playing happily at the edge of the stream. "The rat race in St. Louis seems so far away sometimes . . . almost like another lifetime."

Rebecca studied Zach's pensive profile, trying not to read more into what he was saying than was intended. It *sounded* like he was implying that he'd found something better in St. Genevieve. But he hadn't actually said that. And as far as she knew, he still intended to return to St. Louis when his leave was over and Isabel was gone. Until—or unless—he told her otherwise, she would be wise to remember that this interlude was just an unexpected detour in Zach's life.

"Isabel seems to be having fun," he remarked.

Rebecca looked over at the youngster, who was trying vainly to catch minnows in a plastic cup, and smiled. "Yes. I'm glad you thought of the picnic."

He turned to her then, his eyes thoughtful. "Remember the last time we were here?"

Rebecca nodded. It was the day after their disastrous dinner, the same day he'd told her about Josef's request and she'd offered to help with Isabel. "It seems like a long time ago," she remarked quietly.

"Yeah, it does," he agreed. "But thank God our paths crossed that day! I don't know how I would have managed Isabel without your help. You've been really great with her."

She waved his praise aside. "You would have done just fine. You're obviously good with kids, Zach. You're a hit at the high school, and Isabel took to you right away. I can see why Josef trusted you with her. You make a good uncle."

He turned to look at his young charge again. She'd filled out since arriving, and her cheeks had taken on a healthy glow. Gone was the solemn, wary look that had so often haunted her eyes when she first arrived. Now she seemed like any other carefree almost-eight-year-old. And oddly enough, instead of being the burden he had anticipated, she'd added an unexpected spark to his life. He was going to miss her—a lot—when she went home.

"Believe it or not, I really feel like Isabel is family now," he said slowly. "When I agreed to this arrangement, it never occurred to me that I'd actually grow to love her. I just expected to be sort of a caretaker—keep her fed, clean, safe and as happy as possible under the circumstances. But now . . ." He gazed at the little girl again and sighed, his eyes troubled. "Now I dread the thought of sending her back into that turmoil, even though I know Josef will do his best to protect her." He raked his fingers through his hair and expelled a frustrated breath. "God, why does the world have to be in such a mess?" he said helplessly.

Rebecca swallowed past the lump in her throat, knowing the question was rhetorical, knowing also that there was no answer. She, too, had been thinking more and more about Isabel's impending departure. In three weeks they would put her on a plane and send her home to an uncertain future. It would be the hardest thing Rebecca had ever done in her life.

"I guess we always want to protect the people we love," she reflected softly, "even though it's not always possible. We'll just have to put her in the hands of the Lord and pray that He'll watch over her."

"Uncle Zach! Rebecca! Come see the fish I caught!" Isabel called, hopping from one foot to the other in her excitement.

Rebecca forced herself to smile. "Okay, sweetie." She stood up, then spontaneously held out her hand to Zach. She had been initiating physical contact more and more often lately, he realized with gratitude. He knew that her willingness to reach out to him spoke far more eloquently than words of her growing trust and deepening feelings.

He stood up and laced his fingers with hers, his mouth quirking into an apologetic smile. "Sorry to be so melancholy. I didn't mean to put a damper on the party."

"It's okay. I've been having the same thoughts lately myself. It will be so hard to let her go." Her voice faltered, and she took a deep breath. "I just never realized I could care about someone so much this quickly."

Zach gazed at her, and his eyes grew tender and warm. "Neither did I," he concurred huskily.

He wasn't talking about Isabel anymore, Rebecca realized, her heart soaring at his intimate tone. But before she got carried away she reminded herself that while Zach might care for her, she had no idea just how deeply his feelings ran. She suspected that he was used to casual relationships, where each partner took what they needed and then moved on. And that wasn't her style at all.

But even if he was serious, she still had another obstacle to overcome. In the past few weeks she'd grown comfortable with the gradual introduction of physical contact into their relationship. She welcomed his kisses, waited eagerly for his tender touch. But always she sensed a simmering passion just below the surface, firmly held in check for the moment but clearly seeking release. And when he did give expression to that passion, she was terrified that he would find her inadequate or, worse yet, too frightened to respond with anything but panic.

Even that, however, wasn't her greatest fear. For Zach, these few weeks represented a promise kept, a fling at teaching, a change of pace from his hectic life in St. Louis. He hadn't intended the situation to be permanent. As far as she knew, he still didn't.

And so her greatest fear, the one that haunted her dreams, was that bidding farewell to Isabel wouldn't be the only good-bye she would have to say in the very near future.

"Which present would you like to open first?" Rebecca asked, arranging the colorfully wrapped packages on her coffee table. "Or are you too full?" she teased. Much to the amazement of Rebecca and Zach, Isabel had polished off a plate of spaghetti, a pile of French fries, an ear of corn and two pieces of chocolate cake.

"I think she has a hollow leg," Zach declared, reaching over to tickle her.

"I do not," she told him, giggling as she squirmed out of his grasp. "I was just hungry. And I'm not too full to open presents," she informed Rebecca, eyeing them with delight.

"Then how about if you start with Uncle Zach's?" Rebecca suggested.

"Okay." She reached for it eagerly, quickly tearing the paper off. Her eyes sparkled at the child-sized backpack, decorated with characters from a popular animated children's movie, and she threw her arms around Zach's neck. "Oh, thank you, Uncle Zach! Wait till all my friends at school see this next year!"

Rebecca handed her the next gift, two boxes tied together with ribbon. The first contained a ballpoint pen with Isabel's name engraved on it. "For when you start writing," Rebecca told her. The other held a pink sweater with a smiling teddy bear face on the pocket.

"This is the one we saw in the store the other day," Isabel declared excitedly as she held it up. "I love it! Thank you so much!"

"You're very welcome, honey," Rebecca replied. "Here's your papa's present, sweetie." She reached for the package, which had arrived just a few days before, and handed it to Isabel.

The little girl cradled it in her hands for a moment, then carefully tore off the paper to reveal a beautifully carved wooden box. "I bet my papa made this," she speculated softly, running her fingers reverently over the intricate handiwork. "He's a real good carver." She lifted the lid slowly, and inside, on a red velvet lining, rested a folded sheet of paper and another, smaller package.

Isabel removed the package first and unwrapped it, fishing through the tissue to extract a delicate filigreed gold brooch. The front was hinged, and she flipped it open to reveal a photograph of Katrina and Josef. "This was my mama's," Isabel said, her voice subdued. "She always told me someday it would be mine."

Rebecca blinked rapidly, trying desperately to keep her tears at bay. *Don't cry,* she told herself fiercely. *It will only make Isabel feel worse.*

Isabel withdrew the single sheet of paper in the case and unfolded it, frowning at the words before looking up at Zach. "I'm not very good yet at reading, especially handwriting," she told him. "Would you read it to me?"

Zach took it and smoothed back her hair. "Of course, honey." His voice sounded strained, and Rebecca knew he was struggling with his emotions, just as she was.

"My dearest Isabel," he began. "I am so sorry that I cannot be with you to celebrate your eighth birthday. But I will be thinking of you all day, and hoping you have a good time with Uncle Zach and Rebecca. Wasn't it nice of them to have a party just for you?

"I made you this treasure box, which I hope you will keep always and fill with special things that are important to you. I have given you the first treasure to put in it, the brooch your mama loved so much. Remember how she always wore it close to her heart? I hope you will do the same, my child, to remind you that your mama and I will always be close to your heart, even when we are far away.

"I miss you, little one, more than words can say. You are my sunlight and my joy. Your mama always used to say that God gave us a touch of heaven when He sent you to us, and I believe that she was right. You are a precious gift, and I love you with all my heart. I am counting the days until you are home with me again.

"Happy birthday, Isabel. And may God be with you."

Zach's voice was grave by the time he finished, and he cleared his throat as he slowly refolded Josef's heartfelt note. Rebecca wiped away the tear that suddenly spilled out of her eye, then reached over to hug the suddenly subdued little girl at her side.

"Your papa loves you very much, Isabel," she said, her voice choked. "You're a very lucky girl to have such a wonderful father."

"I know," Isabel replied in a small, quavering voice. She fingered the delicate brooch and stared at the photograph of the smiling young man and woman. "I miss him. And I miss my mama. She was very pretty, wasn't she?"

"She was beautiful," Rebecca agreed. "I think you have her lovely smile, as a matter of fact."

Isabel looked up at Rebecca. "Really?"

"Really."

"Maybe someday I'll look like her," Isabel said hopefully.

"I think that's a very good possibility. Would you like me to pin the brooch on for you?"

Isabel nodded, and Rebecca reached over to secure it firmly on Isabel's sweater.

"They're right by my heart now, aren't they?" she said wistfully.

"Yes, sweetie, they are." She had to get away for a minute, Rebecca thought desperately, or she was going to lose it completely. "Zach, let me get you some more coffee," she offered, reaching for his nearly full cup, fleeing to the kitchen before he could respond.

Even before she reached that sanctuary, the tears were trickling down her cheeks. She leaned against the refrigerator and closed her eyes, her heart tattered, her emotions raw. How on earth could they send this poor child back to the danger and turmoil in her country? And yet she belonged with Josef, who clearly loved her more than anything else on earth. She thought about all the lonely nights he'd spent since Isabel's departure, painstakingly creating the treasure box for her in his silent and empty apartment, and her heart ached. Another tear traced its way down her cheek, and she struggled to stifle her sobs, the back of her hand against her lips. Josef needed Isabel—desperately. But could he protect her? Dear God, what are we to do? she cried silently. How can we ever let her go?

Rebecca suddenly felt two strong arms encircle her, and then Zach pulled her close, smoothing her hair tenderly as he held her. He pressed her cheek against his chest and stroked it soothingly.

"I put a video in," he said softly, his lips against her forehead. "She'll be occupied for a few minutes, anyway."

"Oh, Zach!" Rebecca whispered brokenly. "She's so little. And so helpless. Just thinking about sending her back . . ." Her voice choked.

"I know." His own voice sounded none too steady.

"I'll worry about her constantly."

"So will I." He pressed her even closer, and she hugged him tightly as they tried to draw strength from each other. "I was beginning to think I might enjoy having kids someday, but I'm not sure I can handle the emotional turmoil and worry that goes with that responsibility," he said heavily. "Isabel isn't even my daughter, and yet this whole thing is tearing me up inside."

"I guess that's part of what loving is all about," Rebecca replied tearfully. "Just by caring we expose ourselves to hurt and risk. And yet . . . Isabel has added so much to my life. I wouldn't have wanted to miss that."

As Zach stroked her back comfortingly, Rebecca realized that she felt the same way about him. Even if he left next month, as he very well might, he had given her a precious gift. With patience and gentleness, he had helped her to believe that she could overcome her debilitating fear of physical intimacy and ultimately realize her dream of having a husband who would also father her children.

The only problem was, she couldn't imagine anyone in that role but Zach.

The sound of shattering dishes—for the second time in an hour—brought a frown to Rebecca's face, and she glanced up from the computer in her tiny office at the restaurant. She didn't usually come in on Sunday, but she'd been trying to spend as much time as possible with Zach and Isabel, and so she'd gotten behind on paperwork. Two of her high school wait staff had also volunteered to come in and set up for a special party she was doing tomorrow. But it sounded like her profits were going right down the drain.

She was about to investigate when a tentative knock sounded on her half-closed door and Pete Cramer stuck his head in. "I'm sorry to bother you, Ms. Matthews, but I think there's something wrong with Melanie," he told her, his face a mask of concern. "She looks kind of . . . funny. I asked her if she was sick, but she said no."

Rebecca studied the lanky youth with a frown. He'd only been on the staff for a week, but already she could see that he was a hard worker. He was also very sensitive to people. If he said something was wrong with Melanie, she believed him.

"Are you two about done?" she asked.

"Yeah. We just finished."

"Great. Thanks a lot for coming in, Pete. And ask Melanie to come back for a minute, would you? Just lock the door behind you as you leave."

"Okay."

He disappeared, and a couple of minutes later she heard the front door open and close. Moments later a pale, drawn Melanie appeared in the office doorway, biting her lip nervously. The sixteen-year-old looked nothing like her usual cheerful, smiling self, Rebecca noted worriedly.

"I'm really sorry about the dishes, Ms. Matthews," the girl apologized. "You can just take it out of my pay. I don't mind."

"Don't worry about it, Melanie," Rebecca reassured her. "I'm more concerned about you. You've been working for me for nine months, and I don't think you've ever dropped a plate or glass, let alone a tray. Is everything all right?"

Melanie lowered her eyes and rubbed the palms of her hands nervously against her jeans. "Yeah. I . . . I guess so."

Her tentative tone negated her words, and Rebecca stood up and impulsively put her arm around the girl's shoulders. "I have a feeling that's not quite true," she said gently. "Would you like to have a soda and talk for a few minutes? I'm a good listener."

Melanie considered the offer for a moment, again nervously biting her lip. Finally she nodded her head jerkily. "Okay."

"Go ahead into the restaurant. I'll grab the sodas."

By the time Rebecca joined her, Melanie's eyes were suspiciously moist and her shoulders were hunched miserably. She was obviously deeply upset, but she remained silent, so Rebecca decided to do a little probing.

"Have you had some bad news, Melanie?" she asked quietly. She knew the plant where her father worked was downsizing. Perhaps he was being laid off, which would certainly disrupt the whole family.

The girl shook her head. "No."

Rebecca glanced at Melanie's hand as the girl toyed with the straw, noticing the bruise on her arm for the first time.

"What happened here?" Rebecca asked, laying her fingers gently against the purple area. Melanie flinched and her face seemed to grow even paler. Rebecca realized that the bruise was a clue to her present emotional distress. "When did you do this?" she prompted gently.

"L-last night. I went to the end-of-the-school-year dance."

"Well, I've had a few bruised toes from dancing, but never a bruised arm," Rebecca commented, trying unsuccessfully to induce the girl to relax a little.

"It didn't happen at . . . at the dance. It happened later."

A niggling suspicion suddenly put Rebecca on alert. She reached over and took the girl's hand.

"Melanie, honey, who did you go with?"

"J-Jack Simpson."

"Did he do this?"

Suddenly the girl broke down, no longer able to keep the tears in check. Between choked sobs, she told Rebecca what happened—the excitement of being asked out by one of the most popular boys at school, the fun she had at the dance, the drive to lookout point . . . and the increasingly aggressive, suddenly frightening, advances that she'd fought off as fear had given way to panic. Only the arrival of another car of laughing teenagers had halted the terrifying attack. But the incident had left Melanie shaken and deeply upset.

Rebecca hugged the shaking girl, trying to control her seething rage. "Did you tell your parents?" she asked, struggling to maintain an even tone.

"N-no," the girl sobbed.

"Don't you think you should?"

"I . . . I don't know," she replied helplessly.

"Would it help if I called? Asked them to come over here?"

"I . . . I think so."

"Then that's what we'll do."

An hour later Rebecca stared at Melanie's parents in disbelief after sending Melanie out of the room. "You mean you aren't going to do anything about this?" she demanded, her eyes blazing.

John Lewis rubbed a hand wearily across his face. "Look, Ms. Matthews, Melanie is a good girl and we want to protect her. But Jack is the son of the plant manager, and my job is already in jeopardy. Betty here has medical expenses, and I have four kids to support. I can't afford to take any risks. Besides, it worked out okay. Nothing happened."

"Nothing?" Rebecca's voice was outraged. "Mr. Lewis, Melanie was traumatized last night. An incident like that can leave emotional scars that never heal. And retribution in the workplace is illegal."

"Yeah. So they say. But that doesn't stop it from happening," he replied wearily. "We'll do our best to keep her out of situations where something like this could happen again. And we'll keep her away from that boy. That's all we can do."

Rebecca knew it was useless to press the point, and she watched in helpless frustration as they left, their arms around their daughter. She knew they loved Melanie, knew they meant what they said about doing their best to protect her. But she also knew it was wrong to let that boy get away with what bordered on criminal behavior. What if that other car hadn't driven up and prevented him from finishing what he started? Melanie was lucky. She'd escaped with her virtue intact. But Rebecca knew she could easily carry the emotional scars for the rest of her life.

Rebecca prowled around the restaurant restlessly, too angry to even think straight. She needed to do something to work off her anger, release some of the hyper energy coursing through her veins. Cooking always helped, she thought, heading for the kitchen. A glance at her watch told her she had three hours before Zach and Isabel were scheduled to pick her up for dinner. Hopefully by then she would calm down.

As he passed Rebecca's restaurant, Zach eased his foot off the accelerator in surprise. She'd mentioned at church that she planned to stop by for a little while, but that was hours ago. Why was her car still here?

He pulled up to the curb and parked, then hesitated. He'd been on his way to her apartment, knowing he was an hour early, hoping she wouldn't mind. A friend of Isabel's from Sunday school had unexpectedly invited her for dinner, a movie and a slumber party, and Zach had agreed. He was happy Isabel had made some friends her own age. And, on a more selfish note, he was also grateful for the unexpected opportunity to see Rebecca alone.

Frankly, he was beginning to worry about the lack of progress in their relationship. While Rebecca seemed comfortable with small intimacies, his attempts to get closer to her emotionally made her tense. He could feel her withdraw, close down, put up a No Trespassing sign. And he'd promised not to push. He'd kept that promise, but it grew more difficult daily.

Rebecca had said once that she wasn't a woman who liked to be touched. And he knew, somewhere in her background, there must be a good reason for that. She hadn't chosen to share it with him, which was her right. But he'd hoped that his patience and consideration would eventually make her comfortable enough to trust him, to reveal the secrets of her heart that made her wary.

So far that hadn't happened. And he was running out of time.

Isabel was leaving in two weeks. His leave was over a week after that. He had some important decisions to make, and a lot of those decisions hinged on Rebecca. He couldn't wait any longer to discuss their situation. He'd held off too long already, hoping things would progress in their relationship, but the status quo persisted. Now it was time to find out why.

Rebecca stirred the soup, banged the lid on the pot and then let the spoon clatter to the stainless steel counter. For some reason, making noise helped her vent the anger that still consumed her, even after two hours.

She slammed a pan on the stove and turned on the heat, then paused as an insistent knocking penetrated the other noises in the kitchen. She glanced toward the back door with annoyance, then wiped her hands on her apron and strode over to yank it open.

Zach's smile faded to a frown as his sweeping glance took in her flushed face, clenched jaw and the lines of strain around her rigid mouth. "Are you all right?" he asked without preamble.

"Of course I'm all right," she snapped, glancing irritably at her watch. "What are you doing here, anyway? I thought you were going to pick me up at six. At home. And where's Isabel?"

His frown deepened at Rebecca's uncharacteristic bad humor, and a tingle of alarm raced along his spine. "What's wrong, Rebecca?"

She pushed some loose strands of hair back from her face and glared at him. "What makes you think anything's wrong?" she demanded tersely. "And where's Isabel?"

"A friend from Sunday school invited her to spend the night and go to a movie."

"I thought we were all having dinner together."

"She wanted to go, Rebecca. I'm glad she has a friend. I didn't think you'd mind."

Suddenly Rebecca wrinkled her nose. She turned in dismay and, with a muttered exclamation, dashed toward the smoking pan on the stove. Zach followed more slowly, propping a shoulder against the wall and folding his arms across his chest as he watched her. He'd never seen her this upset. Anger was seething out of every pore in her body.

She dropped the pan into the sink, then turned to the carrots lying next to the cutting board and began to chop them viciously. When Zach remained silent, she looked up at him irritably. "I don't need an audience," she declared crossly.

"I was just trying to give you some time to cool down," he said, striving for a mild tone even as his nerves grew taut. "Do you want to talk about it?"

In reply she gave him a smoldering look, then went back to the carrots.

"Are you angry at me, Rebecca?" he asked quietly.

"No."

"You could have fooled me."

"Sorry," she said shortly, continuing to chop.

"Well, you're obviously angry about something. So do you want to tell me what's wrong?"

There was silence for several long seconds, and Zach began to think she was going to ignore this question, too. But finally she spoke.

"Do you know Melanie Lewis?" she asked curtly. "One of my waitresses?"

Zach frowned. "Yes. She's in one of my classes, as a matter of fact. Why?"

"She went to the end-of-the-school-year dance last night with the son of her father's boss, and he attacked her."

Zach straightened up abruptly, his eyes narrowing. "What do you mean, he attacked her?"

"Exactly what I said." She gave him a cursory account of the incident, her voice shaking with anger. "And if another car full of students hadn't come by that boy might be facing criminal charges right now," she concluded bluntly.

"Is she okay?"

"Physically, yes. Emotionally, I'm not so sure. I talked to her parents about it, but they're not going to do anything. Can you believe that?" she demanded irately.

"I don't know how much they *could* do," he replied thoughtfully. "Those situations are very sticky. We really don't know all of the circumstances. Maybe it was just a misunderstanding."

"A misunderstanding!" Rebecca stared at him disbelievingly, so angry she could barely choke out the words. "She was practically raped!"

"That's a serious charge, Rebecca," he replied gravely.

"It's true!"

"We haven't heard his side."

"I don't need to! I heard Melanie's! I saw her eyes! I know her!"

"I'm not saying she wasn't frightened," Zach tried to placate her. "But maybe she just got in over her head. Maybe he misinterpreted her cues."

"Or maybe he just decided to add another notch to his belt," she replied with cold fury.

"Rebecca, all I'm saying is that we don't know the whole story," he pointed out. "A charge like that could ruin a young boy's life."

"Well, what do you think it does to the victim's?" she shot back.

The conversation was getting way too emotional for Zach. "Look, Rebecca, calm down. You did everything you could. You talked to Melanie. You talked to her parents. They made their decision. There's nothing else you can do."

She finished the carrots and reached for the celery, pausing only to glare at Zach in silence.

"Rebecca, there's a real stigma attached to a charge like this, whether it's true or not," he tried again. "I did a series on date rape a couple of years ago, and it's a murky issue."

She looked at him, her eyes blazing. "Oh, so Mr. Journalist thinks he's an expert just because he wrote a few articles," she retorted sarcastically.

"It was an in-depth series," he replied defensively. "As a matter of fact, it won several awards."

"Well, excuse me. I guess that qualifies you as an expert," she said derisively.

His own temper was beginning to flare. Planting his fists on his hips, he faced her across the counter. "And you are? What makes you such an expert on the topic?" he flung back at her.

She stopped and glared at him, one hand clenched around the knife, the other white-knuckled as it gripped the edge of the counter. When she spoke, her voice was low, but it contained a harsh undertone of bitterness, and it shook with barely controlled rage.

"Because when I was Melanie's age, I came this close," she held up one trembling hand and measured a meager half-inch gap between her thumb and index finger, "to having it happen to me."

Chapter Twelve

For several eternal seconds of quivering, shocked silence they stared at each other across the room, Zach stunned by Rebecca's words, she equally stunned that she'd spoken them.

In a two-second explanation consisting of one simple sentence, Zach finally had an answer to the question that had troubled him for weeks. Now he understood why Rebecca was so afraid to let anyone close. The traumatic experience she'd endured as an impressionable young girl had apparently convinced her that accepting a date carried serious physical risks or, at the very least, expectations of physical closeness. But Rebecca didn't even engage in casual displays of affection, let alone intimacy. With her sensitive nature, that frightening early dating experience would have been a nightmare, one that had pursued her relentlessly through the years. It had taken what should, in the right context, have been a beautiful experience and made it an act of aggression, totally devoid of tenderness or even consideration. No wonder she rarely dated after that, was still so fearful when even a hint of passion surfaced.

As these thoughts raced through Zach's mind, his shock rapidly gave way to anger. How could anyone have hurt this warm, vulnerable, caring woman? he railed silently. His jaw clenched as a cold fury enveloped him and a surge of protectiveness swept over him, so fierce it took his breath away. For the first time in his life he felt capable of doing serious damage to another human being.

Rebecca was aware of Zach's changing expressions, but only on a peripheral level. She was too busy trying to cope with the fact that she'd just revealed her most closely guarded secret. Melanie's story had brought back her own experience with a shattering, vivid intensity that tilted her world out of alignment. The anger she'd vented on Zach had been directed not at him, but at the boy who had scarred her indelibly so many years ago. And it was also directed at herself, for allowing his despicable behavior to ruin her life all these years. It was almost as if a release valve had been flicked open, and all the anger and hurt she'd bottled up inside for almost twenty years had finally burst forth.

As she stared at Zach across the room, trying to decide what to do next, his figure suddenly wavered before her eyes, and the room tilted strangely. She groped for the edge of the counter, then grasped it tightly as she tried to take a deep breath. But her lungs refused to cooperate.

Zach saw the sudden look of disorientation in Rebecca's eyes, took in her white-knuckled grip on the edge of the counter and moved rapidly around the work area, praying he would reach her before she nosedived against the unforgiving edge of the stainless steel work space.

Despite the fuzziness in her brain, however, Zach's movement registered, and a surge of panic swept over her. In a triumph of will over body she fought off the sudden attack of vertigo, backing away from him unsteadily even as she rode the waves of blackness that crashed over her. "Don't touch me," she whispered, wrapping her arms around her body, staring at him with frightened eyes as she willed herself to remain upright.

He stopped a few feet away, sensing that she needed the safety of distance for the moment but poised to reach out to her instantly if she started to pass out. She looked so alone, so vulnerable, so in need of being held. It took every ounce of his willpower to honor her plea when his overriding instinct was to pull her into his arms and hold her until she felt safe and protected and loved.

He saw a shudder ripple through her, and he swallowed convulsively, his gut clenching as burning rage once more consumed him. But comfort and compassion, not anger, were what she needed now, he reminded himself. If she wouldn't let him go to her, maybe he could get her to come to him. Slowly, nonthreateningly, he lifted his hand and held it out to her.

"Let me help, Rebecca," he murmured softly.

She shook her head jerkily. The dizziness was gone, but now she felt oddly weak—and weary. "It's too late," she told him, her voice flat and lifeless.

"I don't think it is. Talking about things can help a lot, and I'm a good listener." When she didn't respond, he took a tentative step forward. "At least take my hand," he coaxed.

She looked down at the strong but gentle hand he offered, then up into his compassionate, caring eyes. Maybe she *should* talk about it. Her secret was out now, anyway. Perhaps the Lord had let her make that slip as a sign that it was time to share her story, to open her heart to this special man. Perhaps by doing that, she could truly begin to heal.

Slowly, hesitantly, she reached out and took his hand, and he enfolded her cold fingers in his warm, reassuring clasp. Gently he urged her toward him and wrapped his arms around her trembling body, stroking her back.

He held her like that for a long time, murmuring soothing words, telling her over and over again that everything would be all right, until finally her trembling subsided. Then, his arm around her shoulders, he led her into the restaurant, to a roomy booth in the corner. As they sat down, he pulled her close, into the protective curve of his arm. Silently he handed her his handkerchief, and she took it gratefully, dabbing at her red-rimmed eyes.

"I—I'm sorry for the way I treated you just now," she apologized tremulously. "It wasn't fair."

"A lot of things in life aren't fair," he said, his voice rough with emotion. "Rebecca, I'm so sorry! I wish I could just erase that whole ugly experience from your life."

"I've wished the same thing thousands of times through the years," she admitted, the catch in her voice tugging at his heart. "But you can't change the past."

"No. All you can do is move on and try not to let it ruin your future."

"That's easier said than done, Zach," she told him wearily.

"I know that, sweetheart," he replied sympathetically. "Sometimes, though, talking it out helps to put it to rest. Do you want to tell me about it?"

She sighed. "I guess I can try. I just don't know where to start."

"Then how about if I play journalist and ask a few questions?" he suggested.

"Okay."

"You said you were the same age as Melanie?"

"Yes. Sixteen. I guess that's why her experience hit so close to home."

"Who was the boy?" Whoever he was, and wherever he was, Zach fervently hoped he'd been made to pay in some way for what he'd done to Rebecca. Maybe that was wrong. But it was the way he felt.

"H-he was the high school football hero. Everyone wanted to go out with him. I couldn't believe it when he asked me to the spring dance, which was the big social event of the season. I thought I was so lucky, to be asked out by the big man on campus on my very first date."

"You mean . . . this happened to you the very first time you ever went out?"

"Yes."

She heard him mutter something under his breath. Though she couldn't quite make it out, she knew from his tone that it wasn't pretty. She inched closer and let her hand rest lightly on his thigh, almost in a gesture of comfort, he thought, a muscle in his jaw twitching. Even in the midst of her own pain, she was attuned to the needs of others. But that was Rebecca. He reached over and covered her hand with his own as she continued.

"We had fun at the dance. And afterward, when he asked me if I wanted to go for a drive, I said yes. I assumed he wanted to . . . well . . . do a little kissing, and I wasn't opposed. I thought it was pretty exciting to have a first date and a first kiss all in the same night. Except . . . except he had a lot more than that on his mind."

Zach squeezed her hand, and she drew a long, shaky breath.

"We drove to Miller's Point. It wasn't the usual make-out place, but I wasn't suspicious. I just figured, being an 'experienced' guy, he'd found a few places that were off the beaten path. I just didn't realize how 'experienced' he was."

She swallowed convulsively, and Zach felt her muscles tense as she continued.

"He had a bottle of wine in the car. I only had one glass, but it was my first experience with wine, so it didn't take much to make me a little 'floaty,' you know? After the wine, he said he knew a great spot that overlooked the river, and would I like to sit there for a while and enjoy the view? I said yes."

She was starting to shake again, and Zach reached over and stroked her cheek, his eyes holding hers compellingly, reassuringly. "It's okay, Rebecca. It happened a long time ago. It can only hurt you now *if* you let it."

"I know." He was right. She had to get through this, deal with it once and for all, so she could move on. "For . . . for a few minutes it was fine. He kissed me, and it was . . . nice. But all of a sudden he got . . . he got really . . . aggressive. It was like he became a different person. His kisses weren't . . . simple . . . anymore. They were . . . rough. I started to get scared, and I tried to pull away. But he pushed me down and just kind of fell across me. He was big . . . and . . . and strong. My arms were pinned down and I—I couldn't move."

Her words were choppy now, her breathing uneven. Zach wanted to tell her to stop, to bury the terrible memories so deeply they would never resurface again. But he knew they would never be put to rest until she dealt with them. The best thing he could do for her was let her talk through the terror and remembered pain, until it no longer had the power to dominate her life. And so he remained silent, stroking her hand comfortingly as she spoke.

"I had long hair, and he . . . he twisted it so I couldn't move my head. The more I struggled, the harder he pulled." She stopped and squeezed her eyes shut. A tear trailed down her cheek and she drew in a harsh breath. "I fought as much as I could, but it was useless. I tried to scream, but he never took his lips off of mine. There wouldn't have been anyone to hear me, anyway. The only thing I could do was pray.

"Then all of a sudden I felt him p-pulling up my dress, and I heard a zipper. I . . . I knew what he was planning to do. Oh, God!" She let out an anguished cry, and Zach pulled her close, his gut twisting painfully.

"It's okay, Rebecca. It's okay," he repeated helplessly, knowing it wasn't but unable to find any adequate words of comfort. Her whole body was shaking, and he could feel her tears soaking through his cotton shirt. All he could do was hold her until she was ready to continue and try to control the rage that burned in his heart.

After a couple of minutes, she drew in several ragged breaths and spoke again, her voice raw with pain, her fingers clutching his shirt convulsively. "I think I . . . I was hysterical by then, because I d-don't even remember clearly what happened next. Except that out of the blue it started to rain. It was a downpour, as if the heavens had opened—almost like a miracle. In any case, it dampened his enthusiasm—and his determination. He took off for the car.

"For the longest time I just lay there. I guess I was in shock or something. But finally I got up and stumbled back to the car. He was waiting for me, none too patiently, aggravated about his rented tux getting wet. He told me to get in. We were out in the middle of nowhere, and I guess I sensed that at that point it would be more dangerous to wander the back roads on foot in a storm than ride back to town with him. Besides, I could tell his ardor, if that's what you'd call it, had cooled. So I got in and he took me home. Can you believe that he . . . he asked me out again, two weeks later?" she said brokenly, the tears still streaming down her face.

Zach muttered another unflattering comment and pressed her cheek more closely to his chest. She could feel the hard, rapid thudding of his heart, could sense his anger in the rigid lines of his body. Oddly enough, her own simmering rage, so tightly coiled all these years, had eased.

Finally Zach drew back slightly and cradled her tear-streaked face with his hands, his thumbs gently erasing the evidence of her tears. "Have you ever told anyone about this, Rebecca?"

"N-no."

"Why not?"

"Because I . . . I was too ashamed. I felt like maybe it was my fault, that I'd done something wrong, encouraged him in some way."

"You don't still think that, do you?"

She shook her head. "No. But it took me a long time to get past that. And I never did get over my fear of being alone with men. That's why the few dates I went on turned into such disasters. I just assumed every time a man kissed me that it would evolve into an attack. I know that's irrational, but I can't seem to control the panic. It just . . . overwhelms me."

"Have you ever thought about counseling?"

"Yes. But I—I've always been too embarrassed to talk about it. And I figured eventually I would get over it. Only . . . I never did."

He stroked her back in silence for a few seconds, then reached up and fingered a few loose tendrils that had worked free of her hairpins and now lay curled softly at her nape. "That's why you always wear your hair up, isn't it?" he asked with sudden insight. "Because he used your long hair against you that night."

She hesitated, then nodded. "Yes. I like long hair, but it seemed . . . safer . . . to wear it up. And this style suits my profession. But I let it down around family and close friends. Like . . . like you," she said, her voice suddenly shy, her eyes downcast.

He studied her for a moment, then decided to risk the question. "Is that all I am, Rebecca?" he asked softly. "A friend?"

He felt a shudder run through her as she drew in a shaky breath. "I . . . I like you a lot, Zach," she replied cautiously. "But I have a major problem with . . . with intimacy. I break into a cold sweat just thinking about it. Touching makes me feel fear, not desire. And no man's ego can take that forever." Her voice suddenly sounded resigned and defeated.

Zach didn't believe for a minute that Rebecca was incapable of desire. He'd seen it flashing in her eyes on any number of occasions. But *she* believed it, and only patience and understanding would convince her otherwise.

"Can I tell you something, Rebecca?" he asked quietly. "I don't think the right man's ego would *have* to take it forever. I've seen the way you look at me. I know in your heart you feel more than just liking for me. You're just too afraid to let those feelings out. But my ego is strong enough to handle your fear until you feel comfortable enough to move forward. I think we could have something very special, you and I. And I also think you owe it to yourself—to both of us—to give this thing a chance."

Rebecca bit her lip as she considered his words. How much progress could she make in three weeks, before Zach left? And the real question was, how much did she want to make? Zach never talked about leaving, or what would happen when he did. Maybe he just wanted to help "cure" her out of compassion and genuine caring. It didn't mean he loved her. But to let the relationship progress and then have him walk out—could she deal with that?

Rebecca wanted to believe that Zach cared enough about her to find a way to keep her in his life once he left St. Genevieve. St. Louis wasn't that far away, after all. If he wanted to continue their relationship, they could manage it.

She closed her eyes, seeking guidance. *Please, Lord, give me a sign. Show me what to do. Do I take a chance on this wonderful man, trust that he cares enough about me to make me part of his life, or do I throw away the possibility for love, let him walk away, out of fear?*

No answer was immediately forthcoming, and she sighed. But when she opened her eyes, her gaze fell on a painting of tulips she'd recently added to the restaurant. It spoke eloquently of spring and hope and new life. And suddenly she knew what she was going to do.

"All right, Zach," she said quietly. "Let's give it a chance."

Zach gathered up the final papers from his desk and shoved them into his briefcase, snapped the clasp shut and glanced around the deserted classroom. It was hard to believe that the last day of school had arrived already.

"Mr. Wright?"

Zach glanced toward the door and smiled. "Hi, Pete."

"Hi. Do you have a minute?"

"Sure. Come on in. I thought everyone had cleared out by now."

"I was just cleaning out my locker." He shuffled in self-consciously, his hands stuck in the pockets of his jeans.

Zach eyed him speculatively, noting the slight flush on his cheeks and the spark in his eyes. He could feel an . . . excitement . . . radiating from the youth. "What's up?" he asked mildly.

Suddenly Pete grinned, unable to keep the good news to himself any longer. "I won the short story contest!" he blurted out, his voice tinged with pride.

Zach's lips curved into a smile of pleasure. He strode toward the boy, taking his hand in a firm grip as he laid his free hand on Pete's shoulder. "Congratulations! Are you the national winner?"

"Yeah. The story will be published next fall. And there's a thousand-dollar prize!"

Zach grinned. "I knew you could do it. You're one of the most talented writers I've ever met."

The boy blushed and looked down. "Well, I just wanted to say that if it hadn't been for you, this would never have happened."

Zach waved his thanks aside. "It's hard to hide talent like yours, Pete. Sooner or later you would have found your voice, with or without me."

The boy frowned and shook his head slowly. "I don't think so, Mr. Wright. I was at kind of a low point in my life, getting involved in some things that weren't . . . well . . . very good. I think you came along at just the right time. You made me believe in myself. I wouldn't even have known about the contest if it hadn't been for you, let alone entered it. And so I just wanted to . . . to say thanks for making such a difference in my life. And to ask if it would be okay for me to keep in touch when you go back to St. Louis."

Zach smiled and squeezed Pete's shoulder. "Absolutely." He reached over to the desk, jotted down his address and handed it to the boy. "I'll be in town for at least another two weeks, though."

"Maybe I'll run into you at Rebecca's," the boy said hopefully.

Zach smiled. "You can count on it."

"Well . . . see you around."

Zach watched him amble out, filled with a sense of deep contentment. Never, in all his years of reporting, had he been aware of making such a direct impact on a single life. And it felt good, he realized. Very good.

Zach propped his hip on the edge of the desk, folded his arms across his chest and gazed pensively out the window at the lush foliage. When he'd arrived in St. Genevieve, in mid-February, the world was gray and dead and cold. Now, at the end of May, it was bright and alive and warm. Much like his heart, he realized. Here, in this small rural town, as a high school teacher, he'd found work that energized him in a way journalism no longer did. He'd found, through Isabel, a new outlook on the world and discovered a surprising paternal side to his personality. And he'd found, in Rebecca, a woman to love.

He thought about the past two weeks, since she'd revealed the trauma that had scarred her heart. He couldn't believe the progress they'd made in just that short time. One by one, Rebecca's emotional defenses had begun to drop away. She was relaxed around him, lighthearted, even affectionate at times. Finally, the scars of the past had begun to heal, and they grew closer day by day. When she faltered, he held fast, and with infinite patience, helped her past the hurdle. It hadn't always been easy, he admitted. He wasn't, by nature, a patient man. At least, he never had been before. But he'd learned a lot about patience this spring, both from Isabel and Rebecca. And patience was the key to winning her heart, he knew.

It was hard to believe his time in St. Genevieve was almost over. The weeks had flown by. He'd learned a great deal, been challenged in countless new ways, discovered an unexpected capacity for love and new dimensions to his personality. The break from reporting had definitely been worthwhile and satisfying on many levels, both personal and professional.

The question now was whether to make that break permanent.

As of this morning, he had the perfect opportunity to do so. When the principal called him into his office before class, Zach assumed it was simply to say thanks and good luck. Instead, he'd offered him a permanent job. Phil Carr would return in the fall, but another English teacher was leaving unexpectedly. Zach had been flattered—and taken aback. The principal had asked him to think about it for a couple of weeks, and then, if he was interested, they could discuss the details.

Zach was definitely interested. Professionally, it would be a good change for him. But ultimately his answer depended on the answer to another, far more personal question: would Rebecca agree to marry him?

Zach hadn't planned to propose just yet. She was only now beginning to feel comfortable with him. But he knew her self-confidence was still at a low ebb, knew she still harbored tremendous doubts and worries about their physical relationship.

Personally, he had no such doubts. He was convinced that in the context of marriage, of a "till death do us part" vow, she would learn to respond, to give full expression to the passion he knew was in her heart. But with the job offer now to consider, he needed to pose the question sooner than planned. Because if he made a commitment to stay in St. Genevieve, he wanted her by his side—permanently.

Zach stood up and reached for his briefcase, his thoughts turning to Ted Larsen's request for a meeting tomorrow in St. Louis. Zach assumed it was to discuss his return to work and his next assignment. Obviously he'd have to put his editor off. But at least the trip to St. Louis would give him a chance to take care of one very important piece of personal business—a trip to a jewelry store.

Zach stared at Ted, his mouth literally dropping open in surprise.

The managing editor smiled at the younger man's dumbfounded reaction. "Don't look so shocked, Zach. You're a top-notch reporter. You deserve this promotion."

"But . . . Washington Bureau chief?" Zach said incredulously, his face still stunned. It was the most coveted job on the newspaper, a chance to mingle with the movers and shakers in Washington, to do in-depth coverage of the events that shaped the nation. "What about Joe?"

"He's decided to take early retirement. I guess he figured that after fifteen years on the Washington beat he's pretty much seen it all. We're sorry to see him go, to be honest. He's done a fine job. But new blood won't hurt, and we're all confident you'll do a terrific job."

Zach felt a surge of adrenaline shoot through his veins. Washington! Press conferences with the president. Interviews with the secretary of state. Access to the most powerful political figures in the world. It was heady stuff. "To say I'm overwhelmed would be putting it mildly," he admitted, shaking his head.

"Then you'll accept?"

Accept? He hadn't even fully absorbed the offer yet. His first instinct was to say yes. But the weight of the ring box in the pocket of his sports coat, resting lightly against his heart, made him hesitate. If he accepted the position, all the plans he'd been making for a far different life would have to change dramatically. Zach knew intuitively that Rebecca wouldn't like the fast-paced, glitzy life in Washington, even if she loved him enough to go. The quieter, simpler style of small-town life suited her. And until a couple of minutes ago he thought it suited him, too, especially if she was by his side.

When Zach didn't respond immediately, Ted placed his elbows on the arms of his chair, steepled his fingers and leaned back, eyeing the younger man speculatively. "I can see this isn't quite as simple a decision for you as I expected, Zach. Would you like to take a few days to think it over?"

Zach nodded. "Yeah. There are some . . . complications."

"Well, just give me a call when you reach a decision." Ted stood up and extended his hand, his grip firm and warm. "Think it through carefully, Zach. Opportunities like this don't come along very often."

As Zach rode down in the elevator, then strolled aimlessly along the street, Ted's words kept replaying in his mind. His editor was right. Some opportunities were rare. Like the offer of Washington Bureau chief. But others came only once in a lifetime. Like winning the love of the most wonderful woman he'd ever met.

Zach detoured into a convenient sidewalk café and mulled over his options as he sipped a cup of coffee. The Washington job certainly offered excitement and the chance to do some of the best reporting of his life. But to take it, he'd have to give up a number of things: satisfying work that he knew, from personal experience, had a direct, positive impact on young people's lives; a life-style that gave him time to breathe; and most important, the woman he loved and the chance to create with her a warm and loving family that would sustain him all the days of his life. That was something Washington couldn't offer. Eventually the excitement there would fade. In the end all he would have to show for his adventure in the nation's capital would be a dusty scrapbook of stories, perhaps a couple of awards to hang on his wall. And those tangible reminders of "success" would be bought at a high price—the price of the life he could have had in St. Genevieve.

Suddenly Zach wondered why he'd even hesitated. Yes, the job offer meant a lot to him. But it meant even more to win one of Isabel's smiles or to feel Rebecca's hand in his or hear the sincere thank-you of a student who had turned his life around. Maybe small-town life didn't have the glitz and glamour of Washington. But he knew with absolute conviction that it was what he wanted.

Zach tossed some bills on the table and rose. "Is there a phone close by?" he asked a passing waitress.

"Sure. Inside. By the rest rooms."

"Thanks."

Zach located it quickly, dialed Rebecca's restaurant, then waited impatiently.

"Rebecca's."

"Rose?"

"No. It's Frances."

"Frances, it's Zach. Is Rebecca there?"

"Of course. Isn't she always? Hold on and I'll get her."

Zach heard her say, "It's your young man, dear," before Rebecca came on the line, and he smiled.

"Zach? Where are you?"

"Still in St. Louis."

"How did it go with your editor?"

"Fine. In fact, are you ready for this? He offered me the job of Washington Bureau chief!"

There was a momentary hesitation, but when Rebecca spoke her voice was bright. "That's wonderful, Zach. When are you supposed to go?"

"I haven't even given him my answer yet."

"Why not? It's a great opportunity, isn't it?"

"Yeah. But . . ."

"Hang on a second, Zach."

He could hear Rebecca conferring with Rose, something about a customer complaint.

"Sorry, Zach," she apologized, sounding frazzled. "It's a zoo here."

"I can tell." He paused, debating how to proceed. He was anxious to talk with her, explain how he felt, but this was clearly not the best place or time. They needed somewhere quiet, where neither would be interrupted. "Listen, I'll tell you all about it when I see you. I guess you'll be pretty swamped until Sunday morning, won't you?" The Friday lunch rush was barely over, and she was probably already gearing up for the dinner crowd. It would be the same tomorrow.

"Yes. You know how Friday and Saturday are."

He sighed. "Yeah. Okay, how about a picnic on Sunday? Just the two of us. Isabel is going right from church to that pool party with her friend from Sunday school. I'll even bring the food."

"That sounds nice, Zach."

Her voice seemed oddly subdued, and Zach frowned. "Is everything okay?"

"Of course."

"You sound . . . funny."

"Just tired. It's been crazy around here."

"Well, try not to work too hard. How about if I stop by for lunch tomorrow?"

"I'll look forward to it. Have a safe drive back, Zach."

"At least I won't have to worry about fog this time," he teased. "Although I can't complain too much. Without that fog, I might never have met you."

"That's true. Listen, I've got to run. I—I'll see you tomorrow."

"Rebecca, I—" The line went dead and Zach frowned, a puzzled expression on his face. Her voice had sounded shaky at the end, like she was upset. Maybe it was just a really rough day at the restaurant, he told himself. Maybe it had nothing to do with him. But for some unsettling reason he had a feeling it did.

As Rebecca replaced the receiver, she forced herself to take a calming breath. She'd always feared the day when Zach would begin making plans to return to his old life. Only she hadn't expected those plans to take him to Washington. Maintaining a long-distance relationship between St. Louis and St. Genevieve was manageable. It was much less feasible if he lived a thousand miles away.

"Is everything all right, dear?" Rose asked, pausing as she bustled by to give Rebecca a concerned look.

"Yes," Rebecca assured her, summoning up a bright smile. "I think I'll go out and talk to that customer who was complaining."

"Oh, he's happy now," Rose assured her. "It wasn't that he didn't *like* the soup. He just didn't understand that it was *supposed* to be cold. But I explained it nicely, and he's happy as a clam now. Even ordered a second bowl."

"Well, that's good news. Thanks, Rose."

Rebecca moved back to the stove and automatically went through the motions of preparing the sauce for the chicken Madeira, that evening's entrée, even while her mind drifted far away.

Rebecca knew why Zach had invited her on the picnic. He was going to tell her that he was leaving. He would say that he cared about her, but explain that this was too good an opportunity to pass up. And she couldn't blame him. Washington offered glitz, glamour, prestige, recognition, a higher profile for his work. What did she have to offer? Her love, certainly. But no guarantee about the ability to give physical expression to that love.

It was true that under Zach's gentle, infinitely patient nurturing, she had made great strides in a very short time. She felt closer to Zach and trusted him more than any man she'd ever known. The bud of her long-dormant passion had begun to unfurl. There had been moments when she really believed that she would overcome her problem.

But even though Zach had never pressed for more than tender kisses there were still moments when the familiar, unreasonable panic response kicked in.

Rebecca sighed. She already knew that Zach was a man of deep passion, who would approach the physical component of love with joy, giving affection freely and without inhibition. And he would rightly expect the same from a partner. She just wasn't sure she was up to the task.

So given a choice between the guaranteed excitement of Washington, the challenge of working in the nation's capital in a prestigious position, versus taking a chance on a woman who might never be able to express love fully, she couldn't blame Zach for choosing the former.

It was, quite simply, no contest.

Rebecca tiredly removed her apron and brushed some stray strands of hair back from her face. It had been a very long day. Saturdays were always busy, but today had been absolutely crazy. She was one server short at lunch, and Rose was out sick. So Rebecca found herself doing all the cooking, while Frances filled in for Rose as hostess. She'd hardly had a chance to say ten words to Zach during lunch before dashing back into the kitchen. Dinner hadn't been any less hectic.

She was just about to grab her purse and switch off the lights when the sudden ringing of the phone startled her. She glanced at her watch, noting the time with a frown. Eleven-thirty. No one ever called the restaurant this late. She dropped her purse on the counter and reached over to pick up the receiver.

"Hello?" she said tentatively.

"Rebecca?"

She frowned. It sounded like Zach—sort of. "Zach?"

"Yeah. Listen, I know it's late, but can you come over."

A rope of tension coiled tightly in her stomach. "Is Isabel okay?"

"Yes. She's asleep. I just had an E-mail from a friend of Josef's. He's—" His voice choked, and Rebecca tightened her grip on the receiver as a feeling of foreboding swept over her. When he spoke again she hardly recognized his voice, it was so raw with emotion. "Rebecca, Josef is dead."

Chapter Thirteen

Rebecca stared unseeingly at the wall as her whole body went numb. "What?" she said uncomprehendingly.

"Josef. He . . . he's dead," Zach repeated in a choked voice.

Suddenly the reality of his news slammed home with a force that sent her reeling, and she groped for the stool, sinking down as her legs turned to rubber. Hot tears stung her eyes and she squeezed them shut, her stomach curling into a tight ball. "Oh, Zach!" she cried, her voice anguished, her heart aching.

"Can you come over?"

It wasn't a question. It was an SOS.

"I'll be there in five minutes," Rebecca promised.

She hung up the receiver and rose, but reaction kicked in with a vengeance. She began to shake, and every nerve ending seemed to be vibrating. She was in no condition to stand, let alone drive, she realized. Even though every instinct told her to get to Zach's side as quickly as possible, she forced herself to sit back down and remain there for a full sixty seconds while she took a dozen deep, steadying breaths. Only then did she grab her purse and run for the car.

As she traveled the short distance to Zach's apartment, she tried to sort through the jumble of incoherent thoughts racing through her mind. What had happened to Josef? Did Isabel know yet? What would become of the little girl now? She was scheduled to go home in less than a week. And how was Zach coping with the news? He sounded bad on the phone. Shocked. Shattered. Lost. Which wasn't surprising. Josef was his best friend. Closer than a brother, he'd once told her. He must be consumed with grief and pain. Rebecca pressed harder on the accelerator. She had to get to him as quickly as possible! *Lord, please help us through this!* she prayed desperately.

Zach was obviously watching for her, because the minute she pulled up he flung open the door. She jumped out of the car and dashed toward him, catching only a quick glance of his grief-ravaged face before he took her hand and pulled her inside. He pushed the door shut with his foot, then silently buried his face in her shoulder, holding her against him so tightly she could hardly breathe. She felt a shudder run through him, and the sound of his ragged breathing made her eyes flood with tears yet again.

For a long time neither spoke. Zach seemed to need the tactile reassurance, the solace, that only her arms could provide. And so she just held him, stroking his back, feeling his desolation as if it was her own.

When at last he drew back, he left one hand resting at her waist while he wiped the back of the other across his eyes. Rebecca was so used to Zach's rock-solid strength and confidence that it tore at her heart to see him so vulnerable and devastated. She reached up to lay a hand against his cheek.

"Zach, I'm so sorry," she whispered, her eyes echoing the pain in his.

"Me, too." His voice still sounded choked, and he shook his head. "He was such a good man. The kind the world needs more of. Caring, compassionate, committed. And now . . ." His words trailed off and he looked down at her helplessly. "Why did this have to happen?"

She tried to think of something to say that would comfort, but nothing came to mind. In the end, she just shook her head. "I don't know," she admitted, her voice breaking.

He sighed, then took her hand and drew her to the couch, pulling her down beside him.

"Have you told Isabel?" she asked.

He shook his head. "No. She's been asleep for hours, and I only got the message about twenty minutes ago. She's one of the reasons I asked you to come over. I hoped that together we could think of a way to tell her. Besides, I just needed you with me. When I got that message, it was like . . . like I had to reassure myself that the other person I care most about in the world was okay. I just needed to touch you," he said with simple candor as he squeezed her hand.

Rebecca looked at him wonderingly. That was the closest Zach had ever come to revealing the depth of his feelings for her. Was he saying that he . . . that he loved her? He hadn't used those words, yet what else could he mean? But her feelings, and their relationship, were a low priority at the moment. She would deal with them later. For now, there were other questions to be asked, decisions to be made.

"Do you know what happened, Zach?" she asked gently.

He nodded. "Josef apparently asked a colleague named Stefan to notify me if—" He drew a shaky breath, unable to say the words. "Stefan said that Josef was working late at their makeshift office, and that a bomb went off. He was . . . killed instantly."

Rebecca shut her eyes and tried to swallow past the lump in her throat. Never before had she been so closely touched by the horror of senseless violence that resulted in the loss of life. A tear trickled down her cheek, and she felt Zach reach over and gently brush it away.

"Oh, Zach, it's so awful!" she whispered, opening her eyes to gaze with shock into his.

"Yeah." He drew a shaky breath, obviously fighting back his own tears, and nodded toward the coffee table. "I got that out of the closet, but I haven't been able to bring myself to open it."

Rebecca glanced toward the large envelope addressed in Josef's hand to Zach. It was the one that Josef had carefully packed in Isabel's luggage, with instructions to open it only if something like this happened. She looked back at Zach and took his hand.

"Maybe it will be easier if we do it together," she said quietly.

He hesitated, then leaned forward and picked up the manila envelope. With one quick motion he slit open the edge and slid the contents, which were held together with a large rubber band, onto his lap. He pulled Rebecca close, and together they scanned the letter on top.

My dear Zachary,

If you are reading this letter, it is because I have been called home to the Lord. Please do not grieve for me, my friend. I am happy now, at peace, and I am once more with my beloved Katrina. All is well with me.

It is Isabel, not me, who needs your sympathy now. In recent weeks, it has become clear to me that without her mother or me here to watch over her, my country will be an inhospitable place for her. It is filled with strife and terror, and while I still believe that things will change, I am resigned that it will not happen during her youth. So there is no life here, no future, for my precious child.

Therefore, Zachary, it is my final wish that Isabel remain in America, the country of her birth, which was always so good to me. I do not expect you to take on the responsibility of raising her. I would not stretch the bounds of our friendship that far. But I do ask that you find her a good and loving home. I have great faith that you will do your best to make sure she is happy and loved.

In this envelope you will find all of the necessary papers—records of Isabel's birth and baptism, of my marriage to Katrina and of her death, as well as letters from my family and my minister, concurring with my decision. Very soon Stefan will send you a record of my death as well. Should you need to obtain any other records or letters, he has agreed to assist you. I have enclosed his address.

I have also included some things that Isabel may find of interest later. Letters her mother and I wrote to each other, photos of her relatives and the house where we lived, some pages from my journal. I believe it is important that she make a new life in America, but it is also important for her to remember her roots.

My dear Zachary, you have my deepest gratitude for all you have already done for Isabel. I hope you will forgive me for placing this one last obligation on you. But I do so, believing that the bond we share will make my request less burdensome. You are my brother in everything but blood, my friend. And I could not have chosen a finer man to fill that role.

I know that this is a difficult time for you. Separation is

always painful. But please do not grieve too deeply. I have had a good, full life. I have done satisfying, worthwhile work. I have known the great joy of fatherhood. And I have loved—and been loved—by a woman beyond compare. No man can ask for more.

So farewell, Zachary, until we meet again. And know that you will always be in my prayers.

They finished reading the note at the same time, and Rebecca raised her eyes to his in silence, her face a mask of grief. She watched him swallow convulsively, saw the glimmer of unshed tears in his red-rimmed eyes, found her own cheeks suddenly damp once again.

"He was a very special man, wasn't he?" she said softly, her voice uneven.

"Yeah." He swallowed again and looked down at the letter once more. "I respected Josef more than any man I've ever met. I know he accepted this possibility, made his peace with it. But I—I'll miss him. And so will Isabel. Dear God, how will we ever tell her that not only is her father gone, but now she has no home to return to?" he asked, his voice anguished.

The idea came to Rebecca suddenly, taking her momentarily off guard. Yet she knew instantly that it was right. She'd always wanted a husband and a family. The husband part still seemed like a long shot. But now, out of the blue, she was being offered the opportunity for a family, the chance to share her life with a child who desperately needed someone to love her.

"Zach."

He turned to her, then tilted his head curiously at the odd expression on her face. "What's wrong?"

"Well, I know this might sound a little off the wall, but . . . well . . . Isabel *does* have a home, because . . . because I'd like to take her," she said impulsively. "I know a single-parent household isn't ideal, but I promise I'll give her enough love to make up for it."

Zach looked into Rebecca's eyes—sincere, warm, loving, compassionate, generous—and his heart overflowed with love for this special woman who cared so deeply and gave of herself so freely. He couldn't have made it through this night without her. And he didn't want to face even one more day until he had her assurance that she would be with him always.

Zach knew the present setting wasn't ideal, nor were the circumstances. But suddenly he knew that this was the right moment to ask the question that would fundamentally affect all of their lives. He reached for her hand, cocooning it snugly between his palms, and drew a deep breath.

"Maybe it doesn't have to be a single-parent household," he told her softly.

She stared at him uncomprehendingly. "What do you mean?"

His lips tilted up into a rueful smile. It shouldn't surprise him that she failed to understand his meaning, he supposed. After all, he'd never told her that he loved her. But he intended to remedy that right now.

"Wait here." He rose and walked over to the desk chair, reached into the pocket of the sports coat draped on the back, and removed something Rebecca couldn't see. When he turned back to her, he held a small box in his hand, and he flipped open the lid as he sat down to reveal a solitaire nestled on a bed of dark blue velvet. "This is what I mean, Rebecca," he said huskily as he held it out to her. "Will you marry me?"

Rebecca looked from the ring to Zach's face, then back again to the ring. Was this a mirage, a dream? Zach had never even said he loved her and now . . . now he was asking her to become his wife? She transferred her gaze back to his face. "Are . . . are you serious?"

"I've never been more serious in my life. I planned to ask you on our picnic tomorrow, but suddenly the timing seems right."

"But . . . but I thought you were leaving. What about the job in Washington? You never said anything about . . . about love. I'm not even sure I'm wife material, Zach. I—I'm defective merchandise." Her words were disjointed, an almost incoherent jumble of thoughts.

He set the ring carefully on the coffee table and then turned to her, his eyes compelling, intense. He grasped her shoulders firmly but gently, so that she couldn't turn away.

"Let's deal with those issues one at a time, okay? First, I'm not leaving. At least, I'm not if you agree to marry me. I was offered a permanent teaching job at the high school, which I'd like to accept.

Second, I'll admit that the Washington offer was flattering. And a year ago I would have jumped at it. But since then I've found something even better. I found a satisfying job here, a life-style that suits me and, most important, a woman I love."

He paused for a moment and searched her eyes. "I haven't told you that before, Rebecca, because I was afraid of scaring you off. I know how you feel about intimacy. I know it frightens you. But as for being wife material, I can't think of anyone who would make a better partner. And don't ever say you're defective merchandise," he told her fiercely, his eyes burning into hers. "You're the most wonderful woman I've ever met. You're compassionate and caring and warm and sensitive and kind and intelligent . . . not to mention drop-dead gorgeous. I know that the passion you're so afraid of is there, locked away in your heart, but yearning to be set free. I'm not afraid that you lack passion, Rebecca. My only fear is that I'll be overwhelmed by it when it's set free."

A warm, glowing elation spread through her as she listened to his words. She believed everything he said, unable to argue with the honesty she saw in his eyes. At least, she believed *he* believed it. And maybe he was right. Maybe she did have an abundance of passion. But she wasn't as convinced as he seemed to be that she would ever find a way to fully express it.

"Zach, I . . . I want to say yes. But I'm so afraid I'll . . . disappoint you," she admitted artlessly, her voice faltering.

"Rebecca, I have only one expectation if you agree to marry me," he told her firmly. "That you love me with all your heart—and for all time."

She felt her throat tighten with emotion. "Oh, Zach, I do! I love you more than words can express! I have for a long time."

His eyes filled with warmth and tenderness—and immense relief. "Then there's no problem," he said easily. "The rest will come in time."

"How can you be so sure?" she persisted. "I've lived with this fear for so long. It won't go away overnight, Zach."

"I don't expect it to."

"But . . . what if . . . if it never does?"

"Rebecca . . ." He sighed and took her hand. "I've finally reached the point in my life where I understand what Josef knew all along. Love is the only thing that really matters in the end. I love you. I want to spend my life with you. The physical side of marriage is important. I won't deny that. But it's only a very small part of our life together. Most of the time it's just the everyday living, the sharing of small joys and sorrows—enjoying the first flower of spring, taking a long walk, even cleaning the house and shopping for groceries. In other words, just being there for each other in a thousand small ways. It's the everyday living that makes a marriage endure and grow stronger as the years pass."

Rebecca blinked back her tears, overcome with gratitude for the gift of love being offered to her by this wonderful, insightful, caring man. Marriage was a huge step, requiring a tremendous leap of faith on both their parts, given her background. But if Zach was willing, if he truly believed they could overcome her problem, how could she say no? He was offering her the life she'd always wanted, and she'd be a fool to walk away out of fear. She would just have to put her trust in him—and in the Lord—and take that leap.

Zach watched her, trying to discern her thoughts, praying that she loved him enough to commit herself to him—in every way. He'd done everything he could think of to make her feel safe and cherished and loved. Now it was up to her. He tried to remain calm as he waited for her answer, but it was a difficult task when his heart was banging against his rib cage, his respiration had gone haywire and his stomach was twisting painfully.

"Can I have a glass of water, Uncle Zach?"

Both heads swiveled in unison to the little girl who stood in the doorway, clutching her bedraggled Raggedy Ann. Rebecca's eyes flew to Zach's in sudden panic. They hadn't yet discussed how they were going to tell Isabel the news—or when. He seemed equally at a loss.

"Why are you here, Rebecca?" Isabel inquired, rubbing her eyes sleepily. "It's not morning yet, is it?"

"No, sweetie."

Isabel walked toward them, looking from one to the other, her face troubled. "Is something wrong?" she asked.

Rebecca turned to Zach and bit her lip, realizing, not for the first time since Isabel's arrival, that children seemed to possess a sort of sixth sense that made them acutely attuned to nuances of emotion. She lifted her eyebrows helplessly, in a "What should we do?" expression.

With sudden decision Zach patted the sofa beside him, moving far enough away from Rebecca to make room for Isabel.

"Come on in, honey. Rebecca and I have something to tell you."

Rebecca wasn't ready for this, she thought in sudden panic. Her emotions were already in shreds. But delaying the inevitable wouldn't make it any easier, she realized. They had to tell Isabel sooner or later, and the little girl already suspected that something was amiss. They might as well get it over with, she thought, trying to control the painful thudding of her heart.

Isabel climbed onto the couch between them and looked solemnly from one to the other. "Is my papa sick?" she asked, intuitively sensing the source of the gloom in the room.

Zach took her small hand in his and smoothed back her flyaway hair, mussed from sleep. "A friend of your papa's sent me a note on E-mail tonight. He had some bad news for us. Isabel, honey, it seems that . . . well, your papa, he—" Zach's voice broke, and Rebecca stepped in.

"Sweetie, what Uncle Zach is trying to say is that the Lord decided it was . . . it was time for your papa to go to heaven."

Isabel stared at her with wide eyes. "You mean he died?"

Rebecca nodded. "Yes."

Isabel clamped her mouth shut and turned away, clutching her doll more tightly to her chest. "I don't believe it. My papa wouldn't leave me alone. He promised he'd always take care of me."

Rebecca looked at Zach helplessly.

"And he will," Zach told her gently. "Remember the note he sent you on your birthday? About always being close to you in your heart, even when he was far away? He still is, honey. He still loves you. It was just his time to go to heaven."

Suddenly Isabel's lower lip began to quiver, and her eyes filled with tears. "But why did he have to go now?" she asked plaintively, her face bereft.

"I don't know," Rebecca confessed gently, blinking to hold back her tears. She slipped her arm lovingly around Isabel's slim shoulders. "Sometimes it's hard to understand why God takes people when he does."

"Maybe Mama was l-lonesome for him," Isabel offered, her voice quavering. "Maybe God knew she needed him."

"That might be," Rebecca agreed.

"But I need him, too!" Isabel cried. "I was supposed to go home next week. Where will I live now?"

Rebecca looked over at Zach. He was watching her carefully, his eyes filled with hope and tenderness and love. In the past few months he had become so much a part of her life that she could no longer imagine it without him. She loved him with all her heart. And she knew that together they could create a beautiful home for each other—and for the precious child that had been entrusted to their care.

Impulsively she reached across the top of the couch and took his hand. His grip was sure and solid and warm. In her heart she suddenly knew, with absolute conviction, that this was meant to be. Her eyes locked on his, reflecting the love and confidence and joy that suddenly overwhelmed her, and when she spoke, her voice was thick with unshed tears. But this time they were tears of happiness.

"You'll live with us," she said softly.

She pulled Isabel onto her lap, and Zach instantly closed the distance between them, his eyes never leaving hers as he draped his arm around her shoulders and pulled them both close. Finally he dragged his gaze from Rebecca and transferred it to the child she held.

"Would you like that, Isabel?" Zach asked, his voice gentle and unusually deep.

"You mean . . . stay here?" she asked.

"Yes. You see, Rebecca and I are going to get married. And we'd like it very much if you would be part of our family."

Isabel looked up at them. "Are you getting married because of me?"

"No, sweetie," Rebecca said quickly, before Zach could respond. She looked over at him. "We would have gotten married anyway." She needed him to know that her decision wasn't based on compassion for Isabel, but on deep, abiding love for him. A slow smile spread across his face, and she knew he'd gotten her message. "But it will be even better if you come to live with us," she continued, turning her attention back to the little girl.

Isabel grew silent for a moment. "I think my papa and mama would like me to do that," she said slowly at last, the tears still welling in her eyes as she turned to look up at Zach. "I heard Papa say once that he wished you had someone like Mama and me to come home to. He said that would make you very happy." Her eyes were serious as she studied his face. "Now you have me and Rebecca. Does that make you happy, Uncle Zach?"

Zach considered her question for a moment, thought about the odd twists and turns of life, with its jolting combinations of deep tragedy and great joy. In one day he'd lost his treasured friend, found a daughter and won the heart of the woman he adored.

Part of him was sad. Part was joyful. But under it all he suddenly felt a sense of peace, a deep contentment, a feeling of coming home. With a silent prayer of thanks, he reached down and touched Isabel's nose, then looked into Rebecca's beautiful, loving eyes and smiled.

"Yes, Isabel. It makes me very happy." He glanced over at Rebecca, and her throat tightened at the love shining in his eyes. "And it feels good to come home at last."

"All right, all right, let's get organized," Sam declared, planting her hands on her hips as she surveyed the dressing room. "Henry, straighten your boutonniere. Isabel, do you need to go to the little girls' room? No? Okay. Rebecca, kindly descend from the clouds long enough to sit down so I can put your headpiece on."

Rebecca smiled dreamily at Sam and did as instructed. Thank goodness *someone* was in charge. She was too wrapped up in being a bride to be of use in any other capacity today.

Rebecca watched in the mirror as Sam securely anchored the wreath of baby's breath and stephanotis, then fluffed the yards of whisper-soft tulle that drifted down the back. When Sam was at last satisfied, Rebecca stood up, and her sister-in-law turned her to face the full-length mirror.

As she did so, Sam recalled a day two and a half years before when she'd done the same with her best friend, Laura. And she thought about the day two years ago when she'd looked at herself as a bride in this same mirror. Three happy endings in less than three years, she mused. Not a bad record, she concluded with a smile.

"So . . . what do you think?" she asked Rebecca.

The bride stared at her reflection in awe. Was that really her, that woman with the radiant face and shining eyes dressed all in white? It didn't seem possible. She gazed at the headpiece of fresh flowers and her cascading waves of russet hair, which tumbled loose and full past her shoulders; the beaded lace bodice of her gown, with its gracious sweetheart neckline; the quaint leg-of-mutton sleeves, which came to a point on the backs of her hands and added a delicate, old-fashioned touch to the gown; the full, satin skirt that swept into a dramatic cathedral-length train.

She truly was the epitome of the traditional bride, Rebecca thought in wonder. It was a role she'd never thought to play, and she relished it with joy and gratitude even as she said a silent prayer of thanks.

"Well?" Sam prompted.

"I guess it's real, isn't it?" Rebecca murmured softly, fingering the clouds of tulle that drifted past her shoulders.

Sam laughed. "Kiddo, you better believe it's real! If you have any doubts, go ask that handsome man who's anxiously waiting for you at the altar." She turned to the audience of two watching the proceedings and angled Rebecca toward them. "Ladies and gentlemen, I give you—the future Mrs. Zachary Wright," she pronounced.

Henry smiled. "I always knew you'd make a beautiful bride, Rebecca. Course, I just about gave up. But the minute I saw Zach, I figured he was the one for you."

"You look so pretty," Isabel said in awe, overwhelmed by the proceedings, reaching out a tentative hand to touch the billowing satin skirt.

"Thank you, sweetie." She nodded toward the brooch that Isabel held carefully in her hand. "Would you like me to pin that on for you?"

"Yes, please."

Rebecca knelt down. "I'm glad you thought about wearing this today," she said softly as she secured it to the front of Isabel's green satin, floor-length dress, an exact duplicate of Sam's. "It makes me feel like your mama and papa are right here with us." She gave the little girl a hug, pressing her close.

A sudden change in organ music sent a surge of excitement sweeping over Rebecca, and with one final, encouraging squeeze for Isabel she stood up.

Sam's discerning gaze swept over her once more, and she gave a satisfied nod. "Perfect," she declared, reaching for her bouquet and handing Isabel hers. "Do you remember everything we practiced the other night?" she asked the youngster.

"Yes."

"Good girl." Sam looked back at Rebecca with a grin and winked. "Knock 'em dead."

Rebecca watched them leave, then turned to her father with a tremulous smile. "Well, Dad, I guess this is it."

"Yep." He cleared his throat and looked down. "I'm mighty happy for you, Becka. Zach is a fine man. I'm only sorry your mother couldn't be here today."

"Me, too," Rebecca concurred softly, her eyes growing misty. "But I have a feeling she's here in spirit."

Henry nodded. "Yeah. I do, too. I know she'd offer you some words of wisdom if she could. I'm not much with words myself. But I hope and pray you and Zach have as wonderful a partnership as your mom and I did, honey. Just remember that marriage is like a roller coaster—lots of ups and downs. But if you stay on track, everything ends up just fine. And don't forget to enjoy the ride."

"I will, Dad. And thanks. For everything."

His eyes suddenly glistened suspiciously, and he sniffed. "Well, honey, you ready for the big walk?"

She took a deep breath and nodded. "It's time." She slid her arm through his and reached for her bouquet, smiling at the springlike combination of white roses and pink tulips. When she'd chosen her flowers, she'd known that tulips weren't traditional for a Thanksgiving wedding. Known they would be out of season. Known the expense would be outrageous.

Known, also, that she had to have them.

As Rebecca and Henry stepped into the vestibule and began the slow march down the aisle, she glanced around at the beaming faces. There were Rose and Frances, in their Sunday best, smiling happily—and just a touch smugly. And Ben, nodding sagely, his bow tie bobbing. Pete was there, too, with Melanie. And Laura and Nick, with their own new daughter, their smiles warm with remembrances of their own special day in this same place. Rebecca felt incredibly blessed to be able to share this day with so many dear family members and friends.

Her gaze shifted to the front. Sam and Isabel watched joyfully as she approached, Isabel looking proud in her "grown-up" dress,

Sam giving her a knowing wink. Brad was there, too, waiting to perform the ceremony that would join his sister and Zach for life. He smiled at her now, a smile of understanding filled with deep affection and happiness. She returned it, thanking him with her eyes for all that he had been to her through the years—a brother, certainly, but even more than that, a friend.

And then her eyes went to the man who had become the center of her universe.

Rebecca's breath caught in her throat as she gazed at him. He looked incredibly handsome in his tux, she thought. Strong. Solid. Steadfast. He had the kind of looks that would make heads turn in any setting, she acknowledged appreciatively.

But it was his eyes that held her spellbound. As Henry placed her hand in Zach's, her husband-to-be smiled down at her. For a long moment they looked at each other, two hearts touching, joining in a timeless way that only those in love can understand. His eyes— tender, yearning, caressing, filled with love and warmth and joy— told her more clearly than words what was in his heart.

And as they stepped forward to recite the vows that would unite them as man and wife, she pledged in her heart to treasure and cherish this wonderful man all the days of her life. For he had already given her what the Good Book rightly described as the greatest thing of all—a deep, abiding love that would last for all time.

Epilogue

❧

Six months later

Rebecca opened her eyes slowly, savoring the sensation of being totally relaxed and at peace. She sighed contentedly as she gazed out of the window at the lush May greenery, enjoying the gentle touch of the warm breeze that drifted lightly over her. Only the melodic song of a bird broke the stillness, and the early-morning light cast a golden glow over the landscape. Since Isabel was spending the Memorial Day weekend with Henry to celebrate the end of the school year, Rebecca had the whole day to share with Zach. Her lips curved into a smile, and a delicious tingle of anticipation swept over her as she turned toward him.

But his side of the bed was empty.

She frowned and rose on one elbow to survey the rumpled pillow, absently adjusting the spaghetti strap that had slipped down her shoulder. Where could he be? She'd been looking forward to a lazy morning in bed, perhaps even a late breakfast on the patio, just the two of them. But it seemed Zach had other plans, she thought disappointedly.

She was just about to swing her legs to the floor when a creaking stair caught her attention. She glanced toward the half-shut bedroom door, just in time to catch Zach peering carefully around the edge. He grinned when he saw that she was awake and pushed the door open with his shoulder.

"Good morning," he greeted her cheerily, smiling at her as he entered.

She stared at him. He was carrying a tray holding a bud vase that contained two pink tulips, a plate of croissants, butter, jam, a pot of coffee and various eating utensils. But what really caught her attention was his attire—shorts and a black tuxedo bow tie. Period.

"Aren't you going to say good morning?" he teased, depositing the tray on the nightstand.

"Good morning," she parroted automatically, her gaze quizzical as she tilted her head. "May I ask what this is all about?"

He stuck his head in the closet and rummaged around, removing two gaily wrapped packages before turning to her with mock chagrin. "I knew it! The magic is wearing off already. You forgot!"

Not likely, she thought with a soft smile. But it surprised her a little that he hadn't. "How could I forget our six-month anniversary?" she chided him gently. "I just didn't expect you to remember. Most men don't think about those things, you know."

His eyes—warm, filled with love, caressing—caught and held hers. "I guess I'm not most men—at least when it comes to you, Rebecca. I've treasured each moment of our marriage and counted my blessings every single day."

Rebecca's throat tightened with emotion as he stretched out beside her, propping himself up on one elbow while he reached over to play with the strap of her gown. As she gazed into his wonderful eyes, she knew in her heart that *she* was the one who had been blessed. She doubted whether many men would have exhibited Zach's infinite understanding and patience, both of which had been taxed to the limit over the past few months. She knew he had often wanted more than she was able to give, but he'd never pushed her. Instead, in his lovingly supportive way, he'd helped her take one step at a time until finally, oh-so-slowly, she'd learned to relax. He had loved her through it all, had never stopped believing and encouraging, even when her own optimism wavered. She owed him a debt of gratitude she could never repay. Except with love. And thanks to him, she had learned to joyfully give full expression to that emotion.

She glanced at the tray, the flowers, the gifts, and her throat constricted with tenderness once more at his thoughtfulness. If she lived a hundred years, she vowed never to take for granted this special man, who let her know every day in countless ways that she was cherished and loved beyond measure. Impulsively she reached over and gave him a long, lingering kiss.

"Happy anniversary," she said huskily.

"Happy anniversary, sweetheart," he echoed, pulling her close to return the kiss. When at last he drew back, he took a deep breath then gave her a crooked grin. "Aren't you going to open your presents?" he teased.

She smiled and snuggled next to him contentedly. "Do I have to?"

He hesitated, then sighed deeply. "I think you'd better," he decided, reaching behind him to retrieve the two packages. "Otherwise I'm likely to forget all about them."

She scooted into a more upright position, reaching for the smallest package first. She tore the wrapping off and flipped open the lid of the jewelry box to reveal a gold tulip on a delicate chain. Her eyes misted as she looked over at him, and he gave her a tender smile.

"That will always be our flower—a symbol of new life and new beginning after a long, dark winter," he said quietly.

"You were my sun, you know," she told him softly. "Your warmth is what brought my heart to life." She reached over and touched his dear face, the tears glistening in her eyes. "Oh, Zach, I love you so much!"

His eyes held hers compellingly, and he reached for her hand, kissing the palm tenderly. "It's mutual, sweetheart," he seconded huskily. "Go ahead and open the other package."

This one was flat, and when she pulled off the paper it was, as she suspected, an envelope. Her gaze fell on the return address and she looked at Zach with eager anticipation. "Is this what I think it is?"

He nodded. "It came yesterday. But I decided to keep it for today."

Carefully, her hands trembling slightly, she opened the envelope and scanned the papers. A feeling of immense relief swept over her, and she closed her eyes, saying a silent prayer of thanks. She'd been confident this day would come, yet there had still been an underlying tension. She and Zach had kept their concerns from Isabel, knowing she'd already dealt with too much uncertainty in her young life. As far as she was concerned, she had belonged to them since the night Josef died. But now it was official. The red tape was finished. Isabel was theirs.

"I thought this would make the day even more memorable," Zach said, smiling at her tenderly.

She set the gifts carefully aside and stretched out beside him. "It makes things feel . . . complete," she reflected. "Like we're really and truly a family now."

"I know what you mean," he concurred, reaching over again to play with a strand of her beautiful hair.

"Zach."

"Mmm-hmm."

"I don't have a present for you. But I do have some news."

"I'm not in the news game anymore," he reminded her distractedly.

"I think you might want to hear this news."

"Actually, I have something else on my mind at the moment," he confessed, reaching down to drop a trail of soft kisses along her collarbone.

"Well, I guess it can wait. I just figured that when a man's wife was going to have a baby, he might want to know right away."

His lips stilled, and then he lifted his head and stared at her. "A baby?"

"Mmm-hmm. You know . . . Small. Pink. Cry and sleep and wet a lot?" she teased.

"A baby? A baby!" he repeated. His tone was incredulous, awed, joyous. "Wow!"

"I just found out yesterday. I didn't want to say anything until I was sure. I hoped you'd be happy."

"Happy? Happy doesn't even begin to describe how I feel! This is . . . this is awesome, as my students would say!"

She laughed softly, a delicious feeling of joy filling her heart. "Yeah. Awesome."

Zach's eyes softened with adoration as he leaned over her, tangling his fingers in her hair. His gaze caressed her, taking in every nuance of her beautiful, expressive face. "Do you have any idea how much I love you?" he asked, his voice catching in a way that tugged at her heart.

"Why don't you show me?" she whispered, her eyes burning into his.

He complied readily, lowering his lips to hers in the silent but eloquent language known to lovers through the ages, and Rebecca gave thanks once again. For the joy Isabel had brought them. For the new life growing within her. And for the gift of this cherished man's love, whose patient nurturing had at last healed her heart.

Zach's heart was also filled with gratitude as he softly gathered Rebecca into his arms. He knew that without this special woman, he might never have discovered the one simple truth Josef had always understood: that love is the only thing that really matters in the end. And for a fleeting moment, just before he lost himself in the wonder of Rebecca's sweet love, he hoped Josef knew how things had turned out.

Because somehow he knew his friend would approve.

Dear Reader,

As I write this letter, I am sitting in my woodland garden watching the world reawaken after the long cold winter. It is a place of renewal, refreshment and enrichment, where the quiet is broken only by the lovely song of the birds. Here, in this special spot, the beauty of God's handiwork can be fully appreciated.

Eight years ago, however, when my husband and I bought this house as newlyweds, this garden was a dense thicket, overgrown and wild. Slowly, year by year, I cut and pulled and dug and planted, always working toward a vision of what it could be, always believing it could be transformed into a beautiful and tranquil oasis. My husband even caught the spirit, adding his own special touch—a meandering stone path. And now, at last, my vision is a reality. But as I have discovered, the garden is, and always will be, a work in progress, one that requires regular tending. Yet the rewards are great.

Love is much like my special place. It requires vision. And persistence. And faith. And attention. But it returns a hundredfold in joy.

All three of my heroines in the VOWS series made this discovery, each in her own unique way. In this, the final book in the series, Rebecca's heart finds new life (much like her cherished tulips) as she discovers the tremendous healing power of love. Writing this story uplifted and inspired me, and I hope it does the same for you as you read it.

This spring, may your life be filled with love—and tulips!

Sweet Charity

Books by Lois Richer
Love Inspired

A Will and a Wedding #8
*Faithfully Yours #15
*A Hopeful Heart #23
*Sweet Charity #32

*Faith, Hope & Charity

LOIS RICHER

credits her love of writing to a childhood spent in a Sunday school where
the King James Version of the Bible was taught. The majesty and clarity
of the language in the Old Testament stories allowed her to create pictures in her own mind while growing up in a tiny prairie village where
everyone strove to make ends meet. During her school years, she continued to find great solace in those words and in the church family that
supported her in local speech festivals, Christmas concerts and little
theater productions. Later in college, her ability with language stood her
in good stead as she majored in linguistics, studied the work of William
Shakespeare and participated in a small drama group.

Today Lois lives in another tiny Canadian town with her husband, Barry,
and two very vocal sons. And still her belief in a strong, vibrant God who
cares more than we know predominates her life. "My writing," she says,
"allows me to express just a few of the words God sends bubbling
around in my brain. If I convey some of the wonder and amazement I
feel when I think of God and His love, I've used my words to good
effect."

Sweet Charity
Lois Richer

Published by Steeple Hill Books™

STEEPLE HILL BOOKS

4 in 1 ISBN: 0-7394-0528-4

SWEET CHARITY

Copyright © 1998 by Lois Richer

This edition published by arrangement with Steeple Hill Books.

There is no fear in love; but perfect
love casts out fear.

—*1 John* 4:18

To my sons Christopher and Joshua

May you always have an abundance of sweet
charity with an added helping of patience. You've
already got persistence down pat!
Love, Mom

Prologue

❧

Dr. Christopher Davis yanked off his green surgical cap and tossed it onto a nearby chair in his office. "Thanks, Macy," he muttered, taking the cup from the hovering secretary's hand and inhaling the fresh-ground aroma. "Traeger's always did make the best Viennese extradark roast."

"They should," she mumbled. "They charge you an arm and a leg for those beans." She ignored his grin. "You'd better drink it fast. The next one is a toughie."

"You mean the abdominal?" Christopher frowned. "Yes, it's going to be rough."

"Jimmy Jones," Macy reminded him with a frown. "His name is Jimmy."

"Oh, yeah. I forgot." Chris shrugged off the reprimand, knowing she thought him heartless. "I can't help it," he defended himself. "This is the fifth operation this morning. We had to start at five because of the power surge last night. Hey, it's Tuesday, isn't it?"

At Macy's nod he continued, "That means there will be interns watching." His shoulders tightened but he refused to show his discomfort. "They usually like watching these abdominal things."

"They like watching *you* because you explain everything to them," Macy told him, grinning as she thrust a single white sheet under his nose. "By the way, your mother has summoned you to dinner tonight. Seven-thirty sharp!" Macy rolled her eyes. "And this fax came in a short while ago. The cover sheet was marked urgent." Quietly she left, closing the office door softly behind her. Christopher sank into his leather chair and started reading.

Dear Chris,

Hey, old buddy! I know we haven't heard from each other in a while, although I have heard rave reviews about your work in Boston. Just yesterday I was talking to our old prof and he said you had resigned. Your timing is perfect, Chris, because I really need your help. Jessica's in her third trimester now, but she's having numerous difficulties. We've been advised to get to Loma Linda ASAP.

I'm hoping you'll agree to fill in for me while we are away. I know this place is nothing like the big city, but I'd sure appreciate it if you could take over here for the next little while. With all your experience, I'm sure you could handle everything easily. The only thing is, I have no idea how long we'll be gone.

Please think about it, would you? And let me know immediately. Thanks, pal.

Dan

Chris scanned the letter quickly, noting that a Dr. Green shared the practice. It took several moments of squinting at the notation below to assemble the patterns into something resembling English. Dan, he recalled fondly, had the worst handwriting he'd ever seen. And that was saying something, he mused, even for a GP. Head to one side, he peered at the odd pen scratches once more. He thought it read, "Jori Jessop is my nurse now and if anyone can keep you in line, it's her. Tall, dark and gorgeous. I think you might even enjoy it here!"

Chris snorted. Yeah, right. He'd known a lot of office nurses in his day and he'd never met one that he was remotely interested in.

Still, he mused, it would be a change. He was tired of these hectic days. He'd finally, at age thirty-six, fulfilled his parents' expectations; attained the status they'd always said he would. In fact, Chris mused, he was on top of his game right now.

And bored out of his mind. Wasn't there supposed to be more to life than working day after day in this cold impersonal hospital; more to life than spending endless days and nights in the operating room? Good grief, he couldn't even remember the patients' names anymore! Life had become one long surgical assembly line.

Which was why he'd asked for a leave of absence six weeks ago. Never mind that he hadn't yet had the opportunity to take it. Maybe now was the perfect time.

"Operating Room Four will be ready for you in fifteen minutes, Doctor." Chris's surgical nurse's voice came through the speakerphone.

Life was bound to be pretty slow in—what was it?—Mossbank, North Dakota.

It sounded like just the place to sit and cogitate. Which was probably all there was to do in a farming community that barely appeared on the map.

Clicking on his computer, Chris peered at the letterhead of Dan's office and then faxed a note to his friend via the modem on his desk, grinning all the while.

At least they had faxes in this one-horse town.

"I know you've had a full day, Dan. But could I talk to you? Just for a moment." Nurse Jordanna Jessop stood waiting for her boss to look up from the chart he was reading.

"Of course, Jori. Come on in." He folded the file and laid it aside. "What's up?"

"I need some advice on something and I don't know who else to ask. It's about my future." Jori kept her eyes focused on her hands and tried to stop twisting them. "The thing is, I've sort of been on hold here, these last few years, and now I think it's time for me to make some decisions."

"You're quitting?" Dr. Dan stared. "But I thought you intended to stay here permanently!"

"No, I'm not leaving. I'm settled here now. That's what I want to talk to you about." She took a deep breath and blurted it all out. "I've decided to have a child."

She peered up at him through her lashes, knowing her friend would be shocked. "I was hoping you could advise me on my options."

"Your, er, options? Jori, are you pregnant?" She could see the sad look in his eyes and hastened to correct him.

"No. Of course not. But I'd like to be. Now, as I see it, I have three choices. I can try to adopt, but the government agency I've been corresponding with didn't seem too hopeful about my chances. Especially since I'm single. Still, I'm not giving up yet. Are you listening?"

"Yes, I'm listening." Dan sounded strange, Jori noted, and decided to make this quick.

"There's also something like a five-year wait if I want to adopt a newborn. And a fast, private adoption is very expensive—and risky."

"Oh, Jordanna, I don't think that's what you want." Dan's voice was full of doubt. "Sometimes birth mothers change their minds. I wouldn't want to see you get hurt."

"Yes, I know. There's also the cost. I'd have to deplete what little I have in my savings to pay for a private adoption. That would leave me with almost nothing if something went wrong with the baby."

"Well, as far as I know, that leaves marriage." Dan grinned happily. "Why don't you try that?"

"With whom? There aren't a lot of available men around here," she said, smoothing the skirt on her white uniform. "And I don't want to move because of my father. Besides—" her full lips turned down "—would you want to date Rodney Little or Gary Norton after you'd seen their medical records?"

"I can't say I'd want to date a man at all," Dan teased. "But I do think there's someone you might be interested in. And fortunately for you he's healthy as a horse. Also tall and good-looking."

"You're not going to trot out that replacement doctor that's coming, are you?" Jori groaned with exasperation. "I told you, I don't want to get involved with some pompous, egocentric surgeon who's doing us all a favor just by agreeing to come to little old Mossbank!" She stood in a huff, frustration making her voice rise. "Never mind! I'll deal with this myself. There's got to be some way I can manage."

"Jori." Dan's voice was soft with sympathy. "Jess and I aren't abandoning you. We'll be back. Just keep the faith, honey. Keep waiting on the Lord."

"The Lord helps those who help themselves." And with that, Jori whirled from the room, chagrin wrinkling her forehead.

"There's got to be a way, Lord," she said to herself. "There's just got to be a way."

Chapter One

"Thank you very much, Mrs. Flowerday. Yes, I'm sure the doctor will be thrilled." Swallowing the burble of laughter that threatened her otherwise solemn facade, Jordanna Jessop carefully lifted the plastic container from the older woman's hands.

"It's the least I can do. We're all so happy to have Dr. Dan's friend here. A doctor needs someone to look after him, keeping such busy hours and all." The warm brown eyes were speculative as she looked at Jori. "He's very handsome, isn't he, dear?"

Mrs. Charity Flowerday shivered delicately. "His eyes are the very same color as the Aegean Sea, I'll wager! And when he stands there in that white coat, well!" She twittered. "It's enough to make your heart speed up, isn't it, dear?"

"I hadn't really noticed," Jori murmured, unwilling to discuss the latest addition to the small town. "It's been so busy, you see."

"Yes, I heard your father went into the home. So sad, dear." She patted Jori's hand affectionately. "And on top of that, I imagine it's hard to get used to a new doctor after working with Dr. Dan for this long. And of course, Dr. Chris is from the city and all. Probably needs a good woman to teach him the ropes." She glanced at Jori speculatively.

"Our Dr. Dan knew about country folks, of course. Such a good man," Charity breathed. "And Jessica is the sweetest woman! I've just been praying as hard as I can for that dear baby." A lone tear trickled down her smooth white cheek until she managed to collect herself, the sweet smile curving her lips once more. "Enough chit-chat! I'd better be on my way. I'm baking pies today. The church bake sale, you know. I do wish this weather would cool off. Bye!"

As Charity Flowerday hobbled out the door, Jori turned away, shoulders shaking with repressed laughter. If she was any judge of character, and she was, the doctor would be somewhat less than appreciative of this latest goodwill gesture from the town's busiest busybody.

She didn't like the allusion Charity had just made to Dr. Davis's need for a wife. Oh, well! Charity Flowerday, Faith Johnson and Hope Conroy were known for their ability to pair off any single adult who came to the district. That was fine by Jori—as long as they didn't include her in their shenanigans!

With her normally unflappable control in place, Jori strode down the hall to the tiny, dull office that presently housed Christopher Davis, M.D. She tapped gently before entering. "Dr. Davis?"

There wasn't any answer. Instead, the good doctor sat studying a file, totally unaware of her presence. For some reason Jori couldn't explain, she was loath to break his concentration.

She studied her temporary boss and the way his golden blond head was bent over the file, hiding his spectacular velvet blue eyes. Her gaze focused on his tanned features, assessing him the way a photographer had taught her to size up a subject. His face was all angles and hard edges, perfectly sculpted with a wide forehead, jutting cheekbones and beautiful lips.

Yep, Jori decided silently, a real lady-killer. Good thing he wasn't her type. Of course, she had known that the moment Dan introduced them.

Big, bossy and boisterous. Jori had cataloged the newcomer right away. Dr. Christopher Davis was not her kind of man. Not at all.

"Yes, Nurse. What is it?" The interloper's deep gravelly voice demanded her immediate attention.

Jori flushed lightly before thrusting out Charity's plastic-boxed gift. "This is for you," she told him, a smirk tipping up the corners of her pert mouth as he groaned loudly.

"Not another praline cheesecake delight," he begged, holding his rib cage in protest. A tiny smile teased the corner of his mouth. Privately, she decided he would be a whole lot more handsome if he made an effort to smile all the time.

"How many is that now? Eight? Ten?" His eyes twinkled across at her.

It really wasn't any wonder the ladies of Mossbank had been in a flap this past week, Jori decided, almost melting under that blaze of perfectly even white smile.

"I don't know. Entirely too many, that's for sure." For some reason his intense scrutiny made her nervous and Jori fiddled with some papers on his desk, bursting into speech when he got to his feet.

"This one will be delicious, though. Charity Flowerday is an excellent cook. It will also be the richest," she warned. Her eyes skittered away from his and then returned for a closer look. "She loves to double the chocolate in everything."

"Hmm, double chocolate," he teased. "A woman after my own heart. How old is she?" His grin made it obvious he'd overheard at least part of the matchmaking schemes currently going on around town.

She ignored that and continued her silent scrutiny. He was taller than she, which was saying something. At five foot ten, few men ever towered over her. Dr. Davis, on the other hand, was about six foot four and all lean muscle. He had the broad strong shoulders women always swooned over, and a wide chest that could accommodate any female's weary head.

"I don't believe anyone can get too much chocolate," he muttered softly. "But this is definitely way too much cheesecake. Do you think there will be any more?"

" 'Fraid so," Jori murmured, shoving aside four other desserts that had arrived earlier that afternoon to make room for the latest addition. "You should never have said Mrs. Belle's was the best praline cheesecake you had ever tasted. It's like you laid down a challenge around here."

"Too bad you couldn't have said something two days ago," Christopher groused, moving to toss one of the less attractive packages into the trash.

"No!" Jori grabbed the thickly muscled forearm, interrupting his attempt at making a basket.

"I wouldn't do that if I were you," she told him seriously, her long fingers tightening as he tried to pull away.

Christopher glanced from her hand on his arm, to her slim body pressed against his desk, to her flushed face.

"Why?" he drawled, obviously curious about her sudden change from quiet, efficient assistant to the disheveled woman who clung to his arm as if her life depended on it.

Jori took the package from him and gently set it on the tabletop once more. "Emery Laser cleans this place every night. His mother is Jasmine Laser." She waited for the light of comprehension, and when it didn't dawn across his frowning countenance, Jori read the tiny card attached to the white carton she had just rescued.

" 'To Dr. Davis, for your kind assistance.' Signed," she said, pausing for effect, " 'Jasmine Laser.' "

"I take it I would be stepping on toes," he moaned, sinking back into his chair, hands tugging the golden strands of his shining hair into tousled disarray.

"To say the least," Jori told him, glad she'd averted disaster. "Chucking that . . . mess . . . would make you an even greater subject of discussion—rather unkind discussion."

"I wish to heck Dan had explained just what I was getting into when he asked for my assistance," Chris snorted, searching for a place to spread out his files.

Dan Gordon had been Mossbank's general practitioner for as long as Jori had been the office nurse. Their working relationship had been a brother-sister one tempered by a lot of friendly bantering. It was something she was beginning to miss with Dr. Christopher Davis. Of course, Dan had been born and raised in a small town and was well used to the unspoken rules that governed the community, unlike his famous, big-city counterpart.

"Look at this place," the new doctor crankily demanded, pointing to the cake boxes of various shapes, sizes and colors scattered on almost every available surface.

"Think of it as proof of your good standing in this community," she told him. "It shows how much you're appreciated. You're lucky they've taken a shine to you."

When a groan of dismay was her only answer, Jori grudgingly picked up three of the earliest arrivals and stuffed them into the vaccine refrigerator that stood in the corner.

"They can't stay there forever, you know," she advised, frowning at his lounging figure. "Sooner or later you're going to have to find a solution to this problem." Jori stared at him curiously, her brown eyes frankly questioning his intent. "What did you do with the rest?"

His blue eyes lit up at that.

"They're safely stored in Dan and Jessica's freezer, just waiting for the soon-to-be parents to come home." His golden brows drew together in a frown. "Although I'm not sure a new mother should be eating that stuff." His sudden grin made her catch her breath. "I'm not sure anyone should." He chuckled at his own little joke.

"Well, then—" Jori started to suggest that he simply add to his private stash, but his deep voice interrupted her immediately.

"Forget it. It's full."

"Sorry, can't help you then," she told him, moving toward the door.

"Can't or won't?" he asked crankily. His blue eyes widened with a new thought. "Why don't you take one of them home? Surely you and your boyfriend could manage at least one of the blasted things."

Jori turned to stare at him. "I don't have a boyfriend and if I did, the last thing I'd feed him would be Emma Simms's cheesecake. It's like sand."

He squinted at her curiously. "Someone who looks like you doesn't have a boyfriend?" His perfect lips slashed open in a mocking grin. "No dreams of marriage and babies, Nurse Jessop? I thought all women dreamed of Prince Charming and white picket fences."

"Prince Charming was highly overrated," she told him, grimly noting how close he'd come to the mark. "And for your information, I already have a white picket fence. Someday I intend to have a child to share it with." Jori immediately wished she had been able to shut up about that.

One blond eyebrow lifted haughtily.

"A child but no husband. Interesting. And how do you plan on accomplishing that?" he inquired softly.

Jori tilted her head back, her face heating with color. "It's not really your business anyhow. Those cheesecakes *are.*" It was rude but she felt compelled to get his focus off her.

He sighed, blinking at the offensive desserts. "Why couldn't they bring roast beef with mashed potatoes and an apple pie?"

Something in the tone of Chris's mournful voice stopped Jori's swift departure. Turning abruptly, her round brown eyes searched his face. "How did you know?"

"Know what?" he asked. His blue eyes surveyed Jori's confusion with a measured glance before she saw enlightenment dawn and berated herself for once more letting her tongue speak too soon. "You are having that tonight, aren't you, Jori?" He inclined his head, his eyes bright as he considered her sulky expression.

"And if there's no boyfriend, there should be lots to share. Am I right?" Bright and eager, his blue eyes dared her to refuse.

Jori exhaled in defeat. There was no point in denying that she'd planned that particular dinner. He would hear about it through the grapevine anyway, since she always made up a tray for Maddy Hopkins. The same local etiquette that demanded he not choose any patient's cooking over another dictated that she invite him for one meal.

Social responsibility. She hated the phrase. With a sigh of frustration Jori accepted her lot. She had orders to be hospitable to Dan's replacement—at least until he returned. She might as well start tonight.

"Six o'clock," she said without preamble and recited her address. "If you're late I'm not waiting."

Turning, Jori strode from the room, frustrated with the situation. She had counted on a quiet evening at home, alone. Time to get her faculties together before she visited her father tomorrow at Sunset Retirement Home. Time to accept that the Alzheimer's had almost taken over and James Jessop would never be the same.

There was no way tonight would be quiet, not with Christopher Davis's loud, booming laugh and even bigger personality. He easily overtook a room, filling it with himself. She had seen it numerous times in the past week. Nobody was immune to his charm, it seemed.

Jori sighed. "I am. I will be."

She had no room in her structured life for anybody like him. If and when she did date, it was always with someone like herself; someone who prized the stable security that life in Mossbank offered. Someone, she told herself, who could see themselves living in the small friendly community in twenty years' time.

Her days of elegant dining and fancy dress were a part of the past and she was glad. She wanted the calm peace that life in her hometown always gave. Acceptance, serenity, tranquility and no surprises.

"There's no way I'm having anything to do with him," she muttered, ignoring her co-worker's amused glance from across the room. Jori snatched the next file up and tossed it into his pickup basket. "Christopher Davis is the exact opposite of what I'm looking for in a husband."

It was highly unlikely that she'd ever get married, Jori assured herself for the third time that week. But if she did, she would opt for a mundane, ordinary trustworthy man who lived in the same small town. They would raise their child in a good, solid home to grow up in and they'd be with James whenever he needed them.

And there wouldn't be any of the disastrous upheavals that had marked her life in the past. She would build a haven, Jori resolved. A place to be who she was without pretense. With her lips set in a determined line, she called out the next patient's name.

No, siree. Dr. Christopher Davis bore just a little too much resemblance to those handsome, pushy, overwhelming men in her past. And look how ugly that had turned out.

It was best to concentrate on building a life for herself here in Mossbank and ignore outsiders. This was her home; these were her friends. They'd stood by her when no one else would.

Supermodel Jordanna Jessop was no more. But Jori Jessop owed the people of Mossbank a huge debt of gratitude, and she had no intention of reneging on that debt.

"There goes Jori home," Faith Johnson murmured to her friends as she sipped another mouthful of the iced tea she had just made. "Such a beautiful girl, but so withdrawn."

"I don't think she's withdrawn at all," Charity commented, adding another teaspoon of sugar to her glass. "If I'd had to deal with that awful young man—what was his name?" She stopped to think and then shook her head. "Well, anyway, if I suffered through all that terrible publicity because of a man who said he loved me, I would be quiet, too."

"She is very good in the office," Hope murmured thoughtfully. "I think Dr. Davis likes having her there, too. When she's busy with a patient, he's always looking at her."

"I don't know how she can work with a man who looks like that," Charity fluttered her hand in the warm spring air. "He has the looks of that fellow in the movies, what's his name? Tom Hanks?"

"Tom Hanks has dark hair," Hope muttered.

"I know but the clean-cut, handsomely chiseled look is the same, don't you think?" Charity's eyes gleamed with appreciation. "We need a few more good-looking men in this town."

"Jordanna has such lovely hair, don't you think?" Hope tried desperately to steer the subject away from men. "So long and glossy. Why, she can even sit on it!"

"My hair used to be near that color," Charity told them. She frowned when Faith laughed. "Well, it did! But it was so long ago, I expect you've forgotten. I was slim and beautiful, too. Once."

"She's having him over for dinner tonight." Faith's soft voice dropped into the conversation.

"How do you know that?" Charity's eyes widened.

"I happened to hear her tell Dr. Davis to be there at six sharp."

"Oh, my," Charity whispered. "That sounds promising."

"It sounds ridiculous," Hope told her firmly. "Jori's merely being kind. There's nothing *romantic* about it." She sounded scandalized. "They are from two different worlds. He's flamboyant, loud and unruly. She's quiet and reserved. Not at all suited."

Faith chuckled. "You've said that before." She grinned. "And you were just as wrong about me and Arthur as you are about those two." Her head cocked sideways. "I think they'd make a lovely couple. I wonder . . ." Her voice died away.

"Well, anyway, he's not staying," Hope mused thoughtfully. "Dr. Davis is only here until Dr. Dan and Jessica return with their baby."

"If they return," Faith whispered. "I've been praying so hard for that wee one. Arthur, too. I'm just going to have to let go and trust that God will lay his hand on their lives."

The three ladies sat quietly in the sun pondering the predicament of their beloved doctor and his wife until Christopher Davis roared past in a racy black sports car.

"He'd better slow down," Charity muttered. "This isn't Boston." She glanced at the clouds building in the sky. "I think there's a storm brewing, girls," she murmured at last. "Perhaps we'd better move inside."

"We should have had our tea at my house." Hope chuckled as she lifted the tray of dishes. "Then you two could have listened in to Jori and Dr. Davis while they have dinner next door."

"What a good idea," Charity agreed blithely. "Why don't you two scurry on over now? It's Arthur's late night at the store and I've got company coming, so you two will be free to eavesdrop all you like."

Faith frowned. "I don't eavesdrop," she murmured. "I just try to help out where I . . . who's coming for dinner, Charity?" she asked suddenly.

Charity smiled and patted her friend's gray curls.

"Oh, just a friend," she told them softly. "A good friend."

"But I want to know who it is," Faith lamented. "You've refused to see anyone that Hope and I have lined up for you even though they were all nice men. Take Frank now. He's—"

"You take him," Charity blazed in an unusual show of temper. "I don't want to go out to dinner with Frank Bellows! He's the *undertaker,* for goodness' sake! What would we talk about? My choice in coffins?"

"Charity, there's no need to get so upset," Hope said placatingly, her hand cuddling the older woman's arthritic one. "Your blood pressure is quite high enough. And after all, we're only trying to help."

"Well, you can help by letting me invite my own men friends for dinner." Charity smoothed her skirt in a motion that both her friends recognized meant her feelings were hurt. "I don't need a man. I'm perfectly happy just the way I am."

"All right, we won't ask you over to dinner with anyone anymore," Hope soothed. "We'll let her pick her own men friends, won't we, Faith?"

Charity's round face had almost regained its usual sunny gleam when Faith spoke.

"But she never picks any men to be with, Hope. Not ever!" Faith's voice rose with indignation. "She's alone in this house all the time. God didn't mean for us to be isolated and alone on this earth." She glanced from one to the other, her green eyes finally settling on Charity.

"Don't you want to share your days with someone else? Don't

you enjoy having someone to talk to?" Faith's wide smiling mouth was turned down as she studied her friend.

"If I want to talk, I have you two," Charity declared. "And you natter on for so long that a body needs a good rest to recuperate. I like my silence. I like to be peaceful and quiet. It's refreshing."

"Piffle," Faith exclaimed. "It's not normal. God has more in store for us than solitude. You're lonely and you know it."

Ever the peacemaker, Hope stood to her feet gathering her belongings. "Come along, Faith, dear. It's going to rain any moment and I don't want to get my new suit spotted. Thanks for tea, Charity. Enjoy your dinner."

"Whoever it's with," Faith grumbled on her way out the door. She raced back in to grab her purse, her face wreathed in smiles. "Hah! You thought I'd forgotten it, didn't you? Well, I'm far too young for Sunset Retirement Home just yet, Charity Flowerday!" And having gotten the last word in, Faith stumbled down the steps and out into the strong westerly wind.

"I'm sorry, dear," Hope murmured as she watched Charity move awkwardly from the chair. "She doesn't mean to hurt you."

"I know." Charity sighed as she watched Faith throw up her arms and catch the first droplets of rain on her tongue. "Maybe she's right. Maybe I have been hiding out here, missing out on life. Maybe it's time I got involved in what's going on around me."

"What are you going to do?" Hope's blue eyes were full of fear.

"Live," Charity told her matter-of-factly. "Maybe I'll ask Howard to take me out for dinner instead of me cooking." Her brow was furrowed in thought.

"Howard Steele?" Hope gaped. "But he's years younger than you are!"

"I know." Charity preened in the full-length mirror hanging in the hall. "Do you think I should wear my black silk?" She twisted and turned in front of the glass, trying to see herself from all angles.

"Black silk? But . . . but that's for special occasions," Hope gasped. "Charity, what is going on?"

"I'm freeing myself. I'm going to be more like Faith—open to new experiences." She pushed her waved hair back into a different style. "No, you're right. The black is too old-fashioned. I think I'll go down to Penelope's and see if she has something a little more in style. A nice bright red, maybe."

"You're going to buy a red dress? To wear on a date with Howard Steele?" Hope sounded scandalized. Her face was a picture of dismay as she watched Charity grasp her car keys and purse and walk slowly to the front door.

"Charity," she asked at last, "are you quite all right?"

"I've never felt better in my life." Charity nodded, motioning for Hope to precede her out the door. "A new outfit, a different hairstyle. It's just the change I need."

"But I liked the old you," Hope said with a perplexed frown.

"Don't say that word again," Charity ordered, moving briskly across the lawn. "You are only as old as you feel and today I feel young and hopeful." To herself she hummed the line from a chorus they'd learned in church last week.

" 'With God All Things Are Possible'?" Faith looked at Hope. "Why is she singing that?"

"She's going to buy a new dress. And change her hairstyle. She's even going to ask Howard Steele out for dinner."

"Howard Steele?" Faith gasped. "But his wife only just divorced him six years ago. And he's younger than Charity. He's got long hair." She added the last as if that were the final nail in poor Howard's personality coffin.

"I know." Hope started walking briskly down the street, grimacing at the darkened spots of color on her pristine aqua suit as the raindrops plopped onto it in fat round splatters.

"Oh, well," Faith murmured, continuing blithely on with her skipping steps. "At least she's getting out of that house. Since Melanie's marriage, she hardly leaves the place."

"I know," Hope agreed. "But it's Howard Steele she's getting out with!"

"It's not what I had in mind, either," Faith assured her. "But the Lord works in mysterious ways."

"Well, this is certainly very mysterious," Hope agreed grimly. She mounted the steps to her home, griping at the inclement weather as she smoothed her hair. "I just hope she doesn't regret her hasty decision."

Chapter Two

"I love this place, Lord," Jori murmured, a grin tilting the full curve of her lips as she viewed her home with satisfaction, enjoying the riot of flowers that always grew in her rock garden. "Even if Dad can't be here anymore."

She refused to let the sadness ruin her evening. Flop, her cocker spaniel, stood wagging his short, stumpy tail inside the wrought iron gate.

"Hi, boy. Did you have a good day chasing squirrels? You look kind of tired."

The dog always knew when she would be home and his routine never varied. After bestowing an enthusiastic swipe across her face with his pink tongue, Flop padded along behind his mistress as she opened the door and entered the comfortable white bungalow.

"Jori, oh, Jori!" Her neighbor, Hope Conroy, was calling from over the white picket fence that separated their lawns.

"Hi, Hope. How are you?"

"I'm fine, dear, just fine. Am I stopping you from your shower?"

Jori was a little surprised to know that Hope was aware of her usual custom of showering right after work. She smiled to herself as she realized this was a large part of the reason she'd wanted to move back home. Everyone knew everyone else and cared about them; there was no pretense here.

"Well, I've got time before dinner."

"I hear you're having a guest. Dr. Davis, isn't it?"

Jori didn't bother asking how the woman knew. Nothing was ever a secret in Mossbank. And Hope was Charity Flowerday's best friend. Little wonder!

"Well, yes," she admitted. "He says he's hungry for something other than fast food so I thought I'd share my roast."

"I thought so. You always have roast beef on Thursdays," Hope murmured triumphantly.

"I didn't realize I'd fallen into such a pattern," Jori murmured, disgusted that her life had become an open book.

"Don't worry, dear. I used to do it myself. All single women do. Especially the organized ones and you've always been organized, Jori. I remember you used to have your marbles stored by color and size. So efficient. I imagine you do the same with your bedding, don't you?"

Jori winced at the woman's admiring smile, wondering when she'd become so boring.

"Uh, was there something you wanted to say, Hope?" she asked at last, hoping they could finish their discussion before Mrs. Johnson moseyed over. Jori loved the woman dearly but Faith Johnson had a habit of rearranging a conversation until no one knew exactly what they were discussing. And today was not a day for more confusion.

"Did you ask her yet?" Faith's high clear voice floated over the fence. "Is she really going to do it?"

"Do what?" Jori asked quietly, studying the flush of embarrassment covering Hope's pale cheeks.

"Well, Faith overheard, that is, er, she thought she overheard . . ." Hope stopped and brushed a wisp of hair out of her eyes. "Oh, this is so embarrassing. I do dislike gossip."

"Just tell me, okay, Hope. I'll try to answer you." Jori patted the perfectly manicured hand gently and watched the even features organize themselves into their usual uncompromising pattern.

"Very well then, I shall." The older woman took a deep breath and then let it all out in one gasp. "Are you really thinking about having a baby, Jordanna? On your own, without benefit of a husband?" Hope sounded shocked and looked scandalized that she'd even said the words.

"I . . . I . . . ." Jori stopped short as Faith came to lean on the gate that adjoined the two properties.

"See, I told you. Look at her face. She's going to do it," Faith chanted, clapping her hands in excitement. "A new baby! Imagine!"

"Just a minute," Jori protested, trying desperately to get a word in. "I never said I was going to . . ."

"I overheard you talking with Dr. Davis," Faith admitted and then clapped a hand over her mouth. Her eyes were huge. "He said it was something to do with a test tube." She stared off into the bright green leaves of Jori's maple tree.

Hope shook her silver blond head. "You can't do it, Jordanna. The good Lord meant for children to have two parents to care for them. You of all people should understand how hard it is to have only one parent around when you need help."

For the third time in as many hours, Jori had to hold her tongue so as not to ask these two nosey women to stop discussing her personal life. She drew a deep breath and prayed for help.

"I'm not going to have a baby," she told them clearly, ignoring the relief that swept across Hope's face. "I'm thinking of adopting a child—one that has no home, no parents and no place to go." She bent down to toss Flop's stick across the grass and then straightened.

"I'm twenty-eight, Hope, and I'm not married. I don't think it's likely to happen any time soon, do you? Considering there are so few single men around Mossbank." She loosed the band holding her hair in a braid and threaded her fingers through the long plait.

"Well, I wouldn't exactly say that," Hope murmured flushing coyly. "After all, Faith and I have both been married at a more advanced age than yours."

"God led me back to Mossbank, I believe that. But He hasn't led any men into my path here and I don't intend to go hunting for one," Jori murmured in disgust, grimacing at the thought. "Mossbank is where I belong and where I want to stay. I have everything I need here. If I can help some child who needs a home and a mother, then that's what I'd like to do.

"I'm sorry, but I have to go now. It's almost time for supper. Bye," she called, striding across the lawn and in through her front door.

After her shower, as she pulled on a comfortable pair of ragged blue jeans, Jori told herself her choice of clothing was in deference to the relaxed atmosphere of her home and had nothing to do with the man who was coming for dinner. Her fingers twitched the hem on a frayed and sleeveless chambray shirt as Jori mentally scorned those ladies who worked so hard at dressing up to impress the new doctor.

"Ridiculous," she muttered to herself. "It's not my style at all. Not that I'm interested," she added, glancing down at the decrepit white sandals which left her toes cooling in the summer sun. "I'm quite content with my life alone, except for Dad, of course."

As she combed out her waist-length hair, Jori brooded on her confrontation with Dr. Davis. He was trouble, that was for sure. And why did he make her think of things long forgotten; things she could never have?

Her eyes slid over the plastic-wrapped gowns in her closet. She could still fit into the elegant outfits that had been part of her daily life seven years ago. Not that it mattered. There was little call for haute couture in Mossbank.

"This is the first time I've had a date because someone is interested in my cooking," she told Flop, who woofed his appreciation. "But that's all he's interested in. And don't go fawning over him, either. You're supposed to remain faithful to the one who feeds you."

Flop obviously understood as he licked her hand before picking up his rawhide bone and heading out of the room. Pushing her hair into a clip, Jori bounded down the stairs, Flop padding along behind.

Everything was simmering nicely in the oven. A fresh garden salad would make the meal complete. Leaving the relative cool of her house, Jori slipped off her sandals and walked barefoot into the lush garden. She squeezed her toes in the moist black loam that was her pride and joy.

Sweet peas, fragrant and multicolored had begun blooming and Jori breathed their heady fragrance. Perfect centerpiece, she decided, snipping a handful. She laid these on the bench at the edge of her plot and then moved over to gather some produce. In her pail she carefully placed furled green lettuce leaves, plump red radishes, three tiny cucumbers, a round onion and a wisp of dill. She was about to straighten up when a laughing voice startled her.

"I must say, this is a side of you I have never really seen before," Dr. Davis teased. "Jori Jessop in the dirt."

"You're early," was the best reply Jori could come up with as she blushed profusely and then prayed he wouldn't comment on it.

Dr. Christopher Davis was dressed in a natty white cotton sweater and blue cotton slacks that showed off his blond good looks to perfection.

As if he needed help, she grumbled to herself. Chris Davis was probably the most handsome doctor she had ever seen. That bothered her.

"I hope you didn't dress up just for me," he chuckled, his quick eyes noting her mismatched clothing.

"No, I didn't," she replied brusquely. "We don't dress for dinner in Mossbank."

When he merely laughed, Jori moved skittishly toward the house, pausing only to hose off the soil clinging to her feet. She wanted to get away from his overwhelming presence, but he followed her into the kitchen.

"I'm sorry. I didn't mean to embarrass you, Jori." His lustrous white teeth flashed his wolfish smile at her. "You look very nice, in a down-home kind of way."

"Yeah, right," she murmured, wishing the evening was at an end already.

"Can I help?" he asked, moving his tall, solid body next to hers at the sink.

Somehow, Jori didn't think he meant to soil his well-manicured hands with dirty garden produce so she motioned toward her small dinette set.

"You can set the table if you want." Her voice was less than gracious, but Jori couldn't help it. He made her so nervous.

Christopher worked quickly, loading the plates, cups and silverware into his arms in order to make the least number of trips possible. Jori winced as her favorite china place settings jostled against each other, but at least he was out of her way. For now.

"I like your house," he offered, still in his friendly jovial tone. "Looks like a real home."

Startled, Jori gazed up at him, intrigued by his assessment. He didn't seem the type to value homes. Before she could reply, Flop sauntered in and wriggled over to their visitor, hips swaying in delight.

"Hello, boy," Chris bent over to ruffle the dog's floppy ears gently, avoiding the dog's wet, pink tongue. "You're a real beauty, aren't you." Surprisingly, the loud voice was soft and gentle as the big man dealt with the enthusiastic dog. "What's his name?" Chris asked, tipping his blond head back to stare up at Jori.

"Flop," she replied brusquely, turning back to her salad. Moments later she felt his big hand on her elbow, turning her to face his shocked look.

"You named a purebred cocker spaniel Flop?" Disbelief flooded his perceptive blue gaze.

"Well, actually his title is Ginger Boy Parkland but I call him Flop. It's what he does best." She giggled, enjoying the look of stupefaction her remark brought.

The dog was obviously perceptive for he chose that moment to drop his plump body onto the floor, his chin resting on his front paws as soulful brown eyes studied them. Seconds later a huge sigh woofed out of him.

"See," she told him in a conspiratorial tone. "It's his trademark."

Christopher shook his head in disbelief. It was clear to Jori that in his exalted opinion, people didn't acquire bloodline animals, have them groomed, teach them dog manners and then bestow a name like Flop.

"Where did you get him?" he asked.

Jori mentally put a guard on her lips. "My dad," she told him shortly, whisking flour into the dark brown beef juices. "He was a homecoming present after I finished nursing school."

She tipped the succulent gravy into an oval bowl and set it on the table with a smack. A platter set to one side bore a small roast of beef, golden brown potatoes and finger-length carrots. She placed the bouquet of sweet peas in the center of the table.

"Everything is ready. Please, have a seat." Her slim hand motioned to the chair opposite hers and she watched as Chris sank into it, licking his lips discreetly.

"I'm really going to enjoy this." He grinned. Those twinkling blue eyes glinted at her. "I appreciate you allowing me to join you tonight, Jori. Thank you."

As if I had a choice, Jori acidly considered replying, but the words stayed inside her head. "I'll just say grace and then we can eat," she murmured.

"Father, bless this food for we are truly grateful for all your blessings. Amen." He murmured an amen, too, and seconds later she watched him tuck into their feast.

It was a small roast. She always had trouble shopping for just herself. Everything came in such large packages and Jori usually got sick of leftovers long before they were gone. Hence the send-out dinners for some of her father's friends.

But, surprisingly, the meal was rapidly diminishing before her eyes. The doctor heaped his large plate full, taking some of everything and then tasting each item thoughtfully, rolling it around on his tongue. When he came to the beef, he closed his eyes in satisfaction, chewing slowly, obviously savoring the rich flavor.

It had been years since she'd watched her father relish her cooking in just that manner and Jori grinned to herself as she tucked into her own well-filled plate, able, for the moment, to dislodge the discomfort she always felt in this man's presence.

"This is so good, a man might even be persuaded to propose," Chris mumbled, his face alight with pleasure as he rolled his eyes.

Jori choked on her water and welcomed his resounding thump on her back to get her breath. Eyes tearing, she stared into his handsome face.

"Isn't that a little extreme?" she gasped, her eyes wide with shock. "Just for a meal?" Surely he wasn't . . .

Her face flushed with embarrassment as she realized he'd been teasing her and she'd fallen for it. Again. Silently, Jori called herself a fool for letting him get to her. It was just that he unnerved her, she told her jangling nerves. She had known he would be trouble right from the start. Jori tipped her head back to glare at him as he burst out laughing.

Jori flashed him a look of disgust before resuming her meal. Fine, she decided. She simply would not converse with the man if he couldn't behave. With a sniff of disgust, Jori pushed away her plate; everything tasted the same anyway. He'd spoiled even this small pleasure with his vibrant presence across the table. She stared at her water glass, intent on ignoring him. And Jori could have carried off her pretended disinterest if he hadn't continued the tomfoolery.

Suddenly he was kneeling beside her, holding the sweet peas under her nose with one broad hand, while the other clasped hers, his fingers warm and tingling. His voice was soft with controlled laughter and his eyes were bright with glee.

"Please, Ms. Jessop. Say you'll marry me. To be able to eat like this with a cook that looks like you, I'm willing to take everything else on spec." His clear blue eyes lingered on her face. "Please say you will."

"What I will do is douse you with the garden hose if you don't stop this right now," she warned him severely, repressing her laughter with difficulty. Her hand tugged away from his and reached out for his half-full plate as she avoided his all-knowing eyes.

"I guess this means you're finished," she murmured sweetly, turning to put the dinner plate on the floor. Immediately, Flop moved in, slurping up the entire contents in one fell swoop of his pink tongue. Jori turned to gaze innocently at Chris's startled face.

"Ready for dessert?" Her voice was soft as butter.

"I hadn't finished, you know." He wasn't laughing now. "And I'm starved." Dark as velvet, Chris's dark soulful eyes beseeched her for sympathy. "Please, ma'am, could I have some more?"

It was such an exact duplication of a recent television commercial that Jori couldn't help the laughter that bubbled out of her. He looked like a naughty little boy with his clear solemn eyes, rumpled blond hair and company-perfect sweater. His big hand stuck out toward her.

"Truce," he offered, waiting earnestly for her response.

Jori sighed in capitulation and got up to find another plate for him. He was back in his chair, eyes downcast when she returned to the table.

"Here. Help yourself." Her voice was resigned to his silliness.

Dr. Davis accepted the dinner plate eagerly and ladled huge amounts of food onto his dish once more. Jori leaned back in her chair, quietly sipping her coffee as she watched him. Somehow he didn't seem quite as bad as she had first anticipated. She ignored the chiding little voice in the back of her mind. After all, it wasn't *that* terrible, having him for dinner, she argued with herself.

And when the nagging voice murmured, *I told you so,* Jori ignored its taunting. Her eyes were busy absorbing the picture of

Christopher Davis, noted surgeon and infamous ladies' man, eating dinner in *her* kitchen. When he finally leaned back in his chair, she was happy to note that very little of the beef remained.

"I have more if you'd like," she murmured, eyeing the remains of the potatoes in the pot. "If you don't eat it, I'll have to reheat it for at least the next week."

"No, thanks! Much as I'd like to, I won't be able to walk if I eat another bite. It was really great though."

Standing, Jori carried away the serving dishes to the sink, poured his coffee and then sat down to sip at her own. Christopher waited expectantly, peering at her from under those disgustingly long lashes. When it was clear that nothing more was forthcoming, he rushed to the heart of the matter.

"Where's the pie?" he asked, glancing around her small kitchen.

"What pie?" Jori was jostled out of her bemused thoughts by his question and she stared at him, uncomprehending. Pie was the last thing on her mind just then. She blushed, remembering exactly what she had been thinking of—that maybe he would kiss her.

Huge blue eyes reproached her sadly. "You mean you lied? You don't have apple pie for dessert?"

Indignation welled up. His nerve was just too much!

"Look, Dr. Davis. You invited yourself here. I didn't say I had apple pie, you just assumed it." She stared at his strong muscular body tipped back precariously on the oak chair that had been her father's favorite. "And sit properly on that," she ordered imperiously before realizing to whom she was speaking.

She was rattled, Jori admitted silently, as little waves of tension skittered up her spine to her neck. And *he* was doing it to her.

"Yes, ma'am!" His big grin split across his laughing face as Chris straightened his chair before reaching out to pat her small hand with his larger one. "It's okay if you don't, you know," he soothed. "The dinner was really great even without that."

"Well, thank you so much. I'm so happy I could be of service," she muttered through clenched teeth.

His good humor was apparently unbreachable. As he sat waiting, the doctor merely kept smiling at her.

The man had gall, Jori mused. There was no doubt about that. And he knew exactly which buttons to push to get her dander up. Jori sighed.

Just another reason why he wasn't her type. Still, he did live alone and if he had been eating his meals at the town's fast-food places, it was no wonder he craved a plain home-cooked meal. Calling herself a soft touch, Jori relented.

"I don't have any apple pie," she said, capitulating at last. "But if you could manage a piece of chocolate cake, I can accommodate you."

It was a thinly veiled hint at the amount of food he had consumed, but the good doctor ignored her jibe with that gracious good humor. His brilliant blue eyes sparkled at her as he kissed the hand he still held. Jori pulled her hand away and tucked it behind her back.

"I was just saying that I would really enjoy a piece of chocolate cake right now," he teased.

Jori sneaked a look at him over her shoulder as she cut a huge slice of the rich dessert. "What you should be eating is praline cheesecake," she muttered snidely.

He pretended to stick a finger down his throat, blue eyes rolling backward as he faked a gagging sound. Jori burst out laughing. The oh-so-sober, very handsome, very famous doctor looked ridiculous.

She set a huge piece of fluffy chocolate cake with its whipped mocha icing in front of him and watched him gobble it up with gusto.

"How often do you eat?" she demanded curiously, stunned by the amount of food he had put away.

"I didn't have time for breakfast today," he told her, shame-faced. He had the grace to look embarrassed as a light flush colored his tanned skin.

"And you didn't have lunch because Mrs. Andrews delivered her baby just about then," Jori guessed. "Did you have dinner last night?"

The big man shrugged his massive shoulders. Jori had to voice her concerns, not just for him but for his patients.

"Chris," she chastised him, only realizing as she said it that she had used his first name. "This practice is a very busy one and you can be kept going for days. You have to make time to eat regularly, or you'll find yourself burned out before Dan gets back. Then what will everyone do?" It was a question she didn't want him to answer.

"Are you worried about me or them?" Chris inquired dryly. It was evident he already knew where her allegiance lay.

"I'm concerned for everyone. If you get sick, you'll toddle off to some expensive hospital in the East and they'll treat you immediately. The people in this town haven't got the money to go to fancy city hospitals. If you leave, they will have no one to help them."

Finished with her spiel, Jori got up and began to systematically clear the table, loading the dishwasher carefully. His fingers on her arm startled her, as did the strength with which he forced her to turn toward him. She was surprised to see his genial face tight with suppressed anger. Blue lightning shot out from his sparkling irises.

"I'm not just playing at medicine, you know," he snapped. "I am fully qualified for most anything that a one-horse town like Mossbank can throw at me." He favored her with a dry look, blue eyes gently mocking. "And I'm not going to cave in if I miss a meal or a night's sleep.

"Don't worry, Jori. All your little farmer friends will be well looked after."

Jori's temper surged upward as the week's tensions of working with him rose to the surface. "If you hate small towns, why did you come here? What is it about this town that you dislike so much anyway, Dr. Davis?" These were her friends and he was acting as if they didn't matter.

"What's the matter, Doc?" she derided. "Afraid you won't get the big accolades in a dinky prairie town? Maybe Boston is where you should have stayed, practicing medicine on people you know nothing about, and care about even less."

"Look, *lady,*" Chris's voice boomed out, loud and exasperated. "I came here on my own to help out a friend who was going through a tough time. I don't have to answer to you or anybody." He snorted derisively.

"It's not my fault that there's nothing going on around here besides a matchmaking game and some bored housewives who think baking a bunch of cheesecakes is going to solve anything."

So he had heard the talk! His handsome face was flushed and angry and perversely, Jori was glad about that, even if she had been elected as one of the contestants in Faith's marriage pool. The man was too full of himself. It was refreshing to see him have to shift out of that smugly superior and condescending mode. She would be more than happy to take him down a peg or two.

"You have eyes, Doctor, but you see nothing. Those 'bored housewives' are extremely busy right now. Many of them hold down full-time jobs off the farm and then help their husbands when they finish. And when those two jobs are done, there's still the laundry, housework and kids to look after."

She glared at him bitterly. "But they took time out of their schedules to express their welcome by baking *you* a cheesecake. Okay, it got a little out of hand. You're supposed to be so smart," she said with a smirk. "Find a solution.

"There are local fairs to attend, 4-H events, auctions, barbecues, dances, picnics and a ton of other things to see and do around here." She waved her hands to indicate the plethora of possibilities. "I suggest, Doctor, that you get to know your patients, find out what their existence is like, before you pass judgment on their *dull* way of life."

In high dudgeon, Jori flounced around the kitchen smacking dish upon dish as she prepared to do battle for her town. Every nerve in her body was on full alert as she whirled to face him.

"The people here are independent and proud. Some of them refuse to leave the land their fathers and grandfathers farmed. They've had to start side businesses from their homes to generate enough capital to let them plant another crop after the first one got hailed out or the last swaths got snowed on.

"They raise their own kids without any fancy psychologists or pricey day cares and mostly without the drug scenes you find in cities all over North America." She risked a glance at him and discovered he was frowning.

"They go to church on Sundays, care about each other and spend lots of time and energy helping out their neighbors. And they maintain decent values in a society where no one cares that seniors are abandoned, rape and assault are commonplace and abusing kids is not unusual."

Jori knew her face was red and that she was yelling, but she couldn't help it. The man deserved to be told a few home truths. Fury tossed all caution to the wind as she berated him angrily.

"They create their own fun by being a community who care about each other. If someone loses a barn, everyone pitches in to build another. If a child is lost, we all search until she's found. That's the way it is on the prairies. You stick together to survive." She shoved a plastic-wrapped slice of cake at him.

"Here's your cake." Her huge brown eyes defied him to comment. "I'm sorry, but I have to ask you to leave. There are some things I need to do right now."

Jori stormed to the front door, ignoring the wagging dog at her heels. She wanted the man out of here. Now. Anyone who was so callous about their patients' welfare should not be part of the only medical team available for miles around.

She yanked the door open and stood grimly beside it, waiting for the eminently eligible surgeon to leave her home. She could see two women walking past her house and groaned inwardly. Mrs. Johnson and Mrs. Conroy. She might have known!

Chris's eyes mirrored his stunned disbelief that anyone should talk to him so peremptorily and if she hadn't been so mad, Jori would have grinned at his shock.

"Good night," she challenged, standing tall and stiff.

Slowly Christopher Davis walked toward the door, still holding his chocolate cake. His blue eyes had softened to a periwinkle tone as he gazed down at her. Then his hand stretched out as his thumb rubbed across her bottom lip. Jori's eyes grew round with surprise and she felt the impact of that light touch right down to her toes.

"You are quite a fierce little thing when you get your dander up, aren't you?" he asked. "Chocolate," he mused, still staring at her.

"What?" Her voice was bemused, disoriented.

"You had chocolate on your lips." With that, Dr. Chris Davis turned to walk through the doorway with that uncaring long-legged grace. He stopped just outside, turned around and fixed her with an amused look.

"Thank you very much for the meal," he offered politely. "I enjoyed it and the company." Bending his lanky form low, Chris rubbed the spaniel's head affectionately. "Bye, Flop." Then he stood tall and straight, his electric blue gaze meeting her dark one head-on.

"Good night, Jordanna Lori Jessop. Dan was right, after all. I am going to enjoy working with you," he added with a grin. And bending down, he placed a very soft, very chaste kiss against her flushed cheek.

Jori barely heard his whispered promise before he disappeared into the dark night.

"I think I might even enjoy getting to know this town of yours."

And there, ogling them from the lawn next door, were two of the town's busiest old ladies. Angrily, Jori slammed the door on his retreating figure. As soon as she came back to earth, that was.

Darn his supercilious attitude anyway. She had returned to Mossbank to live quietly, help out where she could and let her battered world-weary spirit heal. Now, with one kiss, Christopher Davis had threatened all that; rocked her moorings until she wondered if her life really was on the right track.

Shaking her head, Jori went back to the kitchen to clean up the dishes. But the sensation of his lips against her cheek wouldn't be dislodged.

When reason returned Jori berated her foolishly overactive senses. She wished the illustrious blond doctor would have never shown his face in a place so obviously unimportant as Mossbank.

Jori was still frowning when she climbed the stairs to bed.

She closed her eyes tightly, trying desperately to dislodge Faith Johnson's wide grinning smile from her mind.

She wouldn't think about any of it. Not now. She breathed in a few cleansing breaths and then opened her eyes to focus on the moonlit ceiling.

"Lord, you know I don't want any upheaval in my life. I'm not very good at relationships. Besides, I like things just the way they are—calm, unemotional. Please don't send me any more curve balls. I'm not a very good catcher." Satisfied that God would understand her meaning, Jori closed her eyes and drifted off to sleep with a picture of a baseball diamond and a tall, blond pitcher clad in a white lab coat stuck firmly in her mind.

Chapter Three

❧

"I'm so sorry for the delay. The doctor has been detained. I'm sure he'll be here soon, Mrs. Andrews."

Outside it was a glorious July afternoon but Jori noticed little of the beauty of the day. Instead her mind whirled with dark thoughts of retribution. She strove to speak smoothly in order to calm the impatience that was running rampant in the waiting room, unwilling to let her friends see how bothered she was by the city doctor's absence.

"Yes, Mrs. Johnson. The doctor will be with you as soon as he can." Jori gritted her teeth in annoyance as she dialed the hospital for the fourth time without success.

Dr. Christopher Davis was late. Very late. And no one seemed to know just where he was. She doubted he would worry about it too much, given his conversation after their meal together mere days ago.

Meanwhile, she had to face a barrage of patients who wanted to be free from the stuffy waiting room to pick saskatoons, or bale hay, or go to the river for a cooling swim.

"I'm sorry. I can't reschedule you. We're full up. You can wait for an opening if you'd like." Jori listened calmly to the third query from Faith Johnson. Inside, a wild mixture of feelings began whirling around, as she heard the sound of the back door opening.

"You're so much like your mother, Jordanna. I remember her quite well. She was tall like you and willowy thin. When you smile you resemble her the most." Faith stared at Jori happily. "Ruth was always smiling at something, even at the end. Life was so full of joy for her."

Privately, Jori wondered if her mother would have found anything to smile about in this situation. A doctor's office functioned on schedules and adherence to them. Christopher Davis was throwing all her carefully made plans out the window.

When he finally came sauntering into his office, all blond boyishness and charm, Jori's tightly held restraint flew out the window.

"Where in the world have you been?" she growled, protected by the thin office walls, as she slapped down the files in front of him. "These people have lives that don't revolve around your Boston time schedule, you know."

"What's the matter?" Big pools of azure stared up at her as Chris blinked in surprise.

His question was bordering on the ridiculous and Jori let him know it. Hands on her hips she surveyed his relaxed happy grin and blasted away with both barrels, ignoring the intriguing scent of his spicy aftershave as it tickled her nose.

" 'What's the matter?' you ask. Well, I have twelve people waiting to see a doctor who was supposed to be here over an hour ago. The hospital had no idea where you were. You didn't answer either your cell phone or pager. What do *you* think is the matter?" Jori told him disgustedly, his calm manner only infuriating her more.

"Show the first patient in, please, Nurse." He coolly dismissed her without a word, bending to glance at the first on a stack of files that signaled the afternoon's work.

When she didn't move, Chris's tanned face searched her turbulent eyes. His features were composed, controlled; masking whatever was going on inside those innocent baby blues.

"Jori. The patients." His low tone brooked no nonsense. He was pulling rank, and she knew it, but Jori was too angry to argue.

Turning, she marched from his office, snapping the door shut with venom before retrieving Mr. Hunter and Mrs. Johnson from the lounge and showing them into separate rooms.

And so they progressed through the afternoon. Chris asked her for something only when absolutely necessary and Jori answered, polite but cool. By five-thirty, their obvious feud was a hot topic with the only other person in the office, her co-worker, Glenda McKay.

"What is the matter?" the other woman asked, passing Jori in the hall. "I can almost see the steam coming out of your ears."

"You can't exactly soar with the eagles when you work with a big turkey," Jori told her, grimacing as she heard her name barked in that imperious tone once more.

"You're too intense. Maybe he had a good reason," she cajoled.

"Try to get him in for X rays as soon as possible," Chris said as he entered the room. "Also, I want a full blood workup on Mrs., er—" he checked his notes "—Ainsworth."

He was trying to ignore the dark forbidding looks his very attractive nurse had been tossing his way all afternoon. It wasn't easy; he could hardly miss the daggers those big brown eyes were throwing out.

He hadn't meant to fall asleep; not really. But he wasn't used to these maternity all-nighters. Delivering babies was a somewhat new experience for him.

Chris grinned. Who knew what Jori would do with that information, never mind if she found out the rest. He felt as if he were on trial with her already. Dead batteries in the cell phone couldn't be attributed to him, could they?

Of course, Chris reflected as he scribbled a notation on another file, he should have known better than to offend Jori. His patients raved about her constantly—how wonderful, how kind, how sweet, how lovely. He could see for himself just how gorgeous she was. That he had chosen to ignore their thinly veiled hints regarding her single status was obviously his loss.

It was clear that anyone who said anything about Jori Jessop said only good. She was a paragon of virtue, she was a great cook, she could handle emergencies with more aplomb than an army sergeant—the list went on seemingly endlessly.

She was very interesting, too. He had seen that for himself last evening—before Jori had gone from friendly hostess to fiery virago in about thirty seconds, and all without losing that dignified inner sense of self she always projected. Jordanna Jessop was a woman who knew exactly what she wanted out of life, Chris decided. And he was pretty sure she wanted very little from him, at the moment. With a sigh, Chris went to check on yet another patient.

After he administered an injection to one person, checked another's swollen tonsils and conferred with Mrs. Sanderson about her new hip, Chris caught sight of Jori's slim figure hurrying down the hall. A frown marred the smooth tanned skin of his forehead. Why did he have this ridiculous feeling he knew that face?

Chris was positive he'd never met Jordanna Jessop before and yet there was something about her profile that twigged his memory. Maybe it was those dark eyes—thickly fringed pools of sable that hid deep secrets. He knew those eyes. From somewhere.

He wondered for a moment if she didn't look like one of those women who advertised for a makeup company, but quickly decided he must be wrong. He knew very little about the stuff, but he did know that Nurse Jordanna Jessop didn't need anything to enhance her beauty.

She had a healthy glow that lit up her clear creamy skin. Probably due to the pure life she led here in Hicksville, Chris decided sourly, remembering her accusations of days before. Always something going on, she had said.

He was hanged if he knew where the townspeople held these wild shindigs because Chris had heard and seen nothing happening in the small town since he'd arrived. But then, he hadn't been very successful at mixing in with the locals thus far. Maybe he should just ask somebody for help.

Twenty minutes later Chris had learned all he ever wanted to know about the upcoming country fair from a loquacious Mrs. Flowerday. He vaguely remembered the name—something to do with chocolate, he thought.

"Just ask Jori to bring you, dear," the white-haired woman had enthused, patting his hand. "She always comes. Why, Jori's one of our best supporters." She leaned forward to whisper conspiratorially in his ear. "If you can get a bite of her wild blueberry pie, you're in for a real treat. Jori's got a flair for pastry that rivals mine and I'm not bad in that department."

The woman's plump lips had smacked at the thought and Chris's mouth watered at the picture of such bliss. He might even put up with a one-horse country fair for a piece of homemade wild blueberry pie.

"You say it's near here?" He listened as she described the area, understanding not one whit about the Logan or the Neufeld farms. "And she always goes to this fair?"

"Of course. Everyone goes. It's an annual event." Mrs. Flowerday was staring at him as if she couldn't believe Chris hadn't heard of it.

"Well, maybe, if I'm off that day, I'll ask her," he mumbled at last in response to the older woman's urging. "She doesn't like me very much, though." He grinned at the understatement.

"Nonsense! Jori likes everyone. She's an angel of human kindness. Why, there's not a person in this town who hasn't been blessed by her thoughtfulness!"

Yeah, right, Chris thought. So it was only with him that she gave with one hand and scratched with the other. Well, he'd see how thoughtful Miss Jori Jessop could be, he decided, and winced as Jori snapped the next file into his hand.

But three days later Jori was as unapproachable as ever and Chris still had not asked her to the fair. He needed an in, he decided, jogging past her house early Saturday morning, his first weekend off. A young girl stood just inside Jori's gate with a pail of plump red raspberries in her hand.

"Hi," he called merrily, enjoying the run and the feel of the fresh breeze on his overheated body.

But when the girl looked up at him, her eyes were those of a startled doe and Chris grinned to himself. Aha! Just the thing. Report this thief stealing from her garden and Miss Jessop would undoubtedly be grateful enough to agree to his plan.

Wrong.

Jori Jessop was spitting mad when he showed up at her door later that day and she let him know it in no uncertain terms.

"What in heaven's name were you thinking of?" she demanded, her long slim hands planted on the full curve of her hips. Her eyes were honed chips of onyx. He shuffled his feet on her well-trimmed lawn, less sure of his good deed now that he had started this.

"She's twelve years old, for Pete's sake," she griped. "What did you think she was going to do anyway, shoot someone with raspberries?"

Her scathing tone was enough to break the thin line of control Chris maintained. He pulled himself up to his full height.

"Now just a blasted minute, here. I tried to do a good deed and all . . ."

Her face was a picture in astonishment. "A good deed? How, pray tell?"

"Well, how did I know the girl had permission to be there? I thought she was stealing."

Jori pushed the weight of hair off her neck and coiled it around her hand. Chris watched as she closed her big cocoa eyes and counted silently to ten before speaking again.

"At six-thirty in the morning? Get real!" She sighed longsufferingly before enlightening him. "We have a deal. She picks the berries and I pay her. She comes on her own time, when her mother can spare her. She desperately wants a computer and this way she can earn some money."

"Jori." Chris drew in a calming breath as he tried to set her straight. "She wasn't leaving the pail there. She was taking it."

That aggravating woman merely raised her eyes heavenward as she shook her head in frustration. Her eyes scanned around the yard before she hissed at him.

"Shh . . . Be quiet. My neighbors have very sound hearing." She jerked her head toward the house that Chris knew belonged to Judge Conroy and his wife. "I told her to take the berries. I was giving them to someone. Nobody was supposed to know about it."

Chris was completely lost. "Let's see if I've got this right," he mused. "You *paid* someone to pick the berries in your garden so that you could *give* them away? Oh, I see. It's all clear now. Thanks." He smiled at her slightly, peering down his long nose in disdain. The woman didn't make an ounce of sense.

Jori evidently recognized his confusion for she told him flatly, "Just forget about it, okay." Her big eyes glared at him. "And the next time you see someone in my yard, keep walking!"

Jordanna Jessop reminded him of a lily, Chris decided inconsequentially. Tall and slim, she looked delicate enough to break in the slightest wind.

Looks, however, were deceiving. Jori could hold her own any day of the week. Just now her pointed fingernail was back and demanding an answer as she glared at him.

"What were you doing at my house, anyway?" she fumed, her

wide mouth turned downward. Her narrow feet with their bright red toenails wriggled in the grass.

"I, uh, I was coming to ask a favor," he muttered, hoping she might let him down easily, without the acid.

"A favor? What favor?" Jori's tone was less than encouraging, incredulous even.

"It doesn't matter." He chickened out, backing toward the gate. "I'd better go. Sorry if I spoiled things for the girl." He made it through the gate, barely, before her sweetly baiting voice stopped him.

"I've got a blueberry pie just out of the oven." She waited silently, knowingly, like a fisherman with a trout on the line while Chris swallowed again. He turned just enough to catch the shrewd grin on her face and knew he was hooked.

"Look," she offered quietly. "I'm sorry I was so harsh. If you'll accept a piece of pie and a cup of coffee as an apology, I'll try to explain."

"Well, if you put it that way," Chris demurred, his mouth watering. "*I* certainly don't hold grudges."

Cheerfully, he ambled along behind her, prepared to find out everything about this famous blueberry pie. Silken strands of her chestnut hair caught in the morning breeze and blew across his face.

Chris detected the faintest scent of wildflowers before Jori moved away, her hair trailing behind. His palms itched to grasp a gleaming handful. Tamping down the wish, he walked inside Jori's home once more.

"It's so lovely today." Jori waved toward the kitchen. "Why don't we have our coffee on the patio?"

Minutes later Chris had a huge piece of steaming blueberry pie in front of him as well as a fragrant mug of the dark brew she favored.

"I can't believe you bake, too," he murmured, more to himself. But she heard him.

She grinned, patting a wriggling Flop. "Now about the berries." She changed topics like quicksilver and Chris strained to follow, commanding his eyes to stop staring at the slim tanned column of her neck just visible in the vee of her long dress.

"You know Mrs. Selnes?" When his forehead furrowed in

thought, Jori reminded him. "Six kids, three under seven." His face didn't automatically clear so she fed him a little more info. "One of them ate part of a swab last week."

"Yeah, I remember," he agreed sourly. And he did. He wished she would let him forget that unruly mob.

"Well, she has a rather difficult time," Jori told him.

"Ha! That's taking understatement to new limits," he drawled, eyes open wide. "Six kids! That'd give anyone a hard time."

"Yes, well, anyway, Jennifer comes and picks the berries for money to buy a computer. Then I phone Mrs. Selnes and offer my extras. She needs everything she can get her hands on to feed those kids. Her husband is rather useless. I like to help her out. Goodness knows she's grateful enough." Jori's clear forehead creased in thought as she stared straight at him.

"The thing is," she continued, unabashed by his scrutiny. "If she knew I had paid to have them picked, she would insist on paying me and I don't want that." Big as saucers, her dark eyes beseeched him. "Just keep it under your hat, okay?"

Chris nodded slowly. "You mean like the dinner you sent out the other night?"

"How do you know about that?" Jori stared in surprise.

"I stopped in to see the old girl the next evening." He grinned. "Believe me the smell of that roast was memorable."

He chuckled in delight at the dark flush staining her creamy skin once more. She looked slim and very beautiful in the sleeveless yellow dress that flowed to her ankles. Jori's innate grace was apparent when she walked and he wondered again why her face was so familiar.

"I'm impressed," she teased, not quite as acidly as before. "A big-city doctor making house calls. Wow!"

"Thank you, Nurse Jessop. I try." He felt as if he'd finally passed an important test.

"So, what's the favor?" she demanded, obviously anxious to change the subject.

"Uh, the favor?" His mind was addled and Chris had a struggle to organize his thoughts. "Oh, the fair. I wondered if you would take me to the fair." It hadn't come out exactly the way he'd intended, but Chris wasn't going to fuss about that.

His deep blue eyes studied her intently as she digested his request. Her eyes were round with surprise and her pink lips formed a perfect *O*.

"You don't mean the Silven Stream Fair?" she blurted out, obviously aghast at the thought.

"Yeah, I think that's the one. It's some kind of a country fair, isn't it, on today and tomorrow?"

She nodded slowly, as the copper glimmers in her hair caught the sun. A fly buzzed near her face but Jori ignored it.

"Yes, it is, but it's hardly the kind of thing you would be interested in," she advised him. "Very small town, local people sort of thing. Not your stuff at all."

Chris knew he had it coming, but her immediate rebuff still stung, and made him even more determined to figure out just what held her here.

"All the more reason I should attend. I can find out more about this area and its people—what makes them tick." He played his ace where he knew it would do the most good. "That is what you advised, isn't it, Jori? Getting to know the community that I care for?"

He watched her sip a mouthful of coffee that she had laced with cream. Her eyes studied him seriously.

"You really want to go?" Skeptical didn't begin to cover her tone.

He nodded easily. Let her think about it for a moment. He was pretty sure she wouldn't be able to help showing off her prairie town. And if that was the only way he would get to know Miss Jori Jessop a little better, so be it. Besides, if it turned out the fair wasn't everything he'd heard it was going to be, at least he'd get another chance to try her blueberry pie.

"That was excellent," he murmured. "Thank you." Chris scraped his plate clean, swallowing the last bite with relish.

Jori sat silent, peering at him with that probing gaze until he decided to ask the question that had bothered him for days.

"Don't I know you from somewhere?" Her lips curved and Chris read her thoughts with ease. "It's not just a line," he protested, chuckling at her disbelief. "I keep thinking I've met you somewhere, before Mossbank, and yet I'm positive I never have."

"I used to be a model." She burst out giggling at the look of disbelief on his face. "Really. I guess you've probably seen my pictures in some magazines, although I haven't done anything for the last few years."

He studied the fresh oval of her face more clearly and decided that she had the perfect look for a cover girl. He didn't remember specifically, but he was sure now that he had seen her picture somewhere.

"You used to have shorter hair," he muttered, considering the long fall of hair that trailed over her shoulder. Suddenly he stared straight at her, and asked, "Why did you get into modeling?"

Jori didn't try to evade the question. She merely shrugged her shoulders and stated the bare facts.

"My father became ill, he forgot where he was going or what he was doing. Eventually he was diagnosed with Alzheimer's. He needed round-the-clock care. The pay was good, so I took as many assignments as I could to pay for full-time nursing care at home." She glanced up, tears glistening at the corners of her eyes.

"Dad was always less confused when he was at home and so I tried to keep him comfortable there." She stopped for a moment before continuing. Her voice shook. "He got worse in spite of the best nursing I could afford. I was on a shoot, my last one, when they phoned to say he'd hurt himself."

"I'm sorry, Jori. I didn't know." Chris awkwardly stretched out his big hand to cover hers, uncomfortable with her distress.

She smiled through her tears, wiping a hand carelessly across her eyes. "It's all right," she murmured. "He knows the Lord and in his own way he's happy now. Happy and healthy. Even if he's in the nursing home." The assurance in her voice tugged at his heartstrings. "Anyway—" her soft musical voice caught his ear again "—I decided to come home for a while so I could be near him. I finished up my nursing degree, which I had started before Dad got sick, and I've been living contentedly here ever since."

Chris detected the slight hesitation in her words and knew there was something she wasn't saying. "But . . . ?" he questioned, waiting quietly for her to finish.

"Why do you say that?" she demurred, keeping her eyes averted from his. Her slim hands twisted the napkin lying on the picnic table.

"I came back to help my father. Instead I hurt him." Jori's voice was bitter with remorse. Darkly glowing, her eyes stared off into space until she took a deep breath and launched into her story.

"After I'd been home for a week, my fiancé came for a visit. He came to show me some pictures of me that had been published in the tabloids. I had never authorized them, and I don't know where they came from." Her beautiful face was filled with distress as she half whispered to him.

"Everybody saw them. The whole country was talking about my promiscuous behavior." Her face was strained as she steered her eyes away from his. "They were shots, supposedly of me, nude on a beach." Her voice was filled with pain. Chris could only imagine having his privacy invaded so intensely. "They were pasteups. You know—" she motioned "—my head, someone else's body." Her eyes were sad.

"I couldn't have gone back to modeling the exclusive lines if I'd wanted to then. My contract specifically said no nudity." Jori grimaced at him. "It was a clause I'd insisted on and Gaston's held me to it. They said I'd degraded them." The last words came out on a whisper of shame.

"The tabloids made a lot of money from those photos but they practically ruined my life. I couldn't get work. Everywhere I went people stared at me with a funny little smile. It was awful. So I stayed holed up in Mossbank where everyone was as kind as could be. Someone finally admitted that the pictures were tampered photos that had been released without my permission. I sued and the magazine paid but legal costs ate it." Her chest lifted with the weight of her sigh.

"I found justice, but it was too late. My fiancé decided he'd had enough when I decided to stay here. Trace didn't want a small-town hick for a wife. He was my manager and had always encouraged my modeling, especially when the money started to really come in. Trace liked the high life—traveling, the whole thing." Jori thrust out her chin defiantly, her words bitter and hard.

"He announced our breakup in a national magazine that paid him for the story and then he moved on with a friend of mine. Maybe you've heard of her—Sabrina LeClair?"

Chris nodded, remembering the name from some party or another, he thought. But his mind was busy with Jori's story. He could guess the rest. She had stayed here, safe and secure in her little town, away from the prying eyes of the world. And her trust in people had never returned.

Suddenly, she straightened. He watched as a mask fell over the expressive but sad features as Jori pulled back into her shell and once more became the courteous but reserved woman he recognized from the office.

"So, Doctor, I don't know where you saw me, but I suppose that's why I seem familiar." She picked up their used cups and his empty plate and moved through the patio doors to the kitchen.

"I'll take you to the fair if you promise me that you will try to see these people for who they are. They're kind and good and they'd give you the shirt off their backs. I know a country fair is no big deal to you but for some of them, it's an event that they anxiously wait for. Don't spoil it."

Her soft, melodic voice was hard with censure, but Chris let it go. He knew her emotions were still whirling and she needed distance. He decided to give her some space.

"When do we leave?" he asked, bending to tickle the dog lying at his feet.

"I'm going to see my dad this morning so I'll pick you up at one. If you're not ready, I'll go without you." The pain and sadness had left her face. She was a woman defending her town.

"And bring a jacket," she ordered, walking in front of him to the door. "It will get very cool before we get home."

"Yes, ma'am," he answered cheekily, saluting irreverently. "Anything else?"

"Yes," Jori returned, her eyes coming to life again. "Be prepared."

"I'm always prepared," he said, and bent to brush her cheek lightly with his lips. "Thanks for telling me, Jori. And for what it's worth, I am coming to enjoy Mossbank. And its people."

She didn't look at him, but kept her dark gaze fixed on her hands. Chris flicked her cheek with one long finger before turning to march down the walk and along the driveway. He whistled cheerily as he sauntered home.

How about that, he had a date. And with the most gorgeous woman this side of the Rockies. Chris chuckled. He guessed he hadn't quite lost his touch. He hoped!

"What's got your face glowing like the sun on a hot July afternoon?" an elderly lady asked him as he strode past.

Chris stopped and turned, searching his memory for the name.

"I'll tell you, Mrs. Flowerday," he confessed, knowing he couldn't keep it quiet any longer, "I just got myself a ride to that fair we were talking about the other day and it's with my beautiful office nurse."

"Jordanna agreed to take you? Isn't that wonderful?" The little old granny beamed from ear to ear. "She needs an outing with a nice handsome man. You are nice, aren't you?" she asked severely. "I'll not stand idly by while you play with her like that other scoundrel did. I should have smacked him when I had the opportunity."

"No, ma'am." Chris gulped. He stared at her frowning face for a moment and then amended. "I mean, yes, ma'am, I think I'm a nice enough guy."

"Jordanna's the salt of the earth, she just doesn't believe in herself anymore. She's been banged up and bruised by life. Needs a little patience and some love, that's all."

Mrs. Flowerday peered up into the sky and Chris allowed himself a grin as he wondered how Jori would feel about being thought of in that way.

"I won't hurt her, ma'am," he assured the old lady softly and felt the power of those warm brown eyes focus on him once more. "She's been very kind to me, made me feel right at home."

Charity Flowerday snorted derisively.

"Don't try to snowball me, young man," she chided, hitching up her purse under her arm and starting off down the street. "I heard the two of you going at it in the office."

"Yes," he admitted crestfallen as he walked along beside her. "I'm afraid she is rather peeved at me most of the time. She thinks I don't appreciate her little town enough. I'm not sure why it's so important to her." He felt the testing pinch on his biceps and wondered why people always thought little old ladies were weak. He'd have a bruise there from those arthritic fingers.

"Well, you're strong! You can take it," Charity sang out over her shoulder as she veered off away from him. "That indignation is a good sign. If Jori didn't speak to you at all, you'd have something to worry about, now wouldn't you?"

As he rubbed his arm all the way home, Chris decided the woman was probably right.

Probably.

"I'm telling you, Hope, he is attracted to her. Very attracted." Charity beamed at her friends. "I was talking to him and he seemed most interested in Jordanna."

"I'm most interested in who you had over to dinner last night, Charity. Why won't you tell us? Is it a secret?"

"A secret? Oh, my!" Faith breathed softly.

"Hope Conroy, you know blamed well that I hate that word. Faith battens on to it as if it's the next thing to heaven and now she won't give me any peace. Honestly!" Charity rolled her eyes, glaring at her best friends.

"Is it a secret man?" Faith whispered, winking at Hope. "Have you got a secret friend, Charity?" She clapped her hands in delight. "I know! It's Frank, isn't it? He's the secret!"

"You see!" Charity glared at Hope angrily, before huffing into her lawn chair. "No, Faith, it isn't Frank. I'd never invite him to dinner."

"Why not?" Faith demanded in an affronted tone. "Arthur says he's a very nice man. They go fishing together all the time."

"Good! Then Arthur can take him out to dinner. I'm not interested!"

"But why not, Charity? He's a perfectly lovely man. So interesting. Harry says . . ." Hope sank into a thickly padded wicker chair before reaching over to pour out three cups of tea.

"For the fifth time, Hope, I do not care what Harry says!" Charity's voice rose indignantly. "I have no interest in the local undertaker!"

"I just wanted to know why," Hope murmured soothingly. "There must be something that's made you react so negatively."

"You two," Charity sputtered at last. "Why can't you let me alone?" She sat up and straightened her skirt, shifting her swollen ankles onto a nearby rock. "All right, I'll tell you."

The other two visitors leaned in, as if coconspirators in a plan of the utmost secrecy.

"Frank Bellows never says anything."

"Oh, piffle! He's always talking about his life in Australia and the time he spent in Switzerland," Faith cried indignantly. "You can hardly get a word in edgewise when he starts going on about his daughter in Italy."

Charity felt her mouth flop open in surprise.

"He has a daughter? In Italy? Oh." Her face reddened. "Well, I never knew that. He doesn't say a word to me."

"Have you actually talked to him?" Hope demanded, her face drawn into the severe lines she'd used with her students in the past. "Most times I notice you whisk right past him at church. He'd have to hold you down to talk to you."

"That's because I thought, well, that is . . . I wondered if maybe he wasn't . . ." Charity felt her face grow redder by the moment as she searched for the right word. "Wasn't a little . . . you know?"

"*I* don't know," Faith told them loudly. "What does she mean, Hope?"

"I don't know either, Faith. What do you mean, Charity?" There was a hint of cold steel in Hope's sharp blue eyes.

"I thought he was either deaf or a little bit crazy," Charity blurted out at last. "He always stumbles and stammers whenever he says something. I thought maybe he was handicapped!"

"And so you avoided him because of that? Charity Flowerday, I'm amazed at you!" Hope's forehead was furrowed. "I thought we'd all learned our lesson about judging by appearances long ago." She poured another cup of tea for herself and absently added a cube of sugar. "You've probably made him so nervous, he doesn't know what to say," she expostulated.

"He's probably sick to death of being pressured by you two!" Charity glowered angrily at her friends. "I keep telling you, I don't need a man in my life to be happy. I'm perfectly content the way I am. I enjoy solitude. It gives me time to read and think. I'm managing very well!"

"Oh, Charity," Faith murmured, patting the gnarled old hand tenderly as her eyes filled with tears. "Of course you are. And we didn't mean to upset you." She swiped away the tears with the back of her hand and sniffed in a way that brought a frown to Hope's clear countenance.

"It's just that we don't want you to be left out. We've been so happy lately, now that we've found Arthur and Harry and we're worried about leaving you alone too much."

"Besides," Hope added dourly. "Having a man around can make life interesting. And there's always someone to do things with."

"Right now, all I want is to relax and enjoy the sunshine," Charity told them smartly. "If I want a companion, there are several friends I can ask. Or I'll get a dog. *I do not need a man.*"

"Oh, my." Faith giggled. "I don't think a dog could replace Arthur. Especially when he keeps my feet warm at night."

Charity glanced heavenward and sighed. "I already have a hot water bottle," she muttered darkly.

Chapter Four

"Hi, Dad. How are you today?" Jori leaned over to press a kiss against her father's weathered cheek and breathed in the spicy scent of his aftershave. The memories it brought back coaxed tears from her eyes and she brushed them away. Now wasn't the time to get maudlin.

" *'And He said to them, "Why are you troubled and why do doubts arise in your hearts?" Luke 24:38.'* " James Jessop inclined his salt-and-pepper head toward his daughter, his eyes intent in their scrutiny. " *'Fear not.'* " His faded gray eyes studied her intently. "Do I know you?"

"It's Jori, Dad," she murmured softly, clasping his hand in hers. "Do you want to walk in the courtyard? It's nice and warm today."

"All right." Tall and thin, James Jessop ambled to the door, his hand protectively under her elbow. "Mind the step, miss," he murmured.

Jori searched his face, praying that today would be one of his better ones. She needed him; needed to lean on him for a bit.

Her father held out an armchair for her before slouching down in a lounge next to her and closing his eyes to the bright sunlight.

"I love the feel of the sun," he murmured. "It's like heaven is shining right down on me. When it was sunny, Ruth used to say the windows of heaven were open. I miss Ruth."

Jori smiled at this hint that his memory was still there. Somewhere. "So do I, Dad."

She sat quietly, content to be near him as he dozed in the sunlight. He seemed calmer today and she was thankful for that. Perhaps, at last, her father was really settling in to Sunset.

"Hi, Jori!" Melanie Stewart called out from the doorway. "Your dad's having a good day today. He ate quite a big breakfast." She stopped as soon as James's eyes opened. "Good morning, Mr. Jessop. Had a good nap?"

"I wasn't napping, Melanie." James's voice was coolly rational. "I was just resting my eyes. I never sleep during the day. It's a waste of time."

"Of course." Melanie winked at Jori and waved. "I have to get back to work. Have a good visit."

"Jori, dear!" James hugged her tightly. "When did you arrive?"

"Oh, just a few moments ago," she told him. "I just needed to see my dad for a few minutes. How are you?"

"Happy to stare at the beautiful woman my daughter has become," he averred proudly. "And don't frown like that. You are beautiful. Everyone knows it."

"Beauty is only skin deep, Dad. Isn't that what you always used to say?"

"Did I?" James frowned. "Well, I was wrong. I think beauty goes right to the soul in some people and you're one of them, Jori." He hugged her close and then leaned back. "You're not still thinking about that young man, are you?"

"What young man?" Jori pushed the image of Chris's handsomely smiling countenance out of her mind.

"Hmmm. Who makes you blush like that?" James teased, flicking a finger against her cheek. "*I* was talking about that exceptionally dull young man you brought to visit me one time. Travis or something, wasn't it? Who were you thinking about?" His eyes were bright and Jori felt relief that he was still able to connect that much from the past, even if it was terribly hurtful for her.

"It was Trace," she offered quietly. "And no, I wasn't thinking of him at all. We have a new doctor, Dad. I've been working with him for a couple of weeks now."

"Hmmm," James Jessop murmured. "Seems to me I should know that. Who told me? Faith? No, Charity, I think. Somebody told me something about a doctor." The confusion on his dear face was painful to see and Jori patted his hand.

"It doesn't matter. Anyway, his name is Christopher and he's from the big city. He's very famous." Jori wondered why she'd chosen this particular topic.

"Not that famous," a voice murmured from behind them.

Jori whirled around to stare into those bright blue eyes and felt the heat rise in her cheeks at his knowing grin.

"Dad, this is the man I was telling you about, Dr. Christopher Davis. Dr. Davis, this is my father, James Jessop."

"I know him!" James's voice was excited. "Plays chess like a pro." He beamed happily up at them.

"Not nearly as well as you, Mr. Jessop." Chris grinned. "I've yet to win a game."

"You see," her father teased, patting Jori's cheek. "I haven't lost all my marbles." He frowned as her face fell. "None of that, my dear. It was a joke. How can you not laugh on such a wonderful day?"

"Oh, Dad," she whispered tearfully. "I love you."

"Come now, dearest." James brushed his hand over her swath of glistening hair. "I have few enough good days. Let's just enjoy the ones God gives us." His eyes twinkled merrily. "What have you got planned for today?" he asked curiously.

"Actually, Jori's taking me to the fair," Chris said, butting in. "I'd better get moving. She said if I wasn't ready she'd leave me behind." He grinned at the older man. "I think she means it, too."

"Don't pay too much attention to what my daughter says," James advised solemnly. His eyes were serious. "Sometimes she doesn't express her true feelings, but that's because she's been hurt."

Jori could feel Chris's fathomless blue eyes on her, studying her closely. She tried to pretend a nonchalance she didn't feel.

"Oh, Dad." She laughed nervously. "We're not going in to all that old history today, are we?"

But neither her father nor Chris was paying any attention to her. Each studied the other with an intensity that sent little waves of apprehension up her spine. Finally James nodded, as if he'd found what he sought.

"You take care of her," he ordered in a firm no-nonsense voice that Jori hadn't heard since high school. "I don't want my daughter hurt again."

Chris nodded, shaking the other man's hand with a firm grip.

"Don't worry," he murmured. "I won't hurt her." His eyes were speculative as they slipped over Jori's still silent figure, and she felt the old familiar doubts wash over her until his soft words reached her ears. "See you after lunch."

After that, James seemed content to talk sporadically and Jori finally left him in the dining room, ready to sample the barbecue lunch.

"See you tomorrow," she whispered, kissing his cheek. "Take care."

"First Peter 5:7. *'Let Him have all your worries and cares, for He is always thinking about you and watching everything that concerns you,'*" James quoted, smiling at her. "It's a promise, Jori. You can depend on it, you know."

"I know. Thanks, Dad." Jori drove home thinking about those words and trying to apply them to herself. But it made little difference. She still felt the same old apprehensions and qualms assail her. Why didn't she feel the sense of peace that her father did?

"Aren't you there, God?" she prayed at last, as she changed her clothes. "Can't you see how much I need my father right now?" But there was no response from heaven and Jori was left wondering if God cared at all.

"I'm doing this as a favor to him," Jori told herself sternly. "That's all. It's not as if I need a man to complicate my life."

She brought the Jeep to a stop in front of Dr. Dan's house barely two minutes before one. If Chris was ready, they should make good time driving to the fairground. As one of the judges for the children's entries in the exhibits, she liked to arrive early enough to look everything over thoroughly before settling down to reward the best.

It looked as if someone had recently cut the lawn, she mused, glad to see the city doctor was taking good care of their own doctor's home. She wanted everything perfect when Dan and Jessica returned—with their little one, God willing.

When Christopher didn't appear, Jori honked the horn once and then checked the mirror again. Why, she didn't know. What did she care if her hair was mussed or lipstick smeared? Chris Davis's opinion meant absolutely nothing to her, she told herself.

Yeah, right, her heart thumped.

He came strolling out the front door, wearing perfectly creased designer blue jeans and a thin pale blue cotton shirt with a designer logo on the pocket. The blue only enhanced the sapphire sparkle of his eyes.

He looks gorgeous, she decided and then chided her brain for noticing. Dr. Christopher Davis was not her type, Jori reminded herself. Not at all.

Chris tossed his black bag and jacket onto the back seat before folding himself into the front. Then he stared at her curiously.

"Somehow, this isn't what I had pictured you driving," he said, head tilted to one side as he watched her manipulate the steering wheel of her Jeep.

"I didn't know you pictured me doing anything," Jori returned pertly, pulling expertly away from the curb before shifting gears. Her long dark hair whipped behind her in the breeze and she tucked the strands behind her ear.

"Exactly what did you picture me driving, Doc?" The question was only half-teasing, her brown eyes crinkling at the corners.

"Something more sedate," Chris replied and then added, "and stop calling me that. You know my name."

"Yes, sir," Jori replied, tongue in cheek. "Sedate? Thanks a lot. It just so happens that this was a bonus from one of my contracts." She patted the black console lovingly. "I can tell you, it's come in very handy during some of our blizzards. No matter what, Baby and I can always get through."

"Baby?" His blue eyes twinkled with mirth. "You really have a way with names, Jori." His long lean fingers marked off the names. "Flop. Baby. What's next?" His mouth tipped up.

"Makes me wonder about your children's future." His face was wreathed in smiles.

Jori merely turned off the highway onto a gravel road, refusing to answer him. He was quiet for a few minutes and then began questioning her.

"Where is this fair held, anyway?" He searched the waving fields of grain that stretched out around them. "I can't see a thing but this stuff."

"This *stuff* is what pays the bills, Doc. And don't you forget it." Jori's voice was firm with reproof. No one would get away with disparaging her county. When she noticed his wide startled eyes focused on her in surprise, she relented a little.

"We have to weave in and out here for a bit," she told him. "Then you'll see an old barn on one side and a house on the other, just before we cross the river. It's not far after that."

Jori burst out laughing at the look of shock holding Chris's handsome features immobile.

"People come away out here just for a fair?" He sounded confused by the whole thing. Jori could hardly wait for the look on his face when they arrived.

"Oh, a few do." She smirked. There was no way this smug city doctor could understand just what this event meant for the area without having lived here. She didn't want to spoil the effect Jori knew it would have on him.

"This must be the house and barn," Chris noticed, studying the weathered old buildings standing sturdily by. He peered through the window looking for the river. Evidently, the carved landscape gave him a slight clue, but he continued to peer down.

"Where's the water?" he complained more to himself than to her.

Jori pressed her lips tightly together, refusing to answer. As they crested the hill, she watched his blue eyes widen in amazement. There were vehicles parked everywhere. On the sides of the road, in the ditch, beside a row of poplars. Grouped together on any open area of unused field, they numbered in the hundreds.

"Wow," he breathed.

Jori burst out laughing. She couldn't help it.

"Come on," she said, pulling in beside a muddy half-ton. "I hope you remembered sunscreen," she observed, privately thinking that his darkly tanned skin was less likely to burn than her own.

"Yes, ma'am," Chris teased, swinging out of her vehicle.

The shimmering wave of heat hit him flat-out and Jori watched as he caught his breath.

Chris followed her lithe figure down the narrow trail to what he presumed was the fair entrance. Jori walked with an unconscious grace, her long legs bare in the summer sun. He liked her outfit, he decided.

She wore a denim skirt and matching vest that left slim, lightly tanned arms bare. Jori had twisted her hair into a ponytail that flowed down her back like toffee. On her feet she wore canvas flats that kept out the dust. He suddenly felt overdressed.

She quickly paid the two elderly gentlemen the fare posted on a piece of cardboard.

"No charge for the workers, Jordanna," they told her. Grinning, she threw the money into the box on the tabletop. "It's a donation then," she called merrily.

Chris felt her hand on his, tugging him along. "Come on, Doctor," she urged. "I'm late, thanks to you. Don't make it a habit, okay?"

"Late for what?" he asked. Unfortunately the answer eluded him as they walked through an arch of maples to a sight Chris was sure came straight out of the 1800s.

The fairground was set in a huge circular area surrounded on all but the west side by towering green poplars. To the left were a few older buildings. One had a sign on it announcing the Welton School 1958-1977. Beside that stood a long, low building with the word *Exhibits* across the entrance. A broad red ribbon prevented anyone from entering.

Directly in front of him was a softball field where Chris noticed a group of people of all ages eagerly cheering on their teams from weathered bleachers placed on the sidelines. He could hear old-time fiddle music coming from the red-and-white-striped tent behind the diamond. And everywhere there was the smell of horses. Sometimes stronger, sometimes fainter, but always there.

Well, he reflected, it wasn't the World's Fair but it was still pretty interesting. Especially the collection of old machinery puffing and grunting across the way. It looked like some type of tractor pull, but then what did he know about farm machinery?

He felt someone yanking on his arm and looked down dazedly. Jori stood there saying something. He shook his head to clear it before looking down at her again.

"What?"

"I have to go to the exhibit hall to judge the children's work. Do you want to come, or would you rather look around?" She was tapping her foot impatiently and Chris made up his mind quickly.

"I'll go with you first. Then maybe I'll look around." He stared at the people milling about the grounds. "Where did they all come from?" he wondered bemusedly.

Jori giggled, and he decided he liked the sound of her laugh.

"From about a thirty-mile radius. Everyone just shows up when they want. Come on," she urged, trying to hurry him.

She pointed out the bathrooms tucked into the far corner of the grounds. Chris had a sneaking suspicion they were outdoor toilets, although he'd never personally had the opportunity to use one before. My, how his narrow life was being enhanced!

"All the ladies' aid groups offer food for sale to raise money for their charities," she told him. "We'll eat later. They have pies of all kinds here." Jori grinned up at him, her white teeth flashing in the hot sun. "You should be able to pig out to your heart's content."

Chris leered at her playfully, before hugging her shoulders to his big body in a burst of happiness, caught up in the festivities. He did notice that she immediately tugged away from him, and filed that information away for future thought.

Inside the building, it was hot; hotter than outside, he decided. He watched carefully as Jori greeted her friends and then introduced him to those he didn't know. He saw the glimmers of speculation in their eyes and wondered if she was aware of it also.

"I'm going to look around, Jori," he told Jori, who was bent over the sheaf of poems and samples of handwriting submitted for a prize. He touched her arm to gain her attention and noticed that she pulled away immediately but only answered, "Mmm-hmm."

"I'll catch up with you later," he whispered in her ear, deliberately brushing his hand over her back. When she didn't flinch, he moved away, smugly satisfied that she hadn't reacted negatively to his touch. He wondered if Jordanna Jessop would ever thaw out enough to let him hold her the way he wanted to.

Christopher surveyed the room dourly. He gave a cursory glance at the huge cabbages that stood out among the produce displayed, but only because everyone else was. He dutifully smelled the flowers, checked out the ladies' handiwork, the coloring contest and the children's crafts, following the example of those in front.

Then he left, but not before a large woman in a huge straw hat talked him into purchasing tickets for a door prize to be drawn for later in the day.

"What do I win?" he asked innocently.

"A kid," the woman told him, beaming happily.

He had to think twice before he realized she didn't mean one of the human variety. Chris paid for the tickets, sincerely hoping he wouldn't win. There was little room in Dan's backyard for a goat!

Outside, the baseball game was in full swing and he watched from the edge of the stands for a few minutes before deciding to take a closer look at the old school. It was dim inside, with that stale, dusty odor all schools seem to retain.

The old-fashioned desks were a curiosity and he wedged himself gingerly into one until someone else came in. There were initials carved here and there throughout the building and he grinned as he thought of those lovesick kids. A tarnished bell stood atop the teacher's desk, waiting to call the next class to order.

Across the top of the blackboard, the alphabet was carefully chalked in. Underneath, someone had drawn a huge heart with an arrow through. *A.J. and D.S.* Chris wondered idly whose initials they were.

At the back of the schoolhouse, an intense game of horseshoes was being waged between several older men. Chris stood to the side watching until a familiar voice caught his attention.

"Hi, Doc. How's it going?" Aubery Olden stood before him, hand outstretched. As he shook the old man's hand, Chris found himself also checking for other signs. Mr. Olden was one of the few patients Dan had asked Chris to particularly watch out for.

"I'm fine, Mr. Olden. It's a gorgeous day for your fair, isn't it?" The old man's color was good, although he was breathing quite heavily.

They bantered back and forth a bit before Aubery offered him some personal advice.

"If you're after Miss Jordanna, Doc, you will have to take your time. She's a lady who has been depending on herself for so long, she doesn't find it easy to lean on anybody else." The old man coughed loudly for a moment and then grinned. His weathered old face creased with happiness as he spoke.

"But you'll never find a lady more worthy of your love, Doc. She's a fine one, our Miss Jordanna. Looks after everybody without them even asking." He cackled a rasping sound Chris thought was meant to be a laugh. "She ain't too hard on the eyes, either!"

They grinned at each other while Chris's thoughts swirled round and round. As Aubery explained the game, Chris asked himself how the man had known his very personal thoughts. The old gent was cagey in the extreme, but to Chris's certain knowledge, he and Jori had never been together outside of the office, at least not in anyone's sight before. Anyway, the old guy was off the track a bit.

He liked the very gorgeous Miss Jessop, all right. She floated through his thoughts at the oddest moments. He wanted to kiss her, just once. But she backed off every time he even touched her.

Love? Chris wasn't sure he knew what that was. And he was pretty sure that Jordanna Jessop hadn't the least intention of allowing him to get anywhere near that close. He'd seen the flash of interest in her café au lait eyes, of course. But Jori had told him in too many ways to count that her allegiance was with her townsfolk and in her opinion, he didn't fit in. With a sigh, Chris acknowledged that she was right. He was just passing through.

Wandering again, Chris moved over to the children's play area to watch for a few moments. He considered what it would be like to come to a fair like this with your own kids. Surely children these days knew that bigger and better exhibitions could be found most anywhere. Why would they be content to come here?

And yet, as Chris watched, they eagerly participated in the three-legged races and the potato sack races. He watched them follow the one lone clown about the grounds, giggling with delight when Chuckles finally handed them a balloon.

The scene tugged at his subconscious somehow and Chris was deep in thought when long, cool fingers covered his eyes.

"Having fun?" The voice was low and seductive and Chris knew immediately that Mirabel Matthews was behind him. Ducking away, he turned to smile coolly at her.

"Hello, Mrs. Matthews." Chris deliberately addressed her in this manner in an effort to keep their exchange as formal as possible, while praying fervently for Jori's return.

The town's loneliest widow stood clad in the tightest white pants he had ever seen. She wore a top to match in a plunging bikini style that looked vulgarly out of place in the country setting of cotton and denim. Glittering diamonds winked at her ears, deep in her cleavage and on her long-nailed fingers.

"Doctor," she remonstrated, "how can you be so formal at a country fair? Call me Mirabel."

Her arm snaked through his and Chris found there was little he could do to disentangle himself. She was like a boa constrictor, he decided dismally, waiting to squeeze the life out of him. Desperately, he glanced over her shoulder, surreptitiously searching for Jori among those curious folks who ambled past.

"Does this make you long for your own little ones?" she drawled, oblivious to his discomfort.

"What? Uh, no, uh . . . I don't have any. Little ones, I mean." He sucked in a breath of air and tried to extricate himself. "That is, I was just looking, Mrs. Matthews, while I wait for Jori. That's who I came with."

Could he get any clearer than that? Chris wondered. He glanced away from her black-rimmed eyes with their false lashes, trying to avoid the abundant cleavage she was flaunting as he lifted the long, slim octopuslike arm from around his neck and stepped backward.

"Oh, there she is. Sorry, Mrs. Matthews, but we promised to . . ." Chris let the sentence die away as he yanked his arm from her bloodred-tipped manacles and marched over to the woman who stood across the way, grinning merrily from one gold-hooped ear to the other.

"Thanks a lot," he muttered, brushing his shirt down. To his amazement, two of the buttons had come undone. "The least you could have done was help me get away from that barracuda." His voice was accusing but he was quite sure Jori felt no pity.

Instead, her dark eyes beamed up at him.

"Didn't want to interrupt," she said with a giggle. "Seemed to me that you and Mirabel were getting along famously."

"I need something cool," he rasped. "Where did you get that?" He pointed to the orange-colored ice she held in her hand.

"Come on." She tugged on his arm. "I'll show you. After a run-in with Mirabel, I'm surprised that's all you need."

It *wasn't* all that he needed, not nearly. But Chris decided that a triple-decker ice cream might just fill his mouth enough that he wouldn't say anything too stupid. Maybe he'd even be able to carry on a normal conversation.

Jori found a spot in the covered wooden stands where they could sit protected from the sun while they watched the young 4-H riders take each horse through its paces. But even in the shade with a breeze blowing, it was hot.

After they finished their icy treats, the two of them strolled past the booths housing the different ladies' groups who sold their wares to hungry visitors.

A surfboard sat on a bed of air, begging adults and kids alike to try their skills. In the background there was a long, narrow awning under which any who wished to play bingo could sit in the shade and lose money. It was probably the coolest place on the grounds and Chris wondered for a moment if he could learn to play a game he'd never considered even remotely interesting.

Jori, however, was indefatigable. She dragged him past the air house filled with multicolored balls and insisted on spending precious moments in the hot, hot sun trying to placate the crying child whose mother wouldn't allow yet another turn on a ride that made him dizzy.

"Isn't it great? Hi, Mrs. Flowerday. Wonderful afternoon for the fair, isn't it?" Jori beamed at the elderly woman who sat decked out in red gingham under a striped umbrella clipped to the arm of her plastic chair.

"It's just lovely, dear." The warm brown eyes slid over the two of them, widening appreciatively as Chris guided Jori out of the path of several wild youngsters. "You two have a happy time, now," she directed cheerfully.

"We will." They moved on through the growing numbers, pausing to chat with a hundred different people that Chris was positive he'd never seen around Mossbank and wouldn't remember if they came into the office tomorrow.

He wasn't sure exactly how it happened, but when Jori gleefully coaxed him onto the giant trampolines, he went, jumping and bouncing as she dared him to leap even higher. Which he did—just to prove he could, of course.

Laughing uncontrollably and giggling so hard she lost her footing, Jori fell in a heap of laughter, long legs sprawled across the surface, tangling with his. Chris wondered if his blood temperature, which was already steaming while they untangled themselves, would withstand the rest of the afternoon.

"I think I've had enough of that for a while," he said firmly, pulling her away from the center.

"Okay." She bounded over the side. "But it's so much fun. One of these days I'm going to buy a trampoline just for myself."

Lest she drag him into some other trap, Chris steered her away from the three children's rides to the animal barns.

"This is my least favorite place!" He watched as Jori's nose curled in distaste at the strong smells, but she obediently walked beside him checking the pens of sheep, cows, steers, rabbits and pigs. As they walked, Jori explained the intricacies of judging animals.

"Many of the local people prepare their livestock in order to win a trophy or one of the cash prizes sponsored by the town's businesses. Lots of the contestants are children. Oh, just look at this." She pointed.

Her good-natured laughter burst out again when she read the plaque someone had hung on the end of the barn, donating a cash prize for the biggest *bore* shown in memory of their father.

"I wonder if he was a big *bore,* too," she said, chuckling with glee, brushing Chris's shoulder with her hand as she laughingly drew his attention to the words.

The motion, innocent as it was, spread a trail of fire across his chest. It was the first time she had willingly touched him and he was loath to move. But if he hugged her back, would she push him away?

"This is too rich! A bore, for goodness' sake! Oh, I can't take any more."

"Neither can I," Chris agreed. "I'm too hot." He fanned his hand across his warm cheeks, wishing for a sudden rainstorm.

Suddenly sober and strangely aware of his intense scrutiny, Jori realized that she was hot, too. But she wasn't sure exactly how much was due to the temperature and how much to the man standing next to her. Even with bits of straw sticking out of his mussed blond hair, he looked inordinately handsome.

Chris Davis got to her the way few other men ever had. And that bothered her. A lot. It also raised an immoderate amount of curiosity in her vivid imagination. Jori wondered fleetingly what would happen if he ever broke through the shell of reserve she held tightly around herself.

Here, in the center of the compound, it was hotter than ever. All at once Jori thought of her special hideout.

"I know the perfect place," she told him grinning, the image floating into her mind like a mirage. Without thinking, she grabbed his arm, urging him past the throng of people waiting to register for a school reunion.

"Come on," she begged. "There's nothing really happening till after supper anyhow, and we'll be back by then."

Chris made her stand still long enough to collar two sodas and a neatly wrapped plate of watermelon from a nearby refreshment stand.

Jori tugged on his arm, her expressive eyes sparkling in anticipation. "Hurry," she ordered, matching her strides to his longer one.

"What's the rush?" he asked, feeling the trickle of sweat down his backbone. "We'll both die of heatstroke if you don't slow down."

Jori ignored him and whizzed away for a moment to speak to one of the men at the gate before he felt her slim, firm hand digging into his arm again.

"All right, all right," he grumped. "I'm coming."

Chris knew that the Jeep would be a furnace and while she unlocked and opened the door, he held back. When he thought he was prepared, he looked inside. Jori was already in her seat, feet on the pedals, impatiently ready to put the vehicle in motion.

"Get in." She waved.

Chris leaned back in his seat. He had no idea where they were going, but his beeper hadn't gone off yet so he would play along for a while. Groggily, he let his eyelids fall as he savored the light breeze from the dashboard vent.

Seconds later, a hard pinch on his upper arm brought reality back with a slam. Jori's big brown eyes were peering into his, mere inches away. Her face was tight with stress until he looked at her and then her generous smile cut a swath across her face.

"Sheesh, I thought you were dead for a minute there." Her voice was light and airy as she straightened away.

"Come on, I want to show you something," she said, looking like a cat that had just downed the canary. Chris reluctantly stretched himself out of the vehicle, loath to leave the cool confines as a wave of heat smacked him squarely in the chest.

"Leave the car running, I'll just watch from here," he told her. Jori swung the keys on one finger.

"You'll need these then." She grinned, stepping backward. "And I'm going down there."

Chris looked around curiously. They were in some sort of hollow. There were trees all around, creating a kind of hidden alcove. The road they had followed in was not much more than a dirt track. Directly in front of the Jeep was a pool of water fed by a tiny stream.

Jori disappeared behind a bush. A few moments later she emerged clad in a swimsuit. He was half-afraid to look, but curiosity got the better of him and he stared through the overhanging leaves.

He caught his breath as he watched her long lithe figure stride with ease to the edge of the glistening pool. She wore a black swimsuit that wasn't in the least exotic. He could just make out a thin black strap across her back before she plunged into the clear water with a squeal of delight.

Slowly, feeling like the atmosphere was pressing in on him, Chris walked to the edge of the pool. Jori surfaced near him, her dark hair streaming out behind her, her eyes glittering with suppressed excitement.

"Come on in," she coaxed, splashing some water on him. "It's not very cold, but it sure feels great." She dived under the water gracefully, her shiny red toenails the last to disappear. Seconds later she was standing before him again, her chest filling as she gasped for air.

Chris knew Jordanna Jessop was beautiful. She'd been to exotic places, played with world famous celebrities. And yet as this strong vibrant woman with her mane of walnut hair splashed joyfully in the tiny pool, Chris had the impression that he didn't really know her at all. And it was imperative that he find out what lay behind that tough, glossy facade.

He took off his shoes, pausing to stare at her solemnly.

"I can't go in." He sighed. He dipped his toes into the water and then rolled up his pant legs, eager to immerse more of his overheated frame.

"Why not?" Jori stared at him, head tilted to one side. Her long lashes were spiky with droplets of water and they blinked at him innocently. "You look really hot."

He needed her to tell him that! Chris groaned.

"I haven't got a suit." It should have been obvious, he thought. Jori just smirked.

"There's a suit of my dad's in the back of the Jeep. You're welcome to try it if you like. It's a little old-fashioned, but . . ." Her voice died away as she stared at him standing on the edge of the river as if rooted to the spot. Her eyes opened wide and he saw a flicker of something in their depths before she blinked and shrugged her indifference.

"Suit yourself," she called over her slim shoulders, then dashed deeper into the water once more, her body flashing in the dappled sunlight, hair gleaming like a seal's coat.

Chris sat there for about thirty seconds before his hand went to his perspiring forehead. In for a penny, in for a pound. He could hardly wait to sink himself into that pond and feel that coolness lap against his skin.

Seconds later Jori heard a huge splash. And then Chris's blond head surfaced next to her. "Took him long enough," she whispered to herself.

She wasn't exactly sure why she'd brought him here. Sympathy, she told herself. She'd felt sorry for him at the fair. He'd been hot and dirty and totally ill at ease.

No one would ever expect Jori Jessop to go pond dipping with a man, but Christopher Davis was one man who intrigued her like no one else had. He also made her more aware of her femininity than she had ever been. She wanted to know why. And yet at the same time, she was afraid; scared to open herself up to his intense scrutiny.

"Well, Doc," she teased, whipping a hand through the water to splash him in the face. "Great, isn't it?"

Chris's eyes had darkened to a deep electrifying blue. He strode through the water toward her with a look in his eye that Jori knew meant trouble. She backed up as far as she could, but he kept advancing until Jori was treading water in the deepest part of their private pool.

"I said not to call me that," he growled. "Now you'll have to pay."

"Go ahead," she egged him on. "Duck me. I like it."

His big warm palms closed over her shoulders. Then he tugged, bringing her against him.

"That's not what I had in mind," he warned with gleeful menace. "The payment is this."

Without any warning, Chris's head bent to hers. His lips were soft yet purposeful. It was a kiss that was full of unasked questions and tentative responses.

When he finally pulled away, Jori could only hang on to his broad shoulders as she stared up at him. When she finally pushed back, it was to duck her head under the water and swim away from him, as if his kiss meant nothing.

But she couldn't let it go. Something about him, the safe harbor of his arms, made her ask, "Why did you do that? We barely know each other."

Chris shrugged and paddled circles around her.

"I've wanted to kiss you properly for ages," he told her, glittering blue eyes met hers straight on. "You can't deny there's something between us."

He grinned that wide-open easy smile at her and Jori felt her heart turn cartwheels. He looked so cute, so *trustworthy,* standing there soaking wet with that silly smile. She tamped down her inner doubts. After all, she wasn't a model anymore. It wasn't as if someone as famous as Christopher Davis would need to use her.

"You know," he continued, "this country fair thing of yours is hot work." She saw his gaze shift to her mouth. "Why did you bring *me* here, Jori? Do you bring all your dates to this little oasis?"

"I've never brought anyone . . ." Jori's voice trailed away in embarrassment.

Why couldn't she learn some self-control? she asked herself. With heart sinking, she watched the light of understanding dawn in his eyes before they turned a deep navy.

"Well, I'm scandalized." His laughing voice drew Jori out of her introspection. "The always perfect Miss Jori Jessop gave way to the moment and brought her boss to her own private swimming pool. What would the townsfolk think of their favorite citizen now, indulging in such abandon?"

Jori's face was burning. Deep in her heart there was an ache that wouldn't go away. This was a side of Chris she hadn't seen before. He was funny and teasing and lighthearted. All the things she had thought she wanted in a man. Frankly, he was hard to resist in this mood.

Jori turned away, treading water as she strove to regain control.

"I don't do things for the townspeople," she said sharply. "I

came here because it's cool and we can relax and be comfortable."
Jori scrambled to assume her severest schoolteacher look. "I didn't
plan this as some secret assignation, you know. I was just trying to
help you."

She wasn't defending herself, merely stating the facts. It came as
a surprise to hear Chris's low voice in her ear.

"I know. But there's cool, and then there's *cool.*" He grinned.

There was only one recourse and she took it, concentrating on
her swimming.

When she finally stopped, puffing and gasping air into her
starved lungs, Chris sat perched at the water's edge on a huge
boulder, sunning himself dry. She studiously ignored him as she
paddled to the grassy edge and sprawled out on her stomach. The
feathery green blades caressed her skin with a delicate touch.

There was no way, Jori decided, that she was pulling on her
denim skirt while her swimsuit was still soaking wet. Her dip had
left her cool and relaxed and she was loath to break the solitude
and peace of the afternoon. Closing her eyes, she pretended to
relax in the sun, fully aware of the man across from her as he sat
munching watermelon.

"You're self-conscious around me." Chris's soft puzzled voice
carried on the still afternoon air. "I don't understand that. I
thought models would be used to people watching them in various
states of dress."

Chris flopped his long lanky body next to hers on the soft grassy
carpet. His arm brushed hers as he found a comfortable position.
Immediately her armor went up and something inside whispered,
"Be careful."

*So we say with confidence "The Lord is my helper; I will not be
afraid. What can man do to me?"* The old memory verse reverberated through her mind and Jori almost grinned in delight. Talk
about timing!

"You're not a client or a customer," she prevaricated. "Anyway,
it's different here. This is home. And I haven't modeled for quite a
while." Jori twisted her head to look into his smooth velvet eyes,
noticing the way the flaxen mop fell carelessly across his forehead.

"I never was very comfortable around men," she admitted, waiting for that wry look of disbelief to cross his face. She wasn't disappointed.

"I'm sure."

"Look, it was just a job. I needed the money and so I modeled. Some of those assignments paid me very well." She stared straight into his face, daring him to interrupt. "So well, in fact, that my dad got most of what he needed to keep him happy." She gulped down a deep breath and pressed on, needing to get it all out.

"I'm not especially proud of some of what I had to wear, but I did a good job for my clients. Anyway, my father got to spend a few more years happily in his own home. That was the point."

Jori took a deep, calming breath before sitting up slowly, dragging her knees to her chest.

"After I took over his affairs, I found out that he had stashed some money away for my education. I wish I'd known. I would have spent more time with him and less working."

"I'm sorry," he murmured. "I have no right to judge."

Jori stared down at her feet. She'd noticed his large, capable hands soothe a fussing child, or stroke a patient's wringing hands. Now they tipped her chin up to meet his compassionate countenance, strong yet gentle under her chin.

"I think your father is very proud of what his daughter did for him," he murmured, his lips very close to hers. "What man would not have been proud to see the world admiring his beautiful daughter?"

"It wasn't exactly the traditional approach to caring for one's parents," she whispered, mesmerized by his compassionate look.

"Unusual circumstances call for unusual solutions," he whispered. "No one's blaming you for being a model, Jori. Least of all me."

He bent his head slowly and pressed his lips to hers then, and it was unlike anything Jori had experienced before. His mouth was soft and gentle.

Finally Chris pulled his lips away, but continued to touch the silky strands of her hair.

And all the while a tiny voice whispered in Jori's ear. "He will never settle here. He's from the city and that is where he will return." She hated that nagging little voice and its cheerless message.

Thing was, she knew it was right.

Christopher Davis was very good at kissing and he could draw a response that echoed through her body to her toes.

But there was no future for them. She was committed to staying in Mossbank, caring for her father. It was what she'd focused on for months now. And hadn't God directed her home?

So how could she have these feelings for this man? He would leave, move on with his life and then she would be alone. Again. Jori jerked out of his embrace, her cheeks burning as she watched his blue eyes darken.

"Why do you always do that?" he asked, allowing her to slip out of his grasp. "Are you afraid of me? I'm not like your fiancé, Jori. I don't care much about what happened in the past, or your money."

"That's because you have a lot," she told him, her glance downcast. "If you're in this world long enough, you come to realize that there are people who would do anything for money." She glared across at him. "I'm here because I couldn't stand to be around people like that anymore."

He watched her when she plucked a spear of grass and shredded it with her fingernails. The action only made her seem more nervous.

"Like what?" he asked softly. When she frowned, he clarified. "People like what?"

"People who devalue everything that's important. My father taught me to love God and trust him with my life." She laughed harshly. "Believe me, that's not something that you hear much anymore. And I've decided that that was an important heritage. That's why I'm going to stay right here, in this community. This is where I want to live, maybe raise a family, grow old."

"There are lots of communities like Mossbank in this country," he murmured. "Why limit yourself to here?"

"My dad's here," she told him bluntly. "And I have to be nearby in case he needs me."

"But he's in the nursing home! He has someone there all the time. Some days he doesn't even recognize you."

Jori felt the tears well as she swallowed down the lump in her throat with difficulty.

"I know." She hiccupped. "But he has better days and knows who I am. I can't not be there for him."

"Jori, your father has Alzheimer's. He's not going to get better."

Chris shrugged. "I'm no expert in that field, but I do know that these patients don't wake up one morning cured. You're talking about a degenerative disease. Surely, as a nurse, you know what that means."

"Of course I know," she returned angrily. "But I have no intention of deserting my only remaining family. There's nothing out there—" she waved her hand in front of her "—that I want enough to leave Mossbank. This is where I belong. It's where I have to be."

"Nothing to make you leave," he murmured, so softly Jori barely caught his words. "I wonder."

"We'd better get going," she muttered, jumping to her feet. She had to move, to do something that would avoid that knowing look. Chris's blue eyes were bright with understanding. She avoided them. She didn't want to hear him call her a chicken.

She found her clothes and put on her skirt and vest, then turned to find her shoes. As she moved, Jori caught sight of Chris, just standing there, staring at her.

"Well?" Jori snapped, unable to control the exasperation that flashed through her at the notion that she could easily be swayed from her life's plan by a mere kiss. All it would take was a little more of that gentle compassion and she'd start dreaming about a future that was impossible. "Do you intend to stay here?"

"I'm not giving up on you, Jori." The words were quietly spoken, blond head tilted to one side. "You and I have something special going on, you can't deny it. But just when things start to get interesting, you duck out." His wide mouth tightened. "I'm not going to hurt you, Jori." He smiled, brushing one hand down the length of her almost dry hair. "You can trust me.

"You only hurt yourself if you don't live your *own* life. I don't believe either God or your father intended that."

Jori was shaken by his perceptiveness and she let that fear translate into anger. She attacked him verbally while her palms stayed clenched at her side.

"Big deal. You kissed me. The great Dr. Davis! So what?" She snickered. "Am I supposed to be grateful for your attention?" She watched his face darken, a dull red suffusing his healthy skin.

"You kissed me back," he taunted. "You felt the same spark that I did, only you won't admit it. Why, Jori? What do you think is going to happen if you admit that you enjoy being with me?"

In three strides he was standing in front of her. "I didn't force you or coerce you to kiss me, Jordanna Jessop, and I'm sure not going to hurt you. I am not your ex-boyfriend."

Her flashing brown eyes met his glittering blue ones. But what she saw in his eyes only made her more uncomfortable.

"You just shut me out," he murmured. "I thought we'd gone beyond that. I don't scare easily, Jori."

Chris turned away after a few moments and retrieved his clothes. Quietly he slipped them on behind a nearby bush without saying another word. There was a pinched tightness around his mouth, but that was the only hint as to his frustration.

He climbed into the Jeep and sat waiting for her without uttering a word. But Jori could feel his condemnation. She took her time getting into the hot stuffy vehicle.

He was right. She wasn't playing fair. And it was because she wasn't sure what was right or proper anymore. Christopher Davis had mixed up her mind and emotions so badly, she couldn't decide if she liked or hated him more, and she was very much afraid it was far too much of the former.

She sighed. Perhaps she had been too abrupt. They were going to have to work together for the next little while and she owed him at least an apology. Her eyes closed for a moment before she gritted her teeth in determination. She would try again.

"I'm sorry about that," she offered. "I really am just a small-town girl. This is my home and I can't pretend to be somebody else." It didn't come out exactly the way she'd intended so Jori tried again.

"I'm not the sort of person who has a fling with a visiting doctor if the opportunity arises. I'm too old-fashioned, I guess." Jori turned to glance at his stern profile. He still looked mad.

"I want all the things you see in this little town—a family, friends and a neighborhood where you can trust your next-door neighbor." She stopped for a minute and then lest he still didn't get it, blurted out, "The bottom line is, I don't sleep around."

"Who asked you to?" His voice was low and disgruntled. "All I recall doing was kissing you." He turned then to stare straight into her eyes. "Maybe *Trace*—" he laid heavy emphasis on the word "—was the kind of person who expected that, but I'm not him. And why do you immediately assume I'm looking for some kind of a fling? I wish you'd stop treating me as if I have some terminal disease that I'll inflict on this town."

"I don't do that," she gasped in an aggrieved tone.

"Yes, you do," he asserted grimly. "Look, Jori, I like you. You're smart and funny and I'd like to get to know you better." He grinned at her suddenly and Jori let out the lungful of air she held.

"I'm perfectly willing to take it slow while we get to know one another. I want to know things about you like your favorite food, what you eat when you pig out, what countries you modeled in, how you got started." Chris reached out and stroked his hand down the long strands of her shiny tresses.

"We'll take it nice and easy. Just don't run away. Trust me, don't be afraid of me." His soft voice soothed her jangled nerves.

The problem was, Jori reflected, she didn't trust anyone who got too close. Not anymore. And especially not after Trace's desertion. Besides, if he knew the truth about her, Jori wasn't sure Dr. Christopher Davis would want to spend any more effort on getting to know her.

But as she stared into Chris's solemn blue gaze, Jori wondered if perhaps the man upstairs was telling her that it was time to let someone into at least a tiny part of her life.

"Peaches," she told him finally, letting down her guard just the tiniest bit.

Chris looked up from the study he was conducting on her long pink fingernails. "What?" Confusion creased his eyes in perplexity.

"My favorite food—peaches." She smiled at him. "Fresh, ripe and so juicy that it drips down your chin when you bite into it. And I love chocolate."

"Now that wasn't so hard, was it?" his deep voice chided as he smiled at her.

As she sat smiling with him, Jori decided that she wouldn't let herself get too used to him. For her own good. He was a very successful doctor who was just filling in for a friend. When Dan returned, Chris would be gone like the wind. Small towns were not his style; they couldn't be. His work necessitated a city and she had no intention of leaving Mossbank. Perhaps they both needed to remember that.

Jori moved back into her seat and put the Jeep into gear. She drove away from their tiny oasis with resolution. This crazy attraction . . . no, infatuation . . . was only temporary. It would pass, she reassured her doubting voice as they drove toward the fairground. It was just temporary.

Chapter Five

"Faith, have you seen Charity? I've been searching for twenty minutes and there's no sign of her anywhere!" Hope's voice echoed the frustration she felt. She grimaced at the dusty marks on her skirt but no amount of brushing would remove them.

Faith swallowed the last of her double fudge bar and swiped one hand across her mouth in the hopes of removing the traces.

"Charity? Oh, she went off with Aubery. They were going to get an ice-cream cone, I think. One of those triple-decker things." Faith's eyes blazed with happiness. "Don't you just love this fair?"

"Aubery Olden? Oh, no! And why are they eating ice cream at this time of the day?" When Faith began to answer, Hope waved her away. "No, never mind. I don't want to know." She puffed out a breath of air in disgust. "And to think I went to all the trouble of arranging for Frank to join us all for supper."

"Frank Bellows?" Faith shook her head. "You know how she feels about him, Hope. Good heavens, we've tried to get the two of them together often enough, but Charity's dead set against the man."

"I don't understand why. He's a wonderful man and Charity would enjoy him if she'd let herself. She's so stubborn."

Faith wisely refrained from commenting on others of her acquaintance who possessed the same trait and applied herself instead to dabbing at the chocolate smears on her favorite pink blouse.

"I saw Mirabel earlier," she offered as a red herring, smugly happy when Hope's startled glance flew to hers. "She's after our new doctor."

"Mirabel? But she can't be," Hope wailed. "I so wanted Jori to link up with him. She needs someone now that James is in Sunset. She spends far too much time by herself." Hope's blond head whirled around as she searched the crowd. "Where do you suppose Mirabel is now?"

Faith nodded at the refreshment tent on the right. "Chatting to your husband," she murmured softly. "And she's sitting beside mine!"

"I was just coming over to mention that," Charity's voice sputtered from behind them. "Isn't it time you and your husbands had supper? There's the nicest little spot by that hedge over there and I've got a cloth on the table already."

"Charity, you scared the daylights out of me!" Hope pressed a hand to her racing heart before frowning down on the older woman. "I wanted to talk to you about supper," she said. "I was hoping you'd join us."

"I might," Charity acquiesced.

"Come on, Faith," Hope chortled, linking her arm in the other's with a grin. "Let's go rescue Arthur and Harry."

Ten minutes later they were all seated around the red-painted picnic table, plates of cold cuts and salads in front of them.

"I hope you don't mind," Charity said, buttering her roll carefully. "I've asked Aubery Olden to join us."

"You haven't," Hope gasped, spying the old gent making his way toward them. She glanced over her shoulder. "But I asked Frank Bellows!"

"Oh, piffle!" They all stared at Faith's unhappy face. "I suppose it was a bad idea to invite Howard Steele over, too?"

In the end, the seating arrangements had to be revised. Judge Conroy was most vocal in his distaste at sitting four on a side and finally announced that he was moving to the next table. Hope followed him with a backward glance at Charity, who sat happily amid the three men.

"Why don't you go with them, Faith?" she heard Charity offer. "You and Arthur are squished up there like sardines in a can."

"Why did you move?" Hope whispered angrily as Faith sank

onto the seat beside her. "Now we can't hear a word they're saying." She glanced in dismay at the cherubic smile on Charity's round face and sighed. "I just wish you hadn't asked Howard Steele," she muttered in frustration. "He's too young for her." Her face brightened suddenly.

"Ah, hello, Jordanna. Enjoying the fair?"

"It's wonderful," Jori replied, following Hope's glance to the table next door. "Mrs. Flowerday certainly seems to be enjoying herself."

"Yes," Faith grumbled in an unhappy tone as Charity's bright laugh rang out. "She does, doesn't she?"

"I saw you with Dr. Chris," Faith murmured in a low, conspiratorial tone. "You left for a while and I haven't seen him since. Did he have a call?"

Jori felt her heart sink at the curious look in those faded eyes. She pasted on a smile and answered as best she could. "No, Mrs. Johnson. No call. We just left to get out of the heat for a bit. He's around here somewhere." She glanced over her shoulder, as if she were searching for Chris. "I suppose I'd better go find him. We're supposed to have supper together." She waved her hand and moved away before Faith could ask any more questions. "Bye for now."

Chris was deep into a discussion about agricultural practices when Jori found him two hours later. She had deliberately wandered around on her own for a while to give them both some space. After their time at the pond, she needed to regroup, gain perspective.

As she listened to his knowledgeable response on the difficulties with anhydrous ammonia, Jori was forced to smile. It seemed the good doctor knew a lot more about farming than she would have given him credit for. And when he glanced up to grin at her, his sparkling blue eyes negated any progress she might have made in slowing up a racing heartbeat.

"Not a bad looker, is he?" The voice belonged to Amy Grand, Jori's best friend since kindergarten. "You two have something going?" The question was not posed as innocently as Amy's wide green eyes seemed to imply.

"Hi, Amy," Jori greeted her friend. She grinned at Amy's outfit.

Blue jeans and T-shirt, again. "We're just friends. I thought a trip to this fair might open his eyes a little."

Amy smirked saucily before she teased, "Seems to me your eyes are wide-open, too, my girl." She swatted Jori lightly. "It's nice to see, for a change. I thought that heart of yours would be frozen forever!"

Jori wished for the hundredth time that her friend's voice was just a trifle less strident. At this rate, the whole town would be speculating about them.

Jori wished an emergency would set off his beeper and relieve her embarrassment. But she'd never backed down from trouble before and she faced Chris bravely now.

"We've got to be going, Amy," she babbled. "Nice seeing you again. Bring Bob over for coffee tomorrow night. Bye."

It wasn't a great exit but it was the best she could do with those glittering navy orbs daring her to ignore him. She tried to make small talk as they moved toward the grill.

"Sorry about that," she murmured. "Amy always says what she thinks."

"Does she always say it so loudly?" he growled. Jori could hear the dismay in his voice.

"Amy didn't mean anything." Jori frowned. "After all, you are new to the area and very good-looking, so . . ." Realizing what she'd said, Jori slapped a hand over her mouth.

She stopped at the end of the lineup, afraid to meet his gaze, fumbling with her keys. A choking sound made her look up finally. Chris stood behind her trying not to laugh out loud.

"What is so funny?" Jori demanded, hands on her hips.

"You are." He gasped the words out between gulps of laughter. "And thanks for the compliment. I think."

Jori watched him for a few moments and then decided she had gotten off lightly. At least he wasn't mad.

They ate their meal surrounded by a swarm of young people who chatted madly back and forth. There was no need for conversation and not much opportunity if they'd wanted one.

After supper the 4-H youth presented a special routine with their horses marching in formation around the dusty track. Jori sat on the crowded bench with her leg brushing Chris's and tried to concentrate on the patterns that had taken hours of practice to perfect.

"What happens next?" he asked.

Jori tried to control the flutter of nervous awareness that noticed the cowlick on the left side of his head and the way his eyes crinkled at the corners when he smiled.

"There's a talent show now," she whispered back. "Local people who are competing for some of those prizes." She indicated a booth across the way. "The kids have really entered this year because there's a CD player there."

"Are you singing, Jori?" Mrs. Hansen leaned across Chris to ask the question in a voice loud enough to cause several heads to turn.

"No. But I'm supposed to be one of the judges." Jori glanced up at Chris. "I have to move down there." She pointed to where several adults stood around a table placed about twenty feet back from the stage.

"You can come if you want, there are extra chairs. Or you can stay here and I'll meet you after." She waited for him to decide.

"I'll go," he said, inclining his head to the left. "I think I'm a little out of place here." Jori followed his gaze and smirked at the dearth of seniors that had congregated around them on the stands.

"That's one of the best things about a country fair. Everybody fits in," she whispered back.

"I'm judging the singing. You can help if you want. Or leave. It's up to you." She moved down a step.

Her face grew warm as his blue eyes studied her.

He grinned, tightening his hold on her fingers. "I always go home with the woman I came with."

"Well, come on then," she said at last, thrown off by the fatuous grin on his handsome face. "They're ready to start."

"I should tell you that I don't know a thing about singing."

"As a matter of fact, you're tone-deaf," Jori added kindly. She grinned and shook her head at his offended look. "I heard you singing to yourself at the office one day. Totally off-key."

"If my voice is so offensive—" he began indignantly, but Jori just grinned and shushed him.

"The first number is about to come on," she explained. "You'll like it. Just relax and enjoy it. The *guest judge* is allowed."

Four minutes later, Jori knew he was enjoying himself by the way he clapped for the preschool performers. As the tiny sister and brother tucked their fiddles under their arms and took a bow, Chris cheered enthusiastically. Apparently, the crowd agreed for everyone was on their feet.

Once the group had settled down, the next number came on and gave a rousing version of an intricate square dance number that involved full ruffled skirts with stiff crinolines. There was a fourteen-year-old comedian who poked fun at everyone, a ten-year-old piano whiz and two guitar players who harmonized in a Wild West medley that had every toe in the place tapping out the beat.

"These people are all from around here?" Chris leaned over to ask after the fifth entry. When she nodded, he shook his blond head. "There's a lot of hidden talent in Mossbank."

"Didn't I tell you that?" Jori admonished with a reproving grin. Her eyes widened as a young girl with a cropped haircut and tight blue jeans came onto the stage carrying a set of drums. "I was afraid of this," she whispered.

"What's wrong?" Chris stared at her curiously.

Jori grinned and shook her head. "Wait," she commanded with a grin. "Just wait."

There was a two-second interval between the time the announcement was made and the cacophony of thumping, thudding, clanging noise began. Several times Jori glanced over her shoulder, studying the stupefied look on Chris's face before turning back to her notepad and jotting down something in tiny scribbles.

When the silence finally came, it was deafening. The entire assembled throng sat dazed and paralyzed with shock. Jori nudged Chris in the arm and started clapping loudly. Seconds later others joined in until there was a resounding clamor from all around them. The girl calmly picked up her drums and carried them off the stage, her head held high.

"What is the best thing you can think of to say about that performance, guest judge?" Jori hid her smile as she watched his shocked features rearrange themselves in their normal structure.

Chris's eyes were glazed and unfocused as they stared down at her. Finally his mouth opened and whispered something she had to lean closer to hear.

"That it's over!"

Jori nodded and pretended she was writing something, carefully aware of the scrutiny of the townsfolk.

"Just keep that to yourself," she advised softly. "Another small-town rule is that nobody must be offended by these proceedings. Nobody."

"You mean, 'If I can't say something nice, don't say anything at all'?" Those blue eyes were sparkling and clear as they reprimanded her. "I learned that lesson from my nanny a long time ago," he chided her in an aggrieved tone. "It's just as true in the big city, you know, Jordanna."

A young band was announced then and as they crooned a famous country song about young love, Chris's arm slid along the back of her chair. No doubt it was an innocent move. She just happened to be sitting there, next to him. He didn't mean anything by it. Perhaps he just needed to stretch, Jori told herself. But either way, it felt nice to have that strong arm behind her, sort of protecting her.

It was a strange thought. As if she needed protecting, Jori derided her subconscious. She certainly didn't want him to think she couldn't manage alone! But when his arm stayed there through the next three numbers, Jori couldn't ignore the cared-for feeling it transmitted to her weary heart.

It must be nice to have someone to lean on, she thought, staring at the young woman who was arranging her microphone. Somebody to take over the load once in a while.

Reality intruded. Of course, it wasn't likely that any man would want to take on a woman who was tied to this town. Never mind someone with all the doubts and fears she had.

No, Jori decided. She wasn't the type of woman Chris Davis would normally be interested in. She just happened to be here now. Chris was sure of himself and his path through life. He would never understand the misgivings that gripped her each day when she considered her future.

"This one is really good," Chris murmured in her ear, drawing her out of her self-examination. "She gets my vote."

The young woman with the guitar strummed quietly as she sang, her voice building to a crescendo as she told of her love for a young man who had left to find his fortune, and rejected her because she wouldn't go with him. The words were achingly poignant and Jori couldn't help glancing at Chris, assessing his reaction to the song.

There was thunderous applause when the young woman finished. She bowed and then quietly left the stage with many in the audience still clapping.

"She was good, wasn't she?" Chris's voice was full of enthusiasm. "I'd like to hear her again but with a different song. Something lighter."

"I take it you don't believe in love lost," she teased, only half joking.

His eyes were bright and clear as he stared into hers; his voice firm and direct. "I believe that love is a rare and valuable gift that God gives to humans," he murmured, his hand squeezing her shoulder. "If you find it, and many don't, you need to do everything in your power to nurture it, keep it growing. Nothing should be allowed to come between two people who love each other. Nothing."

Jori tore her gaze away from his only because someone on the other side was saying something to her and she didn't understand what it was. As if in a trance, she agreed with the other judges that the young woman was indeed the best performer and deserved the CD player. They went through the list of contestants and awarded a prize to each of them, including the raucous drum player.

"You're giving a prize for that . . . that noise?" Chris demanded in a shocked whisper but his eyes were twinkling in the dusk. "You always play fair, don't you, Jori?"

"I try." She smiled. "There are enough prizes, so why not? It might encourage some future musician." There was more she wanted to say but he hugged her against his big wide chest then and the words got stuck in her throat.

"You're a very special woman, J.J." His lips brushed across her forehead before he set her free and Jori could only hope that it was dark enough that no one in the audience would see.

"J.J.?" She stared up at him in confusion.

"It's my new nickname for you." He grinned. "Makes our friendship more . . . personal, don't you think?"

Jori wondered if things weren't quite personal enough between them, but he gave her no opportunity to comment, wheeling away to speak to one of the youth gathered nearby. Reluctantly, Jori turned away to converse with the other judges, pushing back the longing his words engendered. How close did he want to be?

After the awards were given out, Chris insisted on another piece of pie and Jori gladly accepted the cup of coffee he purchased for her. Many of the younger children had been taken home now and the grounds were quieter as a senior's group played softly onstage. Here and there a few couples swayed to and fro to the old dance tunes of a bygone era.

"I've got to go back to restaurant eating," Chris murmured, licking his lips appreciatively. He patted his flat stomach with a grin. "I didn't eat nearly as much then." He noted the tiny shiver Jori tried to repress. "Are you cold?"

"A little," she admitted ruefully. "I have my sweater in the Jeep but I'm too lazy to go and get it."

"Do you want to leave?"

"We can't go yet!" She stared at him appalled. "The fireworks will be starting soon."

Chris grinned, flicking a finger against the tip of her nose. "Well, we certainly can't miss *that*," he agreed, a roguish look in his eye.

Jori grinned in reproof.

"Stop making fun of me," she ordered. "I happen to like all these small-town traditions. And nothing, *nothing*," she reiterated firmly, "can compare with *these* particular fireworks."

"Nothing?" Chris teased in a slow and easy tone. "Hmmm. That sounds like a challenge. I never could resist a challenge."

She waited, but when nothing more was forthcoming, Jori got up, tossing her cup into a nearby garbage can. "I guess I'd better get my sweater," she murmured. "I'm getting really cold."

They meandered back to the Jeep, meeting people coming and going along the dimly lit path. Chris obligingly pulled on his jacket when she handed it to him and waited with his back turned while Jori slipped into her jeans beneath her skirt, then she removed her skirt. When she'd pulled on her sweater she sighed.

"Mmm, that's better. I was freezing."

"Why didn't you say so?" Chris murmured, inclining his head. He wrapped his arms around her. "I would have warmed you up."

"Oh." There were a thousand things she wanted to say and nothing at all that seemed appropriate, so Jori simply stood there, his arms around her waist, holding still as his mouth lowered to hers.

His gentle kiss made Jori forget all about the country fair and all the people who might see them together like this. His arms were big and solid, yet gentle as they cradled her, and Jori couldn't move. It felt somehow right to be here with him in the dimness of this rustic setting. When he lifted his head, she blinked several times.

"Do you see stars?" she asked in bewilderment. "Blue and red ones with little tails?"

Chris laughed and moved behind her, turning Jori so that she faced the open field. His arms stayed linked around her waist and she relaxed against him when he murmured in her ear.

"Thanks for the compliment, but I think the real fireworks have begun." His lips brushed her hair gently before his chin rested on the top of her head. "And according to a certain nurse I know, they're pretty spectacular."

They watched in silence as the series of explosions rang across the countryside. One after the other, the small puffs of smoke disappeared as yet another blaze of dazzling, glittering bursts lit up the darkening sky. Jori heard his sigh of appreciation as the grand finale, a glistening, wildly colorful waterfall sprayed its sparkling glory across the thin wires that had been rigged earlier.

She hated to leave the comfort of his arms, but streams of people were flowing out from the fairground and Jori could just imagine the speculation if they found her in the arms of the new doctor.

"And that, Dr. Christopher Davis, is the Silven Stream Fair. It's time to call it a night." She eased away from him and dug in her pocket for her keys.

"Yes, I guess it is. Thank you, Jori. I enjoyed it very much. All of it." His eyes were strangely incandescent in the shadows. The gleam in them made Jori nervous. After unlocking the door of the Jeep, she climbed in, conscious of his hand under her arm. When Chris finally got in, Jori couldn't look at him. Instead she drove carefully back over the winding road, ignoring his sudden silence, thinking.

As an instructive experience for a man used to the city, this day had been an unqualified success. But, it seemed that she had learned a few home truths herself. And one of them bothered her. A lot.

She really liked Chris Davis.

"It was nice of you to take me today, Jori," he murmured when they arrived at his home. "I guess I can see why some people want to live here. It must get awfully boring, though. Good thing the city's not too far away."

It wasn't the best thing he could have said and Jori felt that irritating flick of dismay at his cavalier words.

"They stay here because their families, friends and neighbors are here and because they can stop and smell the roses without driving for an hour," she muttered, trying to suppress her frustration.

"But it's so isolated. You have to drive for ages before you can dine out properly. It feels like another world!"

"I suppose you mean because we don't expedite people here like you did in Boston." She emphasized the city sulkily. "In and out without even knowing your patient's name. Well, *Doctor,* in Moss-bank, the guy you malign today is the guy you'll have to do business with tomorrow. You won't find the chilly impersonality of the city here." She tried to stop them, but the bitter words flowed out anyway.

"I suppose that's what you liked most about your work in Bos-ton. You did your thing in the operating room, your patients were gone from your life and you didn't have to think about them any-more."

"Jori, I didn't mean to imply . . ."

"Yes, you did," she sputtered. "You meant that you feel stuck here. Well, it's true in a way. You can't just change things by shift-ing a case to someone else. There's no way to opt out if you don't like Mrs. Newsom's test results. You've got to treat her tomorrow and the day after that until she dies of some horrible disease that no one can cure."

Jori stared at him, trying to remember all the good things about him, but the pain of his words would not abate.

"You can't run away here, Chris. You have to sit and patiently wait until that mom is ready to give birth and whether or not you're ready has nothing to do with it. When she needs you, you'd better be there." She stared at the road and forced herself to speak calmly when all she wanted to do was cry. For what, she wasn't sure.

"If you stay in the rat race long enough, you never take the time to listen, really listen to what your best friend or your sick patient or God is telling you. You scurry away, pretending this or that is more important. And it's not. Nothing is more important than God's voice and lots of times he uses the people in your life to speak."

She barely heard his chilly answer.

"Maybe. But I think hiding out is exactly what you're doing. And sometimes you have to get away from the people in your life in order to carry on." He lunged out of her Jeep and slammed the door before walking around to her side of the vehicle. "Thanks for the day, Jordanna. Good night."

And then he was gone, leaving her to wonder about his words and the obvious pain behind them. He was hurting, although he tried to hide it behind a mask of self-sufficiency. And Jori felt totally unable to cope with it.

"Father, you know what this is about, I don't. Please draw near to Chris tonight. And let him see that you are able to deal with it all, you never grow weary or faint. And please, God, if this thing between us isn't your will, let me know. I'm so mixed up!"

Chris wasn't sure exactly how it happened.

After all, he hadn't really attended a church regularly in years. Except for the odd wedding and funeral. And certainly never one like this. The churches he had known had always seemed such cold, grim places; and once he'd started working, well, shifts being what they were, going to church had been the last thing he'd thought of.

He tried to ignore the voice in his head that snorted he was only here today because of a woman. And yet, here he sat, dressed in a suit and tie, on a polished oak bench, waiting for the service to begin.

It was her fault, of course. Jori Jessop had invited him rather casually one day last week and he'd brushed off the invitation with as much politeness as he could. Not his scene, he'd told her brusquely when the truth was, he didn't want to get any more involved with these people. But when old man Olden had told him Jordanna was singing this morning, Chris had experienced a rapid change of heart.

"Sweet as a bird, Jori is. Sings like one, too. Gonna hear her this Sunday," the old fellow had teased, clearly trying his hand at matchmaking.

"What does she sing?" Chris asked the question before thinking.

But Aubery Olden was nobody's fool and he knew when a fish was on the line. Chris felt like one of those suckers he'd seen the kids catch in the river and he waited impatiently while the old man reeled him in.

"Oh, most 'bout anything she takes a fancy to. Soul, blues, gospel. Jori tries 'em all out sooner or later." As he'd buttoned his shirt the old man's eyes twinkled up into Chris's. "Church starts at eleven," he'd said softly.

He'd been greeted enthusiastically when he entered, Chris mused. He had also been amazed by the grip of some of the elderly parishioners, particularly Frank Bellows. A surgeon's hands were his most important tool, Chris reflected, flexing his hands carefully and deciding nothing was broken.

"We're glad to have you here with us today," the man had said, a warm smile tilting his straight lips. Frank had the soft empathetic voice one expected of an undertaker and Chris knew he'd be good at comforting the bereaved.

Frank showed him to a seat, and for lack of knowing any different, Chris had taken his place, idly watching the assortment of families that filled the rows in front and beside.

When a drooling toddler crawled under the pew in front of him to gnaw on his shoelaces, Chris picked him up easily. The child was a friendly one and grinned happily as he dribbled over Chris's navy blazer. One lone tooth stood out proudly and the little boy used it effectively when his temporary caregiver foolishly allowed the child to play with his thumb.

The frazzled mother rushed up moments later and smiled her gratitude as she ushered the rest of her children into the bench.

"Thank you so much, Doctor," she whispered. "He just gets away from me so fast these days."

"He's certainly a mover," Chris agreed, noting that the rest of her brood looked happily excited to be at the small church. He felt a pang of envy when the father took his place at the end of the pew beside his wife, completing the family unit.

To the left a group of young adults gathered, chattering madly over the worship music of the organ. He saw no signs of wealth on any of them and yet they smiled and talked freely, obviously content with their world. They belonged here and they knew it.

Even the elderly ladies behind him were discussing something with great animation. He was astounded to hear his name moments later.

"That's Christopher Davis, the new doctor." He recognized the birdlike tones of Mrs. Flowerday.

"Filling in for Dr. Dan and Jessica, isn't he?"

"And working with Jori. Now, wouldn't that be a match made in heaven!"

They twittered and talked among themselves as Chris wriggled uncomfortably at their matchmaking. He disliked being the topic of conversation. He also felt guilty sitting in this holy place and scheming to get another date with the lovely Jori.

Plans for marriage were the last thing on his mind these days, especially since he knew Jori intended to stick it out in good old Mossbank! Anyway, permanent entanglements weren't his style. Not at all.

Chris was flipping through the worn red hymnal when someone slid into the seat beside him. Jori. He felt his heartbeat quicken as his lips twitched involuntarily, unable to stop smiling.

"Good morning," he greeted her, tamping down the rise of excitement he felt.

Jori stared at him for several seconds before replying. He could tell she was surprised. He felt sort of shocked himself. Today Jori Jessop looked like a model. Her waist-length hair was loose and free, cascading down her back like walnut silk washed sparkling clean. She wore a slim fitted suit in some reddish color that gave a lovely glow to her cheeks.

The jacket had short sleeves, baring her slim arms to the summer heat. Tapered in, it ended in a point just below her waist. The straight skirt had a small slit in the front where it stopped demurely just below her knees. She wore gold hoops in her earlobes and a tiny gold locket that dipped into the V-neck of her jacket. The total effect was one of ultra-French chic and totally suited her slim tall figure.

Her big dark eyes, fringed by those incredible lashes, shone brightly back at him. "Good morning, yourself. And welcome here."

Chris was conscious of a peace and serenity that pervaded the service that followed. Even the squall of a baby in the back, or the muffled whisperings of two fidgeting youths up front didn't disturb him as he joined in singing the old familiar hymns.

When Jori was introduced, he watched as she moved with that smooth long-legged grace to the front. A taped background provided her accompaniment, but Chris didn't notice it much as he listened to her voice soaring through the stillness of the morning. He watched, totally rapt, as she poured emotion and feeling into her words, drawing the congregation along with her. And when she was finished, he was tempted to clap.

"That was beautiful," he whispered when she sat down once more. Jori merely smiled at him and brushed a strand of hair off her face.

It was then he noticed her hand was shaking. Gently, he covered it with his, squeezing her fingers just a little. And there it lay during the entire sermon. Somehow it made him feel a part of her group. As if, at last, he belonged.

The sermon was short but pertinent; a well-placed talk that described the benefits of belonging to the family of God. As he bowed his head and repeated the prayer's simple words, Chris felt a tingle of electricity in his heart. In this, at least, he belonged, he told himself. He was a part of the family of God.

After the benediction, everyone surged toward the doors, pausing to greet friends and extend invitations. Chris followed, amazed by the warm welcome everyone gave him. He'd never been in a church where everyone was so friendly.

"How's your wife, Jason?" That was Frank Bellows, softly questioning the young man who stood holding a squalling two-year-old boy and the hand of a frightened-looking blond girl.

"She's feeling down today, Frank. That chemo's really taking it out of her." The voice was discouraged and Chris knew why. Tracy Forbes was undergoing one of the strongest treatments available. It was no wonder she was ill.

"You got your spraying done, Jason?"

Chris could see the undertaker's white hand on Jason's shoulder, sharing his sorrow.

"No. I haven't had time. It's Tracy that's important now."

"Course it is, son. Of course it is. Still, you've got to look after that fine crop of yours. I haven't anything on for tomorrow. Do you think the kids would like to go for a boat ride?"

Jason Forbes's face turned up in a smile for the first time that Chris had seen. Relief washed across his young face as he grinned happily. "I know they'd like it, wouldn't you, kids?"

Forbes's two-year-old son's face turned up in a happy smile as he stared at the older man. "Fishin'?" he asked hopefully. "Jody fish?"

"Sure you can fish, Jody. You and Casey both." Frank glanced up at their father. "I'll pick them up around nine, then?"

"It's not going to be too much for you, is it, Frank? It's been mighty hot and you know what Dr. Dan said about getting too much sun." Jason peered down at the pale white skin. "You don't want to get heatstroke."

"Don't worry so much, Jason. I've been taking care of myself for a good long time now. Besides—" Frank beamed "—I might just enlist myself some help."

Chris saw the undertaker's eyes move to where Charity Flowerday stood talking to a tall portly gentleman. Frank's eyes were soft and full of an emotion Chris was loath to identify.

"If she isn't busy with Adam, that is." Frank's voice had dropped to a whisper but Chris heard the dismay in his voice.

"Well then, thank you very much," Jason agreed, pumping his white hand. "Tracy'd be glad of the rest."

"No problem at all. Say, Doc, I'd like to speak to you for a moment, too."

Chris stood where he was, waiting for Frank to approach.

"I was wondering if you might like to go out for dinner one evening?" Frank asked, half-apologetically. "I often eat on my own and it's nice to have someone to talk to."

Chris swiveled his head, trying to keep up with Jori's progress. "I'd like that, Frank. Can I call you?"

"Sure." Frank's gaze narrowed as he watched Chris. "She's beautiful, isn't she?"

"Who?" Chris asked, and then flushed at the look of understanding on the other man's face. "Yes, she is. Unfortunately, she's also as quick as lightning and not too fond of doctors from the city."

Frank laughed and Chris saw his eyes move to Charity once more.

"Yes, I'm familiar with the situation," he agreed. "Somehow they get one picture lodged in their minds and that's all they can see, whether it's reality or not." He turned back to Chris with an uncertain smile. "Maybe we ought to do something about that."

"Yeah. Maybe. Got any ideas?" He watched the older man curiously, noting the sparkle that lit up his grey eyes.

"Not yet. But I'm thinking on it."

"Let me know what you come up with." Chris grinned, shaking his hand. "I'd like to see if it works." Meanwhile, he intended to try some ideas of his own.

Chris waited until Jori was finished speaking to the couple behind them. Then he leaned his head closer to hers, and asked, "Will you have lunch with me, Jori?"

He figured he had given her less opportunity to resist with a crowd of observers around them. He watched as she stared at him, head tipped to one side. When she spoke, it was hesitantly.

"Well, I was going to go for a picnic. You could join me for that, if you like."

"That would be great," Chris replied, thinking about the last time they'd enjoyed nature together.

"There's just one thing you might not like," Jori told him.

"Nonsense." He brushed off her hesitation. "It's perfect weather for a picnic. I'll pick up something and then stop off at your house right after I change. We can choose our spot after that. Okay?"

"Chris, I really don't think . . ." Jori stared at him, her eyes dark with apprehension.

Someone interrupted them and she was tugged away from him in the sudden movement of people. He mouthed the word *later* at her and she nodded, although her forehead was creased in a frown.

An hour later when he arrived at Jori's, Chris found out the reason for her frown. Not only weren't they to be alone, but she planned to bike there. As in bicycle, a two-wheeled vehicle that one pedaled.

"This is Billy Smith. He's in my Sunday school class and today he memorized all the verses for July. So we're going for a picnic." She glanced at Chris's immaculate clothes. "It's okay, you know. If you don't want to bike, we can drive." Her voice was kindly patronizing and Christopher Davis wanted nothing more than to strut his stuff, especially since that freckle-faced kid was ripping off wheelies around him. If he had to prove himself on a bicycle, so be it.

"Hi, Billy. Congratulations." He glanced down at Jori's superior look. "No way, lady. Then you'll be on about my age. If you want to bike, we'll bike." He surveyed the old green model with dismay. "Although, I must confess, I haven't been on a bicycle in twenty or more years, and this one looks like it hasn't been ridden in two decades."

Gingerly, Chris planted himself on the seat and lifted one leg to the pedal. Jori rode around him.

"Come on, Doc," she cheered, giggling merrily. Even Billy joined in, chortling with glee as Chris wobbled and teetered three feet down the drive.

He caught on to the thing, finally. But there was a good chance the tires wouldn't hold him for long and he reminded himself to fall on the grass and not the gravel. Wobbling crazily, he followed her down a rough track of unpaved road behind her house.

As they pedaled along, Billy started singing at the top of his lungs and Jori chimed in. It was clear they were enjoying the day. Chris began to appreciate the benefits of cycling himself, watching Jori ahead of him.

Seconds later he was flat on his back in a patch of weeds alongside the trail. Jori stood over him giggling, her hand outstretched.

"Come on, I'll help you up." Her laughter rang out in the clear afternoon air as the wind whipped the pigtails of hair she had tied up with yellow ribbons. "What happened, Doc?"

Chris took her hand, deciding it was time for a little retribution, especially since Billy had motored on ahead—far ahead. Tugging slightly, Chris was gratified Jori's graceful body landed on the ground beside him. He turned so that he was lying beside her in the weeds.

"I told you not to call me that." He kept his voice low and menacing. "Now you'll have to pay the price."

Jori was still giggling but she stared up at him as she asked carefully, "And what is the price?"

"This," he murmured and gave her startled mouth a gentle kiss. "There are certain advantages to bike riding," he told her.

Jori's dark chocolate eyes opened wide. "Such as?" Her voice was innocence personified.

Chris shook his head. "This," he replied, kissing one of her eyelids closed. "And this," he added, kissing her cheek. Before he could kiss her lips again, his stomach grumbled.

Jori jumped slightly at the low rumbling. "What's that? Thunder?" She peered around his shoulder, searching the clouds. "It doesn't look like rain."

Chris sat up, brushing his hands through his hair. Shamefaced, he met her eyes bashfully.

Jori stared at him for a moment before she burst out in a new fit of giggles. Gathering herself, she stood gracefully, brushing down her clothes.

"What are you doing lying around here, dallying?" she demanded, hands on her curvy hips. "Let's move, Doc . . . man." She had changed the latter only after glancing sideways at him.

"You'd better watch your mouth, miss," Chris advised her. "That's what got us off the track in the first place."

Jori looked at him, frowning, lips pursed. "I don't think it was my mouth you were staring at," she lectured him sternly.

He let her get away with it, standing carefully. Gingerly, Chris mounted the bike once more, intent on keeping his eyes on the road ahead.

"Lead on, Macduff," he urged as his stomach emitted a louder plea for sustenance. Jori, he noticed, suffered no problems from their tumble in the grass. In fact she looked even more beautiful with that flush of pink high on her cheekbones. Her usually candid eyes avoided his as she waited at the side of the road.

"Are you okay, Chris?" He forced himself to look up at her.

"Yeah. But parts of me are more okay than others, if you know what I mean." He patted his hip gently.

Giggling, she rode off, pedaling furiously down the road as if monsters pursued her. Chris heaved a huge sigh and placed his feet on the pedals. He wondered tiredly how far their destination was. Jordanna Jessop and this bucolic country scene wore him out faster than Boston and its eight operating rooms ever had.

In a sunny glade just over the hillside, they found Billy flopped on the ground, chewing a blade of grass.

"You guys sure must be outa shape," he muttered, red faced. "I been here for ages."

"We're older," Chris told him coolly. "We don't like to hurry through life."

Jori raised her eyebrows but said nothing as she spread out their lunch and they hungrily dug in.

"This is a terrible way to eat." Jori laughed as she popped another bite of the fried chicken into her mouth. "Way too much fat." Chris watched her lick her fingers. "But I could force myself to like it."

Billy jumped to his feet. "I'm going fishing. I'll see you later," he said, and took off on his bike.

Chris shook his head when she tentatively offered him the remaining coleslaw and then smirked when she ate what was left. Billy had long since bolted his food and dashed off to check out the trickling brook, so even the last of their shared chocolate bar was hers.

"I don't believe your appetite, J.J. How do you stay so slim?"

"Good genes." She beamed, sprawling on the blanket they had so carefully placed on the ground. "I am stuffed." One long slim hand patted her tummy in satisfaction. Her dark eyes turned toward him, studying his as he sat cross-legged, watching her.

"Actually, I walk a lot. I guess that takes care of most of it. When I was modeling, though, I had to watch every little bite." She sat up and grimaced. "Every ounce counts, we used to say. I decided I'd never eat cottage cheese again."

"Didn't you like modeling?" Chris asked.

"I hated it," she told him starkly. "It's all smoke and mirrors. All anyone cares about is what you look like on the outside," she whispered, playing with the twisted fringe on the blanket. "There are a lot of really bad people in that business but no one sees or cares because on the outside everything looks so perfectly lovely. After a while you start to believe in the hype and you forget who you really are."

Chris watched the sadness swamp her beautiful face. She was lost in past memories. Painful ones, by the look of it.

"What about your fiancé?" he asked softly, not really wanting to know.

"I thought he was special," she told him softly. Her voice ached with sadness. "He turned out to want the same from me that everyone else did. He only wanted what he could see on the surface— the money, the fame. He didn't care about me as a person and because I believed in the lie, I forgot who I was." Jori's eyes met his.

"I let myself trust in those illusory things. I became the person in those pictures. When things altered and my reputation was smeared, I felt as naked as those pictures. As if the real me was exposed and I wasn't anything like the person I'd pretended to be. Trace turned into someone I didn't even know. And then he ran."

Chris could only sit and wait for the calm beauty of the afternoon to wash away the grief he'd just witnessed.

And while he waited, he experienced a feeling of guilt. He had been doing the same thing, he realized. From the start he'd judged Jori by what she looked like. Reality had proven less simple to define. In a few short weeks he had seen that she was gentle and yet fiercely loyal to her priorities, energetic and confident of her future, independent but also curiously attached to this town and its people.

But most of all, Chris thought he could see insecurity beneath all that confidence. She didn't want him to, of that he was sure. But every so often, when she thought no one noticed, Jordanna Jessop the confident, give-as-good-as-you-got woman turned into Jori, the small-town girl. It was a complicated picture.

"Sorry," she murmured after several minutes, clear skin flushed. "Sometimes I get maudlin. You have my permission to give me a swift kick in the keister." Her wide mouth stretched in a grin. "My Granny Grey used to say that."

Chris watched her dark head tip to one side as she studied him. He knew the questions were coming and he dreaded them. How could she possibly understand him when she'd grown up protected in this small, closely knit community.

"How did you get into medicine?" Her coffee-colored eyes sparkled at him. "Did you decide when you were five that your lifelong ambition was to be a doctor, and then scrimped and saved to make it so?" Jori stared at him as if expecting her fairy-tale dream to come true. How little she knew.

"Hardly," Chris snorted, wondering just how much of reality Jori had sampled. In spite of her worldwide exposure and life in the jaded world of modeling, she projected a childish naïveté that Chris had never really appreciated.

Until now.

"I don't think you're really all that interested in my childhood," he muttered, trying to think of another subject.

"Really, I am." Jori rushed to reassure him, wide eyes sparkling. "Tell me."

Chris stared. She was serious. He'd thought to escape with a smart remark or two but she sat there peering at him, waiting for his answer. He sighed and straightened his shoulders with determination.

"In my family, the eldest son was expected to be a doctor. I grew up knowing that I would become something in medicine. End of story." He'd deliberately cut it short—by about twenty years.

Jori wasn't satisfied. He hadn't expected her to be.

"How large of a family?" Why were her eyes so big and shiny?

"Four children—three girls, one boy." There, perhaps that would satisfy her.

"What did your parents do?"

Apparently not. Sighing he let her have the information.

"My father is a professor of biological sciences at McGill. My mother's a chemist. My sister Anne is with a research institute in Boston, Joan is still working on her physics degree and Jayne has just finished her residency in orthopedics. Should we go?"

"Wow."

It was clearly the only descriptive phrase she could think of. He grimaced. At least it was different from the "That's nice," that women usually offered.

"You must be so proud of them all." Jori's sunny tones brought him back to earth. He scowled.

"Why? I didn't have anything to do with their successes." He was curious about this woman, Chris admitted. She had a strangely odd outlook on life.

"No, but I mean, it must be great to share so much knowledge in one family. Christmastime must be a riot at your house."

Chris figured he might as well let her have it all. No sense sparing her sensibilities. Somehow, he doubted she'd ever understand.

"My family doesn't celebrate Christmas, or any of the other religious holidays." His tone was cool and controlled. "We never have."

He knew what she was thinking. What a bunch of cold fish. And Jori was right, they were. He'd always felt the same way about his family. But that didn't mean he liked other people thinking the same thing.

Jori, on the other hand, probably always celebrated Christmas. He could picture her singing the carols, joyously abandoned as she decorated house and yard. He knew she would always have a tree and stockings no matter where she was. Chris was pretty sure Flop would be decorated with a big red bow in honor of the season.

Jori Jessop was everything he wasn't—and a lot of things he wanted. Chris was beginning to realize just what he was missing in his life: a family that was close and involved in each other's lives. People who yelled and hollered at one another and then forgave and forgot. He wanted to be part of a couple who shared every-thing—a bathroom and a bed, and children whose futures were not planned out years ahead of time. Parents who celebrated each child's arrival for the miracle it was instead of mapping out careers for their progeny.

Chris thought back on the thousands of operations he'd per-formed over the years. As always, the Martins came to mind. A couple so bedraggled and quiet, they'd been ignored by almost everyone in the hospital. He'd only seen them because he was checking on a postop gall bladder and Mrs. Martin had passed out in the hallway right in front of him.

It was Christmas Eve, he recalled. Mrs. Martin had been in labor for a number of hours due to the old-fashioned beliefs of a doctor who should have known better. By the time Chris saw her, the woman and child were both in distress.

The cesarean began routinely until she'd begun to hemorrhage. He'd pulled out all the stops to save her. And finally succeeded. Mr. Martin had been overjoyed to see his wife and child alive and relatively healthy. Tears had flowed down his cheeks as he thanked Chris. And when Chris had stopped in to check on the woman Christmas day, they'd invited him to join their celebrations. They had nothing. But they had such love, such joy. They were a family.

"Chris?" The delicate hand was softly tugging at his arm. Chris realized Jori had spoken to him several times.

"What?" His voice came out gruffly and she shrank back. He raked his hand through his hair in frustration, organizing his mind. "Sorry. Did you say something?"

Brown eyes studied him searchingly for several moments. Finally she gave up when he refused to permit her entrance to the dark secrets whirling around inside his head.

"I just wondered if you wanted to leave now."

Chris knew he'd hurt her by refusing to disclose everything. She could probably guess most of it by now anyway. Years of hiding his little-boy wants for a family like the Martins kept him from sharing his pain, however, and he stood immediately.

"Ready when you are." He grinned, forcing a light tone into his voice. Come on, Davis, get with it, he told himself. Get the mask back in place.

She was a good sport, Chris would give her that. She gathered their picnic without a word and stuffed it carelessly into the huge straw bag she carried on the front of her bike. She mounted the old two-wheeler and waited for him.

When he was beside her, she put her hand on his arm, stopping him from going any farther. Her sympathetic eyes met and held his. One hand reached up to push the hair off his forehead.

"If you ever need someone to talk to, someone to listen," she told him quietly, "I'm here." Then Jori called out to Billy and pedaled away down the lane while he stood staring after her.

Chapter Six

"Hi, Dad. How are you?" Jori tugged the thickly padded leather chair a little nearer her father's recliner and patted his hand. "Enjoying the sun?"

James Jessop stared at her, bleary eyed. "Jori?"

She grinned happily, pleased at this evidence that her daily visits were paying off. Her father seemed to recognize her more and more frequently.

"Yes, it's me, Dad. I brought you some pie. Fresh peach." She held out the plate and slipped the plastic wrap off. "Fosters are having their auction today. Do you want to go?"

"Reginald Foster died?" Her father stared at her with disbelief and Jori rushed to correct the error.

"No, Dad. He's moving, remember? Wanted to be nearer Barbra and her girls. In Minneapolis," she added when he continued to stare at her. Maybe it wouldn't be a good idea to remove him from the security of Sunset just yet, Jori considered.

"Oh." James continued to frown for several more minutes before taking the fork Jori offered and cutting off a piece of the pie. "It's good," he said after another mouthful.

"Thanks. I know it's your favorite so I made a couple of them. You let me know and I'll bring some more."

"Apple's my favorite," he told her firmly, pushing the empty plate away. "Always has been. *A word fitly spoke is like apples of gold in settings of silver.*"

"But you always said . . ." Jori stopped, refusing to be drawn. It would only confuse him more.

"Had your snack, have you, James?" Charity Flowerday patted the graying head with a gentle hand. "What was it today?"

But James seemed not to see her. He merely stood and wandered over to the blooming fuchsia plant nearby.

"Oh, dear," Charity murmured, peering down at Jori. "Did I say something wrong? I didn't mean to interrupt, you know."

"Of course you didn't." Jori sighed. "He's just a little confused today."

"Well, we all have those days!" Charity fluffed out the white pleated skirt of her summer dress. "For instance, I thought today was Friday and that I'd meet a friend here."

"It's Thursday," Jori smiled. "And aren't Dad and I friends?"

"Yes, of course, dear." Charity blushed, veering her eyes away from Jori's curious ones. "It's just that I meant a gentleman friend. It's so hard to get any privacy and I thought if we met here we could talk without Faith and Hope butting in."

Jori stared as the elderly woman shuffled her orthopedic shoes back and forth.

"Oh, don't misunderstand me. I love those two girls. We've been through so much together. But I need a little time and space on my own. Without their meddling."

"But you said you were meeting someone," Jori reminded her, frowning. "A man."

If anything, Charity Flowerday's face grew even redder. Her warm brown eyes were shuttered and she looked away from Jori's enquiring gaze.

"I just said that," she admitted at last, her mouth drooping. "I'm so tired of people trying to match me up with someone. Peter was a wonderful husband, but he's gone now and I've accepted that. I don't want anyone else in my life. Not like that. I have more than enough on my plate with Melanie and Mitch expecting." She glanced furtively over her shoulder and then relaxed a little farther into the chair back.

"I know it was silly but I thought if everyone believed I was interested in some mystery man, well . . ." She blushed again. "You know. They'd leave me alone."

"Yes," Jori whispered softly. "I know. But why didn't you just tell Faith and Hope the truth? I'm sure they'd understand."

Charity snorted. "Have you ever tried to get those two to stop once they've made up their minds?" She shook her head gloomily. "It only makes them determined to fix me up. I don't want that." Her voice was firm.

"It would serve you right if I told them." Jori grinned. "After all the matchmaking stunts you three have pulled on everyone else, it seems only fair."

"I can see how you'd think that," Charity murmured, glancing up warily. "But you're young and beautiful. You have your whole future ahead of you. You should have a husband and children." She stopped, staring off through the windows to the fountain spraying in the courtyard.

"That's all in the past for me. I shared some of the best years of my life with Peter and I wouldn't change that for anything, but that part of my life is over."

"You must have loved him very much," Jori breathed, gazing at the sweet face. "I can understand how it must seem that no one can take his place."

"No one can ever take another person's place," Charity agreed archly. "Each of us has our own personal part in the lives of those around us. I didn't mean that. I meant that I can't start reliving my life now. It's too late." She lifted her twisted hands toward Jori. "Besides, who'd want a worn-out crotchety old woman like me?"

"You're a beautiful woman, Mrs. Flowerday." Jori tried to keep the tears out of her voice. "You've given so much of your time and energy and love to this community. Why, no one even notices your hands, except to comment on how much you do with them!"

"I notice them." Charity's voice was so low Jori had to lean nearer. "I look at them every day and feel embarrassed to see how bent and misshapen they've become. And look at my feet." She held out her legs covered in the thick support hose.

"I was once voted the girl with the shapeliest legs, did you know that?"

Jori shook her head.

"No one does anymore. They've all forgotten that I used to be young and beautiful."

Jori was stunned by the admission and couldn't think of anything to say that wouldn't make the woman feel as if she were trying to compensate. She was desperately searching for the right words when, from behind them, James's voice boomed out.

"Man looks on the outward appearance, but God looks on the heart." He stared down at them vacantly, his eyes unfocused.

"Thank you, James." Charity smiled, patting the hand that sat on the back of her chair. "I've told myself that a hundred times, but somehow it just isn't the same."

She stood slowly and straightened, gathering up her purse with brisk birdlike movements that belied the wrinkle of tension on her forehead. "I'm getting maudlin," she said self-deprecatingly. "I'd better go home."

"You could come with us." The soft smooth tones came from behind them and Jori whirled around to see who was there.

Chris Davis stood grinning beside the smaller, more compact frame of Frank Bellows.

"We're going golfing," Chris announced. "Frank's going to teach me the finer points of the game. Want to come along, you two?"

Jori noted the look of longing in the older man's eyes as they moved over Charity's still figure. What could be better to prove to Charity that she was still a desirable woman than to spend the day with two attractive men? The added bonus of time spent in Chris's company couldn't hurt her either, could it?

"We were just saying we needed some fresh air," Jori murmured, linking her arm in Charity's. "I'm going to take Dad to the auction sale this afternoon, but we could go for a round or two until then. You did say you were free Charity," she reminded the older woman.

"Oh, but, I've never been golfing," Charity blustered, a spot of color on each cheek. "It's a long way around the course, isn't it?" She looked doubtfully at them all.

"Yes, it is rather," Frank agreed quietly. "That's why I always take my cart. Don't get so tired then."

Jori recognized the olive branch for what it was—an attempt to make Charity's physical limitation less obvious and realized that Frank really did want to spend time with Charity, whether she knew it or not.

"That would be great, Frank." Jori grinned. "When shall we go?"

"Why, right away!" Frank stared at Charity, obviously a little stunned by his good luck. "May I?" He held out his arm for Charity and that bemused lady slipped hers through it and walked down the hallway without a backward glance.

"Way to go," Chris cheered in Jori's ear. "He's been trying to get a date with her for ages."

"He has?" Jori stared. "How do you know?"

"He told me. Right after he noticed I was trying to get your attention." Chris slipped her arm through his and encouraged her down the hall. "I guess the Lord's looking out for both of us today."

"Oh." It was all she could think of and as she spotted James sipping his coffee and staring out the window, Jori pulled away. "I have to say goodbye to my dad. I'll be back in a minute."

But if James knew she was there, he gave no sign. His eyes were busy watching the flurry of hummingbirds sipping the red nectar from a bottle on the other side of the glass and he didn't respond to either her hug or kiss.

"Everything okay?" Chris's voice was soft with concern as he waited for her down the hall.

"I guess so. I just can't get used to him not noticing me. It's like he's there one minute and gone the next."

"It is the nature of the disease," Chris reminded her. His voice dropped. "And it probably won't get any better."

"I know." She sighed. "I know. Come on. Charity and Frank are probably waiting for us."

The morning passed in an abundance of laughter as Jori and Charity proved they neither knew nor cared about the difference between chipping and putting. Frank's patience was unending but even he shook his head when Jori whacked a ball off the green and far into the trees and shrubs beyond.

"Why don't we just leave it and you can start at the next hole?" Frank offered in his usual quiet tones. "There are wild roses in there and stinging nettles. You'll be a mess."

"No," Jori refused, determined to give the two seniors a few moments together. "I'm not wimping out. You and Charity go on ahead. She's much more adept at this game than I. Doc, you'd better come along. In case I need some medical treatment." Jori opened her eyes wide as she stared at Chris, daring him to back out when she had it all planned.

"Oh! Yeah. Sure." He followed behind her and then squeaked out a protest. "Ow! Jori, put that club down off your shoulder. I have a feeling I'm the one who's going to need the medical help."

Jori turned back just once and that was to wink at Frank Bellows as he stood transfixed on the green.

"Go ahead," she called cheerfully. "We'll catch up."

Frank smiled and nodded and she knew he'd gotten the message.

"Jori, how could you possibly have hit that ball away back here? You must have more strength than I thought."

"More brains, too." She dug around in the undergrowth of ferns and shrubs. "Couldn't you see he wanted to be alone with her? And Frank is exactly what Charity needs right now. Ouch!" She rubbed the sore spot on her brow and found his eyes just inches from her own.

"You sure have a hard head," she muttered, unable to tear her gaze away from his. "I think my skull is cracked."

She stared at the flopped-over lock of hair lying across his forehead, feeling his arms slip around her waist as he leaned a little closer, blue eyes sparkling.

"Can I kiss it and make it better?"

His kiss was like coming home, Jori decided hazily. His arms were like soft clouds of welcome closing around her. There was no threat; she didn't feel pressured as she had with Trace. She felt safe and secure and more alive than she had in weeks. And when at last his mouth moved to her neck she felt cherished.

"What kind of medical treatment was that?" she protested half-heartedly, drawing away as the heat rose in her cheeks.

"It's a specialty of mine," he replied slowly. "I've been doing a bit of research into it lately. What do you think? Is it effective?"

"That depends on what you're trying to cure." Jori chuckled.

"I take my profession very seriously, I'll have you know," he began indignantly. "If I can help relieve the pain and suffering of the masses, I'm going to try."

Jori snorted, appreciating his attempt at humor. Things *had* gotten a little too intense.

"Yeah, right. And the side benefits don't hurt too much either, do they?"

He looked affronted as he picked up the ball and guided her out of the brush.

"Are you implying that I'm somehow in this predicament because of the side benefits? My dear woman, you wound me deeply." He tried to brush the patch of burrs off his pant leg and grimaced when they refused to budge. When Jori burst out laughing, he frowned even harder. "I suppose you think this is funny?"

"I don't know what you mean," she sputtered, walking beside him with a smug air. "I merely came along for a lovely game of golf, out in the fresh air." Her eyes widened when he grasped the club out of her hand with a loud burst of laughter. "What?"

"We're going that way, remember?" He pointed down the fairway in the opposite direction.

"Oh." She peered across the elegant lawns. "Of course," she muttered as if she knew exactly what she was doing.

"Of course," he repeated seriously. But there was an impish glint in those innocent baby blues.

They finally found Charity and Frank on the restaurant patio sipping glasses of iced tea. The two were deep into some heated discussion that stopped short when Jori approached the table. Charity's eyes widened.

"Oh, my word! Jori, dear. Are you all right?" She brushed gently at the twigs and dried leaves caught in Jori's untidy hair. "What happened? Did you have a nice game, dear?"

Jori was about to explain when Chris flopped down beside her, his teeth flashing in the bright sunlight.

"She had a lousy game. She's the worst player I've ever seen," he muttered in frustration. One hand brushed the lock of gleaming blond hair off his forehead. The gesture was totally ineffectual. "I've had easier eighteen-hour days in the operating room," he declared, motioning for a waitress.

"You're the one who insisted on chopping away at that ball." She leaned back in her chair and puffed the bangs off her forehead. "It's really quite a silly game," she announced. "Chasing a stupid little ball around in a circle. I much prefer swimming or baseball."

"You only say that because you don't understand it," Chris counseled. "There is a sequence, a pattern, that you have to follow. You can't just go batting balls around the course willy-nilly. I'm sure some of those you hit belonged to other players."

"Oh, well. They can always find another one. There are hundreds of them in the bush." Jori thought he seemed inordinately worried. She shrugged indifferently.

"Is that where you were, dear?" Charity's voice sounded choked. "You seem to have gotten quite dirty."

"It's filthy out there," Jori told her seriously. "And Chris kept making me change sticks. They're all backward anyway."

"They're not backward," Chris protested vigorously. "How was I supposed to know you're left-handed?"

"Oh, my." Frank sighed. "If I'd only known. I have a set in my garage that has been there for ages. Ever since my daughter left home. She was left-handed."

Jori swallowed her mouthful of tea, shaking her head in disgust. "I don't understand why you need a set," she argued. "One stick works as well as the next to bat with."

"Oh, so that's what you were doing," Chris groaned, shaking his head in disgust. "Batting!"

"He did that the whole time," Jori told the other two self-righteously. "And then when I got a home run, he was all stuffy and rude."

"A home run?" Charity inquired, a tiny smile flickering at the edge of her mouth.

"She means a hole in one," Chris explained, raising his eyebrows at Jori. "Although if you were batting all morning, I suppose technically it was a home run."

"I got it on the fifth hole, too," Jori exclaimed, ignoring his sour tone. "One of the guys there told me that he's never seen it done before."

"The fifth?" Frank frowned. "But that's a really tough one. How in the world did you do it?"

"Don't ask," Chris ordered but Jori ignored him and launched into her personal technique, slapping at the dust on her shorts as she did.

"And so the thing just flew down the hole. I didn't realize someone else was making the shot and when I jumped up and down like that, I guess I distracted him. He sure was cranky." She ignored Chris's snort of disgust and glanced at her watch. "Good grief, I've got to get home and change if I'm going to that auction."

"I was thinking of going myself," Frank murmured. He glanced at Charity and then clearly took his courage in both hands. "Would you like to go, too, Charity? We could have a little lunch here before we head over there."

To Jori's surprise, the older woman readily agreed. "I'd love some lunch. They have the loveliest deep-fried shrimp here. You know, all that exercise has made me quite hungry!"

Jori took a quick second look, but when it seemed that Charity was indeed serious about staying, she got up from her chair and shuffled toward the door. "Thanks for the game. See you at the auction."

"Now that went pretty well, I thought." Chris's fingers on her back propelled her forward.

"What?" She peered up at him curiously.

"Those two." He jerked his head to one side, indicating the senior couple now busily engaged in a discussion. "I knew if he could only get her to sit down and talk, she'd like him. Frank's one of the most interesting men I know."

Jori strode down the street beside him. "I hope that Charity thinks so, too. She's really lonely right now and Frank might be just what she needs."

"A single man, you mean," he derided.

"Nope. Somebody to talk to. She won't come out and say it, but I think Charity is really feeling left out now that Faith and Hope are busy with their husbands. Apparently now they've even started trying to find someone for her and Charity feels that no man would want to be seen with her because of her arthritis."

Chris had one comment and he made it just under his breath. Even so, Jori heard him.

"Women!"

"Well, thanks for walking me home," she said when they reached her front gate. "I've got to go and change before I pick up Dad."

"I'll wait."

"You're going, too?" She peered at him through the tangle of hair that had blown across her face. "Why?"

"Because I've never been to an auction before," he blurted out, eyes daring her to comment. "Why are you going?"

"I'm not really fond of auction sales," she told him, opening the front door and inviting him to sit down with a sweep of her hand. "Especially when it's the Fosters'."

She watched him sprawl in her father's recliner and grinned. Chris Davis overshot the thing by a good foot, his legs dangling out beyond the chair.

"What's so terrible about an auction sale—besides all the junk, I mean?" Chris watched her face close up.

"Auction sales are awful because they always mean we've lost another member of the community. Either through death or because they've moved. And I don't want Mossbank to change," she told him passionately. Her face colored and she glanced away, self-consciously twirling the ends of her hair.

"Reginald Foster saved my life," she told him shortly. "Once when I was ten and then again later when I came home. I hate to think of him moving away from Mossbank. He's been a part of my life for so long." Jolting herself out of her thoughts, Jori turned and started up the stairs. "I'll just be a couple of minutes."

Chris stared at her disappearing figure, wondering at her curious words. This Foster man had saved her life? How?

Jori didn't bring up the subject again and Chris couldn't think of a way to introduce it into the conversation so he let it lapse while they drove to the nursing home. James Jessop was dressed and ready to go.

"Don't understand why Reg thinks he has to leave," he grumbled, fastening his seat belt. "He's the only fellow I know who can fix a piece of furniture so it stays fixed."

"I'm going to miss him, too, Dad," Jori murmured. Chris saw the glint of a tear at the corner of her eye but wisely refrained from commenting on it.

They wandered through the various items set out for auction, pausing now and then as James exclaimed over some tool or another.

"Don't you just love Reg's house?" Jori stared up at the stone walls with the creeping ivy. "It's so solid. It always makes me think of God's love—safe, secure. You can trust it to hold up."

"It doesn't need a bit of work, either," James announced prosaically. "The windows have been replaced. And the doors are all new and solid." He slapped a brick planter with one hand and grinned. "It's as strong as a rock." He turned to Chris. "Jori used to play out there on that lawn. Reg's wife, Gena, would bring her tea for her dolls and they'd pick lilacs and daisies and bring home beautiful bouquets."

"Yes." Jori smiled at her dad. "I love this flower garden. I lugged home all the flowers I could to brighten up the house when Mom was sick. We never had enough room for all these hedges and stuff."

As she trailed past the honeysuckle, Chris watched her delicate nose thin while she breathed in the scent. Seconds later she was bent over a huge yellow rose, cradling it tenderly between her palms.

"And the roses. Aren't they fantastic? I can never get enough roses."

James winked at Chris. "There was a time when she thought dandelions were just fine." The older man chuckled. "It was a lot cheaper to buy those by the tons, I can tell you."

"It does look a lot like a family home," Chris murmured, running his hand over the redwood picnic table and chairs as he remembered his own childhood home. Stiff and formal, it hadn't beckoned like this one did.

"If you close your eyes, you can almost hear the kids rolling in the grass," Jori whispered, her thoughts meshing with his. "Up there in that maple is the most wonderful tree house. Or it used to be. We slept out here on those hot summer nights. I can still hear the crickets."

"It's the kind of home that needs a family," James interrupted, bringing them back to the present. "No wonder Reg wants to move—he must be lonely without Gena."

"Yes, I miss her every day, James. But time goes on and I want to be near my grandchildren." The two old friends slapped each other on the back, laughing and teasing as if time stood still.

"Come on inside," Reg invited. "I've just made some blackberry tea."

As they went inside, Chris watched Jori's bright eyes move to and fro as if searching for something. Moments later he found out what it was.

"Mags is gone, sweetie," Reg murmured softly, his hand brushing over the soft waterfall of Jori's hair. "She was a terrific dog but she just couldn't take the cold winters anymore, I guess."

"Oh." Chris saw the tears form in her eyes. "I guess it all changes, doesn't it?" she whispered to Reg.

"Yes, everything does," he admitted sadly. Then his face lit up with a huge grin. "Even you," he teased, tweaking her nose. "I can't even see the scar."

"What scar?" Chris took his place at the wrought iron table on the patio and accepted the cup of tea he was passed. Reg and James sat peering at Jori, lost in memories of long ago. "Did you hurt yourself or something?"

"Or something," she admitted breathlessly, jumping up from the table. "I'm going to go look around, Dad. You guys can talk about male stuff." With a grin and a toss of her glossy head, she was through the door.

Chris glanced from one man to the other, trying to assess the situation.

"She's never forgotten what you did for her, Reg." James Jessop's voice was filled with something Chris couldn't define. "I doubt if she ever will. I think she's finding it hard to see you go."

"It was a long time ago, James. I did what anyone would have done. It was nothing."

"It was everything," the older man corrected, leaning forward earnestly. "It was her life, her future."

Reg smiled. "Let's talk about happier times."

As they began to rag each other about the biggest trout ever caught, Chris excused himself and went outside. There was something here he didn't understand. And he thought he needed to if he was to comprehend what made Jordanna Jessop so determined to stay in this little town.

"Do you collect china?" His voice was dryly sardonic as he watched her finger the mismatched teacups and saucers. "Is that why you're so determined to stay here forevermore?"

"I never said forevermore," she muttered, flushing at his intense scrutiny. "And I do owe these people a huge debt. They saved my life."

"How?" Finally he would hear the truth behind her reasons for wanting to bury herself in this little town of nobodies.

"Oh, it was a long time ago. When I was little." When he didn't look away she sighed and continued. "I was ten and my friend and I were playing on her farm. There was a stack of newly cut hay and we would jump off the barn roof and into that stack." Her eyes closed, long lashes dark on her fair skin.

"I can still smell the perfume of that fresh hay," she murmured. "Even after all these years."

Chris stood, waiting for her to continue.

"I was a tomboy, kind of a daredevil, I guess. I went a little farther up the roof each time. The last time I went as far as I could and took a flying leap into the haystack. Unfortunately, I missed the hay."

He sucked in his breath at the thought and clinically searched her limbs for some damage he hadn't previously noted.

"What happened?"

"Oh, I guess I bounced off some bales and onto the edge of the cultivator that was nearby. Apparently I cut my head open. I woke up four days later in Minneapolis with my head shaved. Boy, was I mad."

Chris sighed in relief. A few stitches, that was all. Nothing serious.

"They told me that when I hit my head, I'd injured something in my brain that required immediate surgery. The doctor who could operate happened to be in Minneapolis at a convention. He agreed to stay there if they'd fly me in immediately." She shrugged. "He operated and I was fine. End of story."

"I don't think so." Chris drew his eyebrows together. "You haven't said anything about what makes you so indebted to the people of Mossbank."

She was silent for a long time before she replied.

"Reg set up a fund and got everybody to chip in to pay for the surgery and my hospital stay," she told him. "Reg even donated his own blood. My dad was out of work and my mother was sick and we didn't have any insurance left and he was so helpful." Her slim arms squeezed tightly around herself in a defensive gesture learned long ago.

"That's certainly the mark of a good friend," he murmured quietly.

"They did the same thing when my mother died. For months these friends—" her arm waved to the groups of people now browsing the sale area "—made sure that we had a hot meal every night. They cleaned house, washed my clothes and helped me with my homework until my dad could get back on his feet." Her eyes sparkled and shimmered at him, the depths of her feelings obvious.

"I owe them. A lot. It's a debt I can never repay but I intend to try."

The auction was beginning and everyone was moving toward that area. Chris decided to let her go for now. He'd find out more later, he told himself. A lot more.

Chapter Seven

It was one of those days—those crazy mixed-up days when everything happened at the same time. Jori pushed the damp wispy tendrils that had worked free of her topknot off her overheated face and decided to go with the flow. What else was there to do?

First the air conditioner had given out.

"Stands to reason," she muttered to herself, checking the stack of files laid ready for afternoon clinic. "It is the hottest day of the year, after all."

Grimacing, she plucked the sticky nylon uniform from her stomach. It had to be the nylon one, because her washer had died last night in the middle of a load, leaving black grease spots spattered over everything. Nestled at the bottom was, naturally, her coolest cotton outfit.

Then, of course, there was the chicken pox epidemic. Jori vowed every kid in town had it, and all at the same time. And of course, every mother wanted her child checked when the poor little things only wanted to be home, with as little as possible touching their very itchy skin.

Which, for some reason, made her think of Chris. The problem was that his itches were buried deep inside and he wasn't letting anyone scratch them, least of all her. With a brisk shake of her head, Jori dislodged the fanciful thought and forced herself to concentrate on matters at hand, checking to make sure the kits were ready.

"Let's see, we've got a throat culture, remove a couple of sutures, at least two physicals." Jori checked the list again.

"Talking to yourself."

"Aaagh," Jori jumped, pressing her hand to her throat. "Don't do that," she remonstrated with the grinning blond giant behind her. "I'm getting older daily and my heart isn't what it was."

Doc Davis just grinned. "It's not actually my specialty," he murmured, lifting one eyebrow. "But I can perform certain resuscitation techniques if you want." The sun caught the blond stubble on his determined chin as he leaned a little nearer.

Jori's cheeks flushed a bright pink at the suggestive note in his voice.

"Doctor!" She checked to be sure no one had heard him. Thankfully, Glenda was busy arranging her own afternoon and so paid little attention to them.

Chris burst out laughing at her concern. "I didn't realize you were so circumspect. I'll be more careful in the future."

"What future?" Jori kept her head bent, concentrating on the files. That way he wouldn't see the longing in her eyes for the future they would never have.

But he wouldn't let her get away with it. One strong finger tipped up her chin so her dark gaze met his laughing blue ones. He traced the curve of her chin for a moment, his eyes brimming with mirth.

"Oh, I just meant I'll plan it better so next time I'll be able to catch you in a consultation room, or something," he told her, his eyes flashing. Oddly, his skin had flushed a deep red and Jori forced herself to look away.

"Quit flirting, Doctor." Her voice was primly correct. "We have patients to see." Jori snapped the files upright against the counter.

She turned to collect the first appointment of the day, but Chris's hand on her arm stopped any progress she might have made. Jori's round eyes flew to his in surprise. Chris's face was stern with reproof, although his blue velvet eyes caressed her with a sparkle.

"I've warned you several times, J.J. My name is Chris."

"Yes, Doc . . . I mean Chris." She shook her head and strode away while Chris's chuckles followed her down the hall. You couldn't win with the man.

It was appropriate that chaos chose that precise moment to arrive. He was three and well used to speaking his mind; today was no different. His name was Jonathan Grand and he was Jori's godchild.

"Happy bird-day, Auntie Jori," he crowed, alerting the whole waiting room to her milestone. "How old are you?" He chirped the little chorus to the snickers of the roomful of grinning patients.

"Thank you, darling." Jori accepted his hug with aplomb. "I'm twenty-eight, sweetie." She ruffled his brown curls before returning him to his mother with raised brows. "I will get you for this," she promised, teeth clenched in a grim smile.

Amy Grand dangled one jean-clad leg for Jonathan to bounce on.

"I know." She grinned. "That's why I came bearing gifts." With a wide smile, she handed Jori an envelope. "I know you've been wanting to do this for ages, so go for it. Happy birthday!"

Inside were two tickets for a riverboat cruise down the beautiful Missouri River just outside of Bismarck, including a sumptuous dinner for two onboard. Jori stared at her friend, eyes glistening, deeply touched by Amy's thoughtfulness.

"Thank you, Amy. I really appreciate this." They hugged to the benevolent smiles of the rest of the room. Then Jori quirked an eyebrow at her friend. "Two tickets?"

Blunt as usual, Amy blurted out, "For you and Dr. Chris, of course."

Jori figured she might have carried it off if she hadn't turned just then to find said doctor beaming at her over the gray filing cabinets. He nodded, grinning like a Cheshire cat.

Jori turned her back on him. Drat Amy! She had been wanting to ride that cruise for ages, but she wasn't thrilled about having her date chosen for her. Maybe . . . she smiled at Amy kindly.

"Well, thank you for thinking of him, but actually Friday is Dr. Davis's night on call, so I doubt very much that he could . . ."

"Yes, he can." Chris cut in, beaming fatuously. "It's all arranged. He switched shifts just for your birthday."

Jori groaned inwardly. There was no way out, it seemed, not in front of this crowd. She smiled shakily at the room in general, muttered another thank-you and went back to work.

He was getting too close, and she knew it. She also knew there was no possible future for them together. He would leave Mossbank. And she couldn't. Closing her eyes in frustration, Jori counted to ten. It didn't help.

Neither did the beautiful flowers Granny Jones brought from her garden, or the delicious peach pie Zelda Adams had baked. And it was downright difficult to look at another praline cheesecake from Emma Simms.

But when Aubery Olden arrived with one of the beautiful wooden bowls he had so lovingly created from a burl of cherry tree, Jori was forced to relinquish her bad humor. They were kind and generous people, her friends. How could they know she was highly attracted to someone who would leave in a few weeks? Someone she would probably never see again.

"You're something less than thrilled with this arrangement, right?" Chris's low tones brought her abruptly out of her meandering.

They had been driving for twenty minutes and, other than the perfunctory greetings and a thank-you for the iris bouquet, she had purposely said nothing to him as the miles passed.

"Oh, sorry. I guess I was just thinking," Jori hedged nervously. She plucked at the skirt of her turquoise dress self-consciously.

A lot of thought had gone into her choice of clothes for tonight. Jori had wanted to look special since it was Friday night and the boat would be packed with people celebrating. A tiny voice in her head called her a liar. Sighing, she accepted the fact that she had wanted to knock the socks off of one smugly superior substitute doctor.

And Jori was pretty sure this turquoise chiffon thing did it. He had gulped when his eyes took in her figure swathed in the garment with a cinched waist and matching belt. Yards of filmy sheer fabric billowed out in a full knee-length skirt.

"Have you heard anything from Dan?" His deep voice carried softly above the Bach concerto playing in the background.

Jori turned to look at him, shifting comfortably in the T-bird's low-slung bucket seats. A tendril of hair had escaped her tumbling topknot of curls and she pushed it behind her ear.

"Yes, Jessica sent me a card. Apparently, she's been checked in. If she doesn't deliver within the next few days, they'll do a cesarean. I don't think the baby is doing that well."

Surprisingly, her voice was normal and Jori relaxed a little deeper into the seat. She prayed daily for her friends and she just had to believe that God wouldn't let them down when it came to the crunch.

"Dan phoned yesterday to ask me if I could stay longer. Apparently a heart repair on the baby is imminent, although I'm not sure Jess realizes that yet." He glanced at her sideways but Jori faced straight ahead, dreading the question she knew she had to ask.

"And can you?"

Chris turned his dark head to stare at her. "What?" he asked, lost for a moment.

"Can you stay longer?" Jori didn't like asking it, but she had to know. In some ways, it would be easier if he left soon. But her heart soared with happiness when he answered.

"Yes, I can stay as long as I'm needed. My time is my own right now." His tone wasn't welcoming but Jori asked anyway.

"Why did you leave Boston when you were doing so well?"

Chris had known the question was coming. He'd expected it because Jori wasn't the type to ignore significant details like that. She'd want to know everything. But he still didn't have his answer ready. And he knew she'd keep at him until he did. He heaved a sigh of capitulation, searching for the right words.

"Aside from helping out Dan, I guess I had my fill of medicine there. It was a huge hospital and the rotations were fairly spread out, but I felt I needed something different. Something more connected to other people. For now."

There—he had spilled his guts. Let her make what she wanted of it. Knowing Jori, he would bet a tidy sum that she would sense the effort it had cost him to open up.

True to form, she nodded understandingly. "Community, sense of belonging. I think everyone feels it sooner or later." They stopped and parked the car. She linked her arm with his as they stepped onto the waiting boat.

"Well, Doc, here we are." She grinned up at him before moving away to survey the sumptuous dining room with its elegant furnishings.

He tugged her arm gently. "Let's go for a stroll around this tug."

The evening was a balmy one with the sun just setting. Stars twinkled here and there while the lights of the city began to glimmer around them. The gentle motion of the boat was calming and Jori found she was enjoying herself.

In the background, a band began to play old movie tunes. Without much thought they moved into each other's arms and began to sway gently to the music.

"I love this song," Jori murmured as the group segued into "Moon River." She sang along with them for a few bars.

"You have a beautiful voice, J.J. I enjoyed hearing you sing." Chris whispered, the words gently grazing her ear. "And this dress—I don't know if *awesome* quite describes you tonight." He spun her around.

Jori giggled.

"Yeah, I know what you mean." She laughed, leaning back to study him. "You are quite a picture yourself. Especially in that suit." Her dark head tipped back as she studied him. "Yep, sure beats the lab coat."

And that was no lie. His blond good looks were certainly accentuated by the black suit and crisp white shirt Chris wore so comfortably. It was the perfect foil for the blue striped tie that matched the exact azure color of his eyes.

He bowed to thank her just as the maître d' announced dinner. While they waited for directions to their table, Jori glanced around once more. There were a lot of men in the room but she seriously doubted that one of them could hold a candle to Chris. And when her heart repeated that silly little pitter-patter as his arm moved around her waist, Jori made her decision.

She'd enjoy tonight because she doubted there would be another one. Chris would be gone from her life soon and it wasn't likely that she would ever see him again.

Once she made that decision, it was easy to enjoy, even savor, every moment of their time together. They both chose the chef's special for the evening and while they waited, Chris told silly jokes.

"Why didn't the chicken cross the road?"

Jori groaned but he insisted she guess.

"Because she didn't want to get to the other side."

Chris's mouth stretched in a wide grin. "Wrong."

She sat waiting, but Chris just grinned at her. Jori sighed. He was like a big kid himself.

"Okay, I'll bite. Why didn't the chicken cross the road?" Jori just knew she would regret this.

"Because there was a stop sign." His blue eyes twinkled. "Guess who told me that?"

"Jennifer," Jori guessed, naming a young lady who was a glutton for joke books.

"Tommy Banks." Chris chortled just remembering the young boy. "And when I asked him what his favorite book was, he told me he really enjoyed *Parents* magazine because then he could keep up with what the adults had planned."

Jori giggled at the picture Chris painted of the freckled little boy whose precocious attitude she had experienced more than once.

They had barely set their salad forks down when the ribs arrived, redolent with oregano, garlic and lemon juice. The baby potatoes were cooked to perfection and the broccoli spears steamed a bright fresh green. They were both hungry and tucked into the delicious meal with relish. When she could eat no more, Jori leaned back in her chair, replete with the fine meal they had enjoyed.

"This is so wonderful." She sighed, gazing out the windows as the sun colored everything in a rosy glow. "I'm going to have to thank Amy appropriately for this wonderful gesture." She glanced at Chris suddenly.

"And you, too." She blushed. "It was really kind of you to rearrange your schedule this way."

"This is good, but I think your roast beef dinner was better." He rendered his verdict with a haughty tilt of his arched brow. Then he spoiled it by grinning. "And you are very welcome."

During the meal they chatted about Mossbank and its people. Jori was surprised to hear how much Chris had learned about each of his patients in the short time he had been in the town.

"By the way," she asked slyly, "what did you do with the rest of your cheesecakes. Did you really freeze them all?" Actually the problem had been bothering her for days.

Jori giggled as he groaned in dismay. But when a flush of red coursed over his face, she became concerned. She would not have her friends hurt by his insensitive attitude.

"Oh, no!" she moaned, anticipating the worst. "What did you do? Tell me."

His blue eyes met hers, tiny points of light twinkling deep within.

"I wanted to save something for Dan and Jessica. So, I cut one piece from each one and froze it with the appropriate name attached. Then I phoned that kids camp out at Minotka Beach." He grinned. "When I explained my situation to them, they agreed to take the rest off my hands." He held his hands palm up. "*Et, voilà!* It's gone!"

Jori breathed a sigh of relief. Then a thought crossed her mind. "How long ago was this?" she demanded.

Chris stared at her strangely. "Last week. Why?"

"I wondered why we had so many indigestion cases from them." She teased him, beaming with mirth. "Marta, the director, forgot to tell me about the cheesecake."

Jori burst out laughing at the look of chagrin on his face. It was clear that the good doctor had not connected the arrival of his dubious gift with the stomach cramps and other assorted maladies experienced by several of the campers.

Holding up his hand, Chris licked his forefinger and made a number one in the air.

"One for you," he conceded in a grumpy voice that only made Jori's grin widen.

She sipped her coffee while they waited for the dessert cart. The room seemed very quiet all at once, but perhaps the band was taking a break.

When the familiar notes of "Happy Birthday" were played, however, Jori sat straight in her chair. He wouldn't . . . he couldn't . . . could he?

It appeared that he had!

Two waiters carried out a huge cake decorated with fat pink roses. As they moved, the two men sang to the cheerful clapping of the other diners.

Happy Birthday, Jori lay scripted in delicate pink lettering across the glistening white icing. Around the edge glowed a ring of pink-striped candles. Jori would have covered her face but Chris reached out to grasp her hand just then, holding it on top of the table for all the world to see.

The song ended as the cake arrived beside their table. Jori was thankful when the band resumed their musical selections. Her cheeks felt as though they were on fire, but she kept her chin up and met Chris's glance head-on.

"I wish you a very happy birthday, Jori," he said quietly, and then pressed a delicate kiss to the inside of her wrist before allowing her hand to move away.

"Thank you," she murmured, unable to get anything else out. The whole week had been a chain of one surprise after another, but this took the cake, Jori mused. Then laughed. Hah, a pun!

Chris looked at her uncertainly, his eyes narrowed in speculation.

"She overdid it, didn't she?" His voice was quietly sympathetic. Jori stared at him.

"You mean Amy arranged for this?" She motioned toward the monstrous cake. When he nodded, she groaned and laid her forehead on her palm. "I should have known."

"Yes, you should have," Chris's low tones were reproving. "Not my style at all." He stuck out a finger and dipped it into the fluffy white frosting before popping it into his mouth. "Mmm, not bad, though," he told her, grinning.

"What do you mean, not your style?" Jori strove to keep her voice down. "This is exactly like something you would do, Christopher Davis." She had been sure of that once, but now Jori reconsidered.

"Uh-uh. I'm much more subtle."

Jori searched his face. "Yes, you and a steamroller," she mocked. He sat staring at her, perplexed by her attitude. It was clear that the idea had never crossed his mind and Jori felt guilty. "What is your style, then?" she asked, half-afraid of his answer.

His forefinger beckoned her closer. She leaned across to hear his conspiratorial whisper. "I'll show you later."

Dumbfounded, Jori sat wide-eyed and staring until Chris asked for some cake. She cut him a huge piece and a smaller one for herself, going through the motions automatically while she found herself wondering about "later."

They moved outside and Jori sipped her coffee, loath to break into the charming stillness that had fallen. When Chris moved, Jori jerked out of her dreamworld to find him facing her on the narrow bench.

"This is for you," he told her, holding out a beautifully wrapped parcel held together with a tiny bit of silver ribbon. "A very happy birthday, Jori," he offered.

"You didn't need to do this," she murmured, accepting it. "You've done more than enough tonight." Her dark eyes searched his wide blue ones for answers, but got lost studying the tiny smile that turned up the corner of his mouth.

Oh so slowly, Jori slid off the ribbon and the pretty iridescent paper. Inside, a slim black box nestled in white tissue. Holding her breath, Jori slipped off the lid to find a delicate gold chain with a tiny boat attached snuggled into a puff of white cotton. A card read, "To Jori on her twenty-eighth. Chris."

"It's beautiful," she breathed, lifting the tiny weight in her palm. "So delicate and fine. Thank you very much." As she lifted her head, Jori found Chris's eyes much nearer than she expected. She pressed a kiss to his cheek, mere inches from his mouth.

"You're welcome," he murmured before turning his head to meet her lips with his own. It was a questioning kiss. Slowly, tentatively his lips touched hers as if evaluating her response while he waited for her answer.

When she returned his caress, he drew her closer. Jori raised her arms and wrapped them around his neck, happy to oblige his unspoken request.

"Is he the one, Lord?" she prayed silently.

"Jori?" His hands slowed then stopped their delicate caress. His lips pressed softly against the side of her mouth before he pulled gently back, his big hands cupping her face as he stared into her eyes.

"I think we had better go dance," he muttered, closing his gleaming blue eyes for a moment. They popped open a second later when Jori tugged on his hand.

In her palm she held the tiny necklace.

"First, would you put this on for me?" she asked quietly, turning around.

As Chris fumbled with the clasp, Jori drew the wispy tendrils of hair off her neck to give him free access. It seemed to take forever, but finally he turned her around, strong fingers pressing into her waist.

In a trance Jori moved into his arms and allowed him to lead her effortlessly onto the polished dance floor that occupied the upper deck. She swayed to the dreamy music, lost in the feel of his arms around her. She was falling for him. Hard. And the landing, when he left, would be more painful than anything she'd yet endured.

This was wonderful, Chris decided, breathing in her fragrance. Jori Jessop was like quicksilver—strong and supple, gorgeous and ethereal.

But Jori was not his type, he acknowledged grimly in another part of his mind. She was a small-town girl who liked it that way. Her life revolved around her community and she wasn't the type to turn her back on it all for a thirty-six-year-old doctor who had little to offer in terms of stability and even less when it came to family, home and hearth.

Frustrated, Chris glared at his watch. Suddenly he wished the boat would dock so they could get home before he did something really stupid—like tell her his feelings.

Just then Chris felt Jori burrow closer against him and, ignoring his better judgment, he wrapped his arms more tightly around her.

Best make hay while the sun shines, he smiled, thinking of Aubery Olden. The old coot had a lot of sense under all that grime. Perhaps he should listen up. Chris dropped his chin on the top of Jori's piled-up hair. As the faint whisper of her perfume drifted to his nostrils he decided to have another talk with the old fellow. Possibly, Chris considered, he could learn a little something.

"The band is shutting down." Jori's voice was husky, dreamlike. Chris understood that feeling completely.

"I think we have time for a last cup of coffee before we leave this boat." He grasped her hand in his and tugged her over to a table.

Jori sat across from him, staring off into space. "I love this place," she murmured, looking back over her shoulder to the twinkling lights of Bismarck at night.

"Do you come here often?" Chris asked, trying for a neutral subject.

She tipped her head to one side. It was one of her mannerisms that Chris had noticed early on. When she was thinking of something pleasant from the past, Jori always rested her head on one shoulder and closed her eyes. He waited and sure enough, three seconds later her hand came up to twiddle with a tendril of hair. He grinned knowingly.

"My dad used to bring me to Bismarck each Christmas," she reminisced, a tender smile curving her lips. "We always went to the top floor of Enderby's because they had a huge display of animated Christmas scenes."

Her voice was dreamy with the memories. She blinked her eyes, peering absentmindedly into the night.

"I would plan ahead for weeks, waiting to see the tree displays and hear the carolers that strolled through the store, dressed in English outfits straight from Dickens. And boy, could they sing."

Jori turned toward him eagerly, intent on explaining the wonders she'd seen. Chris found himself fascinated by the animation that flew across her expressive face.

"It was totally dark up there, with tiny fairy lights hanging all around. Each scene had its own lighting." Her eyes opened wide as she remembered.

"There was always a pond with ice-skaters," she explained. "And Santa and the reindeer, of course." Her long fingers formed a tent as she thought. "Oh, and Frosty usually walked around, handing out candy canes." Her voice was breathless with delight.

"There was a beautiful Nativity scene with the animals all around it." There was a tiny break in her voice, but Jori recovered immediately, continuing her account. "I especially remember the horse and cutters with kids crammed inside, so happy. The sleighs and toboggans slid down little snow hills and there was always the sound of children laughing."

Chris shared her silence for a few minutes and thought how much he had missed. Jori had such wonderful memories, he mused. It would be something for her to pass on to her own children.

She was speaking again, her voice whispery soft with a tinge of sadness. "I loved the family scene. You know, where everyone gathers round the tree as they open their gifts. I always wished there were more people to share our tree with. Dad and I could have used a family."

Her round dark eyes sparkled with tears. Surprised and touched by the loneliness that threaded through her voice, Chris reached out and covered her hand with his. They sat quietly together for a few moments before he broke the silence.

"Do you still go there to see all that?" He liked to think of her now, wandering through the displays, as enchanted as any child there.

"They don't go to that extent with their decorations anymore.

But I still think the window displays are fabulous. And on New Year's Eve I go to *The Nutcracker* ballet."

"Oh." His one word spoke volumes and Jori's ready laugh bubbled out.

"I know what you're thinking, but *The Nutcracker* is a very special ballet. Dad and I used to go. We would get all dressed up in our very best, go out for a special dinner and then to the theater. I never fell asleep even though it lasted until well after eleven. And each year Dad would give me a nutcracker doll to remember the year." She grinned. "I have quite a collection now."

"You have some lovely memories, Jori," he told her, half-envious.

'Yes, I do." Her voice wobbled a little, but Chris noticed she recovered quickly. "What sorts of things did your family do together?" she asked politely. "It must have been nice to have sisters." He heard the wistful note in her voice and almost laughed.

"I'm not sure you would have enjoyed it," he told her grimly. "My parents are academics. They tried to do a fair bit of entertaining at Christmas so they could work without interruption through the rest of the year." He grimaced, recalling those stiff occasions.

"There were a lot of very formal, very boring dinners where the discussions were usually scientific." Man, he was getting maudlin, Chris decided. He turned his sardonic grin toward Jori.

"Perhaps that's where I began to learn about surgery," he said with just a tinge of bitterness. "Heaven knows I certainly had enough time to dissect anything that crossed my plate."

It must be the dark, Chris decided. Here he was spilling his guts about the worst times of his life to a woman who had experienced the best. This is not the way to end a romantic evening, Davis, he told himself sourly. Unfortunately, he couldn't think of anything else to say.

After a few minutes Jori changed the subject.

"You know, there's a wonderful folk festival near here. It's held in a park and they have some famous names performing at all different times. It's very informal but it's fun. You should go on your day off."

She turned to smile at him and Chris felt an ache in his heart. He couldn't deny it any longer. As he drove down the highway, he acknowledged the truth. He wanted to love and be loved by this woman. He wanted to raise a family with her and grow old together without feeling as if he'd failed someone. He wanted all the dull boring routine things he'd scorned for so long.

But most of all he wanted Jori Jessop by his side for the rest of his days.

The idea was so overwhelming that Chris struggled to concentrate on the last bit of road ahead. He flicked a quick glance at Jori and smiled. She had fallen asleep. Her dark head snuggled against the seat, she had one hand tucked under her cheek. Beauty and innocence, he mused, staring.

"We're home," Chris whispered, his breath blowing the tiny curls away from her face. The night air wafted in the open door and she unconsciously shivered at the chill.

"Jori," he called a little louder, pressing his hand against her shoulder. No response. Shaking his head, Chris lifted her lax body into his arms, carrying her up the walk to the front door. Flop rushed forward to greet them.

"Down, boy," Chris told him quietly. "The lady is sleeping. Let's not wake her."

She was a soft, gentle weight in his arms. If only . . . Chris held her tightly against his chest.

He opened the front door and let himself in, shaking his head at the unlocked door. Carefully he eased his way through the darkened house, climbing the stairs to her bedroom. A night-light was burning, barely illuminating the frilly white mound of pillows.

Carefully, gently, he laid her on them, sliding her arms slowly from his neck. Chris watched as she shifted her hips to turn sideways, snuggling into the soft cushions. Her hands moved together to fold prayerlike beneath her cheek as she sighed once before resuming that slow, even breathing. Dark and spidery, her lashes fanned out against her soft cheek.

Slowly, knowing he would regret it later, Chris bent and placed a soft, featherlight kiss against her lips. They were soft as velvet against his.

"Happy birthday, Jori," he murmured, watching to see if she wakened. When she didn't, he straightened and with a last look, turned and left the room.

But as he slowly drove home, Chris knew that the image would not be removed. It was pointless to pretend. Jordanna Jessop was the one woman who could cool this burning discontent in his soul and help him move into the future with confidence. Perhaps with her at his side, he could overcome the regrets of his bleak past and the worries that yawned gapingly in the future.

But he had to remind himself that Jordanna Jessop was not a part of his future. She couldn't be. They were worlds apart.

Chapter Eight

"Hope Conroy, I will not entertain that nosy group in my home one more time." Charity glared at the two women standing on her doorstep. "They poked through my china, discussed my 'strange' furniture and felt duty-bound to comment on my choice of flowers. I am not impressed!"

Hope swept in through the door, dodging the older woman with an agility newly found on a tennis court.

"You say that every time they come over, Charity. But the ladies' society has to have somewhere to meet and you know you love to watch them quilt." She sat down on the sofa with a whoosh of relief, swiping one hand across her forehead. "Why don't you tell the truth? What you're really mad about is all the questions they asked about your men friends."

Charity flicked the switch on the air conditioner one notch higher, trying to hide her flushed cheeks.

"So I've had a few friends over for a meal. So what? I'm certainly old enough to entertain whomever I like." Her gnarled hands reluctantly poured out two more cups of tea. It was evident to the other two that she was reluctant to say more.

"A few? There were five men over here on Friday night," Faith gasped, peering across at her friend's flower-festooned buffet. "I suppose those are from your suitors?" Her eyes gaped at the surfeit of roses. "Who brought the yellow ones? I love yellow roses!"

"I don't remember," Charity muttered, flushing an even darker

red. "They come as a group and they go as a group; as if they're
attached at the hip." A sigh whispered out through her lips as she
lifted her aching feet to the leather stool. "It's very trying."

"Trying? How can it be trying to have half a dozen men fawning
over you?" Hope shook her head in disgust. "You'd think you'd be
happy to have so much attention."

"I do enjoy their company." Charity sounded embarrassed by the
admission. "They're all very nice men. But I'm not as young as I
once was and sometimes I really enjoy just being alone."

"So? Rest when they're not around. What's the problem?" Hope
peered across the dim room, noting the still-closed blinds. At that
precise moment the doorbell rang and Hope saw the tiredness that
crept over her friend's usually smiling countenance as she shifted
awkwardly to her feet.

"The problem, my dear," Charity muttered irritably as she
limped toward the door, "is that they're always around. Hello, Harold."

"Oh, Charity!"

"Yes, it's me. I live here, remember?" Charity fidgeted from one
foot to the other, glancing over her shoulder to check if her friends
were listening. They were. "Did you want something, Harold?" She
had to ask it for Harold had apparently forgotten whatever it was
he wanted to say.

"Oh. Yes, I did. That is, I was wondering if you're free for dinner
tonight. I remembered you had that leftover beef and I thought
maybe we could go for a drive after, down by the river. You know,
cast a line?"

"I'm sorry, Harold. I'm having some guests over. Two young
friends of mine. They're bringing dinner with them so, I'm sorry,
but you can understand that I couldn't possibly invite you. If it was
me who was making the meal, you know I'd be happy to have you
stay."

"No, no! I understand, believe me." Harold shuffled uncomfortably on the doorstep, his straw hat in his hands. "I'll find something
at the diner. It's just that I was looking forward to your wonderful
cooking." The hangdog look on his face tugged on Charity's tender
heart, but she stood firm.

"Perhaps another time," she suggested quietly.

Harold sniffed miserably, nodded and shuffled off down the driveway. It was all Charity could do not to slam the door.

"Of all the nerve," she stormed, flopping into her chair.

"He was just asking you out," Hope murmured consolingly as she handed her the teacup. "Don't get so flustered."

"He was asking to come for dinner," Charity snorted, slapping her hand on her thigh as the phone rang. "And that'll be another one, looking for a free meal or an open ear to listen to another of those long-winded stories about the good old days. Although I'm hanged if I can remember what was so all-fired good about them!" She glared at the phone malevolently.

"I am not answering that thing."

"But, Charity," Faith blurted, her eyes huge, "that's your gift. You've always listened to other people when they tell their troubles. And then you make them feel better. That's your ministry."

"Not anymore." Her voice was firm. "I'm finished listening to other people. They never take my advice anyhow. From now on I'm going to be quiet and listen to myself. And God," she added as an afterthought.

"She's tired," Hope whispered to Faith. "She just needs to rest. I'll get that," she offered when the phone began its shrill peal once more.

Charity leaned back and closed her eyes, shaking her head in despair. How had it come to this? she asked herself. All she'd wanted was a little attention, someone to notice that she wasn't dead yet. And now she had six, count 'em, *six,* suitors all looking for a free meal.

"It was Aubery," Hope told her. "I said you were too tired to see anyone." She grimaced as the phone started again. "I'll deal with this one, too. This place is like a zoo!"

"There's the doorbell!" Faith jumped to her feet. "I'll send whoever it is away, shall I, Charity?" She sounded eager to dispatch whoever was holding the doorbell down.

"Yes, please," Charity called over the noise, shaking her head as she heard Faith's voice reprimanding her visitors. Curious to know who was there, she hid around the corner where she had a good view of her entry.

"Get your shoulder off that doorbell, Hank Dobbins," Faith ordered. "Do you think the whole world is deaf?"

"Eh?" Hank frowned as he stared at her. "Where's Charity? I brung some bread for supper." He thrust a loaf of semiflattened white bread at Faith, trying to edge past her. "You say something?"

"Turn your hearing aid on," Faith bellowed, glaring at him and pointing to his ear. "I don't know why you bought the thing when it's always turned off!"

"So's I could avoid all the caterwauling you women like to do," Hank told her frankly. "And stop yelling. It's turned on."

"Good. And I don't caterwaul so you can just listen to what I have to say, Hank Dobbins, and don't go trying to ignore me."

Faith didn't budge, standing squarely in the door frame. Short of physically moving her, Charity couldn't see how Hank could get in. She smiled at the scene.

"I didn't come to see you," the old gent informed her with some asperity. "I come to see Charity. To have dinner with her."

"Charity asked me to tell you that she's busy tonight. And tomorrow night." Faith handed back the bread. "So you'd better get on home and butter a slice of this for supper."

"It's that sneaky Tim Carruthers, isn't it?" The old man fumed. "I mighta known he'd try to budge in and get another free meal. Well, he can jest think again! Tim Carruthers, you git out here!" His voice rose as he called out a challenge.

"I am out here, Hank," an amused voice announced behind his back. "If you'd get some batteries for that hearing aid, you'd have heard me coming up the path."

"I got lots of batteries, an' I can hear just fine!" Hank wheeled around and held up his fists. "I'm the one who should be havin' dinner with Miz Flowerday t'night," he announced clearly. "You had yer turn t'other night. So git outta here."

"Tonight's my turn, you silly old coot! You were here last night." Tim shook his head in disgust. "Go home and eat the supper Esther Sue left."

"My daughter's a real fine cook but Esther Sue hasn't got a patch on Miz Charity." Hank licked his lips in anticipation.

"I'm afraid you'll both have to go home," Faith announced firmly. "Charity has other plans for this evening."

"No, she doesn't." Tim edged his way past Hank and stepped up beside Faith. "I made a deal with Aubery for tonight. Cost me plenty, too."

"Are you telling me that you paid someone to stay away so that you could have dinner with Charity tonight?" Faith stared. "But that's ridiculous!"

"I just promised him I wouldn't come to the box social on Friday so he could dance with Myrtle Bigelow. And he gets half of my potato crop. I planted way too much anyhow."

Inside the house, Charity shook her head at Hope's furious gasp of outrage. She placed one finger across her lips and they both listened to Faith's disgusted response.

"Piffle!"

"Eh?" That was Hank, fiddling with his hearing aid again. "What did you say, woman?"

"I said *piffle!* On the lot of you. Now get going and leave Charity alone for a while!" She turned to go inside but Tim Carruthers was standing there. "Well?"

"But what about dinner? I've been waiting all day to taste one of her special dishes. It wouldn't be fair to make me . . ."

"Charity is having dinner with someone else tonight. Now away you go—the both of you!" Faith whirled inside and slammed the door behind her in a snort of disgust.

"That's wood swearing," Hope reminded her, glancing at the solid oak door. "It's just as bad as actually saying the words."

"Maybe. But it's a lot better than knocking those two gray heads together! Honestly!" She stormed into the living room and began gathering up the tea things. "Now what?" She shot the pealing telephone a most venomous look. "Who's left, for Pete's sake?"

"It's Jordanna," Hope interrupted. "She wants to know if this is a good time."

"Yes, it is." Charity sank back into her chair with a sigh of relief and closed her eyes. They opened a moment later. "That leaves Frank Bellows," she told Faith wearily. "Let's hope he's busy with the church board tonight." Her ears picked up Hope's soft voice.

"She's really tired, Jori. The phone's been ringing off the hook and the doorbell's been going nonstop. Can you see if Dr. Chris would come? It mightn't hurt for him to have a look at her. You say he's on the way? Oh, thank you, dear. Bye."

"I don't need a doctor, Hope Conroy." Charity's tone was not friendly. "I need some breathing space."

"Which you will get. I'm sure Jori and the doctor can help you.

It's obvious something has to be done." She grasped her purse as the doorbell rang again. "If that's another male suitor of yours, I'm going to set him straight."

"Well, I am a male," Chris said laughing. "And I can always use some good advice. What's the problem, ladies?"

And the three seniors launched into Charity's predicament, one interrupting the other until the whole story was laid out.

"I can't imagine what I can do," he told them. "But I'll give it some thought. Okay?"

"Is what okay?" Jori stood in the doorway frowning. "Do any of you know that there are two red-faced men arguing outside the gate? What is going on around here?"

The fearsome threesome launched into new explanations.

"I don't know just what it is that I could do," Chris told them. "I mean, I'm new here and so far I've stepped on more than my share of toes. I take it that you don't want anyone's feelings hurt too badly?" He glanced from one to the other of them, pulling out his cell phone as it rang.

"Hello? Oh, hi, Frank. Fishing? Tonight? Hmmm." He glanced at each of the curious faces around him and then smiled a wide grin of excitement.

"Fishing's a great idea. In fact, we were just leaving for the park. Want to meet us there?" He ignored Hope's rolling eyes, Faith's "piffle" of disgust and Charity's slumped shoulders to linger on Jori's frowning countenance and the bag from Hamburger Haven that lay on the floor at her feet.

"Good. We've got dinner so don't worry. J.J., Mrs. Flowerday and me. We need to talk to you about something, too, Frank. About this little plan I've got. Okay." He clicked the phone closed and smiled at the group, his teeth flashing in that tanned face.

"All right now, ladies. It's all set. Charity will have dinner on the lake with Frank and I. We can all relax and talk this situation over. Are you ready?"

They bustled about, gathering a jacket for Charity, a thermos of coffee and three more cups. In the midst of it all, Jori sidled over to the doctor.

"I don't know what you've got planned," she said. "But it better not hurt my friends."

"Trust me," he whispered, his lips brushing her cheek.

She stood back, hands on her hips and glared at him fiercely, except Chris could see the little tick at the corner of her mouth and knew she wasn't mad at all.

"At this point, I haven't got much for alternatives," she grumbled before holding open the door. "You'd better pray this works."

"Oh, I am," he murmured, more to himself. "I'm praying that it works in more ways than one."

Out in the boat in the middle of the lake, life seemed to slow into a wonderfully calm pattern that was completely free of problems and difficulties. Jori watched as Chris turned into the wind, his chiseled face outlined in the waning sun as he explained his plan.

"So if Charity and Frank pretend to be dating and are seen going out together, the others will give up. All her dinners will be promised to Frank and they won't have a chance." His eyes watched the older couple as he whispered to Jori, "I think it just might work. And she needs a break. She looks very tired. The arthritis pain saps her energy, I think."

"I really am sorry about all this, Charity," Frank apologized, his hand tenderly squeezing hers. "We had no right to run you ragged like that. And we should have taken you out instead of making you cook all the time. It's no wonder you're feeling a bit exhausted." His eyes crinkled at the corners. "Although no one would know it to look at you. You look as young as you did twenty-five years ago."

"Why, thank you, Frank!" Charity preened a bit before glancing at the others. "But aging doesn't really give up, no matter how hard you fight it. This Charity is nothing like the one you knew so long ago."

"Of course she is!" He sounded amazed, Jori decided, eyeing the two with a tender glance. "Why, you look exactly as you did then! I remember how those big brown eyes flashed when I corrected that child picking sweet peas in your backyard and howling at the moon. What was his name?"

"Evan Schultz," Charity breathed, a smile tipping up the corners of her lips. "And he was trying his darndest to get into the kids' choir at church."

"Yes, but he had the words wrong. I can still hear him. 'Gee the baloney's good'—that's what he sang," Frank told Chris, winking at him and Jori as he held Charity's hand on his knee.

"What was the song?" Chris looked puzzled at the strange words. "I don't remember a church song about baloney. Or any kind of meat." He turned the wheel and slowed the engine just a bit.

"It wasn't about meat. The words were 'G, double O, D, good!' It was about God and his faithfulness to his children." Charity's laughter rang out over the water. "And Evan couldn't carry a tune in a bucket! That's why I didn't want Frank to hurt his feelings. I knew the child wouldn't get the part."

"I wasn't going to hurt his feelings!" Frank pasted on an affronted look but it couldn't hide the glint of merriment in his kindly gray eyes. "I was going to offer to buy him a trumpet if he'd stop making that infernal noise!" He smirked at Charity.

"But no, you had to assure him he was doing fine and that he just needed to practice! Agh! Thank goodness he took up sports not long after."

Charity giggled like a schoolgirl. Jori was amazed at the change in her. Her eyes sparkled in her flushed face. Her shoulders were thrown back and she giggled happily, leaving her hand wrapped in Frank's.

"She still looks after all the kids in the neighborhood." Frank's voice was soft and admiring. "There's never a kid who can't go to Mrs. Flowerday and find some good advice and a slice of double-chocolate cake to make them feel better."

"You should talk!" Charity grinned. "Who offered to take his boat up to that juvenile camp and tow water-skiers around for three weeks last summer, Franklin Bellows? And then got conned into teaching a class on archery?"

"Okay." he held up a hand. "We're both guilty! But I was trying to make the point that you haven't changed. You're still determined to see God's goodness in people, no matter what."

Jori met Chris's gaze with her own and they both turned away, pretending they weren't listening.

"But I have changed, Frank. This arthritis has crippled me up so badly, I look ugly." She held out her knotted fingers for him to see their twisted disfigurement.

"You look beautiful," he whispered, brushing a strand of gleaming silver off her forehead. "Your skin is as smooth and velvety as an eighteen-year-old's and your nose has the same tip-tilted, smart-aleck angle it's always had." He'd smiled benignly when she blushed.

"And you haven't lost that same lovely glow I saw twenty years ago. That comes from inside, Charity. Not from your hands. From your heart. That's why everyone wants to be around you."

Jori let the wind ripple through her hair as it flew around wildly, her fingers curling in Chris's as they watched Charity and Frank have this special time together. She was so engrossed in Frank's words and the wealth of love in them, that she almost missed Chris's excited whisper.

"What?"

"It's working! She's beginning to see Frank in a new and different light. Thank the Lord! He's been crazy about her for ages." He grinned with delight.

"You mean, you've been matchmaking?" Aghast, Jori could only stare. "Of all the people in this town, you, Christopher Davis, should know how chancy that can be."

"Only if it's done for the wrong reasons and with the wrong people. In this case, I think God means for them to be together."

She stared at him.

"You don't have any fears, any worries?" She shook her head. "I admire you, Doc. You don't have any inhibitions. You just jump in and grab whatever it is you want out of life."

"Yeah, sometimes I do. And I hope you remember that," he whispered in her ear, his arm slipping around her waist. "Some things are worth jumping in after."

And for once, Jordanna felt jealous of a little elderly woman who could cause that glint of loving admiration in her old friend's eye. Jori had been so sure that her ex-fiancé was the man for her, would share those same kind of moments with her.

Instead, he'd publicly exposed her to the world's ridicule by breaking off their engagement and taking off with her best friend. Now she so badly wanted to trust again.

But as Chris's blazing blue eyes searched deep into the depths of hers and she remembered the touch of his mouth, Jori wished, for once, that she could believe that someone could love her again. Part of her wanted so badly to be that one special person to someone else; to have them near, to share hopes and dreams with. To raise a family. And part of her was scared to death to open up to that kind of hurt and rejection.

Maybe it was better to just stay free and clear of it, after all. At least you never got hurt.

You never really live, either, a tiny voice whispered.

The scent of lilacs and lavender was thick in the big airy bathroom as Jori laid back even farther into the deep claw-footed tub. It was the old-fashioned kind that let you put in enough water to really sink into and relax. And boy did she need to relax, Jori thought, grinning.

She had spent the entire day whirling through house and garden, trying to forget the effect a tall, blond doctor had on her nervous system. Consequently, not a weed could be found in the flower beds, vegetable garden, along the walk or within the confines of her rather large yard. Jori had mowed the grass even though ten-year-old Bobby Moore was paid to do it for her. In fact, he had been there only two days before.

The house had been put through a rigorous spit-and-polish regime, from top to bottom. Not a speckle of dust marred the gleaming surfaces in any room. She scrubbed the old kitchen floor to within an inch of its worn life and then waxed and buffed it to a shine that hurt the eyes.

And the worst of it was, it was still only three o'clock in the afternoon!

Jori played with a mound of bubbles and considered what the remainder of the day's entertainment should be. An image of Chris grinning from ear to ear flew into her mind. She shoved it away resolutely. Banishing all thoughts of him from her mind, Jori leaned back once more and closed her eyes.

Unfortunately, he would not leave. And neither would the problem of his presence.

"All right," she mumbled to herself in frustration. "Let's discuss this rationally." She straightened up and glared at the faucet of the tub. "Would a perfectly wonderful doctor who makes pots of money cutting people open and sewing them up, who is inundated with adulation from masses of people telling him he's the best thing since fudge brownies, have any desire to remain in a one-horse country town like Mossbank when his self-imposed sabbatical is over?" Jori snapped the bubbles with her fingers. "Of course not!"

It wasn't a very satisfactory answer and so she tried to reason it out again.

"No doubt he lives in some elegant condo with a pool, weight room and a bevy of drooling nurses for neighbors."

No, she frowned. It was worse to think this way. Jori turned the water on with her toes. "Well, what makes you think he'd hang around Mossbank, then?"

Answer: he wouldn't. Not for any longer than it took Dan and Jessica to get back home and into the groove.

"And you can't leave. You know you can't. Even if he asked you." She squeezed her eyes closed and remembered.

"I'll repay you every dime, every dollar that you've scraped together to send me to school," she'd promised Reg and the men with him tearfully. "I won't renege. You can count on that."

Reg had told her to pay the debt out after her court case had been resolved.

"The town won't hold it against you if you get on with your life somewhere else," he'd insisted. "We never expected you to stay this long."

"I promised seven years," she reminded him. "And anyway, I wouldn't dream of leaving. This is my home now."

Chris's searching blue eyes swam into focus and she could hear his words as clearly as the radio playing in the bedroom.

"Trust me," he'd said.

"I could trust him, I think," she said to herself, trying to wash away the sensation of those arms holding her so gently. "But there's no future in this relationship so just stop thinking about weddings and babies and all that stuff. It's not for you!"

Luckily, the motion picture running across her brain in vivid Technicolor ended there, due to the loud peal of the telephone. Water slopped over the side of the tub as Jori rose hastily grabbing a towel to wrap around her wet body. She scurried into the bedroom to lift the receiver just as the caller hung up.

"Shoot!" Jori tugged on an old chenille housecoat before mopping up the trail of puddles marking her newly polished floors. That job was barely complete when the doorbell rang.

"What is this?" she grouched. "Grand Central Station?"

She yanked the door open to find Chris standing on her front step. The look on his face would have been comical if Jori had been in a mood to appreciate it.

"Oh, uh, s-sorry," he stammered, staring at the gaping V her robe exposed. His eyes flew to her face. Confusion clouded his eyes. "Were you sleeping?"

"Don't be ridiculous," Jori said, horrified that he had to see her in such disarray. "It's three o'clock in the afternoon." She motioned him into the hallway. "I would prefer that the entire town didn't witness me in this ratty old thing," she told him.

Chris seemed amused by her bad temper, which only made it worse. She clenched her teeth at his grin when he spied the ragged bandanna that held up her hair.

"I can go away and come back some other time," he told her softly, watching her face closely.

Jori sighed. She should have gone along with the senior bus trip to Minot and spent her day in the craft store, she told herself tiredly. Perhaps then she would have avoided all tall blond male humans, she muttered inwardly. And dogs, she was forced to add at the sight of Flop's huge brown woebegone eyes peering through the screen door.

"I was in the tub when the phone rang," she explained carefully, as he sat in the huge armchair across from her. She curled her legs carefully under her, making sure they remained covered. "Whomever it was had just hung up when you rang the bell." She shoved the wet stringy hair off her face. "I must look a mess."

Chris sat there staring at her until the color rose in her cheeks. "Well, don't just sit there staring at me! I look terrible."

"No," he murmured softly, "you just look like a little girl getting ready for bed."

Silence yawned between them like a great gaping hole, but Jori couldn't think of a thing to say. His gaze held hers, solemn and probing. She couldn't look away so she stared back, mesmerized by what she saw in the blue depths of his eyes.

The shrill ring of the phone finally broke the spell. Jori picked up the receiver slowly, dazedly.

"Hello, Jori. How was the birthday cruise with the handsome doctor?" Amy's voice bubbled enthusiastically over the line.

It was a little disconcerting to discuss her date with the man in question sitting across from her. Jori decided to skirt the issue.

"Hi, Amy." She cleared the huskiness from her throat and continued brightly. "Thank you very much, I had a lovely time."

Chris coughed just then and she glanced at him from under her lids. He was grinning hugely.

"What you can remember of it, at least," he teased, blue eyes dancing.

"Who's that?" Amy demanded. "I heard a voice."

"I have a guest right now, Amy." Jori frowned at Chris as she spoke. "Can I call you back later?"

"Well, actually, old pal . . ." Jori knew there was something coming when her friend began that con.

"What do you need, Amy?" She sighed, staring at her carpet. This was turning out to be a strange day.

"Uh, well, it's about Jonathan."

Jori tried to think of something to say but Amy was rushing on.

"I need a sitter for tonight. We're going out for dinner." It came out in a rush of breath. Amy's voice was so hopeful that Jori's soft heart caved like mush. "Mom's taking Brit, but she's too old to take on him, too."

Jori could quite understand. Little Jonathan was a terror and he would be no end of trouble but it was the least she could do for her friend, she pointed out to herself.

"Dinner? Wow! Must be some occasion. What's up?" Jori demanded, knowing her friend seldom splurged on anything for herself.

There was a pregnant pause and then Amy's tearful voice came across the line.

"I passed."

Jori shrieked with joy. She grinned, happily including Chris in the pleasure of the moment.

"Way to go, kid!" She cheerfully congratulated her friend. "Do I call you Madam Certified Public Accountant now?"

They laughed and talked and arranged, and the entire time Jori sat there, uncomfortably aware of the handsome doctor seated on her sofa, unashamedly listening.

A thought suddenly occurred and Jori asked her friend anxiously, "Have you got something special to wear?" There was a

murmured response before Jori hooted, "No way. You're not wearing *that*." She stared at Chris searchingly for a moment then nodded as if that settled everything.

"Look, you and I have enough time to scoot over to Mirabel's
and get something really special for tonight. It's my treat." When
the voice on the other end of the line started speaking, Jori's voice
became louder.

"This is my treat and you are not doing me out of the fun. You've
come through for me enough times, Amy."

Apparently she had gotten her way, Chris mused, smiling at the
grin of satisfaction tipping those full lips. Then he sat upright at the
mention of his name.

"Look, Dr. Davis is here. He can watch Jonathan while you and I
go shopping. You would like that, wouldn't you?" She pretended to
ask Chris, then ignored his wildly gesticulating hands and shaking
head. Jori put her hand over the mouthpiece when he told her no,
but after a moment she kept right on talking to her friend as if he
weren't there.

"He'd love to do this for you on your special day," she said
sweetly, glaring fiercely at Chris.

His shoulders slumped. How did she do it? he wondered. She
was always conning him into something. And what did he know
about little kids? Nothing, that's what! Sure, he could give them a
physical, check them over for health problems, or sew them up very
neatly. But he doubted that would be much fun for this Jonathan
kid.

"What time are you leaving?" He heard Jori arranging everything as if he had agreed wholeheartedly. Chris got up and walked
toward the kitchen. He needed a drink of something to keep his
hands busy. Otherwise he'd throttle her.

When he returned, Jori had slipped into white slacks and a blue-
and-white-striped sweater. She was dialing a number.

"Just a minute, Jori," he demanded. "I can't look after a . . ."

She held up her hand as someone answered.

"This is Jordanna Jessop. I'd like to speak to Alex, please."

He tried again.

"Jordanna, I *cannot* . . ."

"Shhh . . . Hi, Alex, this is Jordanna."

Chris wondered at the sudden animation that lit up her glowing brown eyes. A huge grin curved her mouth.

"Great! Listen, Alex, I need a favor. A friend of mine has a very special celebration tonight. I want that window table that overlooks the river, a bouquet of fresh flowers and anything they order charged to me." She listened for a few minutes.

"Good. Oh, and Alex, when they're finished can you get a cab for them." Jori's face was dancing with glee as she gave him the names. "They're going to the Palace but they don't know it. Can you do it? Thank you, you are a sweetie! Okay, bye."

Chris let her enjoy the moment and then tried again.

"Jori, I need to talk to you. There is no way . . ."

Once more she held up her hand and began dialing.

Well, if Jordanna Jessop thought she could bulldoze him into this she had another thought coming. He would darn well wait her out.

"Mrs. Rivers, this is Jori. I need you to pack a bag for Amy and Bob. I've got it all arranged, but I don't want them to know. You're keeping Brit, right? Okay. Well, Jonathan will stay here."

Chris thought she'd never get off the phone, but when Jori finally hung up, he breathed a sigh of relief. Now, perhaps, they could clear this up.

Then the doorbell rang.

"Blast it anyway!" He clenched his teeth in vexation.

Jori's wide eyes stared at him.

"You can't say that around Jonathan," she instructed. "He repeats everything he hears. And for goodness' sake, don't give him chocolate." She opened the front door. "Hi, Amy. All set?"

Everything was happening too fast. Chris felt like a passenger on one of those roller coasters at the amusement park. Everything rushed past and he couldn't quite get a grasp on reality.

Jori's friend Amy was speaking to him. Chris tried to pay attention to her, but tiny hands were pulling on his pants, diverting his attention. He hung on to his waistband with one hand, and pulled the sticky hands away with the other.

"He doesn't need to be fed. And don't give him any chocolate." The woman studied him dubiously and Chris straightened his backbone under the survey. "Jonathan will tell you if he needs to use the potty," she said. Her eyes moved uncertainly over the now stained gray slacks.

"Are you sure you want to do this?" Her question was full of doubt and Chris was about to assure her that he certainly did not when Jori broke in.

"Of course he does, don't you, Chris? We had a lovely time on that cruise and this is our way of thanking you. And, after all, it is *just* Jonathan. Her mom's watching Brittany." Jori's eyes were black hard stones now, daring him to refuse.

When he smiled grimly, the two women moved toward the door, giggling excitedly. Neither one paid him any attention. Jonathan headed straight for the china cabinet.

Chris recognized defeat. He would be graceful, he decided. So magnanimously helpful that Jori would not be able to find fault with him. And then he'd leave. He was pretty sure the kid was here for the evening, so he wouldn't be. It was that simple.

Except it wasn't simple at all, he observed an hour later, staggering under the impact of a three-year-old ball of lead against his midsection. Jonathan laughed uproariously. And launched himself at Chris again.

Chris, however, was not a slow learner and he moved. Too quickly, as it happened. The child banged his head against the edge of Jori's solid oak coffee table and let out a wail designed to bring the cops.

It probably only took a few minutes, but when the racket was finally over, Chris concluded surgery was infinitely less tiring than comforting a crying child who was seriously hurting. He decided to take the boy outside. The dog, that was it!

Chris was pleased with himself. Jonathan could play with Flop. Kids like dogs. Dogs like kids. They'd have a great time.

Except that Flop had apparently met little Jonathan before. The cocker spaniel took one look at the three-year-old and barked. Then he sped as fast as his stumpy little legs would carry him, to the thick growth of trees and bushes behind the house.

"Dog," Jonathan said, pointing. "Me go." As he started after the frightened animal, Chris decided diversionary tactics were needed.

He couldn't very well let the tyke get lost in the woods, Chris knew, but he didn't want a recurrence of that bloodcurdling screeching, either. Chris searched the yard for something, anything! When his frustrated glance returned to little Johnny, the kid was in the garden carefully picking the flowers off Jori's pea plants.

"Flowers," he told Chris, grinning his toothy smile. "Pitty flowers."

"Yeah, kid," Chris agreed morosely. "It's a pity, all right." Sighing, he bent to take the little boy's hand. "Come on, Jonathan. Let's go see cars. Okay?"

The round cherub face twisted in sorrow first. The fat little hands dropped the crushed white blossoms on the ground sadly.

But the word *car* seemed to have some significance. The shiny black button eyes sparkled at his baby-sitter in delight.

"Car, Car," he sang in a cheerful tone. "Wide in car."

Too late, Chris realized what the word *car* meant to this three-year-old. As they walked out the gate, Chris looked to see if Amy's car, with a *baby seat,* was by the curb.

Unfortunately, only his vintage black T-bird, restored and refurbished at an exorbitant sum, sat there. Jonathan seemed delighted. He patted the gleaming rear fender lovingly, and crowed, "Pitty car. Wide in car wif man." Fat little hands imprinted themselves on a wax job Chris had painstakingly completed only this morning. He groaned as the child leaned closer to press a slurpy kiss on his shiny chrome bumper.

"Jon wuv car," he told Chris, smiling happily.

They stood in the hot sun for ages while Chris tried to persuade the little boy to walk down the street for a look at the red sports car parked nearby. But the kid wasn't buying. Jonathan clung to the door handle, persistently saying the same thing over and over, his happy face dropping a little more each time.

"Jon go car wide. Dis car."

Chris picked him up, thinking he'd carry the tiny boy inside, but a wail of distress soon stopped him. Several ladies were entering the house across the street and they turned to peer down their noses at him, heads shaking disapprovingly, obviously concerned by his inability to placate the boy. He set the kid down. Immediately, Jonathan ran back to the T-bird.

"She will pay," Chris promised himself grimly, jaw throbbing as he gritted his teeth once more. "I will make her pay for every single moment of this very long afternoon." He opened the door, resignation in the slump of his shoulders.

"Okay, kid. We're just going to sit in the car, now. Just sit."

The boy scooted across the driver's side and nestled into the passenger's seat. Jonathan was very familiar with what happened next, Chris realized, his heart sinking into his shoes. With great dexterity the kid fastened the seat belt around himself like a pro. His dark eyes shone with excitement.

"Wedy," he chirped.

"Well, I'm not." Chris felt like a grumpy old man, talking to an innocent child like that. But he had reason. Darned good reason to be cranky, he figured.

This was not the manner in which he had planned on spending his afternoon. Not at all! Fleeting thoughts of a picnic, at the beach, in the sun, with Jori, ran rampant through his head. Chris turned to face the little boy. Time for a reality check, oh, great doctor, he chided himself in disgust. Scenario's changed!

"Jonathan. We can't go for a car ride today because I don't have a special seat for you." The kid stared at him, beaming that silly smile. Chris tried again.

"In Mommy's car you have a special seat, don't you, Jonathan?" The child blinked. "Car wide?" he asked innocently.

"No, Jonathan. No car ride." Chris tried to yell above the kid's bawling. "I haven't got a car seat for you."

The child had well-developed lungs for his age, Chris decided, cringing at the shrill bellows. Surely Jori would hear him downtown and get back here, pronto.

When several minutes had passed without any signs of the relief team, Chris took matters into his own hands.

"Okay, kid. You win," he hollered. "We're going, we're going."

The slow motion of the car finally penetrated and Jonathan's crying ceased abruptly. Chris kept it on a sedate fifteen miles per hour and prayed no one would notice he was plodding down the street at a snail's pace, in a racy black Thunderbird whose engine had not been designed for creeping, with a kid next to him who was not belted in according to government specification. Of course, they'd have to be able to see Jonathan first, Chris reasoned, glancing down. This way they'd think he was out by himself. Cruising, no doubt.

"Better and better," he grumbled in revulsion. "Now they'll really be talking!"

Jonathan's happy face beamed satisfaction as he jabbered away.

"Go wide car. Jon like car. Nice car. Pitty." He turned his solemn eyes on Chris, and ordered, "Sing."

Chris ignored him, hoping the child would forget. Fat chance!

"Sing," Jonathan ordered insistently. "Sing."

Chris turned on the radio. There was no way he was going down the street singing. He already had the windows open because he thought air-conditioning would give the kid a chill. Anyway, he couldn't imagine what tune they could possibly share.

As luck would have it, an old country-and-western song was playing. Chris smiled grimly. He'd always suspected that God had a sense of humor, and "coward of the county" described his present condition perfectly.

Jonathan appeared quite happy with the song, though. He crowed away, off-key, as they turned the corner. Chris braked slowly in front of Jori's, noting there was still no sign of Amy's car. He groaned inwardly, but determined not to show it.

"Okay, Jonathan. All finished. Let's go inside, okay," he wheedled.

"Car wide, more." Jonathan was getting angry. Chris could see the little hands curling into angry fists. "Car wide," he shouted.

"Do you want to drive, too?" Chris inquired sourly, raking his hands through his hair.

That was a mistake.

Faster than lightning, the child had released the latch on his belt and landed with a thud on Chris's lap.

"Jon dwive," he agreed cheerfully.

"Uh, I don't think . . ." The little face scrunched up and Chris caved in. "All right!"

And so Jonathan drove. Chris turned the key and the motor purred quietly while his prize car sat in one place and the kid happily turned the wheel left and right to the accompaniment of *Brrrm* and *Rooom.*

Chris let himself relax for a moment, wondering if he'd need to replace his front tires after this grueling workout. His blue eyes narrowed in thought. And he would send the bill to Jori Jessop, he decided. It was the least she could do after setting him up like this.

Still, he considered, if it got him any further beneath that protective shell she always threw up against him, Chris decided it was

worth it. He was definitely interested in the woman, he acknowledged.

And so, as Jonathan drove his car, Chris sat thinking about Jori.
And while a low voice on the radio crooned about her dream lover,
Chris fantasized about his relationship with his office nurse. He
thought of her laughing eyes, that solemn glint they got in them
when she spoke of her past, the way she opened up, just a bit, and
then hid her thoughts and feelings.

"Why me, Lord?" The question stemmed from his need to know
why he'd been presented with a woman who met every one of the
traits he'd deemed desirable in a partner for life and yet seemed
totally unobtainable. "Why *me*, Lord?"

Suddenly Chris felt the insistent tug on his arm. And the warm
wetness soaking through his pants.

He asked the question again, but with totally different intent.

"I haffa go potty," Jonathan advised him solemnly.

"I think you're just a bit late, pal." Chris grimaced sourly as he
stepped gingerly out of the car. His brow furrowed when he surveyed the boy's dirty smeared face.

Great! The kid had snitched a chocolate bar Chris had left in the
cup holder. Now they were both covered with the gooey brown
stuff but Chris wore more of it than Jonathan.

Chris wondered, What next? just as his eyes caught a glimpse of
the dark wet patch creating a highly *visible* circle on the front of his
slacks. He shook his head darkly.

"I concede defeat," Chris informed anyone who was listening. "I
have no pride left," he muttered in frustration. "None."

Oh, she'd pay, all right! Big-time!

After a trip to the bathroom and a change of clothes which Chris
finally found in Jonathan's blue-striped diaper bag tucked discreetly behind the front door, they sat together on the sofa to read
one of the books that had been secreted inside said bag. Chris
wished he'd noticed it sooner. There were enough toys in there to
amuse ten kids.

A few minutes later they were back in the bathroom removing all
traces of a regurgitated chocolate bar that should never have been
eaten. Fortunately for Jori's sofa, most of it had landed in Chris's
lap.

As he surveyed his new pants ruefully, Chris wished he had his own diaper bag. There was a peculiar odor in the air and he was pretty sure he was the source. He dabbed at the expensive fabric as best he could while swallowing thoughts of retribution.

"Vengeance is the Lord's," he quoted self-righteously.

Soon Jonathan's rumpled dark head rested tiredly against his chest as Chris read about Peter Rabbit. No wonder the kid was so smart if he heard this stuff all the time. Beatrix Potter was not one to mince words, Chris decided.

Halfway through the little book, he realized Jonathan had fallen asleep. The child's tiny hand lay on top of his own as the boy snored gently, his chubby body pressed comfortably against Chris.

This is what it would be like to have a son. The words sounded in his brain with a clarity that made his eyes widen. *Here's a demanding little person who depends on you to make his world all right. Someone who needs you to bandage sore knees, read bedtime stories and take for a car ride. Someone who needs you to be there to tuck him in at night.*

Chris had never thought of himself as a father. Never wanted the responsibility. But somehow it seemed perfectly natural to cuddle little Jonathan's body as he lay sleeping. And a feeling of intense longing coursed through him even as the sadness brought reality.

"I'm not the father type," he told that resonant voice. "I haven't got a clue how to raise children except that it wouldn't be the way my parents raised us." Thoughts of happy excited voices debating across the table made him smile. "Mealtimes are fun times," he murmured. "That's the first rule I'd make. And everyone laughs."

A picture of Jori holding a baby in the rocking chair across the room flew into his mind. She should have a family. She was full of warmth and giving and caring. Jori would know the right words to say. She would have the understanding a child would need in this world.

But why did he want it to be his child? He wasn't the type to settle down in a place like Mossbank. He couldn't; he accepted that inevitability as the sun rises each morning. His whole professional career was about maximizing the medical care that he'd been taught to provide. His whole life had been about fulfilling his parents' dreams. And unless there was exponential growth in the future of the little town, he wasn't looking at hanging around. Was he?

In the back of his mind, Chris listened tiredly as his mother's voice droned on.

"You can be the best surgeon in the world, Christopher. People will come from miles to be operated on by you. Your fees will entitle you to the best of everything. You can advance in your field as far as you're willing to go, be among the top brains in the world. You can have it all."

But did he want it all?

Jori pushed open her front door to the same quiet peacefulness that always reigned in her home. How long would she have to wait to hear the sounds of children laughing as they slid down the bannister or swung in the backyard? Would she ever have a child of her own?

Now, however, a tiny frisson of fear coursed through her veins. It was so silent. Where were they?

Stop it, she told herself sternly. Nothing bad has happened. And if it had, Chris would be well equipped to handle an emergency.

All the same, Jori breathed a sigh of relief when she came upon the two of them lying on her sofa, snoring in unison. Flop raised his nose from his comfy position on top of Chris's feet and Jori had to smile at the picture they made. Wistfully, she wondered how Chris's own child would look.

Would his son have that flaxen blond hair and those sun-bleached eyebrows? Would his eyes sparkle with the same navy blueness when he was amused? Would he be as tall and broad as his father?

The pain that shuddered through her as Jori contemplated these and a host of other questions forced her to realize just how deeply she was falling for him.

She wanted to be the mother of his son. Jori calmly accepted her own desires, painfully realizing that it would never happen. Chris would never be happy living in a small town like Mossbank. And why would he?

But while he was here, Jori decided, she would enjoy his company whenever possible. Nothing could come of it, and she would learn to live with that, but she wasn't going to regret that she had grown to love this man.

"Chris." She shook his shoulder gently. When those wide blue eyes popped open, Jori wasn't prepared for the feelings that struck her heart. It took a minute for her to regain her poise.

"You're back," Chris murmured, brushing his hair from his forehead. His eyes darkened as he remembered. "You owe me one," he told her. "More than one."

Jori giggled. She put her hands on her hips, and taunted, "Like what?"

"Supper, for one," he informed her. His blue eyes glinted in the sun.

"One meal for you and Jonathan coming right up," she promised, moving toward the kitchen. She turned in the doorway, tossing a saucy look over her shoulder. "Anything else, your majesty?"

"Yes," he told her. His voice lowered to a whisper. "But I'll tell you later."

It was a promise that Jori rolled through her mind a dozen times as she readied the steaks for grilling. When Chris strolled into the kitchen sometime later, she smiled at the mussed blond hair, dirty wrinkled shirt and stained pants.

"You can shower and change before supper if you want," she told him, eyeing his discolored pants with mirth. "Did you have an accident?"

She kept her tones mildly questioning, which was difficult, because inside Jori was aching to laugh. When his blue eyes glared at her, she moved over to pat his cheek.

"Poor baby," she consoled him. "Did you have a bad day?"

Jori was surprised when his long arms reached out to pull her into his arms. She was even more surprised when his lips touched hers.

"Yes," he answered. "I have had a *very* bad day, but it's getting better."

She wrapped her arms around his neck, still holding the salt shaker in one hand. Her senses were caught on a curious smell. Her nose twitched as she stared up at him.

"Chris?"

"What?" His blue eyes looked at her curiously.

"What is that smell?" she asked, wrinkling her nose in distaste. To her surprise, he backed away immediately. Her hands fell to her sides as she stood staring at him. A flush of red suffused his strong cheekbones. Jori watched the sheepish look cover his face.

Just then, little Jonathan walked into the room. He was mussed and sleepy eyed, clutching his teddy in one grubby hand. As she bent to pick him up, Jori caught the same scent on his clothes. Eyes wide, she turned to stare at Chris.

"It's him, not me!" Chris's voice was defensive. "He stole a chocolate bar, got sick on me and forgot to tell me about going to the bathroom until it was too late." He looked mortally offended, plucking the expensive material away from his thighs. "Unfortunately, he was sitting on me at the time."

It was jumbled, but she got the drift. And she couldn't help herself. Laughter burst from her like a wave in a tidal pool, filling the room with its sound. She laughed until tears ran down her cheeks and then laughed some more. Her stomach ached and quivered with laughter until finally Jori sobered up enough to see the light of battle in his eyes.

"I told you, no chocolate," she reminded him, stifling her glee.

Chris did not look placated. In fact he looked . . . rumpled, she decided grinning.

"I'm sorry," she bubbled, "but it's just the thought of someone, anyone, let alone a child, ruining the great Dr. Chris Davis's p-p-pants . . ." Fresh gales of laughter shook her narrow shoulders as she tried to control her mirth.

Chris marched over to stand in front of her. "It is not funny," he complained. "These were my best pants." He stood watching her set the little boy in his high chair. "In fact, they *were* brand-new."

Jori began feeding the child as he spoke. She was ignoring him, Chris realized. It bugged him.

"Jori," he complained, turning her chin to meet his eyes.

"Yes," she answered, staring at him for a minute before popping another spoonful of food into Jonathan's open mouth. "What did you say?"

"I said, I had plans for tonight. And they didn't include him." His thumb jerked toward the three-year-old safely ensconced in the chair, huge eyes watching them curiously.

"Perhaps next time," Jori advised him, "you should ask me before you make any plans for me." She fixed him with her best office nurse look. "Now, go get changed while I feed Jon. We'll eat when he's asleep."

"Jon not sleepy," the little boy told her seriously. "Jon play wif toys."

"You will be, sweetie. You're going to eat your dinner and after you've had your bath, you are going to bed."

Jori watched from the corner of her eye as Chris lingered in her kitchen for a few minutes, before he strode, muttering, out the back door.

Contrary to his assertions, Jonathan did go to bed and finally to sleep after his dinner and bath, although not without protest.

"Jon not sleepy. No bed."

She had been calm but firm and finally the little tyke had settled down enough to close his eyes and drift off. Jori went downstairs a few moments later, to find Chris had returned and was seated at her kitchen table.

"Whew," she told him seriously. "I was afraid there for a minute that he wouldn't go to sleep and then he would start bawling." She eyed Chris piteously. "You have no idea how loud he is when he starts crying."

Chris surged to his feet. "Yes, I do. I have a very good idea of just how many decibels he reaches with those lungs. When I return to Boston, I am going to have my hearing checked. And I'm sending the bill to you."

"Poor baby!" Jori grinned saucily before she pointed to the array on her counter. "I have seasoned T-bones waiting for grilling. There are new potatoes, fresh green beans, a salad and garlic bread." She smirked. "Will that cover my debt to you?"

"Not nearly! But it is a good start."

And so the evening progressed with neither able to stop the little touches and telling glances they each threw when the other wasn't looking. It could have been a very relaxing evening, except for little Jonathan's peculiar timing. And not once but several times!

Chris had finally gone home, grumbling all the while. But not before he had made Jori wish he was staying. For good.

Chapter Nine

"I wish to speak with Dr. Christopher Davis, Nurse. Fetch him immediately, please." The tall, elegantly dressed woman on the other side of the desk gave Jori a thorough once-over as she impatiently tapped her fingers.

Jori raised her eyebrows at the woman's supercilious tone. Indeed. She wondered where the woman had come from. Her white linen suit was immaculate on a day when the dust was blowing freely across the prairies. Ash blond hair was pulled severely back off her tense face and coiled into some complicated knot at the back. Her face was a study in patrician features with its long aquiline nose, highly defined cheekbones and intense blue eyes. At the moment her full lips were stretched in a thin line across her perfectly made-up face as she waited for Jori to obey.

"Your name, madam?"

"Dr. Charlotte Davis." The smoothly arrogant tones gave the information haughtily. "I am Dr. Davis's mother."

Jori felt the world shift and tilt and wondered why she hadn't expected this. This woman was here to make sure Chris returned to the city.

Somehow she struggled past all that and remembered that Chris would be tied up for some time counseling the young girl in his office on the merits of abstaining from sex. There was no way she was going to interrupt that.

"If you would have a seat, Dr. Davis, I'm sure Chris will see you as soon as he is free." Jori waved her hand toward a waiting room already jammed with patients before glancing down to the appointment book dismissively.

She had pulled a few more patient files from the bulging cabinets before Jori noticed that the woman had not left. She raised her eyebrow questioningly.

"Was there something else, Dr. Davis?"

"I don't think you understand." Her tone was mildly condescending. Jori bristled at the supercilious words.

"I believe I understand perfectly," she insisted quietly. "But perhaps you don't understand that this is a clinic. These patients have made appointments and they are waiting to see the doctor." Her eyes seared around the room before coming to rest on the aristocratic woman standing at the desk. Jori relented only a bit.

"Dr. Davis is attending a patient right now," she told his mother, keeping her voice low. "When he is free, I'll tell him you are here." Her voice was firm. "Now, please be seated."

Dr. Davis sat. Her back was ramrod straight as she perched on the edge of the worn chair as if fearful it would contaminate her.

Twenty minutes later, Jori eased into Chris's office. She watched him as he pored over the next patient's file. After a moment his blond head tipped up, blue eyes crinkling. "What?" he asked.

"Um, well, you see . . ." Jori didn't know exactly why she felt the woman's presence was going to disrupt Chris's concentration on his needy patients, but the niggling feeling of impending doom was there. She tried to tell him quickly. "Your mother is in the waiting room, Doctor. She wants to see you."

The wide grin that had stretched his mouth fell away as he stared at her. His face froze, a chilly look in those gorgeous eyes.

"My mother is here? J.J., she couldn't be. She's working on a top secret project right now." He smiled absurdly. "You must have misunderstood."

"She said her name was Charlotte Davis." She watched the light of recognition dawn. "Ah, I see you believe me now."

He frowned fiercely. "But surely she hasn't come way out here? My father must be working overtime if he's had to recruit her. And I can just imagine what she wants."

Jori stared at him. He said the words to himself, obviously turning it all over in his mind. "But what does she want?"

The comment wasn't directed at her but Jori answered anyway. "I'm sure I don't know. She certainly didn't bother to explain it to me. After all, I'm just the office nurse." Jori shrugged, her eyes carefully studying him. "Shall I show her in here?"

He seemed to pull himself together suddenly, drawing his shoulders up with an inner strength. His eyes were cold as ice when he looked at her, his mouth a thin, straight line.

"No." The word was sharp. "I have a room full of patients. She's the one who always says work comes first." Chris gathered the file together and tapped it against his desk, aligning the papers inside. When he looked at her, Jori could feel the tension crackling around the room.

"You may tell Dr. Davis that I will see her at five." And with that stark statement, Chris left the office to see his next patient as if nothing had happened.

Jori was stunned.

Shrugging, she went to deliver Chris's message, knowing Dr. Charlotte Davis would not be pleased. And she wasn't, but not for the reasons Jori had presumed.

"But, I'm afraid you don't understand, Miss . . ." The words trailed away as the woman stared down her nose.

"Jessop, Nurse Jordanna Jessop," Jori told her, disliking the woman's patronizing tone.

"Very well, Miss Jessop. Apparently what Christopher doesn't understand is that I have very little time at my disposal right now and it is imperative that I see him at once." She issued the edict disdainfully, obviously expecting Jori to race off immediately.

"I'm sorry. Chris did ask me to tell you that he could see you here in the office at five, if you wish." Jori knew that every ear and eye in the waiting room was focused on them. She tried to control the anger raging inside her as the woman addressed her once more.

"*Dr. Davis,* you mean, don't you, Nurse?" It was a very thinly veiled hint which Jori chose to ignore, turning back to her work at the desk.

She was conscious of the woman leaving moments later, but she kept her head bent, filling out the lab forms for one of Chris's most worrisome cancer patients. Just the same, her mind whirled with questions. And with fury.

How dare that woman treat her like some peon!

It was a busy day with a number of drop-ins. Jori flew about, hoping to get the last few letters and notes sent out in the weekend mail. Mondays always presented enough problems. Leftovers from the previous Friday threw everything out of sync.

When Chris's mother returned at five, she ushered the woman into one of the consulting rooms and then crossed the hall to tell Chris. She found him seated, staring vacantly out the tiny window at the sheets of rain that were now falling.

"She's here." It wasn't a question.

Jori nodded. "Room six. Do you want me to arrange dinner for you both?" she asked in a rush, feeling sorry for that lost look on his face.

His blue eyes swiveled over to assess her intently. "I doubt very much if she's staying," he told her without expression. A crooked smile tugged at the corner of his mouth. "But I will be happy to come over for dinner after I do rounds," he teased halfheartedly.

Jori smiled at him, letting him know she knew what he was doing. "Fine," she murmured. "I'm cooking liver. Feel free to bring your mother."

Chris's tongue stuck out at her. "Yuk, that's gross. I hate liver. And Charlotte isn't exactly your typical motherly type." He glared at her. "You might have noticed that for yourself, J.J. I don't think a nice cozy dinner at your place is going to make her ease off."

"Well, what does she want?"

"That's what I'm going to find out." He got up and came around the desk, taking her hands in his.

Jori knew it was stupid and she told herself a thousand times that she was being a fool. She even whispered a prayer that God would make her immune to Chris's laughing good looks. But when Dr. Christopher Davis looked at her like that, she totally lost it, wanting only to wrap her arms around him and keep him away from the woman on the other side of the door.

Chris kissed her nose.

"Now, can't you please make something I like?" he begged piteously, sounding very much like a bratty little boy.

Jori giggled at his downcast expression. "You're a doctor—you should know that liver is very healthy," she lectured.

"It's also full of cholesterol and I can't afford to pile up on that." The light bantering had partially restored his natural effervescence.

Jori gave in gracefully. "Okay. I'll make something else." She blew out a long-suffering sigh. "I think doctors are very spoiled," she noted for his benefit.

"Not all of them, Miss Jessop. Most are far too busy to play silly games." The voice was cool and very controlled. Dr. Davis had apparently given up waiting for Chris and decided to find him for herself. She stood in the doorway glaring at them both.

"I don't think anyone is playing games here, Charlotte. Least of all J.J. and I." Chris's voice was tight with barely concealed anger. His eyes bored into the other woman, who had the grace to flush. "The question is, what are you doing here? And why now? What's so urgent?"

"You are my son, Christopher. Don't you think I should be concerned about you?" Her voice had lightened considerably, Jori noticed, and she now wore a most beguiling smile.

"It's just unusual, that's all. You were never that concerned about me when I was in Boston. I would hardly think you'd have time to even think about me with your new project." Chris turned to wink at Jori, who immediately felt her heart beat a little faster.

"Yes, well, I do wish your staff had not forgotten me in the room like that," the older woman complained. "I've been sitting there for seventeen minutes. I have to be back at the airport as soon as possible. I'm doing an important experiment tomorrow afternoon." She glared at Jori. "Nurses never understand how important a doctor's time is."

Jori blushed and turned to leave. The woman was a stickler for punctuality, she decided grimly. Seventeen minutes indeed.

"Excuse me," she asked the older woman, hoping to leave unscathed.

"Certainly," Dr. Davis moved deliberately in front of Jori. Her ice-cold eyes fixed on Jori's and she gave her orders. "Christopher and I have a lot to discuss. Please see that we are not disturbed."

Jori said nothing. She refused to start an argument with the woman. She wasn't one to be ordered about but there was nothing to be gained by indulging in a power struggle. For once she put a clamp on her lips, moving past silently to go about her usual routine, locking the office doors when the last patient had finally finished dressing. She left at last, tugging her light poplin jacket around her shoulders.

The heavens chose that precise moment to open again and by the time Jori reached her home, she was soaked to the skin from top to bottom. Even Flop refused to do more than wag his tail and bark a little greeting, standing well back so his golden coat absorbed none of the droplets her coat scattered across the braided rug.

"Fair-weather friend," she grumbled at him. He woofed in agreement and went to lie on the hearth rug.

Jori showered quickly before tugging on a fleece jogging suit in a periwinkle shade that she loved. Her hair twisted easily into an intricate coil of interlocking braids and she pinned the ends under so that the effect was one of neatness. Any remnant of makeup had long since washed away and Jori didn't bother to refresh it.

Minutes later she was in front of the freezer, surveying the possibilities for supper. Nothing but hamburger would thaw properly in the short time she had left, so Jori opted for lasagna with the oven-ready noodles. Before long she had it baking in the oven, a small loaf of garlic bread ready to heat and freshly grated coleslaw to accompany everything.

"I don't know what this is about, Father," she murmured, setting the table, "but work it out to your will." She placed the last item on the table and then quickly shut her eyes once more.

"Only, please, please, if he isn't the one for me, make him leave before I get in too deep. I don't know if I can deal with another heartbreak." Embarrassed by the admission, Jori acknowledged inwardly that Dr. Christopher Davis now had in his hands the power to hurt her very badly. And after today, she doubted he had any intention of staying in Mossbank.

The ringing doorbell startled her out of her thoughts. As she yanked open the door, teasing words flew out of her mouth.

"Well, Dr. Davis, it's about time. If you must beg supper the least you could . . ." Dead silence greeted her.

Charlotte Davis stood on the doorstep with Chris's tall figure behind. Neither one looked particularly pleased to be there.

"Jori, I hope you don't mind, but Charlotte said she would join us." His blue eyes begged her indulgence.

As Jori stared at him, she noticed tiny lines of strain radiating from his eyes and around his pursed lips. His shoulders drooped dejectedly. Chris's whole manner was rigidly tense, as if his plans had been rearranged and there was nothing he could do about it. She was about to answer when Dr. Davis broke in.

"Don't be ridiculous, Chris. Of course your little nurse doesn't mind feeding another person." And without batting an eyelash, the woman pushed her way past Jori into the hallway, slipping off her coat as she entered.

Jori straightened her spine. When dealing with rudeness, she decided, one had to face it head-on.

"Oh, please, Dr. Davis, do come in," she invited softly. "And please take off your coat. My home is yours."

The woman had the grace to flush a dull red. Jori picked up the navy trench coat slung over her father's antique oak table and dabbed up the droplets. She opened the closet and stuffed the coat onto a hanger as she spoke. Her voice mellowed considerably when she spoke to Chris.

"Come on, Doc. Hang your coat up, then we'll eat. Your mother is more than welcome to share our feast." She arched an eyebrow at his relieved look. "Does she like liver?"

When his startled gaze met her limpid brown one, Jori could have crowed with laughter. His mouth dropped in surprise before it turned down in a reprimand. But to his credit, Chris said not a word.

Charlotte, however, had already made her way into the living room and was trying to retain her stiff-backed pose in an over-stuffed chair that had been Jori's dad's favorite. Worn and tired, its springs no longer firm, it finally engulfed the slim form in a most unladylike way.

"Excuse me a moment," Jori muttered, trying to stifle the bubble of laughter in her throat. All that pompous stuffiness fell around the woman like ashes as she struggled to liberate her rigidly elegant self from the enveloping folds. "I'll be right back."

In the kitchen Jori gave way to the guffaws of laughter that could only be silenced inside the pantry's thick walls where no one could hear. She was surprised to find Chris pushing his way in moments later.

"Thank you," he breathed pressing a kiss to her forehead.

"You're welcome," Jori answered automatically. Her dark eyebrows flew upward. "For what?"

"For not taking Charlotte up on the gauntlet she tossed at your feet." His blue eyes swept in quick assessment over her. "I like your hair better when it's free," he told her softly, brushing his hand over the coil around her head. "But either way, you're still gorgeous."

"Supper," she murmured at last. "I have to get your supper."

Reluctantly, Chris eased away from her. "You always make all calm and rational thoughts leave my mind," he told her. "I just have to get near you and my mind turns to mush."

"Pretty good stuff, that mush." She chuckled. Her finger pointed to the table. "Dinner's almost ready," she said. "You'd better set another place."

When they finally sat down to dinner, Charlotte Davis looked more severe than ever, watching Chris as he enjoyed the noodles with a gusto that was somehow satisfying to Jori.

"Do you usually eat in the kitchen?" Dr. Davis asked, glancing around. "I suppose one must fit in with the local farm customs."

"Well, yes, there is that," Jori agreed, tamping down her anger. "But generally speaking, I find the kitchen to be more homey."

"What in heaven possessed you to come to this backwater town?" the woman demanded of her son, totally ignoring her hostess.

"I came to help out a friend." Jori listened as Chris quickly told her about Dan and Jessica and their baby. "It's not permanent, Mother," he told her placatingly.

Jori felt her heart drop. She had always known it, of course, but when Chris said it out loud, those words were so much more destructive. She struggled to retain her aplomb as the woman turned toward her.

"Have you always lived here, Miss Jessop?" It wasn't really a question, it was a demand, but Jori forced herself to answer civilly.

"Please, call me Jori," she invited, smiling. "No, not always. I returned a few years ago."

"How can you stand living in such primitive conditions?" The words cut deeply into Jori's pride.

"It's a small town, yes," Jori agreed, "but the city is only a bit away." Her defiant chin went up as she told the woman, "I love it here. I know just about everyone and they know me. We're rather like a large extended family." Jori kept her words crisp and devoid of emotion.

"But my dear, surely you don't intend to stay here, to raise children in this, this Mossbank place? Anyplace less suitable I simply can't imagine. Don't you want them to know the world they will be living in?"

The scorn was evident in her tone and Jori could feel Chris shuffling in his chair. She made a fist under the table and smiled serenely, facing his mother.

"I don't have any children yet," she said firmly. "But if I did, this is exactly where I'd want to raise them. Many of the people who live in rural farming areas are not sophisticated. But they are good people who work hard and care for one another. If the world had more people like them, perhaps there wouldn't be so many problems."

Jori took a sip of her water. But it was clear that Chris's mother was not finished.

"But my dear," she advised in a patronizing tone. "You miss out on so much of the finer things in life here in the—" she stopped at the warning glance from Chris, but went blithely on seconds later "—in this area."

"People always think that anyone who lives in a small town is limited," Jori countered. "But everything is a trade-off, isn't it?" Her hand pointed to the table. "You probably have access to some wonderful wines, but we have pure water from wells that are uncontaminated. And while you can go to the theater or the opera whenever you choose, we *rural* folks can watch a beautiful sunset without obstructions, or listen to the birds twittering in wild areas behind our homes."

Jori stopped to draw a deep breath. Her fuming brown eyes fell on Chris, who was sitting with his face glued to his plate. She thought his shoulders were shaking. She kicked him. Jori was sick of being laughed at by Chris Davis and his mother.

"Just because I live in this area, doesn't mean I'm not interested in what's happening in other parts of the world. I just choose not to live there anymore. More lasagna?"

At the negative shake of Dr. Davis's perfectly groomed head, Jori swept up the empty plates and returned to the table with slices of angel food cake smothered in garden fresh raspberries and thick whipped farm cream. Those distributed, she returned with the coffeepot and poured some for everyone, before plunking the pot angrily onto a cork mat.

The remainder of their meal was silent except for Chris's attempts at lightening the atmosphere. He tried repeatedly to engage his mother in conversation with only limited success. Dr. Davis described the current social scene he was missing out on. She went into long detailed descriptions of her projects that had Jori's eyes glazing over. Charlotte even name-dropped once or twice about local debutantes who had missed him. And through it all, Chris merely sat silent, shifting uncomfortably in his seat.

Jori was disgusted with the haughty woman who sat across from her. At the same time, she remembered her father remonstrating that a guest was still a guest, no matter how ignorant.

Finally, amid the tense, strained mood of the evening, Dr. Davis and her son finished their dessert. Jori could hardly wait to draw a deep relaxing breath and try to ease the strain from her shoulder muscles.

"Please, take your coffee into the living room," she told them both, tired of everything. "You need time to talk and I have a few things to do out here."

"But, Jori, we can't just leave you with all this," Chris protested. He picked up a few dishes and began stacking them in the dishwasher. Jori scooped the remainder from his hands.

"Thank you, but I think it would be best if you and your mother talked in the other room," she said firmly, refusing to give way.

Dark blue eyes searched hers for a long moment. Finally Chris nodded in agreement. He escorted his mother out, but stopped in the doorway.

"It was a delicious meal, Jori. Thank you very much." His big hand brushed over the coil of hair around her head. "I'm sorry Mother upset you."

Once he had gone Jori took out her frustrations on her dishes, leaving two chipped plates and one broken cup. She couldn't help it after the remarks she heard coming from the other room.

"Your training is wasted here," Dr. Davis informed her son. "A GP could serve this community just as well with a third of the training and much less expense than you've caused us."

"Mother, you don't understand. Mossbank gives me back so much."

She'd cut him off, obviously furious.

"Mossbank." She spat the word out. "What is there in this back-water town that has you so impressed? It looks nothing like heaven to me. More like the back forty with those dreadful roads." Jori had grinned but kept her ear near the door. "You'll lose your position, Christopher. They won't hold on forever and then everything you've gained will be lost."

"What 'everything,' Mother?" he'd asked quietly, his voice dull.

"The money, the prestige, the importance of your work. The opportunity to advance—make a name for yourself. Maybe even teach someday. That was always your dream, as I recall." Jori heard the squeak of her father's chair. "Don't you care about those things anymore? Don't you want to be a contributor to society where it matters?"

Jori had wanted to yell that it mattered here in Mossbank. To a whole town and the surrounding community, Chris Davis, M.D. mattered a lot. And to her he mattered more than anyone she'd ever known. But of course, it was none of her business and she highly doubted that he would thank her for interfering.

"Can you imagine what people are saying?" Dr. Davis's voice was low and filled with disgust. "Our son, a surgeon just beginning to make a name for himself, suddenly abandons his life's work to move out here—Nowhereville!" Her voice lowered and Jori had to strain to hear the next part.

"If it's that girl that has you so entranced, there are hundreds of them in Boston that are far better educated and much more suited as your escort."

"How can you say that after Jori invited you here, opened her home and fed you a wonderful meal?"

"Fine, she can cook. So what?" Charlotte Davis had an edge to her voice that brooked no discussion. "The kind of woman you need has to be able to host a dinner for the medical society. She has to be able to hold her own among the rich and elite of Boston, to encourage them to support your rise through the ranks." The contempt was evident in her voice. "That little office nurse would be totally out of her depth."

There was more—a lot more, Jori figured. But she just couldn't listen anymore. She could see all her hopes and dreams driving out of town and her heart sank. Disgusted with herself for eavesdropping, she pulled on an old anorak hanging on the back door, slipped on a pair of duck shoes and went for a walk.

Outside, the cool moist evening air caressed her hot cheeks, dissipating some of the irritation nagging at her. Jori talked to Flop as they walked down the sidewalk. She tried to sort out the variety of emotions that whirled through her mind.

"She's really a piece of work, isn't she, boy? All that haughty posturing. She's certainly pouring on the guilt to try to talk him into going back to the high, muck-a-muck life in the city." She frowned. "I don't want him to go," she told the dog. "I want him to stay here." Flop woofed his agreement.

They walked across the small park that stood kitty-corner to Jori's property. She had played there many times as a child. Cried there, too, when her mother had died, when she had scraped her knees, and when, at eight years old, Douglas Morris had kissed her on the lips. A tiny grin whisked across her lips as she remembered those times.

Flop ran off to investigate the wonders of the park grass, so Jori sank onto the old rope swing and pushed herself back and forth. At last Jori admitted to herself what she had known for weeks.

She was in love with Chris. The knowledge had hung there, suspended in her unconscious until she could deny it no more. It wasn't just his good looks or his handsome physique. It had more to do with the sad, mischievous little boy that hid behind those deep blue eyes, waiting to be freed whenever propriety got lost.

It had a lot to do with the way Chris's big strong arms made her feel secure and the way his very nearness comforted her.

Jori admitted that her love also had a lot to do with the effort he had made to fit in with the community. Chris was a good sport. He had tried hard to get to know his patients and their life-style while clearly acknowledging his deficits in the area of agriculture.

Finally, Jori conceded the impossibility of that love. Chris would return, sooner or later, to his big-city hospital and his wealthy friends. He would resume the cold, impersonal medical practice he'd had before. It was inevitable.

And he should, she told herself vehemently. It was what he loved to do, the reason he had spent years in training and then working in residencies that offered little in monetary recompense and a lot in stress and worry.

Abruptly, the reason for Chris's choice in the field of medicine dawned on Jori. She had heard only a little of his childhood, but it was enough to leave Jori with the impression of a cold, sterile atmosphere. Chris was a person who liked to touch people—a handshake, a pat on the shoulder, ruffling a child's hair. He was always touching her—brushing a hand over her hair, or pressing his long finger against her chin. Jori could only imagine the impact such a frigid childhood would have on a man as sensitive as he.

But Chris had risen above it. In his own way, he had eventually let himself come to care for the people of Mossbank. And in such an atmosphere, he seemed not to need the immunity a large city hospital would have given. For so long Chris had taken care of others while he ignored his own needs. He'd found this place where he could relax, be himself, be accepted. But Jori wondered if his newfound peace would last in the impersonality of the city hospital.

Jori stared at the sodden grass beneath her feet. "I know how much he loves his work." The words came heavily but she said them, nonetheless.

"I know that he's not mine. He never was. He's committed to his life and I to mine here in Mossbank. So, Lord," she sighed heavily, "what am I going to do? I still want to be part of a happy loving family. I want to have children and enjoy them while I'm still young. Do you have another plan for me?

"I love him, God. I never thought it would happen again, but it has. And it's all so hopeless." The heaving sobs finally ebbed away, leaving her drained and lifeless. "What am I going to do now?"

"What's a pretty girl like you doing out on an awful night like this?" The voice was low and filled with laughter.

Jori wheeled around to stare up into a face she barely recalled from high school.

"David? David Andrews?" Jori whispered at the tall lanky man in front of her. "What in the world are you doing back in Mossbank?"

"I could ask the same of you." He grinned, bending to grasp both of her hands in his. "Last I heard you had made it. Big-time."

"I live here now," she told him quietly. "What about you? You were doing something political, as I recall. And married, too!"

His craggy face fell.

"Yes, I was but we split up about three years ago. Marilee

wanted to stay on and move up the fast track but I got downsized and decided to change directions. I'm setting up an office in town and I'm going to practice here. Nothing earth-shattering. Just small-town basic law."

They chatted for several moments before the clouds opened again.

"I'd better get back home. Davey's with a sitter but I don't like to leave him too long. He's my five-year-old son," David explained. "And the pride and joy of my life. Hey, maybe we can go for coffee or lunch sometime."

"I'd like that," Jori murmured, thinking of the woman who had left little Davey with his father. It didn't seem fair somehow. She wanted a child to love and take care of so badly and other women abandoned theirs.

"Good. How about lunch tomorrow?" David's face crinkled in a huge grin. "No sense wasting time."

Jori agreed with a smile, and they arranged a time and place. As she whistled to Flop and headed for home, Jori considered this new turn of events. Maybe this was what God had in mind for her. No doubt Chris with his fathomless blue eyes and big grinning smile was meant for someone else and God had sent David along for her to be with.

"I can be the best darn stepmother going!" A few seconds later she was giggling merrily. She'd only just met David again and suddenly she was a stepmother? "Come on, Flop. The rain's seeped into my brain."

Thankfully, Chris and his mother seemed to have left, and although Jori supposed she should have felt guilty for abandoning them, she relished the opportunity to sink into the hot, bubbling bathwater and soak away her frustrations.

For her, there was no future outside of Mossbank. There couldn't be. If there was one lesson she had learned, it was that she belonged right here. The people who cared about her were here and she couldn't abandon them. She would stay and pay off her debt to them, and lead whatever life God gave her.

"I'll learn how to be satisfied with that," she told herself. "Just like Paul says in the New Testament—I have learned to be content in whatever state I'm in." It wasn't a cheering thought but Jori knew there was nothing else to do.

"Not unless a minor miracle comes along," she whispered to Flop. The phone rang as she was emptying the tub.

"Miss Jessop? This is Lara Mandon. I'm sorry to call you so late, but I knew you'd want to know our decision immediately."

"Yes, I do." Jori crossed her fingers as the woman from the agency cleared her voice. "Am I going to be allowed to adopt?"

"I'm sorry, but no. The board feels that with the shortage of babies and the surplus of couples willing to adopt them, it would be remiss of us to put you on our list. I hope you understand."

"No," Jori said trying to keep the bitterness from her voice. "I don't understand at all. I'm more than willing to give a child a home and you're telling me that I can't. That you don't want to let me have a baby."

"There are several other avenues open to you, Miss Jessop. You could try fostering for the state, although they generally prefer two-parent families. Or perhaps some medical intervention . . . artificial insemination, maybe?"

"I don't think so, but thanks anyway, Miss Mandon. It was good of you to call."

As she replaced the phone, Jori steeled herself against the tears. Her dream of a family had turned to ashes.

Stoically she stood and began straightening the room, pretending that life went on when she felt dead inside. The phone rang again and Jori picked it up listlessly. It was Jessica.

"Hi, Jori. We have a daughter, Liza Jean!"

Jori swallowed her pain and congratulated her friend before demanding all the particulars.

"Well, she was born early this morning. She weighs five pounds, two ounces." There was a long pause and Jori knew something not quite as wonderful would follow. Finally Jessica's tearful voice told her the rest.

"They are going to operate in the morning, Jori. Her heart is defective. The doctors are going to try to repair it right away. Dan and I are sitting here, just waiting." Her friend's soft, tearful voice faded away.

"Jessica, little Liza is going to be fine. You have to believe that. I'll be praying and so will the rest of the town." Jori made her voice firm and convincing. "You and Dan just rest and know that we'll all be here, waiting for you three to come home."

They chatted for a few moments more until Jessica turned the phone over to Dan.

"How's my best nurse?" Jori thought he sounded tired, deflated.

"Oh, I'm just fine, Dr. Gordon, sir. Congratulations, I hear you are a father. Poor little girl to end up with a bossy fellow like you." The banter continued for several moments. Jori hid her own feelings as she fought depression off. Gradually it seeped away as Dan teased her.

"How's my stand-in doing?" he demanded. "I hope he's taken advantage of the good advice I gave him."

"What advice?" Jori asked absentmindedly, pulling a brush through her long hair.

"About you, of course. I told him my nurse was ready for love and he would fill the bill nicely."

Jori groaned, blushing furiously. The words lined up in her head, ready to blast out at him when she heard Jessica's voice in the background.

"Stop lying, Dan. You only said Jori would keep him in line."

Jori breathed a sigh of thanks that she hadn't made a fool of herself. Still, Daniel Gordon, GP, had one coming. In a moment the answer came to her.

"It's okay, Dan. When you get home you will be far too busy changing diapers and eating Emma Simms's cheesecakes. I'm sure you won't have time to worry about my love life." She grinned, satisfied, as she heard his groan in the background. She added the last bit of bait. "Chris's been filling your freezer with them for weeks."

"Jori, that's not fair. You know the woman can't bake . . ."

Jori cut him off midstream, smiling at Jessica's chuckles in the background.

"I have to go now, Dan. I have a hot date to plan and it's *not* with a doctor. Kiss Liza and Jess for me and thanks for phoning."

"Jori?" Dan's voice was soft and consoling. "I know how much you want your own child and that this must hurt you. But if God can look after Liza's medical problems, he can give you the desires of your heart."

"I know." Jori choked down the emotion that gripped her. "It's just that I'm having a little trouble on the when part." She straightened her backbone and tried for a light tone. "I'll be fine. You guys take care of each other and the baby. I love you, bye."

Happiness and sadness vied for uppermost position in her mind as she thought of the tiny baby that hung on to life so precariously. Another family looking toward the future with hope, she mused sadly. And she was still out in the cold.

"Stop feeling sorry for yourself and get on the phone," she ordered angrily.

Her mind breathed a prayer for the baby as she phoned Faith, Hope and Charity who would organize the members of the local ladies' group into a prayer chain. She had to believe that there would be a baby shower when the Gordons returned.

As she dialed, a question whisked across Jori's mind, leaving her shaken and wondering. Would she ever have a new little baby to hold and cuddle and call her own? Or a husband to share those wonderful moments with?

Chapter Ten

Dr. Chris Davis was not looking forward to leaving Mossbank even given the cool, wet weather that had hampered the farmers this past week. The fact that it had also put a blight on his mother's now extended visit had something to do with that.

Not that she had been thrilled to be there anyway, for he knew she'd only stayed longer to insist he give up this work. And with the constant rain, there was little opportunity for him to point out the obvious natural beauties of the area. Not that she was interested.

Charlotte Davis was not accustomed to studying nature in the raw. She spent most of her time in her pristine, climate-controlled lab. Her trip west had been of necessity not for pleasure, she'd told him shortly. A duty she felt compelled to attend to.

"I did not come to this remote community to see the local sights. Your father and I agreed that one of us had to try to bring you to your senses." Her glance through the shabby hotel window had been disparaging. "I came to bring you back to where you belong."

"Well, I'm not ready to leave. Not just yet. Come on, Mother. It's not that far to the city and you might enjoy it if you got to know the locals."

Her straight, severe mouth had curled at that and Chris had known there was nothing to be gained by pursuing the matter. She would fulfill her *mission,* as she termed it, and then return to the work she considered more important than anything: research. Within minutes of entering the lab, Chris knew she would lose herself in the current project and forget about him until something or someone else reminded her of her motherly duty.

He didn't mind. Not anymore, he corrected himself. There had been a time when he had craved his parents' attention, some show of affection; had wished his mother knew how to bake cookies or hold birthday parties; that his father would come out to play catch once in a while.

But somehow, Chris acknowledged sadly, the impossibility of achieving that dream had finally been accepted internally. His parents were not like that. They could not show outward signs of affection with the spontaneity and uninhibited ease he had longed for. To compensate for the shortfall, they strove for excellence in their professional fields and taught him to search for it himself. It was just that work wasn't enough anymore.

Of course they loved him. Chris knew that. Both his parents were concerned about his career. He grimaced as he remembered his mother's caustically cynical remarks regarding Chris's current situation.

"I can't believe you're going to throw it all away," she'd muttered. "And for what? There are lots of women who are just as pretty as your office nurse. And a lot more cosmopolitan in their outlook, I can tell you."

"Mother, Jordanna Jessop was a world-famous, top-notch model. She is hardly small-town stuff!"

"Then why is she hiding herself in the boonies dispensing peace and goodwill? And if you two are so thick, why is she going out to lunch with that young man?" his mother had countered. "She doesn't want you, Christopher. If she did and you decided to go back to Boston, I guarantee she'd follow. Don't sacrifice yourself here."

Chris didn't bother to explain that Jordanna couldn't and wouldn't leave the tiny community. Nor did he want to hear about some new man in her life. The bottom line was that Charlotte wanted him back in Boston. Now. She could not understand his growing affinity with his patients, let alone the unexpected pleasure he derived treating people who had become known entities. How did he expect her to understand someone like Jori? Charlotte couldn't even understand why he had consented to staying here for so long.

"You belong at the General, or somewhere like it," she had told him, mapping his future out in her usual organized style. "There is little call for your specialized skills here. You're wasting your talents."

That, it seemed, was the end of that.

"Mother, these are people with needs every bit as great as those I treated in the city. And if I screw up, or prescribe something that doesn't work, they come back and tell me. It's face-to-face here, personal. There are no huge bureaucratic paper trails to follow up."

Chris made no attempt to tell her that he had been enjoying himself. He knew her opinion very well. This wasn't *important* medicine. Not like the major surgeries he had performed within the hallowed confines of the major hospitals. To Charlotte, these were the little people, and as such, far removed from her milieu.

And in a way, Chris brooded, she was right. He had trained long and hard in order to be qualified to perform the specialized surgeries he had done. And he had enjoyed the work at first. He'd been proud of the success he'd become and the prestige he'd gained. But gradually, his life had become impersonal and cold.

In Mossbank, impersonal would never happen. Oh, some moved out and new folks arrived, but by and large, the majority of people were stable to the area. The baby you delivered last week would be back in periodically for the next eighteen years or so and you could monitor his progress as you stitched and casted and advised.

Chris liked that component of medicine more than anything. That sense of continuity was new and intriguing. And while he occasionally missed the high-tech, fast-paced operating room equipment, he relished the familiarity and friendliness with which his patients treated their doctor. He liked the way Jori treated him even better.

He loved her!

The realization hit him squarely in the stomach, driving away his breath. Chris didn't know why he was surprised. He'd been entranced by her ever since Dan had introduced them. She had only to stare at him with those melting chocolate-colored eyes, or tip her wide, generous lips into a smile and he could feel his knees buckle.

Jori was saucy and beautiful and bright. She glowed with a zest for living that refused to be dimmed by anyone. Her joy in life was as fresh and unspoiled as a child's. She bounded forward, embracing each day with her brisk, no-nonsense attitude that dared him to rain on her parade. And she refused to back down where her principles were concerned.

One of her most steadfast principles was to remain right here in Mossbank. Chris thought he had accepted her decision to bury herself here. Now, suddenly, he realized the personal implication her decision would have on him. Dan and Jessica would come back and he would leave. Alone.

It would be extremely difficult to build a surgical practice here and the travel involved in commuting to a city center didn't bear thinking about. Besides, there wasn't any teaching facility near by.

"It's all right, Mother. You can go back and tell Father I'll be returning to the fold. I've been offered a teaching position in the East. I start as soon as Dan and Jessica get back."

It was amazing how quickly his mother had left after that. In less than half an hour she had packed her rental car, called the airline and taken off out of town like a cat chased by a dog.

"Nice seeing you, Mother," Chris muttered to himself as he strode back to the clinic. "Don't worry about me. I'll be fine."

Now he noticed Jori coming from the opposite direction. She was laughing and smiling at a tall skinny guy by her side. Every so often she leaned down and ruffled the hair of a little boy plodding along beside them, and Chris felt a fist of jealousy clench the muscles of his stomach. That should be him she was with, their child she spoke to. She waved at Chris then walked into the clinic.

But it can't be, Lord. I understand that. I can't ask her to leave everything she holds dear. He slowed up his pace, enjoying the ruffle of wind across his skin. *Her father's getting worse; day by day, week by week, he forgets a little more, and I can't, I won't ask her to abandon him. Maybe in the future . . .* The thought died away. There was no future. Not for the two of them. They would soon be separated by thousands of miles.

He sat on the park bench, lost in his thoughts, until an urgent voice broke through his musings. "Chris, you've got to come right away. There's been an accident!"

He jolted to his feet, a surge of adrenalin racing through his bloodstream.

"It's Jonathan," he heard Jori gasp as she raced beside him to the clinic.

The little boy was whimpering as his mother held him, one hand pressing a spotless white tea towel against his scalp. His eyes were half-open, and Chris recognized the drowsiness of his patient.

"Hi, Jonathan," he called out cheerfully, patting the boy's little hand. Carefully he peeled back the towel, wincing mentally at the gash that yawned open on the child's scalp. He replaced the towel and spoke sharply, hoping to rouse Jonathan enough to keep him awake.

"Jonathan, do you want to go for a car ride?" The child blinked slowly, his huge eyes regarding Christopher solemnly. "Keep him awake," he ordered Jori. "I don't want him nodding off just yet." He turned to Amy Grand, scratching notes on his pad as he spoke. "Did he fall?"

"Yes. About eight feet," she whispered, brushing her hand over the child's small body. "I was working in a flower bed and I'd left a shovel there. That's how he cut his head." Tears flowed down her white cheeks. "Bob's in the field so I piled both kids in the car and drove like crazy." She swatted away the tears and stared at Chris. "He's going to be okay, isn't he?"

"I'll know more after I've had a better look." She tried to stand and he pressed her down. "No, stay there. I want to move him as little as possible. Jori, bring a cart, will you?" He specified what he wanted on it and then left her to get it while he checked Jonathan's pupil reaction.

"You know that I'm a doctor, don't you, Jonathan?" The boy nodded imperceptibly, his eyes drooping. "And I want to help make you all better?" Again the child's head nodded. "Okay then. But I need you to help me out. And the first thing you have to do is stay awake."

"Too tired," Jonathan slurred.

"No, son. You can do it. You're strong." Carefully, Chris lifted away the towel and dabbed gently at the wound on the child's scalp, carefully removing the dried blood and dirt. As he took the swabs from Jori, Chris noticed that her hand was shaking. He checked swiftly, surprised to see how white she'd become.

"I'm fine," she told him grimly. "Go ahead."

One searching look was all he could afford but it told him that Jordanna Jessop would stay the course. He turned back to his patient, all senses on alert.

The injury was a jagged cut from below Jonathan's ear to the back part of his head. There was some swelling, but Chris could not tell much beyond that.

"I want pictures," he instructed Jordanna. "And I'd like them before I suture him. Can you phone the hospital and tell them it's a rush?" She nodded and hurried away while Chris sat down to explain to Jonathan and his mother.

"At the hospital they have this machine that can take pictures of the inside of your head, Jonathan."

"Why?" The question was drowsy, and Chris sat the boy up more solidly in Amy's arms, checking the pulse as he did.

"The pictures tell me whether this is just a plain ordinary cut from a shovel or if you bumped your brain. I want to make sure your brain didn't get hurt."

"What if it did?" Jonathan demanded. "Do you have to cut it out? Auntie Jori said you're a cutting kind of doctoh."

"Sometimes I do that," Chris grinned. "But usually I don't take out brains. Sometimes I sew people up so their insides can't fall out. I think that's what we'll have to do with you."

"Will it hurt?" Jonathan's voice was small and he bit on his lip bravely.

"The pictures won't hurt. But yes, when I sew you up it will hurt. A little bit. But it won't take long and then you'll be good as new. Will that be okay?" He waited while the child thought it over, head tilted to one side as Jonathan considered.

"Can Brit come, too?"

"No." Chris shook his head. "She's too small. Anyway, hospitals are really for people who need help. Did she fall, too?"

Jonathan giggled; it was muffled and short, to be sure, but it was a giggle.

"Brit didn't fall! She don't walk." His eyes were wide-open now as he grinned at his sister.

"What's wrong with her?" Chris pretended amazement. "Does she need her legs fixed?"

"A 'course not!" Jonathan sounded astonished. "Don't you know babies gotta learn to walk?"

"I'll have to study up," Chris promised gravely, lifting the child carefully from his mother's arms. "Shall we go now?"

He waited for Amy's nod of approval and then glanced back at Jori, assessing her state of mind with a clinical glance.

"Maybe Auntie Jori could hold you while your mommy holds Brit and I drive the car."

"Jon dwive?" The little boy's eyes twinkled up at him and Chris felt a stab of something deep within his heart at the trust he glimpsed there.

"Not today, pal," Chris said with a laugh, helping them into his car. "But when Jon's head is all better, I'll take him for a drive. Okay, buddy?"

Jon agreed happily, leaning against Jori's shoulder with a sigh and Chris let his eyes slide up to meet her brown ones, conscious of the woman in the back seat.

"Children suit you," he murmured, shifting into gear. "You should have lots of them." Mine, he whispered mentally and then stopped in disbelief as he saw the huge tears roll down her cheeks. "J.J.?"

"Drive," she whispered, staring straight ahead. "Just drive."

"Jordanna Jessop has a new boyfriend." Faith Johnson smiled triumphantly as she imparted this latest bit of news. When she noticed the skeptical looks on her friends' faces she frowned. "His name is David Andrews, he has a little boy called Davey and he used to live here, so there."

"The only Andrews I knew other than Clarence, was a family that had a shoe store in town. As I recall, their kids would have been much younger than Jordanna." Charity frowned.

"No, dear. That was Anderson. Andrews was the fellow at the seed plant, where they crush canola to make margarine." Hope smiled gently. "They moved when David graduated. He was such an intelligent boy—very good in the debate club, I recall."

"But why would Jori be going out with him? I'm sure she's in love with Dr. Chris." Charity glared accusingly at the other two. "Have you two been matchmaking?"

Faith grinned cheerfully.

"Only for you," she blurted out. "And that didn't seem to work out very well. Not now that you and Frank Bellows are together all the time."

"We're not together *all* the time," Charity muttered, face flushed a dark red. "And anyway, it was just for pretend—at first."

"What?" Hope stared. "Charity Flowerday, what have you been up to?"

With as little detail as possible, Charity tried to explain how it came about that she and the local undertaker spent a goodly portion of each day together.

"He's been very kind," she asserted. "I don't know what I would have done without him."

"You're in love with him!" Faith's faded eyes twinkled merrily. "At last!" She clapped her hands together. "I thought it would never happen."

"Hush, Faith!" Hope caught the glimmer of anger in Charity's brown focus. "Don't tease her. If and when Charity has something to say, I'm sure she'll tell us."

"I *have* something to say," Charity admitted softly. "Frank and I have decided to get married."

"I knew it!" Faith hugged and kissed her friend gleefully. "I just knew you were in love with him."

"I didn't. I thought you said you couldn't stand the man." Hope's perplexed face mirrored her confusion. "As I recall, you said he was boring."

"Well, as we got to know one another, we found we had a lot in common. But I thought we were going to decide about Jori and Dr. Chris?"

"Just one more thing," Faith begged, her face glowing. "When's the wedding?"

"We're having a very small one," Charity cautioned. "Close friends and family, but that's all. At my age you don't have a big celebration."

"Why not? It's a big occasion." Hope frowned.

"I'm not the kind of woman who looks good in satin and lace and I don't intend to wear it, Hope Conroy. I want something plain and simple but it will have to be soon because we want Dr. Chris there. After all, he was the reason we got together and he'll be leaving as soon as Dan and Jessica get back."

"But he can't leave without Jordanna." Hope's usually calm voice was raised. "I thought for sure they'd come to some arrangement, figure out some plan. Anyway, I wanted them to stay here."

"No, he's definitely going back . . . alone." Charity's voice was filled with sadness. "Dr. Chris has been offered a prestigious post in a teaching hospital. He says he's wanted it for a long time."

They sat, the three of them, pondering the situation.

"You say Jori's going out with someone new, Faith?" Charity frowned, scratching her nose.

"David Andrews," Hope murmured. A gentle smile tipped up the corners of her mouth. "He had quite a crush on Flossie Ger-brandt, if I recall. The two of them spent the last two years of school as steadies. I always thought she'd marry him."

"He did get married. But he's divorced now," Faith imparted knowledgeably.

"Is he? How nice." Faith and Hope stared at the strange sentiment coming from their friend's smiling lips. "I do believe I'd like to have some people over for dinner," she whispered with a wicked tilt of her eyebrows. "Flossie's already asked to help me with the wedding. What better time to discuss it than tonight! Now let's see . . ." She thumbed through the church directory, shifting her trifocals a little lower on her nose. "Ah, yes, here it is. New members—Andrews."

"She's doing it again," Faith whispered to Hope. "She's going to try and get them together."

"I know. And while she's busy with that, you and I need to plan a shower for her and Frank. I think a nice couples affair would be a rather pleasant shower."

"Piffle! She's already got her cupboards full," Faith exclaimed. "What in the world would we give them?"

"I think," Hope elaborated slowly, "we might consider a money tree with the funds to go toward a trip to that mineral springs. Remember? It's that spa that's supposed to be so helpful for arthritis. Frank has bad knees, you know. He'd enjoy it, too."

And they whispered and giggled merrily until Charity put down the phone. Her eyes studied them suspiciously.

"What have you two been talking about?"

"The future," Hope told her, jabbing an elbow in Faith's side as that woman started to speak. "And we think it might be a good idea if we have Dr. Chris over for dinner. In fact, we could make it a farewell evening. We've a lot to be grateful for."

Chapter Eleven

Jori knew she was in rough shape. It had been two weeks since little Jonathan's injury but she still couldn't erase the memory of Chris's wonderful skill as he'd soothed the boy. But hearing him say the same thing that was in her heart had made it so much worse. She would be good with kids, darn it! And she wanted to share them with Chris!

Christopher Davis was wonderful with children. He would make a wonderful father. But they wouldn't be her children; they couldn't be. He would leave and then she'd be all alone again.

She couldn't stop the awful message from whirling around in her brain regardless of how hard she drove herself. Alone. Alone.

"I declare, Jordanna Jessop, you look as skinny as a rail!" Jori heard Charity's voice as she got out of her car and walked toward her house. "What are you doing to yourself, child? Is your father worse?"

"A little." She pasted a smile on her lips. "But why are we talking about me? It's the day before your wedding—how are *you* doing? You're glowing!"

"I feel like that, too," Charity admitted. "Once I gave up all my fears and inhibitions and explained to Frank why I was so hesitant to get married again, well, the burden just lifted." She giggled. "Isn't it silly? I thought Frank had stayed away from me because I was all crippled up with this arthritis and now he tells me that he's been in love with me for years. He was just too shy to make the first move." She blushed. "Thank goodness for Dr. Chris."

"Yes, thank goodness," Jori agreed doubtfully.

"How are the two of you getting on now, dear? I know you were beginning to feel something for him. Hasn't it worked out?"

"No." Jori frowned. "It hasn't. He's leaving, you see. And my place is here, in Mossbank. I've always known that."

"Is that why you began going out with David Andrews?" Charity asked waspishly. "You feel Chris is unattainable?"

"Something like that." There was no point in prevaricating, Jori decided. Charity was her friend. It was time to tell her the truth. "I want a home of my own, Charity. I want a family that I can share my life with. But I just can't let myself rely on someone and then have them abandon me."

"And you think Chris Davis would do this?" Charity demanded with a frown.

"He's leaving, Charity. As soon as Dan gets back. And I can't." She straightened her shoulders defensively. "Besides, David is kind and funny. We share things from the past."

"I think he's simply comfortable," Charity muttered, glaring at her knotted fingers. "You're settling for less, Jori. And what's more, you're selling God short."

"I don't think we should continue this," Jori murmured, not wanting to hurt the older woman.

"Yes, we should. And I'll tell you why. David is a nice man. *And,*" she paused expectantly, "he has a son. A cute little child that tugs on your heart strings, whose very look begs for some mothering." She waited for a moment. "But David Andrews is a man, not a little boy. And he deserves a woman who can share his *life* not just his child. Someone like Flossie."

"Flossie? Oh, but she's . . ."

"Been out with him several times," Charity confirmed with a nod of her white head. "And he's been to dinner at her house. I think he really cares for her, or he could. If you'd let him."

"But I haven't . . ." Jori's voice died away at the intent look in Charity's discerning eyes.

"God has something special in mind for you, Jordanna. Something that He's planned since before you were conceived. And if you'll only let Him work in your life, you'll find more happiness than all the manipulation you can manage on your own." Charity wrapped one thin arm around Jori's shoulders and hugged her close.

"But you can't walk in fear, Jori. You can't duck out and take the easy way. You have to learn the lesson before you get the prize. Maybe it's time you stopped trying to control events and let God direct you the way He wants." Her voice dropped to a soft whisper. "God has something He wants to teach you, my dear. Something so wonderful, you can't imagine. And when that day comes, today's trials will seem like nothing."

"You sound like Dad," Jori murmured, glancing down at the gnarled old hands that held hers so lovingly. "He quoted Psalms 30:5 today. *'Weeping may endure for the night, but joy comes in the morning.'"*

"James may have lost bits and pieces of his past but he has kept his wonderful memories of the scriptures." Charity smiled. "And it's true, dear. You may not believe it now but take it from an old lady who's been through the valley. Cling to this—*'You will show me the path of life; Your presence is fullness of joy; At your right hand are pleasures forevermore.'"* Charity moved back a step, her face shining with happiness.

"Let Him show you the path to a full life, Jori."

The wedding of Charity Flowerday and Frank Bellows took place in the local church. It was a brief affair with the bride's best friends escorting her down the aisle, one on each arm. Charity had decided on a lovely cream woolen suit and she carried a small sheaf of deep pink roses.

"I, Charity, take you, Frank, to be my lawful wedded husband. To have and to hold, in sickness or in health, from this day forward, forever more."

The words rang through the tiny sanctuary with a sureness and clarity that brought tears to Jori's eyes. Frank's face was beaming with delight as he leaned down and pressed a hearty kiss against his new wife's lips in a way that made his devotion and great love that evident to the entire congregation.

Christopher had managed to seat himself beside Jori and now his fingers entwined with hers as his blue eyes noted the moisture on her cheeks.

"It's pretty special when it's someone like those two, isn't it?" he whispered softly. "But then," he added, staring at her, "I guess marriage is meant to be pretty special."

There was nothing she could say to that, so Jori contented herself with clapping as the happy couple strolled down the aisle, beaming as they accepted their friends' congratulations. She'd tried to keep him out of her life just as she'd wanted him out of her heart.

"Are you going to use all that confetti?" Chris whispered in her ear. Jori put half of it into his open hands and then eased her way to the front of the crowd surrounding the bride and groom on the cold, windswept sidewalk.

"Best wishes, Charity, and you, too, Frank. I know you'll be very happy together." Hugging the older woman, Jori felt the constriction in her throat and hung on for an extra moment.

"You will be, too, my dear," Charity whispered. "Just keep trusting."

Jori stepped back and raised her arms, sprinkling the multicolored dots of paper over the white heads of her friends.

Just like God's blessings, Jori remembered from some wedding long past.

"All right, everyone!" Faith stood at the top of the steps clapping her hands to gain everyone's attention. "Don't stand around freezing. We have a lovely meal at the senior's hall. It's warm in there and you can visit all you like."

As a group, the townsfolk quickly moved to their cars to drive the short trip to the hall. Jori hugged her coat around her more snugly to shield out the wind and headed for her Jeep.

"Can I tag along?" Christopher stood beside her, his collar up around his ears. "I'd walk but it's too c-cold."

"That's North Dakota for you," Jori agreed, ordering her pulse to slow down. It didn't mean anything; he just needed a ride. "And this is only October!"

"You look very beautiful," he murmured when she pulled to a stop. "Red is certainly your color. Vibrant and full of life."

"Er, thank you," Jori murmured, unable to tear her gaze from his. "You look very nice, too."

"Jori," he whispered as she moved to open the door. His blue eyes were deep and intent as they studied her.

"Yes?" She tried to look away and found she couldn't. There was something so compelling in his eyes. Something that riveted her attention on him and denied her attempt to look away.

"I'll be leaving soon, J.J.," he murmured. "Dan's on his way back and then I've got to go."

"I know. And I can't tell you how much we in Mossbank appreciate this time you've given to us. I've enjoyed working with you, too." Deliberately, Jori kept the conversation on the same businesslike footing she'd used for weeks now. "But I think we'd better go in now. They'll be starting soon." She slid out of her seat and grabbed her purse before slamming the door and moving to the front of the vehicle. Her evasive tactics didn't work.

Chris caught up with her at the front door of the hall, his fingers closing about her elbow. His face was tight and controlled, his lips clamped together. Those vivid blue eyes were cool as they stared at her, but she caught the glint of understanding in his voice.

"We are going to talk, Jordanna. Maybe not here. Maybe not now. But before I leave, I intend to say what I have to say. And you will listen. It's too important to ignore." And then he leaned down and pressed a kiss against her surprised lips before yanking the door open. "After you, ladies."

Jori turned in time to see Faith and Hope sweep through the entry, their grins wide and understanding. With a grimace in Chris's direction, Jori tilted her head and walked through the door, somehow staving off her fury at his temerity.

Still, she mused, hanging her coat on top of another one in the cramped entry, he had kissed her as if he meant it. At least she had that to hold on to.

The reception was unlike anything the people of Mossbank had seen at a wedding before. Tables of food were scattered here and there throughout the hall inviting the guests to snack whenever they wished. There were plenty of chairs for anyone who wished to sit. No stack of presents waited to be opened. The bride and groom had requested no gifts in their invitation in the local newspaper. That didn't stop Harry Conroy and Arthur Johnson from collecting donations from anyone who cared to contribute and it didn't mean that there weren't a stack of cards and a few gag items displayed around the hall.

"The wedding cake is a train?" Chris sounded amazed as he stared at the seven-car confection that sat upon licorice tracks.

Jori grinned at him, catching the sense of fun that prevailed. "Yes, and I understand that it's all edible. Melanie said her mother insisted on it." As they stood staring, a group of small children ventured near, eyes wide as they stared at the masterpiece. Jonathan Grand was among them and it was he who reached out and stole a mint from the caboose.

"He looks good, doesn't he?" Chris murmured. "No aftereffects from his slight concussion, thank the Lord."

"They all look good," Jori told him sincerely. "Thanks to you. You've done a fine job here. I don't know how we could ever thank you."

"I don't need thanks," Chris told her gruffly. "I've gained more from being here than I could ever give. I'll be sorry to leave."

Jori was about to turn away when a sudden scuffling at the entry drew her attention.

"Hey!" A voice she knew and loved called out laughingly. "Can't a couple leave for a few weeks without you folks carrying on like this?"

Dr. Daniel Gordon, M.D., stood grinning in the doorway, his arm around the waist of his happy wife who carried a tiny baby in her arms.

As the rest of the crowd rushed forward to greet the prodigal and his family, Jori turned around, her eyes on Chris's bemused face.

"You knew, didn't you?" She felt her heart drop to her feet. If Dan was home, Chris wouldn't be staying long. There wasn't any point.

"Yes, I knew," he admitted softly. "But you anticipated that from the beginning, didn't you, Jori? My coming to Mossbank was only ever a temporary thing."

As the words stabbed through her heart, shattering all her dreams, Jori turned away, fumbling toward the ladies' room at the back.

No matter how much she'd hoped, how much she'd dreamed, the result was still the same. Chris was leaving.

Why? she begged, staring into the mirror. *Why couldn't he stay here?*

But there was no answer from heaven and other ladies were clustering into the bathroom now. Gathering composure like a cloak around her, Jordanna walked out of the room and toward the entrance. She would trust God with this; at least she would try.

"It's so good to have you guys home," she lied easily. "And this is Liza! Hello, sweetheart." She ignored the pain in her heart and accepted the bundle of softly scented sleeping baby from her friend. "She's a darling, Jess. Just a darling."

Over the heads of the crowd, Jori's eyes locked with Chris's. She saw the need darken their depths and the way his eyes squeezed shut, as if to ward off the pain. Without a word he turned and walked through the door, completely forgetting his coat.

Chapter Twelve

Jori expected the days to drag, but in fact, she was kept busy as the three doctors spent the week catching up. Dr. Green wasn't affected by the transition much, except that he and Dan had grown close over the years, often covering for each other on a special weekend or holiday. The same connection had sprung up between Chris and Dr. Green, and Jori had noticed how frequently Chris had taken over some of the older man's workload. Now that was to be transferred back to Dan which meant checking and rechecking the files to make sure Dan saw the updates of those patients he'd been worried about.

If that wasn't enough to keep Jori hopping, there was a lot of after-hours community planning and organizing going on to welcome the new baby and shower Liza and her mother with an abundance of baby things.

"I'm so glad we had that house cleaned from top to bottom before they arrived," Charity rambled happily over the phone to Jori. "Jessica can have a bit of a rest. Speaking of that, it's my shift with the wee one soon, not that she needs monitoring. Her heart is better than ever. I'd better go." She stopped for a moment and then in a softer tone asked, "How are you doing, dear?"

"I'm praying a lot, Charity. That's all I can do now." Jori carried her dishes to the sink, dragging the phone cord behind her shoulder.

"My dear, that's the very best thing! When you can't see a way through, you have to pray and ask God to open one up."

They had just finished their conversation when the doorbell rang. It was Chris. A tired, pale Chris who stood on the doorstep shuffling from one foot to the other.

"Hi. Can I come in?"

Silently, she opened the door wider.

"I'm leaving tomorrow," he said bleakly.

Jori walked through to the living room dazedly and sank into the nearest chair, telling herself to breathe normally. The time had finally come, as she'd known it would. But now was not the time to be weak and give in to the tears that threatened to spill out at the thought of losing him.

"I'm sorry you have to go," she offered in a friendly but distant tone, her throat clogged. "We've enjoyed having you here."

"I've learned so much from you, Jori. I'm in love with you and I've been trying to tell you for days. But you've been so busy pushing me away, and there's been so much to do with Dan's return, that I let it go. I was afraid to hope, afraid to dream we even had a future."

His face clouded over, his eyes dark with the seriousness of his words. "But now I'm leaving and I've got to know for sure. Do you love me or do I have a bad case of wishful thinking?"

She stared at him. "Love? You really love me?"

He nodded.

"I love you. I've known it for ages. And I think you love me. I think we could have something wonderful together—if you'd give it a chance. Couldn't you come with me?" The whispered words were soft and full of agony. "We could get married right away."

"Chris, I have a contract with this town that I won't renege on. My father is here and he needs the routine of seeing *me,* his one familiar face, every day." She sighed miserably, knowing that wasn't the only reason as the ugly thought of fear outside of this protected oasis gripped her. She could deal with life here.

Grimly she continued. "Besides, I love this town. I've always wanted to raise a family here. I want to savor each moment of my days with people I like and respect. I guess that's the way God made me. This is the place He keeps bringing me back to."

She stood before him and spoke the words as she watched his face tighten with that mask he so often hid behind.

"I've never pretended that I'm the big-city, sophisticated type. That's not me. I'm small-town, old-fashioned." She drew in a deep breath and continued in a whoosh of excuses.

"Besides all that, I don't think I could live your kind of life. The reason I know that is because for a period of my life, I pretended that I fit in, that I had something in common with people I neither knew nor cared about. And I paid the price for it." Jori cleared the tears from her voice and appealed to Chris to understand. "But even if I *could* get past all that and leave my past behind, I still am not free to move."

"Jori, I can't live here. I'm a surgeon. Boston is where I live, where I work."

"I know," she agreed sadly.

He peered up at her in disbelief, a pained smile tugging at his lips. "It's ironic really. I've always thought I was the type who couldn't be part of a family. But now, here, these past few weeks with you, I'm beginning to believe you and I could have the one thing that's always been beyond my reach—love, Jori. Real love. The kind that builds families."

Jori stood staring at him, silently begging God for help.

"Say something. Doesn't it mean anything, that I want you to come with me? That I love you. Or are you too afraid?" he demanded, eyes widening in his intensity. "Too scared to leave your safe, cozy little town and take a chance on life in the real world?" He was angry now.

"You'd better decide, Jori. Are you willing to throw away everything we could have together just because you're *afraid?*"

"I can't leave here, Chris. Not now, anyway." She hated saying it, but there was no other way out, no matter how badly she wanted one. "I'm sorry. I've prayed and prayed but I just don't see a solution. We each have our own paths to travel."

"But I'm in love with you! I want us to have a future. But not if you can't meet me at least halfway." His hands fell to his sides. "I can deal with a lot of things, Jori. But I can't handle that. You're the only one who can find enough strength to let go of the past and embrace the future. I can't do it for you."

Jori felt his words hit her like nails. She was trying! But he was asking her to give up everything!

"But Mossbank is my home," she muttered. "These are my friends. I'm . . ."

"Safe here," he concluded for her flatly. "You don't have to extend yourself one bit more than you want to. You can sit and wallow in the past as long as you want and no one will force you to see that life is passing by without you." His face was white as he gazed down at her.

"We could be there for one another to support and encourage when we needed it," he continued. "We could move ahead with our lives, be somebodies, go somewhere." His voice dropped. "We could have it all. But you have to let go of the past, of the fear that I'll hurt you like he did."

She was shaking, Jori realized. His words and the pictures they'd painted made her long for such a life. But it was impossible. She couldn't give up her father, her town, her friends. Her security, a tiny voice whispered.

"What about my dad? And what do you give up?" she demanded at last, unable to stem the doubts and fears. "Even supposing I could get out of this contract and didn't have to worry about my father, you're still doing your parents' bidding. You're following their plan for your life. What is it that you want, Chris?"

He stood staring down at her for several long minutes. "You," he whispered finally. "And you know your father's not a problem. We can take him with us. But you won't even consider it."

"I'm sorry," she said. "So sorry. But this isn't God's time for us to be together."

"There's a way," he said fiercely, drawing her into his arms. "There is some way for us to be together. I just have to find it. And I will."

Then his lips were on hers and Jori could do nothing but savor his kiss, his tender touch. For tomorrow it would all be gone and she would be alone again.

"You'll move on," she whispered brokenly, trying to hold back the sobs that raged inside. "You'll be a wonderful teacher and your students will take what you know and pass it on to the world." She straightened and pulled away from him, watching his hands fall to his side.

"Go and do the work God's given you, Chris. You'll find someone who isn't afraid to give back your love and you'll be very happy." It hurt to say those words, but Jori knew there was no choice. She had to set him free; make him see that they both had to go on with their lives. Separately.

"I've already found her," he said stubbornly. "The woman I love is you. You just won't accept it."

"I wish I could." It was a prayer from the heart. "But I have to do what I think is right, even if it hurts. And my place is in Mossbank. We both know that you can't run a teaching hospital from here." She swallowed painfully. "Go and live your life, Chris. Be happy."

His fingers had brushed across her cheek, but he shook his head adamantly.

"We will be together," he insisted. "God didn't send me here, introduce me to a wonderful woman who is everything I've ever dreamed of, and let me see what my life could be like with her, just to snatch it all away. I'm going to believe that He has more planned for us." He brushed a quick hard kiss on her lips and then strode to the door.

Standing there, framed in her doorway, his blond head gleaming in the sunshine, Jori heard his low voice clearly across the expanse of the room.

"I'll be back, Jordanna Jessop. Somehow, some way, I'll be back. And we will be together. You just have to trust in that. And wait for me."

And with one last look, he left, leaving a finality and silence behind that tore at her heart. Alone. Again.

It hurt, but she had expected that, Jori told herself. And she had to get on with her life. And try to staunch the flow of pain that haunted her at what she'd given up.

"Medical clinic," she answered the phone several weeks later. A long drawn-out pause greeted her words.

Finally a cool, crisp voice inquired, "Is this Jordanna Jessop?"

"Dr. Davis." Her heart sank at the sound of Chris's mother's voice. "How are you?"

"I'm fine, thank you. I'm calling to extend my gratitude for your hospitality. I neglected to do that and Christopher has remonstrated with me several times."

"You're welcome," Jori told her, pain clutching at her heart. "H-how is he?"

"Christopher is very well, thank you. He has settled into a term position while another surgeon is on leave. It's just temporary, of course, but I can't tell you how happy they were to have him back."

"Oh." Jori couldn't think of anything else to say.

"He is very pleased to be back with his friends and is quite involved in several new projects." It was obvious that Chris's mother couldn't quite conceal the pride at her son's accomplishments.

"At the present he is negotiating with a team from another hospital to improve the surgical technology currently available there. In Australia, I believe. It's a lucrative position, and his father and I are hoping he will accept it. We're both very grateful for the kindness you extended toward our son."

Jori smiled sadly. Kindness, was that all they had shared? She could read clearly between the lines. Christopher Davis had moved far beyond her reach. He'd clearly put Mossbank and her behind him. Don't expect him back, his mother was saying. He doesn't belong there.

Unable to bear the pain of memory, Jori cut the call short, thanking the woman for her duty call and promising she would look them up if she ever traveled east.

Time dragged on. Months passed. Thanksgiving came and went.

"Good gracious," Glenda exclaimed one frosty December day. "Do you realize there are only ten days till Christmas? I've been putting off my Christmas shopping long enough."

"Maybe it's time for you to get away, Jori, even for a weekend," Dan gently advised her later that afternoon, noting the dark circles under her eyes. "You didn't take holidays this year, Jori. You need a break. Go and enjoy yourself for a change. Take Friday off."

Jori nodded her agreement. She took the day off and drove to the city to do some shopping, hoping to drown herself in the business of the holiday. But the busy mothers directing children through lines to see Santa ate at her like acid, and she turned away, unwilling to watch it any longer.

Listlessly, she drove to the old stone church her father had loved and sank into the worn pew as the famous choir began its yearly rendition of Handel's *Messiah.* The joyous message of peace and mercy swelled out, filling the arched building and resounding back to those in the audience. As one, they surged to their feet to the resounding "Hallelujah" chorus.

The wonderful old songs of joy filled her heart as she sang with all the others gathered for the festive celebration. Although there was no one she knew in the crowd, Jori felt her frozen heart melt with the joy of the season. And when several people wished her a merry Christmas, she cheerily did the same.

It wasn't strange or unusual. No one was unfriendly. In fact, she decided, gazing around, there was the same sense of community here that she'd always found in the church at Mossbank. She watched as the little old lady in front of her wrapped her arm through the elderly gentleman beside her. They exchanged a tender smile that tugged at Jori's heartstrings.

Was this what Chris had meant? she asked herself. That wherever they went, they would have each other. That other people and places could be home as long as Chris was there?

When she finally left, Jori carried away a sense of peace tucked within. She drove through the streets, gazing at the gaily decorated homes as a new emotion gripped her. It wasn't fear. It was longing; aching covetousness for a home with Chris and their family.

You'd have to move, her mind whispered.

"You wouldn't be moving away. These people will still be your friends. You'd be moving on *to* something."

Jori felt the aloneness close in on her when she steered back onto the highway. Tears coursed down her cheeks as the pain tore through her lonely heart. She had thrown away the best thing in her life. Tossed Chris away as if his love didn't matter.

"No more," she sobbed to herself in the darkened vehicle. "I can't live in the past anymore. Help me, Lord," she pleaded.

Perfect love casts out all fear. She heard the words through a fog of misery. Her father had said them many times; times when she had been so confused, afraid to venture out into the unknown. *Nothing is as bad as knowing you could have changed things and didn't.*

Her father had been right on the money. If she really and truly loved Chris and wanted to be with him, fear could have no part in it. She had to let him know that place or conditions didn't matter. She loved him; that's all that counted.

The next day she sat at home, wrapping the gift she had purchased for Chris. Jori brushed a finger over the leather-bound volume, a first issue of a Robert Louis Stevenson classic. Dated in the late 1800s, Jori had found it in a dingy bookstore. She remembered Chris's whispered admission from what seemed long ago.

"We never got to read fairy tales when I was a child," he had told her once.

She wanted to remind him to take the time. She wanted him to read them to his own son. She wanted to share those moments, to watch as he took the time his own parents never had. And when he did, Jori wanted to be there.

She wavered back and forth all day, but finally made her decision.

"Dan, it's Jori. I need to ask you something." She waited a few moments and then blurted out her request. "Can I have next week off?"

"What? Why?" he demanded brusquely.

"There's something I need to do," she told him. "Someone I have to see." She waited, tensing as the silence stretched tautly between them.

"I'm sorry, Jori. Glenda has already asked for extra time off. Erma Stant will fill in for a bit but I can't really spare you. How about the week after New Year's? Would that suit you?"

"Are you sure?"

"I'm sorry, Jori. I just can't do it. Where were you going, anyway?"

"I'm not sure. Boston, I think. Maybe Australia." She refused to say any more and thankfully Dan didn't question her any further. "I guess I'll just have to work something else out," she muttered, deflated now that she had finally made the decision to go.

"See you tomorrow," he replied. Jori frowned at the sound of it. Why did he have to sound so darn happy about it?

She sat in her lonely living room, thinking everything out. The house was terribly quiet, the fire flickering softly in the fireplace and Flop snoring at her feet when the telephone rang. She picked it up absently, wondering who could be calling now.

"J.J.?" His voice sounded so dear, Jori's throat clogged up with joy. "Jori, are you there?"

"Y-y-yes," she whispered. "I'm here, Chris."

She heard his sigh, a whoosh of breath over the telephone line.

"How are you?" she asked softly, aching to hear the sound of his voice. "Where are you?"

"In New York. I'm at a conference. I'm presenting a paper." His words were clipped and short. "Jori, I don't want to talk about work. I want to talk about you. I need to know something, J.J."

His voice dropped to a whisper and she just caught the hint of unsureness in it. "I love you, Jori. It's not a temporary thing. It's not going to go away. You're buried deep in my heart." His voice stabbed pricks of pain at her heart while a swelling gladness filled her eyes with tears.

"I keep seeing your face when I go to work, your smile when my patient makes it. I went to church the other day and someone sang. They weren't half as good as you."

"I miss you, too," she whispered, half afraid to say so but overwhelmingly glad that she had when she heard his shout of joy.

"That's what I was waiting for," he bellowed.

"Chris? Are you okay?" She studied the receiver worriedly, wondering if everything was going as well as his mother had said.

"Tell me the truth, J.J. Do you love me?"

Jori could see his face in her mind's eye—his eyes sparkling with mischief, his mouth tilted up, his hair mussed, giving him that little boy look that tugged at her heartstrings.

"We've been all through this," she began.

"No, we haven't. I know all the problems. Believe me, I know!" Chris groaned, but there was a tingle of excitement in his tone that caused shivers to race up and down her arm. "Just answer the question, okay, sweetheart?"

"But . . ."

"Please?"

She couldn't deny that soft, cajoling dear voice any longer. On a sob of relief, she told him what was in her heart.

"Yes! I love you so much that I cry myself to sleep at night. And then I dream of you, and when I wake up I'm lonelier than ever."

There was a long space of silence before he rushed into speech. "J.J., if I can find a way for us to be together, will you marry me?"

The question stunned her and she stared at the black instrument for a moment, wondering if she had made it up in her mind.

"Jordanna? Will you?" The sureness had dropped away now. She could hear the apprehension filling that smooth low tone.

"But, Chris, how?"

"Jordanna, I've been searching for you my whole life and I'm not going to accept that God dangled you in front of me, just to show me what I was missing. No, there's got to be a way. But I have to know that you feel the same way."

"Yes, Chris," she whispered, brushing tears away and straightening her shoulders. He was worth it, she told herself. Chris wasn't Trace; he wouldn't leave her in the lurch. "I love you," she told him plainly. "I would gladly marry you tomorrow if we could get something worked out." Silence dragged out between them until she heard the hiss of his breath against her ear. "I was coming to Boston to tell you that."

"I wish I was there." His voice was soft. "I'd hold you in my arms and never let you go."

Jori got lost in that vision and found herself abruptly jerked back to reality when his disgruntled voice chided her. "Jordanna! Are you listening?"

"Um, yes, I'm here." Her voice was dreamy. She tried to pay attention to what he was saying.

"Then listen. This is going to work out for us. I'm not letting you go. There's a way for us to have our dreams and I'm going to find it, so you'd better be ready, lady. Because when I do figure it all out, I'm coming for you and we're going to be married faster than you can say, 'Dr. and Mrs. Christopher Davis.' "

Jori tried to interrupt but he wouldn't let her.

"Never mind how or when. I don't know that yet." His voice was filled with jubilation. "But I'm going to knock on heaven's door until I get my answer. You get your wedding dress ordered and do whatever else needs doing, because when I come for you, I'm not waiting one day longer than necessary. It might take me days or weeks or months, but we are going to be together, Jordanna Jessop. And don't you forget it."

Jori heard his words through a fog in her mind as happiness washed everything else away. She couldn't have misunderstood him; there was no doubt in Chris's voice.

"I'm giving it over to God, J.J. And you do the same. We can come through this."

"I know we can," she whispered, taking the first tiny step of faith toward him. "And when I get this contract finished, I'll live wherever you want, Chris. I can come back and visit with Dad and Mossbank will always be here." She swallowed hard, ignoring the warning voices in her head, trusting in the love that filled her heart. "I want to marry you, Dr. Davis. As soon as you can work it out."

"Thank you." His voice was barely audible above the clapping sound she could hear in the background, but the joy and relief in it couldn't be mistaken.

"Oh, no! It's my turn. I have to give my speech now! How am I going to talk about suctioning and sutures when all I can think about is you?" he complained with a laugh.

"You can do it," she told him, a sureness ringing through her voice. "You can give the best speech ever. Because when it's over, your mind will be free to start tackling our problem. I'll be thinking about you, Chris. And wishing you were here with me. Goodbye, my love." And gently, carefully, she hung up the phone.

"I will not be afraid," she whispered to herself with resolution. "I will trust in the Lord for His perfect timing and I will wait."

As she turned away, Jori caught a glimpse of herself in the mirror and tried to imagine what she'd look like in a wedding dress and veil.

"Please, God," she prayed softly, "let it be soon."

Chapter Thirteen

Jordanna Jessop was ready. She had her wedding dress; it hung in her father's bedroom, covered by a sheet, waiting for "that" day. She'd been given bridal showers by three local groups and the gifts sat in the basement, waiting for their new home. She'd chosen her bridesmaid, flowers, even the invitations. But although she had spoken to Chris almost every night on the phone, by March she still had no bridegroom and no wedding date.

"He'll be here, dearie." Faith breezed into the office with a smile. "The Lord works in mysterious ways, His wonders to perform."

"Uh, thank you." Jori stared at the woman assessingly. There was something different about her today. A light, she decided. Some inner joy that made her glow beautifully.

"You seem especially happy today, Mrs. Johnson. Is something special happening?"

"Just the spring," Hope Conroy interrupted, stepping into the waiting room with careful regard for the mud on her feet. "She always gets like this in the spring."

"In the spring a young girl's fancy turns to love," Faith misquoted, winking at Jori.

"Did you want to see Dr. Green or Dr. Dan today?" Jori decided to focus on her job. These days it was all that kept her sane.

"Oh, we're waiting for Charity," Faith informed her with a grin. "Then we're all going in together."

"Together? The three of you?" When Hope nodded her agreement, Jori shrugged and made a notation on the book before taking another stack of files from Dan's basket. By the time she returned, the three ladies had disappeared.

It was a relatively slow day so Jori began typing out the forms that lay waiting and tried not to think of Chris's phone call last night. He'd seemed distant, preoccupied. And when she'd pressed him about his location, he'd been vague.

"I'm hopping around a lot," he'd said. "Trying to get things organized. I'm hoping I can be with you soon."

Soon. It was an old line, and frankly Jori was growing tired of it. She'd managed to get through Christmas by spending time with her dad and having a long phone conversation with Chris. He'd spent all of January traveling with a group of medical men in Australia, which seemed hardly fair considering the winter she'd suffered through in Mossbank.

In February, Chris had suddenly decided to update himself on some medical thing that was happening in England and so she hadn't been able to write to him there, either. He wasn't going to be in one place, he said. Moving around a lot.

There had been flowers, lots of them, for Valentine's Day. And a monstrous box of Parisian chocolates that Jori dared not eat in case he came back and she didn't fit her dress. He'd even sent her a necklace, which was wonderful, and she'd thanked him for it. But she would rather have had him.

"If you'd tell me where you'll be, I could arrange to take my holidays there," she had murmured sadly. "At least we could be together for a while. I miss you."

"Oh, Jori! You know I want to be there more than anything. And I will be. I think things are finally beginning to move forward."

But when she'd pressed him on how forward, he'd changed the subject.

"Just be patient. I am coming. Probably sooner than you expect."

"It couldn't be soon enough for me," she told him, stifling the sobs that tried to break through her iron control. "We can go anywhere, Chris. As soon as I'm finished here in September, I intend to find you. And you're not putting me off."

"I wouldn't dream of it!" He'd sounded amused, and Jori had petulantly said goodbye, wondering if he'd changed his mind about wanting her. It was the end of March, for goodness' sake, and nothing, to her knowledge, had changed.

"You can go home early today, Jori," Dan offered, emerging from a consulting room with a grin. "And I'm officially giving you next week off. You need a break."

"No, I don't," Jori protested, frustrated by everyone's good intent. She was alone, she wanted to be with Chris and she needed to keep busy. "I'll want extra time off when Chris comes, so I need to pile up the hours now."

"Well, you're piling up too many hours," Dan informed her sternly. "I know all about the extra shifts you've been putting in at the nursing home. But they won't be calling you this weekend. I've told them that you're to be off for a week." He smiled sadly. "Look at you, kiddo. You're skin and bones. Go home, have a bubble bath and order in some Chinese food. Relax and get some color back into those cheeks. And that's an order. Now, get out of here."

"Yes, sir, Doctor," she muttered gloomily, and shut down the computer dutifully.

"No, leave the filing. I want you to go home and relax. Understand? Liza can't use a baby-sitter who's burned out, you know."

"I'm going, I'm going," Jori muttered, grabbing her purse and heading out the door. "Boy, you've gotten really bossy lately. Must be fatherhood."

"You'll know all about it some day," Dan told her seriously. "Now, get going. And remember, go straight home."

"Yeah, okay." But as she headed down the street, Jori changed her mind and headed for the nursing home to see her father. Maybe he, at least, was having a good day.

James wasn't in his room so she checked in at the nursing station.

"I'm looking for my father," she said clearly. "James Jessop. Can you tell me where he is?"

"He was with the doctor a moment ago. In the television room, I think." The harried nurse turned away to remonstrate with a candy striper who had just knocked some medications on the floor.

"Okay, thanks." Jori strode down the hall, pleased to see her father standing by the window. "Hi, Dad!" She stood on tiptoe and pressed a kiss to his cheek. "What have you been up to?"

"I haven't been up to anything. I don't know why you say that."

James looked in a bad humor and Jori took a deep breath for patience.

"I just meant, what have you been doing. The nurse said the doctor was here." She frowned. "I didn't see Dr. Green leave."

"Doctor? What doctor? Do you see any doctor? I was talking to a young fellow—what was his name?" He frowned, slapping his forehead with one hand. "Drat this memory."

"It's all right," she murmured hastily, and then stopped as James walked down the hall. "Where are you going?"

"It's supper time," he told her absently. "They always eat so early in this place. I get hungry at night." He kept going, walking down the hall, muttering to himself.

With a shrug and a deprecatory smile, Jori left the residence and moved toward home. It was a bad day when not even James wanted to talk to her!

She was almost through her front gate when a shrill, persistent voice stopped her.

"Jordanna!" Charity Bellows stood on the front steps of Hope Conroy's house, her face flushed and arms waving.

"Oh, good. I caught you." She scurried over and moments later had her hand on Jori's arm. "I've goofed, I'm afraid. Or rather, Faith has. She thought today was her turn to cook and she's made the most wonderful supper for my birthday."

"Oh, happy birthday," Jori said in confusion.

"Well, thank you, dear. But you see, the thing is, Frank is taking us all out for dinner and we have this food just waiting to be eaten. Might I bring some of it over for you? You've been working so hard lately and I'm sure you could use a good, hot meal."

"That would be very nice. Thank you, Charity."

"Oh, it's my pleasure, dear." She patted Jori's shoulder tenderly. "I know how awful it's been for you. All this dreadful waiting. It's a little bit like in the Bible, isn't it?"

"I'm sorry. I don't know what you mean." Jori frowned, trying to organize her thoughts.

"Yes, you do." Charity chuckled. "Where it talks about Jesus as the bridegroom coming back for us, his bride, and says that we don't know the day or the hour, but we must be ready at any time. That's just like you and Dr. Davis. It's so romantic."

"Isn't it, though?" Jori muttered dourly. "I'd appreciate anything you want to bring over, Charity. And thank you for thinking of me. I'm going to have a long soak in the tub, so just feel free to walk in and leave whatever you want in the kitchen. And thank you. Thanks a lot."

"You're welcome. I know it's hard," she whispered. "Please don't give up on him. Not yet." Then she turned and walked back to Hope's house.

"I won't," Jori murmured a long time later, drying herself off. "But it's getting so hard to keep believing. Help me, Father."

Jori pulled on a pale peach velour suit that was supposed to be part of her trousseau and started down the stairs, thinking of her dinner. Halfway down, the scent of flowers caught her nostrils and she glanced around, amazed to see huge vases of lilacs and lilies and pansies and daisies scattered around the room. And there, standing in the middle, holding the biggest bouquet of long-stemmed red roses was Christopher Davis.

"Hello, J.J."

She stared at that dear face, soaking in every detail of it, from his blazing blue eyes to his dazzling white smile.

"Don't you remember who I am?" he asked quizzically.

With a shriek of delight, Jori bounded down the stairs and across the room, throwing herself into his arms and hanging on for dear life. She sighed with delight as Chris's strong arms tightened around her and his mouth closed firmly over hers.

"I can't wait anymore," he breathed before his lips touched hers.

Jori knew exactly what he meant. She kissed him back with all the longing she had kept bottled inside for the past months.

"I love you, Jordanna Jessop," he said, his big hands tightening around her tenderly. "I've missed you so much." One hand slipped through the silken length of her hair as he kissed her again and again.

Jori stroked her fingers over his golden head and tanned face. Nothing seemed real, but if this was a dream, Jori was determined to enjoy it and let time stand still.

"Chris," she murmured, staring into his sleepy blue gaze. "Where did all these flowers come from?"

"I brought them. For you." Chris stared straight into her eyes as he spoke. One hand pressed a small package into her hand.

"So is this."

Jori stared at the package nestled in her hands and carefully opened the black velvet box. Glittering brightly, a wide gold band waited inside. It was a perfect match for the engagement ring Chris had sent her for Christmas.

Chris pulled it free and held it up for her to see. His blue eyes stared solemnly into hers. "I'm not waiting any longer, J.J.," he said firmly. "I want us to get married. Right away. I love you," he told her steadily. "Please, say you'll marry me?"

"I—I . . ."

"Do you love me, Jori?"

Jori nodded. "Oh, yes. I love you more than anything, Christopher Davis. More than I thought I could ever love anyone."

He grinned that silly grin she had come to love.

"Then, darling Jori, does it really matter where we live as long as we're together? Isn't that the important thing?"

"Yes, darling," she told him firmly. "It doesn't matter where we live as long as we are together."

And as she wrapped her arms around his neck and returned his embrace, Jori vowed that she would never let anything come between them again.

As she pressed closer to him, she heard the crackle of papers against her ear.

"What *is* that?" she demanded curiously, thrusting her fingers into his jacket pocket. An envelope with Dan's office letterhead lay there and Jori stared at it curiously.

"Oh, that," Chris murmured, tightening his arms around her. "Well, that envelope contains our future, my love." He had a smug, self-satisfied look on his face that Jori didn't understand.

"Go ahead, read it, my darling," he urged, as he sat down on the sofa. "Read it."

Jori pulled out the single sheet of letterhead and attempted to decipher the legalese covering it. She could make out Chris's name at the top, the word *partner,* and Dan's signature below. Hope billowed in her like a sail catching a morning breeze.

"Chris?" she whispered, half afraid to believe.

He puffed out his chest before swinging her up in his arms and dancing around the room.

"You are looking at the newest partner of the Community

Health Clinic located in Mossbank, North Dakota," he told her triumphantly. "I'm buying out Dr. Green's interest."

"But I thought . . . your mother said . . . Dr. Green is . . ." Jori stumbled over all the questions running through her mind. She was afraid to believe her fantasy had come true.

"Yes," he muttered, "my mother." He tipped her chin, blue eyes meeting her soft brown ones. "My mother was wrong about a lot of things. But especially about Mossbank and my future. It's here, with you."

His kiss made Jori forget the questions that seemed so important. Nothing was more significant than the fact that Chris was here, holding her. She did allow one tiny doubt to surface.

"Are you sure this is what you should do?" Jori peered at him anxiously.

"Sweetheart, I've spent years doing what was expected of me. My parents wanted me to go to medical school. I went. They wanted me to choose a specialty. I did. They wanted me to work in Boston and I did that, too, hoping it would satisfy that need I had inside for their love, their approval. But while I was here, I realized that my parents' dreams aren't mine. They never were."

He kissed her nose and leaned back tiredly.

"I was wrong to let them superimpose their belief system on mine. I thought going back and teaching was what I wanted, but it was just another case of accepting other people's opinions over my own instinct." He glanced down tenderly, his hands closing around hers as one finger played with the brilliant solitaire on her left hand.

"By December, I realized that what I wanted was you and what I had right here. But I didn't know how to get it. Those months I spent here were the most satisfying medical moments I've experienced in a long time. I felt like I mattered and I knew that I wanted to keep you in my life. I just didn't know how God was going to work it all out. Now I know. And, yes, I'm sure.

"So, what do you say about marrying me tomorrow?" he offered.

"I just happen to have a week off," she murmured. "Thanks to Dan." She eyed Chris severely, a gleam of suspicion lighting the brown depths.

"Wait a minute," she demanded. "Do you mean to tell me Dan

was in on this?" She was furious at the agony she had been through while her boss had known all along. Her fiancé nodded.

"You mean I sat here, alone, wishing, when he knew all along . . ." Jori slapped at his shoulder in frustration.

"Don't be angry at Dan," he pleaded with her. "It took me a while to realize what I had left behind." His hands tightened around her, hugging her close. "When I did, I wanted to tell you myself. And then, of course, the ladies helped, too."

"What ladies?" she asked.

"Faith, Hope and Charity, of course. They remembered Dr. Green talking about retiring and when they questioned him, found that he hadn't because he'd never been able to find anyone to move here. He didn't want the townsfolk to suffer." Chris beamed at her. "When I phoned him and made an offer, he jumped at it like a trout after bait. Seems his wife wants him to travel and he's pretty keen on the idea himself."

"The Lord works in mysterious ways," Jori murmured, trying to understand it all, but losing the battle when Chris hugged her close.

"Amen," he murmured into her ear.

"Something's burning," she murmured at last, and whisked out of his arms to retrieve a smoking loaf of garlic bread from out of the oven. Fortunately, only the paper had been singed.

As she turned, Jori caught sight of a small hand-painted card on the counter.

"Chris, come and look at this," she called, and found him right behind her, his arms slipping around her waist.

" *'They that wait upon the Lord shall renew their faith. Teach me Lord to wait.'* We think you've waited long enough."

"It's signed Faith and Arthur Johnson, Hope and Harry Conroy, Charity and Frank Bellows."

"Angels of mercy," Chris agreed.

Epilogue

❧

Jori panted through the tail end of the contraction and flopped back against her pillows tiredly.

"That's it," she huffed. "I can't do any more."

"Jordanna Jessop Davis! You've been bugging me about babies for as long as I can remember. And now that you're finally going to get your own, you're wimping out? I don't believe it." Daniel Gordon's stern look flashed above the white surgical mask. "Quitter!"

"Dan!" Chris's blue eyes were hard and cold. "Leave her alone. If she wants to stop—"

"Are you nuts?" Jori snorted at her husband in disgust. "There's no way I'm stopping this. Ooooh! Here comes another one." She grabbed his hand in her viselike grip and leaned forward, pushing with all her might.

"Push!" Dan ordered.

"I am pushing," she hissed through gritted teeth.

"Here comes another one. Push."

And so, summoning the last ounce of her strength from someplace deep within, Jori pushed with all her might.

"Congratulations! The Davis family now includes a son." Ignoring the squalling cry, Dan lifted the red-faced infant and placed him on his mother's chest. "Well done, Jori."

"A son, Chris! We have a son." Jori beamed up at her husband, towering above them. "He looks a lot like you."

"A boy." Christopher studied the baby, noting the perfect fingers and toes and the thatch of flaxen blond hair. He touched the tiny face carefully before patting his wife's shoulder awkwardly. His eyes were dazed as he gaped stupidly at Dan. "I'm a father."

"Yeah, pal, I know." Dan slapped him on the back, grinning like crazy. "Don't you have somebody to talk to now?" At Chris's puzzled look, he jerked a thumb toward the hallway. "Three nosy old ladies and a grandfather."

"Oh, James. Right." Chris leaned down and kissed his tired wife on the lips. "I'm going to tell your father, Jori. I'll be right back."

"Give her a bit of time to rest and get cleaned up," Dan advised softly. "You can stop by later."

It wasn't much later when Chris returned to his wife's hospital room. She was sleeping but woke immediately, glancing at the bouquet in his hands.

"Oh. Thank you," she murmured as she took the flowers from him.

"You don't like them?"

"Of course I like them. They're beautiful," she whispered, accepting his kiss. She hung on when he would have moved away. "I just somehow thought you'd bring roses."

"Roses?" He sounded scandalized. "You can have roses any day of the week, my darling. These are chrysanthe*mums* for a mom— the mother of my son!" He stood proudly before her, his eyes glowing with love.

A beautiful smile lit up Jori's face as she laid the bouquet of flowers on the side of the bed and wrapped both arms around his neck, tugging his mouth nearer hers.

"Quite right, my dear husband. After all, how often does one get to be a mother?"

"I don't know." He grinned, brushing his lips against hers while his fingers tangled in her hair. "But I'm willing to discuss it again whenever you wish."

Faith, Hope and Charity stood for a moment in front of the nursery, gazing at the lone occupant who slept happily unaware.

"This was by far the hardest case of all," Faith murmured, making silly faces into the glass.

"It took some special doing," Hope agreed, allowing her mouth to curve in a tiny cooing noise.

"That's the truth," Charity whispered, pointing toward the baby. "Sent right from heaven." She glanced at the two elderly ladies making foolish, nonsensical gestures at the sleeping child. "But for once I agree wholeheartedly with James."

"What did he say?" Faith demanded, knocking gently on the glass.

"Love bears all things, believes all things, hopes all things, endures all things. Love never fails." Charity quoted the verse with a smile and threaded her arms through each of the other's.

"Come on girls, let's go home. We've done our job here."

And they toddled off into the night, content with all life offered.

Dear Reader,

Isn't it hard to wait? I'm one of those people who shake Christmas gifts as soon as they arrive, trying to figure out what's inside. I detest long lines and delays in traffic because I want to get on with things. And I simply cannot understand people who dillydally, dithering between one choice or another. For me, the choice is quickly made. Did I mention I often make the *wrong* choice?

Perhaps that's why I empathize with Jori. She's so sure she's made the right decision. She's got things organized, her life is going along as it should, and she's ready for the next step—a baby. The trouble is, God seems to see things differently. And when God says "wait," no matter how hard we try to get around it, we have to wait until finally, His perfect will becomes clear to us mere mortals.

The Bible says that those who wait on God will renew their strength. And it further asks God to "teach" us to wait. You know, that's my prayer, too. But I hope He hurries!

I wish you persistent patience in knowing His will.

Night Music

SARA MITCHELL

A popular and highly acclaimed author in the Christian market, her aim is "to depict the struggle between the challenges of everyday life and the values to which our faith would have us aspire." The author of seven contemporary and two historical suspense novels, her work has been published by many Inspirational book publishers.

Having lived in diverse locations from Georgia to California to Great Britain, her extensive travel experience helps her create authentic settings for her books. A lifelong music lover, Sara has also written several musical dramas and has long been active in the music ministries of the churches wherever she and her husband, a retired career air force officer, have lived. The parents of two daughters, Sara and her husband now live in Virginia.

Night Music

Sara Mitchell

Love Inspired™

Published by Steeple Hill Books™

STEEPLE HILL BOOKS

Steeple
Hill™

4 in 1 ISBN: 0-7394-0528-4

NIGHT MUSIC

Copyright © 1998 by Sara Mitchell
Text revised for Love Inspired™ edition

Copyright © 1989 by Sara Mitchell
First published by Accent Publishing under the
title *Walk in Deep Shadows*

The Lord is my light and my salvation; whom shall I fear? The Lord is the strength of my life; of whom shall I be afraid?

—*Psalms* 27:1

With grateful thanks to Linda Phillips and
Dawn Dale-Bartow, for their cheerful assistance:
Linda, for functioning as a go-between;
Dawn, for lending her legal expertise
to bail me out of a plotting snarl.
Couldn't have done it without you both!

Prologue

◆

All eyes in the audience were riveted upon the second of three finalists in the prestigious Jeremy Lake Piano Competition—a young girl still in her teens. Anticipation mounted as the orchestra approached the tumultuous climax of Liszt's Piano Concerto no. 2 in A Major. At the front of the stage, an oblivious Rae Prescott waited, hands poised over the keyboard of the grand piano. Her heart swelled along with the music as she automatically counted. *Five more measures . . . three . . . steady. Don't rush it—now!*

The final crescendo poured from her fingers in a soaring burst of energy. Even after the music stopped, the last notes rang in the packed auditorium. Rae sat, head bowed, hands quiet while her spirit protested the descent into reality. It was over. The competition for which she had practiced and dreaded and anticipated for eleven months was over. The course of her future hovered somewhere between the first measure she'd played—and the decision of the blank-faced judges seated out front.

Then the wave of applause crashed over her. Slowly Rae straightened, lifted her head. Her stunned gaze focused first on Alexi Barinsky, the conductor. He was clapping. *Clapping.* For *her.* Even more incredible—he was *smiling.* Barinsky never smiled at the finalists. Never.

As if in a dream, Rae managed to stand and execute a graceful bow. Then she realized that the audience had also risen, to give her a thunderous standing ovation. A smile spread across her perspiration-streaked face, and she blinked back tears of joy and humility. The applause resounded in her ears, cascading into her bloodstream so that her pulse began to beat in rhythm with the clapping.

Poise wavered when her tear-bright gaze focused on the gaunt figure of Uncle Floyd, applauding so vigorously his thin face above the white Mark Twain mustache had turned the color of a ripe tomato. Everything Rae had accomplished in the last dozen years—from the tentative plunking of childish fingers to this present triumphant moment—was due to her uncle. The smile suddenly filled her face, and in a spontaneous rush of affection she blew him a kiss. Laughter and another storm of applause followed her as she floated gracefully into the wings.

"Miss Prescott?"

Still smiling, Rae turned to two sober-faced men in neat suits who had stepped forward, blocking her way. Behind them, the final contestant brushed by, walking onto the stage to fresh applause. "Yes?" Rae wondered fleetingly who the men could be and how they had circumvented security. She tucked loose strands of the slipping chignon behind her ears and smoothed tired hands down her long black skirt.

"I'm Agent Kevin Davis, and this is Agent John Landis." A shiny badge flashed briefly in front of her face. "We're sorry to intrude at a time like this. . . ."

"You play beautifully," Agent Landis added. A band of red stained his cheeks and the bridge of his nose.

"Ms. Prescott—" Agent Davis paused, sweeping Rae in rapid, faintly regretful assessment "—this concerns your father."

"My father?" As though whisked into a dark soundproofed room, applause and movement ceased. The notes still dancing in her head died in a shattered instant. "I haven't seen or heard from my father since I was four." Her lips felt stiff, and she had to force the words past a constricted throat.

"Yes, well . . . he was arrested late last night, up in Michigan near the Canadian border, and I'm afraid we need to ask you and your uncle some questions."

Chapter One

Colorado Springs, Colorado
Present Day

It was late, a little before ten o'clock, when Rae finally pulled into the driveway of the red sandstone Victorian mansion, home for over twenty years now. With a faint exasperated mutter she turned off the engine and climbed out of her car, juggling a sack of groceries on one hip. The narrow walk leading to the back entrance to the kitchen was completely dark because once again she had forgotten to replace the burned-out lightbulb on the back porch light. *It only needed this.* With the way her day had gone, next she'd probably trip and break her ankle on the uneven sidewalk.

Thin streams of moonlight fought their way through wispy clouds, casting shadows on the driveway and over the lawn. The turrets and gables that made the Prescott mansion a city landmark at this moment loomed more as dark, subtly menacing shapes. Rae paid little attention. For her, the massive pile of bricks, as her older brother described the house, was *home.* Right now, all she wanted was a soothing mug of hot tea before she collapsed for the night.

Choir practice had run longer than usual, since Easter was only three weeks away. Unfortunately, the church choir still sounded less than triumphantly joyful, and Rae's feet dragged as she inched her way up the back steps. As keyboard accompanist for the church, she sympathized with the beleaguered choir director's frustrations, though she had learned to stifle her impatience as well as her training behind a smiling mask. Jerry knew she had trained at Juilliard, knew she had been on the way to the top as a concert pianist—but he didn't need to have his face rubbed in it. Besides, he had far more training than Rae at directing oftimes untrained all-volunteer choirs.

"All right . . . where *is* that key?" she grumbled, fumbling in her purse.

Off to the right, the untrimmed hedge of evergreen bushes stirred, rustling in the brisk night silence. That wretched mutt! Rae thought. She plopped the sack and her purse on the stoop, then peered beneath the shadow-dark bushes. For almost a week now, the stray dog had been wandering around the neighborhood, pilfering garbage and digging holes, eluding the Humane Society while ignoring annoyed residents who shooed him away. Rae had discreetly left meat scraps by the garage a couple of times, though she was careful not to share her softheartedness with the neighbors. Unfortunately, yesterday the animal had tried to bite old Elijah Mortenson, who lived two houses down from Rae.

"Scram, mutt," she called softly. "I'm too tired to be nice, and I'm out of scraps. Besides which, you've about outstayed your welcome around here." Mr. Mortenson might be irascible, but he didn't deserve to be bitten by a stray dog. And the DeVries family across the street had two small children.

There was no response, not even a growl or the sound of retreating paws. For a moment Rae listened, shivering in the cold black shadows of the lightless porch. "That's it," she finally announced. Stepping down, she groped along the edge of the walk until her fingers closed over a rock. "Scram!" she repeated, shooting the rock into the bushes.

Instead of a canine yelp, a rough, bitten-off curse split the night like the unexpected explosion of a shotgun. A dark amorphous figure erupted from the bushes, and a face smeared with black paint turned directly toward Rae. For a frozen second she stared in numb disbelief.

Then the figure took a step toward her. Rae whirled, stumbled up the two porch steps and clawed for her purse. The Mace. Where was the can of Mace she always kept in her purse? Clumsy with fright, her fingers closed over metal and she yanked it out, dropping the purse as she whipped around and aimed the can.

Just as she opened her mouth to scream, the man tore off across the lawn and disappeared around the corner of the house. A few seconds later Rae heard the faint scrunching sound of his footsteps fleeing across the street. The noise echoed loudly in her ears, pounding in rhythm with her stampeding pulse.

A long, trembling moment passed. Finally Rae lowered her arms, gathered her belongings and fumbled her way inside. Methodically she turned the lock, fastened the dead bolt and deposited the groceries on the kitchen counter. Then she forced herself to walk down the long hall to the music store, which now comprised the front rooms of the mansion. All clear. She checked the rooms at the back where she lived. As near as she could tell, the man hadn't broken into the house.

She called the police and made herself a cup of hot tea while she waited for them to arrive.

Officer Nash was a tall, hard-looking man with penetrating brown eyes. He walked through the entire house, including the unused levels. There was no evidence of a break-in, no evidence of even an *attempted* break-in. There was nothing to prove that a prowler existed, though the policeman did point out to Rae that searching the place by herself had been foolhardy.

"We'll keep a patrol check in the area for a while," he promised. "But that's about all we can do right now—hiding in your bushes is not considered a crime, since your yard isn't fenced in." One corner of his mouth lifted. "That foot-high stone wall doesn't count as a fence."

"You mean anybody can skulk around in my bushes, and I can't do anything about it?" Incensed, Rae shook her head, amazed and disconcerted when the world-weary police officer shrugged.

" 'Fraid that's about the size of it, for now."

"What about trespassing?" She glared, trying to get a glimpse past the man's urbane facade. His casual acceptance of the world's unpleasantnesses sent shivers dancing down her spine. Of course, his world and hers had about as much in common as hard metal rock and a Mozart sonata.

Light from the hallway streamed out the open back door, glinting off Officer Nash's badge and the butt of the revolver at his waist where one hand idly rested. He glanced at the burned-out light and frowned. "You ought to fix that," he observed mildly, thankfully ignoring Rae's rising temper. "Ms. Prescott, we'd like to promise safety to all the upright citizens living here, but anymore that's just not possible."

The hot words trembled on her lips. Rae prayed she would manage to keep her lips zipped and the words unspoken. It wasn't as though she'd asked the Springs Police Department for round-the-clock protection. But still . . .

"I've always liked this old place," Officer Nash commented, glancing down the angled hall with its golden oak walls and turn-of-the-century sconces. "I take it one of your ancestors built it, since your surname is Prescott."

"My great-grandfather."

"And you live alone?"

Her chin lifted. "Yes, I do."

"Well . . . just be careful." He started down the porch steps, then paused and looked back. "A prowler's a nebulous call—unless and until an actual crime is committed, there's not a lot we can do." He looked as if he'd like to say more, but he must have sensed Rae's tenuous control and contented himself with a polite farewell. "Call if you need us."

I did call, she felt like yelling. *And a fat lot of good it did.* Taking a deep breath, she forced herself to methodically bolt and chain the door. Why had she had to inherit the tempestuous side of her mother's nature, anyway? Every day Rae struggled against the life-long fear of losing control. The image of her mother during that last nightmarish year loomed in her memory—the screaming frenzies and drug-induced temper tantrums that had terrified Rae and her older brother, Tyler.

All her life, Rae had vowed to be different from her mother. She would never be sweet and gullible—nor turn without warning to a screaming termagant. Never be weak. Never depend or anything or anyone. Except God, of course. It was acceptable to acknowledge God's sovereignty when you were a Christian. Whether a prowler leaped out of the bushes or a policeman patronized her, she was supposed to call on God's help to stay in control.

"I'm fine," she murmured, walking slowly to the tiny galley kitchen, where she stood staring sightlessly at the old-fashioned appliances, the wooden cabinets she had finally repainted last month. "Absolutely no reason to be afraid." Her cup of hot tea—stone cold now, of course—sat on the burnished maple parson's table. Rae very carefully emptied the mug, rinsed it and propped it in the drainer.

Her hands were trembling.

"I'm not afraid." She defiantly turned out the lights and marched down the hall to her bedroom. "I'm in control, and I'm not afraid."

But that night, for the first time since she was ten years old, Rae left a light burning all night long.

Chicago, Illinois

Caleb Myers sprawled bonelessly as a cat in Jackson Overstreet's office as the president of Polaris Corporation explained the reason behind his panicked call. Polaris specialized in space-tracking technologies and at present had a contract with the U.S. Air Force in Colorado Springs.

Two days earlier, the civilian contractor had called to warn Polaris that their system had been sabotaged.

"We're pretty sure it's a virus program," Overstreet said, his face bleak. "The OSI's working it from that end, along with the FBI, but I figured you'd still be the best behind-the-scenes man for the job." The corner of his mouth twitched briefly. "Fortunately, the FBI agreed, probably because of your reputation."

Caleb idly toyed with his watchband. "I'll do what I can, and of course since my contract's with Polaris, you'll have my first loyalty. Professional as well as personal. But you also know interagency cooperation is dicey at best, and an independent is seldom welcomed by any of them. I'll have to be careful and keep my end of things primarily to consulting." He sat back, keeping his uneasiness hidden. He was a private computer security consultant, and he and Jackson had been friends for years. Both men had been around the block enough to know how the game was played, especially in the nation's capital.

But Jack also knew Caleb wouldn't turn down a friend in trouble, no matter how many other agencies were involved—or the personal inconvenience.

"There's not another man or woman on either coast who can

sniff out computer fraud like you, Cal," Overstreet said, almost as though he could hear Caleb's thoughts.

With a deep sigh Caleb sat up straight in the chair and fixed a congenial but penetrating stare across the desk. "Then why didn't you call me eighteen months ago, when you lost that Navy contract? From what you've just told me, the circumstances that resulted in that debacle sound like the same sort of sabotage as the Starseeker case." He studied his friend, carefully wiping any censure from his expression and voice.

"You were in Europe at the time," Jackson answered. "Besides, my own security people are some of the best in the business. At the time we had no reason to suspect any problems beyond faulty technology."

"Until your canceled project with its faulty technology turned up six months later in a rival company—no longer faulty."

"Yeah," Jack agreed heavily. He exchanged a frustrated look with Caleb before turning to pick up a bulging accordian folder from his desk. He thrust it toward Caleb.

"I understand three of the people who worked on that Navy project are also out at Falcon now?" Caleb murmured, leafing through the folder.

"Right. Wilson, Forbes and Fisher." Abruptly the other man jerked upright and slammed his palms on the waxed mahogany desktop. "Cal, they've all been with Polaris five years or more! Not only are they required to update their security clearance regularly, but I pay them enough to keep them in a life-style an Arabian sheik would envy. It's *got* to be someone from the outside!"

"Take it easy, Jack." Caleb stood and strolled around to give his friend a commiserating slap on the shoulder. "Whoever it is, we'll find them. I'll fly down to the Springs tonight, all right? Whatever turns up, you don't want to lose another contract."

"You're mighty right about that. Thanks, man. I knew I could depend on you to keep a level head." Overstreet shook his head. "Even after all these years, you never cease to amaze me, Cal—you and your infernal detachment. We used to place bets, back at the university, as to what it would take to rattle your cage."

Sometimes Caleb wondered the same thing. "Well, let's hope this won't be it." He tucked the folder under his arm. "I'll be in touch as soon as I can. In the meantime, try not to worry yourself into an early grave."

"Sorry about your vacation."

Caleb waved an indifferent hand. "The ocean'll still be there when I can get away, as will my boat. And my folks are used to me not showing up for the annual Easter reunion." He enjoyed going to the rambling old house on the Georgia coast whenever he could, because he knew how much it meant to the family. But this year, Jack's frantic call had been a relief. Sometimes his mother couldn't resist nagging him about his single status, much less his habitual isolation.

"You have the instincts of a caring pastor but the personality of a hermit," she'd complained the last time he flew home to visit. "Why couldn't you have gone to seminary, like your Dad and I wanted you to? At least maybe you'd be *married* by now, instead of chasing crooks all over the earth."

Caleb drove to his apartment with absentminded skill, so used to the maniacal Chicago traffic he could have been driving down a deserted country lane with the same unruffled calm. Three hours later he caught the last flight for Colorado Springs, settling back against the first-class seat with a serene smile for the flight attendant. Her professional aplomb crumbled into blushing promises of solicitude for the duration of the flight. Caleb found himself struggling with the inward battle against cynicism he'd been fighting for what seemed like years. Would the pretty flight attendant have promised the same good service had he been some balding, middle-aged and conspicuously married passenger in an economy seat?

Shaking his head, he forced his mind to the problem ahead of him and his attention to the three Polaris employees whose dossiers filled the accordian file folder—a lot more productive use of his time than fruitless mental conundrums. Human nature being what it was, he figured one or more of Overstreet's handpicked associates—albeit unwillingly—would soon provide the key to the solution of the sabotaged Starseeker technology. *Sorry, Jack,* he whispered to his absent friend. *There's a Judas lurking on every street corner. And as always, the innocent suffer the most.*

Chapter Two

Heavy gray clouds rolling sluggishly over the tops of snow-sprinkled mountains greeted Rae the next morning. The thermometer on the outside of the kitchen window had plunged below the freezing mark. While water boiled for her tea she gloomily watched the clouds swallowing the foothills. There would doubtless be a snowstorm by afternoon.

The weather suited Rae's mood. She stood at the window, sipping tea, thinking of all the tasks facing her today that would have to be dealt with regardless of her mood or circumstances.

After tugging on corduroy slacks and a cowl-necked sweater, she hurriedly ate an English muffin and juice before opening the store. The darkened rooms were quiet, serene. Blessedly normal, as though the terror of the previous night had never occurred. She hoped enough customers would descend before the snow to keep her busy enough to forget last night's incident.

Joyful Noise, Rae's store, specialized in religious and classical sheet music, though she tried to stock a smattering of popular and seasonal songs, as well. She had converted the parlor, living room and a small sitting area to accommodate the store, while leaving enough rooms at the back for living quarters. To conserve heating costs she had closed the upstairs off after Uncle Floyd died. Between the store's income, her salary as the church accompanist and the piano students three afternoons a week, Rae was just able to keep the wolf from the door.

Her brother had finally quit nagging her to give it up and move to New York where he claimed opportunities abounded for an ex-classical pianist and winner of the prestigious Jeremy Lake Competition. "As if you'd know," Rae muttered as she flipped light switches around the rooms. Tyler Prescott might have elbowed his way up the financial ladder to become a successful stockbroker, but what he knew about musical careers wouldn't fill a demitasse cup.

Apparently the threat of bad weather had persuaded customers to run their errands early. When Rae crossed the huge parlor to flip the Open/Closed sign, she was startled to find a woman waiting outside the double oak doors.

"Good morning," Rae said, dragging open the heavy doors after she finally forced the stubborn, antiquated lock to release. "You must be trying to beat the weather."

"It's almost five past nine," the woman snapped, eschewing social pleasantries. A statuesque brunette who looked to be in her early forties, she brushed by Rae and hurried inside, darting a quick, inquisitive glance around the room. Sharpish brown eyes came to rest on Rae. "I don't know much about music—I'm just trying to do a favor for a friend. I need a copy of—" she whipped out a folded piece of paper and glared at it "—Schubert's 'Marche Militaire,' it looks like. Could you hurry? I'm late for an appointment."

"Certainly," Rae returned equably, though her insides always clenched when customers treated her as though she were a personal servant. "That will be in this room." She gestured to the large front room where she kept the classical music, and the woman followed her, hovering impatiently while Rae found the piece.

Rae managed to suppress a smile while she rang up the purchase, but after the customer left, a laugh escaped. The woman had looked at the music as if it was a scroll of Egyptian hieroglyphics.

A few minutes later a couple of music teachers Rae knew from guild meetings bustled in to poke and prod in the bins. Then a young man stopped by to look for some contemporary Christian rock songs he could adapt to guitar. Rae helped him find something with the cheerful efficiency she showed the majority of customers. She tried hard not to hover—the streak of possessiveness might be understandable, but it was misplaced in a retail store.

After three years she was doing better, but there was still that

occasional lost sale because she hated letting people paw haphazardly through what Rae considered *her* music. It was a secret point
of pride that she knew almost to the sheet where every piece of
music was located. When there were no customers or piano students she filled the time by checking the circular displays and the
bins to make sure everything was in its proper place.

The morning passed uneventfully, though Rae heaved a sigh of
relief when, a little before lunch, the tinkling doorbell announced
the departure of a mother with two preschoolers. A man held the
door for them before entering. Rae, busily restoring the scattered
music in the small popular section, glanced back and smiled.

"Be with you in a minute," she called.

"No hurry," the man returned in a pleasant baritone. "I just
wanted to look around."

Rats, Rae thought. Another browser. On the other hand, when
she managed to leave them alone, sometimes browsers turned into
her best customers. Tyler liked to point out in his infrequent communications that she was an idealistic fool to struggle for every
dollar in the unstable market of retailing, especially a market that
depended exclusively on sheet music. Rae would quietly remind
him that at least she had successfully saved the best part of their
heritage, even if he was determined to deny they had one. Not, of
course, that Rae blamed him.

In an almost eerie echo of that train of thought, the man walked
to the small circular alcove and stopped, speaking over his shoulder. "This place is fantastic. Do you know anything about its history?" His gaze roamed appreciatively over the hand-carved San
Domingo mahogany and golden oak woodwork. Finally he turned
and strolled to Rae.

She straightened, wiping her hands on her hips as she studied
this unusual customer who seemed more interested in the woodwork than her store wares. On the surface, he presented a very
attractive male package. Rae's best friend Karen would have been
drooling by now. Ginger-ale-colored eyes framed by uncommonly
thick eyelashes smiled into Rae's. His hair, slightly wavy and unruly
with a lock falling over his left eyebrow, was the color of nutmeg, a
delicious blend of brown and blond and maybe a hint of auburn. In
sunlight it would be stunning.

He was probably shy of six feet but powerful looking, with broad shoulders, long, lean legs and a certain self-assured manner that made Rae feel oddly dominated by his presence in the confining space. Casually she wandered around him and into the parlor area. "I'm very familiar with the history," she said with a smile. "I've lived here most of my life."

"Oh?" One thick eyebrow lifted and disappeared in the unruly lock of hair. "Was it difficult, turning it into a store?"

"Yes . . . and no," Rae answered slowly. "Opening a store was the only solution I could come up with to keep from selling the house."

He nodded, the warm gaze sympathetic. "I imagine the property taxes alone rival the national debt."

Rae shrugged, hiding a sudden spurt of uneasiness. Something about this man—perhaps his very casualness—warned her that the friendly interest disguised an undisclosed agenda. A distinct current radiated from him, filling the room. Rae found herself watching his hands as he unbuttoned his trench coat. Her initial suspicion that he was a house-hungry Realtor faded. Those hands were not the slender, pampered hands of a man who spent his day behind a desk or the wheel of a fancy car. The fingers were long and strong-looking, the blunt fingertips topped by neatly trimmed nails, and the hand was large enough to span at least an octave and a half. *I bet he'd play a mean Grieg concerto,* Rae mused distractedly.

Whoever he was, she didn't believe he had stopped to browse.

" 'I washed m'face 'n 'ands before I come,' " he quoted in a surprisingly accurate Cockney accent. Then he grinned. "*My Fair Lady,* remember? You're staring at my hands like my mother used to when she inspected them before dinner."

Rae was annoyed to feel a blush heat her cheeks. "Sorry. As a pianist, I guess I notice hands. Ah . . . are you a fan of late Victorian architecture?"

There was the slightest of pauses before the man replied. "Amateur league only, though. That staircase is a masterpiece, isn't it?" He ran his hand over one of the elaborately carved griffins guarding either side of the stairs, then glanced at the stained glass window on the landing. "Mind if I go up?"

"I've closed it off," Rae said, then bit her lip at the abrupt tone. She couldn't afford to tell the man to either make a purchase or leave—but the temptation hovered on the tip of her tongue. "It costs too much to maintain when I—" She stopped, unable to believe she had almost blurted out that she lived alone. Last night's prowler highlighted the need for caution, but the undercurrent of poised alertness emanating from this man was almost as alarming as the unexpected intruder.

Rae adopted what she hoped was an expression of professional blandness. "You're welcome to look around the store itself if you like," she said, subtly emphasizing the word *store.*

The bell jangled, and with craven relief she turned to the new customer, an older man who wanted to select a solo to sing at his church. Rae spent the next few moments helping him look, but the whole time she felt as though a peregrine falcon was hovering, waiting for just the right moment to swoop upon her to . . . to *what?* Out of the corner of her eye she marked the amber-eyed man's progress. He strolled about the rooms, hands thrust in the hip pockets of his worn, faded jeans, looking for all the world as if he was admiring the architecture.

When the soloist was paying for his selection, the man came and stood behind him at the counter, slightly back, gaze seemingly lost in the middle distance. But Rae felt the intensity of his interest, and her lips tightened.

She took her time ringing up the purchase, walked with the chatting soloist to the door, then returned to barricade herself behind the counter. "Was there something, ah, *musical* you wanted?" she finally asked, head lowered as she noted the sale in her log book.

Without warning the man leaned over, resting his elbows on the high wooden counter, and Rae suppressed the urge to scoot backward. "Not today." He spoke very gently, but his eyes scorched Rae in a sweeping perusal. "I just want to tell you how much I admire your family home. And—" his head tilted "—to remind you to be careful." He nodded toward the door with the sign stating Private—Keep Out. "You live here alone, don't you?"

The pen dropped to the hardwood floor, clattering loudly on the scarred surface. "Why do you want to know?" Almost unconsciously her fingers began to play a Liszt melody on the countertop.

Shrugging, the man straightened to his full height. "Just wondered. This is a big house, located on a side street. A lot can happen unnoticed—especially to a single woman." Suddenly he grinned, a wholesome, boyish grin that Rae found disarming.

"Wipe the militant gleam from your eye. I was merely making an observation. You *are* a woman. If you do live alone, conforming to the Christian beliefs implied by the Bible verse on that plaque hanging over the fireplace, then you're a *single* woman." The teasing grin faded, and he gave her a somber, penetrating look that would haunt Rae for days. "And you need to . . . be careful."

Rae straightened and regarded him with stormy eyes. "It's none of your business, but I'm perfectly fine. And I'm always careful." Rae stared into the man's amused eyes.

He smiled, a smile so free of artifice and deceit Rae responded in spite of herself. "I'm not here to harm you, Rae Prescott," he murmured. "I've always liked that quote on your plaque myself, but you ought to consider that you might need someone besides angels guarding you in all your ways." There was an electric silence.

Before Rae could gather her scattered senses for an appropriate retort he was gone, the cheerful tinkling of the bell lightly bouncing behind him.

Caleb let himself into the run-down but clean motel room he was renting by the week. He shrugged out of his coat and tossed it on the bed with one hand while the other reached for the phone. After he finished the call, he retrieved a small black notebook from the pocket of his coat, then made himself comfortable on the sagging bed, propping both pillows against the headboard.

For several moments he reviewed his notes, a resigned scowl faintly wrinkling his forehead. Then he picked up a ballpoint pen and jotted an additional note. "Checked out mansion—actually music store. Owner a woman, mid to late twenties. Single. Nervous." The wary gray eyes had watched him even when she was waiting on another customer.

Caleb paused, tapping the end of his nose with the pen. He was irritated when his thoughts stayed on Rae Prescott instead of the Starseeker case. Her slim straight back, stiffening like a poker when he was prowling her store. The way strands of her straight brown hair kept slipping free of the loose chignon she had fashioned, and how she kept tucking them absentmindedly behind her ear with incredibly long, slender fingers. Those fingers should have looked delicate and feminine, but instead they looked graceful and powerful. She was not particularly beautiful, not in the usual sense of the word. But attractive. Maybe too attractive. She was slim and not very tall, but strength and character shone out of her face.

Caleb had never had trouble concentrating before. As Jackson had pointed out, his detachment and ability to focus were legendary. But something about that lady played over his mind like a record needle stuck in a groove.

Lady. *That's* what it was. She reminded him of . . . not a Victorian lady, but an Edwardian one. Genteel, refined but strong. With a temper she was having trouble controlling at the end. Caleb knew he had made her nervous, even intimidated her, but she hadn't backed down an inch. He liked that.

He did *not* like liking that, and with grim determination forced his thoughts to his notebook and the Starseeker case. He'd been blessed with a photographic memory and didn't need to write anything down, but going through the motions usually helped pull together the missing pieces in most of his cases. He flipped back a few pages and read notes he'd made several days before. His scowl deepened as he began to write again. *F. been twice. Innocent or planned? P.M. watch starting tonight.*

He hoped, for Ms. Prescott's sake, that the surveillance would turn out to be boringly routine. He found himself hoping, as well, that she had understood the reassurance he had offered when he paraphrased the verse from Psalms.

Unfortunately, he had a feeling she'd better understood his warning.

Chapter Three

The storm dumped a little over two inches of snow, just enough to turn the surroundings into a winter wonderland postcard. Early the next morning, Rae stood on the back steps gazing into the yard, where sculptured dollops of sparkling white icing coated the low brick wall, the tree branches.

The bushes where the prowler had hidden the other night.

Her smile faded. Then, shaking off the tension, Rae tightened her grip on the handle of the snow shovel and cleared off the steps and a path to the detached garage. She only had an hour before time to open the store. Dry and powdery, the snow flew in showers of sunlit powdered sugar, and the scrape of metal on the walk rang out in the frosty air. Across the street, Mr. DeVries emerged from his house, briefcase in hand, and they exchanged waves. Pausing for breath, Rae watched as his car backed out and drove cautiously down the plowed street. Her eyes wandered over the pristine white blanket of her yard, as yet unmarred by footprints—

At first she couldn't believe it. Dropping the shovel, she took a hesitant step, then tugged off a mitten to rub her eyes. Breath escaping in sharp puffs of steam, she walked with the slow gait of a somnambulist toward the bushes, where a set of faint but definite footprints left a silent, terrifying trail in the snow. They followed the contours of the house and disappeared around the jutting covered porch that used to be the front entrance. Rae tracked them to the brick pathway leading down to the sidewalk that bordered the street. At that point the prints disappeared at the curb, obliterated by the snowplow.

She called the police. Then, oblivious to the cold, she sat on the front steps, arms wrapped around her knees, eyes frozen on the footprints, until the squad car pulled up.

"So I decided the store could wait a few minutes—I needed some old-fashioned tea and sympathy to bolster my courage, even if the tea is cider." Her hands around a stoneware mug, Rae settled into an antique settee in Karen's upstairs apartment. She lifted her gaze to her friend and had to smile.

Even at eight o'clock in the morning, Karen somehow managed to look like a model, in spite of the fact that she was only an inch taller than Rae's five feet four inches. Now—thanks to Rae—she looked more like a model for a murder mystery. Her huge blue eyes were wide with astonishment, and her lithe, energetic body fairly strummed with dismay and indignation. "They told you the same thing they did last time? That there isn't a law against people poking and prying around your house and just to continue to be careful?"

Drained, Rae nodded.

Karen's slow southern drawl was markedly absent. Her arms flapped in a brightly colored caftan. "I think you better move in with me at least for a while— Let me finish, now." She overrode Rae's automatic denial. "I'm only two blocks down so it's not like you'd be abandoning the place to that creep who's creeping around."

Rae's answering laugh was hollow. "Karen, I willingly dropped out of school. I renounced a very prestigious—and lucrative—award. I gave up a career as a concert pianist to keep from selling the Prescott family home. Do you honestly think I'm going to slink away and hide in a corner just because some weirdo is trying to scare me?"

"*Trying,* honey?"

Rae's fingers began running furiously up and down the glass-covered tabletop that stood beside the settee. "All right, so I'm scared. But I'm not going to run." Her expression matched her voice—composed and determined.

With a frustrated sigh Karen capitulated. "She who runs away lives to run another day," she misquoted darkly. For a moment she studied Rae, her glance sliding finally to Rae's hands. "What are you playing?"

Rae's fingers clenched, and she slid them to her lap. "Bach," she confessed. Then, because Karen's blue eyes were starting to fill up with what looked like pity, she swiped the last crumbly Danish and waved it with a flourish. "Don't worry about me, Karen. 'I can do all things through Christ,' " she quoted with some of Karen's dramatic flair. "Oh, all right . . . stop looking at me like that."

She tossed the last of the Danish onto the plate and sat forward. "Seriously, Karen, I'm not trying to be stupid or heroic—I'm trying to be realistic. The police officer told me the guy could be anything from a prankster to a Peeping Tom to a careful cat burglar, since no attempt has been made to break into the house or the store. I've been pulling all my shades at night—always have—so if he's a Peeping Tom he ought to give up soon. If he's out to rob me and he's that determined, eventually he'll succeed, but I can't spend the rest of my life cowering somewhere while I wait for the worst to happen. I want to try and stay as—as normal as possible."

Her hand was back on the table, mindlessly playing a furious but soundless melody. "Maybe," she added flippantly, "God will dispense a few guardian angels to protect me from all those shadows and things that go bump in the night." Unbidden, there welled up in her the memory of a mysterious stranger who had obliquely quoted the Psalm, his voice mellow and warm as golden honey. He'd also told her to be careful.

She had not mentioned the incident to Karen, because in spite of a messy divorce two years previously, Karen was rapidly turning into a rapacious manhunter. "I like men," she cheerfully confessed. "Besides—what's the alternative?" Karen would be after a man like that curious stranger faster than snow melting on a radiator. She would leap onto her second favorite hobbyhorse—psychoanalyzing her friend Rae.

Rae forcefully quelled all thoughts of the unnerving man. Instead she focused on the onerous task of braiding the tangled almost waist-length strands of her hair. She promised herself—not for the first time—she was going to have this mess cut off one of these days when she had the time and money. And courage. "The police want me to remove all of Uncle Floyd's and Aunt Jeannine's keepsakes from the store," she confessed, gratefully accepting the bobby pins Karen dug out of a nearby drawer for her. "Not to mention all of Uncle Floyd's birthday gifts to me. I'm supposed to box everything up, put them in, uh, temporary storage." With jerky motions she secured the braid in a scrunchie she dug out of her pocket. "Substitute 'permanent' for 'temporary.' "

"Well, I've warned you for years that it was asking for trouble, leaving them on display in the store," Karen retorted. She shook her head.

"What good are they if people can't enjoy looking at them? I've gotten lots of compliments, and it keeps the store from looking so . . . commercial." Rae sighed. "Besides, I always hated the way Uncle Floyd hoarded everything away upstairs. Lladro and Limoges didn't intend for their creations to be stuffed inside a box. And the antique Roseville collection—"

"Would bring a thief or dope addict a pretty penny on the black market. It's still a marvel to me that one of your customers hasn't filched anything."

Rae shrugged. "I'm not going to worry about it. They're valuable, yes—but it's the house I really care about, Karen. It's the only part of my past I can be proud of. Sometimes I wish—" She stopped. Usually she kept the inadequacies and her lack of self-esteem safely buttoned up, where not even Karen could reach. The prowler and those footprints had shaken her more than she realized. *Deal with it, Prescott.*

She had a criminal for a father and a mother whose weaknesses had proven greater than her love for her children. All the wishing in the world could not undo reality. So what? Even if her genes were predisposed to run amok, she still had a choice. God had given human beings free will, hadn't He? She could learn from the past, and she hoped God would show a little mercy concerning the future. At least she and Tyler had had Uncle Floyd. He'd done the best he could as a middle-aged widower, loving them as though they had been his own children.

"I'd better go." She stood up, flipping the braid over her shoulder and reaching for her coat. "We both have businesses to run. Tell Sylvia the Danishes were scrumptious. Between the two of you, Gibson Girl is going to outshine every other restaurant in Old Colorado."

"What—not the entire city of Colorado Springs?" Karen wrapped her in a brief hug, but did not badger her any further. Rae was grateful, and after promising to call that evening, headed down the back stairs.

Outside, a small crowd had gathered, waiting to enter the restaurant for breakfast. Rae stepped off the curb to avoid them, accidentally bumping a broad-shouldered man wearing a blue and yellow ski jacket who leaned casually against the eighteen-nineties lamp pole.

Rae apologized but kept on walking, too intent on her thoughts to feel a pair of eyes burning a hole in her back.

Customers were sparse that day, even though the sun came out and melted most of the snow by late afternoon. A retired couple traveling through the area bought a collection of Chopin waltzes and a teacher's choice grouping of short classical works for their granddaughter. The balding, stoop-shouldered man who had been coming in regularly the past several months returned to query her about early editions of Beethoven's works. Apparently he collected old sheet music, though he didn't play himself. Rae found him a couple of Schirmer editions and he departed, pleased. Three giggling teenagers trooped in after school and rearranged almost all the popular music. Fortunately it was also a teaching day, and except for the three teens, her students for once enjoyed Rae's full attention. Most of it, anyway.

The large, sunny room behind the cash register had become Rae's studio. A local music store leased her the grand she used for teaching. The year before she had had folding doors installed, which could be closed whenever there were customers. Her students quickly learned not to waste time even when Rae had a customer. Her ear and training were so acute she could hear and correctly identify the note a chime was playing on a church bell six blocks away. The guilty student who fiddled around playing "Chopsticks" ended up practicing extra scales and arpeggios as penance.

It was a good thing her income was multifaceted, Rae mused late that afternoon after she flipped the sign to Closed. She had made only four sales the entire day. Oh, well. Low sales were part and parcel of retailing, and if you didn't learn to roll with those sporadic punches, you better find another business. Something less stressful—like stockbroking. Rae smiled while she put the store in order. By the time she finished cleaning it was dark outside, the bloodred sunset evaporating into a frigid, frosty evening with typical Colorado abruptness. Rae tucked the last piece of music in its proper place, then moved behind the counter to tally the meager receipts of the day, using only the floor lamp by the cash register for illumination. Its yellowish glow cast grotesque, jagged shadows over the dark room.

At first she didn't notice anything unusual, because the scraping, shuffling noise was faint. When the sound finally filtered through Rae's preoccupation, she froze where she was standing, fingers gripping the money bag holding the day's sparse takings. The sound came again, as though someone was outside in the bushes, underneath the portico window. If that prowler had returned . . .

Rae's hand shot out and yanked the lamp chain. The room was plunged into blackness. Frightened and furious—the Mace was inside her purse in her bedroom—Rae debated whether to call the police or wait until she knew for sure. Out in the street a car backfired, and loud barking erupted from beneath the window.

"Good grief." Rae smacked her palm to her head. "It's that wretched dog again!" She slammed the ancient cash register shut, bitterly aware that her angry response was far out of proportion. At the moment, she didn't care. Stomping and slamming doors released at least some of the tension. Besides, who was there to see? Defiantly, enjoying the loud bang, she slammed the door that separated Joyful Noise from the rest of the house. Yep, that felt real good.

After depositing the money in the hidden safe Uncle Floyd had installed almost forty years earlier, she stalked into her bedroom to change out of the ridiculously expensive six-year-old angora dress she'd worn for work that day. The fresh reminder of her uncle's thoughtless extravagance initiated another surge of irritation.

"Clothes make the man—or woman," he used to tell her, over and over. "If you plan to make something of yourself in the world, you need to dress the part. Making a statement with what you wear is important, so long as you convey the right message." Translated, that meant, *Don't ever dress like your mother used to*.

"But I don't need all these designer clothes," Rae protested.

Uselessly. "Uncle Floyd, you know you don't have that kind of money. I promise not to dress like Mama used to."

She knew why he bought the clothes, knew the burden of shame he carried—and the guilt that haunted him for over two decades. It mirrored her own. "Daffodil" Prescott had died from a drug overdose when Rae was six. Rae knew her mother had displayed a pitiful courage when she showed up with two ragged, crying children on her brother-in-law's doorstep. At the very least, Rae should honor the memory of that courage. But she hadn't, not really.

"I loved my mother—but I don't want to be like her," she announced, hearing the pathetic admission drop with a dull thud into the oppressive silence of her bedroom.

God? Can You forgive me? I don't want to turn out like Mama. . . .

As always, the flash flood of emotion eventually dribbled out, leaving behind a sludgelike exhaustion. Carefully Rae hung the angora dress in the crowded closet, thrust on faded jeans and a sweatshirt and padded down the hall to her private music room.

Control. She had to regain control of her emotions, and her life. That was the answer—and Rae knew of only one time-tested way to establish her equilibrium. Playing her piano. Wraithlike, she drifted to the ebony Steinway grand Uncle Floyd had given her for her high school graduation. It stood in solitary splendor in the middle of the room, welcoming and patient.

Rae sat down, opened the lid, adjusted the bench and began to play. This evening, it was a long time before the music worked its magic.

Chapter Four

Saturdays in the store were usually Rae's busiest days, even in winter when the tourist trade was down and most of her customers were locals. On this particular Saturday a cold drizzling rain splattered the windows all day long, but not even the dreary day dimmed her revived spirits.

It had been a quiet, uneventful week. No stray dogs, no break-ins, no prowlers. Rae's peaceful mood spilled over onto her customers, who bought more than usual. She hummed snatches of gospel songs and contemporary Christian rock while she alternately waited on people who needed assistance and smilingly retreated behind the counter when they wished to browse or seek momentary harbor from the weather.

Late in the afternoon a woman whose arms were wreathed in silver bangle bracelets entered the store, bracelets as well as the store's bell announcing her arrival. "I need a copy of Beethoven's Fifth," she told Rae. "You know—the one with 'Ode to Joy.'" She hummed the first few phrases of the chorus in a low contralto made raspy from too many cigarettes. "You know the tune, of course? It's always been one of my favorites."

Rae opened her mouth to correct the woman, then stopped, opting for discretion in keeping with the amicable atmosphere. Besides, there was something about this customer. . . . "Don't I know you?" she asked as she led her to the classical music. "Something about you looks familiar." Tentatively Rae selected an easy version with "Ode to Joy" printed in large letters across the top, and smiled as she offered it to the woman. "I'm a whiz at memorizing music, but I'm terrible with faces, so if you've been in here before, I apologize. Ah, is this edition all right?"

The woman gave the music a cursory glance. "It's the 'Ode to Joy.' It's fine." She ignored Rae's friendly apology.

With a mental shrug Rae rang up the purchase. She didn't try to chat further. The woman tersely thanked her and left, leaving behind the acrid cigarette odor that had been clinging to her clothes. If the woman returned, Rae thought, maybe she could tactfully point out that "Ode to Joy" was the choral symphony from Beethoven's *Ninth,* not his Fifth.

After she closed the store Rae walked down the street to Gibson Girl, hoping for a chat and early supper with Karen before the dinner crowd descended. It had been five years since Karen converted the turn-of-the-century cottage to a cozy restaurant, and Rae was almost as proud of its success as Karen. She tried to eat there once a week, in spite of the expense. Karen would have gladly fed her breakfast, lunch and dinner daily, on the house, but Rae always refused her friend's hospitality. Decorated in the style of Charles Dana Gibson's "girl" drawings, the atmosphere was both cozy and chic. Copies of work from old issues of *Collier* and *Life* were framed and hung on the mauve-painted walls. Waiters and waitresses dressed in period clothes, and there was an old gramophone scratching out tinny turn-of-the-century tunes.

Rae opened the oval cut-glass door and deposited her dripping umbrella in a ceramic umbrella stand. Mouth-watering odors mingled with the pleasing sounds of voices and clinking silver on china. Sniffing appreciatively, Rae tugged off her gloves and greeted Cheryl, the supper hostess, then shivered when a cold draft blew around their ankles as the door opened behind them. The man who entered shrugged out of his bright blue and yellow ski jacket and hung it on the coatrack as Cheryl led Rae to a corner table for two.

"Looks like your day's been as busy as mine," Rae observed a few minutes later when Karen finally plopped down across from her for a hurried break. "It's only a little before six, and the place is already three-quarters full."

"Where would we small business owners be without Saturdays?"

Karen added, glancing around with an assessing smile. "I'll probably have to leave before I finish, but I want to try Sylvia's split-pea
soup—she's modified the recipe and this is the first night we've
served it."

For several restful moments they chatted, catching up on each
other's weeks while the drizzling rain accelerated to a downpour.
Rae lingered at the table after Karen left, but when the restaurant
filled she wandered upstairs to Karen's apartment, reluctant to return to her isolated house and the omnipresent chores she was too
tired to address tonight. She watched a movie on cable TV—another luxury she denied herself. But when Karen dragged upstairs a
little before eleven, Rae rose to leave. "You're exhausted, and I
have to be at church early in the morning."

She hurried up the street, clutching her wrap coat, head down
against the cold. A relentless wind blowing from the southwest had
pushed the clouds onto the prairie, leaving behind a clear sky and
rapidly dropping temperatures. Streetlights glowed a hazy yellow,
shining on the icy puddles dotting the street and sidewalks.

Rae crossed the dark, quiet street in front of Joyful Noise and
started up the brick path that led to the kitchen entrance. The
towering Chinese elms flanking either side blocked much of the
streetlight, and Rae lifted her head to scan her surroundings. Even
though there had been no evidence of the prowler for over a week,
she wasn't dumb enough to ignore the potential danger inherent in
being alone. On the other hand, she refused to turn into a neurotic
bundle of anxiety afraid to stick her nose outside without a bevy of
bodyguards crowded around her.

Be careful. Unbidden, the quiet voice of the mysterious stranger
whispered inside Rae's head. Shivering, she suppressed a twinge of
uneasiness, although her gloved fingers searched inside her purse
until they closed around the can of Mace. Over the past week she
had convinced herself that the smooth-voiced customer was nothing more than a predatory male who got his kicks from trying to
frighten vulnerable females. When Rae refused to be intimidated
he'd given up.

On the other hand, the persistent little voice nagged, maybe he
really *had* been trying to warn her. Her gaze moved around the
yard, then focused on the front porch and the store.

On the dark shape drifting across the window in front of the religious section.

Someone was inside the store, moving with a soundless stealth that raised hairs on the back of Rae's neck. Her disbelieving eyes zeroed in on a thin beam of light playing over the room. She felt dry-mouthed, and her pulse leaped into a staccato gallop when the pencil-thin light played over the bins of music, paused, then moved across the hall toward the next room.

A wave of hot anger bubbled from the pit of Rae's stomach. She whipped out the can of Mace, her mind racing. If she wasted time running to Karen's to call the police, the intruder would escape. Her best hope lay in surprise—and noise. If she yelled loudly enough to rouse the neighbors—no. This time, she needed to document his presence, sneak close enough to establish visual contact so she could identify the person in a police lineup, if called upon to do so.

Outrage at the violation of her property drowned all warnings. Rae crept toward the front porch, armed with the Mace, eyes glued to the windows. *This* time, the police would not leave with nothing but a polite pat on the hand. If only she could have afforded to put in that alarm system. . . .

Without warning a dark form leaped from the bushes at the corner of the mansion, hurtling toward her with the speed of a charging bull. Caught totally off guard, Rae fumbled to aim and press the button, but she wasn't fast enough. In a single violent swipe the Mace was knocked free, and a pair of brutal hands closed over her forearms. Malodorous fumes of alcohol, tobacco and sweat engulfed her as one of the hands shifted to cover her mouth.

Frightened but furious, Rae bit the encroaching hand, kicking at his legs, stomping on his feet. She twisted, struggling in maniacal fury, and finally managed to free herself. She staggered backward, her breath coming in tearing pants, then turned and ran. But the knee-length boots were awkward, and the assailant caught her before she reached the street.

This time the attacker's hand snagged her braid, yanking her head back so viciously bobby pins scattered and the braid came unwound. His other arm wrapped around her waist, lifting her completely off her feet. Rae felt as if her scalp was being torn off, her body squeezed in two.

"Let *go* of me!" She managed the beginnings of a healthy scream before his hand clamped around her windpipe and he began to choke her.

Rae dug her elbow into a mushy stomach, then reached backward to claw his face with her fingers. The hand choking her moved to her mouth. His fingers dug into her jaw and smashed her lips, crushing her face so she was unable to bite. Doggedly Rae refused to give in, regardless of the pain. A harsh grunt grated in her ear when her flailing hand struck a beard-roughened, fleshy cheekbone. But the vise around her middle squeezed harder, driving out the air in her lungs.

Rae squirmed and struggled, but she was weakening rapidly. Her blurring senses registered the sensation of movement off to her right—the prowler in the store, coming to the aid of his lookout! Rae renewed her struggles in a desperate burst of adrenaline. Red sparks whirled through encroaching waves of blackness. In a few more seconds she would lose consciousness.

"What the—" The guttural exclamation disappeared in a grunt of pain. The hands holding Rae slackened.

She staggered, her limbs feeling curiously weightless, yet weighed down with sandbags. In spite of her willpower her knees buckled, and she collapsed onto the chilly wet sidewalk. Breathing raggedly, head ringing, she sat watching the bizarre events unfold in a dazed state of semiconsciousness.

Two yards away a silent battle raged as Rae's attacker and another darkly clad man exchanged vicious blows. The dull thud of fists against flesh was gratingly obscene. The two men fought in silence except for the harsh sound of their labored breathing and the blows. Suddenly her attacker wrenched free, then turned and fled, his huge body surprisingly fast.

Dizzy, in pain, Rae nonetheless tried to rise, to run—because she at last had recognized the man who had attacked her. The rhythm of his fleeing footsteps, the hunched, shuffling flight, were identical to those of the prowler in her bushes ten days earlier.

Rae's rescuer gave chase, but stopped at the corner of her house and turned back. Rae managed to lurch to her feet, but they refused to obey the urgent order to escape. She stood, swaying, and tried to summon enough air in her lungs to scream if this man decided to turn on her and—

"It's all right. I'm not going to hurt you. Please don't scream." The words were soothing, reassuring, the voice unnervingly familiar. He stopped several yards away. "It's all right, Ms. Prescott," he repeated.

Fresh goose pimples raced over Rae's bruised, stinging skin. *"You?"* she gasped in a painful croak. She recognized that mellow voice with its undertone of a drawl as surely as she had recognized the fleeing man by the sound of his footsteps.

He approached slowly, holding out his hand. "Easy . . . I just want to make sure you don't fall again."

Rae slapped the proffered hand away. "Who *are* you?" Her throat was so raw it hurt to talk. She backed a step, almost falling off the curb, then glared at the man when he started forward. He went still, dropping his hands to his sides.

"My name is Caleb Myers," he said, an inflexible note warning Rae that he was restraining himself with an effort. "I'm a private computer security consultant. If I'd had any idea something like this was going to happen, I would have introduced myself the other day in your store. Ms. Prescott, I'm not going to hurt you—but I *am* going to help you inside. You've had a shock, and you need to get warm."

She hadn't realized until he commented on it that she was shivering almost uncontrollably. "If you really wanted to help, you should have come to my rescue before that—that disgusting creep practically squeezed me in two." She lifted her hand to her scalp. "And tried to pull my hair off."

Tossed by the wind, her long hair swirled over her face, neck and shoulders. Rae held it aside with one hand. A corner of Caleb Myers's mouth suddenly twitched upward. "I was on the second story of the building across the street there," he commented mildly, pointing to an abandoned hardware store. "I got here as soon as I could—didn't even take time to call in reinforcements."

Reinforcements? Rae bit her lip. He sounded more amused than irritated. But maybe it was because he was a . . . a consultant? What was he doing in the old hardware building? It had been vacant for years. Rae pressed frozen fingers against her aching head, trying to think. Unfortunately, she hurt too bad to analyze further. "Well . . ." She tried ineffectually to gather another handful of hair from her face. "Thank you for, ah, coming to the rescue. You're a really great hero. What—"

A sudden gust of wind almost knocked her off her feet, and this time when Caleb Myers's hand shot out to steady her she didn't jerk free. "Maybe we better go inside. My purse—" She stopped, trying to remember what had happened to her purse. She stared toward the porch, and almost panicked. "There was another man. Inside the store." Her gaze swiveled to Myers. "How do I know it wasn't—"

"It wasn't me." The hand holding her arm squeezed, a gentle, reassuring squeeze. "Trust me, all right? You say there was another man? I'll go check. Perhaps if you stay here, under the street-light—"

"I most certainly will not," Rae snapped unfairly, disconcerted by her response to the warmth and strength of Caleb Myers's firm hold—and the explosion of panic at the suggestion that she be left out here all alone. "How do I know there's not a third man hiding somewhere? And why should I trust you? What kind of proof can you produce to convince me that you're not in cahoots with them?" She was talking too fast. *Zip your lip, Prescott, before you really blow it.*

"I'm a private consultant," Caleb Myers repeated patiently. "But right now, I'm . . . lending a hand to the FBI. We've had your place under surveillance for almost two weeks. If you'll allow me to check the premises, we can go inside and I'll explain while we wait for the police."

Had her home under surveillance? Rae's chin lifted. "I want to see some identification."

There was a short pause.

The trembling intensified. She could not prevent her legs from quivering, and all the feeling had left her hands and feet some time ago. But she was *not* moving another step until this gentle-voiced, eagle-eyed man provided her with some proof of his identity, not to mention an explanation for his astounding revelation. She stared into his shadowed face, a little disconcerted because in the shrouded moonlight it looked as though Caleb Myers was *smiling.*

He reached into the back pocket of his jeans and tugged out a worn leather wallet that turned out to be his identification instead of a wallet. "Here." A small penlight appeared as if by magic and shone on an official-looking ID with a badge on one side and a grainy head photo on the other. It stated that he was indeed Caleb Andrew Myers, and a resident of Chicago, Illinois. He had brn. hair, lt. brn. eyes, was 5'11" and weighed 177 lbs.

"Your eyes aren't brown," Rae said. "And there's red in your hair—or at least under the street lamp there's red in your hair, and I saw some that day—in my store."

"The man typing out the information didn't have much imagination," Caleb Myers returned. He added very gently, "Ms. Prescott, I think you need to go inside. I need to check around a bit first, and I'm not going to risk your safety by taking you with me. So. You wait here—under the streetlight where I can keep an eye on you. I'll be back in a minute." He looked at her, and something in his face quashed the last of Rae's protests.

"Hurry."

"I will." He glanced around, his gaze seeming to penetrate even the blackest shadows, then turned to Rae. "Hang in there." He started to say something else, but ended up doing nothing more than giving her shoulder a last bracing squeeze before he ran soundlessly in a low crouch toward the porch.

Rae shuddered when another gust of wind tugged at her coat and bit her ears. She wondered what had happened to her gloves. She wondered what had happened to the can of Mace. Would have been nice, having that can about now. Oh, well . . . perhaps she should sing a song, try to divert her mind . . . hurt to think. Only song floating through her head was a sixties oldie talking about eyes. . . .

She could lose herself in Caleb Myers's eyes. They were an unusual color. Of course, that might have been the streetlight. But the way those eyes looked as if he was smiling even when he wasn't . . . On the other hand, when he cavalierly ordered her to stay put, she'd felt positively immobilized by the stern warning he'd communicated in a single look. Most unfair, for a man to have eyes like that.

She shivered again, and her voice cracked. Maybe singing wasn't such a good idea.

Caleb Myers returned, cupping his hand under her elbow. "All clear outside. I found your purse, with some keys. Will one of these

open the door to your store? I think it's best if we go in that way—
the intruder's long gone."

"Wait." Rae broke free and hurried stiffly across the grass, where
the Mace lay in a patch of moonlit ground. She scooped it up and
returned to Caleb, who watched with the untwitching patience of a
cougar.

He ushered her up the steps and waited while Rae fumbled for
the key. The patient expression did not alter when it took her three
attempts to unfasten the door because she refused to let go of the
Mace.

"It's a shame you weren't able to use that on your attacker," he
commented easily. "Um . . . are you sure you don't want me to
unlock the door? You can keep me covered, if you like."

Rae did not back down. "Very funny. You'll have to excuse me,
Mr. Secret Agent Myers. This is my first brush with the under-
world." The door finally gave way with a protesting groan, and she
stood aside to let Caleb Myers enter first.

"I'm not a secret agent," he pointed out, sounding resigned.

"Fine. Then you won't mind if the first thing I do is call the
police."

"If you hadn't, I would have."

His voice was much too agreeable, Rae thought as they entered
the dark store. On the other hand, she was safe inside, and right
now all she really cared about was checking on Joyful Noise. She
walked across the floor on shaky legs, grateful to be out of the
wind. She turned on the floor lamp by the cash register, immediately checking to see if she'd been robbed. Caleb Myers followed,
shrugging out of a thick fleece-lined jean jacket.

In the more revealing light Rae studied him closely. The wind
had blown his hair into thick, unruly waves all over the sculptured
planes and angles of his face and head. It made him look tough,
rakish and aggressively male. Then she belatedly realized that he
was studying *her,* with such—such compassion pouring from the
extraordinary eyes that a painful blush heated her frozen, chapped
cheeks.

"Unless you think you need to use it on me, I think it's okay to
put that down," he eventually observed, smiling as he nodded
toward her hand.

"Oh." Rae's gaze jerked from his face to the can she still

clutched in a death grip. Blush deepening, she hastily thrust it beneath the counter. Her gaze fell to his hands. One set of knuckles was scraped and had bled slightly.

"Your hand." She faltered, and he glanced at it.

"I'm sure his jaw feels worse." He paused. "Your face is pretty bruised. Does it hurt yet?"

Rae lifted her fingers to explore cheek and jaw, wincing in pained surprise. "Yes." She wriggled her shoulders, took a deep breath. "Tea. I need a cup of tea. I'll call the police, then put on a kettle. Would you like some tea while you explain what you're doing spying on me, Mr. Myers?"

"Call me Caleb," he replied cheerfully. "If you'll show me your kitchen, I'll heat the water so you can look around your store after you call. Don't touch anything, okay? They'll want to dust for fingerprints."

Chapter Five

Caleb filled a tarnished brass kettle with water and put it on an old gas stove top to boil. Then he prowled around Rae Prescott's living quarters while she checked out the store. The FBI guys had already confirmed she had lived alone for the past three years, since her paternal uncle, Floyd Prescott, died. There was an older brother, but no address was available yet.

In a room that looked like a cozy Victorian parlor he found the only photographs in sight. One was of an elderly man with a magnificent snow-white mustache, cane in one hand, the other arm wrapped around a younger Rae's shoulders.

Next to that photograph was a framed snapshot of a lanky man with gangly arms and legs. He was standing by a flashy red sports car, an expression of smug pride on his face. The same brown hair, long narrow nose and stubborn chin as Rae identified him as the brother. Caleb looked on the back, but there was nothing written to corroborate his conclusion. He put it down, smiling. Rae's arms and legs looked just about as long, slender and unwieldy as her brother's. They had probably been teased unmercifully. Rae still moved with a sort of awkward grace, as though she had never quite learned what to do with all her limbs.

On the other hand, the lady had fought off her attacker with a gutsy determination, but the memory still congealed Caleb's blood to ice. He picked up the photo of Rae with her uncle and studied it. Long limbs, long hair, long narrow nose—actually, she reminded him of a long-haired Siamese cat, with gray eyes instead of blue. Her expression was filled with the same combination of intelligence and wariness. Caleb grinned. Of course, *cats* were inherently graceful.

He continued his prowling, tucking away nuggets of information. No pets. Lots of plants. A mixture of antique and modern furniture, most of which needed dusting. Several framed scripture verses like the one over the fireplace in the store. Most of these were from Psalms. The quiet proclamation of her faith in the privacy of her home reassured Caleb. Her faith was more than a carefully orchestrated outward display. Nodding, he moved out of the parlor into another room.

It was her bedroom. A cursory search assured him that it was empty of intruders, though he did lift a brow at her crammed, overflowing closet. The quality of the clothes was top-notch, the majority of the labels those of world famous designers, including a couple that made both Caleb's eyebrows shoot up. All the styles, however, were several years old, some more outdated. Not a single article was new. Caleb grinned at what his three sisters would have said about *that* sorry state of affairs.

So. At some point in the past, Rae Prescott had enjoyed significant material wealth, but apparently those days were long gone. While that could be construed in a suspicious light, Caleb found himself liking her even more because she seemed to have accepted her present circumstances with the same pluckiness she had summoned to fend off her assailant.

Before he left the bedroom, Caleb picked up the phone on her bedside table, verified the line was free and the phone clean of bugs, then made a quick call.

The last room had no furniture except for the biggest grand piano he'd ever seen. It sat in dusty splendor in the middle of the room. Music was piled everywhere. On the floor, in boxes, on the piano, on the bench by the piano . . .

Caleb smiled with self-directed irony, shaking his head as he quietly made his way to the kitchen. He had conducted hundreds of investigations over the years, and most of them involved women at some point. Many of those women had been attractive, even beautiful, but none of them had ever meant anything to Caleb beyond a professional level. He could instantly call up a detailed physical description of any of the women he'd dated casually—and not so casually. Not a single one had ever made his pulse race. Until now.

Rae Prescott was not beautiful, and made no pretensions otherwise, yet for some reason she made his blood pressure shoot skyward every time he looked at her. It was disconcerting and puzzling—and impossible to ignore, because there was a slim possibility that the intriguing Ms. Prescott was not precisely who she appeared to be. *You better watch your step with this one real close, pal.*

When he walked into the galley kitchen, Rae was opening a tin and taking out two tea bags. Her face was pale, hostile, the huge gray eyes smudged with suspicion.

"Did you enjoy your . . . tour?" she asked, dumping the tea bags into a couple of mugs.

"I'm sorry." Caleb took the kettle and poured. "I needed to make sure you didn't have anybody hiding behind a door or in a closet. Did you think I was casing the joint?"

"Yes, I did. Are you going to try to convince me otherwise?"

He put the kettle on the stove and they sat at an attractive maple trestle table. "I think I told you that your home is an impressive place the first time I was here, didn't I? I really like the way you've kept the integrity of the rooms in spite of having to turn half of them into a store."

"Thank you."

She sat there, glaring at him with wavering eyes as if she couldn't decide whether to smile graciously—or fetch that can of Mace.

Caleb sighed. Rae Prescott might be a gutsy lady, but unless he missed his guess, the lady hovered right on the edge of hysteria . . . or volcanic rage. Maybe both. He stared at the distasteful brew while he considered what approach to take to preserve her dignity—and his cover. "I saw your Bible verses, in your bedroom. They're some of my favorites, as well. David was quite a songwriter, wasn't he? Every emotion known to mankind . . . from reverence to rage and everything in between. Somehow he'd figured out that God didn't mind, and would remain faithful regardless of David's mood at the time."

He waited while she slowly registered the implication. "You know, we originally planned to discontinue the surveillance last night. But I had this feeling—now I figure it was God's way of getting my attention—because I told the team I'd watch one more night. Amazing, isn't it?"

She stared at him. "Are you saying . . . that you're a Christian, too?" She searched his face as though trying to crawl inside his brain. "I mean . . . you're not just trying to feed me a line or worm your way into my confidence for your own purposes?"

"Yes, I'm a Christian." He winked at her. "And even if I *had* planned to worm my way into your confidence, I'd think twice about it after seeing you in action against that prowler."

A tentative smile slowly lit the bruised and swollen face.

Caleb fought down the first stirrings of deep uneasiness. Those prowlers might very well be nothing more than a couple of thugs out to rob a vulnerable woman. But he didn't think so. Instinct warned him that they had finally stumbled over the first real lead in the Starseeker case . . . which landed Rae Prescott right in the middle of it all. He forced himself to take a swallow of tea, then smiled across the table. "Will you try to trust me a little now, Rae? It will make the next weeks—and possibly months—a lot easier on both of us."

The police were a lot more thorough than they had been the last two times. Bemused, Rae watched them spill out of the cars, and wondered aloud why they'd sent so many. It was a multiple re-sponse, Caleb Myers told her, in the hopes that the burglars could still be chased down and caught.

Some of the officers stayed outside to search the area, but it seemed as if her kitchen and store were suddenly overrun by a swarm of stone-faced, intent professionals. A couple of men in rumpled civilian suits slipped inside as Rae was giving her account of the assault to a police officer holding a clipboard stuffed with report forms.

After giving his statement and showing his ID, Caleb stayed out of the way. He and two plainclothesmen clustered in a corner of the store, talking quietly. Caleb looked relaxed, casual, as if he was discussing the latest Broncos game with a couple of friends. Every now and then he looked at Rae, but she averted her head each time, uncertain of her feelings toward her rescuer.

The policeman thanked her for her statement and moved off. Rae sat tensely on the stairs leading to the second floor while she watched the activity going on around her. She felt detached, almost anesthetized. Like a fourth-grade boy observing an ant farm. The only time she spoke was to make a rather tart request that they please be careful not to disarrange the music.

After the swarm of police officers finished poking and prying around the store, the sandy-haired one who had written up Rae's account strolled over. He brought along a short, trim man with iron gray hair and shrewd blue eyes. The police officer introduced him as Detective Pete Grabowski. Slowly Rae stood, eyeing both men uncertainly, because Detective Grabowski was looking her over like a piece of fresh fruit at the farmer's market.

"Ms. Prescott," he said in a surprisingly deep tone, "I know you've given Officer Hanley your statement, but would you mind telling me what happened again? Try to remember every detail, regardless of how insignificant you think it may be."

Rae suppressed a long-suffering sigh. "I spent the evening with my friend Karen. She owns Gibson Girl." The detective nodded, so Rae continued without elaborating, though she shuddered at the prospect of Karen's response to the events of this night. "I was walking home a little after eleven—I waited till the rain quit. Just after I crossed the street, I saw someone inside my store."

"You've confirmed that to the best of your knowledge nothing has been stolen?"

She nodded, mouth quirking wryly. "It makes this whole mess more bewildering. What could they have wanted in a music store? I don't keep money in the cash register after I close. . . ."

One of the plainclothesmen who had been conferring with Caleb Myers walked over. Detective Grabowski turned and they spoke in low syllables Rae could not hear. The lines furrowing the detective's head deepened. When he turned to Rae she sensed a coldness, almost hostility.

"Ms. Prescott." He spoke slowly, as if measuring each word. "You live here alone, and you have on display in your store objects worth thousands of dollars. Yet you have taken only the most rudimentary precautions to safeguard them. After the past few weeks I find that extremely foolish."

"I don't have the funds necessary to install the alarms and newer locks your associates recommended." Rae kept her tone civil with difficulty. Why on earth was *she* being made to feel as though she was the one on trial? A hot coal lodged in the pit of her stomach, and she had to clasp her hands tightly together to keep from playing Bach on the stair railing. "Besides, if someone wants to steal anything, they'll find a way regardless of elaborate and or costly protective measures."

"And you would realize a substantial insurance settlement?" Detective Grabowski suggested.

The live coal glowing in her stomach burst into flames. "Detective, I resent your implications—"

"When was the last time you saw your father, Ms. Prescott?"

Rae felt all the indignant color drain out of her face, felt as though she'd been catapulted backward in time to Carnegie Hall. She could almost hear the applause in the background as two hard-eyed men destroyed her world. It was also the same night Uncle Floyd suffered the first heart attack. "My father," she repeated in a dead voice, wrapping her fingers around the top of the griffin's head so tightly her knuckles gleamed bone white.

"I've just been informed that your father, Raymond M. Prescott, is wanted by the FBI for a number of crimes, including extortion and grand larceny," Grabowski said in that cold, level voice that raised welts on Rae's frost-bitten nerves. "Ms. Prescott—is it possible your lack of precaution is intended? That the open display of all these items is so your—"

"How are things going over here, Grabowski?" Caleb Myers was suddenly there, his eyes on Rae as he moved between her and the detective. Rae braced herself. Masculine warmth and power radiated from him with such force she felt suffocated—yet oddly shielded. "Ms. Prescott doesn't look like she's holding up too well," Caleb commented. "Maybe the rest of it could wait until morning?"

"I'm fine," Rae began, yet she did not pull away from the hand urging her to sit down on the stairs. It felt so warm, and she was so cold her teeth were chattering. She was also angry, on a deep, primitive level, and the emotional contradictions left her faintly nauseated. Clamping her lips together, she slid a single swift glance at Caleb Myers.

"She's had a rough time of it," he continued mildly. "Besides, that would also give your people time to gather some mug shots for a photo lineup."

Detective Grabowski suddenly looked a lot less intimidating. "Ms. Prescott claims she wouldn't be able to recognize her attacker. There won't be a lineup unless it's for you, Myers." He paused, then added with the same deliberate lack of inflection, "Ramirez was just telling me about the background check on the Prescott family."

Caleb suddenly dropped down in front of Rae, balancing gracefully on the balls of his feet, his expression intent, probing. "Rae, will you tell me about your father?" he asked, but his voice compelled rather than demanded.

I don't want to talk about my father, she wanted to yell. But fatigue and bewilderment were overpowering the anger, and she felt all her defenses collapsing. She didn't understand this golden-eyed guardian angel who had swooped into her life, turning it completely upside down. She could have fought hostility and suspicion—by the time she entered fourth grade she was a veteran at facing down the slurs and taunts of others. But kindness . . . in the face of kindness she was helpless. "I don't know anything about my father," she admitted stiffly. "He deserted us when I was four."

"You haven't seen or heard from him since?"

"No. The FBI questioned us the last time he surfaced. We couldn't help then, either. My father—" she lifted her chin "—as far as I'm concerned, my father is as dead to me as his family is to him. He's made absolutely no contact that I'm aware of." She turned her head away, furious all of a sudden because the compassion in Caleb's eyes smacked more of pity.

Her gaze fell on a delicate antique hat-pin holder full of assorted pins, perched on top of Uncle Floyd's ancient Victrola. She'd rather have those pins digging into her scalp than be the object of Mr. Magnanimous Myers's *pity.* The sudden uprush of heady temper brought her to her feet to confront Detective Grabowski. "Detective, my lack of security is *not* intended as a flashing neon sign for thieves. In point of fact, I wouldn't realize a penny if anything were stolen. The only insurance I carry is for the house itself. At the time I took out the policy, carrying a personal articles floater was not an option."

A ferocious scowl furrowed the detective's forehead. Looking thoroughly impatient, he opened his mouth as though preparing to verbally skewer Rae. Then he caught Caleb's eye and swallowed the words in an indecipherable grumble. Still glaring at the detective, Rae started when Caleb's hand dropped onto her shoulder.

"Rae," he informed her quietly, "the reason you feel like you're on the wrong end of an interrogation is because you might be involved—unknowingly, of course—in a case I'm working on with the FBI, the OSI and now the Colorado Springs Police Department."

"You're divulging information that might be inappropriate at this time, under the circumstances," Grabowski warned.

Caleb didn't budge. "Your original purpose here, remember, is to investigate a crime committed *against* Ms. Prescott, not *by* her. The fact that her father—a man she claims not to have seen since she was four—is wanted by the FBI may or may not be germane. She deserves more than your suspicions, Grabowski."

"I also deserve an explanation as to why you've had my house under surveillance. Not to mention why you think my father has something to do with the break-in tonight." Rae's lips were stiff, while her knees possessed an unnerving resemblance to water.

She watched Grabowski and Caleb Myers exchange glances and wondered all of a sudden how she must appear to this gathering of stone-faced, cynical men. Hardened professionals who were more accustomed to liars and thieves and muggers than an innocent woman whose behavior vacillated between short-tempered grizzly and trembling mouse. She had taken the time to twist her hair into a chignon before the police arrived, but she knew after a horrified glimpse in the mirror earlier that the only color left in her face was from the swelling bruise. There were dark smudges on her throat, as well.

After an electric moment of silence, Grabowski wordlessly yielded the floor with an irritated swipe of his hand. Did Caleb get his way in everything? Rae wondered.

Just then one of Grabowski's men approached. "We're all through here, sir." The young man had been dusting for prints. He glanced sympathetically at Rae. Grabowski barked out orders and instructions, and the young cop left.

The detective turned to her. His face was not sympathetic. "Mr. Myers obviously feels the need to enlighten you, Ms. Prescott, so I will leave him to it." He paused, then added levelly, "You aren't planning to go anywhere in the next few weeks, are you?"

"Hardly." Rae smiled sweetly. "I don't have enough money for a vacation, either. Perhaps I could burn down the store? I *do* carry fire insurance."

Chapter Six

❧

After the police finally trooped out several moments later, Caleb folded his arms over his chest and settled his shoulders against the wall. Rae turned from shutting the door and almost ran into him. "What happened to the practice of turning the other cheek, Ms. Prescott?" he teased her, nodding at the closed door. "The detective does have a job to do, and in his defense, he doesn't know you any better than you know him."

"My cheeks have suffered enough for one night," Rae retorted, then she sighed, waving a hand. "Sorry. I know you all have a job to do. Normally I control my temper better, but I guess everything sort of overwhelmed me." She glanced at Caleb. "You may have noticed, I have lapses of what my brother irreverently refers to as a prima donna temperament."

"I noticed." He noticed a lot more than he wanted to concerning this young woman. Including the fact that she was trying very hard to maintain a semblance of control when she still bordered on an eruption of Mount Saint Helens proportions.

"Mr. Myers—"

"Caleb." He shouldered away from the wall and stood there studying her in the dim light of the hall sconces. "Call me Caleb, all right?"

Rae inclined her head. "Caleb . . . I apologize for the sarcastic crack I made to Detective Gar—Graw . . . whatever. But—"

"Grabowski. His name's Grabowski, and you don't have to apologize to me, but if you'll take a bit of advice—always cooperate with the police, as much as lies within you." The corner of his mouth lifted. "Even more so, since these guys are all that stand between you and that dirtbag who tried to steamroll you into the ground."

Way to go, Myers. The last thing she needed was a lecture, no matter how deserved. Talk about foot-in-mouth disease . . . If he could have, he would have delivered a swift kick to himself.

"I'll remember." He saw her swallow hard a time or two and inwardly winced at the purpling smudges marring the fine skin. "Caleb, I'd really appreciate it if you could tell me what's going on. I feel like I fell off the tour bus in the middle of the set of one of those prime-time detective shows." Her voice cracked on the last word.

"Why don't we go in the kitchen," Caleb suggested. "It's a lot warmer. I'll heat the water and we can have another cup of tea." His voice deepened with amusement. "I saw all your canisters and cartons. You must stock every kind of tea on the market."

"Tea is a very versatile drink."

He watched her move with wraithlike efficiency around the kitchen, though her movements were stiff and fumbling. Caleb sprawled along the trestle bench, obliging her by staying out of the way, eyes hooded while she struggled to reestablish control of her domain. He wondered how much to tell her, and if what he did tell her would finally shatter that fragile control. When Rae finally set down his mug of tea, then slid into the seat across from him, Caleb offered up a swift prayer for wisdom—and discretion.

"I believed I mentioned working with the FBI at the moment," he began immediately, so Rae wouldn't feel like she had to pry information with a pickax. "Technically speaking I'm still a computer security consultant in the private sector, though I've done a lot of work for most of the government agencies. So when a friend of mine who owns a corporation specializing in the development of state-of-the-art space-tracking technologies called, asking for my help, the FBI agreed to bring me in as a consultant." He grinned sheepishly. "Seems I've acquired something of a reputation in the field of computer fraud and sabotage."

"Ah. Your friend thinks someone is sabotaging the computers in his company?"

"Not exactly." Caleb began fiddling with his watchband. If he was wrong about Rae Prescott, his name would be mud, and his career would take a potentially permanent nosedive. But there was something about those wide unblinking eyes, the nimbleness of her brain. She had followed where his words were going with surprising quickness. "Someone is sabotaging the contract that Polaris—my friend's company—has with the Air Force, and that's where the problem has surfaced. We have reason to believe the individual or individuals are longtime employees of Polaris. That's where I come in—trying to find out who it is."

"So it's just one person?" Rae stared at him. "Is my father—"

"Whoa." He reached across to brush her knuckles with his fingers. "You're getting a little ahead of me here. Right now, let's table the matter of your father, because I don't know any more about him than you." He waited until she nodded. "Okay, then. We don't know how many people are involved yet in the Polaris case. Could be one, could be an entire ring. We have suspects and we're following leads. The OSI—that's the Air Force equivalent of the FBI—is handling the active duty guys, but the FBI gets the rest. Everyone's getting a little shirty, because every official from the defense department down, both military and civilian, is screaming for results." He ran a hand through his hair. "Which is why I'm trying to be . . . ah . . . nice to them all, tiptoeing through the tangles doing my *own* investigating."

Rae sipped her tea. She wouldn't look at him. "I still don't understand why you've had my house under surveillance, unless it's because you think my father is involved."

She couldn't let it go, Caleb realized. Of course, if *his* father was on the FBI's most-wanted list, he supposed he wouldn't be able to let it go, either. He remembered the pain and humiliation in Rae's face when she tried to disavow all ties to the man responsible for giving her life. What, he wondered suddenly, had happened to Rae's mother? Her brother?

"I don't know about your father's involvement," he repeated gently. "The background check's still in the preliminary stages, which is a little unusual and possibly the reason for Grabowski's irritability."

"Background check?" Rae echoed. "The FBI has been checking

up on me—on my family?" The ugly bruises stood out like smears of charcoal on a white sheet as she stared across the table.

Stalling, Caleb took a sip of his drink, struggling to keep a straight face. She had given him some aromatic herb tea that tasted like crushed dandelions. Swallowing an intense desire for a plain old-fashioned mug of hot chocolate, he manfully took another sip of tea, then faced Rae. In for a penny, in for a pound. "It's all part of the reason we've had your place under surveillance," he explained. "One of the suspects has come to your store several times in the last few weeks. Then, on a routine check with the police, we found out about the footprints in the snow. I guess Tray ordered the check after that. He's the FBI agent who's been assigned to head up the case locally— What are you doing with your hands?"

The restless movements of her fingers stopped abruptly, and she wrapped her hands around the mug. "Nothing," she muttered in a stifled voice. Caleb suppressed the urge to cover the nervous fingers with his. "So because one of the suspects in your sabotage case has stopped by Joyful Noise, that justifies a background investigation on my family?"

Caleb winced. "Sounds pretty intrusive, I know—but that's because I can only fill you in on part of the picture." He tilted his head. "I could tell you everything, but then I'd have to shoot you," he quipped, hoping to coax at least a small smile, relax her. . . .

"You're all paranoid!" Rae snapped. She shoved away from the table and stood. "I don't believe this!"

"We have to follow up on any lead, no matter how slim or ludicrous." He sat back, relaxed and peaceable. Nonaggressive. "So far, you represent the best contact yet. The suspect could be coming here just out of a love for music, but it could also be something else—especially after hearing about your prowlers."

"I suppose they're planting top secret information in my music," Rae snapped. "Microchips in the bass and treble clef notes. And don't forget—I'm leaving all my most cherished possessions scattered about so they can help themselves after they plant their information."

"Possibly."

Rae threw up her hands. "That's absurd! I was joking." She hesitated, adding slowly, "You—you're not joking. . . ."

"About the microchips, perhaps," Caleb conceded. "But when

you've been in the business as long as I have, you learn just how creative and twisted the human mind can be. Anything's possible for God's noblest creation." *Careful, Myers. Your cynicism's showing.*

He looked at Rae, whose indignation had disappeared, leaving behind a battered woman who, he observed dispassionately, had had just about all she could take. "I think a good night's sleep will add a little sanity and perspective back in your life."

"If you think I'll sleep a wink after this—"

"Would you like me to arrange for a patrolman to come out for the rest of the night? Under the circumstances, I think I can arrange it without too much official squawkings."

"No. Thank you. I'll just—" She stopped, took a deep breath, her fingers pleating the fabric of her slacks in a restless movement. "I'll be fine."

He stood watching with a frown between his eyes while Rae tried to shore up her defenses. For the first time in years, he didn't know what to do. All his life, he had had to console three younger sisters in all sorts of circumstances, ranging from skinned knees to heartbreak. Nurturing females was as natural to Caleb as breathing, by inclination as well as upbringing. He had a protective instinct as massive and ingrained as the Rockies, which infuriated the women in his life even though he was always the first person they ran to for help.

But he had a feeling if he offered Rae Prescott a shoulder, he'd be lucky to leave with his head still fastened. The lady had been sorely used by the male of the species, and the man who gained her trust would face an uphill battle.

Of course, he'd never been able to resist a challenge—or a puzzle. And Rae Prescott promised both. He stuffed his hands in his hip pockets. "I'm something of a night owl myself," he mused to the ceiling. Then he dropped his gaze to her face. "That's why I told Tray I'd cover the night shifts. Stakeouts are the worst duty to draw. Guys go to any lengths to avoid them, because they're boring, tedious, and it's impossible to maintain a constant vigilance and keep your sanity."

"So why did you volunteer?" Rae asked. She still looked as prickly as a hedgehog, so Caleb merely shrugged.

"My mind is too active to get bored very often. And when I get sleepy, I . . . well, actually I pray out loud." He gave her a sheep-ish grin. "It helps, and we both know the Lord's always awake. At any rate, I'm there until morning. The FBI takes over during the day. I sleep four or five hours, then follow my own leads."

"Why are you telling me all this?"

"Testing the waters," he confessed candidly. "I was working my way around to seeing if you'd like *me* to stick around the rest of the night, since you're uncomfortable bothering the police again." He hesitated, "Rae . . . I'd like to help, if you'll let me."

"Why?"

"Because I owe you one. I blew it earlier tonight—had no idea there was anyone over here until I saw you fighting for your life." Quick thinking, Myers. Plausible, but nonthreatening.

"According to the police, they came in a window on the side. You wouldn't have been able to see even if it wasn't dark." Sud-denly she turned, grabbed the mugs and carried them to the sink. "Thank you, but I'll be fine." Her voice was brisk. "Don't worry about me, Caleb. I'm used to being alone." She turned, produced a tight smile. "I've been alone most of my life. You go ahead—play whatever games you have to play. Dig up whatever dirt you can find on the infamous Prescott family. The door's through there. Good night."

So much for plausible explanations. Ah, well—he'd asked for it, but even so, her rejection still stung. "A cold compress might help the worst of the bruises." He walked to where she stood by the sink, ramrod straight "Take care, Rae Prescott." His gaze touched on her swollen cheek, the purpling bruises at her throat, and his hand lifted as though with a will of its own, his fingers brushing the soft skin just beneath her jaw. "I'll be in touch."

Thirty minutes later, he settled in the nest he'd made on the upper story across the street. He doubted the vigilance was neces-sary, but he knew it was useless to return to his motel when his mind was spinning like an out-of-control CD.

Mom had prayed for years that God would drop a woman in his life who could shake him out of his comfortably nomadic life-style. Well, had that day arrived? Settling in an old automobile seat he'd dragged upstairs, Caleb mentally added up everything he had learned about Rae Prescott since their first inauspicious meeting almost two weeks ago. He was not encouraged. Lord, what could he do to help this very independent, very vulnerable woman who had just been tossed in the middle of a hornet's nest? *And as You already know—I'm going to have to do something . . . so any and all help will be appreciated.*

Matters would become even more dicey if Raymond Meikleham Prescott had decided to return to his daughter's life—especially if that return was evinced in a highly unpleasant, highly illegal manner. Caleb mulled over everything Tray Ramirez had told him and decided that, regardless of the thorns, he had no choice but to try his best to protect the prickly Rae Prescott. Ray—and Rae. Why, Caleb wondered idly, hadn't the man named his *son* after him instead of his daughter?

He checked his watch, then dug in the backpack stashed at his side for a candy bar. While he contentedly munched, he thought about the woman across the street. Right now Rae definitely could not be compared to a sleek Siamese cat. She was more like . . . like the delicate, spindly cat's claw, a wildflower that grew in abundance over the meadows behind his grandparents' Florida panhandle home. Dainty and flimsy to look at, the stems were covered with minute hooked thorns that could lacerate anyone unwary enough to try to pick them. A grin kicked up the corner of his mouth. Next he'd be spouting poetry and sending her flowers and candy.

Rae Prescott. And Ray Meikleham Prescott, her father. The grin faded as Caleb channeled his thinking into official lines. The Starseeker case had just corkscrewed again, and Caleb set his formidable memory to work recalling everything he had read about individuals involved with IOS. If Rae's father was involved, Caleb planned to find out how, and why.

She couldn't sleep. After tossing and turning and watching the clock until the illuminated hands passed the hour of two, Rae threw back the covers. Her fingers fumbled on the floor until they closed around the poker she had placed by the bed. Only then did she turn on the light. For several moments she sat, fighting the fear, the shame . . . the anger. She felt as though she had been emotionally violated, and she didn't know what to do. Finally she jerkily pulled on her robe and made her way to her piano.

For a while she played old gospel songs, hymn arrangements, even the music from the Easter musical. Eyes closed, her fingers flowed over the keyboard, and the music filling the lonely night might have made the angels weep, but it didn't help Rae. After thirty minutes she sighed and rose. It would have to be classical. Nothing else was complicated enough, challenging enough to keep her mind from churning over the events of the evening.

She never knew what prompted the impulse, but for some reason Rae decided to play the choral song from Beethoven's Ninth Symphony—the one that woman had wrongly placed in Beethoven's Fifth. Yeah . . . that would lift her mood. The soaring "Ode to Joy" could also help remind her of God's eternal care, even when His presence seemed—on the surface, anyway—to be as far off as a distant star.

While she was at it, she just might play the Fifth, as well. She could release a lot of pent-up emotion with *that* one.

A brief search through the cluttered piles of music did not yield a copy of either symphony, and Rae ground her teeth in exasperation. She didn't feel like pawing through piles the rest of the night, so she padded down the hall and let herself into the store, defying the ripple of foreboding spiking her nerves. She was perfectly safe, of *course* she was safe.

She glided across the floor to the classical music section, poker at the ready, pausing only to flick on a squat *Gone With The Wind* lamp that had been converted to electricity. Everything looked normal and in order, in spite of the frenetic activity earlier. A smile hovered as Rae riffled through the *B*s in the classical music, remembering how she had followed one of the cops around like an overprotective mother, reminding him to be careful with her music—

The smile froze. Goose bumps roughed her skin in a waterfall of apprehension.

Everything looked normal, on the surface, but something was radically wrong. All her copies of Beethoven's Fifth and Ninth had vanished.

Chapter Seven

"Whaddaya think, Myers? Both father and daughter—it's too much to be coincidence." Tray Ramirez paced back and forth across a threadbare dirty gray carpet, his normally pleasant face creased in a scowl. Thick black hair and an olive skin tone attested to his Latin heritage. "Maybe she's innocent and really hasn't seen her old man in over twenty years. But you gotta admit Ms. Prescott is in this thing up to her dainty little ears."

"I'm convinced the involvement is planned—but without Rae's knowledge. She was blown away when Grabowski dropped the bomb about her father." Caleb's voice was deceptively lazy.

"She could be a good actress."

Caleb shook his head. He remembered with disturbing clarity a pair of gray eyes almost unfocused with pain and shock, a wide mouth that trembled in spite of concerted efforts to keep it still. "I don't think so. She was attacked, assaulted—on her way down when I rescued her." He grinned. He remembered a few other memorable details about Rae, as well. "She also ripped a strip off me for taking so long to get there. Then she grilled me like a veteran interrogator before she was convinced I was on the side of the angels. She was terrified when I made her wait outside while I made sure the premises were safe—but when I came back for her, she was *singing*." Albeit not very well . . .

Ramirez stopped at his desk, white teeth flashing in a reciprocal smile. "I admit she's a little unorthodox. Did you see her stand over one of the police officers and lecture him for not being careful with her music? But I fail to see what her personal idiosyncrasies have to do with—"

"When Grabowski told her about her father I thought she was going to pass out. Not even the best actress in the world could have faked that reaction." Caleb shoved the irritating hair off his forehead, then leaned forward in the chair where he had been sitting. "Tray, she's an innocent victim. We need to protect her, not persecute her."

The FBI agent slammed his hand on the desk. "You tell me how, man! We've had men watching the store—you've been taking the nights for two weeks—and none of us spotted anything!" He paused, adding heavily, "You do realize your timely rescue will raise more questions—with the wrong people. If the Prescott woman is a dupe instead of the victim of assault, your interference is going to make her situation even worse."

Caleb's fingers slid under his watchband and restlessly twisted. "I know. IOS flunkies don't care who gets in the way."

"You're convinced they're behind this? According to my reports, they don't like going after the government." His mouth twitched. "We still have more money and manpower than most of the local cops."

"I know, but the m.o. of the situation out at Falcon is almost identical to the sabotage of a program Polaris was perfecting for the Navy a couple of years ago." Caleb laced his hands behind his head. "The Navy contract was canceled due to supposedly faulty software. Software that turned up later in a company with definite IOS connections."

"I don't like it," Ramirez said reluctantly. "Until we get a definite lead on one of the Starseeker personnel out at Falcon, we're walking in traffic blindfolded and handcuffed."

"I'm going to talk to Rae Prescott again. She might have remembered something now that she's had a night to sleep on it."

"You're sure you didn't recognize the assailant, either?"

Caleb shook his head, and rose. "He wasn't one of the three we've been keeping tabs on, no." He headed for the door, adding very softly, "But you can be sure I'll recognize the gentleman the next time."

* * *

"What do you want?" Rae pulled the folding doors shut behind her, muffling the sound of nine-year-old Angela MacVeese playing a spirited boogie. Her first impulse had been to throw her arms around him and beg him to hold her, just for a moment. Her second, far safer impulse had been to shut the doors in Caleb Myers's face.

Unperturbed by her lack of welcome, he cocked his head toward the room behind her. "A student? You teach piano lessons as well as run Joyful Noise?" He looked relaxed and capable in a heather wool sweater and pleat-front cords—more like a winter tourist than an undercover agent for some federal organization Rae had never heard of. She knew he claimed to be a private computer security consultant, but she wasn't ready to believe him.

Instinctively she'd gone on the offense. "You mean you didn't already know? I'm also the primary accompanist for our church . . . and if you like I can show you my driver's license, although you probably know all that information, too."

He smiled, a dazzling smile warm enough to melt concrete. "Well, I must say I hadn't exactly hoped for the fatted calf, but I didn't expect a verbal assault the next time we saw each other, either." His eyes moved over her in frank masculine survey, then softened. "Not much sleep, huh?"

Rae had a feeling he was memorizing every bruise and every freckle, and blushed. "Not much," she admitted. "As you see, I'm also in the middle of a lesson." Trying to think about teaching, instead of the million or so unanswered questions.

Without warning his hand lifted, and his fingers skimmed with the lightness of gauze over her bruised face. "Hurt pretty bad still?"

The light touch punctured her pride in a single stroke. She had never known, until Caleb Myers burst into her life, how gentle a man's touch could be. "Only when I smile, which is another reason I'm being such a grouch." Caleb laughed, and Rae reluctantly smiled—though it *did* hurt. "Everyone thinks I'm extremely lucky."

"You were, even though I'd call it something besides luck."

She focused on the strong-looking tendons of his throat. "I know," she whispered. *God, why did You have to put a man like this in my path?* A committed Christian, radiating compassion and competence. Regardless of his profession, he was too good to be true, and Rae resolved to keep her distance in spite of her yearnings. Caleb Myers spelled trouble, any way you looked at it. Besides, she had learned by the time she was seventeen that nice men wouldn't risk any kind of commitment with a woman like her. After all, she *might* turn out to be like her mother, her father. Perhaps both.

With a brisk shake of her head, Rae turned around and slid the door open a crack. "Angela, remember to practice feeling the rhythm. Emphasize the left hand a little more. I'll be there in a minute." She turned to Caleb, in control once more. "I do have to go."

"I need to talk to you. Can I stop by when Joyful Noise closes and take you out to dinner?"

"I don't—"

"It concerns your father, Rae."

Though the words were gently spoken, she sensed a force of will behind them that more than matched her own. He was circling her patiently, but if she didn't fall in with his wishes Rae realized he was implacable enough to take her arm and usher her out the door—politely, of course. Oh, well. Why not get it over with? He wasn't asking for a date. He wanted information for his investigation. She had questions of her own. Maybe if she didn't make him beg for his answers, he'd afford the same courtesy to her. Of course, she'd have to dump her whole sordid background in his lap. He probably already knew most of it anyway. She sighed. "Six-thirty, then. And just for dinner."

"Such enthusiasm for my company."

"I'm as enthusiastic as you are."

"Ah." Dancing lights sparked through his eyes. "In that case, it should be a very . . . rewarding evening."

He swiveled on his heel and was out the door before Rae thought up an appropriate retort. The bell laughed merrily at her, and with an impatient head toss Rae went to compliment Angela on her playing.

Two hours later, she gratefully flipped the sign to Closed and was in the process of locking up when a man in a navy blue suit strode swiftly up the steps. Rae opened the door for him and he stepped inside the store. "Ms. Prescott?" He held up a badge. "Detective Jamison. Will you come with me to the station, please?"

Irritated both by his manner and the inconvenience, Rae moved to the revolving popular music display to give herself time to think. "Someone is meeting me at six-thirty," she said as her hands automatically straightened music. "Why do you need me at the station again? I was told this morning that I wouldn't need to come back."

"We brought in a suspect. We'd like to see if you recognize him."

Her hands stilled. "I told Detective Grabowski I didn't think I'd be able to recognize him—it was too dark and happened too fast."

Swift impatience crossed the detective's face. "Nonetheless, we need you to check out the lineup. If you'll come with me, you'll be back in plenty of time for your date." He held the door open.

Rae did not correct his assumption that she had a date. She could see an unmarked car parked at the curb, with a suit-clad driver waiting behind the wheel. "Let me get my coat and purse."

Alarm bells were clanging in her head, but she felt ridiculous voicing them to this aloof, cold-voiced detective. His brusqueness was even more daunting than the detective from last night. Shrugging, Rae gathered her possessions and locked the door. As she climbed into the back seat, she wondered why Detective Grabowski hadn't come himself. Didn't the police observe some kind of protocol concerning who was in charge of investigations? She started to ask, but with a guttural roar the car pulled away from the curb.

Detective Jamison turned to Rae. In his hand was a short, ugly-looking gun, and he was pointing it straight at her heart. The car careened around the corner and down the street. The driver twisted his head around very briefly, an evil smirk on his face and Rae's eyes widened. It was *him*. The man who attacked her!

"I don't think," the bogus detective Jamison stated softly, "that we need to make that trip to the station, do we, Ms. Prescott?"

"What do you want?" Rae asked. Calm. She must remain calm. *This isn't real. It isn't really happening.* She kept her eyes fastened on Jamison.

Her captor relaxed in the seat, but the gun did not waver. "I'm a messenger, Ms. Prescott." Suddenly he leaned forward and the cold barrel of the gun slid lightly over Rae's bruised cheeks, her throat. "A goodwill messenger sent to keep you from acquiring any more of these."

Rae shrank back instinctively, but then the man laughed—and a burst of glorious anger surged through her. "You're making a mistake—"

"Shut up and listen," The man leaned forward, weasel eyes narrowing. "And don't give me any more lip."

Her heart was racing, and she had to twine icy hands in a death grip in her lap to keep them still, but Rae managed to stare coldly back after she gave a short nod. She didn't speak again.

Satisfied, the man settled back with a grunt. "If you want to stay healthy, Ms. Prescott, and you don't want to see that ugly palace of yours burned to the ground, you'll keep your mouth shut about anything you see or hear." He leaned forward again, crowding Rae against the door so that her spine pressed painfully into the handle. "Take my friend here. I know you *think* you recognized him. But I also know that you were mistaken." The cruel thin lips bared in a macabre smile. "You were mistaken, weren't you?"

Slowly, Rae nodded.

"I thought so. Just keep practicing that wide-eyed innocence . . . or next time he won't be as gentle with you."

Rae tried to lick her parched lips, but her mouth was too dry. "Who are you?" she demanded, then flinched when the gun waved a hairbreadth from her face.

"No questions." His head swiveled. "Slow down, you fool!" he snapped furiously. "Do you want every traffic cop in town on our tail?"

The respite from the opaque deadness of his eyes was such a relief Rae drew a shuddering breath. Without thought she lifted a hand to her hair, and the man's head whipped around. Quick as a striking rattlesnake his free hand shot out, the grip biting into her wrist. He twisted it hard, causing Rae to gasp in pain. "Unless you want to be dumped on your back doorstep in a trash bag, keep your hands in your lap and don't move again."

He released her, leaving white and red imprints on her throbbing wrist. Rae didn't move. She couldn't take a breath, couldn't do anything but pray a jumbled entreaty for her safety. The physical assault the previous night had not frightened her as badly as the threat emanating from this walking death machine sitting beside her.

Five minutes later the car pulled into a crowded mall parking lot and stopped in one of the lots with fewer people milling about.

"Remember—" the word reached her roaring ears "—no police, no blabbing. Keep your nose where it belongs, and just maybe it will stay there—in one piece." He leaned across her, opened the door and shoved her out. "And just in case you're lying, we'll be watching you to make sure, Ms. Prescott." The dead eyes bored into her. "Watching you."

The door slammed in her face. The car left, weaving sedately out of the parking lot onto the main street.

Twenty minutes later Molly Ferguson, the music director's wife, dropped her off at home. She smilingly waved away Rae's stammered thanks, her plump face concerned but tactful. "If you change your mind and need to talk give us a call, okay?"

"Thanks, Molly." Rae forced her voice to calmness, but she avoided the older woman's eyes.

It was a little before seven o'clock. Caleb was waiting on the front porch, and so, Rae saw with a sinking heart, was Karen. She might have known her friend would use the opportunity to meet the man she insisted on calling Rae's date, especially when Rae hadn't been out with anyone but Barry Weathering in the past six months.

She clutched her purse and hurried up the brick walk. Caleb's expression, while not impatient, was nonetheless questioning. Karen waved, her fire-engine red poncho practically glowing in the gathering dusk.

"It's a good thing you called and asked me to explain to your date, honey. When I got here Caleb was ready to send for the cavalry or whatever 'cause you weren't here." She flashed Caleb a beguiling grin and poked him in the ribs with her elbow before turning to Rae. "Guess he forgot one of the primary rules—woman always keeps man waiting. Where did you say your car was?"

Rae forced a smile. "Thanks, Karen. You can go back to the restaurant now. I'll tell you all about it later."

Karen's brows lifted. "By all means, excuse me, honey. Three's a crowd and all that." She blew Caleb a kiss. "Nice chattin' with you—ya'll come on down if you want decent food instead of—"

"Karen!"

"I'm going, I'm going!"

After she trotted laughingly down the walk and crossed the

street, Rae gathered her courage and looked at Caleb. "Sorry I'm late." She lifted her chin. "I had to run an errand, and had some car trouble." There. She'd managed, and her voice hadn't even wobbled.

It was difficult to read Caleb's expression in the diffuse yellow porch light she had mercifully turned on before her "trip." He wasn't angry, but something hovered behind the light smiling eyes, something watchful, waiting. He glanced around as if searching the shadows, then put a hand under her elbow.

"Do you need to freshen up before we go?"

Rae stared blankly at him a split second. "Ah, yes," she finally muttered. "I—I do need to freshen up." She gestured awkwardly to the three-year-old suit she'd been wearing when he stopped by earlier that afternoon. The cashmere sweater underneath itched with trickles of perspiration. "I, uh, I didn't take time to change, earlier."

There was a pause, then Caleb said easily, "All right, Rae. Take your time."

She barely suppressed a shudder of relief, though his placid acceptance was unnerving. She hurriedly unlocked the door and fled inside, her nerves twitching, as raw as a fresh-cut slab of meat. *They had said they'd be watching, all the time. Could they hear, as well?*

Ten minutes later, wearing the same suit but a fresh blouse, she was buckled snugly in the car beside Caleb. Her hands lay with deceptive calmness in her lap, but her stomach felt like it was doing cartwheels over her heart.

Over dinner Caleb kept up a light nonthreatening conversation that did not include any mention of her father, Rae's past, or the Starseeker case. Though baffled—since that was ostensibly the reason he'd asked her out in the first place—Rae was grateful for the opportunity to pull herself together. She was almost relaxed by the time they left the restaurant. Caleb Myers could charm the stripes off a tiger, when he chose. Soon, Rae knew, he'd turn on her and pounce, demanding answers, but for now—she needed the respite. Sitting back against the seat of the car, she gazed idly at the passing traffic and stores while Caleb related a funny story about his cat, Sheba.

Then the car pulled over onto a side street and stopped next to the curb. Caleb switched off the ignition and turned toward Rae, one hand dangling over the steering wheel, the other stretching across the back of the seat, only inches from her neck. "Tell me what happened this afternoon." Though spoken quietly, the words framed an order, not a request.

She had known this scene was inevitable, but he'd still caught her unprepared. "I don't want to talk about it." It was a childish response, one of which she was ashamed. Unfortunately, she'd always been a lousy liar.

Caleb heaved a sigh. "Rae, what's happened? Talk to me. Trust me." His hand dropped off the back of the seat and closed around her throbbing wrist. In spite of herself, a gasp of pain escaped. Caleb released her instantly. "What is it?"

"I—my wrist. I sprained it."

"How?"

Trapped, Rae stared at her lap, heart thudding heavily. She would have to lie—or tell the truth. If she lied he would know it, not only because she was lousy at it, but because Caleb Myers was not a stupid man. If she told the truth, *both* of them could end up dead. The fake Detective Jamison had not struck her as a man who issued idle threats.

Chapter Eight

Rae took a deep breath. "I really can't talk about it, Caleb." She looked him in the eye. "I'll tell you about my father, if you like. I know that's the only reason you asked me to dinner, even if you tactfully avoided bringing him up the whole meal."

"Are you in trouble?"

"No more so than I have been since I met you," she snapped pettishly. "Not to mention finding out just because my father is a crook, every law enforcement agency in the country assumes I'm in cahoots with him."

"Mmm." In the muted glow of the dash lights, she thought she saw him smile. " 'In cahoots,' huh? That's a phrase I haven't heard in a while. I think I need to educate you in current cops-and-robbers argot."

Was he *laughing* at her? Control shedding, Rae clenched her hands, though her injured wrist twanged a protest. She wondered what it would feel like to plant a fist in Caleb Myers's handsome face.

"Not everyone assumes you've the same criminal tendencies as your father, Rae—least of all me. I didn't bring everything up at dinner because I hoped we could enjoy a nice quiet meal, relax, get to know each other better." He paused, then finished evenly, "I can see that didn't work. I can also see that you're hiding something from me." There was another, more uncomfortable pause. "If I felt the way you claim all those law enforcement guys feel about you,

I'd be taking you down to the station about now for a bit of intensive interrogation—no, don't freeze up on me."

He ran a hand through his hair, and in the dim glow of a streetlight Rae glimpsed the leashed frustration hardening the angles and planes of his face. "Okay, we'll try it your way for the moment. I'll tell you everything I can about your father, and you tell me as much as you're comfortable with. Fair enough?"

Rae nodded once, unable to speak because her throat muscles felt as though they'd been bound up in piano wire.

After a long moment Caleb shrugged. "Your father was last arrested in San Francisco five years ago," he began, frustration still evident in his voice. "Charge was passing stolen goods. He jumped bond, hasn't been seen since."

"That seems to fit his usual pattern," Rae murmured.

"Do you remember him at all?"

God, You promised to help . . . I don't know if I can do this. It would have been easier to strip naked and walk through fire than sit here in the dark with a compelling, mysterious man who could reduce her to mush with a single look. At least for the moment, anyway, the kindness was noticeably absent. Somehow telling him was easier when he wasn't being kind. "I remember an impression of long hair and some kind of jacket with a fringe. The fringe tickled me and I giggled. That's all. My mother—" she hesitated, finished flatly "—my mother never gave up hoping he'd come back. For some reason, she loved him, even though he broke every promise he'd ever made to her, and finally abandoned her and both his children. I remember climbing up beside her on a window seat—I think we lived in an apartment somewhere in Oregon—and I'd sit there with her while she looked out the window. She was always crying." Her voice sounded harsh, strained. "She tried—I know she tried to take care of my brother and me, but she was . . ."

"It's all right, Rae."

She shook her head. It would never be all right. But she'd resolved to tell Caleb Myers every sordid detail so there would be no misunderstandings. She also needed to deflect his attention from the reason she'd been late for their dinner engagement. "My mother was . . . weak. Uncle Floyd told me once that she was one of the sweetest girls he'd ever met—he'd hoped she would tame my father. But it didn't work that way. I don't think she had the . . .

the inner moral strength, is the only way I can phrase it. She'd believe anything, if it *sounded* plausible. It was the late sixties. I found her high school annual once, when I was playing in the attic. It was before she dropped out, as they used to say. I hardly recognized her. She looked so innocent in that picture, with her perfect pageboy . . . her Peter Pan collar white blouse with the gold initial pin. Just like all the other girls." She stopped, hearing the bitterness rising like bubbles in a soda bottle.

Two blocks away a police siren split the night. Suddenly lights flashed behind them, and seconds later a speeding car roared past, followed by the pursuing cops.

Rae didn't have time to take a breath. Even before the fleeing car squealed around the corner at the end of the block Caleb had grabbed her shoulders and hauled her forward, pressing her onto the seat as he covered her with his body. Then, just as suddenly, the heavy pressure of his weight lifted, and he was pulling her upright again.

The receding siren had almost faded into the distance when he finally spoke. "Sorry about that. When I'm on an undercover job, instinct kicks in, I guess."

Rae felt as though he'd slammed his fist into her stomach instead of smashing her nose against the seat. Somehow in the past few moments she'd forgotten who and what Caleb Myers was, and what he wasn't. *She was as gullible, as naïve as her mother.* "Were you trying to protect me, or prevent me from escaping?" she snapped. "That was the getaway car, of course—only now I'll have to make other arrangements, won't I?" Her voice heated, the anger licking through the words. "I'll have to commend you for your professional instincts. One of them is lying well about your real profession. Computer security consultant? I don't think so. You don't miss a trick, do you?"

"Actually, I seem to have more of a talent for stuffing my foot in my mouth." His hand dropped over her tightly clenched fist. "I didn't mean that like it sounded, Rae. I haven't lied to you about my job. If you'll—"

She yanked her hand free and turned to stare fixedly out the window. "Save it for some other gullible woman. Take me home, please, Mr. Myers," she added, wanting to wound.

He leaned back and folded his arms. "Not until you allow me to explain—and apologize."

"Don't bother with explanations. Apologize, and we can go. I'm sure you've wasted enough time for one evening."

"I'll apologize when you turn around, and I'll take you home when I'm good and ready." Tungsten steel underlay his words, though the quiet voice didn't convey even a hint of anger.

She jerked around, grateful for the darkness so she wouldn't have to see him while he lied to her. Or worse, pitied her.

"Rae, I am *not*—nor have I ever been—an agent of any kind. I've always been as fascinated by computers as I have by people. I want to understand how they work, why they quit working—I can't resist finding solutions, solving puzzles. But my folks wanted me to go to seminary. They thought I'd make a good preacher."

Rae opened her mouth, clamped it shut.

"I agree," Caleb said as though she'd spoken the derisive comment aloud. "I'd have made a terrible servant of the Lord as a preacher. At any rate, eventually I ended up with a consulting firm that did a lot of work for the government. A lot of the jobs dealt with top-secret information. There was risk involved—I had to learn, I suppose, how to think and react more like an undercover agent. I left that company, went into business on my own."

"Why?" Rae ventured after a moment. She was intrigued in spite of herself. He sounded so sincere. *A preacher?*

He stirred. "I . . . like my freedom. I like to decide which jobs to take, which ones I wouldn't touch regardless of the money." He hesitated, sounding almost sheepish. "I don't like to feel . . . chained. By people. By my job."

So. He was one of those. "Less responsibility that way," Rae observed.

"Probably." He didn't sound at all defensive. "Be patient. God isn't finished with me yet," he quipped.

For some reason, his serene acceptance of his flaws made her feel better. Lighter, somehow. Rae studied his face. She wanted to believe him, trust him. Oh, why not admit it? She *did* believe him. "Okay, so you're a hotshot independent. That still doesn't explain your reaction when that police car flew by."

"I wasn't trying to prevent your escape—I was trying to protect you. Instinct again. I have three younger sisters who razz me constantly about my protective instincts." She saw his shoulders lift in a shrug. "You'll just have to deal with it, Ms. Prescott. Besides, I *am* on a job. And after last night, I think you'd be the first to agree there's some physical danger involved. So . . . I apologize if I scared you, but I won't apologize for wanting to protect you."

"Just all part of the job, huh?"

She'd tossed the remark out lightly, but for some reason Caleb went completely still. So still Rae's skin tightened in primitive response. "I won't deny that part of the reason I took you out to dinner was official."

"I never looked at it any other way."

"But that wasn't the only reason I took you out."

"Yeah, right."

Abruptly he leaned forward, so close their noses almost touched and she could feel his warm breath against her cheek. "You have an impressive temper, little cat, but I'm not in the mood to be clawed right now, even though you think I deserve it." His finger stroked her hot cheek once, then he moved behind the wheel. "Let me know when you've got it together again, and we'll . . . talk."

The night closed around them in a dark cocoon. The muffled sound of traffic, the drone of a plane overhead, the nervous rustle of the wind all receded, leaving Rae alone in an increasingly uncomfortable silence. She was trapped. She wasn't immature enough to jump out of the car, much less engage in a losing battle with him by refusing to speak. And she couldn't even yell at him, because she refused to act like her mother.

Humiliation jabbed her, a hot poker to her stomach. She barely knew Caleb, yet she cared about his opinion of her. She didn't want him to think she was as weak as her mother. Another realization slammed into her. Caleb had known about her father. With all his connections, no doubt he already knew all about Daffodil Prescott, as well. Knew about the mood swings, her unrestrained displays of temper. That was why he'd warned Rae to control her simmering emotion. *Lord? Why are You doing this to me?* Right now, she almost would have preferred facing Dead Eyes and his loaded gun.

"I'm willing to stay here all night if you are."

She flinched. "I'm not going to lose my temper," she mumbled.

"I admit to relief." He smiled, a brief flash of white teeth. "Now . . . I know you didn't look on this evening as a date. To be honest,

I didn't either, at first. But something happened during dinner, somewhere between you knocking over your water glass, and spilling pie in your lap." A low chuckle burned Rae's ears. "It's totally unprofessional, not to mention risky. But I've given up denying it. You're not just part of the Starseeker case, Rae Prescott. You're an intriguing, beguiling woman, and . . . I'd like to know you better."

"Why? My father's a criminal. My mother—I never finished telling you about my mother, although you probably already know all about her, too."

"No, I don't, other than what you shared earlier."

The gentleness was back, and Rae swallowed hard, steeling herself against responding. She wasn't weak, wasn't gullible. "Then I'll fill in the rest. After I do, you won't be able to take me home fast enough." She took a deep breath. "My mother was a drug addict." There, why bother to whitewash it? "She never meant to be, of course—she just couldn't help it. After my father left, the last time, she turned to drugs for consolation, instead of the time-honored denials found in alcohol, or even other men. She had just enough sense to bring us here. Uncle Floyd tried to help, but he'd just lost his wife to cancer a year or so earlier, and . . ." Rae shook her head, hating to even speak of the first nightmare years here in Colorado. "My mother died a year after we came here." She stared at Caleb, praying he would revert to the inflexible professional and take her home—yet terrified of that very response.

"I'm sorry. That's a rotten background to overcome. But, Rae—your parents' life-styles don't affect the person *you* are. Nor was their character a reflection of yours, especially now. You're a Christian—surely you know this."

"I know it—sometimes I have trouble . . . accepting it." His calm perception healed, sustained, and Rae relaxed a little. She had forgotten, for a while, the truly miraculous nature of God's love, enacted through the behavior of a fellow believer. So many people called themselves Christians—yet they seldom if ever allowed Christlike compassion to spill from their lives to others. The last of her temper sputtered and died, carrying with it much of the shame of her revelation. Regardless of Caleb's primary agenda, Rae would always be grateful for the gift of his Christian understanding. She managed the first real smile of the evening. "I've mostly accepted my parents, my past. But—"

"But now it's rearing up like a fire-breathing dragon and trying to take a big bite out of you, huh?"

"Well . . . at least breathe its fiery bad breath on me."

They smiled at each other, and Caleb's hand lifted as if he was about to touch her face. Rae was sure she hadn't moved, but his hand stopped and dropped on the seat. "Do you remember the police coming to talk to your uncle once? You would have been about ten. I've read the report from Carnegie Hall, which incidentally was lousy timing."

"It was my father's fault, more than those agents. They were trying to catch him, and the longer they waited the worse their chances. Frankly, I appreciated their tact in waiting until after I performed." Uncle Floyd hadn't, though. Rae had never seen him so angry. "As for that other time, when I was ten—I don't remember. I'm sorry. I know someone came, because I asked this morning, at the station. But I don't remember." She bit her lip. "Caleb? Do you believe me?"

"About that, of course." He sighed. "Did they give you a hard time down at the station?"

"Everyone was very civil, but I don't think they believed that I've had no contact with my father."

"I know." The warmth in the simple phrase stroked her as palpably as a touch. "Rae, I can't tell you too much about the case. But I promise you when I find more definite information about your father, I'll let you know."

"Can you tell me *anything* about what's going on?"

There was a longer pause, and he bowed his head as if in prayer. Then he turned to Rae, and his eyes were very clear, almost glowing in the night. "I can tell you only that it could be even more dangerous than you've already experienced," he said slowly. "I think an organization known as IOS is involved. It's not organized crime, but they're equally deadly."

"IOS?"

His voice grim, Caleb explained. "It started as a bunch of renegade businessmen—powerful, executive-level men who had been fired or laid off. For revenge, a group of them banded together and started sabotaging the companies in a variety of ways—stealing information or technology and selling to rival corporations, manipulating stock. At first it was mostly white-collar crime. This is the third time in three years I've been on a case involving them. It's making some waves at the federal level now. They used to steer clear of anything involving the military. Security is so tight it's not worth the effort. But things have changed."

"What happened?" Rae asked, relieved at the subject change, but increasingly chilled by the implications.

"We're not quite sure, but about four years ago we think there was a major change in policy. Things started getting nasty—a couple of deaths by mysterious causes. Some arson, a case or two of blackmail. The members apparently got carried away by their power."

"Is there one particular man in charge?"

His fingers drummed restlessly on the steering wheel. "Again, we're not sure. By design the whole organization is loosely structured, the secrecy so well-maintained we have little to go on, even after several years. A name dropped here, a letter there—every now and then some sketchy tidbit from a snitch."

I bet I could provide a clue or two. "IOS is a strange name—what is it? Greek? Latin? Or just an acronym?"

He gave her an approving look that was mixed with gravity. "I knew you were a smart lady the first time I met you. You're right on—it's a Greek word, and the simplest translation is *poison*. A corrosive, destructive kind of poison. Whoever came up with it as the organization's name has a brilliant mind, but a twisted sense of humor."

Rae shuddered. "You're right. That's sick." She shifted in the seat. "You're telling me this because of what's happened at Joyful Noise. But my father—" the realization was a knife thrust "—you think it's possible that my father—*no*. He might not care about me, but my father wouldn't hurt me. He couldn't—"

Suddenly Caleb slid over, and his hand came down on her shoulder. "Easy, Rae. Don't borrow trouble, all right? We don't know whether your father's involved, or how, so until we figure that out, the best thing you can do is—" his hand squeezed briefly "—not worry. And trust me." The warm teasing note disappeared. "I won't lie to you. I think you need to be extra careful, even if this turns out to not be IOS. But if they *are* behind it . . . well, they're dangerous. They've had a taste of power, as well as revenge. It's addictive." He shifted, turning so he could see Rae's face in the light of the street lamp. "Power, money, revenge . . . some of Satan's favorite tools."

Rae shivered again, and Caleb's hand slid behind her neck. He massaged the rigid tendons, his touch warm, firm, and Rae almost gasped at the sensations. She had never felt like this before, all jumpy and sizzling on the outside and melting like hot caramel inside. *This is bad, Rae. You're making a bad mistake—possibly the worst of your life. Of his.* "I need to go home."

"In a minute." The hand slid to her chin and gently turned it toward him. "Rae, I know you're hiding something from me. Are you sure you won't tell me what it is?"

Mutely, she shook her head. There was no way Caleb Myers could protect her twenty-four hours a day. And the only way she could protect *him* was with silence. "I'm fine."

"I don't believe you. You've been nervous, even frightened all evening. Knocking over your water glass and spilling pie in your lap might indicate a charming clumsiness on your part—but I think it goes way beyond that." He muttered something indecipherable beneath his breath. "Every time you look at me I want to take you in my arms, shield you from whatever it is that's frightening you—promise you that everything will be all right." He ignored her startled jump. "Believe me, it's not a feeling I'm comfortable with, either. You're blowing my concentration, little cat."

"Thanks. You're not doing much for me, either."

With a chuckle he moved to his side of the car, leaving Rae a tangled mass of regret and relief. Neither of them spoke on the drive home. But as he pulled into the driveway Caleb reached across a restraining hand. "I'll check out your house," he said. "Stay behind me."

Rae didn't protest. In the cold, early spring night the mansion—her home—filled the sky, looking dark, almost malevolent, hiding evil in every corner. She wanted to weep for her loss of innocence, but tears were a sign of weakness, not to mention a waste of time.

Caleb led her up the back stairs and took her key. She could practically feel his body humming with alertness and tension. In a barely audible voice he instructed Rae to stand just inside the door, and she waited—can of Mace at the ready—while he searched the rooms.

He returned moments later, glanced at the Mace, and a grin kicked up one corner of his mouth. "I'm going to check the store," he told her, gesturing for her to follow him down the hall. "Stay behind me, and wait here, at this door, out of sight."

Heart pounding, hands slippery on the can, Rae somehow managed a composed nod. This was the Caleb Myers who had appeared out of nowhere to rescue her, the frowning, deadly professional who looked as capable of protecting her as a sword-wielding Archangel Michael. While it was reassuring to have that protection, it wasn't exactly *comfortable.*

Once again he returned in only a few moments. "You can check to see if anything is missing, but everything looks to be in order, and there's no signs of forced entry," he announced, looking more relaxed.

Rae opened her mouth to tell him about the missing pieces of sheet music, then closed it. She wandered obediently around the store, and the insidious feeling crept over her again. Everything looked normal, in its proper place. Except—

She couldn't prevent the dismayed, clumsy gesture of her arm. Caleb was beside her instantly. "The quarter note there—" she pointed to the shiny brass note mounted on a marble stand "—and that music box. They've been moved."

"How can you tell? The police could have—"

"No." Her voice was firm. "Everything is arranged in a very specific position—I moved them all back after the police left." She met his gaze with a blend of self-consciousness and stubborn certainty. "I'm like that with these. Until he died my uncle gave me a different one every birthday since I was eight years old. I can always tell when someone has picked them up, as you just saw."

"Hmm." Understanding and a disconcerting tenderness lurked behind the watchfulness. "I do see."

More flustered now than she was by the unknown entities who had disarranged her precious keepsakes, Rae turned away, pretending to examine a bin of sheet music. When she felt Caleb's silent approach, she stiffened, but he didn't touch her.

"I'm going to look around again," he murmured. "It'll take a little while. Why don't you make yourself a cup of tea?"

Rae shook her head. "I'll wait."

He spent almost half an hour checking the store for signs of forced entry, wiretaps on her phone and concealed listening devices. There were none. He called someone, his voice soft but persuasive, then told Rae that an extra team would be detailed to watch the Prescott mansion.

Before he left, he stood at the back door for a long, uncomfortable moment, studying Rae. She didn't speak, because a plea for him not to leave her alone was crowding her throat, and she was afraid to open her mouth. Finally Caleb shook his head. His gaze rested one last time on Rae's bruised cheek. "You'll be safe enough," he promised. "But be careful. Something's going on here. Until we know what it is—" he stuffed his hands casually in the waistband of his slacks "—and until you bring yourself to share what you know . . . be careful. Independence is a worthy attribute, but it can be taken to extremes."

Two blocks from the Prescott mansion, Caleb pulled to the curb. After locking the car, he loped down the street, keeping in the shadows and dodging street lamps. The two men in the second story of the abandoned hardware store told him everything was quiet. They had seen nothing, and no one had tried to enter the house. Radio contact with two other undercover men confirmed the report. Caleb sympathized with their frustration and boredom. He had a feeling, however, that it might not last much longer.

His noisy instinct was especially loud. Rae's living quarters were comfortably cluttered and dusty, but she was meticulous to a fault about every aspect of Joyful Noise. If she claimed those two objects had been moved, Caleb was inclined to believe her. But who had moved them, and how had the intruder slipped inside undetected?

The question that nagged him the most ferociously was the one Rae had refused to answer. What had happened to her before he arrived to take her out to dinner?

Chapter Nine

Another week passed. The Easter cantata was declared a success, but Rae shrugged aside the compliments she received for her accompaniment. God's grace alone had been responsible for the brilliance of her playing. Rae's mind—shamefully—had stayed elsewhere.

There had been no sign of the bogus detective or his henchman since the day they took her for a drive, but Rae felt their presence everywhere, even if she couldn't prove it. Her skin crawled from the sensation of being watched.

Caleb had stopped by twice. The last time, he told her he had to go out of town for a few days to check some leads. He didn't say what leads. He had promised to be back by the previous day. Since he hadn't called or come by, Rae had no way of knowing whether or not he really was back in town. She tried not to dwell on the implications of his conspicuous absence.

To pass the time she tried to catch up on bookkeeping and devoted more focused concentration to her students. There hadn't been a lot of customers that week. A lady who was teaching herself piano dropped by twice to purchase more music, and the balding man with thick-lensed glasses who collected old sheet music stopped by. This afternoon he lingered to converse, albeit diffidently.

"I wondered if you would mind if I just rummaged through your music," he asked, mopping his balding head with a folded handker-chief.

Rae wondered why he was sweating. It was twenty-four degrees outside, and the radiators were unable to pull the indoor tempera-ture much above sixty-eight. "Well . . ." She hesitated. In her ex-perience customers who wanted to just look ended up creating after-hours work—and no revenues.

"I won't make a mess," he promised, voice anxious.

He made Rae feel small, so she smiled and told him to help himself. "Let me know if you need my assistance."

One of her favorite piano students arrived about then, and Rae forgot about the funny stoop-shouldered man. He was gone the next time she checked.

The following day proceeded much the same. Caleb still hadn't called or stopped by. Customers were still sparse, though one of them was the raspy-voiced woman who thought "Ode to Joy" was from Beethoven's Fifth. Today her request startled Rae, since she looked as impatient as she had her previous visit. "I'm looking for a piece of religious music," she said. "It's called 'The Lord Is My Light and My Salvation.' Do you have it?"

"Why, yes," Rae replied, wondering if the woman knew any more about this song than she did "Ode to Joy." "That's always been one of my favorites."

The woman did not look impressed. She coughed as she followed Rae, her eyes darting everywhere. She hadn't struck Rae as a par-ticularly devout woman, but then, appearances really *could* be de-ceiving. After paying for the music, she hurried out of the store without so much as a thank-you, and Rae decided to drop the mix-up over Beethoven. Such a strange, almost ill-tempered woman would doubtless not take to correction kindly.

Rae was writing the entry in her log book when the bell jingled and a man wearing the uniform of the phone company sauntered in.

"Got a report that your phone's out of order," he announced.

Rae reached for the phone under the counter. She listened to the dial tone and looked at the man. "There's nothing wrong with my phone. You must have the wrong address."

The man scowled. "This place is Joyful Noise, ain't it? Well, I got orders to check your phones."

Rae stared. "Orders from who?"

"The President of the U.S.," he replied sardonically. "What kind of dumb question is that, lady? Orders from the phone company, okay?"

Rae studied the surly man, suddenly afraid without quite knowing why. He might be a rude serviceman. On the other hand . . . "Why don't you tell me the name of your supervisor and let me call and confirm the order?" She reached for the phone.

He gave her a thoroughly disgusted look. "You want to check my fingerprints, too? Forget it, lady. I got too many other calls to waste time waiting on you." He picked up the metal toolbox he had dumped on the floor. "Don't blame me when your phone won't work."

Well, Rae thought after he stomped out the door. So much for courteous, friendly service. She started to call the phone company anyway, but at that moment a customer entered the store, then the phone rang, and by the time she had another opportunity Rae had decided to shrug the matter aside.

That night she woke abruptly out of a sound sleep. For several moments she lay rigidly in bed, head pressed into the pillow, eyes wide open. There it was again—the creaking of a floorboard somewhere up front. The crawling sensation of danger suddenly jolted her spine like a thousand bolts of electricity, and for a moment Rae was afraid she was going to be ill. Then the anger arrived in a boiling flood.

She tossed back the covers and snatched on her robe, furiously tying it closed over her flimsy silk gown. After grabbing the poker, she tiptoed into the hall. *Not this time.* If they thought she'd tamely sit back while they wreaked havoc in her world, they were in for a rude shock, because regardless of their threats she was *not* going to cower in a corner.

The door to the store was still locked, but even through the thick oak panels Rae could hear the faint shuffling sound. Someone was in the store. Again.

The anger exploded. She lifted the poker over her head, heedless of consequences. "Get out of here!" she shouted. "I'm calling the po—" She stopped, breathing hard. She had been warned not to call the police. "I have a shotgun!" she yelled, resolving to purchase one immediately. "And I know how to use it." Well, surely all you had to do was pull the trigger.

From the other side of the door came the muffled sound of clanging tools and scrambling footsteps. They thudded across the floor away from Rae, and she heard the painful screech from one of the windows, unopened since summer.

Then there was silence.

Rae's arms flopped to her sides, the anger evaporated. Her fingers were so nerveless she almost dropped the poker. Moving on unsteady feet, she made her way into the kitchen and put on the kettle. Then she sat down, flipped her nighttime braid over her shoulder and tried to figure out what to do. She'd threatened to call the police, and she could only hope she'd swallowed that threat in time. Unfortunately, the one about the nonexistent shotgun had been screamed loudly enough for Karen to have heard all the way down the block.

She couldn't handle this alone, and it was the height of stupidity to pretend otherwise.

After a few minutes she went to the bedroom and looked in her purse. Caleb Myers had given her his card, writing down on the back the number of the motel where he was staying. It was two o'clock in the morning. Was he there, and if he was, how would he react to being awakened out of a sound sleep? She knew how she had reacted. *You have the survival instincts of a lemon rind, Prescott.*

The kettle was whistling, but its merry, homey sound dragged across her nerves. She turned off the gas and stood at the stove, holding her hands over the burner, vainly hoping the heat would warm her icy fingers. Her mouth twisted because she couldn't keep them still.

Caleb had more or less told her she was too independent. *All right, Mr. Private Consultant Secret Agent Wannabe Myers, let's see how you react when someone disturbs you unexpectedly.* She dialed the number and asked the sleepy clerk to connect her with his room.

He answered on the second ring. "Myers."

"Caleb?"

"Rae? Is that you?" The calm voice was alert instantly. "What's the matter—your voice is trembling."

"I hate to bother you, but—" she chewed on her lip, then confessed in a tumbled rush of words "—someone broke into the store again. I thought I could scare them off but I was probably . . . I mean, I did a really dumb thing. Can you—"

"Where are you calling from?"

"The kitchen. He ran—"

"Stay there. Turn on all the lights. I'll be there in five minutes. Did you call the police?"

"No!" Her voice was too sharp, and she tried to modify the panicked tone. "I don't want to call the police. I can't. They said—" She stopped, but it was too late.

"Who said?" Caleb asked very quietly.

"N-nothing. I meant—I . . ."

"Don't move. I'll be there in five minutes." He paused, then added, "If you have hot chocolate, I'd rather have that than tea."

Four and a half minutes later she opened the door after his voice softly called out his name, and she recognized the calm, crisp tone. He looked so strong, so capable, that she fought the urge to throw herself into his arms.

Her face must have revealed the childish longing, for he smiled crookedly and held his arms wide. "Come here," he prompted.

She took a step, then stopped, stiffening her shoulders. *If you give in now, it will be even harder after he's gone.* "I'm fine." An even bigger lie than the one about the shotgun.

"Let's go to the kitchen," Caleb suggested, looking resigned.

Rae explained what happened with what she decided was commendable calm. On the other hand, she couldn't bear being left alone, and after a swift perusal of her face, Caleb allowed her to accompany him to the store. He poked around carefully, his expression remote, focused. Then he turned to Rae and gestured for them to go to the kitchen.

"Your phone has been tapped," he said. "Is the one here on the same line as the store?"

She nodded slowly. "An extra line costs too much." Her smile wobbled. "I sound like a broken record, don't I? Actually, the Lord has lived up to His promise about providing my needs, because I have a roof over my head, food to eat, and I can pay all my bills. I hope you—"

"Rae . . . it's going to be all right. I'm here." His hand moved to the pager at his side, then stopped. He cast another of those swift, measuring glances over Rae. "But I do have to leave you for a few minutes," he told her, his voice calm, matter-of-fact. "Three minutes, max. Stay here in the kitchen and drink your tea. Watch the clock—that's a nice one, isn't it? I've always loved the old pendulum wall clocks." He took her arm, led her to the trestle table and gently pressed her down. "Three minutes, and I'll be back. You just sit tight right here. Can you do that for me?"

"Where are you going?"

He didn't answer, just stood above her, the warm ginger-colored eyes shuttered. "I'll be back as soon as I can," he repeated.

Rae throttled the incipient panic. At least she hadn't taken up his earlier offer for comfort. "I'm perfectly all right," she promised. "You can go play all the spy games you want without fear that I'll dissolve into a gibbering idiot. If I can handle being—" She stopped, bitterly aware that she was perilously close to the gibbering idiot label.

Caleb dropped onto the bench opposite. "All right, Rae." He was calm, but firm. "Tell me what's happened. And don't try to fob me off with evasions or a plausible lie." He looked at her. "You're lousy at lying, as I expect you know."

"I wouldn't be much of a Christian if I was good at it, would I?" Rae startled herself by smiling ruefully. Ah, well. Why not admit it? Caleb's presence made her feel incredibly brave. She was a fool on any number of levels, but there was nothing to do now but tough it out. "I've probably behaved stupidly, but then I'm not used to being held at gunpoint."

"What?" All the color left his face. For once the imperturbable Caleb Myers looked completely knocked off balance, and Rae felt a brief sting of satisfaction. It was nice, not being the only one off balance.

"Last week—the night you took me out to dinner." She told the whole story calmly. "At the time I was too frightened to think properly, which of course is what they counted on. I'd do just about anything to keep someone from burning or trashing my home. It's been a week since it happened, and until a few minutes ago I was hoping everything was back to normal." Her hands lifted in a futile gesture. "Which makes me naïve, along with dumb, I know. A cop's worst nightmare." She looked away, swallowing hard. "Have you or the others had any leads?"

"Not until now." His voice was grim. "I trust this time you have a fair idea of what they look like. Grabowski will want to set up another photo lineup at their detective bureau. Can you describe the car?"

Sheepishly Rae shook her head. "It was a—a car." She blushed when Caleb groaned. "I'm sorry. I just never notice things like that much. About all I can tell you is that it reminded me of the kind of car all you undercover types seem to prefer."

"Will you stop saying things like that? I'm a *consultant*." Caleb brushed aside the errant lock of hair dangling over his forehead. "Rae, why didn't you tell me when this happened? I know you were afraid, but—" Mercifully he bit back further words of censure.

She didn't want to look at him. "I couldn't. I should have, but at the time I just couldn't."

After a moment his face softened. "All right. I do understand—but we're calling the police in now." He tilted his head, studied her somberly. "What would you have done if I hadn't been in the motel when you called?"

She shivered. "I don't know." Her chin lifted. "But I would have managed. I yelled through the door that I had a shotgun, and I aim to purchase one first thing in the morning."

The tender look returned, glimmering in his golden eyes and turning her poker of a spine to flimsy straw. "I imagine you would," he murmured. His finger touched the end of her nose. "Don't move. I'll be back as soon as I can."

Chapter Ten

Caleb ran lightly across the street, making no sound as he slipped in and out of the shadows. The two FBI men on duty were as steamed—and perturbed—as Caleb. They notified Grabowski, and everyone converged minutes later at Rae's back porch.

Caleb watched her greet everyone with resigned aplomb. She had combed her hair and twisted it up, and was now dressed in a soft pink warm-up suit instead of her robe and nightgown, for which Caleb was privately relieved. He was still uncomfortable with his feelings toward her, but he had admitted to himself days ago that there was no sense fighting a losing battle. He faced enough of a battle with Rae's insecurities and inconsistencies.

Take right now, for instance—the pale blank face of a DaVinci madonna, with the marks of old bruises faded now to an unbecoming green and yellow. Proud, capable businesswoman and accomplished musician. Vulnerable, terrified young girl, trying to survive her free-fall into a reality no decent human being should have to face. She watched, gray eyes still and dark, while Caleb pointed out the nasty, unobtrusive induction coil planted under the counter. When he described her brief abduction by car the previous week she didn't stir, though Caleb knew she was fighting both fear and humility.

Grabowski looked as if he had been sleeping in his clothes. He was scowling, irritable and short-tempered, though to give him credit, he moderated his response to Rae's lack of wisdom in not calling the police immediately after her abduction. Caleb kept his voice smooth, quietly matter-of-fact as he explained what he knew. All of them held a low-voiced discussion on the difficulty of maintaining a surveillance over a structure with as many angles and sides as the Prescott mansion. Grabowski's surliness flattened out a little, and he questioned Rae with surprising patience.

They fought a brief but furious battle over whether or not to leave the bug in place. Thanks to Rae, the police and the FBI won.

Elbows akimbo with her fists bunched on either side of her waist, Rae stubbornly refused to listen to Caleb at all. "I'm already in danger—and I don't see how I could possibly be more terrified than I was that afternoon last week," she pointed out with what Caleb decided was mule-headed naïveté. "If they find out that— that eavesdropping device is gone, they'll know for sure I called the police."

"What about the phone call you made to me?" Caleb asked, pinning her in an intractable stare. "If anyone was listening, are they going to assume you felt like calling a male friend at two o'clock in the morning for no reason other than to have a chat?" So much for his famous detachment. Right now he was finding it almost impossible to keep from tossing Ms. Prescott over his shoulder and spiriting her away like a Scottish Highlander on a raid.

Rae held his gaze only briefly before hers slid away. He watched her hands move in restless patterns up and down the counter. "I don't know," she admitted finally. "But if you take it away, they'll know for sure I called the authorities. Being threatened was bad enough, but I couldn't stand it if they drove by one night and chucked a firebomb through the window."

"It wouldn't only be the Prescott mansion that suffered," Caleb growled. Little idiot! She might be innocent to the slime buckets and sharks of the world, but she could out-stubborn a fence post. Even though the trait made her difficult to protect, Caleb reluctantly admired her backbone. She definitely wasn't the kind of woman who buckled beneath adversity.

"Ms. Prescott's point is valid," Grabowski interjected, looking as frustrated about the situation as Caleb.

Rae tossed her head. "Well, I'll just make sure I don't conduct any incriminating conversations over the phone." She smiled grimly. "Maybe those guys will even learn something about music."

She stood by the cash register, cornered but game, fighting fear with humor. Caleb felt his insides twist. He wanted to haul her in his arms and kiss those ugly bruises, then her eyes, her mouth. The strength of his emotions amazed and appalled him.

A fresh-faced man with a shock of carrot red hair approached Grabowski. "Rest of the place is clean, sir. But it looks like Ms. Prescott probably interrupted a second placement." He glanced at Rae. "They were going to put it inside one of the music boxes."

Rae's whole body jerked. "Another one?" Her voice rose, and Caleb moved to her side. She turned to Grabowski. "Why are they doing this? Why?"

Her hands flew out, fluttering awkwardly like wounded birds. The long slender fingers, Caleb noted with a pang, ended in short, practically nonexistent nails. *God, please—help me to protect this woman.* Unfortunately, the world seemed determined to rattle her cage, and it was only a matter of time— He stopped the thought.

"Do you still think my father's involved?" she was asking. "Am I still under suspicion?"

"Ms. Prescott," Grabowski began awkwardly, looking uncomfortable.

"I've told her about her father—and I've also told her about IOS." Caleb put his hand on Rae's shoulder. This time she didn't object, and he wondered if she even felt his touch. Her eyes were staring into some private hell, a brilliant, glassy look turning them to black obsidian.

He waited, ignoring Grabowski's impatience, until he felt her relax a little. "Rae, let's look at this from another angle. Think about your customers over the past couple of weeks. Have any of them acted strangely, made unusual requests, looked suspicious? Anything? Think about it as long as you need to before you answer, and don't leave something out because you think it's silly or irrelevant."

While they waited he and Grabowski exchanged looks. Both men were aware that, while wiretapping was a federal offense, the investigation for this incident still belonged to the local police. By rights the detective deserved to be conducting the interrogation, and Caleb appreciated Grabowski's restraint. Over the past weeks they had met together several times, and Grabowski had agreed to let

Caleb handle Rae . . . for the moment. Tonight, the detective's restraint had been pushed to the limit, and Caleb knew it.

Rae finally spoke, though her expression was dubious and she was shaking her head. "Business has been slow," she said. Her hair, hastily pinned, was starting to slip. Caleb couldn't help it. His fingers moved up to her head, pushing the pins in place. Thick and soft, the shining strands smelled like lavender potpourri and fresh linens. So much for detachment.

Rae took a step away, and he dropped his hands. "About the only thing I remember," she mused, faint color washing across the bridge of her nose, "is this woman who wanted Beethoven's 'Ode to Joy,' but she got the right symphony mixed up with—wait."

She hesitated. Grabowski shifted impatiently. Joe, one of the FBI men from across the street, started to say something. Caleb lifted an eyebrow, and Joe shut his mouth.

"What, Rae?" he asked after a minute when he realized she was having difficulty deciding whether or not to speak her mind.

"There is something," she admitted slowly. "But it's silly." A startled look crossed her face, and she smiled at Caleb sheepishly. "But like you said . . . All right." She inhaled, as though steeling herself. "After the first break-in I did discover that all my copies of Beethoven's fifth and ninth symphonies were missing."

Unimpressed, Grabowski snorted. "With all this music, how on earth would you know?"

Rae bristled, and Caleb fought to suppress a grin. "Detective, music is my business. I *know*—you'll just have to take my word for it."

"You probably misfiled them after all the excitement. You were pretty rattled that day."

A faint band of red deepened until two red coins dotted her cheeks. "Detective Grabowski, I may be a little rattled, but *nothing* interferes with running my store. Not thieves or muggers or the entire police department. That music is not misplaced. It's missing."

Caleb dropped his hand over hers, which was moving furiously up and down the counter. The claws were out again, however unwisely. He glanced at Grabowski's face, which was turning just about as red as Rae's. The man was a crackerjack detective, Caleb had determined, albeit a bit gruff. From what the other cops had told him, Grabowski kept himself under iron control and expected the same from others. He would have little patience for Rae's flash-fire temper.

"Grabowski." Caleb fixed a serene but commanding gaze upon him. Without altering his gaze he pressed Rae's fingers one last time, then removed his hand. "Like we discussed earlier, we've determined that they must be using the store as a drop. It's the only explanation that makes sense." He propped his hip on the edge of the counter, adopting a relaxed, nonthreatening pose. "I think Fisher's our man. Joe and Charlie told me he came to the store again this past week. He left empty-handed, unless he slipped something in his pocket." He twisted his head to glance at Rae. "Do you remember selling anything to a man that was small enough to tuck inside a jacket or pants pocket?"

"Not that I recall. I stock stuff with a musical motif like pencils and erasers, key chains, magnets—mostly for little kids. Unless he shoplifted, the man you're talking about isn't anyone I remember selling those items to."

Caleb turned to Grabowski, who like Rae had cooled down considerably. Caleb thought, then mused aloud, "He could have been leaving something behind."

"There's something else." One of the Bureau guys spoke up. Charlie was a good-looking guy in his late twenties, a young Turk who liked to strut but who knew his job. He was staring at Rae with a brooding, calculating look that unaccountably irritated Caleb. "Ms. Prescott is being tailed," he announced, glancing at Grabowski. "And not by us. Are they some of yours?"

Grabowski's eyes narrowed. "Describe the tail."

"Male, average height, slightly overweight. Dark hair, wears a blue and yellow ski jacket or a red plaid lumber jacket. Joe got a picture of him the other day. So far no ID."

Grabowski cursed under his breath. He whipped out his radio and spoke rapidly.

"I haven't noticed anybody like that," Rae said, faltering.

"Why should you?" Hiding his concern, Caleb straightened, jerked his chin slightly and eyed the stairs. The two FBI men started toward them.

"Where are they going? There's nothing up there." Rae darted from behind the counter as they reached the landing. "Just boxes and some old furniture. I keep it closed."

"Relax, Rae," Caleb said, snagging her elbow as she sailed by. She turned to gaze at him with a heartbreaking blend of fear, puzzlement—and wariness. *Don't look at me like that, sweetheart,* Caleb wanted to tell her. *It makes me want all sorts of things I can't afford to ask of you—or do to you—right now.* He contented himself with stroking his thumb over the inside of her elbow, carefully positioning his body so that the gentling caress wasn't witnessed. "It would be a good place to stash a few things, wouldn't it? When's the last time you went up there?"

"We checked it after the first break-in," Grabowski snapped. "It's clean."

Rae's mouth quirked. She stepped away from Caleb, her rejection graceful but final. "It's hardly that. I bet there's three years' worth of dirt and dust all over everything. I keep meaning to go over everything at least once a year, but time sort of gets away from me."

Joe and Charlie returned a few minutes later, dusting their hands on their slacks and sneezing. Caleb and Grabowski met them at the bottom of the stairs for a brief consultation. In a few minutes Caleb returned to Rae, who was studying her dainty ballerina shoes as though they held the secret of the Sphinx in their toes. Caleb waited until she lifted her head.

"It's still—clean." His eyes twinkled briefly. "In one capacity, anyway." He gestured to the watching men. "Rae, the FBI guys are going to give you a number to call in an emergency. It reaches the agents across the street. They have a modular phone set up. We hope you'll feel a little safer." He tried a small smile. "I know *I'll* feel a lot better."

Rae swallowed. "All right. I—thank you."

"Just remember it's for emergencies only. If you can get to another phone to call, do so, since we're leaving the tap on your phone."

"That does make sense," she said slowly, after a minute. "What can I do to help?"

Go on an extended vacation, Caleb wanted to say, but didn't. As it stood, Rae's guardian angels would have to work double time to keep her from dashing her foot against a whole truckload of stones,

because even though he would have liked to become her shadow
. . . watchdog . . . bodyguard, *anything* to keep her safe—he
couldn't. Sometimes acting on faith was blasted difficult. "Just try
to act normally. That means," he elaborated sternly, "that you continue to play the part of a musician, and leave the detective work to
those who have trained for it."

Grabowski had other ideas. "It might help if you start keeping a
written description of every customer, especially if they act peculiar
in any way." He glanced at Caleb. "And keep the information
hidden. Don't leave it lying around for anyone to find. And whatever you do, don't forget to take it out of the store at night."

The phone rang. Rae jumped violently, and without thought Caleb wrapped a protective arm around her shoulders. "Go ahead
and answer it," he told her, giving her an encouraging smile,
amazed when she didn't immediately pull free.

He felt her back straighten, saw her chin rise. The hand that
reached out was calm as a peaceful Sunday morning. On the other
hand, Caleb thought wryly, *his* feelings resembled a Saturday night
play-off game.

"Hello?" Anxiety colored the syllables. After a second her eyes
flew to Grabowski. "No—no, it's all right. I'm fine, Nancy," she
responded with cheerful confidence as her fingers drummed up and
down the counter. "I just thought I heard that prowler again, and
they came to investigate. I'm sorry to cause such drama, but I
promise everything's under control. Yes, it has been something of a
shock . . . I will. Thanks for calling."

She hung up, staring at the phone as if it was a snake before her
gaze moved slowly around the room, stopping on Grabowski. Incredibly, Caleb felt her lean into his chest as though seeking support.

He wrapped his arm around her shoulders and held her as
though her action was the most natural thing in the world. "You
did pretty well for an unworldly musician, Ms. Prescott. And without telling a lie, too."

She seemed to realize all at once where she was, and stiffened.
Caleb dropped his arm but could not resist winking at her. Rae
blushed, swatting him, and everyone in the room relaxed. Then
Grabowski's pager squawked. "I'll be back," he said tersely, and
left to call in by radio.

When he returned a few minutes later, he stood in the doorway for a moment, his grim face looking gray with fatigue. "An unmarked car was stolen from our inventory nine days ago. We just found it. It's probably the one in which Ms. Prescott was abducted. No clues. No prints. It's been wiped clean as a car on the showroom floor."

Chapter Eleven

"It won't look right. Everyone will think you and I—that you're—" Rae threw up her hands in exasperation. "Stop grinning at me like that! You know good and well what they'll think when you show up at choir with me and just sit there."

Caleb shrugged. "I don't care if everyone does think that. In fact, I think it's an idea with a lot of merit."

Rae sighed, too weary to debate the issue. She began the tedious process of closing Joyful Noise for the day, locking the doors, turning the sign, switching off lights. "It's a ridiculous idea founded on a premise too flimsy to be plausible. We both know you're not interested in any kind of dating relationship. Besides which, the whole church is resigned to me being a politically correct, independent, single career woman of the nineties."

"Hogwash. You're an independent, single career woman due to necessity and circumstances, not ideological bent. What puzzles me is why the men in your life are so blind. According to Karen, you've only casually dated the past couple of years, and so infrequently that it barely passes for dating."

Rae began straightening music, not looking at him. "I haven't had time—and it's not exactly as though I'm Delilah enticing Samson. There's also the monumental hurdle of my family ties."

"Few men want a Delilah. Look what happened to Samson. As for your family, I thought we'd settled that already. Frankly, I'm beginning to think you throw your parents up as a convenient barrier."

Rae quit straightening music and produced what she hoped was a sophisticated smile. "Caleb, it's all right. You're not going to hurt my vanity by keeping our relationship strictly professional. I know you and Detective Grabowski and Agent Ram—Rom . . . whatever his name is—"

"Ramirez. Tray Ramirez," Caleb provided patiently.

Rae waved an indifferent hand. "Ramirez. I know you all think I need a bodyguard."

"My interest is not," Caleb replied just as patiently, "merely professional." He subjected her to a lazy, masculine appraisal that flustered Rae completely.

"Caleb, you're embarrassing me," she blurted. She lifted her hands in a sweeping gesture. "Look at me—my hair's a mess because I never take time to have it cut and styled. My nose is too long, my face is too pale . . . and even after all the ballet lessons Uncle Floyd insisted I take I'm about as graceful as a goose. Tyler—that's my brother—he used to call me Spiderlegs."

"I imagine a stockbroker wouldn't have much of an imagination," Caleb murmured, moving to stand in front of her.

Rae froze. "How did you know my brother was a stockbroker?"

He hesitated, then leaned against the music bin, crossing his legs. "Part of the background check. It's been ongoing—I thought you realized."

"Why should I?" she flared. "Of all the sneaky—you could have at least warned me!" Outraged, hurt, she pushed by him. "I'm still a suspect, right? Because of my father! All along, you've been lying about believing me. You don't want to protect me at all—you just want to *spy* on me! See if I have a contact at—at *church.*"

It was always the same. Always. She should have known better, should have listened to her instincts. But Caleb was a far better actor than she'd realized, and stupidly she had trusted him. "It might even be the minister—or Jerry, the music director. I see him all the time, you know—don't *touch* me!" She darted around the bin when he reached for her. "If you think you can trot tamely off to church with me now—"

Caleb followed after her, the golden eyes intent, determined, and Rae realized with a pang that in cat-and-mouse dodging, she didn't stand a chance. Pride and temper gave her the impetus to stand her ground. "Just because I turn into a marshmallow with a touch doesn't mean you can bully me into—mmf—"

With dizzying swiftness his hands tugged her into his embrace, and his mouth came down on hers. As a first kiss, it was extremely thorough, and when Caleb lifted his mouth at last, all she could do was stare into the incandescent brightness of his eyes. Her brain had floated off somewhere in a soggy sea of sensation.

"I've been wanting to do that since the night I rescued you and you chastized me for not getting there sooner." His hands, those warm, clever-fingered hands, lifted and held her face in a tender cage. "You're beautiful where it counts, Rae—inside *and* out. I want you to start believing it. I also want you to believe that I'm not going to let anything or anyone defile what you are."

"You don't know me as well as you think," she whispered miserably. Her hands clung to his shoulders. He felt good—a strong, decent man—and the temptation to accept that strength was powerful because she was weak. Gullible and spineless—trapped in an endless circle. The sins of the fathers—and mothers, it seemed— were unavoidable. God's grace would have to wait for three more generations.

"Hmm . . . well I think I know you more than you think I know," Caleb teased her, nuzzling her nose. "Now pay attention." Her nose received a swift kiss. "I'm your bodyguard because I want to be. It would doubtless surprise you, but half a dozen cops and agents were all vying for the honor." He smiled into her eyes, finishing in quiet satisfaction, "I won."

Rae dropped her gaze to the top button of his chamois shirt. "You won," she echoed. "What you've won, I'm afraid, is a bucketload of trouble."

"Maybe so. But there's a few compensations." His head lowered again. "For instance . . . I need to practice being your significant other a little more in depth." He brushed his lips across hers, then took her mouth in a burning kiss.

If he practiced any better, Rae thought muzzily, she would melt into a puddle on the floor. He ended the kiss, but then his lips traveled all over her face with the softness of a snowflake. Rae wanted to cry from the sweetness of it. She was soaring, caught up in a kind of music she had only been able to create at the keyboard.

After a while, in a warm gust of laughter, Caleb murmured against her mouth, "Don't you think you better finish closing the store? We don't want to be late for choir practice."

Over the ensuing weeks, Caleb became her constant shadow. Rae eventually became accustomed not only to his presence, but the inevitable teasing and bantering they both endured at church. She tried to take each day as it came, tried to let go and let God control her destiny, tried to be a good Christian in the lion-strewn arena of life. Unfortunately, Caleb's attitude only exacerbated her situation. He played the part of attentive boyfriend with convincing realism, to the point that even Karen was won over. He treated Rae like a cherished possession, like a rare, original edition of music, but he was careful not to take advantage of her vulnerability. His kisses were the soul of discretion and respectability. He touched Rae frequently, but seldom with passion.

He was so careful with her that he was almost detached—an actor playing his part. In fact, sometimes he reminded Rae of a chameleon. With her, he was devoted, gently bullying and tactfully unobtrusive. When he talked with the FBI or the police, he slipped into the role of professional agent like feet into a pair of old slippers. Rae was constantly amazed at the level of deference accorded him, since he was assigned to the Starseeker case as a consultant. Probably it was because he seemed to know everything and everybody, from clerks to colonels. His contacts, Tray Ramirez told her once, were the envy of every consulting firm in the country.

In fact, Caleb Myers was . . . perfect. *Too* perfect, and Rae woke every morning wondering if this would be the day both shoes would fall, and his clay feet would be revealed. Just once, she found herself thinking as the days passed, just once she wished he'd lose that infernal self-confidence. That—that annoying *detachment*. Sometimes she wondered if anything every really touched him.

Was that an offshoot of his bone-deep faith—or did he really just not care about anything that deeply?

Rae struggled to emulate his unruffled demeanor. She was convinced that his behavior that day in the store—when he had held her and kissed her and promised her that he really *felt* something for her—had all been an act. So she acted to the hilt as well. Right now she needed someone like Caleb Myers to keep her body healthy, safe from harm. But her heart was her responsibility, and to that end she could remain as *detached* from her feelings as Mr. Myers.

Two weeks passed without incident, and the situation assumed the overtones of a game. Rae pretended she was an ignorant bystander who had never heard of IOS, whose only connection to the FBI was through television shows. The police were distant players, driving their blue and white units around the city streets, nabbing speeders and keeping innocent individuals like herself safe.

On her walks to and from Gibson Girl with Caleb she fell into the habit of surreptitiously trying to pick out which strolling individual had been assigned to tail her. Which car held Agent Ramirez's men. And, of course, who in the never-ending crowd that strolled Old Colorado City were the bad guys.

That was impossible. The gaping tourist with his camera could be an IOS thug. The thick, middle-aged man strolling with apparent enjoyment down the street could have placed an illegal wiretap on her phone. It could even be a woman. After two weeks, Rae was heartily sick of the whole game, and quit pretending that she enjoyed playing cops and robbers. Instead she channeled her energy and focused on her store, her students and her music. When she thought about it, occasionally she prayed for peace of mind.

Toward the end of April, Caleb had to fly to Chicago, then to D.C. He didn't explain why, and Rae didn't ask. While he was gone, on a bright springlike morning with the forsythias bursting in butter yellow blossoms, Agent Ramirez and an FBI agent she had never met came to the store.

"Rob." She put an apologetic hand on the shoulder of her favorite piano student. "I need to talk to these two gentlemen in private." She hesitated. Rob was a gifted, intelligent high school senior who had arranged his schedule to have morning lessons so he could work after school. He was more than capable of watching over Joyful Noise for a few minutes. "Would you mind staying in the store and taking care of any customers? I can't afford to leave it unguarded."

"No worries, Rae." Rob was determined to go to Australia one day. "Take your time." He glanced into the other room. "You're not in any trouble, are you? Those two dudes don't look exactly like they're dying to hear Beethoven or Bach."

"Everything's just ducky, mate," Rae responded, and Rob grinned at her, oblivious to her quaking knees and the icy knot building in the pit of her stomach.

She led the two men wearing their revolvers beneath their suit jackets to her parlor, and wanted to giggle at the incongruity of such alien creatures in the comfortable, cluttered, Victorian-looking room. "Would you like some iced tea, a soda?"

"No, thanks." Agent Ramirez did not smile at her like he usually did. The cola-brown eyes were somber, watchful.

Rae glanced at the other man. He was taller, lanky, with a hard face and lighter brown eyes flicking around the room. "Is something wrong?" she asked into the growing silence.

"Ms. Prescott," Agent Ramirez began without warning, "can you explain who is responsible for the monthly payments you've received in a Denver bank over the last three years?"

He might as well have accused her of *robbing* a Denver bank. "I'm sorry, but I don't have any idea what you're talking about. I don't have an account in a Denver bank. Monthly payments are being made, you say?" She surreptitiously wiped her damp palms on her slacks.

"That's right," the other man confirmed in a gravelly bass voice. "Fifteen hundred dollars a month, to be exact. Deposited in a checking account for Rae Meikleham Prescott."

"You have a nice little pile accumulated," Ramirez observed. "More than enough to negate all the claims you've made about lack of accessible cash."

Rae sank into the old overstuffed easy chair that had been Uncle Floyd's favorite. "I don't know about any money." She looked at her knees. The five-year-old nubby silk designer slacks had a snag. Her whole life had hit a snag. "I have no idea what account you're talking about," she repeated, and pressed her lips tightly together. For once, caution and shock kept her temper under control.

"Ms. Prescott, I know Caleb has warned you that IOS is a ruthless, amoral organization. If they've managed to trap you some way—blackmail, threats of physical violence—you're not going to be safe by keeping your mouth shut."

The tall man stepped to the chair, looming over her. "Are you aware of the possible penalties for committing crimes against the United States government?" he asked, each word setting off tiny explosions of panic deep inside Rae. "The Starseeker program out at Falcon is considered a prototype. The sabotage of it has made a lot of people very angry." He folded his arms across his chest. "How would you like to spend the rest of your life in a federal prison, Ms. Prescott?"

Jackson Overstreet sat back in his chair and crossed his legs. His heavy jowls and broad forehead gave him the look of an aging bulldog. Right now the lines creasing his face were deeper than normal. "You can't be sure you didn't blow your cover a month ago—and that's why the whole thing has bogged down, Cal." He paused, then added, "In all the years I've known you, you've never allowed emotions to get in the way of your investigations before. I appreciate the FBI calling you in, but I'm not too happy right now. Polaris stands to lose more than just money."

Caleb stood in front of Jackson's huge plate glass window, his gaze on the Chicago skyline, hands clasped behind his back. He turned to face Jack. "My emotions aren't getting in the way," he promised. "But I'm not going to apologize for my actions toward Rae Prescott. Top-secret investigation or not, I was not about to be a pharisaical witness to the assault and possible death of an innocent young woman." He watched a commercial jetliner climb until it disappeared in a cloud, then explained with careful neutrality, "And she is innocent, Jack. Tray and I discussed it from every angle. We both agreed that playing the part of boyfriend is a lot easier cover than having a plainclothesman tagging along after her—especially when she spends the bulk of her time in her store or in church, where high visibility is unavoidable. Unfortunately, that's the procedure when I'm not available, regardless of the risk. But on the whole, becoming Ms. Prescott's attentive escort seems to be working pretty well."

Jack's hands slammed on the desk. "Well, now isn't that convenient—that really makes me happy! What are you going to do when your pretended relationship ends up blinding you to the facts? In spite of your assertion, there's still a strong possibility that Ms. Prescott's as dirty as her old man."

Caleb eyed his friend calmly. "I'll continue to do the best job I can—regardless of the facts." He steepled his fingers, deliberately prolonging the pause. "I still don't think Rae's involved criminally, but trust me—even if she were, I can handle it. I want the truth as much as you do, Jack." A fleeting image of Rae crossed his mind, but he suppressed it. He had a job to do, a puzzle to solve, and he refused to cloud his thinking over a woman. Even Rae Prescott. Their separation this past week had been good for him, he decided, because it had given him a needed opportunity to retreat from the dangerous ground upon which he'd found himself.

Overstreet slumped, expelling his breath in a noisy gust. "All right, I was out of line," he admitted. "I know you only want to uncover the truth—it's as much a gospel with you as your religion."

"Faith in Christ isn't a religion, Jack," Caleb informed him with a smile. "And you're not going to get a rise out of me on that tired old chestnut, either."

Overstreet's mouth flickered in response. "I don't know why I keep trying. I guess this whole mess is getting to me more than I realized. But Cal, regardless of your feelings or lack of them for Ms. Prescott, her father's been on the FBI's wanted list for fifteen years. Now you tell me she's been having monthly deposits made in a Denver bank for the past three years, yet you *still* claim she's innocent. Sounds like emotions to me, pal—but then, I could be wrong."

Caleb idly toyed with his watchband. "Rae hasn't heard from her father since she was four. He deserted the wife, Rae and Rae's older brother, as well. I haven't learned all the details yet, but apparently Prescott and his wife were sixties hippies. That whole scene might be looked upon with indulgence nowadays, but I can understand Rae's reluctance to discuss her background." Wounded, wary gray eyes filled his mental vision, and he shook his head to banish the image. "I haven't confronted her about the money yet—Tray just called me this morning."

"It's a little too much to be circumstantial, Cal." Overstreet hesitated, then asked bluntly, "You say you can keep personal feelings out of it, and I believe you, since I've known you over fifteen years. But is there a chance you might have to take yourself off the case anyway? Every time you insist on her innocence in the face of the evidence, it weakens your—and consequently Polaris's—position."

"No." Caleb strolled over and dropped down in one of the leather chairs across from his friend. "I'm convinced the evidence is circumstantial. Rae Prescott is innocent, Jack, but my conviction is based on training and instinct, not emotion." Right then, he still believed it.

Jack wouldn't let it go. "I don't see how you—"

"Okay, let's try it from this angle. Over the past weeks I've gotten to know her, watch her on a daily basis. You've accepted that my Christian faith is real, so you'll have to take my word for this, as well. Rae's that kind of Christian, too, even if she's struggling with it a little right now. She's not one of the Sunday morning bench-warmer crowd—she lives her faith as best she can, which means there is no way she'd *intentionally* involve herself in something illegal."

Jack emitted a rude noise.

Caleb leaned to stare directly into the other man's skeptical eyes. "Jack, do you think *I* could be involved in illegal behavior of any kind?"

He waited, and after an uncomfortable pause Jack reluctantly conceded, "You're the most honest, ethical man I know, and I know you claim the quality of your life-style is because you're a Christian. That's why I backed down earlier. But—"

"Forget the buts. Rae is innocent, a pawn. I'm pretty sure her father is behind it, but his daughter needs our help—not harassment. Give me a little more time, okay? This case has more sides than a prism. I'm hoping to find out about Rae's father when I fly to Washington."

Overstreet picked up a gold pen and twirled it irritably. "All right, Cal. I won't beat the horse to death. Go on—get out of here. Keep me posted on what you find out in D.C." He shook his head. "And good luck in the Springs."

Chapter Twelve

Caleb stopped by his apartment long enough to check the mail and Sheba, who as usual was entrenched in the manager's apartment. Then he packed more clothes, flew to Washington and spent two days with a liaison agent poring over mountainous files at the FBI. He then flew to Colorado Springs, catching the first flight out to make a meeting with Tray, Admiral Vale and Archie Cohen, the civilian contractor from Polaris in charge at Falcon Air Force Station.

After checking into a new motel, he tossed on cords and a light-weight pullover, then drove to Joyful Noise. It was a little before five on a cool, windy Friday afternoon, and in spite of his resolve he realized he was eager to watch Rae's response to his return. Would she maintain the indulgent, distant pose she had adopted these past weeks? He had tolerated the pose mainly because he hadn't wanted her to feel any more trapped than she already did, though several times he'd been tempted to smash the barriers with another mind-blowing kiss.

On one hand, the depth of his feelings made him uncomfortable enough to realize he wasn't ready for what those physical demonstrations indicated. He liked his freedom, liked the lack of responsibility for another person. If he was honest with himself, he'd have to admit that his past unwillingness to invest emotional energy into any serious relationship with a woman was incredibly selfish. On the other hand, what woman wanted to share his nomadic life-style, never knowing where he might be working on any given day? For that matter, what woman would tolerate being totally ignored when he was deep into an interesting puzzle, which—according to his family—was one of Caleb's worst character flaws?

Whoa, there, Myers. Back up, fella. Just because she stuck in his mind like cat hairs stuck to navy slacks didn't mean he was ready for a long-term relationship. Besides, any man willing to take on Rae had to take on the burden of her guilt over her family, as well. The thought of Raymond Prescott was an unwelcome reminder, even though it allowed Caleb to direct his thoughts to more comfortable matters—his job. As he maneuvered through the heavy afternoon traffic, he replayed the conversation in the hall with Tray Ramirez after they'd left the admiral's office. It had not been pleasant, and Caleb was debating what to do when he pulled up in front of Rae's store.

Joyful Noise was closed, though it was twenty minutes before the scheduled closing time. Rae did not respond to his knocks, either on the store door or the back door.

As a child, Caleb had sometimes considered his photographic memory more curse than blessing. Now, sprinting down the street to a public phone in front of a convenience store, he fervently thanked God for the gift. Rapidly he fed in a quarter and punched out the number for the agents stationed across the street from Rae's house.

"This is Myers. What's up? The store is closed." Thankfully Rae had given permission for the FBI to put their own tap on her phone.

"She got a call about some old sheet music—Broadway show tunes, I think. The old lady was leaving town in the morning, so Ms. Prescott closed up early to pick up the stuff."

"Who went with her?"

"Two guys from the Springs intelligence unit are tailing her—she refused to wait for Chuck to go with her in her car. Said it would look too suspicious." Joe's voice plainly revealed what he thought about such gross stubbornness.

Caleb was not used to feeling fear for another person. "What was the address?" A metallic taste trickled down his throat, soured his clenched stomach. "When did she leave?"

The agent played the tape. A scratchy, quavering voice directed

Rae to a house in southwest Colorado Springs. Caleb told Joe he'd be in touch and to check with Grabowski. He borrowed a city map from the convenience store clerk, pinpointed the address and the route Rae would doubtless take.

"You need to buy it?" the clerk asked.

"No." He almost grinned. "I won't be needing it now."

Traffic was appalling—slow, irritating, noisy. Caleb forced himself to remain calm. Grabowski's men were tailing her, it was definitely an old lady's voice—*it wasn't a trap.*

Twenty minutes later he turned off a major thoroughfare onto a narrow two-lane street, his muscles relaxing a little when the traffic finally thinned. A few minutes later he turned onto the street where the elderly woman lived. Eighty-year-old trees lined cracked sidewalks and shaded the small but stately-looking older homes. Several cars were parked on either side, all of them older but well-kept mid-size sedans—except for Rae's mud-splattered hatchback parked halfway down the block. Caleb drove past, mouth softening briefly as his eye caught on the shiny black quarter note painted on the door.

He pulled into a driveway four houses down, then casually reversed into the street. Grabowski's men waited in a medium gray sedan, parked inconspicuously next to the drive where Caleb had turned around. They exchanged brief glances, then Caleb pulled to the curb and parked across the street from Rae's car. After turning off the engine he slouched in the seat, looking as if he might be settling for a catnap. His eyes, however, though almost closed, ceaselessly roamed the surroundings. Adrenaline had kicked his pulse rate into high alert.

Several minutes crawled by, and only two cars passed. Caleb noted the models and colors, then returned his gaze for another sweep of the house where Rae purportedly was visiting. Another car went by. Suddenly, Caleb twisted and glanced out the back window. Not two minutes earlier, that chocolate brown sedan had passed him traveling the other way.

Movement across the street jerked his head around. It was Rae, coming out of the house, her hands clutching a large manila envelope. She smiled at a short, tottering old lady, waved goodbye, then followed the slate path toward her car.

Down the street an engine revved.

Caleb shot out of his car and sprinted across the street even as the sedan hurtled toward Rae like a deadly avalanche. Rae fumbled obliviously with the envelope while she unlocked her door.

Tires squealed, and a hot wind buffeted his back as Caleb grabbed Rae around her waist and hurled both of them over the hood of her car. They knocked against the metal and tumbled in a tangle of limbs into the gutter. Tires squealed again as the car disappeared around the corner.

In the sudden silence, Caleb's ear caught the sound of running footsteps, and he rolled swiftly, shielding Rae with his body. The two plainclothesmen skidded to a halt, faces pale.

"Are you all right?" J.W. asked while MacArthur talked urgently into his radio.

Caleb nodded shortly and turned to Rae, who still clutched the manila envelope to her chest. The backs of her hands were scraped raw, oozing. Her pupils were dilated, her face blank with shock. Caleb swiftly checked for broken bones or a head injury, then lifted her in his arms. "It's all right, Rae," he murmured, carrying her to his car. J.W. opened the back door, and Caleb gently set her on the seat. He searched her face. "Can you tell me if you hurt anywhere? You've got some nasty scrapes on your hands."

She responded automatically, like a wind-up toy. "My knees and my right elbow sting. Probably just scraped, like my hands, and my hip aches." Her mouth curved in a pathetic imitation of a smile. "It wasn't an accident, was it? Guess I'm a popular punching bag for those guys." She stared from Caleb to J.W., back to Caleb. "It *was* IOS, wasn't it?" A shudder rippled over her body.

J.W. glanced at Caleb, cleared his throat. "Ms. Prescott, do you need medical treatment?"

"No. I'm okay. You're not going to tell me, right? Fine." She shoved Caleb, who was crouched at her feet in the open car door. "How nice to see you. Now go away. Thanks for another splendid rescue, Superman. Send me a bill."

Caleb studied her, trying to determine if her fractious temper was shock induced. "Rae, sit here a minute until you've recovered."

"I'm not hurt. I want to go home. I've got some music to catalog." She thrust the manila envelope in front of Caleb's nose.

"Broadway show tunes—classics. *South Pacific, Oklahoma.* They're all in the original covers. I hope they're okay."

She started to open the envelope, and Caleb covered her injured hands with one of his. "Rae—honey. Relax. You're safe now."

"You sure she didn't hit her head?"

Caleb tightened his hold on her hands, keeping her still. Her eyes were wide and strained, still staring blankly, but at least the pupils were evenly dilated. A smudge of dirt smeared one cheek, and some of the pins holding her braids on top of her head had fallen, allowing one of the braids to slip over her ear. "Hold still," he ordered. He released her hands, lifted his to her head. With careful fingers he probed beneath the heavy mass of hair, freeing more pins until the whole mass unraveled across his forearms.

"Now look what you've done," Rae snapped. "It takes *hours* to fix it right." She drew a shallow, quivering breath. Then, "Sorry. I'm all right, Caleb. Really. Just—give me a moment alone. Please."

Caleb stood and backed away. "Sure." He motioned to the detective and they walked to the front of the car. "I don't think she wants us to see her break down," he informed the puzzled man wryly. "In spite of her temper—or maybe *because* of it—she's got this obsession about staying in control, or at least appearing to the world as though she's always in control." He waited until Evan McArthur approached, his normally pleasant black face wearing an intimidating scowl. "Did you get the license number radioed in?"

"I could only make out the first three numbers," MacArthur grumbled in disgust.

"That's okay—I got it." Caleb ignored Evan's astonishment and reeled off the number. *So I memorized the number instantly. Big fat hairy deal.* There wasn't anything they could do about it right now.

Frustrated, still shaken from the encounter, he turned abruptly and slammed his palms against the hood of the car to vent some of his pent-up emotion. It was too much of a risk to pursue the car because neither the police nor the FBI could afford to blow their cover—especially when there was a good chance the incident had been designed to frighten, not kill, Rae. But how many times would the intent be to just frighten, if he kept charging to her rescue? The thought was not a pleasant one. Smoldering, he fought the urge to kick the tires, jamming his fists inside his pockets instead.

"I know how you feel, Myers," J.W. offered sympathetically. "This case is one big headache. We tail her for protection—but we can't follow up on a lead because we can't afford to let IOS know we're tailing her."

He clapped Caleb's back, glanced at his partner. "We better get back—don't need to risk being seen. You sure you can handle Ms. Prescott? She doesn't look so hot." He half-grinned. "Feisty when she's caught off guard, isn't she? I don't envy you the next couple of hours, when the shock wears off."

Caleb shoved his hands deeper in his pants pockets. "I can take care of Ms. Prescott."

The two agents loped down the street, and Caleb shook his head at his confidence. Probably more like arrogance . . . or perhaps pride? Slowly he returned to the other side of the car, wondering if he was about to learn one of the more humbling lessons of his life. Though her hands noticeably trembled, Rae was struggling to braid her hair. Her eyes had focused somewhere in the middle distance, while her lips moved in what Caleb realized was a desperate prayer.

"I need You to help me," he heard her whisper, and he stopped, not wanting to intrude. "Help me remember You've promised to stay with me . . . even when I don't feel You, and everyone else has walked away—*God!* I'm so alone. So . . . scared."

Before he could help himself, Caleb lifted her to her feet and gathered her in his arms, hugging her close. "How ya doing?" he inquired, as though he'd just arrived.

She stiffened. "I'm . . . okay. I think. At any rate, I'm not a child. I haven't asked, and I don't want your—your pity."

"Glad you haven't asked for pity, because I'm not offering any. As for this—" He cupped her shoulders and gave her a gentle shake. "I'm trying to comfort and reassure you, as any, ah, proper guardian angel would under similar circumstances." He dropped a light kiss on her brow. "Doesn't matter whether you're eight or twenty-eight or eighty. You had a rude shock—you need comfort, and so do I, for that matter. You know, if this keeps up, I'm going to have to petition the Lord for a *real* guardian angel to take up the slack." Good, Caleb thought. The light touch was working. He could feel the brittle tension easing, and she was relaxing in his undemanding embrace.

"I suppose rescuing me all the time would get pretty wearing." Suddenly, with an inarticulate little exclamation, she buried her head against his chest, and her hands lifted to clutch fistfuls of his shirt. "I'm sorry, Caleb. I—I'll be all right in a minute, but if you don't mind, hold me. Just . . . hold me, for a few moments."

He gathered her close, bending over her, rocking her while he murmured reassurances in her ear. His hands stroked her hair, her back. A wave of protective compassion so strong it almost knocked the wind out of him washed over him. It was not an entirely comfortable emotion, because though he had felt compassion for hurting souls any number of times in the course of his life, the feeling had never been coupled with physical desire. A desire that multiplied every time he was near her, and even when he was separated by a couple of thousand miles.

Face it, Myers. You're in big trouble. The lady didn't need that complication right now, and neither did he. What she *did* need was understanding and protection. But while he might be able to suppress the desire enough to provide the big-brother understanding she craved, it was humanly impossible for him to protect Rae twenty-four hours a day, regardless of all his skill and professional training.

Chapter Thirteen

"You're a right proper mess." Karen plonked a mug of chamomile tea in front of Rae. "But you say he only kissed your *palms* before he left?"

Rae wrapped her sore hands around the mug and carefully crossed her skinned knee over the unskinned one. Scabs were already forming on all the scraped areas, but between redness and the Merthiolate Caleb so liberally applied, she looked like a refugee from a Red Cross demonstration. There was a new bruise the size of Delaware on her hip.

It was a sunny morning, with balmy April breezes and a predicted high in the sixties. But the hot mug of tea was exactly what Rae needed, and Karen knew it. What she didn't need was Karen's irritating one-track mind. "Karen, do you ever think of anything else? Caleb has a job to do, and just because . . . ."

"Yes?" Karen drawled, one eyebrow raised and her hand resting knowingly on her hip. "Just because the last six weeks or so he's stuck closer to you than eggs on a hot sidewalk, and just because he can't keep from touching you as though you're one of your precious pieces of antique china—even if last night all he did was kiss your hands . . . you're going to tell me his behavior is all in the line of duty?"

She dropped down across from Rae, propping her chin in her hands. "Honey, take it from an old pro. The pair of ya'll have it bad, even if neither one of you wants to admit it. And while Caleb Myers might not be the first guy you'd pick out of a crowd of available men, he's got—" she frowned, then shrugged "—presence is the word that comes to mind. Sort of a quiet power, like a sleeping lion."

Rae sipped her tea and avoided meeting Karen's eloquent gaze. "I'd hate to be around when he got awakened," she muttered, thinking of the expression on Caleb's face when he'd left her the previous night. She sighed, pushed the mug aside and rose. "I better get to the store. It's almost nine."

"How long are you going to ignore what you feel, Rae?"

"Karen, I accepted years ago not to trust my feelings when it comes to men. Yes, I know my rationale is wrong, but this isn't the time—or the man—to try and change for. Eventually, please God, this—this nightmare will be over, but do you honestly think Caleb will stick around? No—don't give me that look. You know I'm right, so be my friend? Let it go. Right now it's the only way I can keep my sanity. I've been mugged, threatened, almost run down—and the authorities suspect me of everything from conspiracy to fraud to sabotage. If I start brooding over Caleb's personal feelings for me and mine for him, I don't think I'd be able to stay in control."

"Great. Lose control. It'd be good for you. You're not your mother, Rae. Even if you threw a teapot across the room, you wouldn't be your mother."

"See you later, Karen. Thanks for the tea."

"I thought you were supposed to let *God* be in control," Karen yelled after her as she started down the steps.

Rae stiffened, hesitated, then kept walking. "He takes care of the big things," she called over her shoulder. "I take care of my life."

She opened the store, her mood subdued, pensive. Karen's words bothered her, even rankled a little. Ever since she was a child, she had determined the course of her life. Never again did she plan to feel the yawning helplessness, the frightening uncertainty that had scarred her early years. A quiet joy and a measure of peace had gradually healed her soul after she accepted Christ as her Savior and adopted His life for the role model she'd never known.

But then Caleb Myers, IOS and the Starseeker case erupted in her life.

Quit brooding, and apply your energy to work. Some things she could change—some she couldn't. One of these years perhaps she'd attain the wisdom to know the difference between them. Until then . . . she checked all the music, dusted the shelves and her treasures and tried to pretend everything was normal. When the bell tinkled thirty minutes later, she looked up from the counter in relief at the young woman with a mop of short blond curls capping her head. "Good morning. How can I help you?"

The young woman smiled brightly, practically bouncing over to the counter. Though at least in her mid-twenties, her manner more resembled an effervescent teenager's. "This is the most awesome store! I heard about it from a friend." She propped her elbows on the countertop, confiding with engaging candor, "Everyone at my church keeps begging me to do a miniconcert, and my friend Elaine promised me you have the best selection of contemporary Christian music in the Springs. So—" she waved her arm "—I need at least half a dozen songs—I've got some, but I'd like to try some new stuff. I'll need the soundtracks, too. You do carry those, don't you? Say, what happened to your hands?"

"I scraped them." Rae came around the counter and headed for the appropriate room. "All the music you'll need will be in here. Why don't you tell me some of the songs you've done, and we'll take it from there?"

A pleasant half hour went by, with a satisfactory pile of sheet music accumulating. Occasionally the customer's attention strayed, her eyes darting around the store as she asked friendly questions. How long had Rae lived there? What was her training? Why didn't she want to move?

Eventually the inquisitive, talkative young woman decided she had enough music. Rae gathered everything up, then tallied the total and waited while the girl rummaged in her purse for the money. "That's a lovely necklace you're wearing," Rae commented. "Very unusual." A fleeting memory surfaced, and she frowned, struggling to capture it. "Are you sure you've never been in here before? For some reason, your necklace looks familiar."

The young woman's hand flew to the necklace, then dropped. "No," she answered, laughing what sounded to Rae a bright, false laugh. "But I'm sure you'll remember me after today, won't you? How many customers buy as much music as I have?" She laughed again, but the eyes watching Rae were narrow, almost calculating, at odds with the throwaway comment.

Rae took the proffered bills and busied herself at the cash register. "Actually, I'm not too good with faces," she confessed, handing back some change. "But your necklace *is* unusual—I haven't seen one like that. Or at least—"

"I have to be going. Thanks for your help." The young woman scooped up the music and walked swiftly out.

Rae shook her head, furious with the serious character flaw she couldn't seem to help, especially now when she needed to be remembering every little detail about people. Detective Grabowski had not been able to hide his frustration and impatience with her lack of observation skills, and even Caleb teased her. Grumbling to herself, she walked to the religious section to straighten the music. Maybe she should enroll in detective school or something. Not only could she better help with the Starseeker case—she could *definitely* improve her customer relations.

She paused, examining her scraped hands. On the other hand, maybe her lack of awareness was the only reason she was nursing a few scrapes instead of lying in the morgue. Sighing, Rae went back to the counter and picked up the phone to call Karen and share the wonderful news of her eighty-seven-dollar sale. She'd also call Jerry at church and chat with him awhile. If nothing else, she could bore IOS to death forcing them to listen to her decidedly nonintriguing conversations.

What she would *not* do was think about her relationship with Caleb.

Caleb pulled up in front of the FBI field office in the Springs, where he had arranged to have a meeting with Tray. He was restless today, his internal radar sending out disquieting signals, and a few minutes later he found out why.

"It's not looking so hot for Ms. Prescott," Tray greeted him bluntly. He indicated a report on his desk, and Caleb picked it up, memorizing the contents while Tray talked. "As you see, Fisher's had two deposits of twenty-five thousand dollars in the past two months—and the same amount has been withdrawn from the checking account in Denver Ms. Prescott claims she knows nothing about."

"I'll ask her about it when I see her later, but I'm not going to push." Caleb stared at the other man. "Cut her some slack, Tray. You and your people have been riding her pretty hard lately."

"I understand how you feel, Myers, but the account *is* in her name." The phone buzzed, and the FBI agent snatched it up, spoke briefly, then hung up. He studied Caleb thoughtfully. "Let's discuss Fisher a few minutes, since Rae Prescott is such a touchy issue."

Caleb dropped into a chair. He'd just as soon not discuss Rae out loud, either, but if Tray thought the issue of her innocence had been settled, the man was in for a rude awakening. "Suits me. What in particular?" He tugged on the lock of hair falling over his forehead while he listened to Tray.

"You're more familiar with computers and computer personality types. Why would Fisher jeopardize his career, get involved with IOS? His record's clean, and his personal life sounds positively dull. Married out of college, divorced three years later. No discernible relationships since. Friends and colleagues think he's your average quiet, retiring-type guy. Nobody's ever labeled him a troublemaker. So why get involved with a vicious gang of traitors?"

Caleb relaxed in the chair, stretching out his legs. "Any number of reasons," he mused, eyeing the ceiling while Fisher's nondescript features floated across his mind's eye. "In Fisher's case, my guess is that it goes beyond money, although that probably figures in it, as well."

"Doesn't it always?"

"It's almost a cliché, isn't it?" Caleb agreed. "Even Aldrich Ames sold his country and countless lives down the river, for love of money." He exchanged world-weary looks with the FBI agent. "Anyway—you've seen Fisher. Unassuming, balding, slight. The antithesis of the Hollywood hunk. I read an article on computer viruses and their perpetrators years ago when viruses first started appearing. At the time, the author theorized about a pattern of personalities he dubbed the 'nerd syndrome.' Granted, the entire industrial world has gone so computer-obsessed that article's probably not viable for the most part. On the other hand, Fisher's history fits the pattern, particularly concerning the poor social integration skills—he had few friends all through school, spent all his spare time with computers."

Tray leaned back, hands over his head. "I got labeled as a Latino troublemaker when I was in high school." He looked at Caleb. "But I didn't turn into a statistic. Maybe Fisher had a lousy childhood—and I'm sorry. But even a self-styled geek can overcome the label."

"People have different breaking points," Caleb murmured. "Cruel name-calling may not break bones, but it has been known to break spirits." He shrugged. "I'm not condoning him, Tray—just trying to walk a mile in his moccasins, so to speak, to better find a way to run him down. Strikes me that he could have devised a virus program as a simple prank that deteriorated to the sabotage. I've cross-checked all Fisher's records, though. Like you say, there's no history of aberrant or malicious behavior." He paused, finishing quietly, "We'll just have to keep digging. I'm as convinced Fisher is involved as I'm convinced Rae Prescott is not. I don't think, however, that Fisher has the personality or profile to mark him as the man in charge."

"What about Ray Prescott, Rae's father?" Tray queried, riffling through some files. He tugged one out and scanned it briefly. "He's definitely got the criminal mind, though his profile doesn't fit an IOS exec. And this name business. Why didn't he name the *son* Ray, Junior?"

"I've had the same question myself," Caleb admitted. "When I put it to Rae, she told me she thought it had to do with the parents' general rebellion against all tradition. Instead of the oldest son, they named the youngest daughter after the father." The two men exchanged looks.

"Makes sense, in a crazy kind of way," Tray said. His fingers fiddled with a paper clip. "There's still something we're missing here, Myers—and a lot of us are convinced it's Ms. Prescott."

"Then a lot of you are wrong."

There was a short, crackling silence, then Ramirez threw up his hands. "I *know* she's the stereotypical picture of innocence. I *know* she's gone out of her way to cooperate." He leveled a piercing look at Caleb. "And I know your emotions have gotten involved. The only reason I haven't demanded that you be thrown off the case is the strength of your reputation. Your objectivity in a case is a byword from here to D.C."

"Thanks. Then perhaps you'll bear that in mind when I continue to reject her willing involvement with IOS? How long since the

Denver guys checked on the signature or signatures that can authorize the withdrawal of deposits from Rae's account?"

"They should get back to me by this afternoon. Dennis Hoffman's our liaison. He's supposed to contact me."

"I'd appreciate the update. I'm heading out to Falcon now to talk with Archie Cohen again. They're still trying to track the virus and how it made it to the mainframe, and I promised to see what I could do. It'll probably take several hours. If I'm not at Joyful Noise or my motel room later, just leave a message with the agents staking out the store."

"It would help if you wore a beeper all the time."

"I'm not a trained pug waiting quietly for the summons of my electronic leash, pal." He rose and headed for the door. "That's one of the reasons I'm content being an independent consultant."

Behind him, Ramirez laughed and called him a rude name. Caleb was almost in the hall when the other man called him back. Caleb suppressed a sigh and retraced his steps.

"What makes you so sure the Prescott woman is innocent?" Tray asked. "I need to write something in my report, and I'd like it to make more sense than Myers's gut instincts." His voice was conciliatory, genuinely curious.

Caleb's hand went to the lock of hair while he tried to decide whether or not to give Tray a pat answer—or the unvarnished truth. He settled on the latter. "Because I can see all the way into her soul when I look in her eyes. She doesn't have the right kind of defenses for a criminal, Tray. She hasn't needed to cultivate any, considering the kind of life she leads."

"Just because she's religious and runs a music store doesn't make her incapable of treachery."

"I'd agree with you if Rae was merely religious," Caleb retorted very softly. "But she's not. She's a Christian." His gaze bore into the confused eyes of the agent. "Think about it, Tray. And while you're at it, think about this. If any of your guys relax their guard, and Rae suffers because of it—I'll be on your back faster than a bolt of chain lightning."

He closed the door with ominous gentleness.

Chapter Fourteen

Rae was sipping tea and reading a how-to book on basic self-defense when Caleb arrived. She waited until he rang the bell and knocked in the distinctive pattern they had devised, then scurried down the short hall to let him in.

"A month ago I would have felt silly taking these elaborate precautions," she confessed as they walked to the kitchen. *Did he know about the bank account?* Caleb gave her one of his looks—the one where his smile lurked somewhere in the backs of those amber eyes, his mouth would soften and one corner tilt. The look that turned her knees and her brain to mush. Rae busied herself by fixing him a glass of lemonade.

"Precautions are never silly, especially in today's world. Sometimes survival—especially for a woman—can depend on a little bit of street smarts." He came up behind her, and his hand brushed lightly over her cheek. "How are you doing? Did all your students and customers make a fuss over your latest battle wounds?"

Rae rolled her eyes, her smile barely forced. "Two students insisted I should be in bed, probably because neither one of them had practiced. Most of the customers were either too polite to say anything, or they didn't care. Karen, on the other hand . . ."

"I don't think I want to hear what Karen had to say," Caleb answered. "She probably thinks we ought to call out the National Guard and have them trail you in perfect formation."

"That about sums it up." Except for her pointed remarks about the nonstatus of hers and Caleb's relationship, Rae added to herself. No way she would bring that up, however. She led the way to the parlor.

"What have you been reading?" He wandered over to Uncle Floyd's chair and picked up the book she had been reading. "Sweetheart, it's impossible to learn adequate self-defense from a book."

"I'm quite aware of that," Rae retorted, her face heating. He knew every trick. Toss out a patronizing comment, but soften it with a glib endearment. Softhead that she was, she knew—and responded anyway. *When was he going to mention that account?* "I'm trying to cultivate my—what was it you said? My street smarts. Beside, it's better than feeling like a sitting duck all the time." She took a sip of lukewarm tea, grimacing, trying to figure out his strange mood. He was, if possible, more enigmatic than usual, and with inward trepidation Rae decided to probe. "Have you found out anything new, Caleb? That you can share with me?"

He sat on the couch and patted the cushion beside him, but Rae sank in the chair, her hands tense on the mug. All the indulgent warmth had fled from his face. "You do know something, don't you? Is it about my father? Or—or something else?"

Caleb took his time responding, propping his elbows on his knees and resting his chin on the palm of his hand. "Rae, will you tell me more about your childhood? There has to be more than you've shared with me, especially concerning your parents, but every time the subject comes up, you shut down like a computer given the control-alt-delete command." The intelligence and gentleness in the amber eyes all but destroyed her crumbling defenses. "Actually . . . I like that analogy of you better than an earlier one I entertained." A corner of his mouth curled up. "You're so determined to stay in control by deleting your past and altering your present circumstances—yet what you've ended up with is a blank screen."

Rae focused on Caleb's fingers. "I don't discuss my past because it *is* irrelevant to the person I am now. It's also very painful, as I've told you before."

"The last thing I want to do," Caleb said, "is to cause you more pain. But, Rae . . . your father *is* involved with IOS. Regardless of whether or not your own involvement in the Starseeker case is incidental or planned, you're still pivotal to the investigation. It would help us both if you'd be more honest and open with me about your memories of him."

She should have known. "I am not a criminal!" Rae sputtered, the sting of betrayal burning deep. "I thought, until now, that you believed me. Believed that my father's illegal activities don't make me a criminal, too. All these weeks—" She surged to her feet. "It's that stupid account, isn't it? Agent Ramirez told you about that account, and now you think—you're trying to maneuver me into admitting—"

She had to stop before her voice broke and betrayed the depth of her hurt. She had learned by the time she was four years old that men were an undependable lot of self-serving egotists, but Caleb had started to change her way of thinking. Until this moment. She couldn't believe she'd been so blind.

You can't depend on anyone, even someone who calls himself a Christian. This must be what Jesus meant when he said that everyone who followed Him would be betrayed, by family and friends . . . by the world. Sometimes she wondered why she continued to put her faith in a God who always seemed to demand more of her than she was capable of giving.

Caleb had risen, as well, coming across to put his hands on her shoulders. "You misunderstood me," he started to say, but Rae pulled free.

"All these weeks, leading me on, treating me like—like I was someone special. Or at least as though I were a decent citizen trapped by circumstances beyond my control." She raked him head to foot in a blistering glare. "But I'm not decent, am I? Why haven't you told the police to go ahead and put me behind bars already, seeing what a dangerous felon you've uncovered with your brilliant mind?"

Caleb stuffed his hands in the back pockets of his wheat-colored jeans and pretended an absorption in the photographs on the table. "Actually, I think your temper is far more dangerous than your nefarious tendencies," he mused. "Especially when you jump to conclusions." His eyes focused on Rae, and their intensity burned a molten gold path into her soul. "I believe you when you say you don't know anything about that bank account, Rae."

Without warning his arms hauled her into a close embrace with such lazy but bewildering speed Rae didn't have time to struggle. One of his hands wrapped around the braid spilling down her back, and he tugged her head until her face was lifted to his. What she saw, flickering deep in the burning brightness of his eyes, flummoxed her completely. Too late, she realized that her wayward tongue had finally stung the sleeping lion one too many times.

"I believe in your innocence totally, little termagant," he breathed, his mouth hovering just above hers. "And I'm spending every hour I'm not with you trying to establish it beyond doubt with everyone else."

"Caleb—"

"But you're going to have to trust me, both as a man—and as a Christian." His grip tightened, and he held her a little way away. "If I can see Christ's love shining out of your eyes, won't you try to see the same thing in mine?" His thumbs began rotating around her shoulders, a caressing motion that threatened to make her knees buckle.

Rae swallowed, dizzy with the sensations bombarding her senses. "I . . . I can't see anything when you hold me like this," she muttered, dazed. Then, with a helpless laugh over her absurd confession, she surrendered, relaxing to rest quietly against his chest. "You don't play fair, Mr. Myers."

A reciprocal chuckle floated past her ear. "How so, Ms. Prescott?" His hand released her braid to cup her cheek, the fingers pressing with restrained tenderness.

Rae took a shallow breath. "I've never known a man like you." Her fingers, graceful only at the piano, lifted to hesitantly touch his hard cheekbone. "Do you really believe that I'm innocent, Caleb?"

She watched the tiny laugh lines at the corners of his eyes deepen. "So much that I put my career on the line over it," he admitted cheerfully, balling his hand to chuck her gently under the chin before he dropped a swift kiss on the end of her nose. In spite of his casual playfulness, Rae felt prickles of heat blossom from her flushed cheeks all the way down to her toes.

"Why?" she asked, unable to hold back the raw vulnerability. "Why would you risk your career for someone like me?"

The teasing laughter faded as he continued to study her upturned face with a solemn intensity. "I've asked myself that question a lot lately," he replied thoughtfully. With almost absentminded gentleness he began stroking fallen wisps of hair from her face. "There's something about you. . . . I feel you pushing me away with one hand—but reaching out with the other. I see the evidence of your faith in the way you've chosen to live, in your inner strength . . . yet I sense a fear, almost as if you're afraid to even trust God to take care of you."

Abruptly he dropped his hands, sat down and took a long swallow of lemonade, then stared into the glass as if memorizing the position of the ice cubes. "To be honest—and I think I've confessed this before—what I feel for you is pretty uncomfortable. But every time I decide to ignore it or push it aside, the feelings just comes back stronger. It's almost as though God keeps using the circumstances to throw us together."

He took a hefty slug of lemonade, then lifted his gaze to capture hers in a look as potent as a touch. "Too much honesty, Rae? We've been playing a game, you and I, these past weeks—me as bodyguard pretending to be boyfriend, you as independent woman indulging the paranoid authorities. Don't you think it's time we faced a few home truths?"

Rae flopped down on the couch next to him. "I suppose," she agreed, though her pulse was racing and every instinct screamed that she was walking into a trap with no escape. "It's silly for me to deny that, physically, I'm pretty much helpless against you, on all levels. All you have to do is touch me." *Rae Prescott, how could you be so stupid, arming him with that kind of ammunition? God? Can You ever forgive me for being so weak? I'm not my mother . . .*

"It's nothing to be ashamed of," Caleb said, his voice gentle. "Physical attraction isn't the sin, Rae. Giving in to it without God's blessing is where most of us run amok. You and I haven't done anything that the Lord would find offensive."

"Caleb, I—" she gestured awkwardly with her hand and knocked the glass of lemonade off the end table where Caleb had put it. For a suspended moment she stared at the spreading puddle. "I don't believe I just did that—yes, I do. I'm certifiable. Absolutely, unequivocably certifiable."

The muttered self-abasement continued while she scuttled to the kitchen and cleaned up the mess. Caleb wisely stayed out of the way, keeping his mouth shut. But at least the mishap accomplished what, in a moment of brutal self-analysis, could only be termed a

Freudian slip. By the time she returned to the parlor, Rae was in control, having successfully throttled the compulsion to confess any further secrets of her soul.

"Yes, I'm feeling pretty mixed up myself," she agreed. "The way I respond to you is doubtless no more than propinquity—or a variation of the white-knight syndrome. Doubtless I'd react that way to *any* man who repeatedly rescued me."

"Doubtless," Caleb intoned, steepling his fingers.

He looked unruffled, relaxed, practically asleep . . . except Rae made the mistake of looking directly into his eyes. Hastily she dropped her gaze. "Never mind. Let's go back to your belief in my innocence. Since you claim to be the only one who thinks I'm *not* part of the whole conspiracy, is the reason for the elaborate setup across the street merely for my protection? Or are your FBI cronies—not to mention the local police—hoping to catch me passing government secrets?" It was a colossal mistake to bait Caleb in this mood, but she had already lost any leverage she might have retained by keeping her mouth shut. "I'll be passing them along to my father, of course, who plans to sell them to the highest enemy foreign government willing to pay for the technology."

"I think we're back to square one," Caleb growled, leaning forward. "Listen to me, and try to take this at face value. Half the reason everyone is so suspicious of you is because of your adamant refusal to talk about your past."

"That's a lot of hogwash," Rae snapped. "Why don't *you* level with *me* for a change? My guilty fate is sealed because of a bank account of which I knew nothing."

Caleb groaned. "All right. All right! I'll level with you. The bank account is a major hurdle, and it's higher than ever, because we just discovered that over the past two months our chief suspect has had two large deposits into one of *his* accounts—with corresponding withdrawals from the checking account opened in your name."

"What?" Rae gasped. A slap in the face would have been less of a blow. "Caleb . . ." Her voice hoarsened. "I have no idea how that account came to be established. Please—you have to believe me. . . ." *It wasn't fair . . . Lord? This isn't fair.*

"I know." The words might have been reassuring, but as always Caleb's focus was unalterable. "And I'm sorry I had to tell you. Can you see how I'm scrabbling for leads? *Any* details you could remember about your father could help, no matter how insignificant they may seem on the surface—no matter how painful an exercise the process may be. A name, a place . . . anything." He waited until she met his gaze. "Rae, help me. Together we can prove your innocence."

"I thought I was innocent until proven guilty." Her fingers played jerkily over the tabletop she'd just cleaned. "I wonder if this is how Jesus used to feel. Everyone kept trying to frame Him, too."

"He also promised the truth would set you free. Yes, it's my opinion that IOS is framing you, but unfortunately that's all I have at the moment—an opinion. And in spite of appearances nowadays, our country's legal system occasionally still tries to operate through the venue of substantiated facts instead of the court of public opinion that crucified Jesus. On the other hand, human nature hasn't changed much in the last two thousand years. So . . . I need your help. Before something worse happens to you than being framed."

Beneath his quiet voice the discordant note of cynicism jarred her ears even as she felt an answering chord resound in her heart. Rae searched his grim face, feeling the bitterness, the despair well up and spill between them in a dark, ugly tide. "I know all about human nature," she finally responded. "Which means that, when IOS succeeds, all your cronies will finally agree that I really was an innocent pawn. They might even be sorry that I had to die to prove it. Maybe I should start planning my funeral now—draw up a list of the songs I'd like played."

Caleb's face lightened, and he slouched in the seat, a slow smile gradually replacing the grimness. "Don't be so melodramatic. Granted, you and your store are being watched for both reasons. We're pretty certain Joyful Noise is being used as a drop. When we figure out how, we ought to be able to pin some concrete evidence on the parties involved." The slow grin turned sheepish. "Should I have said 'substantiated facts,' for consistency?" He shook his head. "Everyone involved really is out to ensure your safety, Rae. But right now, the only avenue open is the one that seems to point to your guilt."

"That's very comforting. In the meantime I just sit around waiting for the next abduction, or a firebomb to be tossed through the window." His quiet confidence irrationally irritated her. Rae stood, her temper flaring because Caleb could sit there looking as laid-back as a cat in sunshine. "I don't like this, Caleb. I need to *do* something, not just sit around feeling helpless, exposed. Staked out like a tethered goat."

"I know. We're working around the clock on it."

"Work faster."

He snagged one of her arms and unhurriedly forced her to sit beside him. "We have a suspect, and it isn't you, so stuff a sock in it, Ms. Prescott." His finger pressed against her lips, then trailed up to tease a wayward strand of hair. "But the situation is actually similar to the one we face with you. We have a lot of hypotheses but still haven't established motive, method or the others involved. All that takes time. Months, but other suspects are also innocent until proven guilty, too, regardless of what our instincts—make that *my* instincts—are screaming."

His arm came around her shoulders. He hugged her to the warmth of his body, and Rae was unable to resist the craven need to sink into the calm and comfort he offered. It felt so good to be held. "I know," she admitted after a long moment of silence. "It's just that . . . I hate feeling like a coward, hate being afraid. And . . . well, I get angry with myself for not being able to claim all the promises God made to take care of us."

His embrace tightened. "I know."

She bit her lip. "I detest feeling so out of control, so unable to do anything concrete."

"I understand *exactly* how you feel."

Rae swiveled her head, puzzled by the nuance of fear she'd heard in that terse acknowledgment.

Caleb feathered a kiss across her forehead. "When I ran across the street yesterday and hurled us both in the gutter," he whispered against her temple, "I came as close to panic as I have in years." She felt his chest expand as he took a deep breath. "Maybe I *should* have trained as an agent instead of specializing in computer sabotage. I'd know more of the tricks of the trade of self-defense. Trouble is, I've also had to face the fact that I can't be here twenty-four hours a day to watch over you, keep you safe."

A lump grew in Rae's throat, and her eyes began to burn. Nobody in her entire life had ever offered to protect her. Abandoned by her father, forsaken by her mother. Pampered by Uncle Floyd out of guilt and pity. Tolerated by her brother, Tyler. Even long and enduring friendships had not offered the promise implied in Caleb's low-voiced confession. Rae tried to speak but couldn't find the words, so she slid both arms around his waist and hugged him.

"I guess," Caleb concluded softly after a while, "that we *both* better start leaning a little more on some of God's promises, hadn't we?"

Chapter Fifteen

Two days later a handwritten note from Caleb was in Rae's mail. *"No time to stop by, and you know I couldn't call. I have a lead on your father, and am flying to Calif. to follow up on it. Be careful, and keep your chin up. P.S. Read Psalm 32:7. Caleb."*

Rae's instinctive response was panic, followed in dizzying procession by resentment, humiliation, anger and—by the end of the day—resignation. For weeks she'd been fighting an internal battle between her heart and her head. For the second time in her life, her head lost. The first time, she had renounced a career as a concert pianist for the sake of the only salvageable part of her heritage. This time, she was falling in love, and she knew the consequences would prove to be far more cataclysmic.

Fortunately, the needs of her customers that day required little thought. Nobody seemed to notice or care about Rae's distracted air. A little before closing time, the bell jangled and the nervous little man who collected old sheet music scuttled crablike to the desk. For some reason—probably because she was already on edge—the man's diffidence rankled today. Rae dredged up a smile. "Hello."

His mouth twitched upward briefly. "I know it's late, but I was wondering if you'd let me rummage a few minutes." He glanced at his watch. "You close at five-thirty? That gives me about ten minutes."

Rae stifled the urge to tell him to try one of the chain stores at the mall if he wanted to poke about. "Were you looking for anything in particular?"

"Ah, not really—I mean, of course I'm always . . . Clementi," he stammered. "I'm looking for Clementi's . . . one of his piano sonatas." He avoided Rae's eye, and his wandering gaze fell across Caleb's note, lying beside the ledger.

Rae followed his glance. Before she could control it, her hand snatched it up, crumpling the stiff paper into a ball. To the casual observer, the note was perhaps intriguing. It certainly hadn't revealed Caleb's identity outside his oblique reference to a lead. All the same, she shouldn't have left it lying about. "Go ahead and look around," she muttered. "I'll finish some work here."

"Thanks." He looked from her clenched hand holding the wadded paper to her temper-heated face. "Problems?" he probed hesitantly.

"No, no. I'm just, uh, out of sorts today." She waved an irritable hand toward the classical room. "You better rummage if you're going to." Mr. Fowler—no, Fisher, he'd told her some weeks back, Rae finally remembered—scuttled off. She remembered his name because of the crablike way he walked. Crab, ocean, fish, Fisher. *Snap out of it, Rae.*

She tried to concentrate on the ledger, but Mr. Fisher kept darting her concerned glances, and Rae made three mistakes in as many minutes before she threw the pencil down. Between Caleb's disturbing note, Mr. Fisher's uncharacteristic interest in it and her uncomfortable revelation earlier, she was about as efficient as a piano missing half its keys. She picked up the offending note, glaring at it. In a wild fit of frustration, she ripped it into tiny pieces.

"Why are you tearing it up? What on earth made you so upset?"

Rae's head snapped up with a jerk. Mr. Fisher had come to the desk and was staring at her with a peculiar expression.

"It was a note. A *personal* note. It made me a little, ah, upset." She swept the minuscule scraps into her palm and dropped them with a flourish in the wastebasket. "Did you find any music you wanted?"

His gaze whipped from the trash to her face. He turned toward the classical music room, then abruptly stopped and looked back at her. "Not today," he replied, his voice as sharp and wary as Rae's.

Mr. Fisher's curiosity might be intrusive, but her behavior

toward a customer was inexcusable. Rae bit her lip hard, then mentally ran through a half-dozen key signatures on the piano. "I'm sorry, Mr. Fisher," she said, her voice contrite. "I shouldn't have snapped at you. I've had a difficult day. But I had no right to take it out on someone interested enough to inquire."

"That's okay." He backed away, his glance moving almost furtively around the store.

Rae frowned. "Mr. Fisher? I really am sorry. Listen, I'm expecting a shipment of music from a store in Aurora that went out of business . . ."

"Um, yes. Well . . . I'll be back." He wiped his forehead, then scuttled out the door.

Restless and keyed up after a lonely supper, Rae decided to run errands. She carefully bolted and locked the back door, resisting the urge to wave at whomever was on duty in the upper level of her detached garage. That novelty had worn thin long ago, but tonight for some reason a dart of fear tickled her back, like skeleton fingers tiptoeing down her spine. She was always watched, never truly alone, and the knowledge taxed already painfully stretched nerves. Her skin crawled every time she left the house. It wasn't just the good guys wearing white hats watching her. Lurking somewhere in the darkness, IOS eyes watched as well.

She turned the car radio to the Christian station she listened to, reminding herself that God always had His eye trained upon her, too. Just as unseen, more often than not even unfelt—but nonetheless there. With sudden resolution, Rae changed lanes, then turned and headed for church. What she needed right now was music, not mindless errand running.

For several hours she played, working on the synthesizer, trying different blends, layering and relayering until she found combinations she liked. Then she moved to the piano, where she practiced for the coming Sunday's music for an hour. By nine o'clock she was tired enough for the last dregs of guilt over her outburst with Mr. Fisher to have dwindled, along with the nagging sense of uneasiness about Caleb's note.

Refreshed, she closed everything up, turned off all the lights, then set the church's alarm system. After she pulled the outside door closed, she lifted the key to turn the lock, which would activate the alarm.

Two men stepped forward out of the shadows.

"Ms. Prescott?"

Rae gasped, choking back a half-scream before it occurred to her that they must be the men assigned to follow her when Caleb wasn't available. "You nearly scared me to death!" she began, and stopped. Both the local police and the FBI were under orders not to approach her in any manner outside of a lifesaving gesture. She clutched the key in her hand, calculating furiously. First she'd have to lock the door, then *unlock* it. The alarm would sound within fifteen seconds if she didn't enter the code.

"If you're planning to rob me, I may as well warn you that I have little cash and no credit cards. If you're going to assault me—I can scream a high C and pierce your eardrums." Her tongue felt thick, unwieldy, and her pulse was racing, but she kept her voice light, almost indifferent. "Well?"

There was a split-second pause before the taller of the two men answered. "Feeling feisty, are we, Ms. Prescott? What a surprise, considering the boyfriend's out of town." His hand moved suddenly, lifting a flashlight and shining it directly in Rae's face. "All the bruises are gone. Maybe it's time to acquire some new ones?"

The other man, short and wide as a bulldozer, crowded Rae away from the door toward a dark corner the outside lighting failed to reach. So much for her grand plan to set off the alarm. A nauseating odor of sweat, cigar smoke and peppermint swirled up Rae's nostrils.

"What do you want?" she demanded, trying to shield her eyes from the flashlight.

The tall man laughed softly, and the sound raised the hairs on the back of Rae's neck. He turned off the flashlight, then casually reached out and enclosed her throat with large, smooth fingers that pressed against her windpipe with increasing weight. "You've made some people very nervous, Ms. Prescott. Just as nervous as me and my associate here are making you." The fingers pressed a little harder, and Rae flinched. At her back, hard hands closed over her shoulders, digging into the tender skin.

"You are nervous, aren't you, Ms. Prescott?" he murmured in a sibilant, seductive whisper.

"Petrified!" Rae gasped out. "You know it. Let go!" Surely they didn't mean to kill her, did they? If so, she deserved it for suicidally determining not to blow the cover of the men who were tailing her. "What do you want?" she asked again, the words emerging as a thin croak.

Another eerie chuckle grated in her roaring ears. "This is a second—friendly—warning, Ms. Prescott. Regardless of what you notice over the next couple of weeks, you better remember to keep your mouth shut. If you happen onto any, shall we say, information, that you're tempted to keep to yourself, let this friendly warning change your mind." The hand squeezed again, and Rae's hands reached up to claw. She might as well have tried to claw an iron pipe. "And," the voice added, "you better not destroy that information."

She was freed and sucked gulps of fresh night air into her depleted lungs. The hands crushing her shoulders in a vise squeezed one last time, and a gust of peppermint-laden breath choked off the gulps of fresh air. "One other matter, *Rae.* You better think up a way to keep your boyfriend's nose out of your business." Peppermint Breath's voice was rough, less polished than the taller man's.

Rae stumbled until she bumped into the brick wall, feeling the cold roughness scrape her elbows and shoulder blades. "My boyfriend?" she repeated hoarsely.

"He might enjoy playing hero, but the next time he comes to the rescue might be his last. Understand?"

Rae managed a jerky nod, but there were no further taunts. The men's bulky silhouettes faded into the night with a noiselessness more terrifying than a thundering herd of wild elephants. Her fingers shook so badly she was barely able to fit the key in the lock to activate the alarm; Rae briefly debated the efficacy of deliberately setting it off, just to see the response of the agents assigned to watch her. Had they even witnessed her latest threat?

After she finally gathered the courage to walk to her car, she collapsed behind the steering wheel and spent several moments thinking. Ever since she had almost been sideswiped the day she bought all that Broadway music from Mrs. Hayfield, Rae had been closely monitored. If Caleb wasn't with her, she couldn't even dash to the 7-Eleven without a discreet escort.

Since no one had charged to the rescue tonight, it was probably because they were willing to take the risk that she wasn't in mortal danger. Obviously the Starseeker case took precedence over a mere individual whose innocence was still questionable. Muttering beneath her breath, Rae started the engine and headed for home. She had just turned off Academy Boulevard when a flashing red light illuminated her rearview mirror. She pulled into a parking lot and stopped.

"What's wrong, Officer?" Rae only rolled the window down several inches. "There isn't a sign preventing a right turn on red at this intersection, and I know I wasn't speeding."

The patrolman responded with a slight smile. "I'm just delivering a message, Ms. Prescott. If you'll wheel into that fast-food restaurant and order yourself a milk shake, someone will happen along who wants to talk to you."

"I'll just bet they do!" Rae snapped huffily. She thanked the police officer, promised to go straight to the fast-food place, and admitted to gratitude in the privacy of her car when the patrolman followed at a discreet distance until she turned into the parking lot.

The only customers in the restaurant left as Rae sat down in a booth at the back. She took a sip of an unwanted milk shake, and waited. A few minutes later a short, compactly built man in jeans and a CSU T-shirt carried his tray down the aisle. Rae recognized the man as one of the detectives who had run to their aid after Caleb rescued her from being sideswiped. Ayers. His name was Ayers. Ha! She'd actually remembered a name. An overdose of adrenaline was good for something.

"Well, hello, Rae! Long time, no see." He slid into the booth opposite her. Without seeming to, his eye roved the deserted restaurant, and he relaxed infinitesimally. After taking a huge bite of chicken sandwich, he turned a shrewd gaze on Rae, studying her while he chewed. "Are you okay?" he asked quietly.

"I'm grateful to still be in one piece. Why the interest now?" Rae asked, now that he had confirmed her suspicion that he and his partner had witnessed the frightening episode but chosen not to intervene. "Where were you hiding out while you enjoyed the show?"

"Close enough to help if you really needed it," the detective promised.

"Oh, really? If they had wanted to stick a knife in my ribs, you could have materialized instantly to prevent it?"

A faint wince crossed his features. He leaned forward. "Listen, Ms. Prescott . . . Rae. It's fairly obvious that right now they don't want to kill you, because they're still too uncertain of your part in all of it. Now, can you tell me what they said? Try to remember exactly, so Ramirez and Grabowski won't override Myers and have you wired every time you leave your house."

Caleb hadn't mentioned anything about that. But then, Caleb rivaled the Egyptian Sphinx for being closemouthed when he chose. Rae shuddered at the thought of having every sneeze or cough recorded and decided that—in this instance, at least—she appreciated his silence. "I'll tell you what I can," she promised Detective Ayer, and dutifully scoured her memory for every detail, faintly apologetic when it was obvious she could provide nothing tangible for the authorities to use.

"It seems," she finished with a twisted smile, "as though my only useful part in this whole mess is to provide local IOS heavies with a punching bag." She stirred the thick shake with short, almost vicious swirls. "I realize you guys are desperate to catch whoever sabotaged that tracking program out at Falcon. But I wish everyone—including those IOS creeps—would accept that I don't know anything! I just want to be left alone."

The detective leaned back, his light gray eyes dissecting her with cool detachment. In that respect he reminded her of Caleb, though the dispassionate gaze lacked the ever-present nuance of compassion Caleb's gaze reflected. And her heart didn't miss a single beat, even though the man sitting across from her was an equally attractive specimen of manhood.

"As long as IOS thinks you might constitute a threat or be hatching some sort of double cross," he told her, "we can't afford to treat you merely as a dupe. Nor can we leave you alone. Especially when there's that account in Denver. And your father."

"It always comes back to that, doesn't it? I don't know why I waste my breath protesting anymore—"

He lifted a placating hand. "I know. Myers insists you're pure as the first snowfall on Pikes Peak, and if it's any consolation, I'm sort of inclined to agree with him."

"Thanks a bunch." Rae glared across the table, wondering what he would do if she kicked his shin as hard as she could with her sturdy Timberlands.

Suddenly he smiled. "You've got guts, Rae Prescott. I'll have to give you credit. Most women would have thrown a screaming fit, back there at your church, and Evan and I halfway expected you to yell for us, since you knew we'd be somewhere close."

"I didn't want to blow your cover." Color crept into her cheeks at his tacit compliment. Okay, so she shouldn't have entertained the notion of kicking his shin. . . .

"We do appreciate that. I know you were scared." He paused, added more gently, "You know, it might help if you gave us the benefit of the doubt, too. If all we were interested in was the case, I wouldn't have bothered to arrange this meeting. I thought it might reassure you."

Most of the adrenaline had dissolved, and all of a sudden Rae was so tired she could have laid her head on the table and fallen asleep. She was also depressed, and toyed with the straw of her milk shake while Detective Ayer finished his sandwich. "Can you tell me if you've found out anything about the man responsible for planting the virus program?" she asked after several moments of silence.

Ayer's head lifted sharply. "How do you know it's a man? And who told you about the virus? Myers?" He muttered something beneath his breath Rae pretended not to hear.

"I assumed it was a man, which was probably archaic of me." She shoved the milk shake aside. "I'm involved in this case whether I invited it or not, and regardless of your need-to-know attitude toward the public, the less I know, the more precarious my safety. Caleb agreed, and yes, he did tell me a little bit about the case." She folded her arms and lifted her chin. "Though not nearly enough, in my opinion. I've also spent some time reading up on virus programs. I'm cooperating as much as I can, and I'd appreci-ate it very much if, in return, you at least pretended to believe that I'm innocent when you're talking to me."

One light brown eyebrow lifted. "I'm beginning to think Myers has met his match in you, Ms. Prescott, ma'am."

"Keep it in mind, Detective."

"How 'bout if you call me J.W. and I call you Rae? If we try hard enough, we might even work our way to mutual respect."

Rae reluctantly smiled, and the atmosphere subtly relaxed.

"You play the piano like a dream," J.W. commented as he polished off his sandwich and balled the paper. "I understand you were planning to go professional until your uncle died."

Rae nodded. "The trouble was, there was no money left after the dust settled, but about the only way I could have established a reputation—and thereby earned a substantial income—would have been to go on the road. I couldn't afford to let the house sit empty." She shrugged. "It wasn't easy, but if I had to make a choice all over again, I'd still keep the place. It's . . . home."

"What about your brother?"

"He couldn't shake the dust from his heels fast enough. He left Colorado when he was seventeen, went back East. I can count on one hand the number of times I've seen him since. We maintain a relationship largely over the phone. He still lectures me over my decision. Calls the Prescott mansion a financial albatross, among other things."

The detective nodded. He studied the pattern on the table, then looked at Rae, a self-conscious smile on his face. "There's a piece you play a lot at night, when Evan and I pull the graveyard shift over your garage. We can hear over the bugs you let the FBI plant in your living quarters. That piece . . . do you remember what it's called?"

Disconcerted, she stared at him. "Um, I play a lot of pieces. Can you hum a little of the one you're talking about?"

Red stained the bridge of his nose and cheeks. "I've got a voice like a cement mixer," he confessed. "The music goes all over the keyboard—sounds like you have about six hands."

"Mmm . . . probably not the Mozart, then. He's complex, not flamboyant. Might be the contemporary Christian, one from a Dino collection, possibly. I do play his arrangements a lot when I'm needing excessive emotion as well as energy." J.W. looked blank. "Let's see, I've been playing 'God and God Alone' a lot." She shoved the empty containers aside and played the opening bars on the table, singing the melody in a soft, clear voice. "Like that?"

"That's it—it's a religious song, then?"

"I think of it as a Christian song, and it's one of my favorites, too." She watched her fingers playing the table a second longer, then quit. "There's also another one that's an older song—one I heard as a teenager, when I first started going to church." She hummed and played on the table again. "That one's called 'The Lord Is My Light.' I guess I've been playing both of those a lot more lately, because of the words—they really help me right now. They remind me that I don't need to be afraid of anything, because God *is* omniscient and omnipresent, able and willing to take care of me." She wrinkled her nose. "Even when the police and FBI aren't."

J.W. shifted. "I never put much stock in that religious stuff," he admitted gruffly. "But I suppose if it helps you cope, I'm all for it."

" 'That stuff,' as you label it, was all that kept me from having the screaming fit you expected at church earlier." A conciliatory smile filled her face, and after a moment, J.W. chuckled in response. "It's odd, now that I mention it. That last song, 'The Lord Is My Light,' has been on my mind over a month now, ever since this woman wanted a copy. She's been in a couple of times, and I never seem to remember *her,* just this necklace she wears. Then I had another customer . . ." Rae shook her head. "I'm rambling—sorry."

"What kind of necklace?"

Rae began gathering the trash. "It was an unusual necklace. I'd never seen one like it—until another customer came in wearing what I'm sure was an exact replica. I probably put my foot in it, because I think I made a comment. I haven't seen either one in a while now."

J.W. leaned across the table. "Describe the necklaces." His voice was level, but an undercurrent of excitement, almost urgency, rippled beneath the quiet words.

A little thrill of warning set her pulse racing. Rae closed her eyes, struggling to remember accurately. "It was silver and turquoise," she replied slowly, "also some pearl-like stone. Old Colorado has similar jewelry on practically every corner. But I'd never seen this particular design. It was unusual enough that I remember it." She opened her eyes wide, excitement building. "There was a large thunderbird at the bottom, with two small ones interspersed with whatever that other stone is on either side." She spread her hands helplessly. "I'm sorry. That's sort of a garbled description. You know how Detective Grabowski grumbles about my lamentable observation skills. But I—"

"You've done great." He was beaming at her, looking so pleased—even smug—that Rae's jaw dropped. His hand reached across and patted hers. "This just might be the break we're looking for."

At Rae's utter look of mystification, he relented. "Occasionally IOS females use that method to identify themselves."

"A thunderbird necklace?"

"Not necessarily *that* necklace—I'm referring to the use of jewelry as the ID code. According to Tray Ramirez, there have been two other recorded cases dealing with IOS where jewelry was used." He closely watched Rae. "Think. Can you describe the women wearing the necklaces? Anything at all?"

Rae closed her eyes again and tried to conjure a picture of either woman, but it was hopeless. She opened her eyes, feeling incredibly stupid. "One was probably in her late thirties—and she didn't know much about music. The other one was young—she bought a whole pile of music, almost ninety dollars' worth. Christian, mostly solos she said she planned to sing."

"Hair, eye color? Weight? Distinguishing marks?"

Rae ducked her head. "I can tell you the music they bought," she offered. "Title, publisher, date of publication and how much it cost. But as far as anything else . . ."

J.W. grimaced. "You're supposed to keep a record of your customers, as well as anything out of the ordinary." He picked up the trash Rae had gathered and stood. "Why haven't you mentioned the necklaces before?" An undercurrent of suspicion had replaced the growing camaraderie.

Rae wearily rose. "It just didn't occur to me," she replied, the words dragging. "At the time, I was being polite, making idle conversation. Now I suppose you think I'm deliberately concealing information."

"One of the things you learn when you've been on the street as long as I have," the detective returned just as wearily, "is that the most angelic face can hide a devil's soul." He looked at Rae. "Myers is a solid guy, for a civilian consultant. I'd be glad to have him at my back any time, in a fight or on a case. So I hope he's right about those guileless eyes of yours. He talks a good story about his Christian faith, and yours. Be nice if it meant more than a bunch of meaningless words."

He nodded once, then sauntered out the door with the wily grace of an alley cat.

Chapter Sixteen

The L.A. precinct office where Caleb sat offered a relatively calm oasis compared to the chaos and noise emanating outside the semi-private glassed-in walls. Drunks, dope peddlers, prostitutes, criminals, victims—all milling around, waiting with apathy or defiance for the system to take its grinding course. No wonder law enforcement struggled against cynicism, Caleb mused—they seldom associate with decent people in their work.

He gloomily contemplated a stack of reports about to slide off Lieutenant Zeingold's desk. Nowadays, with rampant relativism to cloud the issue, he wouldn't be surprised if "decent" people ended up in jail because their so-called standards violated the constitutional rights of everyone who wanted to change the definition of the word.

You're losing it, Myers. How about if you concentrate on the present reality, and try to remember that God's agenda doesn't have to be cleared with you. Caleb shifted his gaze to the man he'd come to see.

Lieutenant Harold Zeingold sipped a lukewarm cup of coffee and ran gnarled, ink-stained fingers through the thinning wisps of his black hair. Deep lines scored his forehead, ran down his nose to his mouth. It was the stubborn, jaded face of a man who had seen and heard everything, and Caleb felt an uncomfortable premonition that he was going to end up like the older man if he wasn't more careful with his thoughts.

"Sorry I can't do more for you," Zeingold offered in a rumbly bass voice, more matter-of-fact than apologetic. "But if the statement we got before he was blown away helps, I'm glad. T-bone was one of our more reliable snitches." He shook his head, shoved the report across the desk and watched while Caleb read the single-page document.

"I'll need a copy of this."

Zeingold waved his hand. "No problem. Keep me posted. Prescott's a sneaky, two-bit hustler, but unfortunately he's gotten himself some good connections. Since they're IOS connections, you guys have your work cut out for you." He leaned back and folded his hands across an ample girth. "Better you and the Colorado police than us. We've had a plateful, these past few years."

"I know," Caleb assented. He twisted his watchband. "I'm pretty sure Prescott will surface in Denver within the next couple of weeks. This—" he held up the statement from the dead informant "—pretty much insures that. I'm concerned about his daughter, though. I'm convinced Prescott is using her. I just don't know how or why, yet."

Zeingold grunted. "Are you still convinced the source leads down here?"

"Fisher doesn't have the personality to spearhead an operation this size. He could be the brains behind formatting and planting the virus, but I think IOS is calling the shots from another city. They wouldn't place any of their top people that close to their victim, especially when it's the U.S. government—and a top-secret project. It's too risky." He smiled ruefully. "Southern California has size as well as anonymity and plenty of targets for milking big bucks, which rates the area pretty high on a list of likely headquarters. Obviously there's others. That's what makes the investigation so tedious and lengthy."

And exhausting. Thankless. Frustrating. "It could just as easily be D.C. or Denver, Chicago or Miami. They might not even *have* a so-called corporate headquarters." He shifted his gaze to the opposite wall. Above cluttered metal desks and rows of filing cabinets, the wall was peppered with maps.

"Neither," Zeingold reminded him dryly, "does organized crime. IOS might not have their power yet, but I don't envy you the task of trying to run them to earth, much less getting a prosecution not based on endangerment or entrapment."

"We'll get as many of them as we can," Caleb promised grimly, even though privately he entertained monumental doubt. "DOD gets pretty hostile when someone messes around with multimillion dollar leading-edge space technology."

Outside the glassed walls, a truculent, slump-shouldered teenager hurled himself into a wooden chair, the violent action catching Caleb's attention. The boy, wearing gang colors, glared with hate-filled eyes at an impassive police officer. Despair lodged in Caleb's chest like a massive boulder. Sometimes he wondered why he didn't just delete his whole career and turn into a beach bum.

Then a picture of Rae filled his head, and he knew why he couldn't give in or give up.

"We're pretty sure," he told Zeingold slowly, "that there's someone in the area instructing Fisher, keeping him in line. They've also sent strong-arm thugs to harass and intimidate Rae Prescott. Any results yet on the descriptions I faxed you?"

"Nope. From what you've been telling me, though, I doubt they'd import dirtbags from this far. Have you checked Denver and Kansas City?"

"I'm flying to Denver this evening."

The door opened and the booking officer poked his head in. "There's a guy out here screaming brutality against Loomis, Lieutenant."

"Who is it?"

"Vinnie. Loomis caught him dealing to a couple of kids."

"Umph." Lieutenant Zeingold grimaced and rose. "Knowing Loomis, he might have done more than read him his rights." He paused, added dryly, "Knowing Vinnie, he probably deserved it. Of course, you didn't hear me say that." He glanced at Caleb. "I'll be there in a minute, Harris."

Caleb stood, as well. "Will you let me know if you hear anything else on IOS? No matter how flimsy or unsubstantiated? The information T-bone provided has been invaluable. I just wish it hadn't been at the cost of his life."

Zeingold shrugged. To the hardened detective, T-bone might have been a useful source of information, but as a human being he'd been a washout, not worth crying over.

It was enough to make a statue weep. Mood glum, Caleb shook the detective's hand. "I better get moving so I don't miss my flight. The sooner I get to Denver, the sooner I can get back to the Springs and we can collate all this information."

Zeingold snorted. "You feeling the heat, Myers?"

"Yeah . . . and I'm starting to sweat. If we don't get some kind of break soon, I have a feeling Congress is going to be screaming for some heads on a platter." He stuffed his hands in the hip pockets of his jeans. "Mine will probably be the first."

Dennis Hoffman, one of the Denver FBI agents, met him at the airport. It was eleven at night, and pouring rain. Hoffman grumbled about the abysmal weather on the long drive to the local Bureau offices as he maneuvered through the surprisingly heavy traffic.

In a conference room littered with paper coffee cups and crumpled cellophane wrappers, they joined the Denver section chief, Bob Taylor. He gestured Caleb to a chair, then slid a file across the table. "Rae Prescott's *brother* is responsible for the checking account," he announced as Caleb sank into the chair. "We finally got hold of him this morning. He hadn't told her about the account because he wanted it to be a cushion if the store bombed." He looked disgusted. "Only Tyler Prescott said *when* the store bombed. Supportive brother, huh?"

"They aren't that close," Hoffman put in. "From what we've learned, Tyler Prescott thinks his sister is too sentimental and idealistic. Not a practical bone in her body. At least he's got enough family feeling to make sure she doesn't end up on the street, homeless and broke."

Caleb rubbed the back of his hand over his mouth and gritty eyes. He had been seventeen hours without sleep, the flight from L.A. had been bumpy and exhausting, and incoming bad weather kept the plane circling the airport for almost an hour. Taylor's revelation poured over his weary bones like the balm of Gilead.

"Thank God," he murmured beneath his breath with heartfelt sincerity. At this point he didn't care if Tyler Prescott had the family feeling of a shark—at least Rae's innocence had been established as far as the Denver account was concerned.

His mouth relaxed into a relieved smile as he rapidly scanned the file. "You're positive the signature on the checks withdrawing the fifty thousand is forged?"

"Yes." Taylor leaned back, absently cracking his knuckles. "It was a professional job—our document examiner's one of the best on the west coast, and she's willing to swear that the original sample was done by a man, which pretty much absolves Ms. Prescott."

"You can sleep tonight, Myers," Dennis Hoffman gibed good-naturedly. "Your girlfriend's off the hook. Or maybe the two of you would rather . . . celebrate."

He was *not* in the mood for this. Caleb shifted slightly, leveling a gelid stare at the agent. After a silent moment of increasing tension, Hoffman shrugged and cleared his throat.

"Sorry," he muttered. "I guess that was out of line."

"Way out," Caleb agreed in a deceptively pleasant voice, and Hoffman backed a couple more steps. "Don't let it happen again."

"The word's out that your interest in the Prescott woman is more than just professional," Taylor intervened. "That's not smart, and you know it, Myers. You're opening yourself up to a sexual harassment suit. And she might have been telling the truth about the checking account, but there's still a good possibility she could be conspiring with her father."

"She's not conspiring with her father." Caleb casually leaned forward and planted his elbows on the table. His voice was low-key, deceptively soft. "As for your concern over a lawsuit, don't be." He looked both men in the eye. "My primary job, like yours, is finding out who's behind the virus that aborted the Starseeker program. But it's also our collective responsibility to make sure that innocent bystanders—like Rae Prescott—are protected. If I can help in that capacity, I plan to do so."

"Take it easy," Taylor counseled. His weary, watery blue eyes analyzed and accepted the threatening aura emanating from Caleb. "No one's implying anything unethical about the Prescott woman or you." He paused, then added flatly, "But you know we're going to dig as deep as we can and follow up on every lead, regardless of the individuals involved. I want to agree with your assessment of her innocence, but until it's established beyond doubt, we can't afford to rule her out."

"I'm aware of that." Caleb raked a hand through his hair. "Whose signature was forged—the brother's?"

"Yeah. He was pretty torqued about it. Especially when we had to warn him it might be his father."

"What did you learn about Ray Prescott, senior?" Dennis asked, his voice and stance back to normal.

Caleb produced the folded sheet from the inside pocket of his jacket. He handed it to Taylor. "A snitch happened to overhear a conversation in a bar between Prescott and an ex-employee of Chem-Con."

"Chem-Con . . . the corporation that pirated, then produced the stolen Polaris technology in that case a couple of years back that you told us about, right?"

Caleb nodded. "It's my opinion that the same thing is happening with the Starseeker technology. I think IOS is after the money and power available upon the sale of the technology more than they're out to sabotage the country's security. T-bone—the snitch—overheard enough of Prescott's conversation for us to establish reasonable proof of the IOS association."

Taylor lifted the paper, read it aloud. " 'I heard him tell the other dude that IOS better come through with the goods. The other dude told him to shut up and never mention the name. He looked around—I saw Prescott put something in his suit pocket. They left.' "

For a long, somber moment the three men pondered in silence before Hoffman spoke.

"Prescott was sighted leaving a restaurant on Colfax Avenue last Tuesday," he told Caleb. "We lost him at a traffic light. He hasn't surfaced since."

"Any more funds disappear from Rae's account?"

Taylor shook his head. "There's only about four thousand left, anyway. Prescott probably wouldn't risk an investigation by depleting the account totally, much less for that trivial amount."

Caleb stretched, then rose with lithe coordination that belied the stiffness of his tired body. "I want to get back to the Springs." For an hour, he'd been feeling uneasy mental twinges—and they all concerned Rae. If God was trying to alert him to something, Caleb planned to listen and take action. "I'm concerned about Ms. Prescott."

Taylor loosened his tie and unbuttoned the collar of his rumpled shirt, then sighed and scratched the back of his head. "You could

be right," he reluctantly admitted. "I talked to Ramirez earlier.
They should have already tightened security around her—there's
no need for you to knock yourself out tonight."

"I'm going to anyway."

"Are you crazy, man?" Dennis sputtered. "It's raining like the
Last Flood, and it's past midnight."

A corner of Caleb's mouth tilted. "Guess I'll just have to hunt up
a southbound ark."

Twenty minutes later, he was headed south on I-25 in an unmarked government car. Soggy with fatigue, eyes rid-rimmed and
grittier than ever, he nonetheless still heard the small voice deep
inside warning him more urgently of pending danger. "Okay,
Lord." He talked out loud to keep alert, squinting through the
rain-lashed windshield at the stygian blackness. "I'm going to need
some help here, or I'll probably end up at the morgue instead of
my motel."

Less than ten miles out of Denver the rain quit, and a weak
yellow moon hovered over the black masses of the mountains,
lighting up the midnight sky.

The crescendoing wail of sirens jarred Rae from a deep but restless sleep. An ominous reddish cast tinted the window, and she
stumbled out of bed, tripping over her slippers as she staggered to
the window. Sleep-clumsy fingers plucked aside enough slats in the
miniblinds so she could peek outside, and the sight brought her to
heart-pounding wakefulness. Her garage was on fire.

The agents! The agents hidden in the loft.

She thrust her arms inside her robe and crammed her feet in
slippers. Praying desperate prayers, she yanked open the back
door. The fire engine whose siren had awakened her was rumbling
to a halt. Men jumped off and ran toward the garage, hoses un-
winding across the lawn behind them. Eyes transfixed on the billowing smoke, Rae hugged the porch railing and stayed out of the
way.

Forty minutes later it was over. No injuries to the agents. Rae
thanked the Lord for His mercies, in spite of the bitter revelation
of the fire's cause. One of the agents who had been on duty—
Charlie?—had slipped her a note so she wouldn't panic. The fire
had been set deliberately—a pile of trash ignited with a kerosene-

soaked rag. Damage was minimal, except for the soot, ashes and puddles of oily water. The agents were safe, and even if the location of this stakeout had leaked somehow, they planned to remain until Agent Ramirez informed them otherwise. She was not to worry. This was just another scare tactic.

Rae thanked the firemen, reassured a police officer that she was all right and woodenly offered a statement to the arson investigator who made out the report. Finally she was allowed to go inside, and out of habit padded into the kitchen to put on the kettle. It was while she was waiting for the water to boil that a disquieting thought drifted into her mind. The fire had been deliberately set— but why? Could there be a reason other than to harass, warn them all of IOS knowledge of the stakeout location?

The fire had provided a good diversion, if they planned— *No!*

Heedlessly Rae ran down the hall, fingers so clumsy in her haste she barely managed to unlock the door to Joyful Noise. *Please,* she prayed desperately. *Please don't let anything have happened.* Her hand went automatically to the light switch and shoved it upward. Then she stood, hand frozen on the switch, while her gaze absorbed the sickening sight.

All her priceless ornaments, the figurines, the china, even the music boxes had been hurled to the floor. Everything lay scattered in thousands of pieces, mutilated, totally destroyed. Only the brass quarter note remained unbroken, gleaming dully on top of the shattered onyx base.

Nausea gushed upward, and a gray veil dimmed her vision. Weakly Rae leaned against the wall, fighting to keep from throwing up or fainting. Possibly both. One fist lifted to her mouth, the other pressed against her chest as if she was trying to keep her heart from leaping out. Her heritage. The best part of her past. All destroyed. Gone forever. She shook her head slowly, hearing a strange keening noise in her ears that she eventually realized was coming from her own mouth. "God, Father God," she whispered over and over. "Help me. I need You to help me."

Chapter Seventeen

Rae called in the police. Regardless of the consequences— merciful God, what else could IOS do that they hadn't done?—she wasn't going to pretend that nothing had happened. Probably IOS was waiting to see if she would do just that. There was even a chance that if she didn't call, their suspicions would be even *more* aroused. The police would certainly question her silence, and if Detective Grabowski discovered she hadn't reported—

She couldn't stand it. The pain, the betrayal and confusion were simply more than she could bear. *God? Where are You?* And where were the men who were supposed to be guarding her and the Prescott mansion?

She dialed the police as if in a trance, having to clear her throat twice before she could speak. "This is Rae Prescott," she told a bored-sounding dispatcher. "My store, Joyful Noise, has been—" She stopped, waited until she had herself under control. "My store has been vandalized."

The voice on the other end transfered her to the complaint clerk, who told Rae a unit would be dispatched to her address. Rae hung up, then stood staring at the phone for a long time. Eventually she turned, looking vaguely around at the mess. Somewhere inside she was screaming, and a deep quivering was working its way out, threatening to explode into hysteria. Busy. She needed to stay busy, do something productive, or she would go mad. And without thought her feet moved across the floor to the bins of sheet music.

Several scores protruded untidily, as though someone had riffled through the music and started to pull individual pieces out, then changed his mind. Rae carefully straightened them, then pulled out a couple of misplaced selections to play while she waited for the police. Destroying evidence never registered in her short-circuited brain.

The piano she leased from the store wasn't *hers,* so Rae wandered trancelike down the hall to her Steinway. *What if they had trashed her piano?* Bile surged in her throat, and Rae gulped convulsively several times. She was afraid to look, but when she flicked on the switch and saw her most precious possession undamaged, waiting for her in dignified splendor, tears filled her eyes. *No. You will not cry.* Her hands scrubbed over her eyes, and she forced herself to take several deep breaths. Then she sank onto the bench, arranged the music she had brought with her and began to play. When she turned the page, a folded piece of paper slipped out and floated to the floor.

Rae stopped playing and picked it up, unfolding it mechanically. Nothing but meaningless notations. Gibberish. Some customer probably using a piece of scrap paper for a marker. With a shrug, her fingers opened and the paper drifted to the floor.

The police arrived just as she lifted her hands to the keyboard, and she met them at the back door. More red lights, only this time, instead of firefighters, the two cars spilled forth what looked like an army of uniforms and plainclothesmen. One of them was Detective Grabowski. So. Her faithful watchdogs must have notified him about the garage. Would have been nice, some detached voice in her brain observed, if they'd noticed the activity going on inside Joyful Noise. She hugged her waist, standing on the threshold, waiting for the onslaught as though she was waiting for the curtain to draw back so the play could begin.

Across the street, the DeVrieses' lights turned on. Nancy had offered to stay with her after the fire, but Rae had persuaded the oversolicitous mother to go home. The last thing she wanted was to be treated like a three-year-old.

"Ms. Prescott? Rae?" Detective Grabowski materialized at her side. He peered into her face, opened his mouth, then shut it. "Are you all right?" he asked after a minute, the normally hard, gritty voice surprisingly gentle. He placed his hand on her arm and ushered her up the porch steps. Inside, he repeated his question.

"Not at the moment," Rae replied with ethereal candor. "I sort of feel like . . . I'm not really here."

Grabowski jerked his head, then steered Rae out of the way. The lab technician and Evan McArthur, Detective Grabowski's second in command, filed past. Another patrol officer loped across the lawn toward the DeVrieses'. A female officer, her rather raw-boned, plain face softened by compassionate brown eyes, laid a comforting hand on Rae's shoulder.

"I'm Officer Dix, Ms. Prescott. Why don't we go in the kitchen?" she suggested. "You can tell me what happened."

Grabowski and Officer Dix exchanged looks, and Rae wondered why they looked so worried. She was all right, under control. She wasn't going to go to pieces on them.

"What's the status on Myers? He was scheduled to fly into Denver this evening," Grabowski said abruptly.

"He hasn't checked in with us."

They both looked at Rae again. At the mention of Caleb's name, Rae's fragile poise wavered. Caleb. She mustn't think of Caleb right now. If she did, she'd lose what little control she had left. The ice-coated fog returned, shrouding her in cold droplets of mist. She stared sightlessly down the hall, praying the mist would never lift. All the *good* memories she had so carefully preserved over the past twenty years were destroyed, lying scattered in millions of pieces all over the floor. She felt as though she had been erased, the essence of her personality crushed. She was nothing—a nobody. And she had nobody to turn to, to restore validity to her existence.

Uncle Floyd was dead. Tyler would say, "Good riddance. Now put the place up for sale and try to make a name for yourself as a concert pianist."

Karen would tell her that there were worse tragedies in life than the loss of material possessions. Divorce, for instance. Everyone at church would reinforce that sentiment. After all, they were just *things.* Rae was lucky to still be alive.

Dear God. *I know they were things, Lord.* But they had helped remind her that beauty could be created even from the ugliness of her past. The pain intensified, because it wasn't valid. She was a Christian. The power of Christ was supposed to have transformed her, maintained her. She shouldn't be hurting so over the loss of material possessions.

Her parents were failures. As a Christian, *she* was a failure.

Rae walked with the step of a somnambulist, into the kitchen with Officer Dix. Until a few months ago she would have proclaimed to the world her unshakable faith in a loving God and thanked Him for His blessings. What had she done wrong, for Him to allow these unspeakable circumstances?

"Ms. Prescott? Rae? Your kettle's boiling away here. Were you fixing yourself a drink before you called?"

The kind voice penetrated her icy reverie, and Rae finally focused on the concerned face across the table. Her silver nameplate glinted in the light. Rae took a shaky breath. "Tea. I want a cup of hot tea." Her lips felt strange, as though they'd been anesthetized

"I'll fix it," Officer Dix said. "Is this the mug you were going to use? It has a tea bag in it. How about if you sit down at your table, and I'll bring it to you. Then we'll talk."

Rae sat down. When the steaming mug appeared in front of her, she stared at it a moment, then looked vaguely at Officer Dix. "Thank you. What did you want to talk about?"

Step by step she was led through the night's events, including the note Charlie handed her during the fire in the garage. The words dribbled out in a slow but steady stream, shorn of emotion, until she tried to describe the state in which she found Joyful Noise. Officer Dix told her again to take her time and calmly waited until Rae could continue.

Detective Grabowski entered as she concluded. He walked wearily over to them. "They did a thorough job of trashing your trinkets, but they didn't touch anything else." He muttered a terse apology when Rae flinched. "I wonder why . . ."

"I'd have to concur with Rae's conclusion that they started a fire in the garage as a diversion," Officer Dix stated. "With all the activity and attention over that, the feds missed what was going on in the store."

"If the feds had been on the ball instead of joining in the three-ring circus, we might have learned some useful information." Grabowski scowled at the toe of his scuffed black shoes. "Nothing could have been done to keep them from destroying the valuables, but at least we might have picked up a lead on the perpetrators."

Rae's chill intensified.

Officer Dix shrugged, rose to her feet. "Can't say I blame those guys too much. You know what a bummer pulling surveillance is. It's impossible to keep your eyes peeled every minute, even without a fire for a distraction."

Headlights flashed through the windows, then disappeared. Into the sudden silence came the faint sound of a car door slamming. Officer Dix slipped her revolver out of the belt rig and moved in front of Rae. Detective Grabowski glided out into the hall, a semi-automatic appearing as if by magic in his hand.

The back door burst open, and Caleb's voice echoed with sharp demand down the hall. "Rae! Where are you?"

Rae's heart had been lying at her feet, a shriveled, lifeless lump. Now it kicked all the way into her throat. Suddenly she lurched up, shoving Officer Dix aside as she hurled herself toward the sound of his voice. Later, she would have time to analyze, question—and regret the revealing response. But right now a force even more powerful than her pain propelled her toward the only man who offered her safety . . . and hope.

"Caleb!" Her voice was choked, the word emerging as a croak. Her eyes fastened on him and refused to turn away.

His hair was damp, shaggy, his clothes impossibly rumpled. His own eyes were bloodshot with exhaustion. But in spite of his obvious fatigue, danger emanated from him in a sizzling current. It electrified every person in the room. He spared Grabowski one swift, comprehensive glance, then turned to Rae. "Rae . . ." The greeting was hoarse, almost guttural.

She faltered to an uncertain halt, hovering in the doorway. Then Caleb lifted his arms, and she fled into them without hesitation. He enfolded her in a protective embrace, and she burrowed against his chest, hands clutching the soft cotton of his shirtfront. She couldn't speak for the tears clogging her throat, her nose, her eyes. The trembling she'd managed to conquer until now surged upward, causing her knees to buckle. Caleb's hold shifted until he was practically supporting her entire weight.

"What happened?" His voice, stripped for once of its low-key control, rumbled above her ear as his hands stroked her hair and back.

"Store got hit by vandals, doubtless courtesy of your IOS pals,"

Detective Grabowski answered. "They trashed all her knicknacks, yet left the music intact. We haven't determined if that was by accident or design. Offhand I'd say they were more out to teach some kind of lesson, bullies taunting, showing their power."

"Did the guys across the street get any pics? How about prints from your people?" Caleb's voice was equally terse, remote, even, but the hands holding her were imbued with warmth and strength. Rae absorbed it like a greedy sponge.

"They're just finishing up," the detective told him with heavily exaggerated courtesy. "But no pics. A trash fire was set in Ms. Prescott's garage to divert anyone who might have been interested in interrupting the party in her store. The feds on duty all felt obliged to join the general commotion at the garage, ostensibly to offer help if needed." Grabowski's opinion of their actions hovered unspoken in the air. "Of course, we wouldn't have interrupted even if the perpetrators *had* been seen. We can't afford to alert them that we've got the place—as well as Ms. Prescott—under surveillance in more than one location."

Then he added in the same dispassionate tone, "Strikes me that a possible motivation for tonight would be if IOS believes she's planning a double cross of some kind." The words hammered into Rae's body like blows.

Her head jerked up and she twisted around, though Caleb wouldn't let her go. "You know that's not true," she denied hoarsely. "Don't—I can't—"

"Shh . . . don't try to talk yet," Caleb ordered. He gently forced her head against his chest. "It's okay," he promised. *"You're* okay. That's more important than the case, or all your keepsakes. They didn't hurt *you* again."

Rae tore herself free, backing away. "You don't understand! Yes, they were things. I know they were just knickknacks and decorative items, inanimate objects. They didn't have a soul—I shouldn't place value in my possessions. My life is more important. But when they destroyed those *things,* they destroyed part of me!" She dragged air into her lungs, stared with burning eyes into Caleb's face. "All those objects were the only part of my past I could look at with pride."

"Rae, that's not—"

"No. Don't say anything else. I know I'm wrong—you don't have to lecture me on my sins. Oh, *God!* I'm sorry. Sorry!" she burst out. "I'm nothing now. He's punishing me because I coveted my possessions, but now I have nothing . . . nothing." She covered her face with her hands.

Then Caleb's hands covered hers and forced them to her sides. His gaze burned into her, the bloodshot amber eyes glittering, so commanding that she went utterly still. "Those objects might have been a reflection of your life, but they were not worth your life. And God is *not* punishing you, Rae." He shook her wrists. "Listen to me. Your grief is legitimate, and God understands. *I* understand. Now, I want you to go wash your face and wait for me in the parlor." The laser-beam gaze searched her face. "I don't want to have to hunt you down, either," he warned, very softly.

He released her and turned to Detective Grabowski. "I brought some info. I'll share it with you after I have a look at Rae's store, if you don't mind. Can you fill me in on everything else that's gone down?" He sent Rae one last, unfathomable look before heading down the hall toward the store, Grabowski at his heels.

Rae stared after them, the icy mist disintegrating into a frostbite of hurt, confusion and despair. Eventually she trudged toward the bathroom. Her face probably did need washing.

Chapter Eighteen

She sat in Uncle Floyd's favorite chair, waiting. Officer Dix poked her head in briefly, and another policeman reminded her that they would need a list of all the destroyed valuables and that she should call her insurance agent first thing in the morning. Rae nodded. She had washed her face, wound her hair up on top of her head and dressed in a warm-up suit, but everyone still treated her as though she was in shock. Her fingers curled, the short nails biting into her palms.

Eventually Grabowski returned. He stood over her without speaking, the lines in his face deeper, his eyes speculative.

Rae straightened her back with a tired sigh. It was obvious the detective had been doing some thinking, as she had. "I suppose you're wondering if I did it myself." She spoke in a remote, indifferent voice.

"The thought occurred to me," he admitted. "Every time I turn around lately, you seem to be in trouble of some kind. I can't help but wonder if it's designed to keep the spotlight on you—instead of where it needs to be."

Even though Rae had anticipated the suspicion, hearing it verbalized exacerbated her already raw state. For the first time, anger stirred, and she lifted her wrists. "Well, why don't you go ahead and arrest me? I might do something really dangerous the next time. Who knows, maybe I'm building a bomb in the basement and I plan to hand it over to my father next week, so he could sell it on the international black market."

"On the whole, I prefer dealing with your temper, but don't you think the bomb's a little extreme?" Caleb's voice, calm yet implacable, cut off Rae's sarcastic flow of words. He walked across the worn Oriental carpet, his gaze locked to Rae's. "What have you been saying to her, Grabowski?"

"Back off, Myers," the detective grumbled. "I'll run my investigations the way I see fit, and you run yours. If I have to question Ms. Prescott, I will."

"Agreed," Caleb assented, and Rae's temper fizzled at the latent threat icing his tone. "But while I'm protecting the lady—and since it involves the Starseeker case—I'd recommend you keep your questions . . . reasonable."

"You wouldn't be trying to threaten me, would you, Myers?"

Caleb smiled a shark's smile. "Not at all. That was by way of some well-intentioned advice."

Grabowski's brows lowered in a fierce scowl, then abruptly he gave a short laugh. "I'm getting too old for this," he muttered, shaking his head. "Have at her, son, but keep in mind what you've learned." He glanced at Rae. "You're right about one thing—I much prefer her in a temper myself, on the whole." Incredibly, he leaned to pat her hand. "Sorry about your things, Ms. Prescott."

After Grabowski left there was a moment of strained silence.

"What have you learned?" Rae finally asked, not looking at him.

"Nothing good," Caleb responded. He leaned over as though he was going to pull her to her feet, but froze when Rae flinched. "Rae, trust me, please. It's going to be all right. I know you're not a criminal."

"Well, you're probably the only one." She swallowed hard. Her fingernails were digging into her palms, but she forced herself to remain calm. "What's the nothing good you've learned? You may as well tell me. It can't possibly be any worse than what I've gone through tonight."

"That's why I'd rather not get into it now. You've had enough. I think it would be best if you went to bed, tried to sleep. Things won't look so black in the morning."

"Don't you *dare* patronize me!" she said angrily, calm forgotten. She stormed to her feet, planting her fists on her hips. "If you don't want to talk, fine. Leave. I don't care. I don't need you, and I'm sorry I threw myself at you earlier. Believe me, it won't happen again." She stopped, breathing hard, reveling in the turbulent feeling crashing through her. At least it reminded her that she was still alive.

Flames licked through Caleb's amber eyes, turning them to hot liquid gold. "Oh, I think it will happen again," he returned. Then he reached out and pulled her close, wrapping his arms around her waist and shoulders. Just as firmly, his head lowered and his lips brushed her ear. "Don't scratch, little cat. I'm wiped out. Seeing this place surrounded by squad cars aged me ten years."

He began to press light, soothing kisses along her neck and across her rigid jaw, and Rae's protest died in her throat, along with the angry hurt. "It was pouring rain in Denver, but I wrangled a car and came anyway," he whispered. "I knew something was wrong—I felt it. I knew you needed me. So even though I'd been on my feet for eighteen hours, I came." A half-frustrated chuckle escaped. "The FBI agents in Denver are convinced I'm a lunatic. Maybe they're right. But over the years I've learned not to ignore that little voice I sometimes hear, somewhere deep inside. I prayed all the way down here." His arms tightened, practically squeezing her in two. "I don't know what I would have done if you'd been hurt . . . or worse."

Incredibly, he sounded almost . . . panicked? It was almost as though he was clinging to Rae as much as . . . well, as much as she wanted to cling to him. Panicked herself, Rae realized that she wanted to sink into him, drown in the mesmerizing warmth he offered. She wanted it with such frightening intensity her knees threatened to give way like wet sand. But she couldn't risk it. Every man in her entire life had always left her, and Caleb was no different. Right now he was relieved that she was safe, that was all. He was a good, decent man. But when the Starseeker case was finally resolved, Caleb would be gone. It didn't matter that she was falling in love with him. Somehow she had to find the strength to stop that free-fall before she hit the bottom.

God was having to teach her many painful lessons. But as she steeled herself against the warmth of Caleb's embrace, Rae realized that watching him walk away was going to be far more devastating than the loss of all the treasures Uncle Floyd had given her.

She turned her head aside from the persistent onslaught of his gentle kisses. *Keep it casual, in control.*

Above all else, she needed to curb her temper.

She laughed, a light, woefully artificial sound, and tried to ignore the enticing pressure of his mouth. "I was just thinking that I'm really doing something wrong somewhere in my life, since God needs such extreme measures to teach me a lesson." For some reason the words were sticking in her throat. "Lately all my prayers seem to sink through the floorboards."

The caressing kisses stopped. Caleb held her away a little, tipping her chin up with his thumbs. "You know better than that."

"I used to think so." Her voice wavered, and the fierce intensity of his gaze softened. *Don't be kind,* Rae wanted to beg. She couldn't sustain the facade against the warmth of his compassion.

"Take it easy, sweetheart," he murmured, the thumbs continuing to stroke her chin. "You've had a rough time of it, haven't you? But it's going to be all right."

She closed her eyes in a vain attempt to keep from responding, but the need for comfort spilled up and out along with a flood of words. "It's gotten out of control, Caleb. My life, the store, this whole situation! Every time I turn around something else happens. I feel like my whole world is the house on shifting sand instead of the house built on rock." A sob caught her by surprise, erupting from her throat. "I had it all planned. Joyful Noise was finally making money. I'd done it, and Tyler would have to eat all his hateful words. I had everything under control. My past couldn't touch me anymore. I prayed so hard, thought God had answered all my prayers. . . ."

"Rae." Caleb wrapped his arms around her and held her close, rocking her, calming her. "You're just not seeing clearly right now. You've forgotten the most fundamental truth of all. God's *unconditional* love. He offers love, sweetheart. It's life that deals out consequences. All these trials . . . well, I don't know why you're having to suffer them, but I do know God hasn't abandoned you." For a fraction of a beat he hesitated before adding gruffly, "I won't abandon you to IOS, either."

She shook her head against his chest, but couldn't bring herself to pull away. "If you do, I might as well make my funeral arrangements." Another watery sob escaped. "It's painfully clear that I'm no good at playing cops and robbers. I don't remember details, everyone but you suspects me of being in collusion with those despicable thugs, and I—I . . ." *Don't do this to yourself, Rae.* "I'm f-frightened all the time. I never thought I'd be a coward. But I am. I am." She closed her eyes in shame and despair.

"Ah, Rae, you're no coward." Gently, inexorably, he lifted her head, and his mouth covered hers, breath flowing across her tightly pressed lips. "You're one of the bravest women I know," he whispered between soft little kisses, and with a last despairing cry her heart gave up the battle.

She lifted her arms around his neck and kissed him. It was either kiss or weep. The deliberate yielding of herself into his care was terrifying, because she did it with the full awareness of inevitable loss. But that vulnerability was still preferable to the humiliation of cowardly tears. Besides, as long as he kept kissing her, she might be able to forget the shattering nightmare of the past hours and the nightmare that waited in the future.

Tomorrow would be soon enough to face the bitter consequences—she had fallen head over heels in love with a man who would disappear out of her life when the Starseeker case was eventually solved. And for the rest of her life, she would be alone.

She had become her mother.

Rae could only pray that God really hadn't abandoned her, because she needed all the divine help He chose to provide.

Karen was helping her clean the mess in her store the next day when the phone rang. Karen looked from a load of smashed glass she'd been emptying in the trash to Rae, who was sitting on the floor of the classical music room staring at the phone as if it was a rattlesnake. IOS, checking up? The police? A customer? Phone solicitation?

Caleb?

"You want me to answer it?" Karen asked after the fifth ring, her drawl more pronounced than usual.

Rae gave a short nod. Before he'd left the previous night, Caleb had called Karen and asked if she could spend the rest of the night with Rae. Alarmed, Karen had flown up the street, bursting on the scene wearing a bright yellow caftan and looking like an enraged canary. Even Caleb had needed fifteen minutes to calm her down.

All in all, Rae reminded herself, her whirlwind of a friend had been a welcome lifeline. She called all Rae's piano students and canceled the lessons, then insisted that the store be closed for at least the day, regardless of Rae's protests. She even handled the reporter from the *Gazette* after Rae's tenuous composure fractured.

Rae nonetheless suffered a symphony of guilt over Karen's involvement in the deepening mess of her life. Now that she'd answered the phone, her friend's voice would be picked up by the IOS phone tap, and Karen would doubtless be investigated by IOS as thoroughly as the authorities were investigating Rae.

Unfortunately, it was too late now. "Hello, Joyful Noise," Karen chirped even as she rolled her eyes at Rae. She listened, a frown growing. "Just a minute. I'll see." She put her hand over the receiver. "Rae, this man claims he's your brother. You want me to ask a few pertinent questions to confirm that?"

Tyler! Rae gasped, her heart leaping in a gigantic thump of gratitude. Awkwardly scrambling up, she bumped her hip on the music bin in her haste. Just as she reached for the receiver, her brain belatedly clicked in. She motioned to Karen, thinking furiously. "Tell him I can't come to the phone right now. Tell him I'm—I'm going down to your place to help—to help plan for some background music for the restaurant. If it's important, he can call me there in a few minutes."

Karen looked baffled, but she relayed the message. "Okay, honey, give," she demanded after hanging up. "Ya got two minutes—then we have to boogie down to my place to supposedly plan some music." She gave Rae a quirky smile. "Y'know, that's not a half-bad idea, as I think about it."

Rae stashed the broom and dustpan in the closet beneath the stairs. "Let's go. I needed to get out of here, anyway." Her skin was crawling. Sometimes she wondered if she would ever feel clean again.

On the way down the street she told Karen about the bugged phone, aware that she was violating official instructions. Karen, with typical emotional fervor, shrieked in outrage, and Rae found herself arguing fast and furiously to convince Karen to keep her mouth shut. Rae shuddered to think of the implications, but she refused to drag her friend into danger wearing the blindfold of ignorance.

Tyler called five minutes after they climbed the stairs to Karen's apartment.

"What's going on?" he demanded irritably. "Why aren't you working in your store? It's ten o'clock out there, isn't it? If you want to run a successful business you can't afford to keep irregular hours, Rae."

Rae smiled, shaking her head. "Hi, Tyler. Thanks for the advice." Her fingers absently played on the countertop where Karen's phone sat. "Why are you calling? It's not Christmas or my birthday."

A long-suffering sigh blew over the phone. "I wanted to make sure you were okay," he said. "Have you, ah, have you talked to the FBI about our esteemed father?"

Rae groaned. "Oh, Tyler—you, too? I'm sorry. This is the biggest mess."

"Tell me about it. I'm sitting in my office, fat, dumb and happy, and some rock-faced fed in a three-piece suit lowers the boom. I'm still reeling from the blow." He covered the mouthpiece and Rae heard him speaking muffled words to someone. When he came on the line he irritably apologized. "Anyway, remember when we set up that Durable Financial Power of Attorney when you were eighteen?"

"The one that gave you legal power to take care of my finances?"

"Yeah. Anyway . . . I opened an account in your name a couple of years back, up in Denver. I didn't tell you cause I figured you'd sink it in that dumb house, and I meant for it to be used as a financial safety net for you."

"Tyler—" Flummoxed, Rae blinked rapidly. Never in her wildest dreams had she expected such a loving gesture from her older brother.

Tyler swept on, hiding his discomfort behind clipped impatience. "Then this guy, this fed, tells me that Dad stole checks from that account, forged the signature and depleted all but a crummy four thou."

"What?" The rush of happiness shattered into shock. "This account . . . it must be the one that the FBI—" She closed her eyes, mentally grappling with the revelations being dropped into her lap like sticks of lighted dynamite. "And it was our father. How . . . did he steal the checks and forge my signature, Tyler? Are you sure?"

"The feds are. I keep the checkbook here at work, locked in my desk. But it's crazy around here, and someone with dear old Dad's experience could pick the lock while I was at lunch. The stolen checks were near the back."

"And my signature?"

"I don't know," he all but yelled. "Quit grilling me, all right? Maybe the bank didn't bother to check. He was depositing the forged check into his own account, not taking cash. Talk to the feds. Let them explain."

"It was our father," Rae repeated, struggling without success to quash the pain of betrayal.

"You bet your sweet little bearish market bottom," Tyler shot back before once again covering the phone to speak to someone else. "Look—I gotta go in a few moments. Haven't you talked to that Myers guy? I spent half the day on the phone with the FBI guys out in Denver, and then Myers rings me up at home a little while ago and rakes me over the coals for not telling you about the account. He told me it's caused you a lot of trouble. If the tone of his voice was any indication, it's a good thing we weren't talking face to face. What's going on between the two of you, Sis?"

Rae laughed a hollow laugh. "I have no idea, brother dear. But I do know that if it hadn't been for Caleb, I'd probably be in jail now."

"Yeah, well, I guess maybe I should have told you about that account," he admitted awkwardly. His voice altered to the defensive whine that catapulted Rae fifteen years back. "How was I supposed to know the old man would surface again after all these years, much less have the gall to pull some of his con tricks on his own family?"

"Don't start that old routine," Rae began, then stopped. "Tyler? Has he ever gotten in touch with you?"

"Not even when he stole the checks right from under my nose. Some father, huh. After a stunt like that, I don't care if I ever talk to him, much less see him. Far as I'm concerned, the old goat's dead." After an uncomfortable pause, he added, "I hate to admit it, but sometimes—especially after this stunt—I wish he was."

"I understand," Rae nodded her thanks as Karen placed a mug of tea and two apple spice muffins on the table beside the phone. "Tyler, did you know the FBI came to Uncle Floyd another time, when we were kids, to ask about Dad?"

"Yeah." He bit the word out. "I knew. I was fourteen. The guys had been hassling me about our background pretty bad. When those two feds came, Uncle Floyd told me to ride my bike to the store for a candy bar, but I didn't go."

Rae's heart went out to the sullen, rebellious teenager her brother had been. "Where did you hide? In that hidden pantry under the stairs?"

"Uh-huh. I heard an earful, too. They wanted him for transfer of stolen goods across state lines, larceny, car theft." There was another long pause before he added roughly, "I never told a soul, but I swore to myself that day I was going to leave and never look back. I was going to make a name for myself, and people would look at a Prescott with respect."

"It was rough on me, too," Rae said gently. "Even if I was too young to really understand. It's hard sometimes, even now. But it made such a difference when I—"

"Don't start all the Jesus stuff again. You know how I feel about that."

"I know. And I don't mean to preach. It's just that lately I've begun to realize how much I *do* depend on my faith. God . . . God accepts me for what and who I am, even when I doubt, or mess things up—" She stopped, impatient with herself. "What I'm trying to say is that I'm learning that God doesn't keep score, and He doesn't hold the sins of our parents against us."

"That's great. Look, I really have to go."

"I know." She wound the phone cord around her little finger, wondering if she should have kept her mouth shut. And yet, even as the doubt surfaced, she felt an elusive sensation of renewed strength flowing softly into her soul. "I don't have all the answers— and I've made a lot of mistakes—but in the past couple of months, I do know that if I hadn't had my faith in God, I wouldn't have made it at all."

"Right. Whatever. Well . . . I just wanted to tell you about the account. Gotta go, Sis."

After he disconnected, Rae still sat, toying with the muffin. The gentle river of peace continued to flow, and after a while a smile spread across her face. Caleb had been right—she really hadn't been abandoned at all.

Chapter Nineteen

"Myers, we spend millions of the taxpayers' hard-earned dollars investigating people to avoid nonsense like the Starseeker sabotage. Now you sit there and tell me that this virus—this logic bomb or time bomb or whatever you called it—could have been planted in the software for over a year? It's unconscionable!"

Admiral Vale chomped on the end of a half-eaten cinnamon stick candy, narrow face mottled red, his eyes hard as stones. "And neither do I like your assertion about the difficulty of getting hard evidence on this Fisher character."

Caleb sat patiently, ignoring the smile Tray was trying to hide behind his hand. They had been called on the carpet over the debacle at Rae's store, the carpet being Admiral Vale's office at Peterson Air Force Base. "Sir," Caleb pointed out when the admiral finally ran down, "you've been aware for two months now of the difficulty in tracing the source of the virus. Thanks to the elaborate security measures the joint services utilize, we at least *have* been able to narrow it down to Fisher."

He offered the angry admiral a placating smile, fully understanding the man's frustration. "I can tell you that my experience with similar cases makes me pretty certain the virus had to be planted from the *inside*. Which means, Admiral, that there was little—if anything—your people could have done."

"The military is trained to defend against *outside* aggressors," Tray reminded him, "not insiders."

"I want Fisher picked up and dealt with now."

"You know we can't do that, sir. We haven't got enough concrete evidence to prove criminal intent, and without it there's no hope of conviction." Tray glanced at Caleb in an unspoken signal for help.

"Don't forget that Fisher is merely a tool—the inside access IOS needed to achieve the sabotage," Caleb continued with the blend of low-key authority and deference that in the past had kept the volatile admiral from erupting further. "We're after the principals, as well, or the whole effort will result in pretty much of a washout. IOS will just recruit someone else." He kept his gaze leveled directly on the scowling man. "Even more to the point, if we don't succeed in cutting off the head of this serpent, they won't think twice about hitting on the military again. The next time, the impact might be more devastating and far-reaching than the Starseeker sabotage."

"You don't need to remind me!" Admiral Vale growled. "These programs are closed systems, complex by nature as well as by design, complete with the latest in safeguards. That's why we could put the finger on the little creep—as you just reminded me, Myers! We'll learn from the incident and adjust security measures accordingly." With an abrupt, unconscious movement his fingers snagged another cinnamon stick out of the jar on his desk. "Unfortunately, criminals nowadays have gotten so sophisticated it's harder than ever to stay one jump ahead. They use the same technology we have to gain access, blast it!"

Caleb opened his mouth, and the admiral held up a hand.

"I've talked to the chief of computer security for the Department of Defense." He stuck the piece of candy between his teeth like a cigar. "He sent his regards, by the way, and promised me you're the best. But, young man, you're going to have to do better than you have been, to convince me."

"I'll do my best, Admiral," Caleb promised solemnly. He saw Tray cover a laugh behind a cough.

"He also assures me," Admiral Vale continued after slicing a censorious look toward Tray, "that any future attempts can nonetheless be detected and contained just as this one, because our technological control is still better than in the civilian sector. We've also implemented a better password-checker program and will be making more frequent data backups."

"Yes, sir," Caleb agreed, though he wasn't assured. "Um, if I may return to the Starseeker case, I need to point out, sir, that if we don't persist in our efforts to uncover the kingpins, Polaris might be out a contract, with both the company *and* the Air Force suffering losses of considerable money and wasted time. IOS will be able to continue to do as they please with impunity."

Admiral Vale slammed his fist on the table. "It's so blasted frustrating! I feel like I'm on a destroyer trying to seek out and neutralize enemy subs—without sonar." His attention returned to Ramirez. "Since Fisher is a civilian, I suppose we won't be able to prosecute him under the Uniform Code of Military Justice. What are our options here, Tray?"

"The Attorney General will be trying for a conviction based on charges of harmful access to a computer." Ramirez leaned back in his chair and laced his fingers behind his head. "Lately we've had a lot more success in those cases." He glanced at Caleb, who nodded. "Also, if there's any way to utilize the Computer Fraud and Abuse Act Congress passed back in eighty-six, they'll go for it."

The admiral heaved a sigh and chomped on the candy. "I don't like all this clandestine maneuvering and namby-pamby political parleying." He quirked a thin gray eyebrow, his mouth curving in a wry half smile. "Guess I've been a military man too long. When the enemy is identified, I want to go after him."

"I tend to agree with you," Caleb murmured. Sometimes it was hard to remember God's admonition that vengeance belonged only to Him. He thought of his feelings after seeing Rae's store the previous night. After the fear, a cold, bloodthirsty rage had threatened to sweep away his civility, as well as his faith. The layers of aloofness that his personality had reinforced all his life had exploded, shocking him to the core. Because of Rae, he knew that his life had been somehow altered forever. It was an unnerving revelation.

"Tell me the latest info you've got," the admiral ordered abruptly, pulling Caleb from his uncomfortable thoughts. "I have a meeting in an hour over at NORAD."

"We think at least two women are involved. No description yet, but we're working on it," Tray supplied. "The Prescott woman happened onto what we think is an IOS identification code used on occasion by their female operatives."

"What about the Prescott woman?"

"We're still monitoring—"

"She's a pawn," Caleb answered, cutting across Tray's answer. "An innocent pawn drawn into this because her father's involved with IOS. So far we've been able to confirm that he's responsible for the funds used to pay off Fisher. He forged Rae's brother's signature to retrieve the funds out of the Denver checking account. The FBI have had a positive ID from the bank employee who gave him the money."

"He surfaced briefly in L.A. and Denver," Tray finished. "Dennis Hoffman told me this morning his car was spotted in San Francisco last night."

"At least, the car he was driving when he was spotted in Denver," Caleb added.

"Do you think he plans to approach his daughter?" Admiral Vale asked. "Is that why there's been no evidence that IOS has moved the drop site?"

Tray looked at Caleb, who contemplated his hands for a long moment. "I don't know," he finally admitted, the syllables dragging out. He lifted his head, met the gazes of both men. "I'm afraid there's a strong possibility they'll try and frame Ms. Prescott. They act like they're still not certain of exactly what she knows."

"And Fisher?"

Caleb stood, a disconcerting restlessness crawling over him. "Fisher doesn't have a criminal mind. He's highly intelligent, but he's not devious. He's been collecting old sheet music for some time, so he doubtless feels comfortable going to Joyful Noise. Possibly he's the reason the drop site hasn't been changed." He pondered the ceiling, thinking, assessing. "Maybe Fisher just dug his heels in and IOS right now is willing to comply. Only Fisher can supply the answer to that." The fear for Rae's safety filled him with ironclad resolution to protect her, regardless of personal consequences.

His gaze returned to the two men, and even the admiral shifted uneasily. "When we nail Fisher, I'll find out the details. If he chose Rae's store deliberately . . . if Rae's father is trying to set her up and IOS harms her person in *any* way—then God help them, and me." His voice dropped to a rustling whisper that seemed to bring down the room temperature by forty degrees. "Because I'll track every last one of them down and nail their hides to the barn door. Permanently."

With the store closed for the day and no piano students, time hung heavy on Rae's restless hands. After she and Karen parted, she indulged in a therapeutic bout of cleaning her living quarters for the first time in six months. When even that failed to help, she made herself some tea, then curled up in Uncle Floyd's chair and picked up her Bible. One of Caleb's notes had mentioned a psalm, and she thought perhaps the comforting words the Psalms always provided might soothe her spirit more than frenetic activity. Besides, it was Caleb who had suggested she read it. If only she hadn't thrown that note away—

The note.

Whispering a soft prayer of gratitude for the guidance, Rae hurried to her music room. She had stacked most of the music into neat piles. She rummaged frantically, scattering everything all over the floor again. Where was it? Had she trashed it without thought in her cleaning frenzy? An explosive sigh of relief escaped when she at last unearthed the scrap of paper, stuffed haphazardly inside the cover of the Brahms sonata where she'd first discovered it.

She studied the meaningless jumble of symbols for a long time, but all she could tell for certain was that they were lines of computer code. Rae's only experience with computers had been a class she had taken at Juilliard that taught a person how to compose music on-screen. One day she hoped to have the funds to purchase a computer, possibly a laptop, to use with her piano students, but until this wretched business with IOS was over . . .

An alarming possibility crashed into her brain. The folded piece of paper might be just that, a worthless scrap of paper some customer had forgotten to remove, used to mark a piece. On the other hand, perhaps one of those women who had worn the matching necklaces had accidentally *dropped* that folded slip of paper into the music while they searched through the bins. If so, and IOS needed the information, it was no wonder they had been hounding Rae so mercilessly!

If they found the paper in her living quarters, obviously moved, her life wouldn't be worth a used tea bag.

She had to alert someone immediately. Clutching the note, she scurried to the bedroom and hastily changed into clean slacks and a three-quarter-sleeve pullover while she determined what to do. Then she folded the note into quarters and stuffed it in her purse. No—too obvious. After a frowning moment, she dug it out and smoothed it into a slimmer shape, then put it deep inside the side seam pockets of her slacks.

She decided to turn it directly over to Caleb. Not only was he the acknowledged computer consultant expert, she could meet him in a more natural fashion to avoid alerting the already suspicious IOS watchdogs. He was supposed to be her boyfriend, after all. Besides, she couldn't very well stroll across the street and wave the paper at the agents on the second floor of the abandoned store.

She forced herself to walk at her normal pace to the garage. Her nose wrinkled at the heavy burned odor, but she didn't spare a glance at the damage as she climbed into her car. Too bad the undercover team had decided to abandon the room over her garage. It was an effort to back out of the driveway, then drive nonchalantly to a small shopping center several blocks down Colorado Avenue, when she knew she risked exposure not only for herself but the team assigned to shadow her. She pulled into a parking spot in front of the grocery store. Once inside, she hunted down a public phone in the back.

Nobody was within hearing distance. Palms damp, she called the number of the agents stationed across the street. "This is Rae Prescott," she announced in a low voice, speaking rapidly. "I need to get to Caleb Myers, fast. Can you tell me where he is?"

"Where are you calling from?" The voice was unfamiliar, the impersonal tone a warning.

Rae wanted to split his eardrums with a shrill scream. "I'm at a public phone," she said sharply. "And I think I might have found a clue." Her eyes cast furtive glances about the store. "I've got to get it to Caleb. He'll know what it means."

"Ms. Prescott, where *exactly* are you calling from? Give me the address, and we'll send someone along. You should have known better—"

"Look, there's no time for this. I appreciate what you're doing, but this information doesn't need to wait until you guys can concoct some fancy little plan so I can pass it to you." She glared at the phone. "Just tell me where Caleb is, and I'll take him the note myself! It will be far less suspicious that way—he's supposed to be my boyfriend, remember?"

"I don't think that would be a good idea, Ms. Prescott. Now, if you—"

"No," she interrupted. "Tell me where Caleb Myers is right now, or I'm going to stroll down the street and announce to everyone who walks by just what's going on on the second floor of the old hardware store." Of course she'd never do such a thing, but they wouldn't know that for sure, considering the reputation she'd earned with her powder-keg temper.

Sure enough, alarmed mutterings grew in the background, but Rae didn't care about their opinion of her right now. She *had* to get to Caleb, had to prove her innocence, and her best hope for accomplishing that lay with Caleb. By turning this note over to him, she would be demonstrating her willing cooperation and, she hoped, finally establishing her innocence once and for all.

"Listen, Ms. Prescott," the agent said in a more conciliatory tone. "Mr. Myers is in a meeting out at Falcon right now. He really can't be reached. If you—"

Falcon Air Force Station. "Thanks! Radio whoever is supposed to keep a tail on me that I'll be headed east on Colorado." She hung up in the middle of the agent's urgent protests, her mind racing.

Since she'd entered a grocery store, she better not leave empty-handed. Hurriedly Rae flung a selection of items in a cart, paying scant attention to either the items or the strange look the cashier gave her at the checkout.

Traffic was light this time of the afternoon, and she made it to the east side of town with no trouble. But a three-car accident at a busy intersection had snarled movement in all directions, and it took Rae ten minutes to finally maneuver past. She wondered if her watchdogs were keeping up, but refused to speculate on the vulture eyes of IOS.

The road to Falcon Air Force Station wound through fifteen miles of almost treeless rolling prairie. Junkyards and occasional houses dotted the road at odd intervals. At one-thirty in the afternoon the road was relatively deserted. Rae spared a brief second to take her first deep breath. She patted her pocket, then almost panicked when she couldn't feel anything. Her fingers wormed beneath the seat belt, searching, and finally brushed against the paper. The loss of that note would have been a bit difficult to explain.

A huge black car roared up behind her, filling the rearview mirror. Rae glanced at her speedometer, which hovered a little above sixty. Her eyebrows lifted. Someone was in an even bigger hurry, and with an inward admonishment at such recklessness she pulled over so the car could pass.

The black car drew alongside her. Rae glimpsed the pale, sinister face staring straight at her, thin lips stretched tightly in a ruthless smile. A tiny shock stung a corner of Rae's brain, but the recognition came a split second too late. Even as she slammed on the brakes the other car swerved, banging against her car's front bumper.

Rae's hatchback hurtled into an out-of-control spin toward a wide, shallow ditch. The world spun violently, a cacophony of noise and speed and a white-hot pain bursting inside her skull. Then darkness.

Chapter Twenty

Faces . . . She sensed faces bending over her. Hands touching her. Rae tried to hit out, tried to squirm away but she couldn't see, couldn't move.

"Take it easy, Rae," a man's voice said. "Stay still, now—you've been hurt."

Something wet and sticky trickled down her forehead into her eyes. Again she tried to open them, but it was like prising the lid off a jar of three-year-old canned preserves. She was semiconscious, but a deep-seated instinct told her that she had to fight, to resist even if they'd blindfolded her and tied her arms. She struggled to lift her arms to find out if she could move them and firm, restraining fingers closed around her wrist.

"Wait a minute," the calm voice ordered. "Wait until you're sentient. Try to move your limbs slowly."

Something soft was pressed against her forehead, and she was tilted very gently back until her head rested against the seat. Rae succeeding in opening her eyes and winced against the light. Pain and nausea rolled over her in a sluggish tide, but she concentrated on keeping her eyes open, blinking until her vision cleared enough to recognize the man leaning over her. Detective Evan MacArthur. His face was full of concern, and beads of perspiration had turned the deep chocolate skin a shimmering ebony in the bright afternoon sun.

"Hello," he said when he saw her eyes focus and register recognition. "Welcome back to the world. Try not to hit me again, okay?" His voice changed, flattened. "Ms. Prescott—Rae. Can you tell us what happened?"

Rae stared at him, mute. Something was telling her she mustn't talk. Couldn't tell him. Pain slashed through her skull. "An animal. I . . . um . . . I swerved. Lost control. Ran off the road," she managed to whisper.

"How's she doing?"

J.W. Ayers, his clever, good-looking face shadowed with worry, appeared behind Evan. The light gray eyes moved over Rae. "I radioed Falcon. Myers is on his way, but I don't think we better wait. She looks like she's in shock."

"Pulse is shallow, rapid—but I think I got the bleeding stopped on her temple. She might be concussed, but there's no broken bones, at least."

J.W. leaned forward suddenly, a frown deepening when Rae flinched. "Look at her throat. Does that look like something the shoulder strap would have done?"

Trembling, Rae shook her head, lifted feeble hands to push them away. "No," she protested, her voice alarmingly weak. "I'm fine. Just lost control." Her vision blurred, and the words suddenly seemed too large to escape her mouth. "Ran . . . off road," she repeated as the two faces swam in front of her, then began a slow slide down a long black tunnel. The voices faded in and out.

"She's scared of something."

"Yeah—whaddaya think?"

"I think we get her to the hospital and hope Myers can find out what it is. That guy could pry the pearl out of an oyster and have the oyster thank him."

"Maybe so, but I have a feeling we're gonna be in deep Dutch with both him and Grabowski but good for letting her get away from us."

"We're not responsible . . . Springs traffic . . . bad scene all the way around, man . . ."

The last pinprick of light vanished, and the men's voices were drowned out by angry bees swarming in Rae's head. She moaned an incoherent protest, then gave in to the bees.

*   *   *

The next time she regained consciousness she was lying on a gurney with a sheet covering her from the neck down. Antiseptic and ammonia smells stung her nose, and a continuous rumble of voices and scraping footsteps sounded somewhere beyond the light green curtain drawn around the cubicle where she lay.

Slowly, cautiously, Rae opened her eyes. Even more cautiously turned her head. And saw Caleb. He stood by the bed, strong and invincible. Caleb.

"Rae." He enclosed one of her hands in both of his, the touch warm, infinitely sustaining. "How are you feeling, sweetheart?"

"Caleb." She tried to smile, tried to speak, but all she could manage was a feeble whisper of his name. Tears welled, and he wiped them away with the backs of his hands.

"Easy, easy. You're okay, which is nothing short of a miracle and the blessings of seat belts."

"What . . ."

He understood instantly. "Your car's a total loss, but you really are all right. Bruised, slight concussion, and tomorrow all your bones will probably let you know about the battle you lost with a ditch." His voice roughened, and the fingers holding hers trembled. "But you're okay. Thank God you're okay."

Rae clung to his hand and tried not to think about the future.

The curtain billowed as Agent Ramirez, Detective Grabowski and a man Rae had never seen crowded around the gurney.

"Glad to see you're not seriously injured, Ms. Prescott," Tray Ramirez greeted her. He slid a black-eyed glance over Caleb. "Think you can answer some questions for us?"

A harried nurse elbowed her way through the cluster of men. "Look, guys, I know you want some info, but the lady here doesn't need to be disturbed."

The man Rae didn't recognize took the nurse's arm, murmured something, then led her outside the curtain. Beneath the sheet, Rae's body had gone rigid, and she could feel the panic beating at the edges of her dazed stupor. Her gaze moved from each of the men, then fastened on Caleb. She didn't know what to do. *Lord? I don't know what to do.*

"Ms. Prescott," Ramirez persisted, his voice determined. "We know you were coming to Falcon to see Myers. We've listened to the tape."

If she closed her eyes, maybe she could fool them into thinking she'd passed out.

"She's hiding something," Grabowski said sharply. "You can see it in her face." He whirled. "Myers—"

"Back off. Give her a chance."

Rae's eyes jerked open, and she found Caleb was shielding her from the others with his body. He looked at Rae, and her heart began to throb in hard, hurtful thuds. She knew that look, knew with fatalistic dread that she didn't have the strength to withstand the implacable force of his will. Uncontrollable shivers rippled through her body. She didn't want him defending her, shielding her. Not now. Not when it could cost him his life.

"Rae, you have to tell me what happened. I know you found something that you wanted me to see. Is that what frightened you?" He leaned closer, searching her face, his gaze sharpening. "What did you find?" He let go of her hand and moved back, as if he knew she needed room. "It must have been pretty important, right?"

Rae stared at him dumbly.

"Ms. Prescott, have you been threatened again?" Detective Grabowski asked. "If so, you need to tell us immediately—unless chasing off toward Falcon with a supposed clue was another diversion?"

"Grabowski—"

The detective certainly knew which buttons to push. With a tremulous sigh Rae squeezed Caleb's hand. "It's all right." She wished her head didn't feel like a dozen jackhammers were drilling away, or that she felt so weak—it would be difficult to divert them. But she had to try and pray the diversion would work. She lifted her eyes to the detective and held his gaze without flinching. "I did find a clue. It looked like lines of computer code, and I wanted Caleb to see it because I knew he would know what it meant." She paused. "And I could also be sure of having the right motive attached to my actions."

"We searched your car, Rae," Tray inserted. "There was no sign of a note." He glanced from her to Caleb. "The contents of your purse were scattered all over the front seat and the floorboards. I guess the impact threw everything out, hmm? Possibly when the police arrived, the note could have blown out when they opened the door."

Grabowski growled something beneath his breath. Rae felt three sets of eyes burning holes in her, and she fought to hide her growing anxiety.

Caleb leaned over, and his fingers brushed droplets of perspiration from the unbandaged side of her head. "*Was* the note in your purse, Rae?" he asked quietly.

"No." With slow, awkward movements her free hand searched beneath the sheet, and her fingers brushed against the paper. The relief made her light-headed, and her eyes burned from fresh tears she was too proud to shed. The three men crowded around the bed, unable to hide their mounting tension. "I put it in my pocket." She withdrew the crumpled note and held it out to Caleb.

He unfolded it, and one eyebrow disappeared beneath the errant lock of hair that always fell over his forehead. "Well, well, well." Bending, he pressed a soft kiss on Rae's temple, winked at her, then turned to the other men. "Gentlemen, I think the case is about to break."

He handed the note to Tray Ramirez. "If I'm not mistaken, what Rae found is part of the commands from the Starseeker program."

He might as well have pulled out an M-16 and sprayed bullets in the ceiling.

"Are you sure, Myers?" Stunned, Grabowski looked from the note to Caleb, then at Rae. "Where did you find this, Ms. Prescott?"

"It was in a copy of a Brahms sonata," Rae said. She passed her tongue around suddenly dry lips. "The one in F minor. Opus five. I was just playing scores at random from some pieces I picked out after my store was vandalized." She kept her eyes on Caleb, praying that he believed her. "The note fell out. It didn't make sense at the time."

She tried to swallow, wishing she could have a drink of water. "I just picked up the Brahms, mostly because a corner of it had been sticking out. I was going to straighten it, then just pulled it out to play later."

"When did you realize it was more than just a random piece of scrap paper?" Tray asked.

His attitude toward her had softened, but Rae still had to force herself to look at him. A glimmer of compassion twinkled beneath the maddening blank-wall look all the agents seemed to have perfected. Rae swallowed convulsively, tears almost spilling over.

"Earlier . . . I was reading my Bible." She colored. "Caleb had mentioned a verse from Psalms in a note he sent me, and that was when I remembered the piece of paper—" she nodded toward the note "—and it occurred to me that it might have been part of a note rather than just a scrap some customer had used to mark a piece of music."

"Where's the music it fell out of? There may have been more notes, or writing on the music itself."

Rae felt her blush deepening into temper at Detective Grabowski's tone, which plainly indicated he still wasn't totally convinced of her innocence. "It's still on my piano," she replied, frost coating the words. "When I realized it might be a clue, I left the house immediately and called the agents from a public phone—I even remembered to buy groceries as camouflage—to find out where Caleb was. If I was planning a double cross or I was part of IOS, I would have destroyed the note, not tried to find Caleb."

"It would have been safer, and far more practical, to arrange to pass the note to one of our men immediately."

"I wanted to give it to someone I trust, who also trusts me," she answered testily. She tried to sit up, hating the vulnerability of lying prone while the obstinate detective towered above her. Pain lanced through her head, but she resisted Caleb's hands when they pressed against her shoulders. She glared at Grabowski. "Well? Would it destroy your reputation if you have to admit you were wrong about me?"

"Easy, Rae." Caleb leaned down again, so close his lips brushed her ear. "Your claws are showing, little cat," he murmured, so low the others couldn't hear.

"I'm willing to admit that your explanation and subsequent actions are plausible, given the circumstances at the time," Grabowski said, ignoring her comment. The ice blue eyes narrowed. "But I'm still waiting for you to tell us why you're frightened, and have been since the accident. According to my men, you tried to fight them off even before you were fully conscious. There have been several times these past few moments when you've been evasive." He crossed his arms. "How 'bout it, Ms. Prescott? If you'll come clean about *everything,* most of my, um, nasty suspicions, shall we say, will be laid to rest."

Rae quit trying to sit up. Fists clenched, her mind scrabbled in tighter and tighter circles, and the pain in her head was almost impossible to ignore any longer. "Detective, I acted frightened because I'd just had the fright of my life. I could have died on that road. On top of that, I've been scared out of my skull most of the past two months. If you want to invest—if you think . . ." She closed her eyes, but that only made her more dizzy. "May I have some water?" she asked weakly. "I . . . don't feel good."

"Quit stalling, Ms. Prescott. I'm still not satisfied."

"I'll ask the nurse if you can have some water," Caleb replied in a soft tone that sent prickles galloping down Rae's spine. "Grabowski. Tray. Let's talk outside." He gave Rae's arm a reassuring squeeze, and she listened to the rustling sound of the curtain as the three men filed quietly out.

When the clucking nurse appeared a moment later with a paper cup of water and a straw, Rae's hands were trembling so badly the nurse had to hold the cup and guide the straw to her lips.

"I should never have let that silver-tongued guy bamboozle me," the nurse said. "They've gone and upset you, haven't they?"

"No, it's not that. It's just all catching up with me." Rae took several more swallows, then asked the nurse to help her sit up. She had just gingerly swung her feet over the side of the bed when Caleb slipped into the cubicle.

Immediately the nurse bristled. "You're going to have to leave. She needs nothing but peace and quiet—"

"That's what I'm here to insure," Caleb interrupted with a lopsided smile that hushed the objections instantly. "I've talked to the doctor, and he assures me that it's perfectly safe to release Ms. Prescott. I'm taking her home."

He turned the potent force of that smile on Rae, and the lance of pain pierced her heart. *Lord, I don't want anything to happen to him.* Why did she have to love him so much?

Without quite knowing how it happened, less than ten minutes later Rae was comfortably ensconced in the seat of Caleb's government-loaned car, and Caleb was competently maneuvering through rush hour traffic. They didn't talk, and Rae sat in a sort of dumb lethargy, floating willy-nilly with the current she was powerless to control. Right now, she couldn't even summon up the energy to care.

A few minutes later her startled gaze flew across the seat to Caleb. "You missed the turn to my house," she protested, fighting to keep alarm out of her voice.

"I know." His reply was calm. "Lean back and rest, sweetheart. We're just going up the road a little ways." The car stopped at a traffic light, and he turned toward her, the light amber eyes deepening to the mesmerizing gold of a tiger's. "Then you and I are going to talk."

Lethargy vanished in a breathless whoosh. Rae's throat tightened, and her heart began to race. He was going to interrogate her, of course. And if she weakened, allowed his powerful charisma and her love to sway her, she would be responsible for his certain death. Yet if she somehow managed to maintain her silence . . . she might be responsible for her own.

Chapter Twenty-One

Bright afternoon sunbeams shot over the top of Pikes Peak into the valley below, reflecting off the incredible red sandstone slablike formations of Garden of the Gods. Caleb turned onto the road leading into the park and drove along the winding lanes until he found a deserted spot to pull over.

When he opened the car door, he took a surreptitious couple of deep breaths and rotated his neck as he crossed to open Rae's door. The next moments just might possibly be the most significant of his entire thirty-two years, and he'd rather be facing a roomful of hungry tigers. The odds of survival were far stronger. His timing, unfortunately, was lousy, but events over the past several hours had forced his hand.

Mom, do you feel the earth moving along with me, all the way back in Georgia?

He helped Rae out, then kept his arm around her as they began walking. She was stiff, her eyes dark and turbulent as a captured doe's. Caleb dredged up a smile, wondering what had happened to his legendary detachment in tense situations. Right now he felt about as laid-back and in control as a bowl of Jell-O balanced on the edge of a rumbling volcano. Too bad he was the Jell-O—and Rae the volcano. *Hey, Lord? Since this was Your doing, how about dosing me up with courage, if I can't have cool?*

"Where are we going?" Rae asked, the question tentative.

"Not far." She felt so fragile, a delicate bundle of bruises and bravado, and she had almost died. Caleb ground his back teeth together and kept walking. "I thought this would be a good place to talk." He shifted her to navigate around some jutting rock and scrub oak.

The road behind them disappeared. He swiftly surveyed the area, and when he neither saw nor heard any sign of other people, he carefully helped Rae sit on a patch of dry ground. After kicking aside a couple of stones and some twigs, he dropped down beside her.

"How's your head? That medicine the doc gave you kicking in yet?"

"Pretty well . . . it still hurts, but it's bearable." She looked around. "Uncle Floyd used to bring Tyler and me here for picnics. We loved to climb the rocks."

"I've been coming here a lot over the past months," Caleb admitted, lifting his face to the warmth of the sun. "It's fascinating—peaceful, but somehow larger than life. Sort of helps me put this whole tangled-up case in perspective." He gave a rueful laugh. "Plus a few other things in my life." Like how he knew for the first time that there *was* something far more important than his work and his nomadic life-style.

Rae glanced around indifferently. "What did you want to talk about?"

He turned to look directly at her, memorizing the determined jut of her chin, the long narrow nose, the splatter of freckles dusting her cheeks. Her eyes.

She was so transparent—and he was in love with her. Incredibly, he could feel sweat gathering on his forehead and hands. He fiddled with his watchband, wanting to play the macho role of caveman instead of this ignoble chess game that he was rapidly losing. "There's a couple of things I need to say, but I want to tell you what I've found out about your father first." Pain twisted his heart at Rae's expression. Then her head bent so all Caleb could see was the shining mass of hair, hastily arranged at the hospital into a sloppy chignon that was already slipping loose.

Before he could help himself, his hands lifted to pull out the pins.

"What are you—Caleb, stop!" She slapped at his hands but it

was too late. Her hair waterfalled down her back, taking Caleb's breath away.

"Helps your headache, though, doesn't it?" He touched her bottom lip with his finger. "And I like it like this. You have beautiful hair."

"I . . . I really am going to cut it all off one of these days." She gnawed on the lip he had touched, looking so uncertain he wanted to cover her mouth with his and banish her feelings of insecurity forever.

"Caleb? My father?" The gray eyes were fogged with shame and worry. "What did you find out?"

Help me to do this right, Lord. "He's one of the IOS couriers," he admitted without dressing it up. Rae had been lied to enough. "He also plays the part of front man, committing grand larceny and a host of other schemes to provide extra funds." He had to touch her again, but only allowed himself to lay his hand over one cold little fist. "Your father is the one who stole the funds out of that bank account in Denver, Rae. I'm sorry."

"I know. I talked to my brother."

"Uh-huh. I suppose you got an earful, since I hadn't had a chance to explain after your store was vandalized."

"It was a shock," she confessed. "But nothing worse than what I've suspected for years. Uncle Floyd refused to talk about him at all, and when I'd question my brother he'd get this horrible scowl and just tell me to shut up. By the time I was fifteen, I figured I'd be fortunate if he wasn't wanted for murder." She looked at Caleb at last, her eyes swimming in tears. "I know it's not supposed to matter when I'm a Christian, Caleb. But it does."

With an inarticulate groan he turned, wrapping her in a close, protective embrace. "I'm sorry, so sorry." He kissed her hair, then pressed his cheek to the soft strands, carefully avoiding her bandaged forehead. "I can't identify with your shame, Rae—but I can share the burden."

He clasped her shoulders, then held her a little way from him. "You're stronger than you realize, you know. All you need to do is reset your thinking knob to a Christian station."

"That's bad, Myers."

"Made you smile, didn't it?" He began stroking her arms, loving the strength he could feel in spite of the delicacy of her bones.

"When you're in over your head—and you are, so you might as well admit it—that's the very time to call on God's help. Let Him provide some of the confidence you think you don't have. It's also time to call on the *human* help—that's me, by the way—for backup."

"I was trying to—and it landed me in a ditch." Her throat muscles swallowed convulsively. "I—it happened so fast, Caleb. And there was nothing I could do. Everything went out of control. And there was nothing I could do." Her fingers lifted to fiddle with the buttons on her blood-splattered shirt, then dropped to fumble nervously in her lap. "These past months have been like that out-of-control car spin. I'm strapped in, totally helpless to do anything to stop the spin." She looked at her hands and tried to smile. "It's a shame there's not a piano close by."

"Ah. Is that how you release tension, regain a little of the control you feel like you've lost? When you're sitting on that bench, *you're* the one in charge?"

She looked bemused. "I suppose. I've never really thought about it that way, but you're right. I do feel like I'm absolutely in control when I'm playing the piano, which is sort of ironic. One of my professors once told me the only time I ever looked relaxed, lost almost, was when I finally mastered a piece and knew where I was going with it."

"How'd you get involved with music, anyway?" He turned her so they were sitting comfortably side by side, his arm still holding her close. Some of that pinched, white look she tended to wear when they talked about her father had faded, though she was still far too pale. He tried for an encouraging smile.

"There was an old upright in the parlor. I used to bang on it. After Mom died, Uncle Floyd would hold me on his lap and pick out tunes. He told me it was the only way he could get me to smile." She looked toward one of the massive red formations, her gaze unfocused. "He got me started on lessons, and the teacher said I had a good ear. Uncle Floyd was delighted and decided I deserved only the best—partly because he was an indulgent, impractical old man, but probably partly out of guilt for the mess his brother had made of all our lives."

She sighed, stretched her hands out and wriggled her fingers. "As you know, I ended up at Juilliard with the promise of a fairly successful career after I won a couple of competitions. Uncle Floyd was so proud—relieved, too. Finally someone in the family was going to make something of themselves. But finances . . . Well, to put it bluntly, my uncle didn't have an iota of financial management sense. I had no idea until his heart attack. He refused to let me help, and by that time Tyler was long gone."

"That was his choice, his responsibility, Rae. Don't carry that burden, as well."

"I try, but you've seen the place. The Prescotts were some of the first to settle this region. Until this last generation, our family was one of the most highly respected in the state. But my father pretty much destroyed that reputation, and even Uncle Floyd was considered something of an eccentric. Tyler couldn't escape fast enough." For a moment she stared fixedly, and Caleb watched the pulse in the hollow of her throat fluttering like a captive bird. "But I cared. I *care*," she said fiercely. "Ultimately, saving the Prescott family home mattered more to me than a career. It's the only decent legacy I have left."

"Don't you realize how much courage that took? Most people with your opportunity would have kissed the place off without looking back, just like your brother did. He ran, sweetheart—but you chose to fight."

A measure of tranquillity softened her face. "Thank you for that. I did a lot of praying back then." She cut him one lightning-swift glance. "It's nice to be able to say that and know you understand. Anyway, I just felt Uncle Floyd deserved more. He took us in, gave us everything, tried his entire life to make us feel like a—a family, tried to make up for what our father and mother were."

"I'd have to say, knowing you like I do, that Uncle Floyd did a magnificent job with his niece."

Color bloomed, and Caleb was entranced. His hand lifted to flick one rose-tinted cheekbone. "You don't have to try and make me feel better, but thanks, anyway," she said, ignoring his intimate gesture. "I've never regretted my decision, and somehow I think God has provided adequate compensation in return." A light laugh tickled Caleb's ears, and the musical sound punched him—hard—straight in the heart. "Even if sometimes my ears flinch when I hear 'Für Elise' butchered, or the choir massacres Mozart . . . the smile on eight-year-old Jennifer's face when she conquers the E

major scale, or the way the sanctuary rings after the choir pulls off
a really good rendition . . . well, I'm content."

He couldn't restrain himself any longer, and cupped her face in
his hands, caressing the fragile cheekbones with his thumbs while
he drowned in the bottomless pools of her eyes. "Y'know something, Rae Prescott? I think you're one special lady."

Her eyelids drooped and her lips half parted. Caleb could feel
her trembling. Control and nobility shot, he lowered his head and
kissed her, and her unguarded response sliced through him like a
flaming sword. He barely retained enough sense to remember her
injured status as he carefully wrapped her in a close embrace.

"Sweetheart," he whispered eventually, kissing the translucent
eyelids, the narrow nose, "I should apologize, I know—we've got to
stop this and talk."

"Don't want to talk . . ."

The words were slurred, almost sultry, and Caleb smiled against
her temple. "Neither do I," he whispered. The corner of his mouth
brushed the edge of the white bandage covering her forehead, jogging his conscience, and a scrap of discipline grudgingly returned.
He pressed his hand to her cheek until she opened her eyes.
"Rae," he said, very gently, "we *have* to talk. I'm afraid your life
may be in danger because of the Starseeker case and your father's
involvement with IOS. So far, they've been playing with you, waiting to see if you could be used. But finding that computer code
changes everything."

She stirred, then went very still. "I know."

"You obviously weren't meant to find it. But because you did, I
don't think IOS is going to be playing with you anymore." He
firmly removed her arms from his neck and set her against the
boulder again, keeping his gaze on her face. "Now will you tell me
what really happened when your car went off the road? You didn't
lose control trying to avoid an animal, did you?"

She shook her head in agonized denial. "Caleb. Don't ask me.
Please."

It was all he could do not to sweep her in his arms, then spirit
her off to the sanctuary of his parents' home half a continent away.
In a deliberate, calming movement, he stretched out prone,
propped on his elbows, and watched a pair of crows lazily circling
above them. After several moments of increasingly uncomfortable

silence in which Rae's hands began their familiar restless playing pattern, he finally spoke. "I can't protect you if you don't level with me."

"I don't care about me!" she burst out suddenly. "It's you. You!"

He picked up a piece of straw grass and twirled it idly. "What do you mean?"

"I can't tell you anything because of what might happen to you. They said—" She stopped abruptly.

"Who said?" he asked, rising lazily to his feet and regarding her steadily. "Who, Rae?" He leaned over and gripped her elbows, tugging her upright.

Instantly she pulled free, standing in front of him stiff and frozen, trapped, her gaze agonized. "I can't!" she moaned. "Caleb—they'll kill you."

"Do you think they'll stop with bruising your throat the next time—or just running you into a ditch?" When he saw that his educated guess hit home, a slow, burning rage he had never felt in his life gathered force deep inside. "Who was it, Rae?" he asked, his voice lethally soft.

Rae backed away, bumping into the boulder.

"They ran you off the road, didn't they?" He followed, crowding her. "Was it the same guys as the first time? They ran you off the road and then they threatened you—warned you to keep quiet?"

After another tension-crackling moment, Rae slumped in defeat. "One of them started to choke me when he couldn't find anything in my purse," she said in a flat, dead voice. "The other one made him quit. Then he said they'd kill you if I tried to identify them. He told me nobody ever double-crossed IOS, and if I tried, I'd lose more than a few lousy trinkets."

He had suspected as much from the moment he heard what happened, but hearing it was like tossing a lighted match onto the gasoline. He wrapped her in his arms and pressed her head against his chest, fighting to control the trembling rage.

"I heard the siren from J.W.'s and Evan's car about that time, but I guess I passed out," she told him, the words muffled against his shirt.

"Rae . . ."

Her arms snaked around his waist and clung. "If anything happened to you, I couldn't bear it," she mumbled in a desperate, broken voice. "I couldn't."

"How do you think I feel about you?" He lifted her head, gazed deeply into her eyes. "Rae, sweetheart—" the words burst free before he could stop them "—I'm in love with you." He felt as though his heart had swelled into his throat, choking off his breath. "I love you."

Incredulous, incandescent joy washed into Rae's face, and two tears finally spilled. Her hands slid from his neck to touch his mouth, his jaw. "Caleb. You love me. . . ." She blinked several times, then musical laughter filled the air. "That's a miracle, because—because I love you, too! But I never thought—I never dreamed—" The words stopped on a breathless gasp.

Caleb lifted her and twirled her around, oblivious to her head and sore muscles, oblivious to everything but the explosion of joy that was rocketing through his body. Then his head lowered and captured her mouth in a passionate kiss that seared all the way to his toes.

"God sure has a funny sense of timing," he mused a long while later, when the first euphoric joy had calmed to a steady, brightly burning flame. "I've known since the first time I saw you that you were different, special—but I was on a case. I kept trying to ignore the feelings, kept fighting them off—telling God I didn't understand why you stuck in my mind like a puzzle I couldn't solve and would He kindly solve it for me. So He did, in a way my mother will be happy to hear. She's been nagging me for years to come home with a good woman."

Rae rubbed her face against his neck below his jaw. "For me, it was your eyes and your kindness. Desire and compassion . . . a potent and irresistible blend." She kissed the pulse throbbing in Caleb's throat and whispered, "Nobody ever looked at me, or treated me, quite the way you did—the way you do."

"And nobody *but* me better look and treat you like I do in the future."

"You mean nobody else can treat me with Christian compassion?"

He kissed her soundly again. "That's what you get for having a sassy mouth."

"I'll try and be sassy more often, then." Suddenly she clutched his shirtfront and pressed her cheek against his chest. The laughter in him died when he heard her sniff. "I just can't believe you love me," she whispered. "I can't believe God would give me someone like you."

The light touch—he had to remember that she responded better to the light touch. "Well, you're stuck with me now, no matter what. And that works two ways, little cat's claw. My mom's been praying since I was in my late teens that God would provide my mate, my perfect helpmeet. I really wasn't ready, much less interested. In fact, I'd about decided God was going to teach me a lesson for not listening to my mother—or Him, so that even when I was ready to settle down, there wouldn't be anybody left. I can't believe God saved *you* for *me.*"

He gently tried to prise her face out of his shirtfront, but Rae resisted so adamantly he gave up and contented himself with running his fingers through her silky waist-length hair. Eventually he felt her draw a deep, unsteady breath.

"I'm not perfect, Caleb," she reminded him in a stifled voice. "I have this temper, if you'll remember. And I'm absentminded and nonobservant except with music—it's my past, Caleb! When your parents find out about mine—"

"Shh. Hush." This time, he wouldn't allow her to hide any longer. "Look at me—no, sweetheart, *look* at me and listen. When you gave yourself to Christ, you gave away your past. All of it, including the pain and mistakes of your parents. And guess what— God is not the God of yesterday, hovering over you with a club to constantly remind you of the past. He's the great *I am.* Think about it, sweetheart—what if you woke up every morning and the day was as fresh and new as our love? No yesterdays, just the promise of today and the hope of tomorrow."

"No yesterdays," she repeated slowly, her nose and forehead wrinkling in concentration. "I'll still lose my temper every day, probably. I keep trying, but I still fail." Her fingers came up to press against his beard-roughened cheek. "But if I'm hearing you right, and remembering my Bible correctly, then for every morning I wake up, I'll have a fresh start for that day. I do love you, Caleb Myers."

"I love you. Don't ever forget either one." Caleb hugged her. "Now—before it gets dark and we get lost trying to find our way back to the car, I'm afraid we have to finish the unpleasant part of this conversation." He covered her hand with his. "Because it's suddenly become even more important to see to your safety and continued well-being."

"No more so than yours," Rae replied. She shivered, and he saw her wince, pain dimming the glow in her eyes.

The sun vanished behind Pikes Peak, throwing crimson streamers across the sky and the world into darkening shadows. Caleb took Rae's hand. "Let's go get something to eat," he said, "and we'll try to come up with a plan of action."

Chapter Twenty-Two

Rae watched Caleb more than she watched the surroundings while they drove through town. A lopsided smile curving her lips probably looked besotted. She didn't care. She didn't care that her head throbbed, or that all her muscles and bones had joined the pain demonstration. *He loved her.* She didn't even care that, buried somewhere underneath the euphoria, terror waited. Caleb would be with her, guarding her not only with his life—but with his love.

Never mind that, at the end of the drive, he would slip into his professional persona and she would slip into hers. They had both shared that golden hour in Garden of the Gods.

"You'll have to wipe that expression off your face if you aren't prepared for the razzing of your life, regardless of circumstances."

"I know." Their hands touched, briefly clung. "I will. I wouldn't want you to be embarrassed. But you'll have to wipe the same expression from your face."

Caleb made a rude noise. "That tears it. My reputation is shot forever. No longer am I the impassive and fearless consultant, able to stare down enraged executives with a single look."

The terror bit deep, jolting in its suddenness. Caleb was knowingly putting his life on the line. *What if IOS succeeded in killing him?* "Caleb?"

He shot her a swift, bracing glance. "Having a reality attack?"

Mute, she nodded, her gaze devouring his face, the shaggy hair and day's growth of beard unable to disguise the strength of character that radiated from him. He drove with relaxed confidence, and although he instantly understood her fear, his eyes—never still—testified to his poised alertness of their surroundings. He might *look* relaxed, but it was deceptive.

Rae struggled to subdue her fear, because the last thing he needed was to have his concentration diluted. *But he's still just a man.* God had brought them together, filled their hearts with love. He wouldn't allow Caleb to die now, would He? "I'll be all right," she said, determined to at least sound as though she had everything under control.

Another jolt sizzled through her, but this time it was one of revelation. She *wasn't* in control. But God was. "Either trust the Conductor or don't play as though you're part of His orchestra," she whispered to herself. "Well, I'm afraid," she amended aloud, "and I'm *trying* to be all right."

"It's all right to be afraid, sweetheart." A long arm snaked along the seat so his hand could massage the back of her neck. "I'm afraid, too—I just know how to deal with it a little better. Sometimes, anyway. Hang on to your faith. God is right here, with both of us. *Whatever* happens, He's here. We just have to try not to think about some of those whatevers, all right?"

"I'm trying, Caleb. But I have to tell you, being a trusting Christian has to be the most difficult piece I've ever played."

The circuitous route Caleb deliberately followed carried them over most of Colorado Springs, but eventually they arrived at Peterson Air Force Base. Night had fallen, though streetlights allowed enough visibility to see much of the surroundings, and several large buildings were illuminated. Curious, Rae was sitting up straighter and looking around. When he asked, she confessed that she'd never been on a military base before, in spite of living in the area most of her life. And—in typical Rae fashion—she'd never really noticed the base's appearance before.

Caleb watched her with secret amusement. "Not exactly what you pictured?" he queried after a few minutes.

"No." She returned his grin sheepishly. "I guess I thought it'd look more like East Germany and Russia during the Cold War era. You know, miles of barbed wire and marching men and guards with machine guns."

"And the only guard you've seen so far is the gate guard, who smiled at you."

"Well, at least the buildings look bland and undistinguished and—military."

"Undistinguished or not, security at this base is tight. Don't be fooled into thinking that just anyone could stroll past that smiling guard or drive onto the grounds for a casual picnic." He was silent a moment. "It's not easy, being part of a volunteer military force during peacetime conditions. The past couple of months I've really come to appreciate the sacrifices these people make." He chuckled suddenly. "I also appreciate Admiral Vale arranging things so we could set up another field office here on the base."

"Why is the location so important?"

His gaze rested on her. "Here on a military base I don't worry as much about walking you into an ambush."

They pulled to a stop in front of a low building with few windows. Caleb glanced swiftly around and stole a kiss as he helped her out of the car. He paid for the indiscretion when Rae bonelessly snuggled against him, and he had to exert every ounce of discipline to keep the contact brief. They exchanged a secret smile, then he ushered her inside the building and down some depressing-looking corridors.

When they entered the room, Tray, Joe Delano and Chuck Livingston, two other FBI agents, looked up from a long table covered with charts, files, and at one end a computer and printer. The men's frowning faces lightened a little.

"Sit down, Ms. Prescott." Tray pulled out a chair. "You look a lot better than the last time I saw you."

Fresh color blossomed in Rae's cheeks, and Caleb suppressed a laugh. He winked at Rae as she sat. "Fresh air'll do that for you, won't it?"

Tray studied them a moment, and Caleb could practically see him analyze, weigh and come up with the correct conclusion. Dancing lights twinkled in the backs of his black eyes, but he kept his mouth shut. When it was all over, Caleb promised himself to reward such discretion with at least a steak dinner.

Once everyone was seated, all levity vanished. Delano handed Caleb a folder, and as he rapidly read the contents his mouth tightened. "Rae," he asked, watching her carefully, "remember when you told the Springs detective—J.W., wasn't it?—about the two women who wore matching necklaces?"

Rae nodded.

"I know you were unable to provide a physical description, but would you try again? I'll help walk you through the process, all right?"

The other agents leaned forward. Caleb knew their collective intensity made Rae nervous, but it couldn't be helped. "Close your eyes," he instructed. "Picture yourself in Joyful Noise. The door opens, and one of those women enters. What do you see?"

Rae obeyed, but after a few moments of painful concentration she opened them again and spread her hands ruefully. "I think the young one was blonde—and I remember smelling cigarette smoke around the other one. But beyond that . . ."

Face expressionless, Chuck Livingston casually flipped over a black and white snapshot and slid it across the table. "What about that?" he asked. "Does that jog your memory at all?"

Rae picked up the picture and studied it. "The face is sort of familiar," she allowed slowly. "But I couldn't swear in court it was the same woman."

Her nose wrinkled, and Caleb found himself wanting to kiss the elegant tip. *I'm losing it.* He ruthlessly tamped down the unwanted emotions and glanced at Livingston. "When and where?" He gestured to the photo.

"Denver, outside the bank where Ms. Prescott's account is. The man has known IOS connections. The woman was followed to the Springs, where she met Fisher in a local restaurant."

"Did they exchange anything?"

Ramirez scowled. "We don't know. They were sitting at a booth, and we weren't able to snag a table that enabled us to monitor any transactions."

Rae was still studying the picture. Caleb's gaze slid over her bent head as he continued talking in a low voice with the other agents. Tray verified that the note Rae had found was, as Caleb suspected, two lines of the Starseeker commands. Archie Cohen, Tray added sourly, had raised unholy havoc when Tray refused to release the note into his custody.

"Wait a minute." Rae grabbed Caleb's arm. Her voice vibrated with shimmering excitement. "Look. See the bag she's carrying? The photo's black and white, and that's why I didn't notice at first, but the more I looked at it, the more I realized there was something familiar about it. The bag—it's from Joyful Noise. It has the big treble clef on it, just like my car."

Tray exclaimed softly, triumphantly, while Joe pounded the table, and Chuck reared back in the chair, relief and satisfaction erasing the deep lines of tension in his face. "We've got them," Tray announced. "We're gonna nail 'em."

Caleb waited until the needed celebration ran its course before he dashed cold water on the moment. Beneath the table, his hand sought Rae's. "You better believe we're going to nail them," he promised, and his tone sobered all three men instantly. "And gentlemen, we're going to nail them *before* they have another opportunity to wreak havoc in Ms. Prescott's life. Let me elaborate. . . ."

Over the next week security was tightened around the Prescott mansion, and Rae was rarely out of Caleb's reach, except at night, when a policewoman disguised as a visiting relative from Oregon was parked in the parlor. For Caleb, the most difficult task was learning to live with the depth of his feelings. He felt as raw, as naked as a newly hatched bird, ricocheting between hovering over Rae and hounding the police, FBI and OSI. Tray finally took him aside.

"Reel it in, pal, or you're going to find yourself pulled off the case entirely," he warned. "This isn't the time to lose it, Cal. Where's that easygoing detachment and laser brain focus you wowed us with last winter?" He punched Caleb's shoulder. "We all share your concern over Rae, but your feelings are interfering with everyone's ability to protect her—including your own."

They were sitting in Rae's kitchen while one of the undercover agents monitored Rae and the store so Tray could update Caleb on the latest developments. Caleb propped his elbows on the table and worried his hair with his hands. "I know," he admitted. "Trust me, I'm not happy with my behavior, either." He looked across the table. "You married?"

"Two years in June."

"How would you feel if it was your wife staked out like the tethered goat?"

"I'd hate it as much as you hate having Rae in that position. But obsessing over it won't get the job done, and we both know it."

"Yeah." Caleb also knew his only hope lay in God's sovereign awareness of circumstances. But he couldn't share that with Tray. The time and circumstances were wrong. *Remember Who's doing the timing, allowing these circumstances, and stop acting like a mule eating loco weed.* On countless occasions he'd self-righteously reminded Rae that God was in control. Now he was in danger of forgetting that fundamental truth.

It wasn't easy, living your faith in a society to whom the Almighty God was little more than a swearword.

"I hear you, Tray," he promised the agent. "Don't worry. I hear you. Besides, I have a hunch things are just about to break wide open."

The following Friday evening, he and Rae were enjoying supper at Gibson Girl. Rae was sharing her ongoing surprise at the sympathetic response on the part of her customers to the vandalism. "And I never realized, until this past week, that half these people even thought of me as a *person,* instead of just part of the store fixtures. But almost all of the customers who have been in before made a point of telling me how sorry they were about all my treasures." She nibbled a flaky crescent roll. "Remember the little old lady who sold me the Broadway music? She stopped by yesterday. You were out at the time. Anyway, her great-granddaughter had told her what happened, so she came all the way over to give me an English ironstone cream pitcher her husband had brought home after World War Two. She wanted me to have it, she said, because . . . because she wanted me to remember that there were still people left who cherished both things and people."

"Thank God for little old ladies. They usually have a clearer eye than the rest of us," Caleb agreed as he lifted his napkin to tenderly wipe stray crumbs from the corner of Rae's mouth. "It's easy to lose your perspective when you become immersed in the evil deeds human beings inflict on the world. You forget the good that still exists. I was thinking about that several weeks ago, when I flew to California."

Rae's head was bobbing in agreement. "I know. Take my customers, for instance. I have this constant internal battle with myself now, trying not to imagine that everyone who enters the store is a criminal just because two female customers turned out to be part of an evil organization." She laughed. "It's so absurd, when I think about it, trying to imagine one of my customers passing government secrets. There's this timid little man—he was in today, as a matter of fact."

She dug into the spinach salad Karen had placed in front of her with a smile and sideways smirk at Caleb. "He's shy and retiring—collects old and out-of-print classical sheet music, if you can believe it." Chewing, she grinned across the table. "Can you imagine someone like *that* being involved with IOS?"

"Was he looking for anything special today?" Caleb asked very casually, though all his senses had leaped to full alert

Rae shrugged, took another bite. "Not really. He did ask me to keep my eye out for a particular edition of Mendelssohn. Come to think of it, I need to give him a call. Some woman called just before the store closed—she wants to sell a bunch of music from an estate sale."

Caleb leaned forward, his mind racing. After a moment Rae blushed, and he realized he'd been staring at her without speaking.

"Do I have dressing on my nose now, instead of crumbs on my chin?" she asked, swiping at her nose with her napkin.

"Your nose is covered only by freckles," he murmured absently. "Sweetheart, do you think there's a chance that Mendelssohn might be in the music the woman wants to sell?"

"I know it is." Her voice was innocently triumphant, electrifying every nerve ending in Caleb's body. "I asked her, so she searched right then while I waited and actually found it. I thought it was really great, and told her I had a customer who was going to be very happy. Isn't that a marvelous coincidence? I've been waiting all afternoon to tell you about it."

"I—" Caleb spoke very softly "—don't believe in coincidence."

Rae dropped her fork. It clattered on the plate unnoticed as she gaped at him across the table. "Caleb?"

His eyes swiftly scanned the nearby diners. "When did this woman say she would bring all the music to your store?"

"This Saturday." Rae bit her lip. Suddenly the gray eyes were dark, filled with uncertainty. "It wasn't a coincidence, was it?"

Caleb shook his head. "No, sweetheart. It wasn't a coincidence."

"But that means Mr. Fisher . . ." Her voice trailed away, and she shook her head in denial. "Caleb, he's so *timid*. He can't be involved."

Right now Caleb could have casually dangled Fisher over a cliff. He might even have dropped him. "Your timid Mr. Fisher is one of the programmers who designed Starseeker. And he's also the one who's been selling the technology to IOS, a piece at a time. You can bet the ranch he's nervous, probably even scared. But he's shrewd, greedy—and after revenge."

Rae shoved her salad aside. "Was Mr. Fisher the one who left that note in my music? The note with all the computer codes I gave to you?"

Caleb nodded. His hand reached across and patted hers, unsurprised to find it trembling. "We've suspected Fisher for months, but I didn't tell you because I was afraid you wouldn't be able to act normal around him." He squeezed gently. "You're too honest. And I hate to have to tell you, but you'll never win an Oscar for your acting skills."

"Apparently Mr. Fisher suffers no such qualms." Though Caleb easily read the gathering temper in her, he was relieved that she was learning to keep it under wraps. She'd even picked up enough these past months to glance around and lower her voice before she spoke. "Caleb—the music. He's using the music, isn't he?"

He nodded, pleased and alarmed at the same time. "Tray and I suspected as much last week, after you told me where you found the computer code. Hoffman—he's FBI, out of Denver—and Grabowski agree with us. We've been racking our brains trying to think of a way to prove it, come up with a way to catch them in the act without further endangering you."

"Isn't all this evidence enough?"

" 'Fraid not. We have to catch Fisher and his IOS contact in the act of passing the information to have any real hope of a conviction."

Restless, feeling the urgency racing through his bloodstream, he stood, pulling Rae with him. "Come on. Let's borrow Karen's apartment. I don't like talking in here. Will she mind?"

"Not at all." Rae favored him with a very dry look. "But if you're thinking of stashing me someplace while you face the line of fire alone, you might as well save your energy. We're in this together—and that's the way we'll stay."

Chapter Twenty-Three

Up in the apartment, Caleb motioned Rae to a chair. He was, she knew by now, in what she dubbed his secret agent mode, though when she'd teased him about it he'd given her a thoroughly disgusted look. "I'm a *consultant*, not a secret agent," he'd growled. Rae cheerfully agreed and let it go. She sat obediently in the chair while he made sure Karen's phone and the apartment were free of any uninvited bugs. But when he placed a call to Tray, she wondered if he thought of himself merely as a consultant.

When this nightmare was all over, they were going to have a serious discussion about semantics and self-perception versus reality.

"I think Rae stumbled onto the system." Caleb spoke to Tray in his normal low, easygoing voice, but she detected the underlying excitement, and in spite of her determination to stay unruffled, she had to sit on her hands to keep from playing a Bach fugue on the chair arm. "Yeah, I'm serious," Caleb was insisting. "I think this is it. Fisher asked her to be on the lookout for a particular piece of music, and several hours later Rae took a call from some woman conveniently wanting to sell a pile of old music." He listened, his free hand twirling the lock of hair that always fell over his forehead. "Mmm. I agree . . . especially when one of the pieces just happened to be the copy Fisher's after."

He glanced at Rae. Smiled reassuringly. Rae wasn't fooled, but even if she couldn't act, she could return a falsely reassuring smile.

Caleb shook his head and turned his back on her. "I know, I know. All we have to do is catch 'em passing the info, and pray it's condemnatory enough for a conviction. Like I said, Tray, if my hunch is correct, this will be the one. Things have gotten too hot, especially after Rae botched things by finding the computer code. What? Where?"

Rae's heart leaped into prestissimo at the exclamation. She rose and hurried over, and Caleb's arm enfolded her, gripping her shoulders in an almost painful vise.

His brows scrunched together. "That makes it even more likely they're winding it up and IOS will hand over the big payoff. What? Next Saturday. Yeah, I know. I don't, either." He raked a hand through his hair. "It's risky, but I think you're going to have to do what I suggested last week and put a team on the second story, over Joyful Noise."

"Caleb, no. IOS will see them—" She clamped her lips together, then relaxed against him, her hand lifting to lightly stroke the hand gripping her shoulder. She could feel his muscles, iron-hard, poised on the brink of violence.

"Don't hand me that. I want to catch them—*all* of them—as much as you do. But I will *not* allow Rae to be placed in that kind of danger. She's a civilian, Tray."

"Now you wait just a minute, Caleb Myers. It's not your—"

He laid firm fingers over her mouth, cutting off the words. "Tray, we'll discuss it later, at our usual time. You can get hold of the others—you might give Grabowski and the Springs intelligence unit a call, as well. Right. I'll see you in a couple of hours." He hung up.

"I won't let you wrap me up in protection like a baby in a blanket," Rae announced belligerently, and pinched the hard muscles below his ribs. "I'm an adult, and I love you. But you can't—"

"Watch me." With a swiftness that left her speechless he hefted her into his arms like a sack of groceries and stalked across the room, ignoring Rae's instinctive struggle. He deposited her at one end of Karen's Victorian fainting couch, then leaned over her, trapping her with his palms braced on either side of her head. "Listen to me, you little tigress. I *love* you. I've never felt like this before, so whether you like it or not, I'll do anything I think is necessary to keep you safe, even if you end up hating me for it. Ya got that?"

His mouth covered hers in a possessive kiss, but beneath the implacable male protective instincts, Rae sensed his turbulent fear. The same fear for her safety that plagued her about *his*. Instinctively she softened, capturing his head between her hands and trying to tell him without words that she understood.

Abruptly he broke the kiss and straightened, cramming his hands in his pockets.

Bewildered, off balance, Rae searched his face.

"Rae, sweetheart, your father was spotted in a bar down on Platte last night."

Numbness cascaded in a river of ice, coating her from head to toe. "What are you saying?" she asked, her voice carefully stripped of feeling. *No. Please, Lord. I don't know if I can stand what I'm going to hear. Help me. . . .*

Caleb studied her a long, unsmiling moment, then expelled his breath in an explosive sigh. "Remember what I told you? That we think he's a courier for IOS? That means he acts like a mailman, picking up deliveries from one location and delivering them to another. If he's here, it's either to pick up the Starseeker technology or to bring in the rest of the money IOS is paying Fisher. Maybe both."

She crammed her fists over her mouth to keep from screaming a denial and closed her eyes. Caleb dropped down beside her, and gratefully she leaned against him. He dropped another kiss on the tip of her nose. "Rae, I'd like to put you on a plane and send you to my folks in Georgia until this is over. I don't suppose you'd consider it? They have a beautiful old place, and all my sisters would visit—everyone will slather you in southern hospitality. You can see my boat. . . ."

Rae kissed him to block the desperate flow of words. "No way," she breathed against his lips after a long time. Even though her eyes were wet, she pulled her head away because she wanted him to see the determination in her face. It more than matched his. "No way will I leave you here alone, with everyone out for your head, because my absence will blow the Starseeker case to smithereens. Because of my father I'm involved up to my neck, whether we like it or not."

She took a deep breath. "He's using me—and my store—as though I was less to him than a faceless drug pusher or some homeless bum he passes by on the street, and it's time I faced that." Even as she spoke the words, she could almost feel the shift deep inside, like ice floes breaking up after an endless frozen winter. Like she used to feel whenever she'd finally *understood*, all the way to her soul, what a composer had felt when he wrote the music she was trying to master.

A tentative confidence stirred, gathering force with each word. Awed, Rae savored the feeling and offered up a grateful prayer. "I'm seeing it through to the end, Caleb—whatever that may be."

"I don't want you to be hurt." His voice was rough, almost hoarse.

"I don't want *you* to be hurt." She threw herself against him. "And we'll both take every precaution, be as careful as your training and my determination allow. But Caleb? Our safety ultimately isn't up to us. Is it?"

His hands clenched in her hair, then he tugged her head back and kissed her again with a tender violence that Rae met—and matched.

It was difficult, she learned over the next few days, to live a normal life when there were two armed men stashed upstairs, figuratively looking over Rae's shoulder and breathing down her neck. Even when she knew they were there to protect her and nail a group of traitors, she found it almost impossible to relax.

For the first time since she could remember, playing the piano didn't help. She had never minded an audience when she was performing onstage, because she was far too disciplined and her love for music had always enabled her to overcome any stagefright. But now, after months of living in goldfish-bowl circumstances, she found that she simply couldn't lose herself at the piano like she used to because she was too aware of those unseen eyes on the second floor.

Without the release of music, she felt lost, restless, in spite of her deepening spiritual maturity. Caleb had been summoned to Chicago by Polaris Corporation, over his strong objections, so Rae didn't have the comfort of his presence, either. She chatted with her customers during store hours, and Lucy, the phlegmatic police matron, in the evenings. But the days crept by, each hour suffocating in its slowness. Paperwork, household chores, even reading her

Bible . . . nothing recaptured that brief moment of affirmation God had showered over her that evening with Caleb in Karen's apartment. And she yearned for more moments like that even as she accepted that part of faith was waiting patiently between those moments.

It was as though she was being tested, her growing faith perfected within the painful fire of divine silence, and denial of every prop upon which she had based her existence.

Unfortunately, her temper began to simmer, bubbling beneath the tissue-thin serene persona she fought to project to the world. More than once she had to fight an overwhelming compulsion to dash outside and scream at the top of her lungs. Maybe kick a tree or the foot-high wall surrounding the mansion. Something immature but infinitely satisfying.

By Friday afternoon she couldn't even pray beyond a constant plea for God to keep her from shattering into a million pieces like her lost treasures. At least Caleb would be back this evening. Lucy had told her so an hour earlier, the placid voice calm, round face expressionless as always. Every afternoon the policewoman, in her guise as Rae's relative, went for her daily "walk," window-shopping in Old Colorado—and maintaining contact with all three agencies—the police, the FBI and OSI. Rae had reached the conclusion days earlier that her personality was definitely *not* designed for undercover work. Her expression would give her away every time, just as Caleb had told her.

It was a gray day, chilly for the first week in May. Instead of sunny skies and mild temperatures, winds with a wintry bite whipped around corners, plunging temperatures into the forties. Sullen clouds slogged over the mountaintops, and the smell of rain hovered in the air.

At a little after three, the store bell jangled, the wind almost tearing the heavy oak door out of Mr. Fisher's hands as he entered the shop. Wisps of mousy hair were tangled all over his balding head. His nose and ears were pink with cold.

"Not much of a spring day out there," he greeted Rae.

"No, it's not," she returned, avoiding eye contact. Her smile felt like more of a baring of teeth. For days, she had mentally rehearsed her behavior for the next time she saw this man and given herself countless silent lectures on controlling her temper. On allowing *God* to control her temper.

Mr. Fisher rubbed his hands together, darting surreptitious looks around the store. "So—how's business been lately? Had, ah, any more excitement around here?" The darting eyes bounced off the healing cut on her forehead.

"The destruction of the entire collection of priceless birthday gifts my uncle gave me over a span of two decades is enough excitement for several lifetimes." Not to mention a paltry thing like abduction, threats, being run off the road . . . Rae looked him straight in the eye. "Most of those objects were irreplaceable. It's almost more than I can bear, unlocking the door to the store every morning now." *Zip your lip, Rae, before you lose it.*

"Oh." Mr. Fisher looked slightly sick, his sallow complexion emphasizing the sharp bones of his face, the prominent Adam's apple above his expensive silk shirt. He glanced toward the bare shelves, just visible through the doorway. "I heard about—I mean a friend of mine who came . . ." He floundered to a halt. "You, uh, you say my Mendelssohn will be in tomorrow?"

"Yes." Rae pretended to look for something under the counter so he couldn't see her face until she regained her composure. She genuinely hadn't realized what a formidable task undercover cops and agents faced, having to hide their feelings all the time. No wonder they all wore those impenetrable masks of indifference.

"What are you doing down there?" Mr. Fisher asked sharply, and Rae's head jerked up with a snap, her hand flailing.

Music, store sacks and her ledger cascaded to the floor in an untidy heap. Rae pressed her fists against her temples and ducked to tackle the mess before she tackled Mr. Fisher.

"I'm sorry." He stood on the other side of the counter, all but dancing on nervous feet. "Here, I'll come around and help pick—"

"No!" Rae interjected, much too sharply. She tried to soften the word with a reassuring smile. "It was my fault. I'll take care of it. You go look around." When he didn't leave, she clenched her hands, casting about in desperation for something else to say. "Was . . . was there another piece of music in particular you were looking for, like the Mendelssohn?"

His complexion turned pasty white, and behind the thick glasses his eyes blinked rapidly. "Why do you ask?"

His agitation was spreading to Rae. *Maybe he was so nervous because IOS had warned him or they were hiding outside in the bushes. Maybe he somehow knew she'd found the code.* "Well, you collect old music," she stammered, standing up, wiping her perspiring hands on her slacks. "I—I just wondered if you'd heard that I had something else. Musically, I mean. You . . . it's just that you don't usually come in on Fridays, and I wondered . . ." She stopped, filled with self-disgust.

Mr. Fisher was backing away, looking as if he expected one of the IOS thugs to jump out at him like they had Rae. "I just remembered—I have an appointment. I'll come back another time. Tomorrow. Right now obviously isn't a good time for you."

He whirled and fled, shoes clattering on the warped oak flooring, fingers scrambling to tug open the door. Cold tentacles of wind slithered across the room in his wake, rustling papers and blowing strands of hair from her face. Rae despised herself, but she ground her teeth and bent to pick up the mess on the floor. If the past six months of painstaking investigation collapsed, she had no one to blame but herself.

A little before five the phone rang. It was the woman who planned to bring in all the music from the estate sale, and she told Rae she wouldn't be able to come in after all.

"There must be some way we can work it out," Rae burst out across the woman's goodbye noises. "Mr. Fi—I mean, my customer will be so disappointed." Heart pounding, she frantically cast about for a more persuasive argument.

"I'm sorry," the cool voice on the other end was saying. "Tell your customer maybe another time."

"Wait—where do you live? I'm—I'm more than willing to come pick the music up." If Caleb had been there he would have ripped the phone from the wall and hurled it across the room. She could only imagine the reaction of all the other listening ears.

There was nothing but dead silence from the other end of the phone.

Rae's hand was slippery with sweat, heart slamming against her rib cage. "I really wouldn't mind," she pressed, praying for a calm, professional voice. "I did promise I would have the Mendelssohn on Saturday, and I hate to go back on my word."

"Just a minute."

The phone was covered, and Rae could hear nothing but the somber ticking of the mantel clock over the fireplace. That and her own erratic breathing.

"You'd have to be here at four o'clock. Can you arrange to close your store early?"

Rae wiped her palm on her slacks. "Where do you live?"

"If you can't be here by four o'clock, your customer will just have to be . . . disappointed. I have an engagement elsewhere."

The woman was obviously not going to provide directions until Rae agreed to the time. "I can be there by four," she answered slowly, reluctantly. *Caleb, forgive me.*

There was another crackling pause, then the woman issued a set of sharp directions, and the fear rolled over Rae in a crescendo as she listened and wrote the instructions on a store bag, her slippery hands ice cold.

"If you're not there by four," the curt voice added, "you'll have made the trip for nothing. I have to leave no later than five after."

"I'll be there."

Chapter Twenty-Four

"I don't care if you plan to bring in the National Guard. It's too dangerous. She's bait for a trap. You know it. I know it." Caleb snagged Rae's eyes in a brief, searing glance. "Even Ms. Prescott knows she's been set up."

The conference room at Peterson throbbed with tension. Not only were Caleb, the FBI and Detective Grabowski present, but a deputy investigator, Sergeant Benthall from the El Paso County sheriff's office, was there, as well. Throughout the night Sergeant Benthall and Tray had been coordinating the deployment of people, studying maps and photographs—and planning.

And throughout the night Caleb had brought to bear every persuasive power, every bribe, threat or plea, argued logically and finally, for the first time in his life, he'd raised his voice, almost yelling. The episode still smarted, not only over the crack in his indomitable calm, but because it hadn't worked. Nothing had dissuaded the men with whom the final decision rested from involving Rae.

Strictly speaking, *nobody* wanted to. She was a civilian, an innocent bystander, and though Caleb's protests were the most vehement, he was not alone in his reluctance.

Detective Grabowski said it best. "Only exigent circumstances allow this," he finally admitted. "I can't think of another case with these unique circumstances, but as of this moment I don't see that we have any better options."

Dennis Hoffman crossed and recrossed his legs. Long and lanky, he looked more like the center for a basketball team than an FBI agent. Right now, he looked like an aggravated, *tired* center. "He's right, Myers. This is our best, possibly our *only* chance to nail at least some of the IOS kingpins, and you know it." He leveled a look at Rae. "Even Ms. Prescott knows it. At least give her credit for being willing to—"

"I don't want to hear another word about sacrifice and the nobility of her motives."

Caleb stalked to the other end of the room, breathing deeply, fingers twitching. The back of his neck burned, and he knew that every person in the room was gawking at him. The realization irritated him like a bad case of poison ivy. Did they think he was some blasted android, some character like Data from *Star Trek: The Next Generation,* a nonhuman devoid of feelings? A man could change, couldn't he? Hadn't anyone in this blasted room—outside of Tray—ever been in love? Caleb's concern for the woman he loved was neither illogical nor unreasonable.

Pivoting on his heel, he stalked to the waiting group.

Rae wrapped her fingers around the chipped ceramic mug one of the agents had scrounged for her. "Caleb, there isn't another way. Besides, it's my fault Fisher spooked, so it's up to me to make amends."

Caleb didn't look at her. She'd said words to that effect in a dozen different ways in the past ninety minutes. And he couldn't change her mind, any more than he'd been able to change Grabowski's or Tray's. Even Jackson Overstreet had reluctantly concluded Rae's participation in the setup was necessary.

Caleb did something then he'd never dreamed he was capable of. He picked up an ashtray full of cigarette butts and hurled it across the conference room. It slammed against the wall, rending the shocked silence with the sound of shattering glass. Then—focusing his gaze on Hoffman and Grabowski—he slammed his palms on the table with such force the table and everything on its surface jumped. Both men instinctively shoved their chairs back.

"Rae's a *civilian,*" he enunciated with lethal softness. "Regardless of her feelings to the contrary—which are due in large part to carefully orchestrated emotional blackmail by everyone in this room—she is *not* responsible for fouling up the case. Hoffman—"

he leaned across the table, spitting the words with the stinging precision of a bullwhip "—you've been especially adept at playing on her guilt. Don't do it again. Ever." His gaze lifted to rake across the group. "Now, why don't we all concentrate our mental faculties on coming up with an alternative plan."

Frozen into silence, the men in the room stared at each other uneasily. Caleb rose to his full height and allowed himself to look at Rae for the first time in ten minutes. Without speaking, she carefully put her mug of lukewarm tea aside and rose. A needle of pain stabbed beneath his skin. She moved as though approaching a cornered wild animal. Did she think he would direct the force of his anger at *her?* Unmoving, he watched her approach.

She walked all the way to him and laid tentative fingers on his bunched shoulder muscles. "Caleb, you can't put the blame on Agent Hoffman or anybody else. I volunteered. I choose to do this of my own free will. It was my decision alone. Mine."

Surprised—and relieved—Caleb felt his tension loosen, and in vague wonder sensed a trembling begin inside his body. Adrenaline. He shook his head, refusing to soften his stance. "Why won't you listen to me, instead of everyone else? You've done enough, Rae. You've had enough done to you. I want you out of it. Now."

"Caleb," Rae said with underlying steel, "you don't have the right to give me that order."

Her eyes pleaded, love burning openly for the others to see, though he knew she wouldn't bring their relationship into the open for fear of compromising whatever authority he still enjoyed. Ha. Lately, his authority was a joke, thanks to the grave, gray-eyed woman who had stolen both his heart and his common sense.

"I'm going to be wired," she reminded him, "and there will be undercover cops and agents positioned all over the place." Incredibly, her mouth flickered in a half-humorous smile. "About like fleas on a stray dog, from what Sergeant Benthall tells me. I'll be fine, Caleb." Her fingers brushed the back of his hand. "You're just going to have to trust me. I'll be fine."

"We don't *know* that." He glowered at her, unreasonably aggravated that *she* was all calm and collected while he stood there breathing like an enraged bull . . . and acting like one. Still . . . "There are so many variables, so many things that you haven't got the training, much less the experience and temperament, to anticipate. In spite of all the bells and whistles and gadgets, there's just too much that could happen that will be beyond our control."

"Then," Rae murmured in a voice only Caleb could hear, "we'll just have to depend on the One who is always in control, won't we?"

He took the gentle counsel like a roundhouse to the gut, and all of a sudden his shoulders slumped. Dropping into the chair, he closed his eyes, wondering if this was how Jonah must have felt inside that whale. His hand reached to press against his temple. After a minute, he looked at Hoffman. "I'm sorry, Dennis," he apologized quietly. "I had no right to behave as I did. I still think I'm right, but—" he glanced at Rae "—so is Rae. She's made her decision, so all I can do now is respect it and try to help her—and all of you—any way I can."

A collective sigh of relief rippled around the room.

"Don't worry about it." Hoffman waved aside the apology. "We're all concerned about Ms. Prescott. But unless she keeps the four o'clock appointment, the Starseeker case is dead in the water. We can't prove Fisher left the program inside a piece of sheet music, and we don't have a positive ID on the woman who seems to be controlling him. Without Rae, the whole case wouldn't stand a chance of making it into court."

Caleb looked at Rae at last. "I know," he answered, his gaze asking forgiveness, betraying fear, admitting defeat. "God help me, I know."

Rae drove south on I-25 toward Pueblo. To her right, rolling hills and water-chiseled ravines covered with scrub and a few trees provided training grounds for Fort Carson. To her left, a winding ribbon of cottonwoods lined Fountain Creek. On that side the terrain was flat, with few hills. Few places to hide.

Beneath the loose knit top she had carefully selected, Velcro held in place a thick belt with its tiny, sophisticated transmitter. The stiff, scratchy contraption tugged Rae's skin, but she ignored the discomfort, choosing to focus instead on the task awaiting her. Caleb had counseled her, over and over, to keep her mind only on what she was *going* to do and what she *could* do—not on the things she couldn't change. His last bit of advice had been the most difficult to heed—avoiding the deadly what-if syndrome.

Her hands were gripped too tightly around the wheel of the rental car she was driving. She relaxed her fingers, one at a time, in a disciplinary tactic she'd learned at school years earlier. The knot lodged just above her breast loosened marginally, allowing her to take a relaxing breath.

"Try not to worry," Sergeant Benthall had told her. *"We'll already have everyone in place long before you show."* He had smiled at her, gold-capped tooth flashing, but the dark brown eyes remained watchful, flat.

Almost ten miles now. The exit should be coming up soon.

"Just be as natural as possible, Ms. Prescott. If the woman gives you a stack of music, thank her and leave. If she dreams up some excuse for not having it, smile and thank her, no matter how implausible the excuse. Then leave." That had been Tray Ramirez, looking serious and grim, his suit jacket tossed aside to reveal the ominous belt rig with the ugly butt of his gun protruding.

Through all the last-minute instructions, Rae had managed to keep her face calm, and even if it hadn't been an Academy Award performance, her relatively collected behavior had won an approving gleam from Detective Grabowski. Inside, of course, she was more terrified than she'd ever been in her life, including the car accident. That, at least, had happened so fast there had been little time for terror.

There it was—the exit the woman had told her to take. Rae flicked on the blinker and headed down the ramp. Perspiration rolled between her shoulder blades, dribbled down her temples. At the intersection, she turned left, crossed over the freeway, then turned onto a dirt road paralleling I-25.

A dust-colored car was tucked in the shadows beneath the overpass, almost indiscernible. The quivering pent-up breath escaped in an explosive puff of relief. Rae swiped at her face, then tried to sing. Her voice warbled into a croak when she belatedly remembered how law enforcement officials would be picking up the sound of her voice. Grimacing, she hushed, playing Grieg on the steering wheel while she searched for landmarks.

There. A dirt road winding east toward Fountain Creek, with smatterings of cottonwoods on either side. She crossed the railroad tracks, dust billowing behind her in a choking cloud. Yesterday's rain had never materialized, and the morning had dawned, in typical Colorado fashion, warm and sunny. Perfect May day.

Rae didn't see any other cars and was almost as panicked as she was relieved, because if *she* spotted them, IOS almost certainly would. There were few places to conceal men and cars in this relatively flat area, which was probably why this out-of-the-way rendezvous had been selected. Clever bunch of criminals. Paranoid, evil, lower-than-a-snake's-belly contemptible . . . criminals.

The vitriolic spate of name-calling helped, though Rae didn't feel the slightest inclination to lose her temper. *"Rae, just remember to keep your temper—stay cool."* In the thick silence of the car, she could almost hear Caleb's voice speaking in her ear, his golden eyes bathing her in loving concern. *"They might suspect you of all sorts of schemes—but they don't know for sure, so they'll wait for your behavior to clue them how to react."*

"I'll remember," she whispered, not caring if the sensitive microphone picked up her words. If Caleb was listening, he would know to whom she had spoken.

"I'll be praying every second you're out there, not only for your safety, but for God's loving Presence to fill your spirit, instead of fear." Rae swallowed. The hard lump was swelling again. She remembered how Caleb had looked just before she had climbed into the car, remembered his parting words, which he'd whispered in her ear as he fastened the seat belt for her.

"Don't forget all those guardian angels that will be surrounding you, since I can't." And then, *"I love you. Please. You have to come back to me."*

A hairpin curve in the narrow, winding road forced her concentration to the matter at hand. Rae slowed, drove carefully around the bend between a stand of cottonwoods and oaks. Off to the right, almost hidden in trees, nestled a run-down house with a For Sale sign leaning drunkenly in the front yard.

"I'm coming up on the house," she murmured. Officer Helen Dix, who had helped position the belt and explain how it worked, had promised that Rae's voice and any others within twenty feet would be picked up. Miles away, in an innocent-looking van, every word would be faithfully recorded.

Rae turned into the front yard—there wasn't a driveway—and the stubborn lump in her throat ballooned to the size of Pikes

Peak. Her hand hovered over the key. She breathed a last prayer and killed the engine. It was time for the curtain to rise, and Rae Prescott needed to give the performance of her life. *For* her life.

The house looked deserted. Sagging front porch, dingy, peeling paint, screen door with the screen ripped halfway out—the place fairly screamed, "This is a setup!"

Rae squared her shoulders and lifted her chin, keeping her gaze on the two windows. They stared back like two blank eyes covered with black patches. *All righty, Rae. Dive in.* With icy fingers that barely felt the rough wood, she dragged open the screen and knocked on the front door.

It was yanked open so suddenly Rae's hand hovered in the air, poised mid-knock. "Hello," she croaked, then cleared her throat and smiled. "I'm Rae Prescott, here for the music?" *There. Much better. Friendly, but professional. You can do this, Rae.*

Suddenly, through the roaring in her ears and the suffocating pounding of her heart, Rae felt an inexplicable sense of calm wash over her. It was incredible, amazing . . . miraculous. She clung to the feeling with every ounce of her being. She might have delivered herself into a den of lions, but power and confidence were flooding her veins in wave after wave. She had never felt this kind of power before, even when she was playing—and winning—in all those piano competitions so many years ago.

The power of God.

She stared into the face of a tall, dark-haired, dark-eyed woman, and she wanted to tell the woman to give it up—she couldn't win this particular battle, no matter what she did to Rae. Then her eyes fell to the necklace draped around the woman's neck, and she dropped with a resounding thud into the realm of foolish mortals.

"The necklace!" she exclaimed with unforgivable stupidity.

Chapter Twenty-Five

The woman's eyes narrowed to slits, and her breath escaped in a hiss. "I knew it." She clamped surprisingly strong fingers around Rae's wrist and tugged her into the room. "All right, you two-timing little schemer, what's your game? Where's the note you stole out of the Brahms?"

Hot color flooded Rae's face. She wrenched her arm free and stepped back. "I don't know what you're talking about. I came here to pick up some—"

"Shut up!" The woman reached forward with a ring-laden hand, her eyes smoldering. "Don't waste your breath. No one cuts in on my turf, do you hear? *No one.* It's been tried before—and it's too bad you were stupid enough to try and pull a double-crossing stunt on me."

"I haven't—"

"I told you to shut up." The glittering eyes raked over her. "You're pathetic. A weak, pathetic wimp. What possessed you to think someone like you could steal Starseeker for yourself? Did you actually think your two-bit innocent act would fool me?"

"I'm not acting!" Goaded, Rae snapped, her tone so furious the woman quit her ranting. "I recognized your necklace—it's beautiful, and I think I told you so the first time I noticed it." In a bold move born of desperation, she attacked, unleashing the temper Caleb had warned her over and over to keep under control. "What's your problem, anyway? I've driven all the way out here—

at *your* convenience—to pick up some music, and in the process I make a harmless comment on your necklace. I'm sorry if that somehow offended you. If you'll give me the music, I'll get out of your hair and out of your life. If I weren't trying to accommodate a valuable customer, I wouldn't even bother at all."

The woman stood motionless, studying Rae as if she were an unfamiliar insect crawling across the floor, which she couldn't decide whether to step on or ignore. Finally she spoke without taking her eyes off Rae, raising her voice slightly. "I think she's lying, Jim baby. Why don't you come on out and see what kind of reaction we get?"

There was silence, then the sound of footsteps scraping hollowly across a bare floor in another room. When Mr. Fisher's stoop-shouldered form shuffled into view, Rae didn't even try to suppress her astonishment. "Mr. Fisher!" she squawked. There. That should have been loud enough for every official in that twenty-mile radius to hear.

Mr. Fisher looked at Rae in sheepish apology. He was practically quaking in fear. "I'm sorry, Ms. Prescott. I never meant—"

"You shut up, too!" the woman hissed. "We've got to find out how much she knows before we clean house and . . . disappear." Her mouth curled in an unpleasant sneer. One ringed finger stroked her cheek with the most exquisitely manicured nails Rae had ever seen. "So, Ms. Prescott, just tell me what you know. I can be reasonable, given enough incentive."

"Larissa, wait a minute." Mr. Fisher's face turned a sickly green. Behind the glasses his eyes were liquid with fear. "You promised that no one would get hurt. I brought the rest of the noncontaminated program. Let's just leave her and go."

"Jim baby, you're beginning to get on my nerves. And your blubbering mouth—" she advanced on the hapless man "—is way too indiscreet."

Good word, Rae decided, realizing that a discreet exit for *her* would be in order. She edged backward one careful step at a time.

Mr. Fisher glanced at her, then hurriedly away—but it was too late. Larissa snapped around. "Don't even try it."

Hmm. The latent menace of the order was unnerving, but Larissa's bulldozing arrogance enraged Rae. She had always despised bullies, especially female ones. They were so crass. "Are you going to run me down? Shall we engage in a catfight? I don't think so—that would be beneath my dignity."

Incredibly, Larissa colored. The nut brown eyes glared, but Rae could see the woman's struggle to bring her temper under control. In a macabre moment of recognition, Rae identified with Larissa's struggle. "Why don't you try to explain what's going on," she persisted. "If I understood, perhaps I could help sort it out." At what point, she wondered, did bluffing become stupidity? "Since it apparently involves Joyful Noise, I'd say I have a right to know."

"I knew I shouldn't have given in to Jim's whining. If we'd moved the drop as I suggested, all this could have been avoided." Larissa glanced out the curtainless window, fingers drumming on the dusty ledge.

"The store was perfect—nobody should have suspected," Fisher mumbled.

Larissa was right, Rae thought. The man *did* whine.

"The store wasn't perfect for anyone but you." Larissa strolled to Mr. Fisher, spearing him with a barbed look of contempt. "You had to feel safe. You wanted—*insisted* on—that store, so what happens now is all on your shoulders. Remember that." She turned to Rae. "I've told you once that your two-bit innocent act wasn't fooling me. You're wasting your time."

Rae affected an indifferent shrug. "All right, then. I know you must be doing something illegal, and I don't appreciate your using Joyful Noise. But if—"

Larissa's face changed. "Don't threaten me, honey. If it hadn't been for your old man, you'd have been out of the picture weeks ago." She watched Rae, then laughed an ugly laugh. "That hits you where it hurts, doesn't it? Your father thought you might be a useful tool, and I suppose for a while he was right. Your father," she repeated. "How does it feel, knowing your own father doesn't care this much—" she snapped her fingers under Rae's nose "—about his own daughter?"

"Larissa, don't," Mr. Fisher pleaded, glancing uneasily at Rae's face.

"If I hadn't been so suspicious that he might be using you to pull a double cross on me, those two visitors at your house would have done a lot more than just threaten you." Larissa moved behind

Rae to block the only door. "Give it up, honey. Just tell me how much you *do* know."

"Why don't you tell me what the two of you—or however many of you are in your little club—have been passing back and forth in my sheet music?" Rae countered, dropping the pretense of ignorance. Larissa's calculated barbs hurt, but not nearly as much as they would have a week ago. Besides, Rae had something far more important to concentrate on right now—her life.

Mr. Fisher's face had turned an ugly shade of mottled red. "You've known, all this time, haven't you? You've *known.* Ms. Prescott, I thought you were nice—I even felt sorry for you because—" He stopped, shooting Larissa an uneasy, sullen look.

Rae regarded him incredulously. "You use my store to steal a top-secret government project, jeopardize national security, and you stand by doing nothing while evil thugs destroy my property. You taunt me about my father, throw his indifference toward me in my face—and *you're* upset with *me?*"

"You don't understand."

"I understand more than I like. I understand the truth, which is more than I can say for you. You don't care a thing about me, Mr. Fisher. You only care that you've been caught with your hands in the cookie jar. But if you think I'll close my eyes to what you're doing, you're in for a disappointment."

"I doubt that," Larissa murmured behind her.

Rae's pulse skittered, but she kept her gaze glued to Mr. Fisher, recognizing the weakest link of the chain binding her in this decrepit prison. "What you're doing is worse than illegal, Mr. Fisher—it's treason. I hope they hang you."

"I don't care about the country—it's corrupt anyway. The government deserves to be compromised—and so does that smug, pompous Overstreet!"

"Fisher—"

He ignored Larissa. "Sitting on his millions, taking all the credit—well, not this time. It's my turn now. This time *I'll* have the money, the prestige. *I* will." He turned to Larissa, his eyes pleading. "Won't I, honey? Just like you promised? I've brought the last of the program with me, like I said I would. Your boss won't have any reason to doubt now. Let's just leave Ms. Prescott and go."

Larissa gave an unladylike snort. "That's right, Jim baby. Leave her here to blab everything to the feds. They've been sniffing around you for a month now, trying to pin some evidence on you."

Fisher swallowed hard. "I don't want anybody hurt."

"You'll look real spiffy in a prison suit."

Desperation flooded his face. He looked like a trapped animal, wild-eyed, searching for a bolt hole. Rae didn't move, afraid to tip Larissa over the edge. Against her waist, the scratchy Velcro belt dug into her skin, a welcome reminder that every word in the room was being monitored. Unfortunately, if Larissa pulled a gun, not a single one of the authorities would be able to crash through the door in time. *Pray harder, then.*

"You won't have to watch," Larissa was saying acidly. "Jules and Romo will take care of it. All you have to do is deliver her to the address I give you." Her voice rose impatiently. "Oh, quit looking like such a rabbit! Did you honestly think we'd leave behind any tale-telling mouths? That's not how it works, baby."

She took a step toward Rae. "We can either do this the easy way, or I knock you out." She studied Rae, and her mouth curved in a little smile. "It's a shame, really. You've got a lot of moxie, for a wide-eyed innocent. But that's the way it is, right, Ms. Prescott? Now—I have a brown belt in karate and none of your dainty Christian scruples, so what's it going to be?"

In a physical confrontation, they would inevitably discover the transmitter. Rae's only hope of rescue lay beneath the folds of her sweater, so she held up her hands in a mock gesture of surrender. "I've been beat up on enough," she admitted.

"I always did admire someone who gives in gracefully," Larissa murmured, stepping closer. "There's a rope in that closet," she told Fisher. "Fetch it for me like a good boy, in case she decides to change her mind."

"Ms. Prescott, she means to have you killed!" Mr. Fisher exclaimed hoarsely.

"I didn't think she wanted to play jump rope," Rae managed to retort. Her mouth was dry, and she began to sink into the choking quicksand of terror she had kept at bay. She tried not to shiver as her arms were wrenched behind her back. Rough strands of rope were wound around her wrists, then her ankles, the coarseness biting into tender skin. Rae bit her lip, focusing on the window and the world beyond. Somewhere out there were a lot of men and women. They would rescue her before it was too late.

Caleb would rescue her.

And if he couldn't, God was with her. He would always be with her, even when Caleb wasn't. She smiled at Larissa. "You think I've given in gracefully," she said. "But you know what I just realized? You're wrong on a number of levels."

"I have to give you credit for stubbornness. Don't make me revise my opinion by this blind persistence in trying to bluff me."

"I'm not bluffing. You're the one who's blind, because you've been wrong ever since the first time you came in my store. In fact, it's because you were wrong that you're in a whole lot more trouble now than you're willing to admit."

Larissa's hand shot out and fastened in Rae's hair, yanking her head painfully. "What are you talking about?"

Her eyes watered from the burning pain in her scalp, but Rae gave look for look. "You don't know the first thing about music," she managed to say between clenched teeth. "You proved your ignorance when you asked for the 'Ode to Joy' from Beethoven's Fifth Symphony."

She heard Mr. Fisher inhale sharply.

"The 'Ode to Joy' is from Beethoven's *Ninth,* Larissa Whoever-you-are," Rae finished, then gasped when the other woman gave her hair another vicious tug. "You were wrong about the music— and you're wrong about me."

"How could you be so stupid!" Mr. Fisher raged. "This whole thing is your fault! Yours! *That's* why the code wasn't in the music that time you kept insisting the mistake was mine. *That's* why you had to send those two goons to try and intimidate the girl and ended up with the police as well as the feds on our tails. That's—"

"Shut up!" Larissa shoved Rae at the raging man, almost causing both Fisher and Rae to fall. "Just take the sanctimonious little nun to this address and get out of here. I'll take the program."

Mr. Fisher cast her a frantic look, staggering beneath the dead weight of Rae's trussed-up body. "My money! What about my money?"

"It will be deposited in your account *after* my people run a test on the whole program." Her voice dripped acid. "So you better take care of her, and you better do it exactly like I've told you—or you won't be around to spend your money, Jim baby."

Her gaze clashed with Rae's. "Say your prayers, honey. Regardless of which stupid symphony that song came from, I guarantee you there won't be any odes to joy where you'll be going."

This time Rae's smile wasn't forced at all. "Wrong again, Larissa. You're wrong again."

Chapter Twenty-Six

❧

"We have to pull her now." Fear coiled in Caleb's stomach, a timber rattler poised to strike. "You heard what Fisher said. They're going to kill her."

The stark words hovered inside the murky confines of the cream-colored van, where he, Tray and one of Benthall's men had been listening to the grim performance a few hundred yards away. He exchanged glances with Tray. With one accord the two men snatched binoculars, then jumped out the back doors. Crouched, alert, they crabbed their way to the front of the van, then belly-crawled along the ground to a position where they could see the house.

"We have to get her out now," Caleb insisted again. Outwardly he was still, his voice a bare rustle of sound. But his insides were molten lava, every nerve ending screaming for action.

Tray didn't move from his prone position. His eyes were glued to the binoculars. "Be cool a little longer, man. You know we can't make our move yet. If this Larissa had planned to ice her, she would have done so by now. It's under control, Cal—Rae's gonna be all right. She's one gutsy woman, your lady."

"I know." Slowly the death grip on his binoculars eased, and Caleb relaxed infinitesimally. "Thanks, Tray."

"Sure. It's going down this time, Myers. Thanks to Rae, we have a fighting chance of nabbing more than just Fisher and the woman." He shifted slightly. "You stick with Fisher, okay? That way, when he transfers Rae, you can move in with the others."

"Yeah." A pebble was gouging a hole in his hip, but Caleb barely noticed. He'd stick with Fisher all right, but more vitally, he'd stick with Rae. His heart had quit beating when she lit into Larissa as though they were two kids on the school playground. He forced his muscles to relax again. "When this is all over, I'm going to haul her to Georgia by her hair and stash her in my boat."

He saw the corner of the FBI man's mouth lift. "I'd say she's done pretty good for a rank novice. You heard her—we should be able to get a conviction on attempted murder as well as theft of classified technology, thanks to Rae's presence of mind. She's got a lot of class, Cal."

Caleb was proud of her, too, but he also knew Rae better than Tray did. She might sound calm, in control, like he did. But the terror lurking in the backs of her eyes could take over at any time. If it did—once again, he stopped the thought, jamming the binoculars against his eyes with enough force to bruise his bones.

It was impossible to relax, especially since they could no longer hear what was going on inside the house. Lying belly-down in the dirt beside Tray, sweat dribbling down his forehead, Caleb struggled to keep his hands steady on his binoculars. He wasn't used to field surveillance, since the bulk of his work took place in the high-tech jungles of multistory office buildings, following paper trails. He kept himself in top physical condition through workouts and jogging, not—as Rae fancifully liked to accuse him—from living the hazardous life of some super spook.

What would happen if he didn't have the skill or the necessary instincts to save her?

You're playing the what-if game, aren't you, Caleb? Let it go, and trust.

He almost jackknifed onto his back, so clearly had he heard the words. His pulse was racing, and he risked a sideways glance at Tray, but the agent hadn't moved a muscle. After a while his pulse returned to near normal, and Caleb realized that a sort of pervasive peace had stolen over him, renewing his confidence. His spirit had soared on the wings of an eagle. A slow, almost invisible smile began and barely tickled the edges of his mouth. He was okay.

The door of the ramshackle house opened. "They're leaving," Tray muttered.

Statue-still, both men watched as Fisher and a tall, dark-haired woman manhandled Rae outside, across the barren, stubbled yard. Her arms were bound behind her back, and the rope passed to her feet, hobbling her so that she was limited to baby steps. Once her knees gave way and she almost pitched face-forward to the ground.

Caleb jerked, his teeth snapping together with an audible click. The powerful binoculars focused directly on Rae as close as if he were standing right in front of her. Pain bleached her face, and he watched her bite her bottom lip. But her eyes . . . under any other circumstances, Caleb would have grinned. Dark, stormy, yet almost serene, she conveyed the heroic acceptance of a martyr. Caleb could tell from the bonelessness of her body, however, that she was creating as much trouble through passive resistance as she could manage, using her captivity with the only means left open to her.

They finally reached the blue sedan Rae had driven, and Fisher opened the back door. Caleb saw Rae's lips move as she offered some final comment. The black-haired woman, Larissa, looked murderous, and all of a sudden her hand snapped up and she slapped Rae across the face.

Caleb half rose, muscles bunched and ready, but Tray's hand pushed him down, his voice brusquely reminding him of the need to stay concealed. "She's all right—just a stinging cheek, Cal."

Caleb nodded. "Sorry." The dispassionate, almost exalted state of perfect detachment and utter confidence continued to pour into him. With the clarity of an avenging angel, he watched. And waited.

Rae was inside the car, across the back seat. Fisher climbed into the driver's seat, and Larissa slammed the door behind him. She leaned in the open window, obviously issuing final instructions, then turned and strode rapidly toward a shed almost hidden behind a stand of willow oaks.

Fisher started the engine, then gunned the car down the dirt lane, a billowing cloud of dust marking his route. Tray whipped out his hand unit, speaking rapidly. "Suspect headed west in victim's car—two-toned blue ninety-five Taurus. License plate Kilo, Uniform, Hotel, three-seven-seven. Male suspect driving."

A wicked-looking black Lexus pulled out of the shed, with Larissa behind the wheel. She roared down the dirt road in the opposite direction.

Caleb and Tray scrambled to their feet, Tray reeling off the info on the Lexus. Hands dangling in poised suspension, Caleb watched the two departing cars with the calm eyes of a patient predator.

"They're far enough away. Let's get moving!" Tray snapped beside him. "We've got tails on them both, so get hold of yourself. You can either come with us in the van, or—" The words were cut off as their gazes met. Tray shivered. "Okay. You've gotten hold of yourself. Try not to annihilate the rest of us in the process."

"I'm only here to protect Rae. Instant retribution would be nice, but that isn't up to me." He smiled. "Too bad."

They tore off down the gully at a dead run. The fleeing cars had shrunk to miniature toys, weaving with drunken haste toward I-25. In their wake, the rolling cloud of dust wafted gently toward the two running men.

"Offhand, I'd say your reputation has been understated," Tray observed between breaths as they sprinted down the wash to the spot where they'd left their cars. "I hope you don't ever decide to come after me, man. The scene yesterday at Peterson was an eye-opener, but this—" They dodged a cluster of tumbleweeds. "Is this what you're always like when you're about to solve a case?"

"Nope. This is what I'm like when I'm protecting the woman I aim to marry." He marveled at the words, spoken aloud for the first time, and wondered again at his incredibly poor timing. On the other hand, he couldn't very well tell Tray that the reason for the restoration of his fabled detachment was that God had spoken to him.

About a hundred yards south, they joined the other agents, Benthall's men and the Springs police. "Did you copy everything?" Tray asked them.

Dennis Hoffman nodded. "Fisher's headed toward the Springs. Benthall's unit will pick 'em up when they hit the freeway. The Lexus is headed south—I've got another car on her tail." He allowed satisfaction to coat his voice. "I think we got 'em."

"Until Rae Prescott is safe, nothing is finished," Caleb observed mildly. He tossed his binoculars to Tray.

Dennis peered at his face and grimaced. "You got it, Myers. I'm with you, a hundred percent."

Tray slapped Hoffman's back. "It's cool, man. Fortunately, he's not after us anymore."

"I'm going after Rae," Caleb concurred. "I want to be there when Fisher tries to . . . dump her."

"Stay out of it, Myers," Benthall warned. "Your part in this is over. It's our business now."

Caleb looked at him. "I don't think so," he replied gently.

He didn't waste time on words, but sprinted toward his car, hidden in the cottonwoods growing thickly along the creek. Behind him came Benthall's furious voice, followed by Tray's matter-of-fact retort. "Get out of his way and let him help," he heard the FBI agent counsel. "He's the best ace in the hole we've got."

That wasn't likely, but Caleb didn't waste time patting himself on the back because Tray thought he was something special. Besides, he knew better. He was calm, in control, all right. But locked deep inside, bound by divine intervention, he was as scared as he'd ever been in his entire life.

He reached the car, yanked open the door and threw himself behind the wheel. After turning the ignition with a savage twist, Caleb gunned down the rutted path that led to the dirt road. Impervious to the damage he was inflicting on the car's undersides, he aimed the hood like a rifle, rocketing over the rough ground in a screaming, teeth-rattling ride.

He rounded a curve, topped the rise—and there was Rae's car, gathering speed as it headed up the entrance ramp to I-25. Caleb watched in grim satisfaction as the undercover cops stationed beneath the overpass pulled out, climbed the embankment and pursued Fisher at a discreet distance.

Caleb rammed his foot on the accelerator. Then he was under the railroad bridge, with the freeway just in front of him. The engine whined, tires squealing as he roared up the ramp at seventy miles an hour. An eighteen-wheeler was approaching in the near lane, but Caleb shot in front of the cab with room to spare. He ignored the warning blast of the truck's airhorn.

Traffic was heavy. He dodged cars with the icy calm of a jet fighter pilot, keeping the speedometer needle hovering near ninety as he wove from lane to lane, simultaneously surveying the road ahead. When the traffic piled up, he finally—reluctantly—eased back on the accelerator. This was no time to have an accident, nor did he have the right to endanger innocent people, regardless of the circumstances.

Scenery passed in one continuous blur, while time stretched, elasticized seconds that seemed to last hours. Two minutes slipped by, then six. The icy calm wavered—he gripped the wheel tighter, forcing himself not to raise his speed. Rae's car was being closely monitored. Fisher wouldn't be able to lose the squad cars, who would be in active pursuit once he hit the city limits. Restlessly his eyes searched the road. He grabbed the radio. "One-X-fifty-one to One-X-fifty. Request position of suspect vehicle."

"One-X-fifty. Vehicle entering city limits. Maintain positions."

He was too far back. Cautiously the car gathered speed, creeping past seventy-five. Almost ten minutes passed. Caleb topped a hill just in time to see the Taurus exit at Nevada.

He noted with abstract astonishment that he was sweating like a racehorse, even though his mind was clear, calm as the balmy spring day, and he was confident of God's sustaining presence here—and with Rae.

Without warning a vivid memory flashed across his brain: Rae lying unconscious on the narrow emergency room bed, her face waxen except for her bloodied forehead. She had looked . . . dead.

Caleb jerked, and the car swerved. He wrestled the car under control, but it felt like an eternity before he wrestled the painful memory away and regained control of his mind. When the exit approached, he was quoting the Twenty-Third Psalm in lightning fast repetitions—an effective spiritual painkiller. He took the ramp too fast, screeching to a standstill at the bottom behind a bright red four-wheel-drive vehicle. Up the heavily traveled street, the car with Rae in it turned right and disappeared.

Caleb grabbed the radio again. "One-X-fifty-one to One-X-forty-seven. Request immediate intercept." Protocol be hanged. He wanted Fisher picked up *now*. Which patrol units were covering this sector? McArthur and Ayers, he knew, were the detectives on site, and they drove an innocuous gray sedan. So where were they?

He was forced to wait to turn onto Nevada while an endless stream of cars chugged past, all with the speed of a dying snail.

The radio crackled. "One-X-forty-seven. Suspect turning right on—" Static garbled the transmission, but not before Caleb caught a bitten-off exclamation.

He finally pulled into the street, but by the time he made it to the corner where Fisher had turned, it was too late. The detectives' car was pulled to the curb, and Caleb slammed to a halt behind them, then sprinted to the car. "What happened? Where's Fisher?"

"Get in with us. Tell you on the way." Evan slapped a fist-size portable siren bubble in place while J.W. spoke rapidly into the radio. Caleb barely had time to slam the door before they tore off in pursuit of Rae's car.

"Fisher did an illegal U-turn, practically got wiped out by a truck." MacArthur threw the words over his shoulder, his face grim, savage. "They stopped in front of that alley, another car pulled up, and a guy jumped out. He grabbed Miss Prescott, tossed her in the back of the car and took off."

"They're headed west on Colorado," J.W. added. He spoke into the radio again. "Responding code three—we're westbound on the avenue and attempting to intercept suspect vehicle. Request code one and assistance." He twisted his head and caught Caleb's eye. "She'll be okay," he promised, trying with little success to sound confident. "There's at least four units responding, not to mention the feds and OSI."

Caleb nodded grimly. He watched the stores and cars and people without seeing them while his fingers fiddled with his watchband. Calm . . . control. It was still there, allowing him to sit quietly, but the detachment was nowhere to be found.

At this moment, he was utterly powerless—but God wasn't.

He had lost all control of the situation—but God hadn't.

He didn't know if Rae would be alive or dead the next time he saw her—but God did know.

Over the past endless hours that knowledge had sustained and fueled Caleb, keeping him sane. He would carry the memory of that audible voice to his grave, along with the awesome power that had coursed through him then. But right now the voice was silent, and Caleb's knowledge offered cold comfort when his heart was bracing itself to be destroyed.

Chapter Twenty-Seven

Terror circled Rae like a pack of frenzied pit bulldogs. She could tell from the sounds of traffic that they had entered a city—was it the Springs or Pueblo? Were the good guys keeping up? *Where was Caleb?* Clamping her teeth together, she worked to free herself in spite of maniacal driving that was tossing and bouncing her all over the back seat. She was afraid to reason with Mr. Fisher—much less plead—for fear the distraction would precipitate a serious accident.

Good, Rae. You're worried about being involved in a car accident when this guy's driving you to your execution?

She unclenched her teeth and took a deep breath. "Hey! Mr. Fisher! You don't need to do this!" she yelled over the seat. "Please . . . while there's still time. Stop the car, toss me out. Don't do this!"

Mr. Fisher ignored her.

Rae shouted louder, talking nonstop as fast as she could, not caring what she said or sounded like. Her only intent was to distract.

Suddenly the car slammed to a halt, almost throwing her onto the floor. Rae squirmed, struggling to reposition her trussed body closer to the back of the seat. Without warning Mr. Fisher was looming over her. His face was slippery, flattened out, like melting wax. Behind the ugly glasses his eyes were fixed, glittering.

"Shut up!" he screamed. "Just shut up! I have to do this! I don't have any choice!"

He turned, and the car shot forward. Outside, brakes shrieked. A horn blasted angrily.

You always have a choice, Rae thought, wondering if she should keep shouting. Well, what did she have to lose? "You always have a choice!" she yelled, furiously sawing at her wrists. "You always—"

Once again the car turned abruptly, this time so violently she was flung first against the seat, then onto the floor when they slammed to a halt. The door was yanked open. Hard, urgent hands grabbed her, hauled her out. Fear and anger exploded. Rae twisted and squirmed, opened her mouth to scream. The attempt ended in a choked gasp when she was flung into the back of another car and her head struck a glancing blow on the door handle.

"Get moving," a dead-fish voice ordered. "The little chip head's brought company."

Rae knew that voice. Shaken, stunned into immobility, she lay across the seat. *Lord . . . Lord—help me.* She knew that voice. She would hear it in her sleep the rest of her life.

He turned to gaze over the seat. "You don't learn, do you, Ms. Prescott?" he asked, then smiled. He'd smiled like that the day he had run her off the road, then throttled her. All the time his hands were squeezing, squeezing, he'd been smiling.

If I throw up now, I'll just die, Rae thought, swallowing convulsively. A hysterical giggle crowded into her throat. She *was* going to die. Surely she would have been rescued by now if the cops—if Caleb—had been able to keep up. No. *No!* She didn't want to die— wasn't ready to die. Not like this. Not like—

"Cops on our tail." Panic coated the driver's rough voice. "Where'd they come from? What'll I do?"

"Lose them," her nemesis ordered without inflection, his head jerking around, away from Rae.

Relief flooded through her. For several precious seconds all she could do was lie on the seat, blinking back tears of gratitude while her fear-knotted muscles slackened and began to tremble. Then, buoyed by a resurgence of hope and fresh determination, she once again set about the task of freeing herself. She could do it. She *would* do it. She just had to concentrate, ignore the pain, the fear.

Focus. "You'll never make it to the top if you don't focus," her piano coach used to remind her, over and over.

The apostle Paul had promised she could do all things through Christ. Paul had been in prison, and God released the chains. Maybe . . . *Focus, Rae. Do what you can, and let God take care of the rest.*

"They're getting closer!"

"Turn on Thirtieth. Take the road into Garden of the Gods. We'll lose them and dump her there."

So. They had brought her home. Home to die. *No! Don't think it. Focus!*

She had five minutes, maybe less.

Blood trickled, dripping between her fingers onto the seat. Her wrists burned, throbbed. Pain shot into her shoulders, insistent, weakening her will. *Renew my strength, Lord.*

Caleb, I love you. Where are you?

Outside the window, huge red monoliths rose in Rae's blurring vision. Garden of the Gods. The mountainous boulders protruded from the gray-green earth like dorsal plates on a gigantic stegosaurus. Jurassic Park. She was going to be eaten by a dinosaur. *Stop it, Rae! Focus!*

The car swerved into the park entrance on two wheels, throwing Rae across the seat.

"Be careful, you fool!"

Rae's little finger slipped free of the rope. Her heart jerked once, then tripped over itself when the man turned to stare into her face with his dead pits of eyes.

"Say goodbye, Ms. Prescott." He shifted his body, preparing to reach over the seat.

Rae froze, eyes locked to his. She shook her head, heart hammering, unable to speak.

The car fishtailed wildly. Cursing, the man grabbed the seat to keep from being thrown against the driver. The two men began arguing, a furious exchange of curses and forceful gestures as Rae's killer was forced to give terse directions to the panicking driver. *He wasn't looking at her right now.*

Rae waited a fraction of a second, then tugged on the ropes in a burst of desperate strength. Her ring finger slipped past, then her thumb. Tears poured down her cheeks, blinding her. She scrubbed her face against the rough fabric of the seat as she gave one hard tug. Her right hand flopped free, dropping uselessly behind her like the hand of a—of a corpse.

Sirens keened in the distance, drawing closer, promising help. No time. They wouldn't be there in time. She was going to—

Focus, Rae! Rae . . . you can do this. It's all right. Focus . . . and fear not.

The control poured over her in a cataract of warmth and power. Urgency still flooded her, but her mind had somehow grown clear, detached from the terror. She felt as though she had just stepped onto the stage at Carnegie Hall, and yet somehow the feeling was different. Rae kept her gaze on the two men, while behind her back she worked her fingers, ignoring the pain because she needed to use them. *Play an F-sharp scale, Prescott, that'll limber those fingers. Count while you're doing it, to keep the rhythm. Count seconds. Five, ten . . .*

"They're practically on our tail—we gotta dump her now!"

"Take that side road—" No longer cold and flat, his voice rapped out the words, control slipping. "There—there, you fool! We'll lose them and dump her at the bottom of— Hey! What the—"

Rae attacked like an enraged Doberman, teeth bared, eyes trained on nothing but its prey. She hurled herself toward the driver, hands clawing his face, scratching at his eyes. Even as he automatically lifted his hands, Rae was grabbing the steering wheel. She wrenched it to the right as hard as she could.

The driver was screaming in her ear. Hands tore at her wrists, her waist as the world disintegrated into a kaleidoscope of whirling sound and color. Swerving like a drunken rocket, the car crashed against a guardrail, spun halfway around, then pitched headfirst down a scrub-choked ravine.

I love you, Caleb. Love you—

She drifted to earth slowly. The roller-coaster motion had stopped. All the yelling and screaming had stopped. *Dead—or dreaming?* Had to be one or the other, because in the midst of the overpowering silence and stillness, she could hear Caleb's voice right next to her ear.

He was talking to someone. The words . . . She needed to listen so she could understand. Wait—was that her name? But he sounded upset, choked. As though he was . . . crying? Why? *God? Am I dead?*

"No, you're not dead, Rae. Thank You, Lord, dear God—no, sweetheart, you're not dead. . . ."

Oh. Caleb was telling her she wasn't dead. Rae tried to move, tried to force her uncooperative eyelids to open.

"Rae, it's all right. It's over. You're all right. Please wake up and talk to me, sweetheart. Rae, I love you. . . ."

Like a curtain lifting, strength and full consciousness returned. Rae opened her eyes, blinking in the bright afternoon sunlight. Caleb! She was alive—and Caleb was here. His face, white and gaunt, rimmed with dust and lines of fatigue and worry, had never looked more beautiful.

A smile tickled the corners of her mouth, spread irresistibly. *She was alive!* And the man she loved with all her heart was alive, as well—and holding her as though he would never let go of her. "You're late again. What took you so long?" she tried to tease, but the words emerged in more of a hoarse croak.

Tortured eyes widened, searching her face. He stared at her for almost a full minute without speaking, his pale cheeks hollowed, mouth a compressed white line. Gradually the gauntness faded, and lights began to twinkle in his eyes. A smile crept across his face. Finally he began to laugh. Then he hugged her and buried his face in her neck. "Rae, sweetheart. Thank You, Lord. Thank You," he whispered in her ear, the phrases blurred, running together in a rhapsody of relief.

After a long time he lifted his head and covered her face with kisses. "I got here as soon as I could," he murmured, laughter in the words as he tenderly mimicked the ones he had spoken months earlier. A lifetime ago. "Guess my timing wasn't much better than when I was on the second story of the hardware store across the street, was it?"

Rae's giddy smile wavered, almost turning upside down. "But you're here. You're here, Caleb. I love you."

"Myers! Hey, Myers! The ambulance is on its way." Tray Ramirez slid down the embankment, skidded to a halt next to them. "How is she? Cal—how's Rae?"

Rae shifted her gaze to the other man. The imperturbable agent sounded almost as shaken as Caleb looked. "Believe it or not, I think I'm fine."

"It was a miracle," Caleb concurred. "No broken bones. She's conscious—talking." Rae saw with astonishment that his eyes were wet. "She should have been—"

"Well, I have a few injuries to complain about," Rae hastily inserted. Her eyes were stinging. "Nothing that a little more Merthiolate won't heal, though." She lifted a raw and bloodied wrist to flick the lock of hair on Caleb's brow with unsteady fingers. "But since Caleb's so good at patching me up, I won't need an ambulance. And I *sure* don't need a hospital."

"Well, I'm taking you there anyway. *I* need to be sure," Caleb said.

The plea in his eyes belied the dictatorial statement. Rae didn't argue. She glanced at Tray. "What about—"

Caleb put his hand to her cheek. "I'll tell you all about it later, okay?"

"Everything's cool, Rae," Tray put in. "Don't worry about a thing." He looked at Caleb. "Take her by the hospital, hero. I'll keep everyone's attention elsewhere. You can bring her in tomorrow for the debriefing."

All of a sudden Rae became aware of the activity churning all around them. Lights flashing, radios crackling, movement. Voices talking in subdued, efficient tones. The emergency was over, danger neutralized. *It was over.* Rae looked into Caleb's eyes, and abruptly the world fell away into a deep indigo twilight. She was alone and safe. Safe in the arms of a man who loved her. *Loved* her.

Safe, as well, in the arms of a loving Father who loved her. Loved *her.*

Her heart began to swell in a symphony of music. She knew, deep inside, that the melody playing in her heart was music that would last a lifetime no matter *what* happened in that lifetime. God's music, she had learned, was like that. Better even than Mozart. Better than Caleb's laughter, though she would always be especially grateful for the joyful sound of it. *Thank You.*

She looked at him and smiled. "Will you do something for me . . . right now?"

"What is it, sweetheart?" He held her closer. "What do you need? You hurting somewhere?"

"Not exactly." She squirmed, grimacing. "Just that . . . can you *please* take this wretched Velcro thing off my waist before we leave? It's driving me crazy, irritating my skin." Heart full, Rae watched laughter fill his face again. Then she added, her voice breaking a little, "I don't mind telling the police and the FBI and the OSI . . . the *whole world* how much I love you. But I've had enough eavesdropping in my affairs for a while."

"I think that might be easily arranged, Ms. Prescott."

He deftly removed the equipment, then lifted Rae into his arms and stood. She tried to peek over his shoulder, to see the car.

"Caleb, what about—"

"Tomorrow, sweetheart. I'll fill you in on everything tomorrow." He tightened his grip, then began picking his way along the scrub- and rock-choked ravine. The path was difficult, the climb steep— but his arms never relaxed their protective hold. And his feet never stumbled.

Rae closed her eyes, laid her head on his shoulder—and relinquished control.

Chapter Twenty-Eight

They drove to Peterson the next morning through an unrelenting downpour, but Rae wouldn't have cared if the weather had dumped a six-foot blizzard of snow. For the first time in months—in her life—she had slept like a baby all night long. Surveillance was being maintained awhile longer, as a precaution, and Caleb had refused to leave until Lucy was competently ensconced in the parlor for the night.

Didn't matter to Rae. Eventually the surveillance teams would leave, as would Lucy. Even Caleb might leave. Come bedtime, Rae would still be able to lie down in perfect peace. She knew, with a more profound assurance than she had ever known, that she would *always* be watched over.

But not by *human* eyes and ears.

Snugly fastened in her seat belt next to Caleb, she savored the delicious sensation of being alive. Of being . . . free. "I've learned some things about myself," she announced when Caleb stopped at a red light. Rain pounded the windshield, turning the city to a colorful tear-streaked Monet painting.

"What things?" Caleb asked, slanting her a possessive glance. His hand slid across to brush her gauze-covered wrist.

Rae held her bandaged wrists up, studying them while she talked. "For one thing, I learned I really *don't* have to be in control for things to work out all right." She smiled a little sheepishly. "All these years I've tried to be such an obedient Christian. I thought I was—well, *helping* God by taking charge of my life. He gave me a will, a brain, all that stuff."

"Yeah," Caleb agreed. "All that stuff. And then?"

"You charged into my life."

"Literally," he added helpfully, chuckling when she swatted his arm.

The light changed to green. Rae sat back with a contented sigh, eyes half-closed, listening to the swishing tires, the rhythmic clack of the windshield wipers and the incessant drumming of the rain. "I learned," she murmured dreamily, "that life is more rewarding when I leave the driving to the Lord." Another quiet chuckle from Caleb. "You know, you taught me the true nature of God's unconditional love—you really never cared who and what my parents were, did you?"

"Nope. I cared that *you* were burdened. But God's presence in your life, in your heart, was obvious to me from almost the beginning. All I wanted to do was to prove your innocence in the Starseeker case. After I learned about your father, I wanted to prove your innocence to *you.*"

"I'm never going to see my father, am I?"

He hesitated, then answered gently. "Probably not, sweetheart. He's gone to ground again and might not surface for another five years. If he'd wanted to see you, meet you—he would have done so by now."

Rae closed her eyes. When Caleb squeezed her shoulder, she sighed, turning her cheek to rub the back of his hand. "Thank you for being honest. I—it helps. I suppose there's always going to be a hurt little girl inside of me somewhere, wishing my father had loved me. That my mother— Well, never mind. I'm trying hard to let God's love change those feelings instead of trying to work through them by myself and—" she gave a rueful laugh "—continuing to fail."

"I know. If it helps, you're not the only one who's had to learn a few hard lessons." They stopped for another red light, and he removed his hand. "God has a way of blasting us out of our securities and comfortable preconceptions so we *will* depend completely on Him, doesn't He?"

"I would have preferred a gentler method than IOS."

"Mmm. But if it hadn't been IOS, you might never have come to terms with your father."

For a while they were both silent. Rae had a feeling, from the lines pulling either side of Caleb's mouth, that his thoughts had tumbled briefly to the nightmare of the past twenty-four hours. "I guess we seldom appreciate how precious the life we have is, until we realize— Caleb?" She stopped, gnawing on her lip.

"What is it, sweetheart? Don't you know by now you can tell or ask me anything?"

"You might think I'm . . . ascribing wishful thinking, or hallucinating—I don't know. It's something that happened when I was in the back of that car, tied up." She saw his hands clench on the wheel, and a muscle jumped in his cheek. "I'm sorry," she recanted, contrite. "It's nothing. I shouldn't have reminded you— us."

"Don't be silly." He glanced at her, then turned into a parking lot and stopped the car, set the brake. "What happened, Rae? Tell me now, before we get to the base. I need to know." He reached out, touched her cheek with his fingers. "I need to know," he repeated.

She searched his face, seeing the love shining nakedly, and with a little laugh threw up her hands. "I heard God speak to me," she admitted in a rush. "In the car. I was about to panic and I heard— Caleb? What? Why are you looking at me like that?" She grabbed his arm. "Caleb, I warned you that—"

He crushed her against his chest, stifling her words. Against her ear his heart thundered like the rainstorm, and he was holding her so tightly she could barely breathe. "Caleb, you're going to suffocate me." The crushing hold instantly softened, but he wouldn't free her. His hand came up to cradle her head, and then he began to speak, the words low, so full of emotion goose bumps sprang up all over Rae's skin.

"If we're crazy, then we'll have to be crazy together. Fools for Christ," he whispered. "God . . . spoke to me, too. It's amazing, isn't it? We talk it, believe it . . . but until something like this happens and we *experience* the absolute reality of His presence— it's just blind faith. But then . . ."

"I once was blind, but now I see. Amazing grace."

"Do you know a song for everything?"

"Just about." She burrowed comfortably against him. "Deal with it, Myers. I'm a musician."

"Mmm. I have a feeling—" He stopped, and Rae felt a chuckle build strength until it tickled her ears in a puff of laughter. "Yep. I have a lot more feeling than I ever realized." He tugged her head up and kissed her. "Thank God for feelings, even if my reputation's just been permanently revised, updated. Reprogrammed."

"Do you know a computer analogy for everything, Myers?"

"Just about." He kissed her again. "Deal with it, Prescott. I'm a computer security consultant."

"Are you *sure* you're not a secret agent?"

He groaned, set her away and started the car. "I'm sure of a lot of things, Ms. Prescott." He pulled onto the road. "I'm sure that I love you. I'm sure—now, especially—that God really does have perfect timing to go along with His perfect love. Perfectly demonstrated by the miraculous changes that have occurred in both our lives."

"Caleb Myers . . ."

"I'm sure that Admiral Vale will rip a strip off *both* our skins if we're late for the debriefing."

"I'm sure I'm going to commit an act of violence to your person if you don't stop teasing me." She shook her fist mock-threateningly at him. "Tell me that you're just a consultant. Now."

"I love a tough woman. What happens if I don't tell you what you want to hear?"

Her heart leaped in a not-quite-comfortable somersault. He *was* teasing her, wasn't he? "I'll throw a real-live temper tantrum? Take out an ad in every major U.S. newspaper highlighting everything I know about you?" Her voice faltered. "Caleb?"

They turned into the road leading to Peterson Air Force Base. Caleb stopped to show the gate guard his ID, then they were on their way. Caleb didn't speak until they reached Admiral Vale's office and parked the car. He pocketed the key, unfastened his seat belt, then reached over and unfastened Rae's. "Come here, sweetheart," he ordered, very sternly.

Rae's mouth went dry, her euphoria faltering. He looked so serious all of a sudden, even though his eyes were still smiling and the corner of his mouth kept trying to curve upward. Even though they had made no vows to each other, no commitment beyond admissions of mutual love . . . She prayed her deepening faith would help her survive—never knowing. "You are, aren't you?" she whispered, her voice tremulous.

His head tilted, and his eyes narrowed. "Do you honestly think I might have lied to you?" he asked, taking her shoulders and turning her until their gazes were only inches apart. "Little idiot," he murmured lovingly after a long moment where she forgot to breathe. "I can see I have my work cut out for me the next half-century or so."

"I— *What?*" She gaped at him, dizzy and more breathless than ever. "What did you say?"

"Hmm. I think what's more important is what I meant, isn't it?" His fingers went to her chin and held it still. "I love you. You love me. We both love the Lord. I want to be part of your life forever. In my book, Rae Prescott, that means marriage. What does it mean to you?"

"I—I . . . you want to marry me?" Her voice rose to a squeak.

Incredibly, an expression of wonder filled his face, followed by wry amusement. "Yeah, I do. Another miracle, of sorts. I can't think of anything more I want out of life, Rae Prescott, than to marry you."

"But—my father . . . The Prescott family isn't . . . I mean . . ."

He stopped the halting words with a tender kiss. "Then my offer is the perfect solution to the problem you seem to have with your name." The amber eyes glowed even brighter. "Change it to Myers." He glanced swiftly at his watch, and the wry amusement deepened. "It's a good thing Christ will be the head of our family. I think I might have discovered an ongoing problem with my sense of timing concerning you."

"I think I could learn to live with that," Rae managed to say, all of a sudden floating higher than a weather balloon. "If you can live with my faults, I can live with yours."

"Is that a yes?"

Lids drooping, she slanted him a provocative look. "I'll tell you," she promised sweetly, "*after* you tell me what your job *really* is."

He gave a shout of laughter, pulled her close and bent to whisper in her ear. Then, hand in hand, they went inside for the debriefing.

*   *   *

Admiral Vale's office was crowded. Rae recognized most of the people. Tray Ramirez, Detective Grabowski, J.W. and Evan, Agent Hoffman. Caleb introduced her to the others—the FBI Denver section chief, the civilian contractor who headed the Starseeker program out at Falcon, Admiral Vale.

Overwhelmed, a little intimidated, Rae let the contractor, a nervous medium-size man with cowlicks all over his hair, shake her hand until she was afraid he would squeeze it off.

Admiral Vale clapped her shoulder with so much force only Caleb's swift reflexes kept her from pitching into a wastepaper basket.

"Young lady," he boomed, pointing a striped candy stick at her, "The U.S. Space Command, the Air Force—and our country—owe you an aircraft carrier-size thanks."

"I didn't do anything," Rae protested. "It was Caleb who pulled all the pieces together and figured it all out."

Everyone grinned indulgently at her. Rae gave up and sat gingerly in a chair J.W. held for her. Assorted bumps and bruises were singing an anvil chorus this morning, but she wasn't about to complain. She was alive, relatively sound—a miracle in anyone's terms.

"Can someone finally tell me the details?" she asked, her gaze moving shyly over the room. "I want to know. I think I *need* to know. For . . . closure?"

"Fill 'er in, Ramirez!" Admiral Vale ordered with a wicked grin. He winked at Rae. "Young woman, don't tell *anyone* a word of what you hear in this room, or I'll have to have you shot at dawn."

Rae swallowed a gasp of laughter, her gaze flying to Caleb.

"I've already threatened her with that one," he said, enlightening Admiral Vale. He dropped into the chair next to Rae's. "Sorry 'bout that, sir."

"Feel free to quote me anytime, son," the admiral equipped before leveling an unnervingly intense gaze upon Rae. "I reckon I won't worry over the matter as long as you're as staunch in your faith as Myers here is. Proceed, Mr. Ramirez."

Tray gave Rae an encouraging look. "Anything in particular you'd like to know first?"

"Mr. Fisher," Rae said without hesitation. "Is he . . . He's not—"

"He's alive and in custody," Tray promised. "We caught him at the airport—he's agreed to turn state's evidence. Larissa Holman, the woman who engineered your attempted murder, was his contact with IOS. Fisher was an easy enough mark for her to lure in, then trap. She used a combination of flattery and the promise of money followed by the inevitable blackmail and threats."

"A black widow spider," she observed with a shudder. The men exchanged quick grins, which Rae bore good-naturedly. "Did you catch her?"

Ramirez hesitated, glanced at Caleb, who nodded. Rae tensed, clenching her hands in her lap, and felt Caleb's close over hers.

"She's dead," Tray revealed flatly. "Car spun out of control in a high-speed chase down the freeway. She tried to exit where there wasn't one. Car flipped six times. She wasn't wearing a seat belt."

"Oh." Rae looked at the table. Larissa had been committing reprehensible acts of evil, but that was a terrible way to die.

"Rotten luck," Dennis Hoffman put in, then added callously, "means a dead end to tracking down IOS."

"Um . . . what about the other two men?" Rae asked after a moment. "The ones Larissa hired to— Well, what happened to those guys?"

"Grabowski's men were there first." Tray nodded to the detective, and he met Rae's carefully bland expression with a sour smile.

"They won't be going anywhere for a while," he assured her. "The one called Romo has a broken collarbone and a concussion. Jules broke both legs and a couple of ribs. Amazing, truth be told, that all three of you weren't killed, considering what that car looks like." He peered at Rae. "Did Myers tell you that Jules, the driver, is the reason you're relatively unscathed? You were pinned between him and the seat. His body protected you from the front, and the car seat from the rear."

Rae stared at him, then at Caleb. "How . . . ironic," she managed to say eventually. "Does he know?"

The detective shrugged. "Doubt it. They were both still unconscious when the ambulance took 'em off. If you like, I'll be sure to pass the information along, right after they're informed that they're to be tried for attempted murder.

"Among other things," Caleb murmured. He squeezed Rae's cold fingers.

"Were they from IOS?"

"Probably." Tray Ramirez took up the narrative again. "Neither one of them is talking right now. We'll find out, though. And—" this with a quick grin to Caleb "—within reason, we'll see that you're apprised. Fair enough, Myers?"

"Fair enough," Rae said tartly before Caleb could speak, and everyone laughed.

Agent Hoffman slid a piece of sheet music across the table. "You might be interested in that, Ms. Prescott."

It was the Mendelssohn. Rae freed her hands, then slowly flipped the cover open. A single sheet of paper with a few terse sentences typed across the middle covered the first page of music. "Your time has run out," Rae read aloud. "We require the rest of the program within seventy-two hours. Otherwise, no additional funds will be deposited in your account. Your association will be terminated. Permanently." Rae carefully laid the ominous paper down. She wanted to wash her hands all of a sudden. "Charming." She suppressed a shudder. "Was it meant for Mr. Fisher?"

Caleb nodded. "Sent him right over the edge. He'd been passing the Starseeker program a few lines at a time, remember?"

"I remember."

"IOS apparently got impatient," Tray continued. "Larissa Holman sensed everything closing in. She leaned on Fisher. So when he came into Joyful Noise the other day and *you* were so nervous, he was petrified that everything was about to go up in smoke.

"Everything did," Grabowski put in, very dryly. "Thanks to the courage of a woman who took a lot of abuse from a lot of different sources the past few months." He stretched his arm across the table. "Mostly from me. I'm eating my words, Ms. Prescott. And may I say that I'm relieved to have to do so?"

Coloring, Rae shook his hand. "You had cause. If it helps any, I've come to understand the difficulties *you* have to face, being constantly surrounded by liars and murderers and the like. Human beings at their worst. I was looking at my potential customers more as potential criminals myself!"

The maganimous gesture had been difficult for her to make. Then the harsh lines in Detective Grabowski's face softened, and for a fleeting moment gratitude and respect gleamed out of his eyes. It was enough. Rae ducked her head, her blush intensifying.

But there was one more thing she had to do. A ghost she had to lay to rest once and for all.

Rae looked at Agent Ramirez. "Caleb has helped me understand that I'm not responsible for my father's actions. But I would like you to know that I'm sorry about all the trouble he's caused." She paused, struggling to keep her voice even. "If I have helped your investigation, I'm glad. I hope . . . I hope you'll be able to view the Prescott name in a *little* more charitable light."

The men looked uncomfortable, awkward. Tray cleared his throat. "I don't think that will be a problem."

In a graceful move Caleb rose to his feet, then tugged Rae to stand beside him. "Perhaps," he volunteered with a sideways smile at Rae, "this is as good a time as any to make an official announcement of another kind."

"Caleb!" Rae said out of the side of her mouth. "What are you *doing*? Timing. You need to think of your execrable timing . . ." She began to sputter as his grin widened. He turned her so that her back was to the room. His hands rested on her shoulders. "What about waiting on the Lord? What about God's perfect timing? What about letting God control your actions? Your—"

"What Rae's trying to confess in her own charming manner—" Caleb's honey-smooth, commanding voice easily overrode hers "—is that she likes *my* name a lot better than Prescott. Since I'm an honorable fellow, I offered to share it with her. On a permanent basis, of course." He kissed her indignation into blissful silence.

Laughter and good-natured heckling filled the room. Someone produced cups and a couple of cans of soft drinks. Amid congratulations, hugs and teasing kisses, Rae toasted her new fiancé—and spilled half the drink in her lap.

"Might as well get used to it." She giggled as Caleb resignedly helped mop up the mess. Rae dabbed the front of her blouse and skirt with paper towels, too happy to care about her habitual clumsiness.

"When's the big day?" Tray asked, a huge grin on his face.

"Haven't a clue," Rae began, at the same time Caleb announced, "As soon as possible."

She pressed a kiss to the corner of his mouth. "I *do* know what our processional's going to be," she informed the others. "Beethoven. The 'Ode to Joy.' "

"The one from his Fifth Symphony?" Caleb inquired teasingly.

"I thought the 'Ode to Joy' was from Beethoven's Ninth," Admiral Vale commented, his booming voice perplexed.

Fresh laughter erupted from everyone, and Rae threw her arms around Caleb. "Who cares?" She smiled at the circle of indulgent masculine faces. "We'll have them both!"

Dear Reader,

I started out writing *NIGHT MUSIC* as entertaining romantic suspense—which incidentally, I hope it proves to be! But somewhere along the way, Rae and Caleb took over, the struggles they face against the conspiracies of evil men broadened, until they were struggling with themselves and their faith as well. It's incredible to me how much God really does care about we fumbling, fallible humans. Even those who insist, like Rae, that He can "take care of the big things. I take care of my life."

Because Rae is a professional musician (and the author is sort of an amateur musician), song pervades *NIGHT MUSIC*, from Psalms to Beethoven and a whole lot in between. Caleb points Rae to Psalm 32:7 . . . she plays a piano selection based on Psalm 27. Then there's Beethoven's *Ode to Joy*, which figures prominently in the plot.

Yet sometimes, even a writer who loves words has to concede that . . . there are no words to adequately convey the depth of God's unconditional love. But when I listen to a stirring rendition of Mozart's *Ein Kleine Nachtmusik* . . . or old hymns played on a hammered dulcimer and Autoharp, well . . . I feel God's loving presence. Actually, perhaps my hope for *NIGHT MUSIC* can best be summed up in a homily I read once: God gave us music, that we might pray without words.

May whatever songs you sing bring you closer to the joy of His presence.

Colossians 3:17

Sara Mitchell

P.S.
Beethoven's *Ode to Joy* is featured prominently in this story—by design. Twenty-seven years ago my husband and I chose it for our wedding processional!

Promises To Keep

Books by Jane Peart
Love Inspired

The Risk of Loving #1
Promises To Keep #43

JANE PEART

Award-winning and bestselling author Jane Peart grew up in North Carolina and was educated in New England. Jane and her husband now reside in Northern California, which is often a setting for her novels.

In more than twenty books and her bestselling Orphan Train West series, Jane has brought to readers the timeless themes of family, faith and committed love.

Promises To Keep

Jane Peart

Love Inspired

Published by Steeple Hill Books™

STEEPLE HILL BOOKS

Steeple
Hill™

4 in 1 ISBN: 0-7394-0528-4

PROMISES TO KEEP

Copyright © 1998 by Jane Peart

Be strong and of good courage, do not be afraid,
nor be dismayed, for the Lord your God is with you
wherever you go.

—*Joshua* 1:9

Part I

Chapter One

It was the kind of day San Franciscans like to boast about. A brilliant postcard blue sky, the sun sparkling on the Bay where boats, their sails billowing in the crisp wind, bobbed like toys. Seated at their table in the rooftop restaurant at Ghirardelli Square, Valerie Evans and her little girl, Megan, watched the Chinese kites being flown from the marina below and floating into view. They were unaware that they were being observed with more than casual interest by a man at a nearby table.

He had noticed the child right away. About four or five years old, she was enchanting, her cherubic face haloed by a cloud of golden hair. Garth Hasten whipped out the sketchbook he always carried with him and began to draw, his pencil moving swiftly with professional skill.

"Look, Mommy," the child exclaimed, scrambling up to her knees on her chair, pointing to the colorful soaring kites. "Could I get a kite like that?"

Her mother was about to reply just as the waitress came to take their order, blocking Garth's view of the child. His pencil halted. As she studied the menu, the mother was in his direct line of vision. Quickly he turned the page and started a new sketch. She was not beautiful, not in the classic sense, the jaw too strong, the mouth too wide, but her face had an individuality that made it interesting to an artist. She had taken off her dark glasses and he saw her eyes. Under even brows, they were large, hazel maybe or gray. And there was something in them that he couldn't quite capture. Her high-lighted brown hair fell from a center part curving just below her ears where tiny triangular earrings hung, glistening when she moved her head. They were her only jewelry except for a wide gold wedding band and a heavy gold link bracelet from which dangled several charms. When the waitress left, Valerie caught Garth's intense gaze. Immediately she stiffened, frowned, turned away, obviously annoyed.

He got up and walked over to their table, holding up his sketchbook so she could see his drawing of Megan. "Forgive me if I made you uncomfortable. Let me introduce myself. I'm Garth Hasten, an illustrator of children's books. Your daughter is such a lovely child I couldn't resist making a quick sketch of her."

Startled, Val glanced at the sketch. She had to admit it was very good. Professional. However, she did not like the idea of a stranger watching them like that for whatever reason. She looked away from the sketch and up to the man. Actually, he didn't look at all threatening. His expression in his tan, lean face was pleasant. There were laugh wrinkles around his very blue eyes. With his tousled thatch of graying brown hair and beard, and the Irish-knit sweater he was wearing, he gave the appearance of a roguish seafarer.

When she made no comment, Garth explained, "I'm doing a series of illustrations for a new book of fairy tales to be published by—" here he mentioned his publishers, a firm well-known for producing award-winning children's books. Seeing she recognized the name, he was encouraged and went on, "I wonder, would you be at all interested in letting your daughter model for me?" He dug into his pocket and held out his business card.

Val shook her head. "No, I'm sorry, that would be impossible."

Garth waited another minute, then said, "I understand your reluctance, but I can give you all kinds of references, professional, character, whatever. My phone number is on my card." He glanced down at Megan, who was looking from one to the other of the adults during this conversation. "It's just that this little girl would be an ideal subject."

"Mommy, it's a picture of me!" Megan exclaimed. "See, it looks just like me. Can I have it?"

Garth glanced at Val who seemed to be hesitating. He raised his eyebrows. "If your mother gives permission." He then said to Val,

"I'd like her to have it." Unable to say no, Val inclined her head. Garth smiled, tore the page from his sketchbook and handed the picture to Megan. "There you go, young lady."

"Thank you," Megan said shyly.

Garth turned back to Val. "If you should change your mind, you can reach me or my rep at either of these numbers."

"Thank you, but I'm sure I won't change my mind," Val replied icily.

At that moment, the waitress appeared with their order. There was an awkward few seconds. The waitress stood waiting while Garth's hand was extended, holding out his card.

There was nothing Val could do but take it. Without reading it, she dropped it indifferently into her handbag. Deliberately, she indicated to the waitress to set down their plates.

"Sorry to have bothered you," Garth said, then went back to his table, left a tip and walked over to the cash register.

Val slipped her dark glasses back on and watched as he left the restaurant. What a strange incident, she thought, then looked fondly at her daughter. No wonder Megan had attracted the artist's eye. She was a picture. Dainty, pretty, like a doll. Except . . . Val sighed.

Their reason for coming into the city had not been merely for a special treat. Today they'd had an appointment with a specialist recommended by their regular pediatrician. Val turned over in her mind what Dr. Melton had told her. Megan's hearing was getting worse. Eventually, she would probably be totally deaf. It was unreal and so unfair.

Val dreaded telling Kevin the doctor's diagnosis. Kevin had an aversion to any kind of physical disability. Val remembered how he'd once told her he hated to be around people with any kind of medical disorder. "I'm just no good at it, don't ask me why. It just makes me uneasy somehow." During their marriage, Val had accepted that about him, hiding her own occasional headaches, minimizing a bad cold.

Megan's hearing loss had not been evident at first. Some slight inattentiveness, a lack of concentration. Gradually, Val realized Megan simply could not hear unless she was spoken to directly. Then began the round of specialists. Lately, the hope they had at first began to fade.

Of course, she would have to tell Kevin even though she knew what his reaction would be. Explosive. Anger. As if it was anyone's fault.

After finishing their sandwiches and sodas, they went to a shop on the lower level that sold Chinese kites and bought one for Megan. Then they went to the parking garage where Val had left the station wagon. With Megan happily buckled in beside her, she eased down the ramp and out onto the street, then headed for the Golden Gate Bridge and the Marin suburbs.

They merged into the flow of freeway traffic and then took the Mill Valley turnoff. After making a boulevard stop, she turned at Meadowbrook, heading up a narrow winding road lined with eucalyptus trees, and drove slowly around curves up the hill. She pulled into a circular driveway just as a black Porsche backed out of the double garage. Val braked alongside.

A deeply tanned man, with stylishly groomed dark hair and neatly trimmed mustache, leaned out his open car window and, with the engine still running, asked brusquely, "Well?" Val just shook her head. Kevin's mouth tightened, but he said nothing. He stared ahead for a few seconds, then said, "I'm on my way to play racquetball at the club. I won't be home for dinner. I have a meeting tonight. I'll go in from there." He gave a small salute, shifted gears and swerved the car around, then, with a spit of gravel, roared out of the driveway.

Val sighed. She knew Kev's moods so well. Better that he bat some balls in vigorous activity than pace and prowl around the house in fury and frustration. He was tightly wound, a high-energy workaholic. She would have liked for them to be able to sit and talk quietly about Megan's prognosis. She wished she could unload some of her own anxiety. If only that was possible. But with Kevin . . .

Val got out of the car and held the door open for Megan. She looked up at the modern cedar-and-stone hillside house. Paid far too much for it. Had they really needed such a big, expensive house? For just the three of them, since Kevin had made it clear he considered their family complete. But he'd convinced her a good address was important.

The sound of wild barking greeted them as they started up the steps to the wraparound deck. Flynn, their huge black-and-tan

Airedale came bounding down the steps from the deck. He circled them, yelping ecstatically, his tail wagging furiously, racing ahead of them, then clumsily wheeling and leaping back to be sure they were following him.

Inside, Megan called, "Harriet, we're home!"

Their weekly housekeeper, a gray-haired woman in a flowered housedress, came and stood in the archway leading from the kitchen into the hall.

"Any calls?" Val asked.

"Only Miss Grant, Mr. Evans's secretary," Harriet replied. Over Megan's head, she lifted her eyebrows inquiringly. "I s'pose there weren't any good news?"

Harriet knew about Megan's doctor's appointment. She had come to work for them when Megan was a baby and loved her dearly. Harriet had always been a rock of support to Val, who had no family of her own to lean on or confide in when the doctor first gave her the report of Megan's problem.

A faithful churchgoer, Harriet had enlisted her prayer group to pray for Megan. "We're a bunch of real prayer warriors," she'd told Val, assuring her they had added Megan's healing to her list of heavenly requests.

" 'Fraid not." Val sighed. "By the way, Mr. Evans won't be home for dinner. So since it'll just be Megan and me, you might as well leave early, Harriet."

Val picked up the mail on the hall table and carried it with her into the living room. Walled with windows, it had a spectacular view of the hills, which were beginning to show the first gold and bronze tinges of autumn color.

Slipping her feet out of her leather flats, Val curled up in a corner of the curved coffee-colored sectional sofa. There was nothing much in the mail. She started to sift through the few envelopes. Mostly ads, two catalogs. Kevin must have already gone through it, taken the important stuff. She put the rest on the coffee table, then leaned her head back against the velour cushions. It had been a long day and a discouraging one. If only she had someone to talk to about Megan. Even if Kevin were here, he wouldn't have wanted to talk about it. He would probably have shut himself up in his den with the work he always seemed to bring home.

Val closed her eyes, rubbing her temples that were beginning to throb. This was not the first night recently that Kevin hadn't been home for dinner. He hadn't said anything at breakfast about having to go back to the bank. In fact, he had planned to take the whole afternoon off and play racquetball. Something must have come up. Harriet said his secretary had called.

Megan wandered into the room, followed by Flynn. She went over to the bookcase where her games and toys were kept on a lower shelf, got out one of her puzzles. She plopped down on the rug, emptied out the pieces and began to work on it. Flynn stretched out beside her, his big head and paws as close to her as possible, his eyes slavishly adoring.

Soon Harriet, in her coat and wearing an incredible purple knitted hat, appeared at the living-room arch. "Well, I'm on my way."

"Good night, Harriet, we'll see you on Thursday." Val smiled.

"Night, Harriet!" Megan chirped.

"Good night, sweetness." Harriet blew her a kiss.

A few minutes later, they heard the chugging sound of Harriet's old sedan's engine reluctantly start, followed by a grinding shift of gears as she went out the driveway and down the hill.

The house was quiet, peaceful. Again Val wished Kev was home. It had been a long time since the three of them had had dinner as a family or spent the evening together.

The sky began to blaze. The oncoming sunset sent a brilliant light into the room. It fell on Megan, who was all concentration as she fitted the pieces of her puzzle together, turning her light hair into golden satin. She was such a pretty child and so dear. Val wished Kev would spend more time with her. Val frowned. Kev worked too hard. He was so ambitious, so eager to move up the corporate ladder. But other things were important, too. She wished she could make him see that. Megan was important, especially now. They would soon have to talk about how they could best help her if, as the doctor predicted, her hearing loss became more severe. Make some decisions about her schooling, her future. Yes, she and Kevin must talk about it.

They never seemed to have a chance to talk about things. Kev seemed to have so many evening meetings after banking business hours. Unwanted, a nagging thought intruded. Had it just been since Rhonda became his secretary that Kevin had started working later and later?

An image of Rhonda came vividly. Val had met her for the first time a few months ago. She had stopped by the bank because she and Kev were going to lunch and then pick out birthday presents for Megan. Rhonda was undeniably attractive, tall, masses of auburn hair, a good figure that her knitted dress showed off to advantage. She'd been very pleasant to Val, effusive, actually. Seated as she was at the entrance to the loan officers' desks, Rhonda would make a good impression on the bank's customers.

Val quickly thrust back her stab of suspicion. How silly to imagine Rhonda had anything to do with Kev's frequently being late. Kev explained that a great deal of the bank's business was done outside the bank, after hours. This sometimes necessitated meeting a potential client or bank customer after work. "It's a good idea for them to see you in a different setting. Get to know you on a more personal level."

Still, Val didn't like it. Life should have definite compartments. There should be a better balance between work and family. She wished Kev felt that way. Moving up the corporate ladder was the most important thing to him. "Later, when I've really made it. There'll be plenty of time." This was his argument whenever Val brought up the subject. But time was quickly going by. Megan's childhood was going quickly, too. . . .

"All done!" Megan exclaimed. "See, Mommy, got it all put together. Isn't it nice?"

"Yes, darling, very nice. Ready to have supper?" Val uncurled herself from the sofa and stood, searching with one foot for her shoe. "Are you hungry? Since Daddy isn't coming, we'll just eat in the kitchen, okay?"

"Is he going to Rhonda's?" Megan asked.

Astonished at the question, Val halted, one shoe on, the other dangling. "Rhonda? How do you know Rhonda, honey?" As well as she could recall, there hadn't been any occasion where the little girl might have met Kevin's secretary.

"With Daddy."

"Oh, did Daddy take you by his office?" Val asked. A few days ago, she'd had a dental appointment and Kev had volunteered to pick Megan up at play school where she went three days a week.

"No, on Saturday."

"Saturday?"

"You know, Saturday, when you went out with Emily."

Val remembered that Kevin had reluctantly agreed to take Megan to the park when the sitter had canceled at the last minute. "Oh?" Val waited, then asked, "So where did you see Rhonda?"

"We went to Rhonda's 'partment. It has a swimming pool. We sat on her balcony. We could see people swimming. But I didn't have my bathing suit."

Why hadn't Kevin mentioned taking Megan to his secretary's apartment? Unless it wasn't important. Or maybe it was too important. Either way, it bothered her. She glanced at Megan. She wanted to ask her more, but she wasn't going to pump their child about it. But she didn't like it. She didn't like it at all. She intended to ask Kev about it. There was probably some simple explanation.

But Val didn't have the chance. Something much more serious happened. She waited up until ten. Then she took a bath, got into bed and read until midnight. Kevin still hadn't come home. At one, her eyes drooping, having read the same sentence over several times, Val turned out the light and went to sleep.

She was never sure what awakened her. But she sat up suddenly, fully awake. She sensed rather than heard movement in the house. Aware that Kevin must have come in, Val reached for her robe, thrust her feet into slippers and went down the hall to the living room.

Kevin was sitting on the sofa, his head lowered, holding a half-empty glass of amber fluid in a glass, a bottle of whiskey on the coffee table in front of him. As Val walked in, he raised his head, turned and looked at her. Immediately, she knew something was terribly wrong.

His face was ashen under the tan, giving him a haunted look. Staring at her from deep hollows, his eyes were full of fear. For a moment, Val couldn't find her voice. Her throat felt tight and sore. She couldn't seem to draw a breath. Finally, she managed to ask, "Kev, what is it? What's happened."

He took a long swallow of the liquid in the glass, draining it, then gave a hoarse laugh. "I'm finished. It's all over."

"What do you mean?" Val moved toward him, feeling she was treading on quicksand. "What do you mean?"

He lifted the bottle and poured another few inches into his glass, then held it up as if studying it. "I've blown it, that's what. Embezzled. Hundreds of thousands in bogus loans. I was going to put it back, every last cent of it, if I'd only had a little more time." He took a quick sip, shook his head. "Time, that's all I needed. But the bank examiners arrived." He laughed harshly. It sounded more like a grunt or a groan. "They never give any advance notice. I just got word that they were there . . . Well, it's too late now."

Her knees began to tremble, grow weak. She sat down at the end of the sofa and began to shiver. Long, deep shudders shook her body.

It was the beginning of a nightmare, one from which she couldn't wake up. It was the beginning of a whole new chapter of her life, and the end of another.

Chapter Two

Val felt as if she were sleepwalking as she entered the courtroom. She took a seat in the front row of the spectator section behind the table where Kevin's lawyer, Brad Hensley, was going over some papers. He turned, briefly acknowledged her with a nod, then went back to whatever he was reading.

This was it, Val thought. This was what they had finally come to after all these nightmarish weeks. Kev had refused to have a trial. He thought his chances would be better if he pleaded guilty and threw himself on the mercy of the court. He felt sure if he declared his remorse and assured the judge of his firm intention of repaying every cent of the money, saying that he had never intended to keep any of it, that he had used it to take care of the temporary shortfall from some unwise investments, he'd most likely get a suspended sentence and probation.

That was his story. Val wasn't sure Brad believed him, but that's the way he had presented Kev's case to the judge. And today he would be sentenced.

Kev was so sure his own sales skills would work in court the way they had worked in most areas of his life up until now. To Val, it seemed total madness not to call character witnesses, former employers, fellow workers who could vouch for him, provide some defense. But, as usual, she had been unable to talk Kevin out of anything he had decided to do.

At least there'd be no jury filing in, giving her, the wife of the defendant, curious looks. Suspicious ones, too, probably thinking she must have known what her husband was doing.

Val stiffened. The adage, "tarred with the same brush" came to mind. She had already felt the scorn and heard the whispers of their neighbors. She had little pride left to hang on to now. She smoothed the skirt of her blue suit, ran her fingers along the braid trim of the jacket. She'd purposely worn this outfit. Blue was Kevin's favorite color; that's why she had chosen it this morning. Nervously, she touched her hair. Kevin liked her naturally light brown hair highlighted, so she'd had it done the day before. Although she certainly couldn't afford it.

Actually, she couldn't afford much of anything anymore. After Kevin's arrest, their checking and savings accounts had been impounded. Creditors had lost no time repossessing all their belongings: furniture, Kev's elaborate exercise equipment, golf clubs, TVs, cars. The house, of course, which Val discovered Kevin had mortgaged to the hilt in a desperate effort to recoup some of his losses, went with everything else. Nothing was left that she could sell for cash. Not that she would have wanted anything that had been purchased with the money Kevin embezzled, she thought bitterly.

While Kev was in the county jail awaiting his trial, Val had lived on the small insurance policy her parents had left her. But that was almost gone. The only other money available was a few hundred dollars in traveler's checks from one of their last trips she had never cashed. And those wouldn't last long.

When a door at the side of the courtroom opened and a police officer brought Kevin in, all thoughts of herself vanished. The look on Kev's face struck Val to the very heart. He had a terrible set expression. His eyes looked empty. His glance in her direction merely grazed her and he turned quickly away. She had hoped to send him signals of support, but there was no chance. He took his place beside Brad and the two murmured together for a few minutes before the bailiff announced in a loud voice, "All rise," and the judge entered.

Afterward, Val remembered little else other than the judge's deep voice asking, "How does the defendant plead?" then Kevin's answer, "Guilty." She had then expected Kevin to launch into his own defense. But it didn't happen. Had Brad persuaded him otherwise or had the die already been cast? All she clearly recalled were the words "seven to fifteen years." She felt her whole body sway as if from a severe blow, then her knees sagged and she had to grab onto the railing in front of her to steady herself. A wave of nausea left her weak and dizzy.

Slowly the reality of the sentence hit her. If Kevin served the full term, he would be forty-seven, she would be forty-five, and they would be middle-aged, half their lives gone. Megan would be a grown woman!

Val was to be allowed fifteen minutes with Kevin before he was taken away, driven upstate to the prison where he would be spending the next years of his life. Dazedly, she walked out into the lobby. Out of the corner of her eye, she thought she saw Mr. Carson, Kev's immediate boss at the bank. If he saw her, he pretended not to, quickly averting his head. He must have caught some of the flak when the discrepancies and false accounts came to light in his department, "on his watch." Ironically, Val recalled his former jovial demeanor, the hearty greetings that were usual when they met at some bank party or other social function. He had always declared loudly and often to any and everyone that "they were all a big family." He'd clap an arm around Kev's shoulders and tell her heartily, "This is my boy. We have great plans for Kevin, Mrs. Evans. He's our shining star." Now, he wouldn't even meet her gaze.

"This way, ma'am," a bailiff said, beckoning her.

Before she could follow, Brad Hensley approached. Stiffly, he thrust a manila folder at her. "There are some documents in here you'll need to look over, Val. If there's anything you don't understand, you can call my office. However, I believe it's all self-explanatory." He looked so uncomfortable, Val almost felt sorry for him. He mumbled something that sounded like, "Really sorry about this, Val." Then he turned and made a quick exit out the courthouse door.

Glad to be rid of us, Val thought. Not that she blamed him. Who wanted to be seen associating with a thief, or even the wife of one? She felt sure some people suspected she had known what Kev was doing. Spent the money herself.

The bailiff was holding open the door to a room down the hall for her. She hurried toward it.

Kevin was standing with his back to the door, staring out the barred window of the small, bare room into which she was ushered. He turned at her entrance and her first impulse was to go into his arms. But he hadn't opened them. In fact, he stood rigidly, his arms close to his sides. His glance went over her head and she realized a guard would remain during their last meeting.

"Kev," she said, her voice cracking a little as she went toward him. But as her arms went around him, she felt him stiffen.

He moved out of her embrace, then took her by the wrists. His expression was grim. "Listen, Val, there's not much time and I have some important things to say."

His intensity frightened her. His brusqueness hurt her. But maybe he was afraid to show any emotion, afraid to look weak. Kev was always conscious of his impression on other people. Even an officer of the court.

"Do you understand? There are things I want you to promise."

She nodded, knowing at this point she would have promised him anything. Anything that might somehow take the desperation out of his eyes. But she was unprepared for what he demanded.

"First, you've got to divorce me."

"Kev, you can't mean that!"

"I've never meant anything more. Next, you've got to take Megan and move somewhere away from here, even out of the state, if possible. Change your name. You've got to start a new life for the two of you where no one knows you and no one can connect you with me. Understand?"

"But, Kevin . . ." His fingers gripped more tightly, hurting her slender wrists. "I don't want to divorce you, Kev. This isn't a life sentence—"

"It might as well be."

"But you may not even have to serve the whole term. There's good behavior—no prior record—"

"Look, Val, believe me, I know. I've discussed this with Brad. There's a whole big political thing involved in the justice system right now. White-collar crime, they call it. Don't let them get away with it. This judge is up for election. If nothing else, he wants to make an example of me. This is a high-profile case in his district. So I'm not going to get any breaks." Val's wrists began to throb from the way he was gripping them. "Well, do I have your promise?"

Tears came stinging into her eyes. "Oh, Kev, please don't ask me to do this. When you get out, we can—"

"Haven't you heard anything I've said?" Kevin interrupted her. "Do what I say." He let go her hands and flung her away from him, then took a few steps toward the door where the guard stood impassively.

"Wait, Kev." Val caught his arm, "Yes, of course I'll do whatever you want. Please, don't be angry."

He half turned back. "Promise?"

She nodded, her throat too constricted to speak.

"Okay, then. Remember it's got to be a complete break. I don't want Megan growing up with a con for a father." His voice rasped.

Val knew he was fighting his own emotions. She went over to him, put her arms around his neck and clung to him, tears streaming down her face. Over Kevin's shoulders, she saw even the guard looked distressed. It struck her that in spite of having to perform their duty, these people were human. No matter how many similar scenes they must have witnessed, they could feel the pain of such partings.

Kevin's hands pried her clasped fingers loose and he pushed her away. To the guard, he said, "I'm out of here. Let's go." Val was sobbing now. She pressed both her hands against her mouth as she watched Kevin leave with the deputy.

This couldn't be happening, Val screamed silently. But it was. That truth finally hit her. She slumped into one of the wooden chairs, weeping uncontrollably.

Chapter Three

Val woke up as the gray light of dawn filtered through the slats of the venetian blinds. Struggling out of the grogginess of exhausted sleep into which she'd fallen, she raised herself on her elbows and looked around the unfamiliar room.

At first, she couldn't figure out where she was. Then she remembered and came fully awake. The shock of what had happened yesterday brought it all back. She closed her eyes as if to block out the horror. But it was impossible. A deep shudder went through her. There was no escape. The events of the day before took shape in her mind. After she left the courthouse, she'd booked a room at a downtown hotel, then gone to pick up Megan at Harriet's house.

Megan had stayed with Harriet for a few days before Kevin's court appearance. She had kept Flynn, too. Harriet's husband was a disabled vet, confined to a wheelchair, and when Val wondered what they would do about the dog after they left Meadowbrook, Harriet had offered to keep him. "He's been company for Lew," she told Val. "He's here by himself most days when I'm out working. He's really taken to him."

Flynn was just one more thing that had to go. Val was doubtful if she could find a place to live with a child, much less a dog. A dog as large and as used to having room to run as Flynn. She had already made phone calls about rentals and discovered that children and dogs were liabilities for most places she could afford.

Val wasn't even sure what that was. She had to find some kind of job. And soon. She would have to support herself and Megan. But how? She hadn't worked since before Megan's birth. And then only as a saleswoman in a gift shop boutique. What did she have to offer a prospective employer? Val was grateful to Harriet. It made Megan's parting with Flynn easier knowing Harriet would take care of him.

Val pulled on her robe, slid her feet into slippers, fighting desperately the sense of desperation that threatened to overwhelm her. At the window, she peered through the slats of the blind. Just across the square stood the brick courthouse. She shuddered and turned away from the view. Her gaze went to Megan.

The little girl was still asleep, hair spread tangled on the pillow, rosebud mouth partly opened, plump cheeks resting on dimpled hands. She seemed untouched by all they had been through. Thank God she was free from all Val's anguish and anxiety. Completely trusting that her mother would take care of her. Little did she know the panic with which Val awakened, the fear that had been Val's constant companion for the past weeks.

Megan thought everything was an adventure. Even when Val had told her they were moving. She helped pack up her toys, books and games to be put in storage until they knew where they would be living, what they were going to do. It was then that she had showed Val the sketch the artist had made of her. That day they had been in the city at the rooftop restaurant in Ghirardelli Square seemed so long ago. Val had almost forgotten about it in the wake of all that had happened since. In fact, it was that very night that Kev had told her about the embezzlement. She had not had the slightest premonition that afternoon that their world was going to come crashing down around them.

There were so many things to decide, so much to face.

What did she do now? Where did she go from here? For the first time, she really confronted the question of what her next step would be. Somehow she had lived on the false hope that Kevin might receive a short jail term, even a suspended sentence, but now she knew that wasn't going to happen. There was no one to tell her what to do.

She took out the file folder Brad Hensley had thrust into her numb hands. Brad's demeanor had been cold, businesslike. It was hard to remember he had once been a friend. His whole attitude toward her had changed. As if he thought what had happened to them was contagious and he wanted to avoid contact. Yesterday she had been too upset to look inside the folder to see what he was talking about. Her mind had been on Kevin, the sentence the judge had just handed down. Far stiffer than Brad had led them to believe. If Brad had really worked for Kevin, would her husband have received less than the maximum in a state penitentiary?

Well, it was over now. No appeal of the sentence was possible.

With shaky hands, Val opened the folder. Divorce papers were the first thing she saw. So Brad had been in on this decision, as well. She shuddered. No matter what she had promised Kevin, this seemed a horrible solution to their problems. She put it aside and went on to the other legal papers on which her signature was needed.

What were her two most pressing needs? A place to live and a job? Slowly, Val began to understand why Kevin wanted her to change her name, to take Megan and move as far away as she could from this small community where they were known. Kevin's conviction had made the papers. If she applied for a job with Kevin's last name, prospective employers might identify her as his wife. Maybe they'd even think of her as an accomplice who'd lived on stolen money! And who could she give as a character reference?

For the first time, the awful reality of her situation struck Val. When the court had sentenced Kevin, it had sentenced her, as well.

A feeling of despair swept over her. She looked around the drab, impersonal room. Anonymous, she thought, that's what we have to become. Her gaze landed on their suitcases, which she had just dumped at the door the night before, not even bothering to unpack anything but Megan's nightie and her own, their toothbrushes and toothpaste. Until she figured out what to do, they would have to stay here.

Wearily, she opened the biggest suitcase and took out some of the things to place in the dresser. As she opened the top drawer, she saw the Gideon Bible. It surprised her until she recalled she had heard of the organization whose main ministry was placing a Bible in hotel and motel rooms. At the same time, she felt a pang of guilt. In all this terrible time, she had prayed only desperate prayers. Prayers without any real sense of direction, just tortured cries for help, wrung out of a bewildered mind, a broken heart. But she hadn't even felt help would be forthcoming. They were in trouble. Big time. But she had no real faith they would be rescued. "You reap what you sow" was the kind of phrase that came to her. Kevin had sowed a lot of bad seeds and they were reaping them. Even as the truth of that came to her, it was no comfort.

Val took out the Bible. Her grandmother, she recalled, had always said the answers to life were in the Bible. If they were, Val knew she needed some answers now. She opened it, turning the pages randomly. Was there some direction, some guidance for her within this ancient book? Something for now? Some of the Psalms were familiar, but as Val's eyes searched them, nothing seemed relevant. She came to Proverbs and as she turned the pages her gaze stopped at Chapter 3, Verse 5. "Trust in the Lord with all your heart, And lean not on your own understanding; In all your ways acknowledge Him, And He will direct your paths."

That made sense. Val felt somewhat apologetic. Why would God even want to listen to her prayers? Although she had always gone to Sunday school as a child and, until she met Kevin, attended her church's youth group, it had been a long time since she had sought Him. After Megan was born, she had often suggested to Kevin that they find a church to go to as a family. But Kevin had not been interested and she had not pursued it. As usual, it was easier to go along with Kev than confront him. Another thing for which she blamed herself. In a way, it seemed hypocritical to come to God now that she was in such desperate circumstances.

Still, what other resource did she have? Holding tight to the book, Val closed her eyes and prayed, *"Dear God, I need direction. I don't know what to do, where to go. Unless You show me, I am at a loss. Please help me. I promise I'll always be grateful."* It seemed an inadequate prayer, but it was the only thing she could think of to do.

Megan stirred in her sleep and Val put the Bible back in the drawer. When Megan woke up, they got dressed and went down to the coffee shop. The little girl skipped along beside her, swinging Val's hand. She was happy about all the exciting new things they were doing, like sleeping in a hotel, eating breakfast out.

On a nearby table someone had left a morning paper and Val picked it up. While Megan happily drowned her pancakes in syrup, Val glanced through the want ads not knowing quite what she was looking for. The paper covered a wide area and jobs were advertised in many of the smaller towns in the southern part of the state. Suddenly, a name seemed to jump out at Val, one that instantly brought back memories. Seawood. "Popular restaurant, formerly Le Chalet, under new ownership, now hiring waitresses for the coming season."

Seawood was a small town halfway between San Francisco and Carmel, a picturesque resort about a hundred miles down the coast. Years ago when Megan was a baby, Kevin had come home one day driving a shiny British sports car. With a broad wink, he told her he was test-driving it. At least that's what he had told the dealer. "Come on, honey, let's go." Although Val hadn't thought it quite honest to pretend to the salesman that he was thinking of buying it, Kevin had shrugged off any protests. "Who knows, but someday we'll be buying one like this. Anyway, why pass up a chance to drive a sweet number like this with a ten-thousand-dollar engine?" He grinned. That grin of his usually melted her resistance to any of Kevin's ideas. Persuaded, Val hastily called her regular sitter and they took off. To Carmel.

It had been a glorious day and they had driven, top down, along a beautiful span of scenic highway, on one side towering hills dark with Monterey pines and on the other, the ocean exploding dramatically against the rocky cliffs.

They'd had dinner at Le Chalet, a French restaurant whose menu Val couldn't read and whose prices she didn't dare look at too closely. Kevin had ordered a gourmet meal with an assurance that even then amazed Val. Before their dessert came, Kevin excused himself. When he came back to the table, he placed a key beside Val's plate. "Guess what? We're staying over." He held up a hand as Val opened her mouth to ask about Megan. He'd called the sitter, made arrangements for her to spend the night.

The fairy-tale cottage was reached by climbing a path up a wooded hillside behind the restaurant. It seemed to cling to the rocks high above the ocean. There was a fireplace and a canopy bed. Kevin had ordered another bottle of wine and they sipped it while sitting on the little balcony. Val worried what this would do to their budget, but Kevin wouldn't let her even guess.

"Just think of it as a second honeymoon, babe." That was always Kevin's excuse for any impulsive weekend trip or unplanned vacation. Their life together had been a series of second honeymoons, Val thought ruefully. The trouble was they'd never settled down to a real marriage.

Val remembered that time with a mixture of nostalgia and regret. Maybe she should have protested his extravagances more. Especially when they couldn't possibly afford it. Like that weekend.

She really had to take some of the blame for the way they had lived. She had always wanted to please him, but why? Because she was afraid of his sudden shifts of mood, his temper. It was much easier, pleasanter, to go along.

Val's attention went back to the Help Wanted ad.

"Now hiring for the coming season: attractive, personable young ladies as waitresses for restaurant in small coastal community. Top wages, pleasant working conditions, good benefits. For interview contact Manager, Eileen McDermott." A post-office box and phone number was given. "Seawood, CA."

Val read the ad over again. Maybe seeing this ad was some kind of sign. Maybe it was God's way of providing for her and Megan. Of course, she wasn't an experienced waitress, but they had not prefaced the job as requiring experience. Val had worked in an ice-cream parlor part-time when in high school. Not the kind of job to qualify her for one in a large, busy restaurant. Still, she had the feeling that she ought to follow her hunch. Or, maybe, this was the answer to her prayer? "Trust in the Lord . . . and He will direct your paths." Maybe He was directing her path. She needed to find a job and a place to live. And right away. They couldn't stay in the hotel indefinitely. She had to make a move. One step at a time, they always said. Well, she'd take that step, Val decided, tearing out the ad.

After returning with Megan to their room, she sat at the phone and dialed the number.

A pleasant-sounding woman's voice answered, identifying herself as Eileen McDermott. Val asked if there were still openings for waitresses and was told yes. An interview was set for ten the following morning. "And what did you say your name was?" Mrs. McDermott asked.

For a moment, Val was caught, then she swallowed hard. "Valerie, Valerie—" a slight hesitation "—Madison." That was the first time she'd used her maiden name in years.

Val's hand holding the phone felt clammy with nervousness. She took a long, dragging sigh. She hated any kind of lying. She was just following Kev's orders.

Val quickly packed up their things. She didn't give herself a chance for second thoughts, knowing doubts could creep in and she might change her mind. The next step was the bus station where she purchased tickets to Seawood. An underlying excitement had taken the place of the uncertainty. The woman on the phone had sounded very nice. Perhaps Val could convince her to take a chance, despite her inexperience. She was scared, but at least she'd made a decision.

As the two of them settled into their cushioned seats in the bus, the huge vehicle rolled out of the terminal and lumbered toward the freeway. This was another new experience for Megan, who pressed her snub nose to the window and bounced up and down. They were on their way to a new life, whatever that was. Val had one bad moment when she spotted the sign, Mill Valley Next Exit. How often had she taken that turnoff. That was the past, that was over, she reminded herself as she watched the sign slide past as the bus roared along the freeway.

They'd been so happy when they first moved to that house. Kevin's enthusiasm had soon overcome Val's initial resistance to its location, size and all the new furniture. Even the hiring of Harriet to houseclean had seemed an unnecessary expense. But Kev had insisted. "We're moving up, babe." The promotion to new accounts at the bank had just come through and his future had looked very bright. In fact as he was fond of singing to her, whenever she protested, "Everything's coming up roses." And it did seem that way. Only Val didn't know it was on borrowed time and that time would soon run out.

And she had to admit they had been happy there for three, almost four years—until Kevin's arrest and the resulting shock waves that reverberated through their affluent neighborhood. Overnight they became anathema to their friends and neighbors. They'd quite pointedly turned the other way if she happened to see them in the small shopping center. After that the phone never rang, except for a few crank calls—until she had the number changed. No one ever came by or dropped in. It was as though suddenly she'd ceased to exist. Val knew they would all be relieved, the sooner she was gone the better. The morning of Kev's court date when she left the house for the last time, she'd stood at the end of the driveway, waiting for a cab. Val was sure she could almost feel hostile eyes boring into her.

It had all been so different before. The friendly get-togethers, the sharing of child care and carpooling, helping each other give kids' birthday parties, the backyard barbecues, the Sunday brunches on someone's flower-bordered patio. They'd been part of the upwardly mobile young marrieds. Now, they'd become invisible to everyone. The morning of the sentencing, Val had left Megan with Harriet, who was the only one who had stood by them all these weeks. In the old days, before anything had happened, it would have been natural for Val's next-door neighbor, Emily, to keep Megan. But she had not spoken to Val since the news broke.

Val felt a tug on her sleeve as Megan asked a question, and glad to pull her mind back to the present, she answered it. Megan kept chattering and pointing out things as they traveled. It was a welcome diversion for Val and kept her from dwelling on their hazy future. After a while, Megan got tired. Val pushed up the armrest and Megan put her head on her lap and curled up on the seat. As she smoothed the child's silky hair, Val wondered how tomorrow's interview would go.

Finally, the bus stopped in Seawood. Val got their luggage and went into the small station. At the snack bar, Val ordered a couple of hamburgers and then checked into the small motel across the street. The room was spare but clean and had a small black-and-white TV. After Megan fell asleep, Val took a shower, shampooed her hair. As she set it, she surveyed herself in the bathroom mirror. What she'd been going through in recent months plainly showed. She had lost weight and there were what seemed to be permanent circles under her eyes. Makeup would help. She just hoped she could manage to look "attractive, personable and young" enough to be hired as a waitress at the restaurant now renamed The Seawinds.

The next morning, Val found out from the motel manager that the restaurant was located about three miles away. Too far to walk from the center of town. So after they ate breakfast, Val hailed a taxi. When she gave the driver her destination, he remarked that it was one of the "classiest" places in the resort town. "The new owners redecorated, renovated it to a fare-thee-well. Course everything's kinda slow right now, but when the season opens I bet it'll be popular. People don't mind driving someplace they know they'll get good food and the atmosphere's right."

"I'm hoping to get a waitress job there," Val volunteered.

"That a fact? I've heard the McDermotts are nice folks to work for," he said as he pulled to a stop in front of a rambling, low-roofed rustic building built on a projectory with a sweeping view of the ocean. As he leaned back over the front seat to open the rear door he said, "Well, good luck."

I'll need more than luck, Val thought, whispering a prayer. If she wasn't hired, this trip would have been for nothing. She was sure this little town did not have that many other job opportunities.

Mrs. McDermott, an attractive woman in her late forties, with prematurely silver hair, greeted Val warmly. Her genuine, friendly manner put Val at ease right away. She gave Megan a cup of cocoa while she poured two cups of coffee for them. She opened the interview casually by telling Val that she and her husband had owned a number of restaurants, the last one in San Francisco. But it had been a hectic pace and they'd decided they wanted a less stressful life. So when they heard that this restaurant, closed for a few seasons, had come on the market, they'd bought it and moved to Seawood.

"We're pretty laid-back." She laughed. "That's why we're only open five days a week and then only for dinner. My husband loves to fish, so this gives him plenty of time. I stay busy managing the restaurant. Now, tell me about yourself," she invited Val with a smile.

As truthfully as she dared, Val told her she was raising her daughter on her own, that she hadn't had much recent experience as a waitress but was more than willing to work hard and learn.

"Well, I don't see why you wouldn't work out just fine. You're pretty and smart and the work isn't too difficult. You'll have plenty of chances to get the hang of it. We have an orientation week for new employees before we open, which isn't until after Memorial Day. Then we expect to swing into our busy season right up until Labor Day. By that time you'll be experienced." She laughed.

Just then, the front door opened and a tall, gray-haired man walked inside. Mrs. McDermott's face lit up. "Oh, here's my husband."

The man was casually dressed in a plaid flannel shirt and blue jeans, and his weathered face was deeply lined. He had a wide smile and twinkling blue eyes. He spotted Megan immediately. "Well, hello, little lady, who are you?"

"I'm Megan." She looked up at him with a dimpled smile.

"Tom," Mrs. McDermott called, "come over here. I'd like you to meet one of our new waitresses, Valerie Madison."

Val almost said Evans automatically to correct her, then caught herself in time.

"Hello, nice to meet you. Does that little charmer belong to you?"

"Yes, that's Valerie's daughter." Mrs. McDermott turned to Val. "Tom adores children. We have two grandsons, but they live back east so we don't get to see them often or have much chance to spoil them." She handed Valerie a printed application. "This is merely a formality. Just need your Social Security number, that sort of thing."

"Then I have the job?" Val asked.

"Yes, of course, and since you just got into town, you're looking for a place to live, right?"

Val nodded, amazed at how things were falling into place. "Yes, I'm staying at the motel in town, but—"

Mrs. McDermott smiled. "Let me pull a few strings." And she picked up the phone. After some banter with the person on the other end, Val heard her ask, "Are you still renting those cottages out on the far end of Beach Road? Good. I've got a renter for you." After she hung up, she wrote something down on a slip of paper and handed it to Val. "They're not fancy," she said. "Just basic. It's a part of the town that never developed. The developers ran into some problems with the coastal planners or something and Bob bought up all the cottages for back taxes. Got them for a song and rents them cheap. Anyway, being off-season, the rent will be even cheaper. Bob will probably give you a deal. He'll be happy to get one off his hands. Something he doesn't have to worry about. Much better to have a place occupied. And it's walking distance to here and to some small shops, the post office, grocery."

Val thanked her. "You've been very kind."

"We're glad to have you on board," Mrs. McDermott told her.

When Val went outside with Megan, she was surprised to find the taxi still there. The driver was reading the newspaper behind the wheel.

"Got the job, did you? Thought so."

With a start, Val realized Seawood was a small town. And like in any small town, nothing much went unnoticed. She would have to be extra careful about what she said and who she said it to if she was going to protect Megan and herself from being identified.

"Where to now, miss?" the driver asked, folding his newspaper, then holding open the rear door for them.

She told him about the rental and he took her right to the Dobbs Realty office. It had been a long time since anyone had been as friendly and helpful as this man and the McDermotts. Even so, Val warned herself she still had to be cautious.

The driver told her that he'd wait.

"You're sure?"

"Yep, haven't got another fare anyway."

After Val left the office, the same taxi drove them to the motel to collect their bags and then out to the cottage she had just rented. The driver kept up a running monologue all the way, telling her the same story as Mrs. McDermott had with more embellishments about the "hotshot" developers who had bought the property ten years ago, hoping to make a "quick buck" but who then had dropped the whole project.

Mentally, Val winced. This could well be the ill-fated investment Kevin had been enthusiastic about. But like so many of his other schemes, it had petered out. It seemed a strange coincidence. But then lately, her life was filled with a series of unexpected incidents.

"Them cottages are not up to code, did Bob tell you that?" the driver asked. "No heating, no electricity? Couldn't pass the state building laws. Bob probably told you they were built for summer rentals. The season is short here on this coast, but as I said, it just never took off. But you'll be okay. Most of the year we don't get too much cold weather, and they have stoves—wood-burning ones. Think you can manage?" He looked at Val in his rearview mirror, raising bushy eyebrows.

She nodded, praying she could. The Realtor had told her the same thing, so when she bought groceries, she had also purchased kerosene for the lamps that were in the cottage and a box of Presto-logs for the stove. What neither Bob nor the taxi driver nor the grocery clerk knew was that whatever the conditions were she had to manage. At that kind of rent, somehow she would. The two months rent she had to pay in advance left her just barely enough to get by until she started working. She'd been lucky today. She had a job and a place to live. That was more than she'd had yesterday.

The cab turned off the main road onto a rutted one that dipped down parallel to the ocean. Five small, gray frame houses with slanted roofs, widely spaced from each other, were the only buildings in sight. The taxi braked to a jolting stop in front of the first one, a weathered shingled cottage. There was a badly listing fence with a sagging gate that led into a sandy front yard scattered with ice plant and thistles. Val disguised her dismay. It was more dilapidated and forlorn than she had imagined. Nonetheless, they were here.

She was fighting exhaustion as she paid the driver, then thanked him for carrying two of her suitcases up to the porch while she staggered in her high heels with the other two bags and the groceries. With a sinking heart, she watched him drive back down the rutted road and disappear. Suddenly, she felt alone and abandoned.

Megan, however, was delighted with everything. She squatted down and sifted the sand through both chubby hands. "Look, Mommy, it's just like my sandbox at home only lots bigger."

Thank God for Megan, Val said, meaning it like a prayer. Without her, she would have given in to despair.

Inside, Val did a quick walk-through of the practically bare rooms. Whatever it was, it's home for now, Val told herself firmly. She would make the best of it. She was determined.

She had gone on enough camping trips with her parents to be fairly adept at getting the small two-burner gas stove lighted to heat a can of tomato soup. That done, she got a fire going in the potbellied stove. It gave out an amazing amount of heat once it caught. Again, it was Megan's cheerful presence that kept Val from giving way to the hovering fear that seemed to lurk in the shadowy corners of the empty rooms.

She made up the beds and gradually Megan wound down. Yawning sleepily, she climbed into the little cot in the bedroom. Val had tucked her in when all at once Megan's eyes popped wide open and she said, "Prayers, Mommy."

Val was stricken. She'd completely forgotten. A little child shall lead them, Val thought guiltily. Hastily, she came back and knelt beside Megan.

Clasping her small hands together and closing her eyes, Megan began, "Thank you God for our nice little house and the beach just over the dunes. Bless Mommy and Harriet and Flynn." Megan halted, a little pucker in her forehead. "You think Flynn misses us, Mommy?"

"I'm sure he does, darling, but Harriet promised she and Lew would take good care of him, so don't worry."

"Can we have him soon since we've got a new place? There's lots of room for him to run here, don't you think?"

"We'll see, darling." Val gave the answer she used to hate to hear from her own parents. But there was no help for it. She couldn't make a promise to Megan she couldn't keep.

Megan squeezed her eyes tight, and folding her hands again, she added, "And God bless Daddy, too." Those words were like a sharp knife in Val's heart. How much did Megan know? What had she gleaned from everything that had been going on around her all these weeks, hushed conversations, telephone calls, the changes, the appearance of strangers, the absence of friends?

God bless Daddy. The child's innocent prayer echoed in Val's mind. Oh, Kevin! Why did you let this happen?

Val leaned down and kissed Megan, holding her in a tight hug for a minute. It took an effort not to let the tears that pressed the back of her eyes fall. "Good night, precious," she whispered as she kissed her again before she left the room. A minute later, she looked in and Megan was sound asleep.

It was then the awful loneliness descended. Val shivered as if from a freezing wind. She huddled by the stove far into the night. Finally, it sputtered out, and not wanting to use more of the logs than necessary, she crept into bed. But she couldn't get warm. The cold seemed to penetrate into her bones. She buried her face into the pillow, smothering her sobs, not wanting to wake Megan. Her misery was deep and terrible. Even so, Val realized whatever she was going through could not compare with what Kevin must be enduring. *Oh, God, help him, please,* she moaned a quiet prayer. A man like Kevin could go mad, locked up in a cell like an animal in a cage. *Have mercy, Lord.*

Chapter Four

❧

Val got up carefully so as not to awaken Megan. It was early, but that wasn't unusual for her now. She hadn't slept well at all during these past few months. After tossing and turning half the night, her sleep distorted by dreams, she would wake up before dawn. She'd told herself that it was her worry about Kevin that kept her awake. Once the initial shock was over, she'd hoped her insomnia would get better.

But now there were new anxieties. She would be on the brink of sleep when suddenly the fact that she and Megan were completely alone in the world would bring her to instant wakefulness. She would lie there trembling, realizing they were without family or friends, miles from everyone and everything familiar. No backup. No support, emotional or financial, available if anything happened. An emergency of some sort. Frightening possibilities flashed through her imagination. What if she got sick or had some kind of breakdown, what would happen to Megan? Val would look over at the little girl sleeping so peacefully and a fierce determination would follow. She refused to give in to that fear. She reminded herself that at least now they had a place to live and she had a promise of a job. She had to be strong for Megan's sake. They would make it, please God.

Shivering in the damp chill of the unheated cottage, Val put on her robe and hurried out to the front room to get the stove going. After nearly a week's practice, she had become better at getting a fire started. The small stove provided a good amount of heat for the place and she could also cook on it if she didn't want to use the gas stove. It was amazing what you could get used to, Val thought as she filled the kettle with water to boil so she could make coffee. How much she had taken for granted before in her home in Meadowbrook. A flick of a switch and within minutes the house would be comfortably warm. An automatic coffeemaker set the night before would have fresh coffee waiting when she came into the kitchen.

Val didn't allow much mental wandering back to the old life, but sometimes comparisons were inevitable. But every day she gained a little confidence that things were going to work out. Each step she took on her own gave her the courage to take the next one. She was doing her best to accomplish what Kevin had asked—to build a new life for herself and Megan. She measured instant coffee into a mug, poured in the boiling water, stirred it until the crystals dissolved, then took it over to the window and looked out.

It was beginning to get light. The wind off the ocean was chopping the gray-blue sea into haphazard waves. Seagulls in search of breakfast were gliding and dipping in a kind of frenzied ballet. Glancing to her left, down the stretch of winter beach, she saw smoke coming from one of the other cottages. It was the last one in the staggered line of weathered shingled houses.

Vaguely, she wondered who else had come to this isolated place at this time of year. It didn't really matter. Val knew that she couldn't risk friendships. One thing led to another on the slightest acquaintance. People expected a certain amount of information about your background, where you'd come from, what you were doing. Although Val had always liked getting to know people, that was something her present circumstances didn't allow anymore.

Again came the clang of her own prison door. It might be invisible, but it was nonetheless real. Her promise to Kev had shut out the possibility of her having any normal contact with other people, no matter how casual. She would have to guard against the temptation, simply out of loneliness, of getting friendly with anyone. It would be so easy to let something slip. And she had to protect Megan at all costs. That's what Kevin had wanted. Correction, *insisted* on her doing.

Val remembered how she used to worry that Kev didn't spend

enough time with Megan, play with her enough, pay enough attention to her. Afraid, that, maybe he didn't even love her enough. Especially after the problem with her hearing was discovered. Yet it was his concern for Megan that had prompted his adamant insistence on Val taking her someplace where no one would know about him. Surely, that must prove how much he did love her.

Val turned back from the window and looked around the room. The shabbiness of the place was even more depressing in daytime. There were the usual beach-rental castoffs: a wicker set consisting of a love seat and two armchairs, a table, a couple of straight chairs, a lopsided bookcase. It needed brightening badly. It wouldn't take a whole lot or cost much to do. Val had always been sensitive to her surroundings. She decided that living in this drab, barren cottage would drive her crazy if she didn't do something about it.

Just then, Megan woke up and called from the bedroom, "Mommy, what can we do today? Can we go to the beach?" Val smiled. Megan wanted to go to the beach every day since they had come to the cottage. She came running out in her nightie. "Please, Mommy, can we?" she begged, hopping from one foot to the other.

Val grabbed her up in a hug, swung her around. "It's still pretty cold, honey. But we're going to have a fun day. Today we're going to go shopping and get some pretty curtains and maybe new bedspreads and some pillows. You can pick out the kind you like, okay?"

Megan had never before been consulted on decorating and the idea was a new and exciting prospect.

Very much aware of her dwindling funds, Val felt this was not an extravagance but a necessary expense. An investment in her well-being. She had noticed a variety store between the Realtor's and the post office so that's where they headed. It was only a short walk to the center of Seawood and Megan was a merry little companion.

They found some café curtains patterned with sunflowers and several toss pillows in bright patterns. Megan chose pink chenille bedspreads. To her relief, Val found their combined purchases totaled little more than fifty dollars. She was satisfied that whatever the cost it was well worth it. How little it took to make a child happy, she thought, watching Megan skip happily ahead of her down the street.

On the way home, they stopped for fish and chips at a small fish market and ate at a picnic table outside in view of the ocean. A pale sun had come out and the sea was a deep royal blue with bobbing whitecaps.

"I love it here, Mommy," Megan said suddenly. "Can we stay here forever?"

Val's heart contracted. Forever? Forever is a long time. How do you measure forever? For her, even five years, the soonest Kevin could come up for parole, seemed forever. Even the weeks since his arrest seemed forever. But she managed to answer Megan's question. "Well, darling, we'll certainly be living here for a while."

Brightening up the little cottage helped a lot. So did a change in the weather. The morning fog seemed to burn off earlier and they began to have longer sunny afternoons, which more and more they spent at the beach. Megan never tired of digging in the sand, hunting for shells or poking at sand crabs. They took long walks along the edge of the water, playing tag with the tide, picking up driftwood. Where the beach rounded a rocky bend, they discovered a sheltered cove that they claimed as their own special place.

Sometimes, when watching Megan running back and forth from the ocean back to the sand, her golden hair flying behind her in the wind, or hunched over a tide pool, earnestly studying the tiny sea creatures, Val would feel a wrench. How sad that Kevin was missing so much of Megan's evolving little person. She knew that was futile thinking, even harmful. She had to go on. Live in the present, not dwell in the past, nor in pointless regrets. Take one day at a time.

One thing she could not push aside, or think about without concern, was Kevin's total lack of communication. She had done everything he asked except for the divorce. She felt he had made that decision under extreme duress. Val was convinced it was a wrong decision. It was the act of a man desperate and despairing. Hadn't they promised each other "for better or for worse"? Well, this was the worst either of them could ever have imagined. She prayed he would change his mind when he had time to consider it. He would want her to wait for him.

Val had read that men in prison need one thing more than anything else. Hope. Hope that someone would be waiting when they'd done their time. That they would have something, someone, to come back to, to help them make a fresh start, turn over a new leaf. Val wanted to give Kevin that.

So she had written him several letters. So far he hadn't answered. But she wasn't willing to give up. He had to have a period of adjustment to prison life. Then maybe he'd allow himself to think of her and Megan, to miss them, to long for some connection. That's what she was praying for, was trusting would happen. If the loneliness she was experiencing was sometimes more than she could bear, what must it be for Kevin? Kevin, the energetic, outgoing person she knew, one who loved having company in, going out. The confinement of prison, the enforced company of hardened criminals—it must be terrible for him.

But he didn't write. Day after day, Val watched the blue-and-white snub-nosed mail truck go by, never stopping at their mailbox. They never got any mail. Except some circulars marked Occupant. That shouldn't seem strange. No one knew where they were even if there had been somebody to write. Val decided not to request a box at the post office. She would have had to fill out an application supplying all sorts of information. She'd also heard that small-town post offices were the center for local gossip. Val didn't dare have people in Seawood speculating about her.

She wondered if Kevin had any idea what lengths she was having to go to keep her word to him? More and more Val realized she had been sentenced along with Kevin to her own kind of prison.

Chapter Five

Val assured herself that things would get better once she started work. Once they had some regular routine to their life and a weekly paycheck. And they did.

For one thing, she was too tired at night to lie awake and worry. The job at the restaurant gave a structure to her days. The McDermotts were great employers. There had been a preseason orientation week for the new staff. The other waitresses were friendly and pleasant. Most of them had had more waitressing experience than Val, but she found them ready to help her learn the ropes.

Best of all, Val found a good sitter for Megan through Colleen, one of the other waitresses. Her sister was a young mom with two small youngsters. She was eager to earn the extra money and Megan needed the companionship of other children. Val dropped Megan off at Sue's house on her way to work and picked her up on the way home. Things were working out much better than Val could have hoped. Except for one important thing.

There still was no word from Kevin. He had not answered any of Val's letters. Every week she wrote another one, begging him to let her come see him. But day after day she checked the mail and there was nothing. It had been two months now since that awful day in the courtroom. Surely the loneliness must be getting to Kevin. Maybe her letters had been too reassuring, maybe he thought they were doing okay, that he had done the right thing and was determined not to make contact. Val turned all the possibilities over and over in her mind. Nothing made sense. How could Kevin just eliminate them like pressing Delete on a computer?

Finally, Val wrote to the prison asking for information on visiting schedules. She then wrote a second letter and addressed it to the warden's office, explaining that she had heard nothing from her husband and asking for a progress report.

After she mailed it, Val felt frightened and guilty. Kevin had been almost violent that day when he insisted she was to forget him.

Since high school, Kevin had been the most important person in Val's life. She had loved Kevin almost from the first. He was a street-smart kid from the wrong side of the tracks in their small conservative California hometown. His boldness attracted her, while at the same time, she also saw a vulnerable, insecure side of him that drew her sympathy and love.

Her schoolteacher parents had strongly objected to and tried to discourage their relationship. But their opposition only fueled the fire of their romance. They had continued to see each other secretly and the summer after Val graduated high school they eloped. Val's parents' attempt to have the marriage annulled was abandoned, but the estrangement from their daughter and her husband lasted until their deaths a few years ago.

Two years ahead of Val in high school, Kevin had excelled in sports. He'd been a track star and won an athletic scholarship to college. Upon graduation, he'd been recruited into the executive-training program of one of the large Bay area chain of banks. He had made rapid progress, moving up with successive promotions to the position of a loan officer at one of the branches. In that position, Kevin was able to indulge his expensive tastes. His personality, always brash, by thirty-two had become supremely self-confident. Although some people thought him arrogant, Val made excuses for him because she understood that his behavior masked leftover insecurities from childhood. However, it was the reckless side of him, the side that liked taking chances, gambling, that in the end brought him down. Success had come too soon, too easily.

After sending off the letter to the warden, Val lived on hope. Three weeks dragged by and there was no reply. Then one day she found a letter in her mailbox. It had a return address she did not

recognize. It wasn't from the prison. Curious, she tore open the
envelope, drew out the typed, single-spaced letter. The signature
identified the writer as Chaplain Scott, the prison chaplain. Her
letter had been referred to him by the warden.

Your husband is having an unusually difficult time adjusting to
prison life. For some men the adjustment is more severe than
for others. This may be the case with your husband. It sometimes takes six months or more for a man to finally accept the
fact of being in prison and decide he has to make the best of
his term of imprisonment. The only advice I can give you is to
be patient. I have tried to talk to him, but he refuses to discuss
with me his reasons for not writing to you. When your husband
has completed the required probationary period before he can
receive visitors, you will be notified.

In the meantime, perhaps if you continue to write the kind
of loving, supportive letters you indicated you have been writing to him, in due time he may reply.

If I can be of any further assistance to you, please feel free
to write to me.

Val replaced the letter in the envelope. She felt let down, discouraged. In spite of the chaplain's suggestion, it seemed pointless
to continue trying. Was Kevin even reading her letters? Would he
continue to hold out? For all her disappointment, deep down inside Val a spark burned, a small, persistent flame of hope.

Once, Kevin had loved her. Their physical passion had been real.
He had always had the "you and me against the world" attitude.
That couldn't have changed. He couldn't have forgotten all that
they'd been through together. They had weathered other storms,
hurdled obstacles even to be with each other, to marry. This was
the biggest challenge—the biggest tragedy—they'd ever faced. The
words "seven to fifteen years" rang in Val's memory. Could their
marriage somehow survive this? She shuddered.

Val put the letter in her dresser drawer. Every once in a while
during the weeks that followed, she'd take it out and read it. The
possibility of change, the hope the chaplain had held out, was like a
life raft. She clung to it the way a drowning person clutches at a
straw. After all, it was all she had.

Chapter Six

After Memorial Day weekend, the restaurant was busy, but the work was not all that hard. Seawood was actually off the beaten track. Most people coming south from San Francisco were on their way to Carmel, the ones going north heading up into redwood country. Only the most leisurely of travelers, not in a hurry to get anywhere particular, took the off-ramp from the freeway and discovered The Seawind.

Val's hours gave her lots of quality time with Megan. As they went into summer, the long, lovely days were perfect beach weather. She'd pack a basket of snacks, a thermos of lemonade, then the two of them would walk down to the little inlet they'd begun to call their "secret cove." There they would spread out a blanket and Megan would play happily in the sand, building roads, tunnels and castles, running into the shallow water, then carrying back her small bucket of water. Sometimes, Val brought a magazine or a paperback to read, but mostly she would watch Megan.

Children are marvelous, she thought. How quickly they adjust to new circumstances. Megan seemed content and secure. All Val had told her was that Kevin had to be away for a while. That seemed to satisfy her. She didn't seem to miss him and rarely mentioned her father except in her nighttime prayers. To Val, that seemed a shame, but that's the way Kevin had wanted it. Megan's precious days of early childhood were something that could never be replaced. Even as Val watched her, she was changing from day to day.

This time was slipping away just as Megan's sand castles were washed away in the surf. And Kevin was missing them.

By summer, the other three cottages were sometimes rented for weekends. One family came for a week. Most of the time they were empty. Better accommodations for vacationers could be found in other places nearby. But as far as Val could tell, the cottage at the far end, the one she'd seen smoke coming from, remained unoccupied. She never explored that part of the beach. It would have meant passing by the other cottages, perhaps running into one of the renters. She still avoided even the briefest conversation with anyone other than the people at work.

As the weeks went by, Val began to lose hope that Kevin would write. She continued her weekly letter to him although she was finding it harder to fill more than a page. There was less and less to say. There was no more heartbroken pleading, no declarations that she disagreed with his decision. Little by little her spark of faith began to flicker and go out.

On the surface, their life seemed as smooth as the sea on a windless day. No one would ever have guessed the emotional turmoil that was always just under the surface. Megan was happy and as friendly as a little puppy. She soon became the restaurant's pet. The other waitresses called her their mascot while the chef was always sending treats home for her, little lemon tarts or iced petits fours. The McDermotts doted on her almost as if she were one of their grandchildren. Tom always wanted Val to bring her by before she took her to the sitter's. Both McDermotts were so kind Val began to feel guilty she hadn't told them the truth about Kevin. What would they say if they knew she was living a lie?

The atmosphere at The Seawinds was so friendly, the food so delicious and the staff trained to treat customers like visiting royalty that the tips were more than generous. Val was able to stash away a nice nest egg that she hoped would tide her over the months when the restaurant was closed for the season. She hoped she could find some other temporary job; even a part-time position would help. She wasn't looking that far ahead yet, but she knew Seawinds would close in November. The McDermotts went to Mexico for several months until the restaurant reopened in the spring.

Because she was busy with work and had gradually given up any hope of hearing from Kevin, Val was totally unprepared for what happened toward the end of August. Another letter came from the prison chaplain. Almost afraid to open it, Val finally read it with mixed feelings. The chaplain said Kevin seemed to be making some progress toward adjustment but that he continued to find him uncommunicative and still refusing to discuss anything personal. Kevin had passed the six-month probationary period and was now allowed to have visitors. However, he advised Val not to come unless Kevin himself wrote and requested it.

Val read the letter through twice, then once again more slowly, letting the impact of each word sift through the jumbled thoughts crowding into her head. If she waited until Kevin wrote and asked—that might be never! She knew how stubborn Kevin could be. Even if he wanted her, Val felt sure he would not write and ask.

The letter had come just before Val left for work. She put it in her apron pocket where it lay like a burning coal all during her shift. Later, when she got home, she read the letter again. Finally, she decided she had to go see him. Maybe when he saw her she would realize what a mistake it was to cut himself off like this and insist that they divorce.

But how was she to get some time off to travel the considerable distance to the state prison? And how would she explain it to the McDermotts? Val knew she could trade hours with one or two of the other waitresses, but it was the peak of the season. The Seawinds was always filled with hungry customers. It would be like that until after Labor Day, some of the staff warned. If she was going, she would need at least two full days off. How could she ask without telling Mrs. McDermott the reason?

It was Kevin's day in court all over again. Val tried to control her nervousness as she lingered at the end of the shift, waiting for an opportunity to speak to Eileen McDermott. The dinner crowd had gone, the busboys were bundling up tablecloths, stacking up plates, and there was a clatter of trays and murmur of voices as they talked and joked with each other. Mrs. McDermott was behind the cash register. Val watched for the right moment to approach her.

"May I talk to you privately for a few minutes?" she asked in a low voice.

"Sure, Val, what can I do for you?" Mrs. McDermott smiled.

Val couldn't help wondering how long the smile would last when she knew that Val's reason for wanting time off was to visit her husband in prison. She glanced uneasily around, then whispered, "Do you think we could go into your office. I don't want to be overheard."

Mrs. McDermott looked puzzled, but she agreed at once. "Of course." She led the way into her small, cozy office behind the dining room. She sat down on one of the two chintz-covered armchairs and gestured to Val to take the other one. "Now, Val, what's on your mind? You look mighty serious. I hope you're not going to tell me you're quitting?" She gave Val a wary look.

"No, not at all, Mrs. McDermott. I love it here, I like my job. It's just—I need some time off, but first, there's something I should have told you in the beginning."

Telling the facts turned out to be a great deal easier than Val had anticipated. Eileen McDermott listened with a thoughtful expression. Val's voice rose and fell and became breathless as she poured out the whole awful story. Tears came perilously close and she struggled to hold them back. When she finished, she saw only sympathy and concern in the older woman's eyes. Instead of being shocked or judgmental, she just gently scolded Val for thinking she wouldn't understand.

"Of course you can take the time off, Val, and I think you should go."

Val couldn't bring herself to tell her that Kevin didn't want to see her, that he might even refuse to see her once she got there. She was too relieved that her employer had been so understanding and there would be no problem about taking time off. Not only that, but Mrs. McDermott insisted Val leave Megan with them and save baby-sitting fees.

"You know Tom will be tickled to death to have her. Now, it's settled. You go ahead and make your plans."

The night before Val was to leave, she nearly lost her nerve. It had been six months since that dreadful day in the bare little room in the courthouse when Kevin had brutally shaken off her embrace, violently demanded she get a divorce. She had no idea how he would react when she showed up at the prison. Well, ready or not, it was a chance she'd have to take. In her heart, she felt it was the right thing to do. Give them both another chance.

Val studied herself in the mirror. Kevin would find her changed.

She had lost at least five pounds, which, on her small frame, made her look almost thin. She had stopped highlighting her hair, letting it return to its natural brown color. Not able to afford the expensive styling she used to get, she had cut it herself. Very short. With almost daily dips in the ocean before she went to work, this length was much easier. But would Kev like it?

What should she wear for this visit? She hadn't worn anything but her uniform, and jeans or shorts or a bathing suit for months. Kev had always been highly critical of her appearance, telling her what he liked and what he didn't like in no uncertain terms. She wanted to look her best no matter what. It would be especially important when he saw her for the first time in all these months. After trying on first one thing and then the next, she finally decided on a blue, washed-silk shirtwaist dress. It was Kev's favorite color and wouldn't wrinkle badly in her small suitcase.

Val stopped fussing over her own appearance long enough to get Megan packed up and the next morning, she took her to the McDermotts. Megan was thrilled with the novelty of staying over with the McDermotts. After Val kissed her goodbye, she went happily hand in hand with Tom down to his boat.

"Don't worry, she'll be fine," Eileen assured her and wished her a good trip. Val thanked her again, then hurried off to where the northbound bus stopped.

Chapter Seven

On the long bus trip, Val had a lot of time to think about what she would say to Kevin. She didn't even know if he had read her letters or just torn them up. Maybe it didn't matter. Maybe she should have written to the chaplain, telling him she had decided to come, then he could have prepared Kev for her visit. Maybe she should phone his office at one of the rest stops? Maybe, maybe, so many things. But maybe none of it mattered? She was on her way now. There was no turning back.

Her stomach was in knots most of the way. The hours of travel seemed endless, the bus crowded and the trip a jolting one, up twisting mountain roads, long stretches of highway bordered with brooding wooded hills as they got closer to the isolated site of the state prison.

At last, early in the evening, they reached the town above which the penitentiary was located. It was dreary beyond description. Fog swirled eerily as Val made her way down the dingy main street to a small hotel the bus driver told her was about the only decent place in town to stay. She thought he had looked at her with something like sympathy mixed with curiosity. When she asked him directions, she felt her face grow warm. Did he know why she was here in this town at this time of night? And what difference did that make? It was just her own sense of shame. He probably brought busloads of relatives of prison inmates here all the time. It was nothing new to him. Her private agony meant nothing to him.

Worn out from the long bus ride and nerves, Val fell into an exhausted sleep. She woke up long before it was time to catch the local bus up to the prison. Val knew about that from the brochure on visiting procedures she'd received when she wrote for information. As she dressed, her heart was beating so fast she could hardly breathe. She brushed her hair, put on lipstick with a shaky hand. In the bathroom mirror, under the glaring light over the sink, she looked deathly pale. She dusted on blusher. Okay? She kept trying to see herself through Kevin's eyes. Then she shivered. That was the best she could do.

Outside, she walked across the street to the bus station and bought coffee at the snack counter. It was weak and tasted terrible in the paper cup, so she only took a few sips. Was it time yet? She glanced down at the dainty diamond-chip wristwatch Kevin had given her when he got his first promotion at the bank. It was too ornate to wear at work, but Val had worn it today thinking Kevin might like to see it on her.

She looked around at the other people in the station. There were several women of various ages. A few sat together, talking in low voices. A few sat apart, faces set in misery. Were they all going up to the prison, too? Most were poorly dressed, worn-looking. Val turned away. She shouldn't be staring. She was embarrassed for them. A core of bitterness she rarely admitted stirred inside her. Resentment that Kevin had put her in this position. Humiliation seared her. Why should she feel superior to these women? She was in exactly the same situation they were.

The door to the loading platform opened and a driver announced, "Bus now boarding." There was a general movement as the passengers in the waiting room, mostly women, gathered up bundles and packages, then started toward the door. For a minute, Val hesitated. She didn't want to file out there with the others, admit she was going to the prison to visit an inmate. Then quickly she felt ashamed. Whatever she was feeling, what Kevin must be feeling all these months was worse. She straightened her shoulders and walked out to the bus.

From the bus window, the outline of the huge gray prison loomed ahead like a medieval fortress as the bus wound its way up the narrow road. The facility had been built on a cliff overlooking the ocean to provide maximum security for prisoners who might think of escaping. When it had been built, the word was put out, and since then the legend had grown that no one ever escaped from this penal institution. That bleak view was what Kevin had to look out at every day. That is, if there was a window in his cell.

The bus stopped at the prison gates, and everyone filed down the aisles and out. Val realized she had been right; all the passengers were on the same mission. Visitors. She wondered if the wives of prisoners had some kind of distinguishing mark? Something that identified them as indelibly as the numbers stamped on inmates' clothes. Or maybe they were only recognizable to a fellow sufferer.

Even though the day was warming, Val kept shivering, had to press her lips together to keep her teeth from chattering.

At a wire-windowed enclosure at the gate, they had to present identification to a uniformed guard. From there go through a metal detector before passing through the gates into an inner courtyard. Here they went single file through a door marked Visitors into a large empty room with wooden benches along one side. A half-glass partition divided the room. On the visitors' side were shelves, a telephone and a straight chair. The guard indicated they were to sit down until the name lists were checked, inmates who were to receive visitors notified.

They waited for what seemed at least half an hour. No one spoke. Even the women who had been murmuring together at the bus station were now wrapped in a tense silence. No one more than Val. She glanced around. Probably most of these other women were expected. Their husbands, boyfriends, brothers were looking forward to seeing them. Her case was different. Her hands clenched compulsively. Suddenly, an electric bell shrilled, causing her to jump. Through the glass, she saw a door on the other side open and a line of men in drab prison garb filed into the room.

Val held her breath, searching for a glimpse of Kevin among them. Then saw him and suppressed a cry. She half rose, waving her hand. The guard barked out the names and motioned the women forward as prisoners moved into places on the other side.

Kev was scowling. Val was sure he had not been able to figure out who his visitor was. Maybe he thought it might be Brad Hensley, his lawyer. When he saw her, his eyes widened, he flushed a deep red, then his mouth settled into a straight line. But he walked to the seat as she hurried to the window opposite.

Nothing could have prepared Val for what prison life had done to her husband. It was the physical changes in his appearance that were the most shocking. He looked much older. His eyes were dull, the eyelids puffy. The tan he cultivated so diligently had faded, replaced by a grayness that almost matched the rough denim shirt. Kev had always been a "fitness freak," maintaining his body with rigid discipline. Now there was a slackness about him; he looked soft, pudgy. He slumped into the chair. Somewhere, Val had read modern prisons had exercise rooms where prisoners could work out, pump iron, keep in shape. Was this another of the options offered to inmates that Kevin had refused to take advantage of?

Val tried to conceal her dismay at the way he'd deteriorated. She took her place opposite him, picked up the phone and said huskily, "Hi, darling." Kevin did not pick up the receiver on his side. Instead, he folded his arms across his chest, his expression like stone. He avoided making eye contact. Val tried again. "Please, Kev. We must talk."

Reluctantly, he lifted the phone. Between clenched teeth, he said, "I told you not to come."

"I know, Kev. But I had to come. Darling, don't you see what you're doing is wrong? Wrong for Megan, wrong for me, wrong for you. Please, try to understand, I can't let you blot us out of your life like this."

"I thought I made it clear I didn't want you to come. You should have done what I told you," he said harshly. "It was stupid of you to think I'd change my mind." His expression hardened. "Brad— my lawyer—" he almost spit out the word, so Val guessed he must have met with some recent coldness from his onetime friend "—tells me you haven't returned the divorce papers. I want you to sign them."

"I can't sign them. I don't want to end our marriage. Listen, Kevin, it's going to be all right, I promise you. I did what you asked. I moved out of town to Seawood. Remember Seawood? Anyway, I'm using my maiden name so Megan is protected and I've got a job and a place to live. We're doing okay. Of course, we miss you terribly, and when you're free—"

"I'll never be free of the stink of prison. It will cling to me for the rest of my life. Don't you realize it's over for us? For you and me? Things will never be the same. Don't you get it? Or are you too stupid?" he shouted. Val saw the man on the other side of Kevin glance at him. The guard walking back and forth along the line of prisoners halted, watching him.

Val winced. She knew that when Kevin was angry or upset he said things, terrible things sometimes, things he didn't mean, things he was sorry for afterward. Half the presents he gave her were offered in apology for some tirade or other. She'd learned to expect both. The explosion, then the remorse.

If she just remained composed, kept Kevin talking, maybe she could calm him down, make him see how important her coming was for all of them, their future. But she didn't have a chance. Kevin leaned forward, his face very close to the glass partition, the phone next to his mouth.

"Now listen, Val, I want you to do exactly what I say. Don't delay any longer on the divorce. I don't want you to come here again. Ever, understand? You're young and smart and you'll make it. I want you to be free. You'll meet someone and get married again—"

"No, no, you're wrong, Kev. I won't. I don't want to. I—"

"Shut up!" Kev yelled. Stunned, Val drew back, almost dropping the phone. Kev's voice was so loud everyone could hear it in spite of the partition. "Didn't I tell you not to come here? Don't you ever come back or try to see me again. You hear me? And you sign those papers, you hear?"

With that, Kevin slammed down the phone, then stood, pushing back and knocking over the chair. It crashed onto the concrete floor. Without a backward glance, Kevin flung himself away and stalked to the door leading back to the main part of the prison.

Chapter Eight

❧

The buzz of other voices, magnified in the high-ceilinged room, halted abruptly, everyone shocked into silence by Kevin's outburst. Val sat there, paralyzed. She felt the blood rush into her face. Kev's fury had lashed like a stinging whip. Dazed, she somehow managed to get to her feet, then stood for a minute, dizzy with humiliation. Mercifully, the other visitors looked away, resuming their own conversations while she headed blindly toward the exit.

The outer door was opened by the guard and Val brushed by not knowing whether he looked at her with contempt or compassion. She hurried down the long corridor and was given clearance to leave from the security guard at the next door. She walked stiffly to the gate where another guard drew back the bolt and at last she stumbled outside into the glare of hazy sunlight. She let out a long breath not realizing she had been holding it. She stood uncertainly, not knowing where to go, what to do. She wasn't sure when there would be another bus back to the small town. She'd just have to walk down to the bus shelter and wait. One was bound to come along in a while.

She was too numb to cry. She felt bruised by the brutality of Kevin's reaction. His rejection had been total. Wobbling a little on her high heels, Val went down the steep hill. It was almost funny. She had only worn these pumps because Kev had always liked to see her in high heels. A pale sun struggled through the overcast. It was turning into a pretty day.

As Val made her way to the bus shelter, her mind was trying to make sense of it all. It seemed incredible that out here the sun was shining, flowers blooming along the roadside, birds singing, people driving by in cars and RVs, going on vacation. How could life continue so normally when hers had fallen apart? Her heart twisted in pity for Kev and all the men who, for whatever reason, were locked inside the prison where the sun never entered, where life was grim, gray, hopeless.

When she reached the bus stop, she saw that another woman was already seated there. She looked like she might have been shedding a few tears but glanced the other way as Val took a seat at the other end of the wooden bench.

Everything about the visit had gone wrong, Val thought. She'd meant it to be so different, even rehearsed being cheerful and positive. And it had all ended so badly. The tears she hadn't shed now began to rush into her eyes. She'd even forgotten to show Kev Megan's crayon drawings. She hadn't had a chance.

She opened her handbag and fumbled for a tissue. She pulled out her compact, powdered her nose and freshened her lipstick. In the mirror, she saw the other woman looking at her. Val put her things back in her purse, then looked back at her. Their glances met and they measured each other slowly. Then, as if instinctively acknowledging they were in the same boat, the woman nodded and smiled faintly. A few minutes later, she got up and moved over to sit beside Val. She jerked her head in the direction of the prison.

"You been up there to see your man, too?"

"Yes," Val answered.

"Awful, isn't it? For weeks you look forward to coming and when you're face-to-face you wish you hadn't come. Sometimes Jack's okay, but other times . . ." Her voice trailed away and she shook her head. "It's all so unnatural. If we could just hold hands, if he could touch me." She sighed heavily. "I love my husband. A lot. But I don't know if a marriage can last with this kind of physical separation."

Val tensed. What this woman was saying came from her heart, from a depth of experience that she herself was just entering.

"I'm sure he wonders the same thing. And I know his biggest fear is getting out and not having anyone to come home to. I know from the way he acts sometimes when I visit that it's been getting to him. Every so often he breaks down when I'm there, tells me that night after night he lies in his bunk wondering where I am, what I'm doing, and if I'm being faithful. It's torture."

She took out a pack of cigarettes, offered it to Val, who shook her head. Then she reached inside her handbag for a small lighter, flicked it and lit her cigarette.

"Jack's in on his second offense, this time car theft. Would you believe he smashed up the car before they arrested him? Now he's seeing the prison psychiatrist to see what makes him do it." She inhaled deeply and blew the smoke out with a bitter laugh. "Maybe I'm the one who should see a shrink. I must be nuts to love a guy like him."

She smoked silently for a few minutes and Val studied her. She was probably Val's age or even younger, pretty in a kind of flashy way. Her hair was blond, with help, and she wore a great deal of makeup. Maybe that was the way Jack liked her to look and dress. Maybe she was just like me, Val thought sadly, trying to please her man. Maybe that's why we ended up with the kind of men we had.

"Jack's forty now, he'll be nearly fifty by the time he gets out. He's not learning any skills in prison. I don't have a clue as to what he'll do when he does get out. An ex-con has a hard enough time getting any kind of job. But an ex-con who's almost fifty with no skills, well, the outlook for a guy like that is probably zilch."

Her words struck Val with their harsh truth. Kevin would also be an ex-con when he got out. He must know that, too. That might be adding to his bitterness, his depression. Kev had always gotten by on his looks, his charm, his self-assured can-do attitude. Prison had been the ultimate defeat.

The woman was speaking again, almost as if to herself.

"I don't know if I can stick it out. When I think of eight more years. Making this trip once a month to see him for an hour or less. Especially after a bad one like we had today. I don't know whether it's worth it." She shook her head vigorously, causing her red plastic hoop earrings to swing. "Yeah, sometimes I really wonder. The loneliness, the hopelessness . . . I don't think those guys, the judges who do the sentencing, realize they're sentencing the wives and families of those men to the same amount of time. And I begin to think, wouldn't it be better to cut your losses and try to make a new start while you're still young enough . . . ?"

Her voice trailed off because just then the bus came into view and they boarded. There weren't two seats together so they each found a separate seat. In a way, Val was glad. The other woman's words had echoed hollowly in her heart. They mirrored her own half-formed conclusions about her own situation.

However, when they got to the bus station in town, the other woman was standing on the platform waiting for her. "You wouldn't want to go somewhere and talk some more, I guess?" she asked doubtfully.

Val didn't want to seem unfriendly, but she knew it wouldn't be a good idea. She was already depressed enough. What purpose would it serve for either of them? They had the same problem and they each would have to handle it the best way they could.

"I'm sorry, but I can't," Val said gently. "Someone is taking care of my little girl for me and I think I better take the next bus home. Thanks anyway."

The woman nodded as if she understood, then shrugged. "Well, so long and good luck," she said, and walked away down the street where a neon sign blinked Cocktails.

Back in the bus station, Val realized her head was pounding. She remembered she hadn't eaten all day. She couldn't have eaten anything. Even now her stomach was in knots from her emotional stress. She bought a small box of aspirin and got a soda from the soft-drink dispenser to wash two of them down. Hopefully, she could sleep on the bus back to Seawood. She didn't want to think or even feel. Oblivion sounded like a wonderful escape after all she'd been through.

Chapter Nine

By the time the bus pulled into Seawood, Val was bone tired. She had not been able to sleep on the bus as she had hoped. She felt wired. Over and over she replayed the scene with Kevin, his words repeating themselves again and again in her brain. If this was what he really wanted, then what? She wondered how he could still love her or Megan at all and be able to insist that they break all ties so coldly, so irrevocably. What did she do with the rest of her life? Hers and Megan's? Of course, there was no immediate answer.

Shaky, sick, almost feverish, Val was shivering when she got off the bus. She called Eileen McDermott from a pay phone and asked if it would be all right for Megan to stay over until the next day. Mrs. McDermott assured Val that it would be fine.

"As a matter of fact, she's already in her pajamas and watching TV with Tom. I was just about to serve them both ice cream when you called." There was a slight pause, then she asked, "How did it go?"

"Not great," Val answered. From Val's tone of voice, Eileen must have guessed how weary she was and didn't ask any more questions.

"You get a good night's sleep," she just said, "and we'll see you tomorrow. Don't worry, Megan is as happy as a little clam."

"Thanks, I can't tell you how much I appreciate—"

"Don't try." Eileen cut her off. "It's been our pleasure. Megan is a doll."

Val let herself into the dark, empty cottage and closed the door behind her. Alone, she didn't have to put on a good front or be brave for anyone. It was then the whole horrible experience kicked in and she began to shake uncontrollably. In spite of the warm evening, she felt cold. Moving like a robot, she went over to the stove, crumpled up some newspaper, threw on a few wood chips and stood there, her arms wrapped around her upper body, until the fire caught hold. She pulled up one of the chairs in front of the stove, hunching there trying to get warm and to figure out what she was going to do, how to put the pieces of her shattered hopes into some endurable whole.

Over and over in her mind, Val went through all that she had wanted to say to Kevin. To tell him that she'd done most of what he had wanted her to do except for the divorce. She'd moved to this remote little spot, changed her name, given no one, not even Harriet, a forwarding address. There was no way anyone connected with the bank or our old neighborhood could trace them here. She was an ordinary single mom, working as a waitress, raising a little girl by herself, doing the best she could. Nobody except Mrs. McDermott knew she was the wife of a convicted embezzler. No reason why after Kevin served his time, they couldn't move somewhere else, start their life together again as a family. It didn't make sense to break up their marriage.

Of course, Val had already had this imaginary argument with Kev, dozens of times. That was what she had hoped she'd be able to convince him of in this visit. She had thought these months apart would have been so miserable that he would agree. Now, she had to face the fact that in spite of all she'd said to him or written, in her letters, which he may or may not have read, he stayed stubbornly convinced that he was right in what he had demanded.

It was a complete rejection of everything Val had believed in. Kevin was trying to wipe out the past as though it had never happened, to deny their love as if it had never existed. She had been madly in love with Kevin, had rebelled against her loving parents in order to be with him. He had been the center of her life since high school. He and Megan had been her world.

Even in their darkest hour, when the missing funds were discovered and Kev told her he had taken the money, she had stood by him through the ordeal, suffering for him. She had never considered, even for a moment, running away from the disgrace, the nightmare of it. She had believed in those vows they had taken so long ago—"For better for worse . . . till death us do part." She could not easily give up her faith in their meaning.

Through the little grate in the stove, Val stared into the fire, watching the flames leap. Almost hypnotized by the dancing light, she seemed to hear a voice. *But isn't this a kind of death? Kevin is trying to kill your marriage, your love. When love dies, doesn't that end the marriage?*

After a while, Val stood up, went over to the window and looked out into the night. Far away, she could hear the roar of the surf crashing against the jetty. Suddenly, she was gripped by the idea of running out there, plunging into the sea and letting the waves wash over her, blotting out the hurt, the pain, the despair. She shuddered and turned back into the room. That was sick thinking. Self-destructive. *God forgive me.* Of course, there was Megan to think of, plan for, take care of. She was what was important. She and Kevin had brought her into the world. She was their responsibility. And now hers. Alone. She had no one to depend on. No one was going to rescue her. She had to be brave and resourceful. But most of all, she had to pray.

Val reported to The Seawinds an hour before her shift began in order to have time to take Megan to the sitter's. But Eileen McDermott took one look at her and ladled out a bowl of thick, creamy clam chowder and stood over Val while she ate every spoonful.

"No offense, Val, but you look like you could use some more time off. It must have been a grueling trip and certainly no picnic. Besides, Tom has taken Megan out fishing with him, so why don't you take the rest of the day off?" she suggested. "Colleen will be glad to take your shift. Only the other day she told me she'd welcome some extra hours. She's saving for college tuition in the fall. Okay?"

"That would be good," Val said gratefully. "Thanks, Mrs. McDermott."

"I think you can call me Eileen, Val." She patted Val's shoulder. "Most of the staff do, you know."

"Thanks, Eileen."

Relieved that Eileen had been sensitive enough not to probe for any details about her trip to see Kevin, Val promised to be in the next day as usual and left.

Back at the cottage, she changed from her uniform into some jeans and an old pullover and walked down to the beach. Deep in troubling thoughts, she walked without any real awareness of the direction and soon found herself out by the old stone jetty at the end. She went along the narrow stone path that jutted into the sea, feeling the salt spray from the dashing waves on her face. She sat down on the edge and tried to make sense of the visit, of what Kevin's mind-set was and what she should do now.

She realized how much their separation had changed her and how little Kevin's imprisonment had changed him. Oh, physically he had changed, but his basic character had not. He had a habit of rewriting facts, shaping them to his own benefit. After the awful disclosure of the embezzlement, Kev had gone through a period of maudlin self-pity. Normally a moderate drinker, he had begun to drink heavily those terrible days. He had wept, but not tears of repentance. Remorse, yes. And worst of all, he'd shifted the responsibility, rationalizing.

To Val's horror, he'd said over and over, "I did it for you, babe. You and Megan. I wanted to make a big financial killing. A lot of people I knew were getting rich. I had tips I thought were foolproof. I was going to make us secure for life."

Val hadn't contradicted him. What would have been the use? He always knew better. Maybe she should have said, "Don't blame me, Kev. Blame yourself." But it seemed cruel to kick someone who was already down. Now she wished she had. Maybe she could have helped him see the truth.

She had to accept that Kevin meant it when he said he wanted them out of his life, that he wanted no reminders of a life that was over. When he got out of prison, whenever that happened, he wanted to make a fresh start on his own. Maybe she and Megan reminded him of his failure.

There was no point in looking back. No thinking about what might have been. No one could change the past. She had to build a new life without Kevin. For her own sake and especially for Megan's, and the sooner the better. Not just for the next few years but for the foreseeable future.

"It's over." She said the words with only the seagulls to hear. Somehow saying them out loud fortified her resolve. She took a deep breath and looked at the ocean. It was a dozen shades of blue, the sun scattering glittering lights like golden sequins on the rippling water.

She remembered that awful day after the court hearing in the hotel when she had, in desperation, sought help in the Gideon Bible. That same verse she'd looked up afterward in a Bible she'd found and bought in a thrift shop in town. She had often read it, seeking reassurance that she was not, after all, alone. Out of the chapter of Joshua the words, "I will be with you, I will not leave you or forsake you," came into her mind. If she could just believe that. Trust that promise. She would be okay.

The world was so beautiful. She was so blessed to be here, to be young, healthy, to have Megan. A spontaneous prayer of thanksgiving rose from Val's heart. She was really not alone.

Gradually, a kind of calm overtook her. The fog that had veiled her thinking slowly began to lift. The afternoon ebbed into the glow of the setting sun.

Val stood up and started back along the jetty and onto the beach toward their cottage. She felt a sadness for what had gone but a new hope about what might lie ahead. She lifted her head and started running. She was leaving her old life behind like her footprints in the sand. Soon the incoming tide would sweep in and all traces would disappear. A sense of confidence overtook her, the feeling that somehow things would work out. . . .

Part II

Chapter Ten

The summer season was at its peak. The restaurant was crowded. Word of mouth about The Seawinds had resulted in more and more tourists "finding" it. Much of the increased business was due to an item that had appeared in a popular travel writer's column in the leisure section of the *San Francisco Chronicle*. Eileen had read it to the staff with a mixture of pride and surprise.

" 'If you're in no hurry and want to meander down the coast and spend a delightful day having a delicious meal in a charming seaside restaurant with a spectacular ocean view, there's no better place than The Seawinds. . . .' " With mock apprehension, Eileen said, "This may mean more work now that we're on the gourmet map."

It also meant the waitresses were paid overtime and the tips increased, which no one objected to and nobody minded. Colleen was going back to college in the fall and every extra penny Val earned was welcome.

Gradually, Val recovered from her experience visiting Kevin at the prison. She stopped thinking about how long it might take before Kev got out. For a long time, she couldn't get rid of that last image of him, his angry, sullen coldness toward her. Eventually the pain became bearable. It was no longer an open wound, raw and aching each day. Scar tissue was forming and slowly the healing process began.

In the fall, Megan would enter kindergarten. The doctors had told Val that until her deafness became so acute as to require special training in signing or lip-reading, it was thought better to "mainstream" the child in a regular school.

The Seawinds would close when the McDermotts went to Mexico, and although Val knew she had a job there when the restaurant reopened, she needed some income during the months they would be gone. She needed to find a temporary job. She didn't want to use up all her savings from the extra tips she'd earned at the height of the season. She would stay in the cottage, since there was no other place offering such reasonable rent. So Megan would be enrolled at Oceanview Elementary, in the next town over from Seawood.

In order to register her, Val had to produce Megan's birth certificate. It was when she was looking for it that Val came across her unsigned divorce papers. She had thrust away the folder with the accompanying letter from Brad Hensley because she could hardly bear the sight of it. Now, she took it out and reluctantly waded through all the legalese. Soon all the whereases and therefores started to blur. Impatiently, Val shoved the folder back into the drawer, making the excuse to herself that she'd review them some other time when she wasn't so rushed. Even as she told herself that, Val knew she was just putting off the inevitable. It just seemed so final. Once she signed those papers, there was no way back. It was the end of all hope. A hope that still lurked somewhere in the regions of her heart.

Labor Day weekend The Seawinds was booked solid. People were savoring the last days of summer vacation and every shift had tables filled to capacity. After that, the crowds gradually diminished and the staff breathed a collective sigh of relief. It had been a wonderfully successful launching of the restaurant and the McDermotts were already talking expansion. They had spoken to an architect about building on an addition and would probably spend their Mexican "vacation" making plans.

The season was coming to an end. The few renters of the other cottages had gone home, packing up their beach umbrellas, their plastic coolers, their Frisbees, beach balls and surfboards, leaving the beach deserted during the beautiful, long, sunny afternoons. Val realized she had gotten possessive about the beach and was glad to have it to herself again.

Megan, however, missed the children she had had a chance to play with during July and August. But when she started kindergarten she would soon have plenty of children to play with, Val reassured her. Val had taken Megan with her when she went to register her. She explained to the principal about Megan's hearing loss.

Mrs. Elwood listened sympathetically as Val told her that, according to the doctors, the deafness would be progressive but gradual. "Nowadays," she remarked, "it is considered best to mainstream children unless their disability is marked and would prevent them from participating or contributing in class." She glanced at Megan, who had been seated at a small table with a puzzle during the interview. "Your daughter seems bright and alert. I don't see any reason that would keep her from enjoying kindergarten. But I'd like you to meet her teacher and have a chance to talk to her about Megan."

She introduced Val to Miss Pierson, a young, pretty brunette with warm brown eyes and a wonderful smile. After a brief explanation, she began a short conversation with Megan, who responded with her usual spontaneity. Miss Pierson then turned to Val. "I don't see it as any problem."

"Megan's a very responsive little girl," Val volunteered. "I find if I speak directly to her, she has no difficulty. At a little distance, she doesn't always seem to hear me."

Miss Pierson nodded understandingly. "I'm sure it will work out just fine, Mrs. Madison. My sister's a special education teacher in southern California. I'll ask her if there are any suggestions she might have about later on." Then taking Megan's hand, she led her into the bright, cheerful kindergarten room, showed her all its colorful posters, the dollhouse, big building blocks, low round tables and little chairs, also modeling clay, even small easels for finger painting. Megan was very excited at the prospect of starting school and the experience had been a happy one.

From there they'd gone to the one department store in Oceanview where Val splurged on some new outfits for Megan. Then she let her pick out a lunchbox and a colorful padded rug for rest time and story hour. It was fun for both of them. However, on the first day Val took Megan to school, she was surprised at her mixed feelings. When she left her at the gate of the kindergarten playground she felt tears crowd into her eyes. Megan had gone happily into her new adventure. Yet for Val it seemed another letting go. Another page she was turning in life. Again, turning it alone.

Val walked back home on the beach instead of on the road. Along the California coast, the weather in autumn is often at its best. The days are bright and sunny but the mornings are usually cooler, with fog and the fog rolls in earlier and earlier in the afternoons.

As Val took the path off Beach Road over the dunes down to the beach, she was surprised to see smoke curling from the chimney of the cottage at the very end of the beach. It had remained empty all summer. Val had been so busy with work and getting Megan ready for school she had not noticed any activity down there. With the rest of the cottages empty, abandoned for the winter, it seemed strange to realize it was occupied.

A week went by, then two. The restaurant was now only open weekends. The staff was reduced, and Colleen, Val's closest friend among the waitresses, had left to go back to college. Val had applied and gotten a part-time clerking job at Murphy's hardware store in Seawood. Working mornings, Val had her afternoons free to be with Megan.

One day after work, she met Megan at the school bus stop and they went to have milkshakes before going grocery shopping. It was Friday, payday, and Val stocked up on canned goods. She didn't realize she had bought too much until she carried out two heavy bagloads and they started walking home.

They took the usual route, it had always seemed a shortcut, but now Val wished she'd stayed on the road. The sun had suddenly disappeared, and a chill wind blew in from the ocean as they trudged along the water's edge.

Bent on getting home as quickly as possible, Val didn't notice Megan playing her favorite tag game with the incoming waves. That is, until Megan asked plaintively, "Can I take off my shoes, Mommy?"

Her arms aching from the heavy bags, Val turned around. "No, of course not. It's getting too cold to go barefoot."

It was then Val saw that Megan had got her canvas shoes soaked by walking too close to the water.

"Oh, Megan!" Val said sharply, feeling tired and cross. She could feel the edge of a can tearing through the bottom of one of the paper bags.

"But they feel all icky and they squoosh when I walk," Megan wailed.

"Well, that's too bad. You should have watched where you were walking and not gotten them wet." Val started walking again. "Now hurry up, the sooner we get home the sooner you can take off your shoes. Come on."

They continued on, Megan lagging behind. Val shifted the bags carefully, trying not to let the ripped one tear any more. But there was no stopping it. It fell completely apart and its contents—cans, cereal boxes, potatoes and apples—spilled out onto the sand.

"Oh, no! Megan, come help me!" Val called frantically, as she tried to catch a can of tomato juice rolling down toward the ocean.

Just then, a man seemed to appear out of nowhere, eerily emerging from the drifts of fog swirling around them. Val was too busy trying to retrieve her groceries even to register surprise.

"Can I help?" he asked.

She flung out her hands helplessly at the remnants of the paper bag, her scattered groceries. "Oh, please! I'm in a mess."

He began scooping up things randomly and setting them some distance from the incoming tide. "It looks like we caught everything before it got washed out to sea." Then, pointing in the direction of the last cottage on the beach, he said, "I'm staying over there. I could run up and get another bag for you or I could take you home in my car if you live around here."

Val glanced at him gratefully. "A bag would be a big help. I haven't far to go."

"If you're sure, then. I'll run up and get a bag. Be back in a jiff." She watched the tall figure sprint up the dunes and disappear into the cottage. So he was the mysterious renter.

There was something vaguely familiar about him. He had probably dined at The Seawinds sometime during the summer. She was trying to place him as one of the diners she might have served when he returned with a sturdy string bag.

Megan slipped her hand into Val's and asked in a stage whisper, "Why couldn't we take a ride, Mommy? I'm tired."

Val frowned and squeezed her hand warningly.

But the man had overheard her and smiled at Megan. "I'd be glad to give you a lift."

"No, thanks just the same. We live just down the beach." Val pointed to their cottage, now dimly outlined in the thickening fog.

Efficiently, he placed all the groceries into the string bag and slung it over his shoulder, saying, "I'll carry this one for you. I was out for a walk anyway."

"That's very kind of you but—" Val began, but the man just grinned and started walking.

"No problem," he said.

The wind off the ocean encouraged them all to quicken their pace. Even Megan. Her attention was fastened on the tall man who'd appeared out of the fog. When they got to the wooden steps that led over the dunes to the side of their cottage, Val stopped and reached for the bag of groceries he had carried for her. "Thank you very much."

"Not at all. By the way, since we are neigbors, I'm Garth Hasten."

He didn't seem to notice Val's slight hesitation. After his help it would have been rude not to introduce herself, too. "I'm Val Madison, and this is—"

But before she could finish, Megan was already introducing herself. "I'm Megan, I'm in kindergarten, the morning session. Miss Pierson is my teacher and I can tell time and tie my shoes and print my name."

"Megan," Val remonstrated gently.

But Garth laughed and said directly to Megan, "That's wonderful."

"If you'll wait a minute, I'll empty this and give you back your bag," Val said.

He dismissed the idea with a shake of his head. "No need now. I can pick it up some other time. It was nice meeting you." He took a few steps, then looked back and said, "Well, so long, hope to see you both again soon." Then with a wave he continued down the beach.

Val stood there for a few seconds, watching the tall figure as he strode away. Maybe she should have asked him in for a cup of coffee after he had come to their rescue and been so helpful. But what would she possibly have to talk to him about? What would they have in common?

From the look of his expensively casual clothes, the stonewashed jeans, the cable-knit sweater, his reasons for renting one of these cheap cottages were not the same economic ones as hers. No, it would have been awkward if she asked him in.

"Come on, Megan," she said, and with Megan wearily trailing behind in her soggy canvas shoes, they went up the rickety wooden steps and into the house.

When she let herself in, the house seemed particularly empty, depressing in an odd, indefinable way.

Megan plopped herself down on the floor and began tugging at her wet shoes, complaining, "I don't see why we couldn't take a ride."

"Because I've told you over and over we never accept rides from strangers." Val spoke with exaggerated patience.

"But he wasn't a stranger. He's our neighbor," Megan replied. Val glanced at the little girl. She started to explain further, then decided that to Megan her reasoning made perfect sense. Instead, she just said, "Go change your socks, honey, and I'll make us some cocoa."

Val busied herself in the kitchen. But as she started putting away the groceries, she felt an unexpected urge to cry. How stupid, she thought, biting her lip. She suddenly felt an aching loneliness. Why? Because someone had been kind to her, helped her? In the past months, she had learned to do so many things because she'd had no one else to depend on, but she was tired. She longed for what she dared not admit she missed—someone to lean on, some-one to care about her. . . .

From Megan's room, she heard the tinny sound of the little hand-cranked record player they'd found in a thrift shop along with some story records. Megan had learned to do without television and playmates after school. She had adjusted to their new life. Why couldn't *she?*

After Megan was asleep in bed, Val determinedly got out the speed-writing book she'd written away for from an ad she'd seen in a magazine. Someday she might need to look for a better-paying job to support them. An office job. Later, if Megan needed special tutoring or had to attend a special school for the deaf, it might cost a great deal. She had to think ahead. No one else was around to depend on but herself. Sure, Megan was only in kindergarten now, but time went fast and she should be prepared.

For some reason, Val found it hard to concentrate that evening. Her mind tended to drift off to that chance encounter with the neighbor. There was something about him . . . The eyes? The smile? He seemed genuinely kind and friendly. But Val couldn't afford the luxury of friendship.

Finally, she gave up trying to study and went to bed. Yet she was restless. There were many nights, even when she was really tired, that she couldn't sleep. She'd lie there, tense, as though waiting, listening . . . For what? The step that never came, the laughter of a shared joke, the warmth of companionship. That night, the loneliness she usually kept at bay seemed painfully intense.

In the last cottage down the beach, the kerosene lamp burned brightly. Garth Hasten was busily setting up his work space. He'd been out of the country for several months and only been back in the States a couple of days. He'd wasted no time but driven down from San Francisco eager to get to his beach studio. He was energized in spite of the fact he should be experiencing jet lag.

Everything was just as he'd left it months before. His drawing table, placed in the front room at the windows, had a view of the beach and ocean. Meticulously, he set out his brushes, his paints, checked his stacks of sketchbooks on the shelves built under the windows. He was full of enthusiasm and anticipation. But he knew it would take him days to settle in enough to really work.

Idly, he picked up one of his sketchbooks at random and glanced quickly through it to see if any of his sketches would be usable for this new project. He discarded it and picked up another, noting the date on the cover. He always dated his sketchbooks, noted where and when he'd used them. San Francisco, almost a year ago. He started turning the pages, then lingered at one. A woman's face. Ghirardelli Square, the rooftop restaurant, a brilliant fall day, the sun on the Bay, the Chinese kites against the vivid blue sky. He studied the sketch. He'd done it rapidly, no time for details, just an impression. But he had caught something in her expression, something that had remained with him for a long time afterward. Since then, of course, he'd done hundreds of other sketches. He'd almost forgotten her. Until today. The woman on the beach.

At first glance, he wasn't certain about her, but he was sure it was the same little girl. He had not forgotten the child who he'd thought would be perfect for his Goldilocks illustration. The woman, however, looked different now, thinner, her hair a darker brown and cut casually short.

He thought back to the day he had first seen them both. The woman of his sketch had the aloof blond-goddess look of Grace Kelly. Dressed simply but expensively with understated good taste. Her dark glasses had given her an aura of glamour, mystery. But when she had taken them off, her eyes, gray, shadowed by dark lashes, had looked . . . haunted?

He had started to say something today on the beach. Haven't we met before? Too clichéd. He had stopped himself. It was foolish to think she would have remembered him. Their encounter had been awkward. He had acted impulsively, asking her for permission to use the little girl as a model. Naturally, she'd been suspicious, protective of her child. He'd been coolly refused, he remembered ruefully. Dismissed, actually.

But what were they doing here, in this out-of-the-way beach town, living in one of these isolated cottages?

There was some story there. Something must have happened to bring them to this place. He was curious and he still would like to paint the child.

Surely their paths would cross again. It seemed too much of a coincidence not to be significant. Maybe they'd become friends. Anything was possible.

Chapter Eleven

The following Saturday, Val and Megan took a picnic to their special cove. It was a perfect day. The cove was sheltered from the wind and there was a sandbar that stretched far out so that Megan could play safely in the water that curved into the sandy beach.

Megan was a child of the sea. She was never happier than when she was at the beach, building roads and tunnels in the sand, running back and forth with her bucket. Val had brought along her speed-writing manual, thinking she would practice. However, after a few distracted moments, it lay in her lap unread. The ocean was too beguiling, with its ebb and flow, providing her endless fascination. She was lazily daydreaming when suddenly she heard Megan saying, "Hi."

Startled, she raised her head to see Garth Hasten, the rescuer in the grocery disaster. She immediately felt a twinge of guilt. She had not as yet returned his string bag. She had no excuse, she had just put off taking it back. She tried to think of what to say. At the moment, he was squatting on his heels beside Megan, looking with interest at the castle she was building, giving her his complete attention.

There's a man who loves children. The thought flashed through Val's mind. Not everyone knew how to interact with them, but this man did. Even as she was thinking this, he stood up, turned and smiled at her. Then, accompanied by Megan, he walked toward her. He was carrying a fishing rod, and a well-worn creel was slung by a leather strap over one shoulder.

"Hi there, Mrs. Madison," he greeted her. "I've had some real luck this morning. Could you use some fresh fish for dinner tonight? I've got way more than I can possibly eat."

Fresh-caught fish were a treat anytime. Val's grocery budget, usually limited to basic staples, rarely included such delicacies. Even at the risk of becoming more indebted to this man, it would have seemed rude to refuse his generous offer.

Evidently mistaking her hesitation for something else, he grinned. "They're all cleaned. All they need is to be dipped in a little egg and cornmeal, some butter and a hot frying pan."

"You must be quite a cook," Val managed to say.

"Bachelors have to be or they'd starve." He laughed. "So, how about it?"

"Well, yes, thank you, that's very generous of you."

"Good, I'm on my way home. I'll put these in some ice and bring them over later."

Uh-oh, Val thought, watching him walk away. Did that mean she'd have to ask him in? She didn't want to start anything with this stranger, handsome and congenial though he seemed to be. It would just complicate her already complicated life.

She purposely lingered down at the cove longer than usual, telling herself it was because Megan was having such a good time and the day was so warm, so beautiful. Actually, she was avoiding another encounter with Garth Hasten that might prove awkward.

At last it was time to pack up. When they got to their cottage, on their porch was a small plastic container with the fish packed in ice. On it was a note. "Enjoy, GH." To her own chagrin, Val felt a small pang of disappointment to have missed him.

That evening, they had the delicious fish for supper. Later, when the dishes were washed and put away, Val settled down to read Megan her bedtime story. It was a familiar one that Megan often requested and Val found her mind wandering even as she spoke the words. Her feelings about their new neighbor were mixed. In one way, she was drawn to him; in another, she was leery of becoming too friendly. It was Megan who made a surprising statement that caused Val to rethink her attitude.

As she was getting ready to say her prayers before getting into bed, the little girl said, "I think I'll add our neighbor to my God-blesses tonight, Mommy. He's nice, isn't he?"

"Yes, he is, honey," Val answered. Afterward, she thought Megan was right. Garth Hasten had been nothing but cordial and helpful. Why did she feel somehow threatened by his entrance into their lives?

It wasn't until a week later that Val saw Garth Hasten again. Every time she noticed his string bag hanging on the hook by the kitchen door, she reminded herself she must return it. Somehow she felt shy about doing so.

"I'll wait until a day when Megan is with me and we're walking into town," Val promised herself aloud. "I really must do it before he stops here, asks for it." Although that seemed unlikely, the thought of Garth Hasten's towering figure arriving at her cottage door was unnerving. His appearance was so masculine, his manner so self-assured. Silly as it seemed, she didn't want to encourage an acquaintanceship with their attractive neighbor.

A week went by. Almost every day, Val saw Garth Hasten walk past her cottage. Sometimes he had fishing gear with him; other times he just strolled leisurely along the ocean's edge. She was tempted to run outside, return his string bag. But then she hung back. She didn't want him to know she often stood at her window, half-hidden by the curtain, and watched him go by. She had succeeded in cocooning herself all these months, keeping her real identity a secret, not inviting even the staff at The Seawinds to be friends. It was safer that way.

As it turned out, she ran into him again purely by accident. She had taken Megan to catch the school bus and was walking back to the cottage along the beach. It was a beautiful morning, the sky clear, the sun bright, the ocean deep blue, the air tangy with salt. As she went along, she was thinking how lucky, in spite of the circumstances that had brought them to this spot, they were to live here. More like, blessed, she amended. More and more she had come to believe that God had directed her steps, just as she had prayed that desperate day after Kevin's sentencing.

"Mrs. Madison." At the sound of her name, Val whirled around and saw Garth Hasten striding up the beach behind her. She halted to let him catch up with her. "You're out early, too, I see," he said. "Mind if I keep you company?" Without waiting for an answer, he just started walking alongside her. "Boy, what a great day? Look at those whitecaps. We're sure having some weather, aren't we? The best I've ever seen this time of year and I've been coming down here every fall for years."

That caught Val's attention. Why had he chosen this particular beach? Val couldn't guess.

He talked easily, unselfconsciously. "I feel so alive here. There's something special about this place, don't you agree? Unspoiled." He glanced over at her as if for confirmation.

Knowing her reasons were far different from his, Val didn't answer. Garth didn't seem to notice, just went on talking, saying he'd gotten up at dawn, walked down to the dock, ate breakfast with some of the fishermen.

Finally, they neared the place where she usually cut over the dunes to her own cottage and she halted. "I still have the string bag you lent me. Would you wait here a minute while I run up and get it?"

"There's no hurry. You can stop by any time you and Megan are out and bring it over."

Val hesitated. "Well, if you're sure?"

"Yes, any time. I'm usually there. Well, so long." With that, Garth went on down the beach.

Val climbed the rickety wooden steps leading to her cottage. As she went inside, Val was irritated with herself. Garth Hasten must think her a real dud. *What's the matter with me? I can't even carry on a decent conversation. I never used to be like this.* Of course, she knew it was because of the awful events that had changed her life forever. Wouldn't she ever get over it, be normal again?

A few days later, before walking Megan to the bus stop, she folded the string bag and stuck it in her jacket pocket, intending to make a quick stop at Garth Hasten's cottage on her way home. If he wasn't there, she could easily leave it wedged into the screen door. She wouldn't have to knock or anything, just leave it there, she told herself. Then felt annoyed by all this fuss. Why was she making such a big deal about such an ordinary errand?

The wind off the ocean was brisk and she walked with her head down, bent against it. That's how she happened not to see Garth coming from the other direction.

He greeted her with his usual good humor. Taken by surprise, she stammered, "I—I was just coming by your place to—"

"Good!" He didn't let her finish. "How about coming in and having a cup of coffee? I just made a pot and while it was brewing came out looking around for some driftwood."

Val knew it would be stupid to refuse. Still, she paused uncertainly.

Garth said in a gently teasing voice, "I won't bite, I promise. I've been down here for three weeks and I haven't had any company at all. I just walked to town and bought some fresh bagels. Please come and share them."

His smile was so genuine, his voice so friendly, Val realized it would look silly not to accept his invitation. After all, as Megan had pointed out, they were neighbors.

Inside Garth's cottage, Val looked around with interest. It had exactly the same floor plan as hers, but it was decorated in a unique style. All along one side of the front room, there were built-in bookcases filled with books, shells, odd pieces of driftwood. Then she saw the drawing table at the windows.

"Why, you're an artist!" she said, turning to look at him with a mixture of awe and surprise.

"Yes."

She looked at two framed seascapes, then at a stack of unframed canvases stacked against the wall. "Are those yours?"

"Yes."

"Why didn't you tell me you were an artist?" she asked. "It seems like something you'd tell someone right away."

"Maybe. Sometimes it puts people off." He paused and looked at her skeptically. "Should I have told you?" He grinned. "Maybe if I had, you wouldn't have come here. You know the old line that goes, 'I'd like to show you my etchings.' In my case, my sketches." He gave her a teasing look. "You wouldn't have come, would you?"

She had to laugh. "Oh, I don't know, maybe not. But it's wonderful. To be talented, I mean."

"Everyone is talented in one way or another. Mine just happens to be my livelihood."

"How marvelous to be able to work at something you love."

"Don't you?"

Val shrugged. "I'm a waitress at The Seawinds. It's not exactly what you'd call a talent."

"That depends. I've had some great waitresses and some surly ones. It certainly makes a difference to the enjoyment of a meal." Garth went into the small kitchen area at the end of the main room. Val heard the clatter of cups, of cabinet doors opening and closing. She went to look out the window. "You have a fantastic view from here."

"Sure do. On a clear day I can see past the jetty, out to the lighthouse." He came out from the counter divider bringing an aluminum coffee carafe. "Come sit over here at this window. There's another view down to the end of the beach. I can see your cottage from here, just at the curve of the inlet."

She sat down at the scrubbed oak table in the alcove. Sure enough, she could see their small weathered cottage behind the dunes. In a few minutes, Garth brought a tray to the table, set down pottery mugs and a basket of bagels, a jar of marmalade and a crock of butter.

Val took a sip of the delicious coffee. "Mmm, this is wonderful. Freshly ground, gourmet, right? I've forgotten how good real coffee tastes. I use instant since I'm the only one who drinks—" She stopped abruptly. She hadn't meant to say something like that, give away her single status so quickly.

Garth picked up on it immediately. He stirred sugar into his coffee, looking at her directly. "Then there's no Mr. Madison?"

Val felt breathless as she always did when she had to hedge the truth. She took another sip of coffee before answering in a low voice, "No."

"Actually, that's what I've been trying to find out. Hoping to find out. I mean, I've seen you and Megan a lot. Even before we officially met. Remember the grocery fiasco?" He smiled broadly. "I've seen you walking by. Then that day on the beach. Naturally, I couldn't help wonder. I mean, obviously Megan had to have a father. What I guess I'm trying to ask is would it be okay for me to ask you to go out with me sometime?" Val's shock must have shown on her face. Garth put down his coffee, his expression all concern. "Sorry. Did I say something out of line?"

She shook her head. "No, not at all. It's just that I haven't been going out—yet."

"I should have asked first. Are you divorced, or is he . . . dead?"

Later, much later, Val was to remember her moment of truth. Or rather, untruth. At the time, it hadn't seemed that important. After all, everyone at The Seawinds, except Eileen and Tom, thought she was separated. But, right then, as Garth's steady gaze held hers, she had felt trapped. Still, he was someone she'd really just met. He'd told her he was only staying until December. After that, he would leave Seawood. She'd never see him again. What difference did it make?

Besides, Kevin might as well be dead. That's the way he wanted it, wasn't it? In that split second of decision, Val justified her answer.

"He's dead."

"Has it been long?" Garth asked next.

"Almost a year," she said tightly, wishing desperately she'd never come here for coffee, never gotten into this whole mess. It would be rude to get up and leave at this point. Escape. Common courtesy required her to finish her coffee, carry on some kind of conversation. She glanced at Garth and saw that he was looking so anxious she felt sorry for him.

"I'm sorry. I shouldn't have asked. Forgive me. I always seem to be starting out on the wrong foot with you."

"What do you mean?" she asked, puzzled.

"You don't remember, do you?" Garth paused. "San Francisco, about this time last year. The rooftop restaurant at Ghirardelli Square. I asked if you would allow Megan to model for me. I'm the artist who did the sketch of her."

Val put down her mug and stared at him. Slowly, the incident floated back into her memory. Of course, the sketch of Megan, the bearded man who had come to their table.

"That was *you?*" she demanded. "But you don't look the same."

Garth rubbed his jaw. "I've shaved off my beard."

Val scrutinized him. "Yes, now I vaguely . . . ." Her voice faded as a more vivid memory took its place. That was the day—the terrible day—she had learned what Kevin had done. Everything else that happened that day had simply disappeared. Except for that one awful reality. No wonder she hadn't recognized Garth Hasten.

"Look, I don't know how to apologize," Garth said. "Maybe I should have told you right away, that first day I met you on the beach. Told you who I was and that I recognized you . . . well, actually, I recognized Megan first." He paused. "You've changed a little yourself."

Self-consciously, Val touched her hair. "Yes, I know. I wore my hair differently then." She spoke slowly through stiff lips. Her voice seemed to be coming from a long way off. It was such a strange, fantastic coincidence.

"It's none of my business, I know, but why are you living here? Seawood is a long way from Marin."

"I wanted to get away from things. Make a new start," Val said. That at least was the unvarnished truth.

"But I've heard when you lose someone you love, you need the support. Is it a good idea to isolate yourself from people who care, could help, and live so far from family and friends?"

"There is no family, nor any friends." Val's mouth twisted slightly. "No people who care."

"No one?" He stared at her, making Val feel even more uncomfortable. "That's hard to believe."

"Believe it," Val said, and stood up. "I really have to go. Lots to do before time to meet Megan."

He walked with her to the door and opened it for her. "Look, have I messed up things impossibly between us or can we be . . . friends? I'd like that very much."

"Of course."

"I'd really hate it if I've offended you. I didn't mean to."

"It's all right, really." He was blocking her way out and she wanted to leave badly. It had been a mistake to come here. She'd talked too much, told this man too much. He moved away, giving her room to pass.

"I have to go up to the city for a few days on business. But when I come back, could I see you, make some plans?"

"I don't know." Val began to feel suffocated. She had to get out of here.

"I'll call, then, may I?" he persisted.

"I don't have a phone. I really have to go," she said, and stepped out onto the porch. "Thanks for the coffee," she said over her shoulder, then hurried down his wooden path, over the dunes and onto the beach, without looking back.

Chapter Twelve

Val was breathless when she reached her cottage. Hurrying inside, she shut the door behind her and leaned against it feeling suddenly dizzy. After all she'd done to conceal her identity, her past, her careful cover had been blown. Garth Hasten had recognized her. This man, of all people, to come to this out-of-the-way place. It was unbelievable.

She closed her eyes for a minute. The details of that day that she'd pushed to the back of her mind now came rushing back in agonizing detail. Taking Megan to the specialist in the city and receiving the bad prognosis. Then later, the revelation from Kevin about the embezzlement. It had been the worst day of her life. She wanted to forget it forever. Now, it was impossible.

She had forgotten all about that incident with Garth Hasten in the restaurant. And here he was in Seawood. Wanting to be friends.

All during the next week, Val ventured out very little. The weather turned gray and foggy. That was excuse enough not to go down to the beach. Of course, her real reason was to avoid Garth Hasten. When she walked up to meet Megan's bus, she went along the seawall instead of the beach.

Sometimes when she was standing at the window facing the ocean, she would see him striding along the edge of the water. Often he seemed to slow his walk below their cottage and look up. Her heart strangely pounding, Val would step back so as not to be seen. Then he'd walk on. He never came up to the cottage door.

When a few days went by and she didn't see him Val recalled he had told her he was going up to the city. She missed seeing the lights in the cottage at the far end of the inlet. It made her feel lonelier than ever, more isolated.

Then, one Friday night at the end of her shift, Eileen asked Val to take over the register. She had a long-distance call from her daughter back east and wanted to talk to her. Val was just adding up some receipts when a familiar voice asked, "Good evening, Mrs. Madison."

Val looked up. It was Garth Hasten. "You're back!"

He was wearing a tweed jacket, button-down shirt, a great-looking tie. He looked very handsome. "Is it too late to be served?"

"No, I don't think so. . . ." She felt two things at once—unexpected pleasure at seeing him and a concern that she might show it.

Just at that moment, Eileen came out of her office and saw Garth. "Garth Hasten!" she exclaimed. "What a happy surprise!"

"Hi, Eileen," he greeted her. "Where's Tom?"

"Watching TV, but wait until I tell him you're here." She turned to Val. "We knew Garth in San Francisco when we had our restaurant there. He was one of our favorite customers." She looked back at Garth. "I guess you've been holed up in your beach place painting, haven't you? It really is great to see you." Again she turned to Val. "Why don't you show Garth to a table and I'll tell Johnny."

"You brought Johnny down here with you?" Garth said in surprise. "No wonder you're on the map. You've been written up in the *Chronicle*." To Val, he explained, "Johnny's one of the best chefs in northern California."

"Will it be sole or salmon, then?" Eileen asked.

"Sole will be great, thanks, Eileen." When Eileen went in search of her husband and to place a dinner order for Garth, he turned a disconcertingly direct gaze on Val. "And how have you been? And how is Megan?"

"Fine, fine. We're both fine," she answered, feeling her face warm, her heart beating faster. She fastened the receipts with a paperclip and placed them in the register drawer, realizing her hands were shaking a little.

Garth leaned his elbows on the counter beside the register and said, "I missed you. You and Megan."

Val looked at him, wondering if her expression gave her away, revealed that she had missed him, too. But Tom came in at that

moment and greeted Garth heartily. While the two men were talking, Val slipped out through the kitchen, got her jacket from the
employees' lounge and left.

She hurried down the road to the sitter's house to pick up
Megan. It was irrational to rush out like that, but she had not
wanted to linger at The Seawinds.

She had been taken aback by Garth's sudden appearance, even
more by her own reaction to seeing him again. His obvious interest
in her was unnerving. There wasn't room in her life for anyone
else. She had all she could handle.

Later, after Megan was tucked in, Val went to the window in the
front room and looked out. There were lights in the last cottage. It
was then Val realized she had missed Garth Hasten and she was
glad he was back in Seawood.

The next day was Saturday, a cold gray morning. Megan was
happy, excited because today she had been invited to spend the day
with a friend from her kindergarten class. Ever since school started,
she had talked endlessly about a little girl named Bonnie. "We're
best friends," she had announced almost from the first day.

At the open house for parents, Bonnie's mother, seeing Val with
Megan, introduced herself. "I'm Chris Faraday, and you must be
Megan's mom. I guess you know our girls are inseparable. I wonder
if you'd allow Megan to come spend the day with Bonnie next
Saturday? I couldn't find a phone listing for you or I'd have called.
I thought I might take them to lunch and to Playland Park?"

Val felt the urgent tug on her hand and looked down into
Megan's upturned eager face. She had overheard the invitation.
While she'd resisted making friends herself, she knew she couldn't
deprive Megan of the normal pleasures of childhood or keep her in
the prison *she* had created for herself. No matter what, Megan had
to have her own life. So permission was given and plans made. The
two little girls were ecstatic.

Saturday morning, Val walked with Megan up to the service station on the highway above the beach where they had arranged for
Mrs. Faraday to pick her up. That had been Val's idea. She felt self-
conscious about anyone coming to their shabby little cottage. She
was ashamed of feeling that way, knowing it was false pride. However, Mrs. Faraday reminded Val of her former neighbors in
Meadowbrook; she was well-groomed in the casual style of young

California suburbanites. Val still wasn't comfortable with her present situation in comparison with the life she had lived before. The life Chris Faraday was probably living.

The Faradays' shiny station wagon was waiting. Mrs. Faraday had a friend with her who was going along. She introduced her, then told Megan to hop in the back seat with Bonnie, and with a wave they drove off. Val stood watching the station wagon disappear down the road, feeling suddenly deserted. That was the sort of thing she and Emily used to do together. Pack the kids in the car and take off for a day at the zoo or park or beach. For a few minutes, Val felt the desperate longing for a friend, for an afternoon lunching or shopping at the mall. It had been so long since she'd done anything frivolous or simply fun.

She turned to start walking back to the cottage. Fog was drifting up from the beach so that even the ocean was blocked from view. It felt depressing. Val wondered how she would fill the hours ahead today without Megan's cheerful little presence.

She thrust her hands into her jacket pockets and headed down the sandy hill. Thinking of the day ahead alone was bad enough, but that thought dragged up the bleak picture of the years ahead. A lifetime ahead.

Val wasn't sure how long she'd been walking, lost in her dreary thoughts, when she saw the dim outline of a figure moving toward her. The beach was deserted. Val threw a quick look over her shoulder. No one else was in sight. The sounds from the highway behind her were muted by the dense fog. For the first time since she had moved here, Val felt a clammy fear slide over her. She stopped. The urge to turn and run in the opposite direction was strong. But she wasn't sure exactly where she was in relation to her cottage. The figure moved steadily closer. As it came nearer, she let out a sigh of relief. She recognized the man breaking through the swirling mist.

It was Garth Hasten. Her relief was rapidly replaced by a flash of embarrassment. She remembered that she had run out of the restaurant the other evening without even saying goodbye. He must think her terribly rude.

When he was about five feet away, he greeted her jovially, "Well, if it isn't my neighbor, the elusive Mrs. Madison. All these sunny afternoons we've had lately, I've looked for you and Megan on the beach, but you were a no-show. Now, here you come out of the fog."

She couldn't think of anything to say to that. Although his voice had a teasing quality, Val guessed from the expression on his face that he knew the truth that she had been avoiding him. For a minute, the roar of the unseen ocean and the harsh cries of the gulls were the only sounds in the awkward silence that fell between them. Val fumbled with the zipper on her jacket, then pulled the hood up over her head, shivering in the wind.

"Looks like we're the only ones braving it out today," Garth said, "except for the gulls. Of course, they're foraging for food. Which isn't a bad idea. I was just going in search of some myself. It's a perfect day for a bowl of clam chowder. Would you and Megan join me?"

"Megan's gone for the day. To lunch with friends in Oceanview."

"Then why don't you come along? Since we're both on our own. I don't like eating alone, do you?" He smiled and took a few steps to come beside her. He took her arm and turned her around. "Besides, I'd enjoy the company. I've been holed up alone most of the week and it's getting to me." He laughed, and before she realized it, they were walking together toward the fishing dock.

Half an hour later, sitting opposite Garth at a table in the steamy dockside diner, spooning delicious, thick, creamy chowder, Val wondered why she had resisted. There was a warm, friendly atmosphere here. Voices and laughter of the commercial fishermen and the "regulars" provided a pleasant background. Her uncertainty about going with him soon disappeared. Garth's casual, forthright manner made being with him easy.

He told her he had been seeing people in San Francisco related to his art business, and now that all that had been taken care of, he had to settle down to the real work.

"It's all very well being taken out to dinner, complimented on the last book I did and picking up a few royalty checks. Now I have to produce. You're only as good as your last book."

"I've seen some of your work," Val said shyly. "At Megan's kindergarten there are several of the books you've illustrated. Megan happens to love the one about Petey, the squirrel who lives in the tree outside Buddy Bascombe's house and observes all that goes on inside from his little hole."

"Well, how about that." Garth seemed genuinely pleased and surprised. "I did that one at least five years ago. So it's still around?"

"And being read and loved by children. You should feel proud."

"I do. It's very rewarding to know something you do makes someone happy."

"How did you get started as an illustrator? I mean, it must be very difficult to get assignments, isn't it?"

"Yes, until you have a track record. You have to serve an apprenticeship. Get known, recognized. Then it's also luck. Hard work. I peddled my portfolio for a number of years before I got my first real break. I did lots of other things in the meantime before what I'm doing now. Worked for an advertising agency. Hated it. I like being on my own. Choosing my own work."

He paused. "I had a mentor. Actually, two. One of my art teachers thought I had promise. And his wife. They took me under their wings. Angel wings." He laughed. "Fed me a lot of times when I probably would have gone hungry. Saw me through the disappointments. Millie, that's Don's wife, was particularly wonderful. She had a saying, 'When one door closes, another opens.' I've found that to be true. You never know what's in store for you around the next corner. No matter how you plan your life."

Val thought she could say amen to that. If Garth had any idea how her life had changed, turned upside down, he'd be even more convinced of what he was saying.

Afterward, Val couldn't remember how long they remained there talking. The waitress came, refilled their coffee mugs several times, but they were scarcely aware of it. Of course, it was Garth who did most of the talking. He seemed to realize this. "I'm sorry, I've been talking your ear off, haven't I? You must think I'm a complete egotist." His smile was somewhat sheepish. "And I really want to know about you. That must be pretty obvious. I've been hoping for a chance like this. Just to spend some time with you, reassure you. Whatever impression you may have gotten. I'm really quite harmless."

Val laughed. "I know."

"Yes, but that first time I *was* pretty brash, presumptuous, asking you to let Megan model for me."

"First impressions can often be wrong," Val said, smiling.

"My first impression of you wasn't wrong." Garth looked serious. "I thought you were beautiful, charming and somehow mysterious."

"Mysterious?" Val felt the color flow into her face.

"Yes, as if—" But Garth didn't get to finish whatever he was about to say because the waitress came with the check. It was a welcome interruption for Val. They were treading on dangerous territory.

They walked back along the slate gray beach. Coming from the other direction, his cottage was the first one in the row. They stopped just below it and stood there for a few minutes.

"Would you like to come up for a while, toast your toes in front of my fire? The afternoon is still young." His eyes were hopeful.

Val knew Megan wouldn't be back until after five. It was tempting, but she decided it wasn't a good idea. She could imagine the intimate setting, shut off by the fog, sitting together in front of the Franklin stove, the conversation perhaps verging off into the more personal. No, it was dangerous. Too dangerous.

Val shook her head. "No, thanks, I better get home. I have a lot of catching up kind of things to do this weekend. Then I have to go meet Megan."

Garth looked disappointed but not defeated. He insisted on walking with her to her cottage. At the door, he said, "Maybe, you could come and bring Megan another time? She'd probably enjoy seeing the original paintings of some of the illustrations she might have seen in the books you mentioned."

"Yes, I'm sure she'd love that," Val said, thinking how considerate and sensitive of him to include Megan. "Well, thanks for a really enjoyable afternoon."

"Thank you for coming." Garth took her hand and held it for a minute. Again, he seemed to be about to say something more. Evidently he thought better of it and instead said, "Be seeing you. Tell Megan 'hi' for me." Then he went whistling down the boardwalk and the fog closed behind him.

Val went inside. She felt happy and also vulnerable. She had enjoyed the unexpected afternoon with Garth Hasten, maybe more than was safe.

Chapter Thirteen

Without Val's fully realizing it, that day spent with Garth marked a definite turning point for her. It was as if a burden had been lifted and she could take a deep breath. She had been afraid to let her guard down, to be close to people, fearing it might endanger her careful plan to hide from the past. But the more time she spent with Garth, the more comfortable she became.

It happened so naturally—the chance meetings on the beach, the walks, the conversations, the times he joined her and Megan on sunny afternoons at the cove. Over the next few weeks, Garth Hasten became a part of their life. For the first time in months, Val discovered that she woke up in the morning not dreading but looking forward to the day.

He was true to his promise of having Megan and Val over. One Friday afternoon, they came home to find a card from Garth stuck in their screen door. It was painted with his own artwork; clowns and cats and pumpkins were scattered in profusion along the border of an invitation for them to come to lunch on Saturday.

"Can we, Mommy, can we go?" Megan asked, jumping up and down with excitement. Val had told her what Garth did. Megan had used her *Petey the Squirrel* book for her show-and-tell day at kindergarten, proudly announcing that the man who had done the pictures was her neighbor.

Upon arriving at his cottage, Val saw that Garth had gone to a great deal of trouble. He had decorated the table with colorful mats and used bright Fiesta china. He had prepared food that any child would love—hamburgers on buns, French fries, a platter of finger-size crisp veggies, a creamy dip, large tossed salad with chocolate cake for dessert. He spent time showing Megan his paintings, then opened a large trunk filled with stuffed animals, rag dolls, wooden toys of various kinds, the props he used in his illustrations. She was in a child's wonderland.

Leaving her to explore the contents, Garth went over to Val, who'd been watching them. "Megan is really special, Val. She's so bright. She's unusually attentive. She listens so intently to everything I'm saying."

Val hesitated, then decided why not. "Garth, one explanation may be that she has impaired hearing." He looked startled, so she went on, "The reason she listens so carefully is so she won't miss anything. When we were first told about her loss of normal hearing, the doctors suggested that we speak very slowly and distinctly to her. When she was little, I used to hold her face by her chin and be sure that I had eye contact before I spoke."

"I'm sorry. I would never have guessed." Garth turned to glance at Megan, who was having the time of her life with two puppets. "It must have been a blow to you and your husband when you found out."

Val remembered Kevin's reaction—anger, bitterness, blaming God. She thrust the memory away, trying not to shudder. It had seemed so inappropriate at the time. When she'd tried to talk to him about it, he'd become even angrier.

Garth was looking at her expectantly.

"Yes, it was," she answered.

"Can something be done, an operation?"

"No, they don't suggest that. Just to be prepared as the loss becomes more acute. Later, we may start her signing. But people who lose their hearing after they have their language, who've heard sounds, voices, music, the normal noises of life, have a much easier time learning to read lips, speak."

There was a look of such compassion in Garth's eyes that Val almost wanted to confide in him more. It was so comforting to talk about Megan, how wonderful it would be to share her anxieties, her concerns about her future. But that would be a mistake. To confide all that would only weaken her. Garth was just passing through her life. In a few months, he would be gone and she'd still have to carry on alone.

This all went through Val's mind in seconds. Before she could fully absorb the meaning, Megan came over to her with the picture she had been coloring while Val and Garth talked. As she always did when she wanted Val's undivided attention, Megan thrust the paper right in front of Val's face and tapped on her knee at the same time.

"Look, Mommy, look. See, I drew a picture of our house." Val took the paper and held it out so she could see it better. Megan had drawn a house with a deck, a gray-haired woman standing beside the front door and a little girl playing with a dog in the yard. A car was in the driveway and two other figures, a man and a woman, were standing beside it. At once, Val felt a chill. It was their house in Meadowbrook, not the little beach cottage. At the same time, Val was conscious that Garth was leaning over her shoulder also looking at the drawing.

"That's very good, Megan," he said. "It really is, Val."

Megan looked pleased at his comment. Then a small frown puckered her brow and she asked earnestly, "When is Daddy going to come get us? It's been a long time."

Something cold and hard clutched Val's heart. All she had ever told Megan was that Daddy had had to go away for a while, maybe a very long time. Caught in the lie she'd told Garth, she felt trapped. Her mouth went dry. Megan rarely mentioned Kevin even though he was always in her God-blesses at prayer time. Val assumed she had forgotten that there ever had been another life in Meadowbrook until here in her drawing were all the missing pieces of that life—Harriet, Flynn and Kevin.

It was Garth who saved the moment. "Is that your dog? What's his name?" It switched Megan's focus immediately.

"Yeah, that's Flynn. But I didn't draw him very good. He's big and brown and black and his coat is really rough."

"Dogs are hard to get right. I have trouble with them myself," Garth said. "Come on, I'll show you an easy way to draw one." He got up and led Megan over to his drawing table, and for the next half hour, they were busily involved drawing dogs.

Weak with relief that the sticky moment had passed, Val felt grateful for Garth's instinctive tact. However, she wondered if, or more likely when, Garth might ask her if Megan did not know her father was dead.

Chapter Fourteen

Even though Val didn't feel she could confide fully all the circumstances of her life to Garth, she decided to appreciate his friendship while he was staying in Seawood. Val knew that friendship was all it was, and all it ever would be. Since Garth seemed to accept these unspoken limits and never tried to push their relationship beyond casual companionship, Val relaxed.

The pleasant autumn weather lingered, and they spent happy hours on the still-sunny beach. They often shared dinner, alternating at Garth's cottage and at theirs. Garth was so tender with Megan, so patient. When they were at his cottage, he provided her with reams of drawing paper, pencils and crayons and colored felt markers. He always took time to explain things to her and let her borrow the books he'd illustrated.

October soon turned into early November and there was a week of stormy weather. The coastal winter had begun. The restaurant was closed. The McDermotts were getting ready to leave for Mexico. They planned a big farewell party for the staff, encouraging each of them to bring a friend. Val debated whether or not to ask Garth. He knew the McDermotts and she knew he would be welcome. But she wasn't sure she wanted any speculation among The Seawinds group about their relationship. It was Eileen herself that settled the question for Val.

"Of course, you'll bring Megan." She pulled a sad face. "Tom and I are sure going to miss her. Our daughter and grandchildren are coming to us for Christmas, but Megan is special." It warmed Val's heart to know the McDermotts loved her little daughter. She started to ask Eileen about bringing Garth, but her employer surprised her by saying, "Why don't you ask Garth Hasten to come with you two? I know he's a kind of workaholic, but he probably gets lonely and would like a chance to get out and be with other people."

"Okay, I'll ask him," Val said, glad that the decision had been made for her.

Garth accepted at once. He seemed very pleased to have been asked.

At the prospect of the party, Val realized she hadn't been anywhere, done anything like that, in over a year. The idea of getting dressed up was strange and rather exciting. The only thing she wore other than jeans and a sweater was the maroon poplin jacket worn by the employees at the hardware store and her waitress uniform. On impulse, she bought herself a new dress. When she'd taken Megan over to Oceanview for a dental checkup, she'd spotted it in the window of a small shop. It was on sale. After she tried it on, it took little urging from the salesclerk to convince her to buy it. It was a simple, classic design, with long sleeves, round neck, gently flowing skirt. Uncluttered, the kind of dress she preferred. Kevin had gone for more sophisticated styles, like slinky sheaths awash in sequins. Her hair had been fair for so many years that it had never occurred to her to choose something this shade, a deep apricot. But with her hair now its natural brown, the color was really becoming.

As she got dressed the night of the McDermotts' party, Val found herself humming. The dress fitted perfectly and the color was great, but it needed some jewelry to accent it. Val had sold most of the elaborate, expensive jewelry Kevin had given her over the years for much-needed cash. She'd kept only a few pieces that had sentimental value for her. She opened her dresser drawer and brought out her jewelry box. As she lifted it, she caught a glimpse of the blue legal folder underneath, and froze. She knew it contained the still-unsigned divorce papers. With one hand, she pushed the folder back farther out of sight. She wasn't going to think of that tonight, nor of Kevin, nor of any of the ugly past.

She opened the lid of the jewelry box and examined the contents.

All that she had kept was a string of freshwater pearls, a coral necklace and a few pairs of earrings. She decided on the coral strand and small coral cluster studs. Then she saw the charm bracelet.

Kevin had given it to her in high school when they were the "in" thing. He'd had to pay for it in monthly installments out of the salary from his after-school job as a bagger in the local market. But it was fourteen-karat gold. Nothing cheap for Kevin.

She had loved it back then and each of the charms he had given her throughout their romance. The tiny pair of roller skates signifying their secret meetings at the skating rink, a tiny graduation cap marking her graduation two years after his, the tiny replica of engagement and wedding rings, the little cradle celebrating Megan's birth. All milestones in their life together. But after a while, Kevin didn't give her any more charms. He gave her other pieces, bigger, showier, more expensive.

Val replaced the bracelet, covered it with the velvet cushion that also hid the wide wedding ring she didn't wear any longer, closed the lid of the jewelry box and put it back in the drawer.

She studied herself in the mirror. She liked what she saw. It was much more "her" than she had ever seen before. The *real* her. The woman she really was, not the polished image Kevin had wanted her to be. For the first time in many years, she felt excited and happy.

Just then, Garth's signal knock sounded at the front door. Val heard the patter of Megan's feet in their brand-new patent leather shoes on the wooden floor as she ran to answer it, calling as she ran, "It's Garth, Mommy! Are you ready for the party?"

As ready as I'll ever be, Val said to the woman in the mirror. She grabbed her coat and went to greet Garth.

At The Seawinds, all was festive. Chef Johnny had outdone himself with a fabulous buffet, beautifully presented. Turkey, ham, salmon mousse, creamed potatoes, asparagus, five different kinds of salad, fruit compote, lemon cake, pecan pie. A selection of wines, pineapple punch, coffee. It was a lavish feast such as one he might have put on for a gala society affair in San Francisco. Several people had brought their children, too, so Megan had others to play with while the adults relaxed and thoroughly enjoyed themselves. Val realized what a friendly bunch her co-workers were and that she would miss them when the restaurant was closed. Garth seemed to fit right in as if he had been one of them and found it only natural to be there.

The McDermotts were looking forward to their restful time at their condo south of the border, but as the evening came to a close, Tom waxed a little nostalgic. He had everyone form a circle to sing "Auld Lang Syne," promising that they'd be back in March to open the restaurant and hoping that everyone would return to join them.

On the way home, Megan fell asleep in Garth's car and he carried her into the cottage and to her bedroom. She stirred sleepily as Val undressed her and tucked her in.

"Wasn't it fun, Mommy?" she asked drowsily. "The most fun we've had in a long time, wasn't it?" For some reason, the child's voice had a plaintive sound that went straight to Val's heart. Had she somehow infected her little girl with some of her own melancholy? Unintentionally, of course, but it had somehow been a shadow on their life. Then and there, Val promised herself that she was going to consciously try to change. Megan deserved more, deserved a mother who was optimistic, positive, and a childhood as happy and worry free as possible.

When Val went back out to the front room, Garth was standing at the window looking out at the sea. The frosty-looking moon was shining on the water, shedding a luminous light on the rippling waves.

"Come here, Val, this is too lovely to miss," he said without turning around. She went and stood beside him. She felt his arm go around her shoulders and pull her close to him. She drew in her breath. She felt a shock of delight at his nearness and a strong, sweet emotion rose within her.

It had been so long since she'd been this close to a man. So close she could smell the tweedy scent of his jacket, feel the strength of his fingers tightening on her arm through the material of her dress. For a few seconds, she longed to let her head rest against his shoulder, let him hold her, comfort her. Comfort? She wasn't sure what she meant by that. She just knew it was wonderful and she wanted it to go on and on.

"Val, Val," he said softly, caressingly. He moved as if to turn her around and into his arms.

The tenderness in his voice alerted her and she stepped away, her heart hammering in her throat. Danger zone, something warned. Garth pulled her gently back to him, put his hand under her chin and lifted her face so she had to look at him.

"Val, I've been wanting to do this all evening," he said. "I've been wanting to do this for weeks."

He leaned down and kissed her, a kiss whose sweetness she wanted to savor and which she reluctantly ended.

"Val, I—" Garth started to say, but she placed her fingers on his lips, shook her head.

"No, Garth, please. Don't say anything."

"But why? I want to tell you how I feel—"

"Please don't. I don't want to hear it."

"Why not? Don't you know, haven't you guessed that I—"

"It's too soon, Garth."

"Too soon for what? To say that I care for you? That I know I can make you happy?"

She didn't answer, just shook her head.

"Or do you mean too soon since . . . after your husband?"

That seemed the simplest explanation. How else could she possibly explain that it would be fatal if she took what he was saying seriously, flung herself into his arms, into the safety and security of this good, dear man, and let him love her? She had lied to him. She was living a lie. And Garth was so honest, so open, so loving. It shouldn't have happened. She shouldn't have let it happen.

"Just try to understand, Garth. I can't say any more."

Garth sighed, frowned, then said, "All right, I won't press you, Val. But someday . . . someday soon, you'll have to let me say it and you'll have to listen."

He let go her hands and she walked with him to the door.

"Good night, Val," he said, and waited for some response.

"Good night, Garth. Thank you for everything."

After he left, Val pressed her hands against her flaming cheeks. She was trembling. It had been close. All her feelings for Garth, the feelings of which she had been vaguely aware had rushed to the surface tonight with his touch, with his kiss. Val closed her eyes, squeezing them tight, and from the corners tears rolled slowly out. It would have been so easy, so lovely, to give in, to let Garth take her in his arms, love her. No matter what she felt, this was not in her plan. Her life did not include sharing love. She had too many secrets. If Garth knew, he would despise her for not being honest. She had skated too close to the edge, she had to back off, before everyone would be hurt.

Chapter Fifteen

The days following the McDermotts' farewell party were filled with contradictory emotions for Val. What had happened between her and Garth disturbed her. It should never have happened. It was her fault. She had given in to the impulse of the moment. The longing for companionship, comfort.

She had been aware of her growing attraction to Garth Hasten. As their friendship had developed, she saw in him all the things she admired in a man—intelligence, consideration, sensitivity along with a strength that was masculine without being macho. He didn't seem to feel the need to prove anything. He was just himself. The more she had come to admire him, the more she was drawn to him.

Was it love? Perhaps, not yet. But she had to be honest. It could easily become love if she allowed it to happen. The trouble was that she wasn't free to love Garth or anyone else. Legally, she was still married. And she had lied to Garth about that. That troubled her most.

He had been so open with her and she had kept the deepest, most important thing about herself a secret.

Before she could let anything more develop between her and Garth, her marriage to Kevin must be dissolved. The divorce papers were still unsigned. Val felt the most wrenching indecision at the thought. How would Garth react when she told him the truth? Because that's what she had to do or . . . or what? Run away?

Again? She was done with trying to escape from the past. She wanted a normal life for both Megan and herself.

After a third restless night, feeling groggy from lack of sleep, Val dragged herself out of bed. She went through the motions of fixing breakfast and walking with Megan to meet the school bus. Then she walked back down the beach and headed toward the cove. Her head ached from the inner confusion, the indecision that racked her brain and bruised her heart. Over and over she asked herself questions that seemed to have no answers. No right answers anyway. Were there any right answers?

Should she do what Kevin had demanded? Sign the papers, get it over with once and for all? If she did, then she would be free. Free. That word had a strange, unpredictable ring. She hadn't really been free since the first time she saw Kevin.

He'd been coming down the hall in high school, with his stocky, muscular body, a swagger in his walk, his head held in a defiant way. He'd stood in front of her and her friend, Ellen, on their way to class and boldly asked her, "Where do you hang out after school?"

Hang out? Even then, she could only imagine what her school-teacher mother would say to that kind of talk! Why had she let Kevin take over her life? Was it the novelty of opposites attracting? Or rebellion against her sheltered environment, conservative parents? Had they been, as her mother had tried to point out to her, "unequally yoked" even from the beginning?

"It will never work," her father had said. "Oil and water. You're too different, come from too different backgrounds. You're a smart girl, Valerie, be sensible." Both parents had begged her to stay away from him. All their dire predictions had fallen on deaf ears. Val was infatuated. She hadn't listened. She'd gone headlong into disaster.

Disaster? The description startled Val. Had her marriage been a disaster? She tried to think back, to remember. Scenes flickered one after the other like slides in a projector of her mind. Incidents, events, parties, celebrations, arguments, excitement, birthdays, anniversaries, romantic occasions. Kevin elated, Kevin moody, Kevin angry . . . Theirs had been a turbulent relationship. But they had loved each other. Hadn't they?

Lost in her own confused thoughts, Val walked to the end of the inlet, then turned back and began going in the other direction. The ocean was sluggish, a pewter color. The sky, heavy with gray clouds, matched her dreary mood. She walked along, head down. Today Megan was going home with Bonnie after kindergarten, so there was no need to hurry home. Val trudged on, not knowing how long she'd been on the beach. Then, suddenly, she found herself at the foot of the narrow wooden steps that led to Garth's cottage. She stopped and looked up toward the small weathered house.

Even as she did, his door opened and he came bounding down the steps toward her, calling her name as he ran. As he approached her, he was smiling. "I've been thinking about you all morning," he said. "I was trying to decide whether to come and get you, snatch you away from whatever you were doing." Then as if he saw something in her expression that troubled him, his smile faded. He put both hands on her shoulders and looked deep into her eyes. For a full moment, they simply stood there not saying anything. "Is something wrong?" he asked.

How could she tell him it was their relationship, her growing feelings for him that were troubling her? That lately she had become aware of how much she looked forward to their times together. After all she'd been through, she'd wondered if she would ever be able to feel again, even to love, but getting to know Garth had answered that question. Val realized that a man like Garth was someone she could trust and love. There was something special about him that gave her the hope that the kind of relationship she had always longed for but wasn't sure was possible could indeed exist. Now that realization frightened her.

"I just made a pot of coffee. Come on," Garth said, taking hold of her hand and pulling on it gently.

Val hesitated for just one moment, then wordlessly she went with him over the dunes, up the steps of the cottage.

Inside, the fire in the stove crackled. Garth helped her off with her jacket. He poured coffee for both of them and placed the mugs on the table. "I want to show you some new sketches," he told her. "My idea for a new book. They're rough, but I want your opinion. As you'll see, I used some of Megan. I did it—" he grinned "—without your permission, I'm afraid. I did them one afternoon when we were at the cove. Later, when I was looking at them— well, it all just came together. With the right words, they could be made into a picture book that would teach kids about shells and tide pools. Anyway, I'd like to see what you think."

He brought his sketchbook over to the table and Val began slowly turning the pages. Garth was certainly a skilled artist. Even though he had identified them as rough, the drawings were exceptionally good and he had caught Megan perfectly. Val's eyes misted slightly as she saw how he had captured the movements of her tiny body, her delicate profile as she bent over a tide pool, examined a shell.

"These are wonderful," she said finally.

"I haven't submitted them to my agent yet, obviously. I want to do a couple of finished paintings, then present the proposal." He added almost shyly, "I hoped you'd like them."

"I do."

They spent more time discussing the layout of the proposed book, Val contributing some ideas that Garth enthusiastically agreed he could incorporate in the text. He refilled their coffee mugs several times and neither was aware of the passage of time. Finally, Garth closed the sketchbook and pushed it aside. "Thank you. Your suggestions were great. I should give you credit as my collaborator when it's published." Impulsively, he leaned over and kissed her lightly.

Somewhere far away, she could hear the pounding of the surf and yet it all seemed unreal. Nothing seemed real. Then reality broke through. Startled, Val drew back.

"I have to go. I shouldn't have come."

"Don't say that, Val. Don't spoil it," Garth protested. "I tried to tell you before that I feel we were somehow meant to be together. Why else would our paths have crossed for the second time?"

"I don't know. I never meant for this to happen."

"Neither did I. But it did. We can't deny what we feel." He caught her hand. "I care a great deal about you, Val."

"Don't say that," Val said sharply. She pulled her hand away and stood up.

"But it's the truth," Garth protested.

Val walked into the middle of the room. Her back to him she said, "Please, don't tell me that. You don't know me—you don't know anything about me . . ."

"I have to go." She whirled around, eyes wide, desperate. "Where's my jacket?"

Garth went over to her. "Okay, okay," he said gently. "Everything's all right. I didn't mean to rush you. We'll take our time. Get to know each other longer, if that's what you want. If that's what it takes. Can't I hope? Can't you let yourself care for me?"

"You're far too nice, Garth." She shook her head. "I don't deserve it." Tears started rolling down her cheeks.

"You deserve a great deal more," he said very softly. He leaned to her and wiped away the tears with his thumbs. "Please don't cry. I want to make you happy."

She looked up at him, wondering if it was possible to be happy? Could she allow herself to be happy? She glanced at her watch. "Oh, no, I have to go. Mrs. Faraday will be bringing Megan back. I have to get up to Mitchell's service station to meet her."

"Let me drive you," Garth offered.

"No, I need to walk. Get out in the fresh air. Clear my brain," Val said. "I feel all mixed up."

Garth held her face in his hands a moment longer, gazing down at her.

"I really do have to go, Garth," Val repeated, fighting the urge to stay with him.

He laughed softly, then held her a little longer, reciting the old nursery rhyme, " 'Ladybug, ladybug, fly away home. Your house is on fire and your children alone.' " Then he released her. "Okay, I'll let you go for now."

Out in the wind, Val ran along the ocean where the tide had left the sand hard, then scrambled up the dunes to Beach Road. She was out of breath from running when she saw Mrs. Faraday's station wagon come in sight.

Val thanked Bonnie's mother and waved as they drove away. Taking Megan's hand, she started back down the beach to their cottage. Megan chattered about her day with her friends, then looked up at Val and asked, "So what did you do all day, Mommy?"

Immediately, Val felt a rush of guilt. She thought of the hamper of clothes she had meant to take to the Laundromat, the list of groceries she should have brought with her. To say she had been with Garth most of the day would only bring more questions. Again she thought of what had happened between them.

She looked down at Megan's little face. And she saw Kevin's deep blue eyes. They were expecting an answer. In that moment, Val was struck by her features. Undeniable. The eyes, the shape of her nose—Megan was Kevin's child and Val was still legally married to her father. No matter what she felt for Garth Hasten, before their relationship went any further, she had to end her marriage to Kevin. Val felt a painful twinge. That was the real question. Was she ready to end her marriage—free herself forever?

Chapter Sixteen

All the next day, Val's thoughts were in conflict. She had to admit her feelings for Garth were strong. But she also realized she wasn't free to indulge them. Not free because of her own indecision. Not free because she hadn't used the key she'd been given to unlock her own imprisoned heart.

Things were still unresolved the next morning. She was dressed for work and in the kitchen making coffee when a tap came on the door. It was Garth. She opened it wider for him to come in, but he shook his head. "No, Val, I just stopped by to tell you. I wanted you to know that I have no intention of pressuring you or pushing our relationship any further than you're ready to go." He looked at her intently. "I care very much about you. And Megan. I don't want anything to ruin what we already have. You'll set the limits. That's what I wanted you to know. I want to be your friend. More than that, if you want it, too. But only then."

"Thank you, Garth," Val murmured. She felt almost over-whelmed by such honesty, his generosity of heart.

He smiled then. "Just so it's understood. I don't want to lose you, okay?"

"Okay." She smiled in return.

After he left, Val knew she had to tell Garth her real situation, tell him the truth about Kevin, that he wasn't dead but in prison. It wasn't fair to let him go on thinking . . . what? That she was available? She would just have to find the right time. It wasn't something you just blurted out.

Good intentions are one thing; carrying them out another thing entirely. Days passed. The opportunity never seemed to present itself, the time wasn't ever quite right. Garth was now finishing up a project, several illustrations for a book with a January deadline looming. With Val's work hours, her regular everyday life as a single mom, their time together was limited.

A stormy Pacific-coast November ushered in a surprisingly mild December. Mornings were sunny and often the afternoons were too, although short. On such days, they managed to take long walks on the beach, usually accompanied by Megan, who had formed a strong attachment to Garth. Val noticed this with both pleasure and pain. It was the kind of relationship she had wanted Megan to have with Kevin.

That had never happened. Kevin had never spent the time with his child that Garth seemed to enjoy. Kevin was too impatient, and especially after they learned about Megan's deafness, he'd seemed to lose interest. That seemed a harsh judgment on a child's father. Sad as it was, Val had to admit it was true. Sometimes watching the tall man and the little girl, their heads bent together examining a tide pool or walking along swinging hands, Val had a fleeting dream wish—that this caring, special guy was Megan's father, the kind of father the little girl deserved. Val knew it was probably wrong of her to think such thoughts. Still, the contrast between Garth's relationship with Megan and Kevin's was too glaring not to notice.

Before school closed for the holidays, Megan's teacher sent home a note with her inviting them to the Christmas program to be held at her church in Oceanview. She wrote, "The Sunday-school children will have their own performance, and from what my sister tells me, it should have special interest to you and Megan."

"Would you like to go?" Val asked Megan after reading the note.

"Oh, yes, Mommy."

Arrangements were made for them to meet Miss Pierson outside the church and sit with her and her family. When Garth heard about the plan, he insisted on driving them. "It'll be a long bus ride and probably cold," he insisted firmly, cutting off any argument on Val's part.

As they pulled up outside the church, Val impulsively asked, "Would you like to come in with us?"

There was a moment's hesitation, then Garth asked, "Do you think it would be all right?"

"I don't see why not."

"Okay, I'd like to." He circled the parking lot for a space and pulled in. Val noticed he had on a shirt and tie. Maybe he had hoped he'd be invited to come along with them. She was glad she had. From the looks of the assembled congregation, it was a family sort of activity. Miss Pierson, waiting just inside the door, greeted them and was introduced.

The church was festively decorated with swags of evergreens. Bunches of crimson-berried holly hung over all the tall, narrow windows. Clusters of red bows were tied at the end of each pew. A tree trimmed with gold stars, strings of glittering beads and topped with a gilt angel, stood majestically at the side of the altar.

Sitting beside Garth in the darkened church, lit by dozens of red candles, Val felt a wonderful warmth she had never before experienced. Kevin had never gone to church with her. Not that it was an excuse or a reason, but little by little in the years of their marriage, she had given up going herself. She glanced at Garth, then at Megan, and she had a sense of completion, a rightness about the three of them here together in God's house.

She did not have a chance to delve very deeply into her feelings because the program was beginning. There was a rustling, a shuffling of feet, the murmur of children's voices, followed by adult sounds of "Shhh." Then the piano struck the first notes of a familiar Christmas carol and two lines of little boys and girls from five years of age to about seven or eight, marched down the aisle and took their places in double rows at the front of the church. The girls wore red dresses of various styles, the boys white shirts with red bow ties. A young woman, evidently their Sunday-school teacher, stood facing them.

With a nod from her, the children all took big breaths and began to sing. "Away in a manger, no crib for His bed, the Little Lord Jesus . . ." The high, sweet, piping voices, a little off-key, rang out. But it was the other thing they were doing that caught Val's attention. They were signing, their small hands forming the beautiful gestures of the language of the deaf. Val drew in her breath. She felt Garth's hand take hers and squeeze it. Val looked down at Megan, who was watching spellbound.

When the carol was over, the teacher turned to the congregation and asked, "Would you like to sing the next hymn along with us? It's one I'm sure you all know and the signs are very simple. I'll go through it once or twice, then we can all sing it together."

The pianist played the tune through one time as the teacher demonstrated how to sign the words, "Jesus loves me, this I know, 'cause the Bible tells me so."

Val heard Garth's deep baritone rise along with her higher voice. "Yes, Jesus loves me. Yes, Jesus loves me." He was joining right in as if he had been doing it all his life. She would have to ask him sometime about his church background. They had never spoken about spiritual things. . . . She felt there was much more to learn about this man.

From Garth, Val turned to look at Megan and saw to her delight that Megan was signing along with everyone else and seemed to be thoroughly enjoying herself.

Everyone was invited to the parish hall for coffee, punch and cake after the service. Miss Pierson came up to them. "How did you like the program?" she asked Val hopefully. While they chatted, Garth wandered away hand in hand with Megan. Out of the corner of her eye, Val saw them in conversation with two ladies, one she recognized as the pianist. What on earth were they talking about? And how did Garth explain his presence here with Megan? Curious, Val asked Megan about it after they'd gone home and she was helping her get ready for bed.

"What were you and Garth talking to those ladies about?"

Megan dimpled and said, "They thought he was my daddy."

Val felt a small, anxious twinge. "So what did you tell them?"

"I didn't tell them anything. Garth did." Megan gave a little bounce on her bed before getting under the sheets.

"And what did he say?"

"He said he was a friend of the family!" Megan laughed. "Wasn't that funny, Mommy? A friend of the family!"

"Well, he is, isn't he?" Val said rather breathlessly as she tucked Megan in.

"He's more than that, Mommy." Megan frowned.

Again Val felt a little twinge. How much had Megan noticed? What did she think about Garth?

"Oh?"

"You know. He's our neighbor."

Slightly relieved, Val kissed her daughter good-night and put out the lamp. Once more, she felt guilty for not leveling with Garth about Kevin. Sooner or later, she had to do it. Then and only then, could she make some decision about her next step.

That night, she got out the blue legal folder and read over the divorce papers. To sign and file them, she would have to return them to Brad Hensley, and he in turn would have to notify Kevin.

With the holidays coming, it somehow seemed the worst time to do this. Christmas must be the bleakest time of year for all prison inmates. She shoved the folder back in the drawer again. She couldn't do that to Kevin. Pour salt on the open wound of his despair.

Kevin had always made a big deal about Christmas. Not the religious part but the decorations, the presents, the glitz. They always had to have the most lights in the yard, the showiest wreath on the front door, the tallest tree in the neighborhood, sparkling with ornaments and shimmering tinsel. Every year they gave a party right before the twenty-fifth so that people could see the piles of gaudily wrapped gifts under the tree. It used to embarrass Val when she heard Kevin boast to some of their guests about the presents he was giving her. It was always something splashy, extravagant, something she didn't need or even want.

Poor Kevin. What would his Christmas this year be like? In spite of what he'd said, Val thought she'd send a small package to him, things the prison wouldn't prohibit. Some of that Danish chocolate he liked . . . How could Kevin object to that?

This Christmas would be nothing like their Christmases in Meadowbrook. However, Eileen had told Val earlier that she and Tom wanted to give Megan one of the dolls from the "Americana Collection." "I'm a doll collector myself. And these are so special," Eileen laughingly confessed to Val. "Since I don't have a granddaughter of my own to give one to, indulge me, please." Of course, Val and Megan had both seen those dolls, but the price tag was way too much for Val to consider. When Val protested, Eileen had quickly contradicted, "Now, Val, we insist. We want to do it. In fact,

I've already ordered it out of the catalog. Just think how happy she'll be on Christmas morning."

Val knew Megan would be overjoyed. So she had gratefully agreed to the gift. She had put away a few other small things for Megan, as well. There would be a doll bed and a set of tiny dishes, a new dress. They would have a table tree with homemade decorations, string dried cranberries and popcorn, and make a star out of aluminum foil.

It was Garth who came up with the most wonderful holiday plan. "I want to take you and Megan up to San Francisco for the annual production of *The Nutcracker.* I was thinking of a matinee, on a Saturday or Sunday. We'll have lunch at some fancy place and see the store windows and decorations and have one heck of a time. How does that sound?"

"It sounds fabulous!" Val exclaimed. "I know Megan will love it." Val was deeply touched at his having suggested something like this that they could share together with Megan. "Thank you, Garth."

It was a special day. San Francisco at Christmastime was a magical place. The streets were beautifully decorated; store windows had creative displays, scenes from favorite Christmas stories, with life-size puppets representing characters out of Dickens or some other famous holiday tale. The sound of carols filled the air as the revolving doors opened, sending the familiar melodies out into the street. Valiant Salvation Army workers rang their bells, shoppers thronged the sidewalks with their bulging shopping bags from which rolls of bright wrapping paper emerged. There was a marvelous Santa Claus to be visited and Megan got to sit on his lap and whisper what she wanted. Her eyes were shining as she rejoined Val with the candy cane he had given her. She skipped between them, holding on to both their hands as they walked toward the restaurant where they planned to have lunch before going to the theater.

The Nutcracker was fantastic, with its wonderful costumes, music and dancing. Megan was totally enthralled. She sat on the edge of her seat between Val and Garth, her face reflecting her absolute joy. She hardly moved throughout the entire performance.

Driving back to Seawood through the dark night, the little girl was quiet, still wrapped up in the enchantment of the ballet. When they got home and Val was putting her to bed, Megan said dreamily, "I wish I could have a dream like Clara's, Mommy."

"You can have your own dream, sweetie."

"Today was sort of like a dream, wasn't it?" Megan said as she climbed under the covers.

"Yes, darling, it was." Val kissed the flushed cheeks.

And it had been. Val couldn't remember being as happy for a whole day as she had been today. Almost guiltily, she remembered she hadn't thought of Kevin once. It had seemed so perfect, so complete, just the three of them.

Garth was heating them some cranberry juice in a saucepan on the woodstove when Val came out of Megan's room.

"All settled?"

"Yes, and she's one happy little girl. Oh, Garth, how can I thank you? Megan had such a wonderful day. One I know she'll never forget."

"It was wonderful for me, too, Val." He stopped stirring, ladled out a cup of the steaming beverage and handed it to her. She took it and sat down in one of the wicker chairs. He stood looking at her before taking a seat in the chair opposite. "I felt like a family," he said, then added, "Did you?"

Over the rim of the cup, Val met his gaze. Was this the time to tell him? Tell him that, yes, it had felt that way to her, too? But she didn't have the right to feel that way.

"Don't answer that," he said before she could get her thoughts together. "It was an unfair question." He paused. "So, let's talk about Christmas. I'm going to have to go to New York the week after, but we can have a good, old-fashioned Christmas." He launched into some ideas and plans.

Not wanting to spoil his enthusiasm as he outlined his plans, Val let the moment she might have told him about Kevin slip by.

Garth insisted on bringing the turkey for their Christmas dinner. Because neither of their cottages had an adequate stove to do the job, he decided to have it roasted at a bakery in Oceanview that specialized in holiday catering. Val was to furnish the vegetables and salad. Of course, when Garth showed up on Christmas morning, he brought much more than the bird. Val looked on in mock astonishment as he unloaded bag after bag, all kinds of fruit, oranges, apples, a pineapple, bananas, candy and ice cream and a bottle of sparkling cider. He also had several gaily wrapped packages for Megan.

"Oh, Garth, you're a regular Santa Claus. You're making a believer out of me." Val laughed, delighted but somewhat taken aback. She had only a small gift for him, a desk calendar, and Megan had made him a pencil holder at school out of papier-mâché and painted it herself. "You really are too kind," Val said as they looked over at Megan, who was happily playing with her new doll, pretending to read to her from the big, beautiful book Garth had given her.

"Not kind at all. I get a great deal of pleasure doing things for you and Megan." He reached over and took Val's hand. "Don't you realize that, Val?"

For a minute, Garth's gaze held hers as if searching for some answer he desperately wanted to hear.

She hesitated and almost spoke, but he quickly dropped her hand, got up and went behind the kitchen divider, saying, "Let's open the cider. It's a celebration, isn't it?" He worked at the cork.

"I guess so," Val said.

"Not sure? Well, come over here and I'll tell you." He poured out the bubbly liquid into glasses he'd brought and held one out to her.

"What are we celebrating, besides Christmas?"

"Do we really have to have more of a reason other than we've found each other?" Garth asked in a low voice.

Involuntarily, Val looked over her shoulder at Megan. But she was completely engaged in the tea party she was having with her doll.

"I don't care if Megan knows how I feel about you," Garth said, raising his glass in a toasting gesture. "I'd like the whole world to know it."

"Garth, there's something—" Val started to say, but Garth shook his head and put down his glass on the counter.

"I almost forgot," he said. "I've got a little present for you."

"But you've done so much already . . . the turkey and all the fixings and Megan's gifts."

"This is a special one. Just for you." He reached into his jacket pocket and brought out a small square box. It was wrapped in shiny gold paper and had a gauzy silk bow. It looked like the size jewelry might come in. Val took it warily.

"Go on, open it," Garth directed.

Val untied the ribbon with trembling hands and lifted out a gray suede box. When she opened it, she met Garth's smiling eyes and couldn't help smiling, too. It was a gold pin in the shape of a ladybug, sparkling with tiny red stones outlining its distinctive markings.

"Remember, 'Ladybug, ladybug, fly away home'?" he asked gently.

How could she forget the day she'd run home, her heart pounding, escaping what she was feeling. Fled for her life, actually.

"Yes, I remember," Val replied. They looked at each other for a long moment. In that look was all that was unspoken but could no longer be denied.

The undercurrent of excitement between them permeated the rest of the day. Everything seemed to glow. With each glance, each casual word or touch, the heightened feeling increased. As they talked, joked, everything seemed touched with a kind of magic. They were more loving toward Megan. They played checkers and did a puzzle with her and laughed easily over everything.

At last it was time for Megan to go to bed.

When it was time to say her prayers, Megan jolted Val by asking, "Do you think Harriet gave Flynn an extra big bone for his Christmas dinner?" Val was startled. Megan had not mentioned their dog or Harriet or their life before Seawood in a long time. That didn't mean the child hadn't thought about them, of course. Did she also think of Kevin?

That idea sent a chill through Val, taking some of the shining happiness of this day from her. As she groped for something reassuring to say in response to Megan's question, Val was acutely conscious that Garth was waiting for her in the other room. But suddenly the shadow of Kevin was there, intruding in whatever future they might have.

"Sweet dreams, sweetheart." Val kissed Megan, turned on the night-light and went to the door. Her hand on the knob, she hesitated. She knew Garth was waiting, waiting for this moment when they would be alone. Her heart quickened. She had to head off whatever he had hoped for, what she herself longed to do. She opened the door and went out into the front room. Ignoring the eager look on his face, she went straight past him to the stove. There she stood holding out her suddenly cold hands to its warmth. Behind her she heard his footsteps, next she felt his arms go around her waist. Immediately she moved away, "No, no—"

"Why not, Val? We can't deny our feelings for each other any longer."

Val closed her eyes, held her breath, desperately trying to recall the words of Scripture that she had tried to memorize. "God is faithful, Who will not allow you to be tempted beyond what you are able." But they seemed hollow in the face of the great temptation of the moment, the need, the longing for love and safety she knew she could experience with Garth.

She felt his hands on her shoulders, his breath in her ear, as he whispered, "Don't be afraid, darling. I love you. . . ."

She felt a sob rise in her throat. With tremendous effort, she broke away, shaking and breathless. More real than ever, she felt Kevin's shadow—tortured, trapped, hovering. She could feel the shackles of the love that still bound her, ones from which she could not break free. It was no use. No matter how she tried to block out his image, it was impossible.

"What is it, Val? What's wrong? Did I do something? Say something? Answer me."

She shuddered, then slowly turned toward him. His expression was puzzled. Indecision gripped her. Was this the time to tell Garth that her husband, who instead of being dead as she pretended, was alive? That she had lied? In that split second, Val knew it was too late; her lie was now forcing her into another. To deny that she loved Garth. She had dug her own pit from which she couldn't see any escape.

Garth gave a deep sigh. "Well, I guess I misread the signals again. I wanted a commitment from you. I love you so much. . . ." There was discouragement and defeat in his voice. "You're not ready to break with the past, are you, Val? That's it, isn't it?"

She couldn't answer. She felt too ashamed at what she had done. Lied, let him care, let him hope that something was possible between them. She forced herself to look at Garth. Saw naked pain in his eyes, the reflection of his wounded heart. Should she try to explain that it wasn't his fault, nothing he had said or done? It was because she couldn't free herself from a love that kept her prisoner.

Val put out her hand to touch his arm, but Garth had already moved away. He stood, picked up his sport jacket, slung it over one shoulder, then turned to face her.

"Well, I can't compete with a dead man," he said tightly. Then, without another word, he walked to the door. His hand on the doorknob, he turned back. "Goodbye, Val." Then he was gone.

The bang of the door resounded in the silent cottage. The echo of that door's slam would ring in Val's ears for a long time.

Chapter Seventeen

The New Year Val had looked forward to was ushered in by a fierce Pacific storm. Rain rattled the windows of their cottage, wind howled around the corners, penetrated the thin walls. The ocean looked dark, angry, as turbulent as Val's emotions.

Christmas had come and gone and she had not heard from Garth. A hundred times the accusation he had flung at her had resounded in her mind. "You're not ready to break with the past, are you, Val?" The sound of the door banging behind him echoed in her aching heart just like his parting shot. "Well, I can't compete with a dead man."

Every morning since, Val had looked out her window down the beach to Garth's cottage. But there was no spiral of smoke from the chimney, no lights at night. She walked along Beach Road to check, saw that his carport was empty, the car gone.

She felt crushed. She hadn't realized how much Garth had come to mean to her. Maybe it had taken this. Garth had left Seawood without even telling her, without even saying goodbye, without her having told him the truth.

The weeks that followed passed slowly, filled with regrets, longings and the vague hope that Garth would relent, that he would come back, that somehow things could be straightened out between them. Even after she had told him, would he ever forgive her for lying to him all these months?

Maybe it wasn't meant to be after all. Maybe their lives had been too different. Maybe she came with too much baggage for any relationship. Maybe Garth was right. Maybe she couldn't break with the past. Maybe it was just her and Megan against the world that Kevin had thrust them into. Maybe she shouldn't dream of the possibilities of anything else. Just play the hand she'd been dealt.

The fact that she'd brought this second heartbreak on herself didn't help. Much as she tried, the oppressive loneliness descended again. Megan was vocal about missing Garth. She asked about him constantly. But Val had no answer for her persistent "When is Garth coming home?"

January dragged into February and two important things happened that directed Val's attention from her own heartache. Megan brought a note home from the school nurse saying that during a routine hearing check, it was noted that Megan's hearing loss was acute. She recommended that Megan see a specialist. Of course, this was no shock to Val. She had been warned that the hearing loss was progressive. Megan had adapted so well and compensated in so many ways for her deafness that Val realized she had, too.

Now the question was, should she take her to San Francisco to see the doctor they had consulted before? She felt sure he would only repeat his diagnosis, make the same suggestions to prepare Megan for total hearing loss that he had before. She decided to talk to Miss Pierson, Megan's teacher before making any further decisions. She made an appointment to see her.

The teacher was sympathetic. "Megan is so bright and is always so attentive, especially at story time, it would be hard for anyone who didn't know her to tell she's hearing impaired." She went on, "I did talk to my sister during Christmas vacation. She said it would be a good idea to start teaching her to sign. But since she already has language and understands, it would be a natural progression to help her practice reading lips. Both skills for someone like Megan would be valuable." Before Val left, Miss Pierson suggested, "I wish you and Megan would come to our church some Sunday. As you know from the Christmas program, we have a wonderful lady who signs when the choir is singing. It's really lovely. I think you'd enjoy it. And it might be a way to start Megan on signing, to learn hymns."

Val thanked her and thought the suggestion a good one. The very next Sunday, she and Megan took the bus to Oceanside to

Miss Pierson's church. As the teacher had told them, the signing of the choir's hymn selections was beautiful. After the service, Miss Pierson waited for them and introduced them to the choir leader who signed. She gave Val a small booklet with pictures of the hand movements for signing so that they could practice at home.

This proved a special shared experience for Megan and Val. Each evening at supper and bedtime, they signed to each other. They made a game of learning together. It seemed to bring them even closer.

The worst time for Val was when Megan was asleep. That's when the little cottage seemed vast and empty. Curled up in front of the stove, bundled in a thick sweater, she tried to study her speed-writing and business math. But it was hard to concentrate since her mind kept wandering. The eerie sound of the wind didn't help and the fog that sometimes enveloped the house made her feel cut off from the world. Alone. Hard as she fought the depression, it seemed to creep over her like a smothering blanket.

The second thing that happened, unlike the progress of Megan's deafness, was totally unexpected. She received a letter from the prison chaplain. It was a shock. She had heard nothing since her disastrous visit in the summer. As she opened it, she was a little apprehensive, thinking he might have been angry that she'd rejected his advice about not visiting until Kevin asked to see her. The chaplain's letter was brief.

He merely stated that Kevin had sat in on a couple of his group sessions. He felt this was an indication that Kevin might eventually accept counseling. Even if it didn't, the chaplain observed that Kevin's general attitude was less hostile, less withdrawn. He didn't mention whether Kevin had said anything about the Christmas box she'd sent. Of course, she'd heard nothing.

The news from the prison chaplain brought a mixed reaction. One was that it brought the past rushing back. All the things Val had deliberately tried not to think about, tried to forget.

She sat holding the letter for a long time. Kevin was not dead as Garth believed. He existed. He was a living, breathing human being, no matter what, no matter that he never wrote, never communicated. The second reaction Val had was that it didn't really matter anymore. The truth was that not hearing from Kevin didn't hurt as much as not hearing from Garth.

* * *

Val was glad when the McDermotts returned from Mexico in March and preparations began for the reopening of the restaurant. She was happy to see them and they were eager to see Megan and hear about her winter. They had brought presents for Megan—some maracas, gaily painted wooden gourds—and a beautiful embroidered blouse and a pair of dangly silver earrings for her.

"We missed you two," Eileen told Val, hugging her. When Val told them about taking the business course, Eileen suggested she could work part-time in the office. "I could use some help. It would be great if you could do some of the filing, correspondence and billing."

It seemed a wonderful opportunity to hone her new skills. It meant adjusting her hours, dividing the office work from her waitressing shift and making additional arrangements for Megan. But the extra money was helpful. Val squirreled some of it away in a special savings account. It appeared certain that later on Megan would need some specialized training or to attend a private school.

The season was under way and again Val's life took on a pattern—work at The Seawinds in the restaurant and then in the office. She felt that at last she was gaining some confidence in her own abilities, not only to cope but to exercise some control over her circumstances.

Then one night, after Megan was asleep, there was a familiar knock on her door. At first, Val thought she was mistaken, that she imagined she'd heard it. Then it came again, and she jumped up from the table where she'd been studying and hurried to the door. There stood Garth.

"Garth!" She could hardly manage his name.

"Hello, Val." His voice was husky.

"When did you arrive? I didn't know—"

"I just got here. I drove down from the city. I've only been back in California a few days. I couldn't wait any longer. I had to come. Had to see you." He paused. "May I come in?"

"Of course." She opened the door wider and he stepped inside.

"I'm so glad to see you, Val. I passed your cottage on the way to mine but didn't see any lights. I was afraid . . . thought you might have moved—"

"No, I'm still here. We're still here. The Seawinds is open. I'm working there again." Her words were tumbling over each other. She was excited, happy, scared. Her heart was thudding.

"Val, there's so much I want to say, but first, I have to ask . . ." He paused. "Forgive me?"

"For what? There's nothing to forgive."

"Yes, there is. I was insensitive. I tried to push things. I should have understood. Given you more time before . . . well, I know that now. I hope it's not too late. I left angry, hurt. I guess I wanted it so much—wanted you and Megan in my life, wanted to have it all. I thought it was what you wanted, too, but . . ." He hesitated. "What I'm trying to say is this, Val, I want things to be on your terms. Okay? You name them. I'll go along with them. If friendship is all it will ever be, I'll live with that. I don't want to lose you. Give us another chance?"

The tears that sprang to Val's eyes blurred Garth's anxious face. She was too moved emotionally by all that he was offering to speak. All she could do was nod.

Everything changed after Garth came back into Val's life. She had learned the truth that you never know how much you value something until it is lost. Garth's return was like the sun breaking through heavy clouds. He brought warmth and laughter, his own zest for life, flowing back into theirs. Megan was overjoyed.

It was a wonderful spring and summer. They spent part of each day together; hours at the cove where Megan would play happily while Garth sketched and Val sunbathed. Sometimes they cooked Garth's catch over a fire, sheltered by the dunes. Garth taught Megan how to make s'mores—toasted marshmallows squashed between chocolate grahams—and they became the dessert of choice at the beach. They sang old camp songs from both Garth's and Val's childhood. Afterward, Megan would curl up on a blanket and go to sleep while Val and Garth sat watching the driftwood fire.

Other times, they alternated supper at his cottage or theirs. Megan was a part of everything they did. Garth began to learn sign language and made it even more of a fun game. He was always thinking up things for them to do together. He was so thoughtful of her, suggested taking her to the carnival at Dorado Beach and watching the big fireworks display at Harbor Beach on the Fourth of July.

For Val, it was an inevitable comparison of what kind of father Kevin had been with the possibility of what kind of father Garth might prove to be.

Val was so happy that summer that she ignored the underlying problem beneath their growing closeness. Garth's quiet strength, his stable character, his always knowing what he wanted to be and achieving it—was also in marked contrast to Kevin's.

Although the word "marriage" was never actually spoken, it was always there between them. Val knew Garth was impatient for their friendship to grow into something more, but true to his word, he remained patient and accepted Val's unspoken terms.

Suddenly, she knew that she was in love with Garth, passionately in love with him. That the one thing in the world that would make her happier than she ever dreamed of being would be to marry him. He was everything she wanted, a man she could admire, trust and deeply love.

Now she realized that she had to tell Garth about her marriage. And, the time had come to make a decision about signing the divorce papers. She had avoided the problem long enough—too long perhaps. But now that she knew that she loved Garth, that their relationship was so much more than mere companionship, Val also knew she had a responsibility to him, and to all involved. Including Kevin.

Kevin. The thought of Kevin came back often. At the end of a wonderful day when she'd fallen asleep at night, Val would sometimes wake up with a start wondering about Kevin. He was still her husband.

From the distance of nearly two years, Val could now view their relationship, their marriage, with different eyes. Now she realized she had married a boy who had never grown up, a seriously flawed man. She had heard the attorney and the judge in court describe him as a person of poor moral judgment who was incapable of discerning right from wrong, who had rationalized his crime as poor timing rather than wrongdoing. He had taken a calculated risk and lost. If the odds had been different, he'd told Val, everything would have worked out. He hadn't seemed to realize even when she'd visited him in the county jail before the trial, that embezzling funds was a criminal act. Like everything else that had ever gone wrong in his life, he wasn't to blame.

She had been purposely blind to his faults. Why? Had she just married too young? Was she afraid to admit she had made a mistake, been stubbornly determined to make a bad marriage work? A kind of old-fashioned "you've made your bed, now lie in it" sort of mentality? But she didn't know any different. Hadn't really known any other man. Until now. Meeting Garth had changed her viewpoint of what a relationship could be.

Now she knew what she needed, what Megan needed, what neither of them had ever received in full measure from Kevin because he simply couldn't give it.

So what was keeping her from legally ending the marriage? Why were the divorce papers still unsigned?

It often kept Val sleepless knowing she should have told Garth about Kevin right from the beginning. And she certainly should have told him when he first came back to Seawood. Why did she keep putting it off? The answer was she feared Garth's reaction when he learned that she had lied to him. He would lose all respect for her, all trust in her. And though Val knew she'd deserve to lose his good opinion, she also knew how much her confession could hurt him, and she recoiled at the idea of hurting him.

The long days of summer moved on and still Val vacillated. Everything was so perfect. But as August drew to a close, Val knew she couldn't wait any longer.

Chapter Eighteen

The very next afternoon before she went to work, Val got out the blue legal folder that contained the divorce papers. Her feeling of guilt at not telling Garth the truth weighed heavily on her conscience.

She winced, remembering the reaction of one of their best friends in Meadowbrook, Dave Moore. After the news broke, she had come face-to-face with him at the shopping center. She would never forget his expression when he saw her. His eyes had narrowed, his face had twisted, and he'd almost spit out the words, "Don't tell me you didn't know what Kevin was up to. Any wife was bound to know. In my mind, you're every bit as guilty as he is."

Val was sure Dave was not the only one who felt the same. She was branded with Kevin's guilt. Would Garth find it just as hard to believe? Would he also doubt that it was possible to live with a man and not know him at all? She had only seen the shadow of the man, not the real person Kevin was. If she had . . .

The old panic rose within her again. Would she never be free of it? Would it always be there somewhere, lurking like a coiled snake ready to lunge at her?

Yes, she knew she should have leveled with Garth right away. But how was she to know what they would become to each other? And how do you say to someone you've just met, "Oh, by the way, my husband is serving seven to fifteen years in the state penitentiary for embezzlement." That's some conversation starter, a real icebreaker. Val shuddered. She couldn't go back, undo anything. What she did now was the important thing.

She opened the folder, and on the top of the first page she read the title, Petition For The Dissolution Of Marriage. She turned the pages, skimming the legal terms she did not understand, moving along until the words began to dance and waver. Impatiently, she wiped away the unwanted tears. It was all so cold. Another legal document swam into her mind, one that had the same two names on it but instead read, Certificate Of Marriage.

It seemed to have nothing to do with her, the starry-eyed bride she had been at eighteen, standing beside Kevin in the tacky wedding chapel in Las Vegas. Nonetheless, he had bought her an orchid corsage and she had meant every word of the vows she repeated in a young, breathless voice. "I, Valerie take you, Kevin, to have and to hold from this day forward, for better for worse, for richer for poorer, in sickness and in health, to love and to cherish, till death . . ." Death. That's what she had promised. "Till death" not "dissolution."

Val sat down, holding the folder in suddenly trembling hands. She had wanted a good marriage. Given everything to make it so, tried to make Kevin happy. She never dreamed that anything would happen to make it impossible for her to keep those vows.

She wasn't sure how long she sat there, wrapped in the past, incident after incident, memory after memory, floating into her mind. All at once, she glanced at her watch. She'd be late for work if she didn't hurry. She shoved the folder back in the drawer. Tomorrow. Tomorrow for sure she'd sign the papers, mail them to Brad Hensley. Then she could face Garth, tell him that it would only be a matter of waiting a few months, then she'd be free.

Eileen greeted her as she rushed in a little flushed from hurrying. "Where's Megan?" she asked.

Sometimes Val brought Megan along as Tom doted on the little girl and was always happy to have her watch TV with him or sit near him while he worked on his boat.

"Garth took her to supper at the Dock Café. They're great pals, you know."

Eileen raised her eyebrows. "I know. We've all noticed. I think Tom's a little jealous."

"You're kidding," Val said, surprised.

"Yes, of course," Eileen said, grinning. "But we're all wondering when you two are going to set a wedding date."

Val looked startled. She had no idea she and Garth had been the subject of speculation among The Seawinds folks. She glanced around to be sure none of the other waitresses who were setting up their tables could hear her, then said in a low voice, "Eileen, I haven't got my divorce yet."

It was Eileen's turn to look shocked. "You haven't? What on earth are you waiting for?"

Val had no answer for that. Eileen went on, "I thought Garth was in a hurry. He sure seemed to be when he was talking to Tom and me."

"Garth has talked to you and Tom about us?"

"Yes, he has." She patted Val's hand. "I know he thinks you're a widow. We won't say anything to make him think otherwise. When and how you tell him is up to you. But you must know he's crazy about you, Val, and nuts about Megan." She paused, then said thoughtfully, "It's probably none of my business except that I care about you and Megan. Very much. And I think Garth is a prince of a fellow. His kind of man is almost extinct these days. So my advice is don't make him wait too long."

Val knew Eileen was speaking straight from her heart with only the best of intentions. And she was going to work things out. There was plenty of time, she told herself.

Val thanked Eileen and went to get her station ready for the early diners who would arrive at five. But as she took orders, and served, she was completely preoccupied. She was just coming out of the kitchen with a tray of desserts for her first table when she saw two couples coming in the entrance. One of whom she recognized. The Talbots, her former next-door neighbors in Meadowbrook. Val almost dropped the tray. For a stark second, the two women stared at each other. Emily's face blanched. It was Val who finally gained her composure enough to say quietly, "Hello, Emily."

"Val!" Emily gasped, looking as if she'd seen a ghost. Her husband turned a deep red when he realized who the waitress was. Jack had been one of the most verbal to condemn Kevin after his arrest. Val knew he had forbidden Emily to have any contact with her. In better days, Jack had spent a lot of time on their patio drinking Kevin's imported beer and trading jokes.

The other couple looked puzzled. They knew something strange was going on but didn't know what. Suddenly, Val knew there was nothing that could be said other than acknowledging each other. She didn't have to explain anything. There had been a time when they were as close as sisters. She and Emily had traded recipes and maternity clothes, borrowed teacups and missing baking ingredients. Now they had nothing to say to one other.

"Nice to see you," Val murmured, then moved past them to save Emily the embarrassment of introducing her to the other couple.

Later, Val chanced a look across the room and saw they were seated at another waitress's section. Somehow she got through the rest of her shift. She couldn't help but wonder what their dinner conversation had been. The neigborhood scandal starring Kevin might have provided something juicier than the steaks they'd ordered. As much as she tried to tell herself it didn't matter, Val felt keenly the old agony of lost friendships, ruined reputations and shattered lives.

When her shift ended, Val hurried outside to wait for Garth and Megan. She didn't want Emily to see either of them or Megan to see her. It would have all had to be explained and Val wanted to tell Garth about everything in her own time and place.

The season was coming to a close again. The McDermotts were getting ready for their winter vacation in Mexico. Since Labor Day the restaurant was only open on the weekends. During the week, Val worked in the office, getting all the billing done and helping with the final bookkeeping and correspondence. At the end of one morning's work, Eileen handed her a generous check.

"This is way too much," Val protested, staring at the amount.

"Nonsense. I couldn't have accomplished this much without your help. Use it for something special for yourself, Val." Her eyes twinkled merrily as she added, "But promise you won't get married until we get back. I want to give you and Garth a fabulous wedding banquet and reception."

"Oh, Eileen!" Val laughed and they hugged. She didn't mention the divorce was still not filed. She knew Eileen would be shocked at her delaying for so long. Val pushed back the nagging question in her own mind about why she hadn't yet done it. She thanked Eileen and left. Garth and Megan were waiting for her at the cove. They were going to have a cookout that evening. Val was to stop at the cottage and pack the rest of the food into a basket to bring down for their picnic supper.

As she walked home along the beach road, Val thought how especially lovely this fall had been. It was a beautiful day. The ocean stretched out in at least five shades of blue and there wasn't a cloud in the sky. Garth had said there would be a full moon that night. That meant they could stay down at the beach until late. Val smiled to herself, looking forward to the evening ahead, as this was the nicest time to swim and then they could build a driftwood fire, toast marshmallows. . . . Later, she remembered that she didn't have a hint or clue that anything would mar this happy time they'd planned together.

The blue-and-white mail truck passed her on the road and she waved at the driver. She was surprised to see him stop at her mailbox. She never got any mail other than the junk marked Occupant. But before going down to the house, she stopped and checked. She found a long white envelope with a return address she immediately recognized. She shivered as she drew it out. It was from the prison chaplain. She tore the envelope open and unfolded the single typewritten sheet. Her eyes raced down the page.

It has been a long time since you have heard from me and an equally long time since I have received an inquiry from you as to your husband's progress. You will be glad to know there has been a remarkable change in your husband over the past few months. This should encourage you to try for another visit.

I have had the opportunity to discuss your last one and Kevin expresses some remorse over the way he reacted to your coming. In a number of one-on-one sessions I have been able to have with him, he feels that he has severed his relationship with you. That the divorce he demanded has erased any possibility of reconciliation.

His attitude toward rehabilitation is encouraging. He has attended the group meetings regularly and has availed himself of some self-help tapes from the library and is working out in the gym. In other words, I see a positive change.

I want to encourage you to keep communicating with your husband. An inmate who has a stable relationship on the outside has a much better chance of rehabilitation and eventually applying for parole.

There was more, but Val stopped reading. Her hands turned to ice. She walked down the dunes, slipping and sliding as she did until she reached the front porch of the cottage. There she sat down because her legs were so wobbly. A dull throb began in her temple as her mind filled with questions. Now what? Why now? Just as she thought she was turning a corner, heading for a new life, the past rose up and slapped her down. Kevin remorseful, wanting a reconciliation? Kevin expressing regret for his actions? All the things she'd yearned for in the first miserable months of his imprisonment were happening now. When it was too late. Too late? For him? For me? Too late for the wonderful things Garth was offering? Garth! Val's hands clenched, crumpling up the envelope.

She felt dizzy, put her head in her hands, moaning. If only she'd signed the divorce papers, mailed them. By now, Kevin's lawyer would have filed them. It was almost two years. It would have been final by now. Kevin would have received his copy and they would have been divorced. She would have been free.

The sun shifted direction and hit her eyes. Val put up her hand to shield them. How long she'd been sitting there in a kind of daze, she didn't know. She pulled herself to her feet, hanging on to the porch post, and went inside. Moving mechanically, she packed the picnic basket, filled two thermoses, one with milk, one with coffee, put in the hot dogs, buns, mustard, relish, marshmallows, cookies. Then she changed into her bathing suit, got sweaters for both her and Megan for later, picked up towels and a blanket, stuffed them into a large canvas tote.

Before she left, she smoothed out the wrinkled envelope containing the chaplain's letter and put it in the drawer on top of the blue legal folder. Then she went out of the cottage and headed for the cove. Resolutely, she made a decision. *I'll think about this tomorrow, decide what to do tomorrow, but at least we'll have this day.*

Chapter Nineteen

Val saw Garth and Megan before they saw her. Both were standing at the water's edge. Garth was helping her with the small fishing rod he had bought for her and she was casting her line. She heard Megan's high lilting laugh and Garth's deep voice as he coached her. Val winced. Her chest felt tight with pain. How could she possibly give this up?

As she stood there watching the two of them, Val became sharply aware of the passage of time. Megan was almost seven. She had grown so much this past year. The pink bathing suit new at the start of the summer was now faded, almost too small for the long legs and little-girl skinniness that had replaced the baby plumpness of last year. It didn't seem possible that they had been at Seawood for almost two years.

Garth turned, saw her and waved, smiling. "There's your mom," he told Megan, and she turned, too.

"Look, Mommy!" She shook her fishing line, a big grin on her face.

"I see, darling!" Val called back over the lump rising in her throat. Megan was so completely happy.

It would have been a perfect evening if Val hadn't had such a heavy heart. The burden of what she had to tell Garth hung over her like a black cloud. Megan managed to stay awake long enough to see the huge pale moon rise over the sea. Then she'd been content to be wrapped in a blanket while Val and Garth remained basking in its silvery glow.

After a few minutes, Val drew a long breath, ready to tell Garth what had to be told. She knew there was no easy way to break this to him. However, before she had a chance, Garth said, "I have some great news. I didn't want to say anything about it in front of Megan until I'd checked it out first with you."

"What is it?" Val asked, glad of the temporary reprieve.

"I heard from my agent in New York today and he's negotiating a contract for illustrations for a book that's to be published both in France and this country. The bonus is that the background is to be Paris!"

"You mean you'll be going to Paris?"

"No, Val, we—you, Megan and I—will be going to Paris. For six months or maybe a year! Isn't that wonderful? We can be married and spend our honeymoon in Paris . . . city of lights, city of lovers!" He leaned over and kissed Val on the tip of her nose. "Well, aren't you going to say something?" he teased.

"I'm speechless," she managed to murmur.

Garth started to kiss her again, but she turned her head.

"Garth, I have to tell you something."

"Okay, but don't frown." He smiled.

"Garth, I'm serious."

"So am I. Very serious. Seriously in love." He put his arm around her shoulder to draw her close, but she stiffened.

"Please, Garth, I haven't told you the truth about something important. I know I should have long before this, but I didn't, and now I don't know where to begin."

"You haven't got a passport? Well, that's no problem. We can fix that."

Val's heart sank. Garth was so elated, this was going to be much harder than she'd thought. "Listen, it's not about passports or Paris, or maybe it is. I don't know exactly where to start."

Garth looked puzzled. "The beginning's usually a good place. But, Val, don't feel you have to tell me anything about your past you'd rather not. I don't want to know anything that's going to make you unhappy."

"It does make me unhappy, but you've got to know. We can't

make any plans. At least not right away. I should have told you before this. You see, I'm not free to marry you."

A blankness came over Garth's expression as if what Val had said didn't register. He looked at her as if she'd been speaking a foreign language.

"I'm not a widow like you assumed, like I told you." Val swallowed hard but continued. "My husband is in prison. He's serving a sentence for embezzlement. He wanted me to divorce him, but I never did. I just couldn't bring myself to do it. He wanted me to build a new life for myself and Megan, move from the community where we'd lived, where we were known. That's how I happened to come here, why I used my maiden name. He didn't want to see me, to communicate in any way. I went once. He was furious with me. Since then we haven't—I haven't seen or heard from him for over a year."

She stopped, took a long, shaky breath. "Then I met you. It changed my life. I was so lonely, desperately lonely. But I never dreamed we'd . . . fall in love, that we had any kind of future together." A sob broke her voice. "Oh, Garth, I'm so terribly sorry. I should have told you long before this. It was wrong not to. I guess I was afraid. . . ."

The tears came then and the racking sobs. Garth's arms went around Val, cradling her against him. His hand smoothed the back of her head as it lay on his shoulder, his voice soft, comforting, as he soothed her. "It doesn't matter, darling. Don't cry, please. It's all right. It's going to be all right. You can still go ahead, get your divorce. Here in California it only takes a matter of weeks. Everything can be taken care of and then we can get married."

Sniffling, Val pulled away. "Oh, Garth, if only it was that simple. There's more. I got a letter from the prison chaplain. Kevin has changed his mind about wanting Megan and me out of his life. His whole attitude has changed . . . he's working in the programs with the goal of getting paroled." She gulped back more sobs. "The chaplain says it's important for an inmate to have the possibility of returning to a stable home, loving relatives. It will go a long way in impressing the parole board to grant Kevin a parole."

Garth was silent, his face set in grim lines.

"The chaplain says if Kevin knows I'm waiting for him, it will make all the difference."

"But that's unfair. Why should you be sacrificed? The man kicked you out of his life, forced you to start over, work at a job you weren't prepared for, struggle along bringing Megan up alone. Now, he can't expect to have everything again. Just because he needs you to get out of prison."

"It's not exactly like that, Garth. Kevin hasn't contacted me himself. It was the chaplain who wrote—"

Garth was bristling with anger. "Who is this guy to tell you what you should do with your life?"

"He's just a man trying to do his job. Help prisoners get their lives back together."

"What about you? What about me? Are you going to let a letter from some guy we don't even know change everything? Unless . . ." Garth hesitated as if he could hardly bring himself to ask the question. "Or do you still love your husband?"

Val flung her hands out helplessly. "Love? Not the way you mean. I did what he wanted me to even though I didn't think it was right. But you can't just wipe out twelve years of your life as though they never existed." She paused. "I care what happens to him. Yes."

Megan stirred, murmured in her sleep. Garth leaned over and pulled the blanket more securely around her. Then he turned back to Val. "Does she know about this?"

Val shook her head. "No. She rarely talks about Kevin anymore. A child forgets soon. He never wrote or anything. I just told her Daddy had gone away. Kevin used to travel a lot. She was used to it just being the two of us. Certainly now she is. Except that now she has you, too."

Garth got up abruptly and stalked down to the ocean's edge. Val could see his tall figure silhouetted against the silvery moonlight, the ocean a rippling, glittering backdrop. Then she thought of Kevin. No matter what she did, everyone was going to be hurt.

Garth walked back and forth for a long time. Then he came back to Val. He sat down beside her again and gently took her hands in his. "We don't have to talk about this anymore tonight. We'll sleep on it. Then we can decide what you'll do."

Silently, they gathered everything up. Repacked the picnic basket, folded the blanket, towels. Then Garth lifted Megan and carried her up the beach, over the dunes and into the cottage. Val followed him, set down the basket, the other things. Garth came out of Megan's bedroom where he had laid her gently on the bed. He came over to Val, took her into his arms and held her for a long time. She could feel his heart beating against hers and she closed her eyes, wishing none of this had happened, wishing . . . wishing . . . She sighed. Remembered the song from an old movie. "A wish is a dream your heart makes." If she could just wish them all into her dream of happily ever after . . .

Garth's voice brought her back to reality. "Nothing has to be decided right away. I have some work to get out in the morning, but I'll come over later. Things will look better in the morning, you'll see. We can talk then."

She looked up at him and nodded. Then he left. Drained of all emotion, Val lay down on the couch in the front room. Garth had made it sound as if what she did would be a joint decision. But she knew, in her deepest heart of hearts, that it had to be her decision and hers alone.

Chapter Twenty

"Mommy, why are you sleeping out here?" Megan's anxious little face close to hers awakened Val. She raised herself on her elbows, pushed back her hair and tried to focus sleep-heavy eyes to look at the child peering down at her.

"I guess I just drifted off out here, honey." Val sat up. She pulled herself to her feet, feeling cold and stiff, her neck aching from the awkward position in which she had finally fallen asleep. Slowly, the agonizing scene with Garth came back to her. Her mind felt fuzzy. What had she decided? Then she remembered. Nothing. It was all still a terrible unsolved muddle.

Megan skipped out to the kitchen area, calling back over her shoulder, "Are we going to the cove again today, Mommy? You said we could."

Val heard the sound of the kitchen stool being moved, cabinet doors opening then slamming shut, the clatter of dishes and the rustle of dry cereal being poured into a bowl.

"Can I have cocoa for breakfast? I can make it myself." The refrigerator door clicked and Megan's voice continued. "Guess what, Mommy? Bonnie's cat is going to have kittens and she said I could have one of them when they get bornded. Is that okay with you? I'd like a gray striped one like the mama cat. Except her four paws are white. That's why they call her Boots."

Val clenched her teeth. The sound of Megan's sweet, high voice was grating on her pounding head. Her impulse was to beg Megan to play quietly with her dolls in her room for the morning, allow her to get some more sleep. But with the need to make a decision hanging over her, Val knew she probably couldn't sleep anyway. Out in the kitchen, she groped in the cabinet over the sink for the bottle of aspirin and gulped down two while trying to oversee Megan measuring cocoa powder into a saucepan and adding milk from the carton without spilling it all over the counter.

"So can we, Mommy?" Megan persisted.

"Can we what, honey?"

"Go to our cove."

"Oh, yes, I guess so." Every nerve in Val's body longed for peace and quiet to think, to plan, to come to some conclusion.

She made herself some strong coffee and sipped it standing at the window. The whole coast was a misty gray-green, but even as she watched, the thin veil lifted and a bright sun came out, revealing the long stretch of beach. It was going to be another beautiful day after all. Maybe it would be a good thing to be down at the cove.

Their cove was tucked between large, overhanging cliffs; a crescent of sandy beach curved from the dunes. The rocks formed natural tunnels that filled rapidly when the tide was coming in. This morning, the tide was out, leaving a wide margin of wet gray surface, perfect for sand-castle building. Driftwood and kelp were strewn on the beach swept up from the last high tide.

Val felt as though she was moving in slow motion as she staggered up over the dunes and got settled with the blanket spread out, the picnic basket and thermoses. By the time she had stretched out on her stomach, her chin on folded arms so that she could watch Megan, the little girl was already filling her bucket with water.

Val thought of the day before when all three of them had been down here together. Without Garth, something was definitely missing. What was she going to do? The things that had kept her awake most of the night now seemed to be slipping out of her grasp. She felt too weary to figure out anything. The scene at the prison when she'd visited Kevin rose up in vivid detail. She saw his face, twisted with bitterness, eyes shuttered with resentment, his whole body bristling with anger. Could he have changed? Really changed, as the chaplain indicated? Val shuddered even though the sun was prickling her back with hot needles.

Then she thought of Garth, of the wonderful future he was offering them. She squinted her eyes against the sun's glare, looked down to the water's edge, where Megan squatted on the shoreline. Almost as if aware of her mother's gaze, the little girl turned and waved. Val waved back. Megan loved Garth. He would be such a great father. . . . *Oh, dear God, how can I make the right choice?* Any choice she made would hurt someone. Who had the most claim on her? Megan? Garth? Kevin?

The answer that came seemed to lead her—drag her—down a dead-end road she had traveled before. Back to a time of waiting, of being unable to see whatever was at the end of it. There was no guarantee that Kevin would be paroled even if she did stay with him. If she gave up a new life with Garth, Kevin might still have to serve his entire sentence, and then what? She would have lost the chance for a kind of happiness she knew now she had always wanted but never imagined was possible. And she would have lost it for Megan, too.

The sun playing on the water was dazzlingly bright. Far out on the horizon, a freighter moved slowly. The surf swirled in foamy circles onto the sand with a measured rhythm. Val felt her eyelids grow heavier, droop. The need for sleep was almost overpowering. She glanced at Megan now industriously piling mounds of sand into a huge pyramid. Val blinked and stifled a yawn. The urge to close her eyes was irresistible. She put her head down on her folded arms, thinking it would be for just a minute.

Suddenly, she jerked her head up. Shivering, she sat up. The sun had shifted and she was now completely in shadow. The wind off the ocean was cool. Wide awake, she got to her knees, then stood. Megan was nowhere in sight. A jolt like an electric shock went through her when she saw the empty beach, saw Megan's sand castle collapsing in the wake of the inrushing tide.

"Megan! Megan!" she shouted. But her voice was carried away by the roar of the waves. She ran forward, stumbling in the softer sand of the dunes, down to the beach where Megan was playing just a few minutes ago.

A few minutes? Had she been asleep for twenty minutes or more? Panic gripped her. Could Megan possibly have been swept out to sea? Had she been kneeling, her back to the ocean, been caught by a wave she didn't see? *Oh, dear God,* Val silently screamed, *I shouldn't have taken my eyes off her, not for one second.*

She waded into the water, calling Megan's name, the waves lapping around her calves, then her knees. Her child's name became a frantic sob. "Oh, God, please, God, don't let anything have happened to Megan. . . ."

Just then from behind her, she heard, "Mommy, Mommy, here I am!"

Val whirled around, nearly losing her balance in the pull of the strong current. Then she saw her. Megan was standing on top of one of the rocks on the shelf of bluffs above the cove. How she had ever climbed up that far, Val didn't know. But the fact was, she was there. Val ran through the surf, gesturing wildly, calling, "Megan, don't! It's too high up there. Come down."

But Megan only waved and turned back, continuing to climb. With a sense of horror, Val realized the little girl couldn't hear her. Megan was usually obedient. She wouldn't have deliberately disobeyed her mother. She just didn't know how dangerous the cliffs were. She had thought it was an adventure. Something out of *Swiss Family Robinson,* the abbreviated edition Garth was now illustrating and reading to Megan. She had been captivated by the daring exploits of the children of the shipwrecked family. That's probably what was in her mind when she ventured up the steep slope. Val knew she didn't realize that she would have to come down, the descent just as perilous as the climb had been.

Concentrating on trying to get Megan's attention, Val was unaware of her own situation until she felt a pulling rush of water from under her feet, the sucking sensation of the waves on her bare legs. The tide was coming in fast. Just as this realization hit, a hard wave knocked her down and there was a swirl of sand and shells. Grappling for a foothold, she struggled to get back up but only half succeeded when another big wave struck.

Gasping for breath, Val tried to run into shore but was caught as the wave broke, hitting her hard and sending her down as the water rushed over her in a thundering crash. On her hands and knees now, she managed to crawl then stagger to her feet and make the shore before another incoming wave could wash over her. Her palms and knees were scraped by sharp pieces of shell. But that didn't matter. All that mattered was getting Megan down safely and then getting away from the cove before the tide came in and cut off their escape.

At last she made it to the bottom of the cliff. Yelling at the top of her voice, she called again, "Megan, Megan, come down at once. The tide's coming in. We've got to hurry and get out before we get caught."

Megan turned with a look on her face that stopped Val from saying anything else.

"I can't, Mommy!" she wailed.

"What do you mean, you can't?"

"I'm scared. It's too high. It's too far down."

Val bit her lip. Out of her own fear, she nearly said, You should have thought of that. Of course, she didn't. As slowly and calmly as she could manage, Val directed, "Stay right there. Don't move. I'll come get you."

There was no time to argue, no time to hesitate. Soon the narrow channel leading to the other side of the beach would be filled with the churning ocean water sweeping in with the tide.

Chilled from her soaking and urged on by fear, Val ran over to their things and shoved her feet into her thongs. They weren't climbing boots but would be better than trying to cover the rocks in her bare feet. She ran back to the foot of the cliff. She could hear Megan crying now. The little girl had realized her predicament. Val called up to her, "Don't worry, honey. I'm coming, just hold on."

Slowly, Val picked her way up the rocks, breaking a couple of fingernails as she grasped for handholds to pull herself up. Above, Megan's crying got louder.

Val tried to soothe her. "Don't move, Megan. I'm coming." At last she reached the little girl and Megan flung herself on Val, nearly toppling them both. "Wait, honey, we're going to have to go piggyback. That's the only way Mommy can climb down and carry you."

Val swiveled, holding on to Megan until the little girl was positioned on her back, her legs straddling Val's waist, her arms in a strangling grip around Val's shoulders and neck.

"You're choking me, honey!" Val pleaded at one point. But Megan's clasp didn't loosen. The child was too frightened. Somehow, Val never knew how, they inched their way down the cliff. The feel of sand on her feet was welcome. She set Megan down gently and looked around. The waves were higher and coming in with increasing speed. "Come on, Megan, we've got to make a run for it. Grab everything you can. Then let's go."

The water was getting deep as they waded through the arch formed by the gigantic boulders that served as the entrance to the cove. Val held tight to Megan's hand with her one hand, carrying their picnic basket in the other, the blanket over her arm. Megan was carrying one of the thermoses, but as the waves churned under their feet, she dropped it and it disappeared in the waves. "It doesn't matter," Val told her, pulling her along.

At last they reached the beach on the other side, and with a safe expanse of sand between them and the incoming tide, Val stopped to catch her breath, and reassemble their belongings. Megan was shivering violently. Her lips were blue. Val wrapped the blanket around her, but it was damp and didn't give her much warmth.

"Come on, darling, we'll have to hurry and get home. We'll pop you in a warm bath right away or you'll catch a terrible cold. Try to run, okay?"

Just as they were struggling up the last few feet of the dunes in front of the cottage, Megan tugged on Val's hand and said plaintively, "I'm sorry, Mommy."

Val's heart melted. "It's okay, darling, we've both learned a lesson. Once you've had a bath and some hot chocolate, we'll both feel better."

A half hour later, Megan was bundled up in front of the stove, both hands clutching a mug of creamy cocoa. It was only then Val realized *she* was still in her wet bathing suit, her hair dripping. The supply in their small hot water tank had nearly run out by the time she got into the tub herself, and instead of warming her, the tepid water chilled her more.

No matter what she tried—cups of steaming tea, changing into a warm sweater, wool slacks—Val couldn't seem to get warm. Along with the outer shivering, an inner trembling began. It was the belated realization of the danger both Megan and she had been in that day.

She was still cold, yet feverish, when late in the afternoon, Garth showed up. When she told him what had happened, he frowned. "You mean you think Megan didn't hear you at first?"

"I called and called, then when she realized where she was, she turned and looked down. That's when she saw me. I'm not sure she heard me before then."

"Do you think her deafness is getting worse? I thought I noticed it, too, but I wasn't sure. Her not hearing you could be dangerous. More dangerous than today." Garth's frown deepened. "Maybe we should make an appointment with a specialist, have her checked. Possibly some kind of hearing aid would help."

Val's heart turned over. Garth had said "we" as if it was both their responsibility. Garth was so dear, so concerned. His love for Megan was apparent. She covered his hand with her own. "Yes, maybe we should. I feel so guilty. I should never have gone to sleep. Taken my eyes off her."

"It's all this unnecessary tension—that letter, all of it has upset you. You're not yourself. Not thinking straight. No wonder . . ." His mouth grew grimly tight. Val knew he was suppressing a lot of what he was feeling, thinking.

She was now beginning to feel too ill to talk about what was foremost in both their minds. It would be no use to go into it any further tonight. Although she protested she'd be all right, Garth insisted she go to bed. He would take care of Megan, feed her supper, read to her and tuck her in, which Megan was delighted to hear. Gratefully, Val agreed and left them to go to bed.

She woke in the middle of the night aching in every bone, with a throbbing head and a heaviness in her chest. The next morning when Garth arrived to check on them, she could only speak in a hoarse whisper. There was no question but that she should remain in bed. Garth took over. He brought lemons, vitamin C tablets and chicken broth. Then he took Megan to school. He also called Val's manager at the hardware store, where she had resumed her job from last winter, and told him that Val was ill and unable to come to work. He reappeared every hour or so and Val was only vaguely aware of his coming and going. She slept deeply, grateful that Garth was in charge, glad to relinquish Megan's care to him, too weak to feel any guilt.

Two days later, Val woke up clearheaded and rested. She heard the sound of movement in the kitchen area and Megan's and Garth's voices. Soon Garth appeared at her bedroom door with a tray. "Good morning, sleepyhead." He grinned. "Feeling better?"

"Yes, thanks to you. I think I might live." Val sat up, pushed her pillow behind her back. "How can I ever repay you for this, Garth? It was beyond the call of duty or friendship or anything." She shook her head. "You were wonderful taking care of me and Megan like this."

"Don't you know that's what I want to do? Keep on doing? Taking care of you and Megan for the rest of our lives?"

His words brought back the fact of the letter from the prison chaplain. The one that had brought about their crisis before she became ill. Now, as their eyes met in a loving gaze, Val remembered. She drew back the hand she had held out to Garth.

His smile faded as if he knew what had happened. He set down the tray on her lap, then drew an envelope out of his shirt pocket and laid it alongside her cup and saucer. "This came in yesterday's mail."

Val glanced at the return address and recognized the handwriting. It was Kevin's. She looked up at Garth.

"I'll take Megan to school. Give you a chance to read this in private. When I get back, we can talk."

The little house seemed unnaturally still after they left. Or maybe Val's heart was pounding so loudly so that it silenced every other sound. Blocked everything out while she opened Kevin's letter.

It was written in his familiar style. Staccato sentences, lots of dashes.

Dear Val,

I'm not sure I'll have the guts to mail this when I finish writing it—not after all I've done and put you through—but the chaplain and the prison shrink both think it will be therapeutic for me to do this—and who am I to argue with them?

I understand the chaplain has been in touch with you over the past year and he thinks you may be willing to forgive and forget. I don't know if this is true or not—I wouldn't blame you if it isn't. But I've always been one to take a risk. So I guess that's what this letter is—a gamble.

I've been going to the group encounter sessions. They're pretty rough. Nobody lets you get away with anything. Everyone says what they think. The counselor who leads the group says the seeds of how we turn out are sown early in our lives, the reasons why we act like we do, do the things that get us in here. Not that I'm like most of the other guys. My childhood wasn't rougher than some of theirs. I had a lot going for me at one time. I just got off track somewhere. It might have all worked out. But that's another story.

The real point of this letter is to tell you I do care about you and Megan—whatever I might have said—whatever you might have been led to believe.

I want you to know I'm not counting on anything—and I'm not holding you to anything. I know you didn't sign the divorce papers even though I thought that's what I wanted you to do, told you to do. The chaplain says that means something—does it, Val? Maybe things could work out for us if I get released early, get a parole—the chaplain says there's a good chance of that. First offense—no prior record—I'm turning into a model prisoner. How about that? The point is that an inmate who toes the line—follows the rules—that's considered good conduct in here.

The big thing is if a man has a stable home life on the outside, there's a real chance for rehabilitation—that he won't repeat the offense he's serving time for. That kind of guy is much more likely to get a parole. These prisons are overcrowded with real criminals—they'd like to get rid of some of the ones who are not a danger to society. Anyway, if you still have any love left in your heart for me, we could start over and be together as a family again—I'm hoping this is how it is. It's up to you, Val. I won't blame you if you've had it but I thought you'd want to know I've changed my mind—about a lot of things. Well, I guess that's all for now.

Yours ever,
Kevin

Val let the letter drop out of limp hands, leaned her head back against the pillow and closed her eyes. The man who had written this letter was a new Kevin. Kevin was never the kind to look at himself, to examine his motives or explain his actions. Reading this letter, Val thought of how hopeless she'd sometimes felt in their marriage. How she could rarely express her real feelings. She recalled all the hurts and misunderstandings, the times she'd been filled with resentment, angered by Kevin's indifference toward her or Megan. Now he was bringing into the open some of the things they'd never talked about. Why had it taken this terrible experience to make him see reality?

Val knew the letter had at least accomplished one thing. It had brought her to a decision. She had to go and see Kevin again. See this new Kevin. Judge for herself if this was for real. Maybe discover what she could not read between the scrawled lines of this letter.

Time had not blotted out hurtful memories, all she had been forced to face, handle, manage on her own. It had been nearly two years. If Kevin had changed, so had she. They were no longer the same two people they had been. The question was, how much had they changed? Were there now irreconcilable differences—as the divorce petition stated—for them to be together ever again?

Val had to find out. Before she made any other decision. She would have to see Kevin. The only thing she dreaded was telling Garth.

Chapter Twenty-One

❧

They didn't have a chance to talk until early that evening. It wasn't until after Garth had fixed them all supper, Megan had been read to and tucked in bed. Wrapped in a blanket, Val was propped on the couch in front of the stove, where the fire Garth had built earlier crackled cheerfully.

As gently and as reasonably as she could, Val broke the news that she had decided to visit Kevin again. That she felt compelled to do so. Garth's reaction was what she had expected.

"Why did this have to happen now? We were so happy." His jaw set, he leaned forward clenching his hands.

Val longed to reach over, comfort him in some way, but she didn't dare touch him. Her own emotions were too precarious. It would only make things harder. She knew now what she had to do. "I have to go. Don't you see that?"

"If you feel that's what you have to do, of course." Then Garth said firmly, "But you're not going anywhere until you're completely well."

"I know. Besides, I'll have to write first, find out when I can come, the visiting schedule, that sort of thing." What she didn't mention was her own determination to be careful not to give Kevin any false hope.

Another silence followed. Garth kept staring at the fire. Val watched the light from the flickering firelight cast interesting shad-

ows on the rugged contours of his face. Garth cleared his throat as
if what he was going to say was difficult. He turned toward her.

A muscle in Garth's cheek tightened visibly. "I don't want you to
go."

"I know, but there's no other way. I'd never have any peace if I
didn't."

Garth pounded his fist into his palm. "*Why?* I keep asking myself
why."

"It's all my fault," Val said miserably. "I should have told you
about Kevin, told you the whole truth right from the start. Then
none of this would have happened."

"No, sweetheart." Garth was beside her in a second, kneeling on
the floor. He took both her hands in his and looked at her. "It isn't
your fault. My falling in love with you would have happened anyway. Something started the first time I saw you and then when I
met you again, that day on the beach." He shook his head vigorously. "No, you and I, we were meant to be. I thought so then. I
still think so. I'm tired of all this talk, this confusion we're feeling.
It's not fair and it's not right. No matter what, I'll go on loving
you."

Val touched his cheek with her hand, relishing his strength. She
pushed away her guilty feelings. If only she'd done what Kevin
wanted in the first place. Now she would be free. Free to love
Garth. But fair or not—and whoever said life was fair?—the promises she'd made to Kevin still stood. Slowly she moved away from
Garth, walked over to the window and looked out. How calm the
sea looked today, unlike her own troubled soul.

Ten days passed and Val moved through them like a sleepwalker.
On the surface, things were the same although she and Garth
treated each other with extra gentleness, extra consideration. Val
meticulously avoided any physical contact with Garth. She knew
Garth was exerting the same control. They waited, like two people
on the precipice of a mountain, for word from the prison. When it
came, there was a feeling of anguished relief. At least now they had
a time and a date.

When Val showed Garth the letter she had received back from
the chaplain, he read it, then looked at her, his deep-set eyes full of
anxiety. Impulsively, Val put her hand over his. "Oh, Garth, I'm so

sorry for what this is doing to you. I've really messed up your life, haven't I?"

"Don't say that. Don't even think that." He frowned.

"But it's true. You would have been so much better off falling in love with someone with a less complicated life."

"Val, I love you. There couldn't be anyone else."

"Hasn't there ever been?" Val asked.

From the first, they had simply taken each other at face value. Val had avoided talking about her own past, did not want to answer questions Garth might ask, and so had been afraid to ask Garth about his. Naturally, she had wondered about it. Someone as attractive and interesting as Garth must have had a past, must have seen other women.

He had no reticence about it. He was forthright and casual as he told her, "Of course. In college, like everyone else. They were short-lived romances. Then I was so intent on my career there wasn't really time for a serious relationship. When that got underway, there were times when I was attracted to someone. Once or twice it even looked like it might lead somewhere. Then I'd find I was saying a lot of things I didn't mean, going places I didn't like, doing things I wasn't much interested in doing." He paused, a slight smile lifting the corners of his mouth. "At the risk of being really corny, can I tell you I think I've been searching for someone like you all my life?"

Val smiled at him with a kind of wistfulness. "Maybe a little corny, but very nice."

Things moved very quickly after Val got the letter stating Kevin was looking forward to her visit. But what to do about Megan for the two days it would take traveling back and forth? Val knew the only way would be to take the McDermotts into her confidence again.

If Garth's reaction could have been anticipated, Eileen's was even more negative. "But why now of all times? I thought you and Garth were making plans. Why jeopardize your future, yours and Megan's?"

"I have to go, Eileen. I know it's hard for anyone else to understand. But that's the way it is."

Eileen pressed her lips together. "My grown children tell me I shouldn't give unsolicited advice, but, Val, I really feel this is a mistake." When Val made no reply, Eileen sighed. "Okay. I've said all I'm going to say. And of course we'll keep Megan. Does she know where you're going and why?"

"No, I want to wait and see if . . . well, see and talk to Kevin first. I'll just have to cross that bridge when I come to it." Val knew that was an unsatisfactory answer but the only one she could give right now.

She decided not to say anything to her daughter about her father. Not just yet. So much hung in the balance. She would know what to do or not to do after she'd seen Kevin.

The night before Val was to leave, Garth went with her to take Megan to the McDermotts. Then they drove over to Oceanview and went to a small Italian restaurant for dinner. Neither of them had much of an appetite nor ate very much. They talked very little, just gazed at each other across the candlelit table, heart-heavy with all that was unspoken. Afterward, they returned to the beach practically in silence. Garth parked on the road above Val's cottage. He cut the engine, then turned to her. Without a word, she touched his cheek with her hand. Then she flung open the door and ran up the path, her vision blurred by tears.

Chapter Twenty-Two

The next day as Val waited for the bus out to the prison, everything seemed strangely familiar. I've done this before, Val thought with a sense of the ridiculous bordering on hysteria that she knew was inappropriate.

But everything was exactly the same as the first time she'd made this trip to visit Kevin. Even though this time he was expecting her, wanted her to come, Val had the same panicky sensation. She felt the perspiration gathering on her hands, felt the frightening breathlessness, the terrifying pounding of her heart. She felt sandy-eyed from not having enough sleep.

She had not been able to sleep last night either in the cheap motel where she'd checked in upon her arrival. When she gave up trying after a night of tossing and turning, she had showered and dressed.

She started to pin the small jeweled ladybug pin Garth had given her at Christmas on the lapel of her cornflower blue jacket. Then decided not to. Kevin might ask questions. He always noticed such things. She held it in her hand for a few seconds, then slipped it into her handbag. It made her feel unhappy to do it. As if she was abandoning Garth.

She went out into the early-morning stillness of the street. Besides the bus station, the only place open where she could get a cup of coffee was a diner. Inside its white tiled interior, the glaring fluorescent lights burned into her sleep-hungry eyes. She forced herself to nibble on a stale sweet roll and swallow a little coffee. Then she went back to her motel room to wait out the next two hours before it was time to catch the prison bus.

Again she was struck by the sight of the others waiting for the bus. Bound together on this common journey yet separated by private pain. There was an older woman with sad, dark eyes carrying a covered wicker basket, which, Val knew from her previous visit, she would not be allowed to carry into the visitors' section. It was probably filled with nothing more than home-baked goodies, perhaps favorites of the man she was coming to see. However, it would be checked for drugs or anything that might be made into a weapon. It might never reach the person for whom the contents had been baked so lovingly. Val glanced at the woman sympathetically. Whoever she was visiting—husband, brother, son—he had done his share of etching the deep lines in her face.

Suddenly, a thought struck Val. How would she look in fifteen years? How would she seem to younger women waiting to go up to that gray stone fortress on the hill? A wave of nausea swept over her. But she managed to control it. She looked away quickly and saw the bus coming.

She maneuvered the high step carefully, thinking she had been foolish to wear high heels. She had done so automatically, remembering that Kevin had always preferred her to wear them. What difference did it make? The point of her coming was not to please Kevin. But as they neared the bus stop near the prison gate, she took out her compact and checked her image.

Kevin would find her changed. The hairstyle, the color, all different. Still tanned from the summer, she wore much less makeup now. No eyeliner and only lip gloss. She liked the way she looked, felt it was her real self. Maybe that was one of the biggest changes in her. She wasn't trying to create someone else's image of how she should look or dressing to please anyone but herself these days. For the first time in years she felt she knew who she really was. And she liked it that way. A smile touched her lips. Garth seemed to like it, too.

Val also knew there were changes in her that had nothing to do with how she looked. She snapped the compact shut. With a screech of brakes, the bus jerked to a stop and the door swung open. At the gated entrance, an armed guard checked identity cards, then in a single, silent file the visitors were let inside the compound to make their way to the next guarded station.

Since Val had a pass to see Chaplain Scott as well as to visit an inmate, she was led past the visitors' room, down several corridors, through several bolted doors. Her teeth clenched as she waited for a guard to unlock each one, then afterward she heard it clang and the bolt shoved back.

She was ushered into a drab little office with a couple of golden oak armchairs and a window with heavy steel mesh obscuring the view, then told to wait. She tried to relax by taking deep breaths, flexing her fingers. But her hands were so moist she had to keep wiping them on her skirt.

"Mrs. Evans?" a pleasant male voice said, and Val jumped. "Sorry, I didn't mean to startle you. I'm Chaplain Scott."

Val stood up, dropping her purse as she put out her hand to shake his extended one. There followed a few minutes of confusion as they both bent to pick it up, retrieve the spilled contents.

"Won't you please sit down?" The chaplain pulled up the other chair and seated himself, smiling at her as if theirs was an ordinary kind of visit. Not a matter of life or death.

Val looked at the man whose letter had brought her here, made such an impact on the life she had made for herself since her last visit to the prison. The man who had evidently had such an influence on Kevin.

He was not handsome, his chin too prominent, his nose too large, his hair balding.

But his eyes were extraordinary, light blue, almost luminous, and he looked directly at her as he spoke. These were truth-seeking eyes, truth-telling ones. Instinctively, Val knew she could trust whatever this man said, whatever he told her. She tensed as he began to speak.

"I want you to understand that a possibility of your husband's parole is just that, a possibility. It's a long process and requires a lot of recommendations for the applicant. The one that has a great deal of bearing on whether an inmate is granted parole is what will happen when he gets out. If there's a chance of returning to old companions, old haunts, old temptations, his chances are not very good." Chaplain Scott paused significantly. "However, if he'll be returning to a loving home, a good environment, people who care about him and will support him in turning over a new leaf, well, then, it improves the likelihood of his getting paroled."

His keen gaze lingered on Val. She twisted the straps of the purse in her lap.

"The board only meets three times a year, and since they just met last month, it will be another four before they hear any new appeals. Another test of patience. Think you're up to that?"

"I don't know," Val said. "I honestly don't. It's a new idea. I'll have to wait until I see Kevin, talk to him myself."

"I don't mean to probe, but I can see you don't have the same attitude you had before. From your letter, I got the impression you were willing to wait for Kevin no matter how long it took. Have things changed? Have your feelings for your husband changed?"

Val couldn't lie. Not with those honest eyes looking penetratingly at her, as if they could see into her very heart.

"No, not exactly. I mean, I hoped Kevin was adjusting better, accepting the situation, but . . . yes, I guess you'd have to say things have changed. It's been almost two years. On my own a good part of that time, I've had to change." She took a long breath. "And I've met someone. Someone who means a great deal to me now. We met when I'd lost all hope that Kevin wanted us . . . me and our little girl. He didn't answer any of my letters."

Again Val took a breath that was almost a gasp before she went on. "A wonderful man, a good, intelligent, caring person, wants to marry me. He would provide a secure home and be a loving father to Megan."

She let this sink in for a moment before going on. The chaplain was leaning forward, listening attentively.

"The problem is, I never did what Kevin demanded at first. That I divorce him. Somehow I could never bring myself to sign the papers so that they could be filed and end our marriage."

"What does that tell you? About your own feelings? About the divorce?"

"That legally I'm still Kevin's wife, that I'm not free to marry."

"I wish I'd known this before I sent that letter," Chaplain Scott said thoughtfully. "I wouldn't have got Kevin's hopes up, encouraged him to write to you."

"He thinks everything is the same?"

"Well, he's pretty sure of it. He told me you were high school sweethearts, that your relationship has always been a good one . . ." The chaplain hesitated. "What does the other man think of all this?"

"He's upset, of course."

"And your little girl? Does she know there's a possibility of her daddy coming home?"

"No, I haven't told her anything." Quick tears came into Val's eyes. "I wanted to wait until things were clearer." She flung out her hands helplessly. "I don't know what to do. What's right or what's wrong. Whatever choice I make, somebody will be hurt." She looked at Chaplain Scott. "What do you think I should do?"

"I can't make that choice for you, my dear. What concerns me is Kevin. If he finds out you're not willing to provide him the support he needs to get a parole, that you won't be waiting for him when he gets out, whenever that is, it will be a blow. A real setback." Chaplain Scott looked grieved. "He has placed a great deal on his belief that you still love him. I don't know what finding out that someone has taken his place in your affections and in your little girl's, well . . ." He shook his head.

"But is it right to penalize us for what he's brought on himself? It just isn't fair."

"Life seldom is," Chaplain Scott said sadly.

Val got up, walked over to the window and looked out through the mesh. She could see the corner of the prison yard where the inmates took their exercise or mingled in the short recreation time. Beyond were the towering granite walls, the coiled rolls of barbed wire and an electric fence. Beyond them were the rolling California hills, still covered with golden poppies and purple lupins. Beyond all this was freedom. Her freedom. To love and live unafraid, cherished, protected by a wonderful man. She felt a wrenching desire to take that freedom. To run out of this grim place and never look back.

But she knew she couldn't. If Megan was her only consideration, there would be no contest. Garth was clearly the more sensible choice of a father for her child. His gentleness, his interest and patience, his concern for Megan, were so much greater than Kevin had ever shown. But for Kevin, Val's feeling was less analytical. He had been a part of her life ever since she was fifteen. . . .

Why now did the words of the wedding vows they had taken

come back to haunt her? Even though they had been spoken in the gaudy atmosphere of a Las Vegas marriage mill, to Val they had eternal meaning. She and Kevin had been joined together "in the sight of God" in a union that was to last forever, come what may, no matter what.

Val turned back from the window, faced Chaplain Scott. He was sitting, head bent forward, chin resting on folded hands, almost in a pose of prayer. Had he been praying? she wondered.

"I'm ready now, I think," she said.

"You've made your choice, then." It was more a statement than a question. He must have known, Val thought, that I never really had a choice. Maybe that was why she'd never signed the divorce papers. Somehow, underneath it all, she knew it would take more than her signature for her and Kevin's marriage to be over.

Chaplain Scott rose to his feet. "Good. Come on, I'll take you to Kevin."

They had only fifteen minutes together because this was not a regular visiting day. Kevin had to be released from his work detail in order to see Val. As Val saw her husband approach accompanied by a guard, Val thought he looked physically better than the last time. He'd been working out in the prison gym, and even in the baggy jumpsuit he wore, he looked trimmer, his bearing more energetic.

Through the glass enclosure, Val saw the look of hope in his eyes as he picked up the communicating phone.

"It was good of you to come, Val," he said.

"I wanted to see you."

"You got my letter?"

"Yes, that's why I'm here."

"Forgive me?"

She waved her hand as if that was unnecessary. There was no point in responding to that.

"How's Megan?" he asked next.

"She's doing well."

"I guess she's grown a lot. How about sending a picture?"

"Sure. They took them at school in the spring."

"You're looking good, Val. Good? You look wonderful." Kevin bit his lower lip, leaned closer to the glass. "It's so great to see you, Val. When I get out of here, I'll make it up to you."

Val felt a clutch at her heart. How could he make up for what was lost? Ever?

But Kevin rushed on, "Val, I've got so many plans. Did Chaplain Scott tell you there's a really good chance I can get paroled? Well, when I do, I have some fantastic ideas . . ."

Val realized the chaplain was right. Kevin was already building a larger-than-life picture of what it was going to be like when he got out. Dangerous? Maybe. But she knew it was his way of surviving. Without dreams, without big ideas, or if his hopes were dashed in here, Kevin would die.

Still, it frightened Val to see that glimpse of the old scheming Kevin, the Kevin who wanted to get the best of everything, of everybody, whatever it took.

There really wasn't much more to be said between them. Val felt the words she spoke, the replies she made, were all automatic, on the surface. The real things were too deep, too heartbreaking, too important to say in this environment. Then time was up. She had to leave.

"Will you come again?" Kevin asked.

"I'll try."

The bus ride back to Seawood passed in a sort of peculiar blur. Val felt as if she were viewing a TV program, scenes of the prison, the interview with the chaplain, then her brief visit with Kevin, superimposed on the fleeting landscape. Over and over she reviewed that strange yet hauntingly familiar time with Kevin. A Kevin subtly changed by his prison experience, yet basically the same. Her own reaction was detached. She didn't feel anything. Not love, not resentment, not bitterness, only a kind of emptiness within.

For some reason, the bus pulled into Seawood forty minutes ahead of its scheduled arrival. She had called Garth from a phone booth before boarding the bus so he could meet her. His voice, tight, tense, had asked, "How did things go?"

"I'll tell you when I see you," she had replied. And hung up. She hadn't wanted to go into anything on the phone. She wanted to wait until she could tell him face-to-face.

She got off the bus and looked around. There was no sign of

Garth. Of course, it was earlier than he'd expected her. All at once,
Val felt terrified. She couldn't bear to face Garth, tell him what had
to be told. That she was going to stay married to Kevin. There was
only one choice for her to make. To say goodbye.

Chapter Twenty-Three

"I can't believe you mean that." Garth's voice was rough. "I can't believe you're going to do this to us. To Megan."

Val knew it was going to be heartbreakingly hard to tell Garth her decision. However, she had not really anticipated the violence of his reaction.

When he arrived at the bus stop to meet her, they simply went into each other's arms. Val closed her eyes, allowing herself the fleeting moment of feeling loved, safe. But only for that one fleeting moment. It was too dangerous. She backed out of Garth's embrace, avoiding the puzzled expression on his face.

"Eileen's keeping Megan overnight. I'll take you home," he said quietly. "I went by earlier, lit a fire. It should be warm by now." He took her small bag, then helped her into the car.

They stepped inside the cottage and Val saw the fire, the bunch of bronze and gold chrysanthemums in a pottery vase on the table. There was something savory simmering on the stove and the sharp fragrance of fresh coffee. She smiled gratefully at Garth. All these thoughtful touches welcoming her home.

Garth moved toward her. She could tell he wanted to take her in his arms again. "So glad you're back. I missed you."

Then before she could stop herself, she blurted out, "Garth, I told Kevin I'd wait for him."

Garth stepped back from her, a look of disappointment and shock on his face. "You don't mean that."

"It's true," Val rushed on. Once she had started, she might as well let it all out. "I talked to both the chaplain and the warden. They both feel it's the only thing that will keep Kevin sane, keep him alive in that place. The hope that there will be something for him when he gets out. Or even sooner. They said he had a good chance of parole and that having me waiting was part of his rehabilitation—"

Garth muttered something under his breath, a combination of swearing or a moan, Val didn't know which. Then he burst out, "I knew that man would talk you into it—play on your principles, make you feel guilty, make you feel responsible. Well, I've got news for them. It isn't your responsibility. Kevin is where he is through his own fault, not yours."

"You don't understand, Garth. Nobody talked me into it."

"Oh, you're so naive, Val. You were taken in for all the years you were married to that guy. You said you had no idea what he was doing. He's clever all right. Now he's counting on your pity." He started to pace, then spun around, fists clenched, and declared, "Well, I won't give you up."

"Garth—"

"No, Val, no! I'm not going to let you do this. Whatever the rationale. I won't let you throw your life away like this. Be a martyr. Make a sacrifice of yourself and of me. I know you love me. No matter what they told you or what they persuaded you to agree with up there. I'm going to fight it."

"Nobody made me do anything, Garth. You must understand—"

"No, I don't have to understand. Why should I? It's my life you're dealing with as well as your own. And Megan's. I love you too much to let you go by default. It doesn't make sense. We—you, Megan and I—we're becoming a family. More than you ever had with Kevin. He forfeited his right to you two years ago. He was the one who wanted the divorce, right? He gave you up. Now, for his own purposes, he wants you back. No, I won't let him do it. He's not going to ruin all our lives."

"Garth, it's my fault. I should have done what Kevin wanted me to in the first place, and I should have told you the truth to begin with. I blame myself for everything."

"That's all in the past, Val. I'm not talking about what's past."

"But don't you see, Garth? It's the past that's the problem. I'm a prisoner of the past."

"You don't have to be a prisoner, Val. That's what I'm trying to get you to see. It's possible for a prisoner to escape."

"But I made promises—"

"Promises under different circumstances. At a different time. Did Kevin keep his promises?" he demanded. "He deceived you, deprived you, threw you out into the world to fend for yourself. What do you owe him?"

"I'm not talking about that. Maybe you don't understand that I made a new promise. Up there at the prison. I promised Kevin I'd wait and when he got out we'd make a new start."

At last the whole truth was out. Garth seemed instantly sobered by this statement.

"Do you realize he may have to serve his entire sentence?" Garth's voice was harsh, angry. "Do you know how slim his chances for parole are? The wheels of justice turn slowly. There's been a lot of discussion lately about the courts being soft on crime. The public is very aware of this, watching politicians, demanding tougher sentencing, prisoners serving out their complete sentences. Have you considered that you may have promised to wait for a man who will be totally different from the man you knew? A stranger to Megan. An aging man, hardened by prison, his association with fellow prisoners. Have you thought of that beyond some emotional decision, some sentimental ideal that it's your duty?"

"Oh, Garth, don't. I did what I thought was the right thing, the only thing. I couldn't turn my back on Kevin if there was any way I could help. If I deserted him now, I don't know what he'd have to keep going."

"He should have thought of that when he stole all that money," Garth said bitterly.

"How long is he supposed to pay for his mistake?"

"The law has pretty much decided that, hasn't it?" Garth retorted. "But they didn't sentence you, too. Val, why should you be punished? Or Megan? Have you thought of what this is going to do to her? To suddenly have a father after all this time? Are you going to tell her that her father has been in jail? I don't think you've really thought this through."

"Oh, Garth, I have. I've thought of little else for the past few days. Give me credit for that." Val's voice cracked a little. She felt exhausted not only from her journey, but from going over and over all that they were now discussing. "All I know is that Kevin needs me."

"I need you, too," Garth said morosely.

"Not the way Kevin does."

There was a long silence. The only sound was the crackling sizzle in the stove, and the intermittent banging of a shutter somewhere on the house. Garth inclined his head in that direction as if the noise annoyed him. Then he turned back to Val. "Val, you can't give your life like a gift to someone," he said seriously. "Please don't make the mistake of thinking because Kevin tells you he's changed, things will be different when he gets out. You have no more guarantee of that than the possibility of his parole. You may be wasting your youth, your happiness, your life, on a slim chance that he will change." He sighed deeply. "Not just yours, but mine and Megan's, too."

Val put her fingers on her suddenly throbbing temples. "Stop, please, Garth. I've made up my mind. I know what I have to do. There's no use arguing."

In a few strides, Garth was beside her. Holding her shoulders, he turned her to face him. His voice was edged with desperation. "Val, don't do this to us."

Her sobs came then and she covered her face with her hands.

Feeling Garth gently drawing her close, Val pulled away. The urge to let him comfort her was strong but she had to be stronger. For both their sakes. In his embrace, all Val's resolutions would weaken. All her brave words seem meaningless. How much she wanted to allow him to ease her pain, hold her safe. Yet, she couldn't allow it. Not now.

She heard him murmur, "Don't cry, darling. We'll work it out. I promise you, we'll find a way."

She listened, but all the time she knew what path she'd be taking. There was no going back. In Garth's embrace, anything would seem possible. But the irrevocable truth was that she had promised to stay with Kevin "for better for worse" and those vows still bound her.

After a long while, Val's tears were spent. She found some tissues and wiped her eyes.

Nearby, she heard Garth sigh. "You're exhausted. We won't talk anymore tonight. We can't make sense out of anything at this point." He tenderly stroked her hair, then said, "Get a good night's sleep, Val. I'll be over tomorrow morning. We'll figure something out."

Tired as she was, Val had difficulty falling asleep. There was too much on her mind. Things she could not explain to Garth. He had an answer to all her arguments and they were valid. There was one thing he could not answer, nor could anyone else. How could they build their happiness on someone else's misery? The only answer was in Val's own conscience. Whatever anyone said or thought, Val knew what she had to do.

Chapter Twenty-Four

Val woke up, looked at the clock. It was nearly six. The fire had gone out and the house was cold. Shivering, she got up, made coffee. The past three days seemed unreal. Only the inevitableness of what she must do remained clear. She would have to go away. Someplace where Garth wouldn't follow. There had to be a clean break, otherwise . . .

Val didn't trust herself. If she stayed in Seawood, it was only a matter of time before her resistance would break down. She and Garth were already on thin ice. She had felt it so strongly the night before. From somewhere in her deepest soul, the Scriptural warning came back to her with new, relevant meaning. Matthew 5:28. She and Garth had wanted to do more than just look at each other with desire. She had never before felt tempted. There had never been another man until Garth.

She must get out of harm's way before she was destroyed. She knew her own weakness. It would ruin everything they had together if they took something they weren't free to take. If she divorced Kevin now, she might wipe out any chance he had of getting paroled. If she married Garth, how could she ever forget the price that her longing for happiness would cost Kevin? She just couldn't go through with it. Before that happened, there was only one thing to do. Escape.

Chaplain Scott and the prison counselor had both pointed out to her how her presence and support would work on Kevin's behalf when he came up for parole. It could be the deciding factor. She had given them her word. She couldn't go back on it.

Once, Garth had promised he was willing to continue their relationship on her terms. But they had moved far beyond that first attraction. Their love for each other could no longer be denied. She didn't even trust herself and she loved him too much to expect him to.

Garth's familiar knock on the cottage door startled her. She was even more surprised to see he was wearing a corduroy sport jacket, shirt and tie. He looked haggard, as if he hadn't had much sleep, either.

"Come in, I have coffee made."

He shook his head, held up one hand. "No, thanks, I can't. I'm flying to L.A. today on business. I've been putting it off, but I think I might as well go and get it done. It will give us both a few days to think things through."

Val was taken aback. She had somehow expected that they would spend the day together, talking more. But maybe this was better.

"I just wanted you to know that I love you, Val. I know we can have a wonderful life together. I can't persuade you against your will. But I think—I hope—when you've had time to weigh everything, you'll realize what we have together is worth fighting for. At least, I'm willing to fight for it. There's so much to gain and everything to lose if . . . ."

He pressed his lips together. She could tell there was more he wanted to say but couldn't decide whether to or not. He glanced away from her, down toward the beach. When he spoke again, his voice was rough with emotion.

"What we can give to Megan is worth more than some promise you made under emotional stress." He stood there for another long minute, then said, "I love you, Val."

"I love you, too," Val replied, thinking, You'll never know how much.

When he was gone, all the tears she had kept back while Garth was there burst out. She wept as if she would never stop. Sobbing, she threw herself on the couch, burying her face in the pillows. Finally, spent and shaken, she lay there thinking, This is the way it feels when your heart is breaking.

It was a physical pain as well as an emotional one. It was then she decided she couldn't wait until Garth returned. It would be too late. She wouldn't have the courage to go. She had to leave now. She got up, stood uncertainly for a few minutes in the middle of the room, wondering what to do first. Of course, she must tell Garth why. Write him a letter. Put it all down in writing so he could not argue her out of it. Yes, that was the best way.

She got out paper and pen, sat down at the kitchen table and began to write.

Dearest Garth,

By the time you read this, I shall be far from here. Please forgive me for hurting you by doing it like this. I would hurt you far more if I stayed. I love you and I always will. But it's impossible for me to remain here and be true to myself and what I've promised.

I take full responsibility for what has happened. I blame myself for giving you a false impression of my situation when we met. I became tangled in my own web. But as you've said so often, the past is the past, I can't undo anything. I just ask you not to hate me for messing up your life.

I know you don't understand why I can't desert Kevin at this point. I just can't cut the ties that still bind me to him.

I will always be thankful for having known you, proud that you loved me and wanted me. I will be forever grateful for your loving my little girl and becoming a part of our lives. I'm sure she will never forget you.

I could go on and on writing about all the things about you and our time together that I'll remember and cherish for the rest of my life. I will just close now and say God bless you, Garth, and thank you for all you've done for me and been to me.

Goodbye,

Val hesitated before she signed her name. Somehow the words she'd written seemed cold, stiff. And yet to pour out all the deeply felt love she had for him, the things she might have whispered in his arms, would only hurt him more. Quickly, she folded the letter, slipped it in an envelope. She would put it in his mailbox when she went up to the McDermotts' for Megan.

She packed Megan's clothes and her own, ironically in the same four suitcases she had brought with her that night two years before. She had not acquired many new things and only replaced clothes that Megan had outgrown.

She then took out the strongbox in which she kept her cash. She had never opened an account at the local bank because of all the information that had to be put on an application. In a way that was lucky. There would be no unnecessary delay. She counted it out. She had accumulated a good sum in all these months. There was enough for bus fare to San Francisco—from there she could decide where to go—and enough to live on for a few weeks until she got settled, found a job. She was trembling with nerves by the time she got everything together. She took one long, last look around the little cottage that had been their home, that had held so many times of happiness as well as of sorrow. Now they were off again, like two Gypsies, to find another place to hide for who knew how long.

Of course, Eileen tried to dissuade Val from going.

"Don't be a fool, Val! Don't turn your back on a man like Garth, a chance for real happiness. I've been around a lot longer than you have and I know you two have something special. Think what this will do to him. And what about Megan? She loves Garth. Please, listen to me, Val. Believe me, if you do this, you'll regret it."

"Eileen, I have to go. I've thought of it from every possible angle. This way, we'll get over the hurt faster. If I stayed, we'd both be dying by inches knowing that eventually I had to keep my promise to Kevin. Don't you understand?"

Eileen sighed. "Maybe you're right. But where are you going, where will you be?"

"I don't know for sure, Eileen. Besides, I can't tell you. That way, you won't have to lie to Garth if he tries to find out. And he mustn't find out, Eileen. One thing you've got to promise me, that if I use The Seawinds and you and Tom as a reference for another job, you won't tell Garth. Promise?"

Reluctantly, Eileen agreed. Her eyes welled with tears as she helped Megan get dressed while Val called a cab to take them to the bus station in Oceanview. Eileen hugged them both hard and, at the last minute, stuffed a wad of bills into Val's hand.

The taxi honked, and after another quick hug, Val grabbed their suitcases and they ran out to the waiting car, through a light rain. As the cab made the turn onto the highway, Val took a last look back at the rustic restaurant building and then down to the gray beach, the crashing breakers, the wheeling seagulls, until they all were enveloped in mist. Then she turned and, for the rest of the ride, stared straight ahead.

At the bus station, Val went to the ticket counter and determinedly purchased two one-way tickets to San Francisco.

Megan didn't grasp the full impact of what they were doing. Val knew she would have a great deal of explaining to do later on. For now, Megan was happy as they boarded the bus, ready for a new adventure.

It wasn't until they were on their way that Val took the money Eileen had pressed on her out of her wallet and saw six fifty-dollar bills. Val nearly broke down then and there. She was leaving not only the man she loved but the dearest, kindest friends she had ever known. Would she ever be that happy again, anywhere?

Part III

Chapter Twenty-Five

❧

When word came from the prison that Kevin's parole had been granted, Val found herself emotionally unprepared. Although it had been a possibility for the past ten months, the news still came with an unexpected suddenness.

The call had come on Monday from Chaplain Scott saying that Kevin would be released at noon the next Friday. Could she come to the prison to pick him up?

"Of course," Val had replied through stiff lips. When she replaced the receiver of the kitchen wall phone, she slumped weakly against the sink, gripping the metal edge of the counter to steady herself.

"It's too soon," she thought irrationally. *I'm not ready.* Not ready to begin life again with a man from whom she'd been separated for almost three years, a man she had tried to put out of her heart and mind, a man she wasn't even sure she still loved.

Quickly she reminded herself that it wasn't too soon for Kevin. He'd been increasingly impatient every month when she'd gone to see him. He'd been irritable, nervous, constantly cracking his knuckles in clenched hands. She'd leave after a visit, feeling uneasy, upset. She tried to explain away Kevin's snappishness with her. She was reminded of all the other times when he'd lashed out at her. Become angry over some small incident or something she'd failed to do. Kev had a short fuse, always had. And, of course, he was under severe tension. It was understandable, she told herself.

She looked around the sunny kitchen trying to make sense of the phone call. It seemed to come from some faraway, foreign place. Far removed from the peaceful life she'd found in Spring Valley. This small northern California town, deep in Redwood Country, was where she and Megan now lived. Coming here had been happenstance.

It had been a last-minute decision, actually. After heartbrokenly leaving Seawood, Val had been uncertain about the best place for her and Megan to go. Living in a city would be expensive and finding a safe area to live, reliable sitters for Megan when she was at work, would be difficult. So when they reached San Francisco, Val extended their ticket farther north. It would be a greater distance from Seawood but closer to the prison situated on the Oregon border.

That decision had been a good one. They'd found a nice duplex at reasonable rent and within walking distance to school for Megan. Val had found two part-time jobs, one during Megan's school hours, the other a billing job she could do from home for a local catalog company. They had joined a church and Megan had made many friends and was happy.

Now with Kevin coming back into their lives, everything would change. Once more Val thought, *It's too soon.* The thing that terrified her was this, was it too late for her and Kevin to build a life together?

The rest of the week went by with frightening swiftness. As Val hurried around getting everything in readiness, she felt time was rushing by, hurtling her forward into an unknown future.

Mrs. Ellerbee, the fiftyish widow, who lived on the other side of Val's apartment, was more than willing to keep Megan. She had become a friend and confidante in the months Val had lived next door. She had grandchildren who sometimes visited her on weekends and Megan was perfectly comfortable with the arrangement. In the past months, little by little, Val had talked to Megan about her father, told her that he might be coming home to live with them again. With a child's astonishing flexibility, Megan seemed to accept that without a qualm. The fact that he would be home in a few days seemed only natural.

Val wished she had the same attitude. The closer Friday approached, the more inner turmoil she felt. She couldn't sleep, or eat. Then at last it was Friday.

Val's hands gripped the steering wheel of the secondhand compact she had bought a few months before. Merging into the flow of traffic on the freeway, Val's heart pumped wildly. She slid in a tape hoping some of the Amy Grant songs Megan loved and had learned to sing would be calming. It was a bright, beautiful spring morning and she knew she should be feeling happy. Yet a thousand doubts clouded her mind. She remembered the last conversation she'd had with Chaplain Scott on one of her recent visits to Kevin. He'd been waiting for her and asked her to come into his office.

"I know Kevin thinks his parole is a done deal," he'd told her, "and his optimism is better than the depression he went through. But it's never a certainty, although his chances are immeasurably improved by your standing by him. I just don't want to hold out any false hope that if and when he gets out, everything's going to be perfect, that you will live happily ever after. Unfortunately, it's been my experience that even if an ex-convict is lucky enough to find a job, many of them get restless in a routine, ordinary situation. The everyday life that they've fantasized about in prison begins to look pretty dull. That's when some find it hard to resist the temptation to look for the easy money they may have found in illegal ways . . . the very things that landed them in prison. I hope this won't be the case with your husband."

Strangely enough, the chaplain's caution had come right on top of that day's visit. Kevin had been talking enthusiastically about the correspondence course he had enrolled in by mail.

"Real estate is where the big money is these days. There's a regular gold mine in land investment and development. The second-home trend is really booming. There are a lot of people in big jobs making huge salaries that take early retirement and want to get out of the big cities, want homes in scenic environments, out of the rat race and urban problems. Northern California and Oregon are ripe for this game."

Val had not thought much about that since. But somehow recalling the chaplain's warning coupled with the memory of Kevin's enthusiasm made her a little uneasy. Instinctively, she had a hunch that Kevin wouldn't be satisfied with a salesclerk's job at a department store such as the ones Val saw advertised in the local paper.

She parked her car several yards from the prison in sight of the guardhouse and gate. Her hands were sweaty and she had to keep wiping them with tissues. This was it. The end of the endless waiting. Calm down, calm down, Val ordered herself. The strain was like a wire pulled excruciatingly tight. It was hard to breathe. The shriek of the prison's noon whistle split the air. Val tensed, eyes riveted on the prison gate.

Then she saw it open and a man stepped out through the narrow doorway in the heavy steel gate. She pushed open the car door and got out. She waved. "Kevin! Over here, Kevin!"

Kevin put the six-pack in the refrigerator, let the door slam. He pulled the metal tab on one can with a swishing sound. Then he swung one of the kitchen chairs out from the table, turned it around, straddled it. Leaning his arms on its back, he took a swallow of beer, then looked around.

"Believe me, baby, I'll soon have us out of this dump."

Val swallowed back an indignant retort. Kevin had only been out a week, but he'd found fault with everything in the little duplex she had worked so hard to spruce up for him. The fresh café curtains, the row of African violets blooming on the windowsill, the framed Renoir prints on the freshly painted walls, the new bedspread in the bedroom they now shared. Everything had been scrubbed and polished to a gleaming shine.

It will take time, Val reminded herself. But trying to heed the chaplain's advice was difficult. She had been on her own for a long time. Now Kevin was back, running the show like in the old days before anything had happened to change things. She had tried to remain calm, cheerful, but it wasn't easy.

"Do you have a credit card?" he asked. "I can't apply for one yet. But I need to get some new clothes. Gotta look sharp. Image is everything." He took another swig of his beer.

Val picked up her handbag, got out her wallet, took the credit card and handed it over to Kevin.

"What's the credit limit?" he asked.

She told him. She felt guilty that she was reluctant to let him use it. She always paid off the balance every month, so no interest charges had accrued to make the payments too large. She had used it only to get new mattresses for the beds, a microwave and a small

TV when they first moved into the duplex. But Kevin was probably planning to go on job interviews now that he had had a chance to get settled. Just being out of prison was a big adjustment.

"Have you some interviews lined up?"

It seemed a reasonable question. She wasn't prepared for Kevin's explosion.

"Stop nagging, will you? I'm not going to line up at some employment office, if that's what you mean. I've got my own plans. Big ones."

Val was startled at his reaction. There hadn't been any justification for his angry response. Soon after that, Kevin took the car keys and left.

He came back late. Val had already fed Megan her supper and was in the kitchen washing up when he returned. He was loaded with packages and bags bearing the logo of a well-known men's clothing store. He was wearing a striped shirt, raw-silk sport coat, Italian loafers. He looked like the old Kevin. "Wow!" was all Val could say.

Kevin was obviously pleased with himself. He went into the bedroom and Val heard dresser drawers being opened, the closet door being pushed back. Kevin was evidently putting all his new purchases away. Val could only imagine what her credit-card bill would list when it arrived at the first of next month.

She tried not to feel resentful. Kevin needed the boost of self-confidence some good-looking clothes would give him. His self-esteem had been ground down to zero in prison. Buying all these expensive clothes could be considered part of the expense of his rehabilitation. Probably it was well worth it.

A few days later, Kevin announced that he was going to drive to San Francisco to meet a friend, a business associate.

"Someone I know?" Val asked, wondering if Kevin had been in touch with any of his former colleagues at the bank.

"No." He sounded sullen. "If you must know, it's a guy I met in prison." Val's shock must have shown because Kevin snarled, "Don't give me that sanctimonious look. It doesn't mean he was in for murder. White-collar crime, remember? Jerry had a run-in with the IRS, some tax problem, that's all. But he's a sharp fellow. He can put me in touch with some of the people I need to connect with in real estate."

They were in the kitchen, and Megan, dressed and ready for school, came in just then and said, "Mommy, I need my lunch."

Kevin said, "Don't interrupt, Megan. Your mother and I are having a conversation." Val saw at once that Megan hadn't heard him, for she went on talking. Kevin evidently didn't realize that and yanked the little girl by her shoulder, turning her toward him. "I said don't interrupt."

Megan looked frightened, bewildered. "I'm sorry, Daddy."

"Kevin," Val protested, tapping her ear with her forefinger in an attempt to explain.

Kevin gave her an irritated glance and demanded, "What?"

"I'll tell you later," she said, and handed Megan her lunchbox, leaned down and kissed her, then took her by the hand and saw her out the door. Returning to the kitchen, she managed to say in a calm voice, "Kevin, Megan didn't mean to interrupt. She didn't hear us talking when she came in."

Kevin scowled. "Is she worse? Maybe we should investigate a school where she'd be with other handicapped kids."

"Handicapped? Megan isn't disabled, Kevin!" Val struggled not to lose her temper. She kept her voice even. "She gets along per- fectly well where she is. Her teachers are very complimentary about how attentive she is, how well she participates—"

"Okay, okay. End of discussion." Kevin pushed back his chair, slammed his coffee mug down on the table, then stood up. "I've got to get going. I'm renting a car. A new model. Can't be seen driving a clunker. You'll have to go with me to the car rental, sign it out for me. I don't want to fill out an application for one while I'm on parole."

Upset at how he had treated Megan, Val said, "Kevin, we have to talk. About Megan."

"Not now, Val. I haven't time." With that, Kevin walked out of the room, leaving Val smoldering. They would have to talk. She started to clear the table. Indeed, there were a great many things they had to talk about.

Kevin picked out a long, sleek, luxury rental car and Val, against her better judgment, signed for it.

Kevin had said he might stay overnight in San Francisco in case the talks went late or Jerry wanted to take him to meet someone. Val was still upset about the scene that morning and did not comment. As she drove her own car back home, she thought this adjustment to living together again was far harder than she had anticipated.

Kevin was jumpy and on edge most of the time. He watched TV with his finger constantly on the remote, switching channels as if nothing could hold his attention. His sleep was disturbed with nightmares. He would wake up often, then take a pillow and blanket and spend the remainder of the night on the living-room couch. After their first night together, which turned out to be a failure, they had not regained the physical intimacy that had been such a big part of their relationship before. His relationship with Megan, for which she had such high hopes, was also disappointing. After an initial rush of excitement, Kevin resumed his distracted, indifferent attitude toward her. He seemed annoyed by her deafness, which he seemed to have forgotten about.

More and more, Val wondered if she had done the right thing. More and more, her thoughts returned to Garth. What had he done when he read her letter? Where was he now? It was useless to go over and over it all again. She had done what she thought was right at the time. It had to work. She had to try harder. "Dear God, help me," she whispered.

When she met Jerry Meisner, Val thought, *I don't like him.* There was something about him that made her recoil. He was too smooth, too quick with a compliment, his laugh too forced, his smile phony. Something about his eyes . . . Val disliked being so critical of the man Kevin had introduced her to at the airport. But there it was. She couldn't help it. Kevin was excited, up. Val hadn't seen him so positive and confident since he'd gotten out of prison. There was the old spring in his step, the ready wit and spontaneous enthusiasm. No wonder Meisner's associates wanted someone like Kevin as their sales representative.

They were flying to Lake Tahoe for a big bash, a party to be held at the model home Meisner's construction company had built—one of the many they hoped to build and sell on lakeside sites. It was going to be a grand affair—food and wine and sales talk. Kevin would be in his element.

Val had mixed feelings as he gave her a quick hug and kiss before the two men, still talking, walked into the terminal to board the company's private Cessna. Kevin glanced over his shoulder once and, seeing Val still standing there, gave her a jaunty wave.

That night, Val and Megan had supper alone, and Val sat on Megan's bed to read her a story. "This is nice, isn't it, Mommy? Just you and me," Megan said as she cuddled close. Val hugged her. She knew Megan was sensitive to the tension that Kevin's presence made in their little house, where once it had been so cozy and relaxed.

Val settled Megan down for the night, then took a long bath and went to bed. She wondered how the party at Lake Tahoe was going and if Kevin had made any sales. If he was successful, would he want them to move to Tahoe? What did the future hold for them? Before anything was decided, she had to talk to Kevin about Megan. Their little girl was eight now and they would have to make some plans if her deafness was increasing.

After her bath, Val was too tired to watch TV. Instead, she read for a while, then went to sleep.

The persistent peal of her doorbell brought Val awake. A glance at the bedside clock told her it was nearly six. Had Kevin come back already? Forgotten his key? She grabbed her robe, flung it around her shoulders and ran barefoot to the front door.

Somehow she knew, even before anything was said, when she opened the door and saw the two highway patrolmen, tall and erect in their crisp uniforms, standing on the steps.

A private plane with four passengers had crashed upon takeoff from the Tahoe airport. Kevin was one of the passengers. They were sorry to inform her that there were no survivors.

Chapter Twenty-Six

The summer Megan was ten, Val made arrangements for her to attend Girl Scout camp in the Santa Cruz Mountains. Even though she would miss her terribly, Val knew it was important for Megan to become more independent. Happy and excited as she was to go, at the last minute, right before boarding the camp bus, Megan ran back to give her mother one more hug.

In the years since Kevin's death, Val had tried not to be overprotective of the little girl or allow her to become too attached. Especially because of Megan's deafness, Val knew it was important for her to be exposed to different experiences.

Val had taken some accrued vacation days to get Megan ready for camp. She was in no hurry to go back to their duplex, which would seem empty with Megan away. So after seeing her daughter off, Val decided to drive to Carmel. The picturesque little town with its art galleries, boutiques and quaint shops was only a little farther down the coast.

After finding a parking spot, Val strolled leisurely along the winding streets whose sidewalks meandered around trees that gave a leafy shade. The display window in every store she passed offered something to make her take a look and decide whether to go inside or not. However, it was a sign outside one small gallery that brought her to an abrupt halt. It read, New Paintings By Garth Hasten.

As she stood there staring at the name, the world seemed to stop turning. Though she was unable to move, her feet rooted to the pavement, her pulse pounded, her heart raced. Was he here? Should she go inside or turn around now and leave?

Finally, curiosity won over hesitation and Val walked inside. Garth was one of several artists exhibited in this gallery. Familiar as she was with his technique, she recognized his at once. Representational, yet there was something new, a freer style, as if influenced by the French Impressionists. The scenes of country landscapes and villages convinced her that he must have gone to France after all. Without them. Val thought of the happy plans he'd made that day by the ocean. Plans that had disappeared like a drift of fog.

There were eight paintings in all signed by GH, but no paintings from the sketches Val knew he had made on the beach when the three of them were all there together. He'd made dozens of sketches of Megan, hoping to use them someday in a picture book with the seashore as background. Megan in her skimpy pink bathing suit she had long since outgrown, standing in the foamy shallows, stooping to examine tide pools, kneeling in the sand, industriously creating her towered castles. What had he done with them?

"May I help you in any way, madam? Are you interested in any of these paintings?"

Val slowly came back to the present at the sound of the question. She turned to see an exotic young woman wearing dangling silver earrings and a black-and-gold leopard-patterned dress regarding her curiously. The gallery manager, she guessed.

"Are you familiar with the artist's work?"

"No, not exactly. I mean, yes, I admire his work. But I'm afraid I couldn't afford any of his paintings."

"He's really quite remarkable in that he's primarily an illustrator of children's books. Few artists make that transition to fine art, but Garth Hasten has. His paintings are much in demand." She gestured to the ones in front of them. "Most of these are sold. See the small red dots in the corners? We had an opening for him earlier in the summer when he was down here. It was very successful."

"I'm glad to hear it."

"We could sell everything he paints. But there are some he's reluctant to part with. In fact, we have two he wouldn't let us put up for this show unless we put NFS stickers on them."

Something made Val ask, "May I see them?"

The young woman hesitated. She seemed to be making a mental calculation. If this wasn't a serious buyer, why was she interested and should she take the time with her? Of course, one never knew. Even with her experience with art collectors, she was sometimes wrong. She glanced around the gallery. There was no one else wandering through at the moment. It had been a slow afternoon. So she said to Val, "Certainly, come this way. We hung them in the annex so that only the most ardent fans of his would seek them out. Especially since he refuses to sell them, it doesn't seem practical for us to display them in the front of the gallery."

The two paintings struck Val's heart with an impact she couldn't have anticipated. One was a long view of a curved beach and walking along the edge were two figures, one of a woman, the other of a little girl. Even though the figures were viewed from behind, Val knew they were of her and Megan. The other one was of a child bent over, holding a seashell in one cupped hand against the background of the ocean, the frothy scallops of water swirling around her small, bare brown feet. There was no doubt. It was Megan at six years of age.

Memories crowded in, making her almost weak with regret. She managed to ask in a husky voice, "Does Mr. Hasten live in Carmel?"

"No. I'm not sure where he lives. He's rather reclusive. I know the gallery owner had to go through his agent to persuade him to do this exhibit. He must travel a good deal. All these current paintings are from a year he spent in France."

Val moved away. She was afraid the young woman would notice the tears that gathered in her eyes.

"Would you like to sign our visitors' book. Be on our mailing list?"

"No, thank you."

"Please take one of our brochures."

Val picked one up off the table at the entrance as she went back outside again. She walked down to the next corner to an outdoor café. She sat at an umbrellaed table, ordered a caffe latte and opened the colorful brochure.

"Garth Hasten, well-known illustrator of children's books, has long been hailed as a fine artist. The current exhibit is a collection from paintings he did while spending a 'vagabond' year traveling in France."

A tightness formed in Val's throat as she read. Those were the months that were to have been their honeymoon. She tried to imagine what that time had been like for Garth. Overall, the paintings had been light, filled with sunshine, flowers, arbors and cottages, old stone churches and rolling hills. There was no hint of melancholy or unhappiness in the artist who painted them. A spontaneous prayer welled up in Val's heart for Garth, blessing him.

As she had done daily since they parted, she prayed that the wounds she'd inflicted on Garth had healed, that he had forgiven her and not blamed her for what she had done.

Val left Carmel and started north again. Back on the freeway, seeing the sign, on impulse she took the Seawood turnoff. She wasn't sure why. She'd learned the McDermotts had closed The Seawinds and retired for good to Mexico. She had written them once, a brief note after she and Megan were settled, but had put no return address on the envelope. Since she didn't have their Mexican address, she hadn't been able to let them know about Kevin's death. She was sure they had also lost track of Garth.

The little town of Seawood looked deserted, not much different from the first time she'd seen it. Progress had passed it by. The businesses that had held on precariously while The Seawinds was open had closed up shop, probably moved into Oceanview, twenty miles away.

Val drove down the rutted beach road and parked above the cottage that had been her and Megan's home for nearly two years. It looked more weathered and forlorn. Its roof sagged, the rain gutters rusted and bent. Not a sign of life anywhere. Drawn by some unknown pull, Val got out of the car. The day had darkened since she left Carmel. Here, clouds hung ominously over a steel gray choppy ocean. The entire stretch of beach looked abandoned. Didn't even summer people seeking a cheap place to vacation come here anymore?

She had a strange feeling of déjà vu. It was just such a day when she had first arrived here herself. She remembered her dismay at seeing the cottage she had rented. How she had dreaded starting a new life in such a place. And yet she had come to love it. Even on a day like this, the sea, the beach, held a beauty, a fascination for her.

She had eventually been happier here than any other place in her life.

Scattered wisps of fog blew up from the ocean. Val breathed deeply of the tangy salt air. She walked down the warped wooden path onto the dunes and then to the beach. There she slipped off her flats and stockings, tucked them in the pocket of her jacket and walked down along the beach to the water's edge. She felt the delicious sensation as the water curled up in between her toes and she dug her feet into the wet sand. She began walking. Gradually, the feelings of calm and peace the ocean had always brought to her soul began to come over her. Oh, how she had missed it all, the smell and sight and feel of the air, sea, sand. She experienced a lightness of heart as she went on, the sensation of a homecoming after a long time away. It seemed so right to be here. She wondered again if God had brought her here the first time and now, had drawn her back.

She stopped to look out at the ocean and saw two solitary surfers in wet suits riding the waves. She stood there long after the surfers had beached, raised their boards over their heads and started walking down the sand in the opposite direction.

Had they found our old cove? Our special place? Val wondered. Would they build a driftwood fire in the shelter of the dunes? Were they lovers? Would they wait for the moon to rise and look into the firelight and dream their dreams—the way she and Garth had once done?

Val walked on, more slowly now, remembering the past, the golden days of the second spring she had lived at Seawood. Then suddenly, she became conscious of a tingling along her spine, a quiver of awareness that she was no longer alone on the beach. She turned away from the ocean and looked up.

On the cliff above, outlined against the gray sky, was a man's figure. Something looked familiar about the set of the head and shoulders. She felt a clutching sensation in her heart. Could it be? Was it possible? As she stood there watching, he made his way down onto the beach. He was striding toward her purposefully. Then he broke into a run and there was no mistake. She knew who it was.

Yet when he was a few feet away, she heard herself say, "I don't believe it."

Even as he came closer, she felt that she must be dreaming. Then he smiled and said, "I've just made coffee. Will you come up and have some?"

The invitation was a replay of a dozen other times as well as the dialogue in a hundred dreams come true.

"This can't really be happening," she said again when at last they were seated opposite each other in the window of Garth's cottage. "I never thought you'd still be here."

"I couldn't bring myself to leave. Somehow I thought, hoped, prayed, that someday you'd return. So I come down here for a few weeks, try to paint—"

"I've just seen your new paintings in the gallery in Carmel."

"The ones I did in France?"

"Yes, and . . . the others."

She noticed a subtle change in his expression, then Garth reached across for her left hand, lifted it and examined her fourth finger. "No wedding ring? You didn't go back to your husband after all?"

"Kevin's dead, Garth." Garth's eyebrows lifted. Skeptically? Val realized he was considering the lie she had told him before, the one that had caused them both such pain. She felt ashamed, remembering. "This time it's true."

Quickly, Val explained the circumstances of Kevin's parole and what had happened to him.

"How long ago?"

"Two years."

"Then why . . . ?" Garth frowned, letting his unspoken question hang between them. "Why didn't you get in touch with me?" he finally asked.

"I'm not sure. Maybe because I was afraid I had hurt you too much. That you were well rid of me. I thought you must have met someone else by then, maybe even married. Besides, you had gone to France—"

"I would have come back. Don't you know that, Val? If I'd known, nothing would have kept me from coming." Garth's hold on her hand tightened. "I've never stopped loving you, Val. I can't tell you how empty my life has been without you and Megan."

It seemed incredible to Val. That those long, lonely years had ended with this remarkable reunion. She could still hardly believe it was real until he had gathered her into his arms . . . until she felt the warmth of his lips on hers as she welcomed his kiss.

"My darling," Val heard Garth's voice say over and over as he held her close. There would be time, she knew, when all this could be explained, when all the pieces of the scattered puzzle would be picked up, examined, reexamined and put together at last. There was so much to tell, so much time to make up for, but they had all the time in the world. They had forever.

Together they went to pick Megan up from camp. When the little girl saw Garth, there was hardly a moment's hesitation before she ran and flung herself into his outstretched arms.

He swung her around, then set her down, and she turned happily to Val, saying, "Oh, Mom, where did you find him?" They all laughed, and as Val's gaze met Garth's over Megan's head, she knew that at last she had found the man who would share with her all the joys, responsibilities and struggles of raising a child. A man she could trust and love.

She had been alone so long. And now she was being given a second chance. A second chance for a new life, a new love.

In September at the Wayside Chapel, a small church set deep among the redwoods, Val and Garth were married. It seemed the appropriate and the perfect place for a wedding. Polished beams of glowing wood overhead led to the altar behind which were three arched windows overlooking a beautiful valley. Through the glass, two stately redwood trees rose side by side, soaring into the sky. Above the altar on a cross beam were carved the words, "Faith, Hope and Love and the greatest of these is Love."

As she and Garth joined hands to repeat their pledges, Val knew that these spiritual principles would guide and direct their life together, strengthening their commitment to each other in the sacred promises they would keep forever.

Dear Reader,

Novelists take readers into the high points of their characters' lives, the dramatic events, the intimate moments, the life-changing decisions. We create situations forcing our characters to make important choices. We imagine how they will react by the qualities, flaws, weaknesses and strengths we give them. That is why I love being a writer and why I am particularly pleased for the opportunity the Love Inspired line gives me to portray identifiable characters in realistic ways as they face serious challenges.

Few women will ever have to confront the problem Val does. However, in telling her story I asked myself what would I do faced with her choices. I asked the questions:

How committed are most people to their marriage vows?

How binding do they consider them when the partner wants out?

What is the individual's responsibility no matter what the other person does?

Is marriage simply a contract, or is it a sacred promise?

Do values really matter?

These are some of the issues I hope you will find as compelling as I did writing this book.

With best wishes,

Jane Peart